THE BRANDED ROSE PROPHECY

TRACY COOPER-POSEY

STORIES RULE
EDMONTON • ALBERTA

This is an original publication of Tracy Cooper-Posey

This is a work of fiction. Names, characters, places and incidents either are the product of the author's imagination or are used fictitiously, and any resemblance to actual persons, living or dead, business establishments, events, or locales, is entirely coincidental. The publisher does not have any control over and does not assume any responsibility for third-party websites or their content.

FIRST EDITION: December 2014

Cooper-Posey, Tracy
The Branded Rose Prophecy/Tracy Cooper-Posey—1st Ed.

Romance—Fiction
Paranormal – Fiction
Fantasy—Fiction

ONE WORLD

Chapter One

Modern **humans** (*Homo sapiens* or *Homo sapiens sapiens*) are the only extant members of the hominin clade, a branch of great apes characterized by erect posture and bipedal locomotion; manual dexterity and increased tool use; and a general trend toward larger, more complex brains and societies.

Wikipedia

Charlee was ten when she met her first non-human, but another twenty years would pass before she truly understood Asher's nature. She was very young, despite growing up in the Bronx. That first day, though, she did figure out two facts about him. One, he owned a wicked sword that vanished at will. And two, what he did was heroic even though a man died and it was not Charlee he saved. Her own rescue would come much later, after the fall of New York.

Their first meeting happened in early September, on a sultry night with no breeze for relief. The air was so still that the smell of dust rose from the sidewalks to tickle the inside of Charlee's nose. Her feet inside her old Chucks throbbed from contact with the baked concrete as she hurried along Trinity Avenue.

The sun had finally slipped behind the buildings sometime after seven, a ball of angry red and orange, sending down the street long shadows that merged into twilight. Nothing moved, not even the leaves drooping overhead. It was like the whole world had paused to take a collective breath of relief now that the cool of the evening could descend.

It was still warm and close despite the dark. As Charlee headed northeast along the street, she could feel the air colliding with her damp skin, reluctantly parting to let her through.

Water, she thought, as her throat clicked with dryness. She should get some water for Chocolate, to go with the food she had brought. She started to look for a faucet. If this had been Cauldwell Avenue, she would have known exactly where one was, but she didn't know Trinity very well. It took her a block out of her way, from school to home, but she had come this way a week ago when she had spotted a large group of

4

Lightning Lords blocking the way on Cauldwell. The gang had been lolling about on the sidewalk, leaning against the fences that bordered this section, brooding gazes scanning the street and pedestrians.

Two weeks ago, three teenagers had been found in the alley behind the Chinese supermarket at the top end of Cauldwell Avenue where it ran into 160th Street, their bodies riddled by machine gun fire. Residents in the closest buildings had seen nothin' and heard less, but the talk at school was that the teenagers, who all went to Herbert H. Lehman high school, had given the gang too much attitude as they walked past them.

Better to walk an extra block than risk making the Lords angry.

Using Trinity Avenue was the reason she had met Chocolate, which made up for the inconvenience. Charlee thought of him as she scanned the homes and their yards, looking for a free faucet. His brown eyes had been so big in his face that for the first time Charlee really understood what people meant when they said someone's eyes were as big as saucers.

She had known he was homeless straight away, which had made her sad. How could anyone turn him out? One look into his big eyes and she could see he was gentle and kind, even though he made a noise in his throat when she got closer, a sound she had just known meant "stay away." But there was hope in his eyes, too, so she had spoken to him.

They had become friends almost instantly. Charlee had found him somewhere to bed down for the night, then she had returned right after supper, the frankfurts she had not eaten wrapped in greaseproof paper in her pocket. Chocolate had been so grateful, gulping down the two frankfurts in about ten seconds, that she had felt guilty for not bringing more.

She had returned every night since, bringing what she could from her supper plate and anything the rest of her family left untouched, which wasn't much. Chocolate had been waiting patiently each time she arrived, giving her a welcome so warm that her heart had lifted.

When she reached the alleyway she still had not spotted a faucet, but she couldn't spend more time looking for one. She didn't want to be away from the house for much longer. Her mother never checked on either her or Lucas once they had escaped to their rooms after supper, as she preferred to stay at the kitchen table with her favorite brand of beer. Her father, though, might look in while she was away and find her room empty. It was much more likely that Lucas would come to talk to her before he went to bed himself, as he sometimes did. It was amazing that he had not discovered her gone this past week. Although if he did discover her gone, she could talk him into staying silent about it in return for her silence over the magazines she had found under his mattress.

The air seemed even thicker in the closed-in, narrow alley. The shadows seemed darker, but even before she reached the bend where the alley turned around the corner of the apartment building it hugged, she heard Chocolate in the dark ahead of her. He had caught her scent and was pleased to see her.

"Chocolate? Here, boy," she coaxed, digging into her dress pocket for the plastic bag. She extracted the bag carefully, for it was half-filled with watery stew. "You're prob'ly not gonna like all this," she told Chocolate, easing the bag open. "But it's real good stuff, so you chow down, okay?"

Chocolate inched closer. He was a light shadow in the dim light. His patchy fur looked washed out even in Charlee's limited experience. His tail was wagging, swaying his whole body, but he still took a careful step at a time toward the open bag, not quite cringing. He was ready to bolt at the slightest hint of danger.

Charlee had to keep hold of the bag, or it would spill its contents. Until tonight, she had opened the bag then stepped well out of Chocolate's way, letting him approach the bag without her standing over it. Last night, once he had become involved in eating, she had taken a step closer, then another, until she could crouch down next to him. Chocolate had shied, ducking, but the power of the food had brought him back to the bag and as he ate, she stroked the fur between his ears softly, thrilled that he trusted her enough to let her touch him.

She hoped that tiny amount of trust would let her hold the bag for him now. "C'mere, boy," she whispered. "Come and get it."

Chocolate was quivering with eagerness, but still hesitant. He stepped closer. He didn't shift back and forth the way he had the first night they'd met, torn between the smell of the food and safety, but he still took his time thinking about it until, finally, he pushed his nose inside the bag. Apparently, she was worthy of trust.

Charlee was enormously pleased, but she held still and grinned in the darkness. "*Good* boy. Smart boy!" she told him. She would have tried to pet him, but she had to hold the bag with both hands so he could get at the stew.

"Hey, chickita. Whatcha think you're doing, huh?" The soft inquiry came from behind her, shocking her with its unexpectedness.

Charlee looked over her shoulder, then bounced to her feet in one powerful movement that she would never have been able to make if her heart had not been leaping as it was. She almost swayed on her feet, feeling sick and weak.

She and Chocolate were tucked into the sharp corner of the alley where it turned, next to some banged-up garbage cans. The section of the alley that ran into the street had been behind her. She faced it now, and it was full of dark shadows and warm air. Ranged across the width of the alley were four men. Boys in age, but experience had made them old before their time. They wore clothes that weren't quite the same in style, but were identical in intent: jeans, black tanks and silk shirts over the top. Their shirts were all hanging open to show a small fortune in thick gold necklaces, at least three apiece.

Lightning Lords. She would have become afraid if her heart had not already been zooming up near the clouds somewhere. They had snuck up on her while she was busy coaxing Chocolate to eat.

One of them, one of the ones standing in the middle, was a pace in front of the rest. He was the one who had spoken, she guessed. He was staring at her. A smile pulled at his lips but there was a hard, cold light in his eyes that didn't match the smile. "Huh, chickie?" he prompted her.

"I ain't doin' nothing," she said. It was a weak defense, but she couldn't seem to think straight.

"Looks to me like you're doin' plenty," he said. "Dontcha know that thing could be filled with rabies?"

Charlee didn't know what rabies was, but just the name sounded horrible. She made a mental reminder to find out what rabies was, the next time she was near a dictionary or in the library. She kept her face still, so he wouldn't see her ignorance. "I'm just feedin' him."

"We gotta hurry, Lonzo," one of the others murmured. "They'll be waiting."

Lonzo waved away the reminder with an impatient motion of his hand. He didn't shift his gaze from Charlee or Chocolate, who was nosing at the last of the stew in the corners of the bag. Chocolate didn't like the newcomers, but the food kept him anchored. His whole body was stretched backwards, like he would be gone in a second if only the stew wasn't there.

"Feedin' that mutt is a waste of time, anyways," Lonzo told her. "It's a stray. It's gonna die inside a week or two. If a car don't get it, another dog will. You're better off doin' it a favor."

She didn't know exactly what he meant by doing Chocolate a favor, but she could guess at his general intention. Anger sprouted. "Don't you dare touch him."

One of the boys chortled then choked it back. The others grinned, including Lonzo. Again, the expression didn't reach his eyes. They were dead. Muddy black eyes that let nothing out. He took a step forward. It brought him very close to her.

Chocolate lifted his snout a few inches, his interest in the meal instantly gone. He growled in the back of his throat, a deep sound that Charlee had never heard before. He wasn't backing up.

"Shh…" she told Chocolate quickly.

"You givin' me an order?" Lonzo asked, his voice soft. The low sound made her heart gallop all over again and she shook her head quickly.

"Sounded ta me like you was tellin' me what to do."

She tried to swallow, but her throat was too dry. The sick feeling swooped back, and sweat popped on her temples and prickled under her arms. She could hear her heart in her head, booming loudly. "I wouldn't," she told Lonzo helplessly.

"'Course you wouldn't." He was calm, even friendly. "'Coz I can do anything I wanna do. Want me to prove it?"

She shook her head quickly.

Chocolate was still growling. His top lip lifted, baring his teeth. It looked frightening, but *his* eyes were warm with feeling.

Lonzo moved quickly, catching Charlee by surprise. He took another long stride forward. His heavy steel-toed workboot that had never seen a moment of anything resembling work planted itself on the crumpled plastic bag, and the bag popped as the air was squashed out of it.

Then he shifted his weight forward, his trailing leg swinging viciously. The toe of his boot caught Chocolate in the rib cage just behind his front leg, down low where the ribs ended.

Chocolate howled. It was a terrible sound, one that would stay with Charlee the rest of her life. The sound was loud, keening. It pierced her heart, making it hurt. It stopped her brain for a moment, so that she simply froze.

He kicked him. Mother Mary…he kicked Chocolate. It was the only coherent thought she had.

But the moment of frozen surprise didn't last. Heated emotion rushed up from her toes, filling her with a fury stronger than anything she had ever experienced. While Chocolate staggered away from Lonzo with a limping gait, his howls shifting to pain-filled yips, Charlee drew in a breath that seemed to fill her lungs with white-hot energy. "How dare you!" she cried and leapt at Lonzo.

Lonzo was just starting to grin, delighted at the effectiveness of his kick. He was level with Charlee in the alleyway, so his flank was turned toward her. He was a small man, barely over five and a half feet, while Charlee was tall for her age. She pushed herself off her feet and up into the air, her arms held out toward him, her fingers spread.

She landed against his shoulder and momentum threw her around so that she slammed against his back. She wrapped her arms around his neck in a purely instinctive search for anchorage to hold her up.

Then she shifted her weight so one arm could keep her in place and began to thump her fist against his chest and shoulder and the side of his face. The whole time, she was screaming, her anger driving words out of her that she didn't pause to put together. "You fucker! You goddamn fucker! You kicked him. You hurt Chocolate and he didn't do a thing to you. Listen to him, listen to what you did!"

When his fingers gripped her forearm and tried to pull it away, she realized that she was choking off his breath.

....*good, I hope he dies...I hope it hurts, hurts like hell...* The thought was calm, coming from a quiet place in her mind that she didn't recognize. It was the same place that was analyzing the strong cologne Lonzo wore, disliking both it and the aroma of stale sweat beneath it.

More hands were on her arms and curling around her neck. The others were stepping in to rescue their leader. They were going to yank her off him.

Her anger was subsiding and now there was room for other emotions. Fear touched her. If they pulled her off Lonzo's back, they would beat the crap out of her for attacking him.

She stopped trying to hit him with her fist and wrapped both arms around his neck, gripping her forearms to cement her hold. She tried to get her legs around his body, for the extra strength it would provide. One of them grabbed her ankle in a painful grip, wrenching her leg backwards. "No, you don't!" came the cry. "Grab her foot, for fuck's sake."

"Kill the bitch!" Lonzo croaked. He was leaning forward. Staggering.

Through it all, through the shouting, the curses and her blood thundering in her ears, Charlee could still hear Chocolate somewhere in the dark, whimpering in pain.

She closed her eyes and hung on as best she could. They were pulling her backwards by the grip on her legs, while Lonzo pushed forward. There were three of them behind her, all grown men. They would break her grip any second and then...and then she would have to just take what they dished out.

But Chocolate was no longer in sight, which meant they would never catch him. The cool, calm corner of her mind was grimly satisfied.

"*What d' fuck?*" came the cry from behind her and at the same time, one of her ankles was freed.

There was a sound, a grunt of pain. It was not dissimilar to the painful wheeze Chocolate had made.

"Fucker!" one of the others cried.

Her other ankle was let loose and now she was hanging from Lonzo's neck, her full weight pulling her forearms up tight against his throat. She hung only for a second, then hands gripped her middle and plucked her away like she was a piece of lint. Her arms were ripped from around

Lonzo's throat.

She was placed gently on her feet, facing the back of the alley. Instantly, she spun to face the gang, to see what had pulled her from Lonzo.

Two of the gang were sprawled on the stony tarmac, one propping himself up with an arm while the other hand pressed against his stomach, lying very still. The third was running toward the street, his silk shirt flying out behind him like a short cape, his slightly bowed legs pumping hard.

Gutless creep. Charlee could feel her nose wrinkling in disgust. She turned her head to look farther down the alley, on the other side of the bend. She had a perfect view down both lengths.

Lonzo was facing a giant standing in the middle of the alley. The giant had his back to Charlee. She didn't know if he was really a giant, but he seemed *huge*. He stood a foot higher than Lonzo and from behind, his shoulders were really big, too. He seemed to glow in a dull way, but she didn't stop to wonder why, for Lonzo was staring at the man, his lips curling back like Chocolate's had done when he thought he was in danger. He was reaching under his shirt. Under and behind.

"He's got a gun!" Charlee warned the glowing man, for she had felt the shape of the pistol tucked into Lonzo's jeans when she had been hanging against him.

The man didn't back away. He didn't seem to react at all. He stood quite still. One hand was tucked into the pocket of what looked like perfectly normal trousers, as far as she could tell in the thickening dark.

Lonzo pulled out the pistol. It looked really big, too, and made Lonzo's hand look small. But his fingers curled around the handle with familiarity, the long forefinger resting against the trigger. He didn't point the gun at the man. He held it pointing up into the air, not quite threatening.

"Really *not* a good idea," the man said.

Lonzo just grinned.

"I heard what you did to the dog," the man said, not sounding even a little bit afraid of Lonzo or his gun. "You don't get to walk away unpunished for that, but if you put the gun down, then you *will* walk away."

"I'm walkin', man," Lonzo said, hiking the gun up an inch to draw attention to it. "You can't stop me."

"But if you don't put the gun down," the man said, speaking as if Lonzo hadn't said anything, "then that changes things. I can't guarantee you'll walk anywhere if you don't."

Lonzo snorted. "Says you."

"Think it through," the man encouraged Lonzo. He sounded like he was almost begging Lonzo to reconsider.

Lonzo brought the gun down and pointed it. Not at the man. He held it sideways, like the gangsters in the movies. Charlee's breath jammed up in her throat, because he was pointing the gun at her.

Lonzo grinned at the man. "Gotcha, asshole."

The man sighed.

Things happened very quickly after that and it was only later, when Charlee recalled the next few seconds over and over, rebuilding the fractional parts of those seconds into the right order, that she was able to put it together with any coherence. The big man pulled his hand out of his pocket with a tiny swishing sound. His hand was held in a fist. In the dark, she thought he was holding something.

Then, suddenly, he *was* holding something. It was a sword. A real, honest-to-goodness sword, with a long blade that pointed up into the night sky.

The blade didn't stay still. Lonzo spotted it and made a sound that Charlee could barely define. The snort/exhalation held some surprise, but there was happiness there, too. A primal glee over the man's attack. Lonzo swiveled the gun to point at him.

The blade moved with a high singing note, then Lonzo dropped the gun and gripped his wrist with his other hand, his eyes and mouth turning into almost perfect circles. Charlee smelled a hot, coppery scent and knew what it was without confirmation. Blood.

"End this now," the man urged Lonzo. "Walk away."

Charlee licked her lips. Lonzo wasn't the type to walk—or run, like his gang friend had. Besides, his other two Lords were still there, watching. The one that had been lying still was sitting up now. Lonzo glanced at them and Charlee knew he wouldn't leave. Not now.

She wanted to warn the man, but before she could think of what to say, or draw breath to speak, Lonzo leapt at him, a switchblade in his left hand. The blade glinted in the little light still left. It swung, reminding Charlee of the way Lonzo had swung his boot when he kicked Chocolate. It was the same fast, powerful arc.

The man spun in a tight circle. Again, much later, Charlee recalled seeing him twist around and at the same time his arm, the one that held the sword, brushed aside Lonzo's forearm, deflecting the knife as it swung around to meet the spot where the man had been standing less than a second before.

Abruptly, the man was *behind* Lonzo. His free arm wrapped around Lonzo's shoulders, encompassing them easily and holding him still. The tip of the long sword slid up under Lonzo's chin, puncturing the skin…and kept going, sliding easily like a knife through soft butter.

Lonzo jerked, his whole body stiffening. Then he relaxed in the man's grip, making a soft sighing sound.

"Holy Mary, mother of god…" one of Lonzo's friends whispered. "He scragged him. The fucking dude just scragged Lonzo."

Charlee could feel her heart trying to ram its way past her ribs. The *ease* with which he had moved was fascinating in a black, bad way.

The man was facing the remaining pair of Lords over Lonzo's still shoulder. "I gave him every chance to end it before this moment."

The silent one of the pair glanced at the other.

"If you speak of this to anyone, I will find out. Then I will find you," the man added. "Do you doubt that?"

The first shook his head. The second spat on the tarmac.

The man jerked his sword out of Lonzo's skull. It made a wet, sucking sound, and Charlee clapped her hand over her mouth, holding in any noise she might make. Lonzo crumpled to the ground at the man's feet, his face scraping across the pebbles and dirt.

"Take him and do what you do with those you deal with. I don't want his body surfacing later for the police to examine. I will be upset if that happens. Do you understand?"

The first of them, the talker, crept forward on his hands and knees and grabbed Lonzo. The second stirred and helped him pick Lonzo up. They started backing down the alley toward the street, Lonzo hanging limp and crumpled between them.

"The *other* way," the man directed. "Away from public eyes."

They hesitated, looking at him fearfully. Charlee knew they didn't want to get too close to him and he stood in the middle of the narrow alley, blocking their way.

"Move it," he growled at them and stepped aside, giving them room to pass.

They shuffled past him awkwardly, their burden slowing them down. Then they hurried along the alley until the dark swallowed them up and all Charlee could hear was their slow, dragging steps.

It left her alone with the man and his sword.

Chapter Two

Kine IPA^(key): /kaɪn/ [kʰaɪn];
Related to Middle English _kin, kyn, ken,
kun_, from Old English _cynn_ ("kind, sort,
rank, quality, family, generation,
offspring, pedigree, kin, race, people,
gender, sex, propriety, etiquette"), from
Proto-Germanic *_kunja_ ("race,
generation, descent")…
from _Darwin's Dictionary_, 2017 Edition.

Asher put his sword away, barely thinking about the quick movements that reduced it and slid it into his pocket. They were moves he had practiced over and over, tearing good garments and slicing his hip and fingers open, until he had reached this automatic process. He was so good and so fast at it now that most humans weren't able to follow what he had done.

The young girl was standing very still, staring at him with enormous dark eyes, in a pale, thin face. It looked like her hair might be flaming red in daylight. It spilled over her shoulders in a wavy, tangled mess. She looked ready to bolt at the merest hint of danger.

Asher knew why she hadn't already faded away like any normal New Yorker would have as soon as they could get free of the trouble they were in. So he held out both his hands to show her they were empty and addressed the issue head on. "Where did the dog go?" he asked her gently. "Do you know where he lives?"

She blinked and her throat worked as she swallowed. "You…k-killed him!"

"I had no choice." Asher glanced at the paling fence that separated the alley from the houses behind it. In the dark, he could see the silhouette of a crow sitting silently, watching them. As he looked, another fluttered down and settled next to the first, folding its wings with a snap.

The birds told him he was running out of time. "We need to hurry," Asher told the girl. "Quickly, now. Where will the dog be? We need to make sure he's okay." He jogged her memory with a deliberate prod. "What did the…" Then he remembered the name the others had used. "What did Lonzo do to the dog?"

The girl flinched. She blinked again and this time her gaze focused upon him. He had caught her attention. Good.

"What did he do?" he coaxed. He kept his voice low, but didn't know why. Little girls, even boys...he had no experience with children at all. But she was frozen like a cornered animal, rigid with fear. Perhaps that was why he was using gentle, soothing tones. He'd had plenty of practice dealing with frightened creatures of all types. Torger had been a vicious stray once, too.

The girl's eyes gradually lost their fear as she looked at him. "He kicked Chocolate," she said. "He *kicked* him!" Her indignation rose, squaring her shoulders and firing up her temper.

Asher clamped down on the fury that touched him. *I should have bled him out slowly, instead.* But he didn't say it. The girl was calming down, but saying that aloud would remind her of her fear and ruin the shallow peace he had built. Instead he said, very gently, "Well, he can't do that again. Not to any dog, or anyone."

Her eyes widened again. This time, it was surprise. Then her head tilted as she studied him openly and frankly. "No, he can't, can he?" He could see she was exploring the idea of raw justice and consequences in this new light, but he didn't have time to let her deal with it. The birds were gathering thickly along the fence now, but she was too preoccupied to notice them.

"Where would...Chocolate be?" he urged her, recalling the name she had used. "We need to find him and maybe take him to an animal shelter, if he needs help."

She looked around. "This is where he lives," she said simply, with a shrug.

"Call him. If he lives here and you're his friend, he'll come when you call."

"But he doesn't know it's his name. It's just what I call him."

"Dogs are very clever," he assured her. "He'll know your voice. Call him."

She looked around in the dark. "Chocolate!" she called softly. "Here, boy!" She didn't raise her voice. Her instincts, which had been sharpened by the last few minutes, were making her cautious. "Here, Chocolate!"

There was a soft whine from farther down the alley. The dog shifted. Asher could barely see his shadow, tucked in among the deeper dark. "There." He pointed.

The girl crouched, making herself smaller and less threatening, although there was very little of her to start with. She held out her hand and coaxed the dog with soft calls. Asher stepped away from her, giving the dog the room he wanted.

The dog limped over to the girl and thrust his nose into her hand. He licked the palm, whining softly. Asher could hear the pain.

He moved slowly closer until the dog took notice of him, then held out his hand for him to sniff. The dog's nose wrinkled as he sampled Asher's smell. Then he licked his finger. His tail shifted slowly from side to side. Asher had been approved.

He ran a hand over the dog's back, getting him used to his touch, then very gently along his sides. Wiry hair slid under his fingers, stiff with dirt and neglect, almost bald in places. He leaned closer to examine him and gave a soft laugh. "Chocolate is a girl," he told the human girl soothing the dog.

"He is? She is?" The girl pressed her lips together. "I don't know how to tell boy dogs and girl dogs apart. Is she gonna be okay?"

The dog had flinched when he had run his hands over her flank, just behind her front leg, but she hadn't recoiled or made any sound in reaction. "I think she is okay," Asher decided. "No broken bones."

"You sure?" the girl insisted.

He'd seen hundreds of broken bones in men, horses, dogs and all manner of creatures. War was destructive for more than the combatants. "I'm sure," he told the girl, putting all the confidence he could muster into his voice.

The birds on the fence shifted in unison, like they did when they were swarming. The dog turned her head, spotting them. A low warning growl issued.

Asher patted her head and stood up. "I'm going to see you home," he told the girl. "Did you sneak out tonight?" It was an educated guess. A girl this young wouldn't normally be allowed to roam the streets by herself after dark. But anything was possible. She had the thinness and unkempt look he associated with the children of broken families. Or with no families and no one to give a damn about them.

The girl hunched in on herself. "Are you gonna tell on me?"

"No, but I am going to make sure you get home safely." He glanced at the birds, silent witnesses watching without movement. The pressure to move, to get away from ground zero, increased. "Come on," he said, urging her to move back down the alley by taking a few steps toward the street.

She stayed still. "What about Chocolate? They're gonna come back, you know. They'll come back and they'll find her and they'll be angry about what happened."

Asher agreed with her. "Bring the dog," he said shortly. "We'll find somewhere for her to stay."

* * * * *

Once they were out on the street and had merged with the few pedestrians, Asher relaxed. Chocolate trotted along beside the girl as if she had always belonged there.

The girl looked up at Asher. "What do I call you?"

She hadn't asked for his name, as most humans would. Instead, she had asked what she should use as a name for him. Interesting. "You can call me Asher."

"Like a tenement fire?"

"Like a tree," Asher said truthfully.

She wrinkled her nose, trying to fit his name into what she knew about trees. "Ash tree?" she asked doubtfully.

"Yes."

"They called you a tree?"

"Better than being named after a cow shed."

She giggled quietly and Chocolate gave a little skip next to her, her tongue lolling. "A cow shed?"

"Do you know anyone called Byron?"

"Is that what Byron means? A cow shed?" She grinned. "That explains why Byron at school is always in a bad mood. Do names always mean something?"

"Nearly always."

"Even mine?"

"What is yours?"

"Charlotte. But everyone calls me Charlee."

"They call you Charlee because they care."

She snorted doubtfully. "You don't know my folks."

"If they didn't care, they wouldn't call you anything at all. Strangers call you Charlotte, right?"

"When they know that's my name."

"People who think they're friends, that they have the privilege because they're friends, they're the ones who call you Charlee. So that's the meaning of your name for them. That you're a friend."

"Friend?" She sounded incredulous.

"It's not a direct translation, like my name. But that's the baggage that goes with your name."

She thought about it for a few steps, her lips pursed doubtfully.

The farther they walked from the alley, the better he felt. But there was still one big problem he had to deal with. Pulling her and Chocolate away from the battlefield created a problem. She had seen him fighting, although on his personal Richter scale of battles, this confrontation barely registered. But she had seen the sword. What to do?

They had turned the corner into 162nd and were heading for Cauldwell, when Charlee gave him the hint he needed.

"My house is just up there." She pointed, suddenly shy. No, not shy. Cautious.

He wondered why she was wary now, when she had been almost free-spirited once they had left the alley. His dispatch of the gang leader, Lonzo, didn't seem to have made any negative impact on her at all. He recalled her reaction to his suggestion that karma had caught up with the boy. Did the idea of Lonzo getting his just desserts make it alright in her eyes? Were all kids that resilient? He didn't know.

"I have to go in the back way," she added.

Ahh... He mentally sighed. Now he understood. She had crept out secretly earlier in the night. Now she needed to sneak back in and was hoping he would cooperate. Any other adult would insist on talking to her parents or guardians, if she had them. This was a relatively peaceful neighborhood. The chances were good she had someone who was technically watching out for her, even if they were actually asleep at the switch.

Or perhaps she was too sneaky for them.

"Do you steal out of your house a lot?" he asked.

She bit her lip, her eyes big, as she assessed him, trying to determine where he was taking the conversation and therefore what the best answer would be to get him to work with her.

Asher slowed, giving himself time to resolve this before they reached the house she had pointed out. "If you tell the truth, I'll tell the truth," he told her. "Deal?"

She turned to face him, her back to the row of wrought iron and wooden fencing lining the footpath. The houses were square and small. Despite their tiny proportions, they were still jammed up against each other. Many of them had common walls. It was New York's version of the terrace housing the Brits put up with. From one of them, he couldn't tell which, Blondie was urging everyone to call her, at the top of her lungs. It made him wince. If he was going to listen to music at that volume, he'd much rather listen to *The Wall*, which Pink Floyd had just released.

Chocolate sat down next to Charlee, her shoulder brushing Charlee's calf, as if it was the natural place to be. Charlee shrugged and answered his question. "I don't go out very often. Mostly. But I found Chocolate, y'see." It sounded like the truth. She was keeping her side of the deal.

"I guess you've learned how dangerous it is, sneaking out."

"Could've been really bad," she agreed. "But it wasn't, coz of you."

It brought them very neatly to his dilemma. "You watched it all," he said, easing into it.

She licked her lips. He could almost feel her caution rising. But she honored their agreement. "Yeah," she said, her voice low.

"You saw…" He took a breath. This was harder than he thought it might be. *Laun* defined his life and shaped the secrecy that was part of it. She had seen his sword and him using it. Normally a situation like that had only one outcome. Why had he even pulled her out of the alley? He should have left her there and waited for them to come as they always did. They would have dealt with Charlee as they did any human who learned of them.

"You mean I saw your sword," Charlee finished for him. "The magic one." She said it matter-of-factly, like an adult would say "your camcorder, the black one."

Asher stared at her. She had accepted the sword's disappearance. Just like that. No questions. No disbelief or vain attempt to rationalize away what she had seen.

He drew in a deep breath. Her absolute acceptance made this much easier for him to arrange the compromise that would save both their hides, if he could just get past his own reluctance to speak the words aloud. In that respect, Charlee was way ahead of him.

"The magic sword," he made himself say, agreeing with her. His voice dropped as he said it, and he fought the need to look around and see who might be eavesdropping on their conversation. He felt foolish, using the childish words she had used. *Just say it, you idiot*, he raged at himself. They had a deal. Truth for truth. "You seeing my sword puts you in a different sort of trouble, Charlee. You and me, both."

She didn't look worried, or scared. She considered him for a moment. "You had to save Chocolate," she pointed out. "The gang didn't give you a choice."

It wasn't what he had expected her to say. He wasn't sure what he had thought she might respond with, but this adult reasoning was a surprise. Her reaction stepped right over the questions he presumed she would have. *Who says you have to keep it secret? What sort of trouble am I in?* Even a protest over how unfair it was would have been more in line with what he knew of kids and their fierce focus on their own concerns.

"They won't see it that way. But I can't talk about that," he added. "Just like you can't talk about this. Any of it." He looked her in the eye, confident that she would understand this part of it. "Just like you don't want me to talk about you being out of the house without your folks knowing."

Charlee stood still, thinking it through. She was a slim, straight girl with long legs. The nimbus of coppery red hair looked almost kinky. Her skin was very pale, as if her hair had stolen all the life and color from it. Her head came up to just under his shoulder. He judged she was around ten or so, but figured he was probably wrong. What did he know of kids?

Her dark brown eyes refocused on him. "Another deal?" she asked, then kicked up her leg behind her and slapped at a mosquito on her ankle. Chocolate stirred and her tongue lolled.

Asher felt relief. She had understood. "Another deal," he confirmed. "But this is a grown-up deal, Charlee. You can't even tell your best friend at school. No one. Not ever."

She just stared at him, taking it in.

Asher wasn't satisfied. "What I did to that kid…"

"He wasn't a kid. He was a gangster," she said instantly.

"What I did," Asher insisted, for she *had* to understand the gravity of this, "it was bad."

"You saved Chocolate."

"But if the people you know, your friends and family, if they had seen what I did, they would be shocked and angry at me." It was a wild over-simplification of what they would really do, but it would make the point.

"You killed him," Charlee said, using frank truth once more. She shrugged. "He kicked Chocolate."

He blew out his breath. "What do they do to people who kill other people, Charlee? I know you know this."

Her eyes seemed to be enormous in her face as she came up with the answer. She spoke slowly. "They go to prison. Sometimes…worse." She pressed her lips together. Then, "But…Chocolate," she added helplessly and bent to stroke the dog's soft fur between her ears. Chocolate panted happily, shifting on the warm concrete.

"That's what the people you know would do," Asher said. "But the people I know, Charlee, they would do much more than that."

Her eyes seemed to grow even larger. "Are you in a gang?" she whispered. In her small world, people who did such unspeakable things, people who could do more than execute criminals, were in gangs.

"I can't tell you any more," Asher replied. "It would make things even worse for you. I just need to know that you understand the deal and why you must keep it."

"Tell no one. Forever an' ever. I got it."

Asher let out his breath slowly, controlling his reaction of deep relief. "So let's find somewhere for Chocolate to stay, then you need to climb back in your window."

They turned and walked slowly along the path, discussing possible homes for Chocolate and the last of his worry over the incident drained away. She was a child, but he trusted her to keep her word.

It never occurred to him that he might be the one to break the deal.

* * * * *

Asher watched Charlee shimmy up the external plumbing at the back of her house and disappear through her bedroom window, before heading back to Cauldwell Avenue, where he could hail a cab. There was no point in going home now. Because of the battle, they would be expecting him at the hall.

The cab dropped him off on Pearl twenty minutes later. For the last thirty-two years, the way to the hall had been from Pearl, although the entrance had been relocated a dozen times over the last century or so, using one of the three sides of the building with street access. They had tried using the alley between the building and its neighbor as an entry point, but that had lasted for only five short years. It was easier to blend in with the locals using a street entrance.

He bypassed the elevator and took the stairs. It had been too long since he'd been to the gym. He needed the exercise.

The stairs stopped two floors short of the top of the building, although there was nothing that would tell a human visitor—or an official inspector—that there were two more floors above.

Asher punched in the code. The buttons were unmarked. Anyone with legitimate business on this floor had to remember the pattern and hit the right ones. He pushed his way out into the foyer beyond. The guard of the day looked up briefly as the fire door opened, saw him, and returned his gaze to the narrow section of the foyer where the elevators emerged. No one could select the elevator button for this floor without a security code, just like the fire exit door, but tailgaters were always possible.

When Asher passed the guard, he murmured his name in acknowledgment and got a nod in return. The guards were not encouraged to talk while they were on shift, although if a human did manage to get past the security codes and wandered into the foyer, the guard would turn into a congenial and chatty stranger willing to help them find how to get to where they needed to go (*"no, not on this floor, ma'am. I'm pretty sure the dentist surgery is on the third"*) and would shepherd them back into the elevator, all without the human even suspecting they were being guided away from exploring.

The foyer was empty of anyone but the guard, who sprawled on an old leather armchair, ostensibly reading a magazine.

Apart from the narrower section of the foyer where the elevators disgorged passengers, the passage was really a big, almost square, room. The green linoleum was a sea of dark smoothness. The well-waxed and cared-for surface always gleamed. During daylight hours the light came through the high arched windows at the end of the foyer opposite the elevators, to fall on the linoleum. At night, the floor reflected the radiance from three big chandeliers overhead. They were heavy wrought iron creations and yellow cylindrical shades clustered thickly on the ends of their metal branches.

The fire escape door was at the same end as the arched window, tucked into the corner. There were no other entries or exits from the foyer, except one. Opposite the row of leather club chairs ranked against the wall, where the guard was currently sitting, were the doors to the hall.

They were big commercial five-panel doors. They had started out as oiled teak but now they were dark with age and the impact of many hands pushing against them. The bottoms were chipped and scratched by shoes and boots. They were utterly ordinary and modern doors, designed to blend in with the portions of the building that humans were allowed to see. The handles were industrial grey steel, curving in minimalistic arches. The doors gave no hint of what lay behind their bland facade.

Nevertheless, Asher's spirits never failed to lift when he saw them. Once he stepped through them he could become himself.

He thrust out his hand and pushed against the right-hand door of the big pair, swinging it open.

Scents peculiar to the hall washed over him in a swirl caused by the movement of the door. They brought to mind quick flashes of impressions and sensations: the cool touch of mead in his mouth, and the dusky smell of hide stretched over frames. The sound of laughter and music from the many, many feasts he had attended. The raw touch of cold air from the open fire vent.

He didn't have to recall the yellow light that infused the air, for it bathed the wide steps in front of him now, flickering with a warm glow. He looked up. The walls, which were made of rough-cut timbers that had been worn to smoothness over the years, held a pair each of flaming sconces. Their flames barely moved in the still room. They ran on gas, but when the hall had first been built, the flames had fed on oil-soaked rags, just like the lamps in the First Hall.

Asher could remember any number of occasions when the steps in front of him had been choked with people climbing slowly up to the main level. There were other times when friends had lingered on the steps, pulled to one side to talk earnestly or lightly. Many of his memories included friends holding horns and cups, their faces flushed by the mead.

There was no one lingering on the steps tonight but at the top, where the stairs gave way to the hall itself, two more guards stood facing the other end, their backs to the stairs. Asher had never made the mistake of thinking the guards had failed to notice his arrival, despite their lack of reaction.

He climbed the stairs quickly and stood at the top. One of the guards turned his head just enough to see him and confirm his identity. Asher nodded at him and murmured his name. Unlike the guard out in the foyer, these guards were wearing traditional clothing and leather armor, helmets and shields. Their spears stood taller than them.

Asher looked around, checking to see who was in the hall. The room stretched out before him. It was over one hundred feet from where he stood to the other end where the dais was located. The tall, carved chair sitting on the dais was empty. The walls soared for twenty feet, pushing through the upper floor of the building to the roof.

When they had first designed the hall, just over a hundred years ago, they had reached back to their common roots for inspiration. Asher suspected that most of them had wanted a reminder of older, more human times, even though such an idea had not been mentioned. No one spoke of the Descent. They had used words like "traditional" instead, and so the hall had been built.

The long walls of the elongated space were curved so that they bowed out in the middle. They were lined with the same once-rough wood palings that lined the stairs. Every twelve feet or so along their length, sconces flickered. Three tiers butted up against each long wall. The first was knee-high, a comfortable sitting height. The second was waist-high and the third breast-high. Each tier was wide enough for a table and benches, and the top tier was dotted with both. The tables on the top tier were never removed. For a feast, more tables would be added to the lower tiers.

Marching along the front of both lower tiers, massive pillars that had once been trees rose to the roof. Where each pillar touched the roof, heavy beams radiated out around them, making starred patterns of support.

The hall was so wide that despite the tiers on either side, there was still a good thirty feet of clear space in the center, at the widest point of the room. In that respect, the hall differed from the narrow *langhaus* of his childhood.

There were several women working in the hall, all of them Amica. One was running a motorized cleaner over the floor. Two more were sweeping tiers and straightening up the tables and benches. He recognized them, although he could not name but one of them. The one whose name he knew was tending the firepit and he strode down the hall toward her. Erica lifted her head as his footsteps echoed up from the tiles, and gave him a small smile of acknowledgment.

The tiles were a concession to modern living. If they had maintained the rigid standards dictated by *tradition*, the floor would be dirt and the fire would be fueled by wood. But in the middle of New York, endless supplies of firewood would draw attention, as would sandy footsteps leading out of the building.

Erica straightened up from her crouch over the massive firepit as Asher drew near. She was wearing yoga pants and a T-shirt with the sleeves rolled up to her shoulders. Her hair was pinned up on top of her head. Her hands and the lower half of her forearms were covered in black grime.

The firepit sat in the center of the room. It was the length of one of the tables and just as wide. The edges of the pit were protected by flat stones, which thrust jagged teeth up to calf height. The floor of the pit was also stone, although this had been mortared and was flat and featureless.

What looked like a bonfire's worth of logs and stumps were scattered artfully across the pit, hiding the gas burners strung throughout the fake logs. The fire was never extinguished and wouldn't be for as long as the hall was able to welcome the Kine. But right now, two of the sets of gas burners had been turned off, leaving the one on the far end still flickering over the logs. It allowed Erica to clean the logs and the burners that were unlit.

She carefully brushed stray hair out of her eyes with the back of her wrist, but still left a smear behind. Her smile was warm. Friendly. "Stallari," she said, using his official title, which was proper for within the hall.

"I'm looking for the earl. Is he in his quarters?"

"I believe he is waiting for you there."

Asher held in his reaction. Just for the slightest moment, for the merest heartbeat, he felt a mild irritation. The constant sense of community and the peculiar sensitivity that the Kine had for the wellbeing of all in their ranks meant a decrease in personal privacy and an uptick in the level of accountability each of them had to all others. Normally, that intimacy was reassuring. Tonight, it did not sit well and he knew why. *You're trying to hide something from people who can sense when you're in trouble.*

Unhappy, he made his way to the doorway just off to the side of the main dais. It punched through the tiers, into the wall behind. Normal electric light shone through from the opening, spilling onto the same formerly rough planking that made up the dais.

Wafting faintly through the door were the sounds of one of Roar's beloved operas. If he was listening to opera, he was in a bad mood.

Asher headed for the doorway. Time to face the music. Pun intended...but it didn't make him feel any better.

* * * * *

When Charlee slithered through the half-open window onto her bed, no one thrust open her bedroom door, demanding to know where she had been. Nothing had changed since she had slipped out just over sixty minutes ago. Her homework was still sitting on her bedside table. The lamp was still on. Her Janet Jackson poster still hung on the wall with one corner rolling over, casting a shadow over Janet's face.

Charlee's pink floral jeans, which she had worn today and would wear again tomorrow, were lying across the foot of her bed.

Downstairs, she could hear the sound of the TV. Southern accents. Her father was watching *Dallas*. That meant her mother was probably in the kitchen, sitting at the table with her glass in front of her, lined up next to her cigarette packet and the glass ashtray she used.

Charlee shucked off her clothes and wriggled into her nightgown, moving as silently as she could and staying away from the center of the room where the squeaky board was. As she dressed, her father started to cough. The rasping hack started off as they all did, with a few soft barking noises. Then it got hold of his throat and lungs and squeezed, and the sound changed and became something that made Charlee wince and wonder if her father wouldn't rip out the back of his throat and spit it up.

But he always got control of the cough. She waited for him to clear his throat with another noisy rasp, then silence, except for the soft sounds of Bobby Ewing complaining about something.

Nothing had changed…but everything had.

She flung back the covers—it was too warm to lie beneath them—and settled into bed with the sheet pooling around her hips and her pillow propped up between her and the head of the bed, cushioning her back. She opened her homework up and stared blindly at the equations, until the black text blurred and all she could see was fuzzy grey lines and squiggles.

Everything had changed, including her.

Magic was real. Heroes were real. She thought of all the things she had not believed until tonight. She had learned the so-called truth about Santa Claus four years ago, when Lucas had tried to explain why there had been no Christmas tree that year, or any year since, and why her gift from Santa had come wrapped in newsprint and twine, as that was all he had been able to find. Since then she had gradually worked her way through the children's pantheon, dismissing it all: fairies, pixies, witches and demons. Puff the Magic Dragon. Aslan. The tooth fairy didn't put money under pillows and steal teeth. Stepping on cracks didn't break anyone's back. Halloween was just a great way to collect more candy in two hours than she saw for the entire rest of the year.

What was true and what wasn't?

Magic was real and heroes wore suits, with their ties pulled down and the top button unfastened. Heroes came with shockingly blond hair and very blues eyes. If she had ever thought she might meet a real hero, that wasn't what she would have expected of him.

Heroes did come with special weapons, strange names and packed to the brim with secrets, which lined up with what she knew about heroes from the comics and the one time she had seen the *Superman* movie.

A gentle knock sounded and she refocused on the door, blinking her eyes.

"Charlee?" Lucas called.

"'kay!" she called back just as softly.

The door opened, letting the light from the bare bulb in the corridor fall onto the carpet, then her bed, making her blink. Lucas slipped in and shut the door. "Hey, Einie." He kept his voice down.

Lucas was five years older than her. In the unspoken way that families communicated their history, through comments and pictures, and passing reference, Charlee had pieced together an understanding that Lucas had been an unplanned child, but welcomed, nevertheless. She had been created five years later, in an attempt to 'fix things' between her parents. She wasn't entirely sure how she had been expected to fix anything, and that was probably why she had failed, for the relationship her parents had looked nothing like the marriages Charlee had read about and seen on TV. Their house was mostly silent except for, lately, her father's coughing.

Charlee adored Lucas with a pure affection that was unsullied by his big-brother attitude. She understood—and this knowledge also came to her in small fractions over time—that Lucas mostly tried to fill the gaps their parents failed to cover. But he was only fifteen, so taking care of Charlee usually meant bossing her around.

Lucas was one of the best-looking fifteen year olds she knew. He had missed out on their father's red hair. Instead, he had inherited their mother's pitch black locks, which he kept fashionably long and curling around his collar. He had grey eyes that looked colorless in the right light. They were surrounded by bristly lashes. Lucas' glance had turned more than a few of the girls at school into giggling wrecks.

But Lucas didn't seem to be interested in girls. He wasn't into boys, either, or so the school gossip network assured her.

To Charlee, Lucas always seemed to be older than he really was. He knew things that other fifteen year olds, the very few in whose company she had ever been allowed to spend any time, seemed to not even care about. The things they *did* care about Lucas didn't seem to be interested in. Girls. Music. Movies. Ditching classes. Failing courses. Drinking.

He was her big brother, different in his way from most other people Charlee knew. Just as she was different in her own way.

Lucas crouched down next to her bed, and looked up at her. The conical sea shell he wore around his neck on a thin black leather band reflected the light of her lamp in a pearlescent, pretty way. It was very white against his tanned flesh.

"You doin' okay, Einie?" he asked. Einie was short for Einstein. He only called her that when no one else was listening. That was because he meant it.

"I'm good."

"You've been awful quiet tonight."

She pressed her lips together, holding in her secret. She couldn't tell anyone. No one at all, not even Lucas.

He touched her math book. "Calculus?" he asked.

She rolled her eyes. "I'm only ten," she pointed out. "It's algebra."

"You're a real smart ten. I didn't get to algebra until I was in junior high. Is this something Mr. Baxter is teaching you?"

Mr. Baxter was their neighbor. He lived two doors down, on the south side of the house. If anyone should be called smart, it was him. He worked at the New York library, the big one by Central Park, with the lions. He had been teaching Charlee extra courses on top of her school curriculum for the last two years, something that both Lucas and Charlee had failed to mention to their parents.

"He gave me the book to read, if I wanted to."

"Pretty big book," Lucas observed.

"It's interesting."

He rolled his eyes and stood up. His Pink Floyd T-shirt was snug over his shoulders and chest and hung loose around his waist. Lately, she had started to notice in a distant way that his body was more like a grown man's, and less and less like the tall, skinny big brother she was used to. She had noticed and pushed the knowledge aside. The idea of Lucas changing (*and not loving me anymore*) was uncomfortable.

"Amanda Gooseman said I was to say 'hi' to you," Charlee said, reaching for something, anything, to shift her thoughts.

Lucas frowned. "Gooseman?"

"The girl with the blonde hair down to her butt."

"Pigtails, right? I remember her."

"She doesn't wear pigtails anymore," Charlee assured him. "She's going to junior high next year. You'll see her then."

"Maybe."

Charlee grinned. "She'll make sure you do."

Lucas grinned back and for a moment he was just her skinny brother again, sharing a moment where they both understood each other perfectly. "Don't stay up late," he told her as he turned toward the door. "You've got school tomorrow."

"I was just gonna turn the light off."

"Going to," he corrected and opened the door.

"Yeah, that, too."

He rolled his eyes at her as he shut the door behind him.

Charlee closed the unread math book and put it back on the stand, then turned out the light and settled down for sleep. She stared up at the ceiling, where light from the first floor of the neighbors directly behind them, the Clancy family, was dappled by the leaves of the big maple that grew against the fence between them. The shadows of the tri-pointed leaves moved gently.

And perhaps they're not shadows, but the souls of tree elves escaping for a night's adventure.

What was real? What wasn't?

He'd saved Chocolate. She remembered that and smiled into her pillow. Whatever hero he ended up being didn't matter, after what he'd already done.

Everything was changing. Even Lucas.

Tomorrow, she would do what she could to figure out what else besides magic was real after all.

Chapter Three

Gudherleifr
Compilation of Old Norse "gud" – *god*,
"herr" – *army*, "Leifr" – *descendent*.
Customarily reduced to Herleifr.
From *Darwin's Dictionary*, 2017 Edition

Asher pushed the door to Roar's apartment open without knocking. The music was making the door vibrate against its hinges. A knock wouldn't be heard.

He winced as the door opened and the music jumped in volume. It was almost a physical assault.

Brighter light spilled out into the corridor and he stepped in and shut the door. No need to disturb anyone else still in the hall.

Roar had been using the earl's apartment since the hall and the offices were built in late Victorian times. The apartment took up most of the south side of the top floor. It had been laid out in an open studio style, long before studios had become chic. The windows along the south wall were monstrous double-hung openings that even in winter spilled sunlight onto the polished floorboards, warming them.

Roar had been living alone for a long time, but he had never lost the domesticity that Meggy had imparted. The apartment was clean and tidy. At the far end, Japanese silk screens hid the bed and the ensuite.

The middle section of the rectangular apartment was the kitchen area. A big dining table sat between the kitchen counter and the windows, but it was used more for informal meetings than eating. Roar did most of his eating sitting on the sofa, a modern habit he had picked up with ease.

The big leather sofa and the reclining armchair were at this end, where Asher stood just inside the door. They faced the windows, for Roar had never bought himself a television. The windows were not all they faced. The big floor speakers that were attached to the powerful sound system were placed so that anyone sitting in the middle of the sofa was positioned to hear the music issuing from the speakers in ideal ratios.

Music was what Roar obsessed about instead of watching television like a normal human. The hall and offices took up the rest of the two floors the Kine had commandeered, so his was the only residential apartment in the building. He could pump up the volume with impunity and the only possible neighbors he could offend were those across the street in the buildings opposite. As Roar kept the windows closed most of the time, even that danger was minimal.

Roar wasn't sitting on the sofa. Instead, he was standing behind the kitchen counter, adding cream to a coffee mug. There was only one mug, so it had to be for the other person in the room.

Eira was propped on one of the broad windowsills, holding the sleeve of the record currently playing. She had been reading it, but now she was leaning back against the glass, simply listening.

As Regin, Eira resided in the longhouse under Tryvannshøyden, in Oslo, but she was a frequent visitor to this hall. She was tall, for a woman, and had the sable black hair and olive skin that characterized those from the Appenine peninsula, for she had been born a Roman when Roman citizens and the armies that protected them were the most feared and respected in the known world.

Eira had been a part of those armies, but she was Regin now. Her long legs were stretched out, her ankles crossed, one boot heel digging into the rug under the table, keeping her propped up. She was wearing close-fitting trousers that were tucked into the boots, and a jacket that looked vaguely military in style and cut. She wasn't just listening to the music. She was watching Roar with her dark eyes.

Asher moved farther into the room, not just to move out of the aim of the speakers, but also to draw their attention with movement, as calling out would be useless against the soprano currently wailing about her lost love in strained German.

Both of them looked around, seeing him, as he headed toward them. A furrow appeared between Roar's brows. He strode past Asher and lifted the lid on the turntable, then picked up the arm and put it back on the bracket.

The cessation of the thundering orchestra was almost a relief. Asher let out a long, slow breath. "Mozart?" he guessed, for the very little he knew about opera he had picked up unwillingly from Roar. Mozart was a German-speaking composer.

"Wagner," Roar answered. His full mouth lifted in a grimace that held some amusement. "*Götterdämmerung.*"

Even Eira smiled at the irony. *Götterdämmerung* was the German equivalent of Ragnarok.

Roar moved back to the kitchen, picked up the coffee cup and held it out to Eira. "Would you mind very much giving me a few minutes alone with Asher?"

She took the cup, her eyes narrowing as she glanced at Asher. She would have felt the crisis just like any one of them, but if it was discussed in front of her it became an official matter. "Should I worry?" she asked Asher.

He shook his head. "Not in the slightest."

She gave him small smile, then sent a much warmer smile toward Roar. "I want to soak up some warm air while I'm here, anyway. It's still cold in Norway."

"You always say it's cold," Asher replied.

"That's because it always is."

"Roman," Roar said in a way that made it sound like an epithet, but he was smiling.

"Northman," she shot back in the same tone. She gave Asher another neutral smile. "Excuse me," she murmured as she headed for the apartment door, still carrying her coffee cup.

Roar waited until the door was closed once more, then cocked his head at Asher. "What happened?"

"Nothing," Asher said. "It was a misunderstanding."

"A misunderstanding," Roar repeated flatly. "It didn't feel like a simple misunderstanding."

"It was a few gang members, looking for trouble. I sorted it out."

Roar crossed his arms. His square jaw flexed. "When they got there, there was nothing to recover. Why didn't you stay there?"

Caution flooded him. Asher crossed his arms, unconsciously copying Roar. "What the fuck is this third degree about?" he demanded, letting his voice rise. "I said I dealt with it. It's done. Over. No consequences. That's why they found nothing."

Roar didn't move. His blue eyes narrowed. As Asher's older brother, he had the same eyes, but his hair was golden, rather than white blond.

"What is it you're not telling me?" Asher added. "You weren't this concerned when I had that run-in with the gang last year."

Roar looked surprised. "It was the same gang? Did they come looking for you?"

"No. I told you. It was pure coincidence. Nothing to worry about."

"But you drew your sword," Roar said flatly.

Asher's heart squeezed. "No, I didn't," he lied.

"Blood was spilled," Roar countered. He—all of them—would have sensed that the battle had escalated to blood-letting.

"The punk had a knife," Asher replied. He shrugged. "He regretted drawing it."

Roar grinned. The expression seemed to be pulled from him unwillingly. "I'm sure he did," he said. His arms dropped. "Why the fuck you live in that god forsaken armpit beats the hell out of me."

"So you've said. More than once." Asher relaxed. A little. "I like the

Bronx." There was more of a family and suburb feel to the Bronx that didn't exist in lower Manhattan. "I like the people."

"And the gangster accents." Roar turned back to the kitchen. His movement signaled that the cross-examination was over. He had been satisfied. He pulled two glasses out of the overhead cupboard and a bottle of Johnny Walker from another and cracked the seal. "You could have called and let us know there was nothing to worry about," he pointed out.

"You complain I don't visit enough and now when I do, you complain I don't call instead." He took the glass Roar offered him. He wasn't a scotch drinker, but if Roar was offering he'd take it.

"You know what I meant," Roar replied, swirling the half-inch of liquid in his own glass. "Battles unsettle everyone."

"It wasn't a battle."

"It still provokes the same concern. Gods' teeth, Asher! After so long, I still have to explain this to you?"

So, he wasn't going to be allowed off the hook after all. But Asher knew that now, Roar was talking to him as his older brother. He'd put aside the earl trappings when he'd turned to pour the drinks.

Uncomfortable about the evasions and lies he was generating, Asher sought to change the subject. "So...Eira stopped by. Again."

Roar's jaw flexed. Then he tossed back the scotch in one large gulp and hissed at the back-flavor. "It's customary to check in with the big hall. They are troubled by the same crises we are." His expression told Asher he wasn't clear of this yet.

"They have runners for that, same as we do. The Regin running errands..." He raised his brow.

Roar looked away. "She gets restless," he said flatly.

"Don't we all?" Asher murmured and swallowed half of the scotch. It bit the back of his throat with a peaty tang that he breathed out.

Eira had been a soldier and mercenary, one of the highest paid warriors in the history of Rome. She had won impossible victories for employers across Europe and been described as unstoppable, until she had met her match in battle late in the first century. Even then, Rome had been crumbling and her fame had been lost among the rubble and chaos the barbarian conquerors had left behind.

As a seasoned warrior, it was reasonable that Eira would miss the feel of her sword.

Asher still did not properly understand why she had first sought the company of the man who had defeated her. Why she continued to do so was silently understood by everyone, except perhaps Roar himself. The collective agreement of silence on the matter meant Asher could not directly ask him.

He drained the rest of the scotch and put the glass back on the counter. "Thanks," he told his brother.

"Another?"

Asher shook his head. "I must stop in at the restaurant. Ylva will be worried."

Roar's brows came together, as they always did whenever Asher spoke Ylva's name. It was a milder version of the same reaction any of the Kine had when her name was spoken—a mild to moderate irritation at being reminded of that bleak moment in their history.

Roar poured himself another healthy shot and put the bottle back in the cupboard. "Business is well?" he asked.

"Well enough," Asher replied. He turned his wrist and looked at his watch. "The evening rush will be over by the time I get there, so...."

"You've been missed at council," Roar said.

Tired irritation pricked at Asher. *Not this again*, a voice whispered in his mind. "I have to go," he said firmly.

"You always do have to go." Roar swirled the scotch again. "Will you be here for the next one?"

"You know what my life is like. I'll see."

"Your human life is not the real priority."

"My *human* life? You're talking about the only life I have. *My* life!"

"You have a responsibility toward the Kine—" Roar began.

Asher held up his hand. "Don't start on this. Please."

"You continue to put us in jeopardy. There is always trouble. It surrounds you like metal filings around a magnet. We're always cleaning up your messes."

"Not tonight," Asher said with some satisfaction, although the implied lie—and all he had not said about tonight—prodded at his conscience. "If you didn't insist on maintaining *laun* as tightly as you did...if we came out, then tonight would not have happened. They would have known who I was and left me alone."

He didn't know for sure if tonight would have happened even if humans knew of them, but this was an old, even geriatric, subject and he could feel himself sliding into the worn channels of argument and counter-argument like a ball dropping into a chute. There was nowhere to go from here but down the familiar slope.

"*Laun* preserves us," Roar countered. He was breathing hard. This was an old disagreement for him, too. Asher even knew what he was about to say...and not say. "If humans knew about us," Roar added, "they would not be kind. They wouldn't understand." Asher knew he was thinking about Meggy, but he would never speak her name aloud.

That was eight hundred years ago! Asher wanted to cry. But the same prohibition that stopped Roar from speaking of it halted Asher, too. It was all the fault of *laun*. Secrets, silence, collaborative hiding...it kept most of their lives buried. The habits of secrecy made not talking about matters that *should* be spoken of easier.

But even that argument was old. Roar never let the sense of it register. Denial was a fine, fine tool of statecraft, Asher thought bitterly. He drew in a slow, hard breath, trying to let his anger dissipate. "I'm going," he said shortly.

"Yes," Roar agreed flatly.

As always, Asher stalked from the hall with his temper stirred and all the old frustrations churning, making themselves felt anew.

He needed a drink. Something other than scotch. He needed to forget, but forgetting was not a human luxury the Kine enjoyed.

* * * * *

Asher remembered what he had forgotten as soon as he walked into the restaurant.

Jessica was sitting at the bar, a highball glass containing one of her disgusting whiskey sours in front of her. The pretty brunette was bowed over the padded front of the bar like she had been there for a while.

Ylva was in the dining section, leaning over a table of regulars that Asher vaguely recognized. She straightened up when she saw him and her gaze flickered toward Jessica. She didn't smile until she looked down at the diners once more.

Tiredness gripped him. Everyone wanted a piece of him tonight. Everyone was pissed at him. Jessica wasn't good at holding back her feelings, so this was going to be a round and a half of acrimony, but in her case, he was guilty as charged.

He took a breath, bracing himself, and crossed to the bar and slid onto the stool next to her. "Jess, I'm sorry."

She straightened up with a snap. "I've been here over two freaking hours! Where were you?"

"Did you eat? Can I get you something?" he asked, lifting his hand to catch Bernie's gaze and beckon him over.

"No, I don't want anything to eat, you fucking moron!" Contrary to the power of her words, she kept her voice low. Intense. It had been that low register in her purring words that had first caught his attention. But that attraction had waned, possibly long ago. Jessica, like most of his life, had evolved into a habit. Ingrained and overlooked...until now.

"I'll call a cab for you," he said, the tiredness spreading through his shoulders and the back of his neck, making them ache.

Jessica's eyes widened. "You're getting rid of me."

TRACY COOPER-POSEY

"It's late," he pointed out. "You've got work in the morning."

"It's past nine. I *waited* for you." All the sultriness in her voice had fled.

"Jess, I'm tired, and this is not the place for this discussion." Ylva had warned him more than once about conducting his personal affairs in front of customers.

"When, then?" she demanded. "You're always here, or somewhere where I can't find you. You're never at the bank and you told me that was your real job. And you're never home!"

"I have a complicated life."

She laughed, and there was bitterness in it. "What's the complication's name?"

It's nothing like what you think. The words were there, tempting him to speak them aloud. But that would push the discussion (*argument*) onto dangerous ground.

He thought of the beginning of his evening. The child with the dark eyes and direct way of speaking about...things. *Truth for truth.* That had been the deal.

"Charlee," Asher said flatly, staring Jessica in the eye. "Her name is Charlee."

Jessica grew still. She had been reaching for her purse where it sat on the bar next to her elbow, but even that movement halted. She turned her head to look at Asher once more. Her eyes were wide.

Wounded.

"But I *love* you," she whispered.

Asher's gut tightened. He cast about for a sane response, something that wouldn't hurt, that would make this alright for her. But there was nothing. Then he realized that it didn't matter. The hurt had already been ladled out. The truth was going to hurt, no matter how he gave it to her.

So he looked her in the eye again and shook his head gently.

Her eyes welled with shining liquid and one tear dropped from her lashes. "Asher..." she whispered. It was loaded with pain.

Asher got to his feet and waved Bernie over. The barman hurried up. "Call a cab, please," Asher told him. He reached past Jessica, who still sat motionless, and grabbed a pile of paper napkins off the bar, pushing them toward her. "Come on," he said, taking her arm. "Let's wait for the cab outside."

She tore her arm from his grip. "*Don't.*"

"Don't what? I'm just going to see you home."

"You're *handling* me. Like you handle everything. Nothing touches you, does it?" She sucked in a breath that hitched and dashed her tears away with the back of her hand. "One day, someone will get past all your

34

armor. I hope you're hurt. I hope whoever it is *kills* you." She straightened up. She was only average height, which put her head just past his shoulder. "I wish I could be there to see it."

There was nothing he could say aloud. Nothing he could say would ease this for her. So he stayed silent.

But even his silence hurt her. Her face tightened. "Asshole," she breathed and headed for the door without looking back.

"Well, at least she didn't crack the glass over your head, like Maria did," Ylva said, next to him. She had glided up in her silent way while Asher watched Jessica leave.

"Sorry about the public performance," Asher told her. "It blew up too fast."

"I think you're the only one surprised that it blew up in the first place," Ylva said gently.

He looked at her, startled.

Ylva smiled and tucked her hand under his elbow. "Come on. You need coffee." She led him back to the bar and asked Bernie softly for a cappuccino. Bernie hurried away to do his boss's bidding as Asher tiredly lowered himself back onto the stool. Ylva perched next to him, her long legs under the hostess gown stretching down to the floor. She was still a beautiful woman, although her face was lined now. The hair that had once been a deep, dark brown was shot with grey.

The signs of aging in her had bothered Asher greatly when he had first seen them, but now he barely saw them. What he did notice, over and over again, was how...well, *happy* she was. Nothing seemed to remove the contented, quiet aura that surrounded her. The invisible cloak of joy had not always been there.

"How's Jerry?" Asher asked.

Her smile shifted and grew warmer, making her eyes crinkle and dance. "Bored," she admitted. "I'm tempted to tell him to go get a job, but I don't think anyone would give him one at his age."

Bernie slid the coffee in front of her and she pushed it over to Asher. "Drink." She looked at Bernie. "Thank you."

Bernie was smart. He knew he was dismissed. He nodded and moved toward the other end of the bar.

Ylva folded her hands in her lap. "You've had a busy night, haven't you?"

Asher put the cup down. "It's nothing. I'm fine."

Ylva nodded, accepting his assurance. "That's what I told myself when I felt it. You're the best I know at what you do. But still...I worry."

"Join the club," he muttered. It was purely a figure of speech, but after Roar and Eira's concerns and the talk (*argument. The first argument, you mean*) with Roar, he didn't want to have to soothe yet more ruffles.

"That's a club I was kicked out of a long time ago," Ylva replied. Her tone was light, but the reminder made him wince.

"Sorry," he said, as gently as he could.

She gave him a smile, this one tinged with something he couldn't name. Regret? Sadness? It didn't seem sad. Ylva never seemed sad. But for a moment her smile...drooped.

She got to her feet and he knew she was shaking the moment off. "Do you want to see the monthly balance sheet? I have it on my desk. The accountant sent it over this afternoon."

"Can we do it some other time?" he asked.

"Of course." She said it smoothly, the good business manager diplomatically dealing with her cranky, tired boss. "I'll keep it to one side until you're ready."

"Is it good news, at least?"

Ylva's smile was full of good cheer, this time. "I don't know what it is about you, Asher. Every business you start just...blooms."

"It's the quality of the managers I hire," he said flatly. "I find only the best."

Her cheeks tinged pink. "It's a shame your love life can't match your business success. I have a friend—"

Asher groaned.

"What?" she demanded.

"You always have a friend. Jessica was a 'friend', remember?"

"How else are you going to find anyone to keep you company?" Ylva asked reasonably.

"I'm a grown man. I think I can find women all by myself."

Ylva tilted her head to one side and put a hand on her hip.

"Besides, I've already found someone," Asher lied. It would stop her from parading more women past him.

"Really?" Her voice was flat with disbelief.

He reached for the same construct he had given Jessica. "She's a redhead. Doesn't hold back when she speaks. Truth or die. Big black eyes."

"Truth, hmm?" Ylva thought it over. "Does this redhead have a name?"

"Charlee."

"And does this Charlee have anything to do with tonight?" Ylva asked. It was a penetrating question, and Asher almost jumped guiltily. If he wasn't so exhausted from all the anger he had been deflecting for the last few hours, he would have.

He reached for the denial, the negative answer. But this was Ylva. He couldn't flat out lie to her. Evade, dodge and misdirect, yes—hell, that defined his entire fucking life and every one of the Kine, too—but he couldn't lie to her face.

Instead he got to his feet, like her, and looked at his watch. "I'm going home. I need a shower and I really want to sleep."

Ylva gave him another small smile. "I'm sure you do."

* * * * *

Dairy, meat and produce were delivered each morning to the restaurant. One of the sous chefs inspected the orders before accepting delivery, then started up the kitchen routines for the day, prepping for the lunch rush, while Ylva and Pierre, the head chef, didn't come in until late afternoon. Every now and then Ylva liked to arrive unexpectedly early, to check on activities at odd times of the day.

After a restless night of fractured sleep shot with images of Asher lying bloodied on the battlefield, Ylva dressed and went in around noon. She checked on the daily inventory, talked to the sous chef, and settled into her office to tackle the paperwork Asher hated. He was at best an absentee owner and left very nearly all of the restaurant's concerns to her, while he dealt with the other demons in his life, but at least he acknowledged his lack of involvement, as he had last night. Ylva had earned a small fortune over the last forty years, controlling a series of start-ups for him. Constantly starting over, risking everything yet one more time, gave life a degree of spice that she would have missed otherwise, so she didn't in the least mind his absence.

Around four in the afternoon, she stirred and went out to the bar in search of coffee, to stretch her legs and clear her head, instead of having it brought to her desk. So she was sitting in sight of the front door when it opened a few minutes later, letting in warmth and afternoon sunlight.

A young girl stepped hesitantly into the restaurant and paused by the hostess's podium, looking around. She looked nervous, her big eyes wide and apprehensive. Her big dark eyes.

Ylva took in the bright red hair that seemed to spring upwards from her head before the sheer weight of it pulled it down toward the ground and swiveled on her stool toward the girl. "Can I help you?" she asked, lifting her voice enough to reach her.

The girl licked her lips. "I'm looking for.... Does Asher work here?"

Her dark eyes and red hair had braced Ylva for the girl's answer; otherwise she might have been surprised. Instead, she felt a touch of amusement. "I know Asher," she told her. "But he doesn't work here. Not exactly." She beckoned with her hand. "Come closer. It's alright."

The girl walked past the small group of sofas, heading for the bar.

Her glance fell on one of the set tables on her left. The dishes and cutlery from the last lunch customer still sat, forgotten, on the snowy cloth. Ylva made a note to ask a waiter to clear the table as soon as she spotted one.

The girl stopped five feet away from the bar and licked her lips again.

"It's alright," Ylva repeated. "The bar isn't really open and I'm just drinking coffee. Why are you looking for Asher?"

"You know him?"

"Very well."

The girl studied her, tilting her head to one side just a little. "You're lucky."

Ylva blinked, surprised. Then she considered the girl's observation frankly. "I think I am," she agreed. "Are you...is your name Charlee?"

The girl smiled and the expression lit up her face, her eyes. It seemed to highlight her glowing hair. "He told you about me."

"Not exactly." Ylva held back the rest of what she had been about to say, that Asher had omitted a bagful of details, the sort of details that had left Ylva thinking he'd met another doe-eyed beauty that would try to own him, gripping tighter and tighter until he was forced to pry her from him. He had let Ylva imagine the complete antithesis of this child standing before her.

"Is he here?" Charlee asked.

"Not at the moment."

All the brightness in the girl wilted. "Oh."

"Tell me why you're looking for him," Ylva told her. "I might be able to find him for you."

Charlee shifted on her feet awkwardly. She gave Ylva a small smile and a shrug. "I feel really stupid about it." She said it like it was a confession.

Humor touched Ylva again. "Charlee, I've heard more stupid stories about Asher than you've had hot dinners. I don't think you could surprise or shock me."

Charlee tilted her head again, considering her. Then she slipped the backpack she was carrying off her shoulder and dug into one of the outside pockets. "He gave me a card last night. One of those little ones. It just had a phone number on it. In case I needed his help again."

"He helped you?"

Charlee hesitated. Ylva could almost see the caution touch her. "Yeah, in a way," she said. She held up the business card.

Ylva recognized it as one of several that Asher used. "That's the number at the bank," she said.

Charlee nodded. "I went there after school, but the lady at the desk at the front—"

"The receptionist," Ylva corrected, almost automatically.

"Yeah, the receptionist. She wouldn't let me in. She said to try this place here, so here I am."

The last two words came out sounding like "eye-yam." The girl's Bronx wasn't as strong as some Ylva had heard. Their dishwasher's accent was so thick she often wanted to giggle at the rich hoodlum images it provoked. Charlee's accent hadn't been audible at all when she had first begun to speak. She must have been concentrating, masking it. Now she was relaxing a bit more, it was emerging.

"You need Asher's help again?" Ylva asked her.

The girl shook her head and dug back into the pocket again. This time she withdrew a larger white sheet. There were hand drawings on it and some block letters filled in with crayon. Ylva spotted the first word and put it together. A home-made thank-you card.

"I wanted to give him this," Charlee explained. "But he's hard to find."

"He can be," Ylva agreed heartily. She held out her hand. "If you give it to me, I'll make sure he gets it."

Charlee didn't hand the card over. She was looking around the restaurant, at the brass fittings, the ornate ceiling, the silk wallpaper. "He doesn't work here?" she clarified.

"He's sort of a manager," Ylva said. Which was a truth of a kind. Not handing over unnecessary knowledge about another of the Kine was automatic. It came without thought. She didn't know what Asher had told the girl about himself, so anything she said might contradict what the girl knew about him. Better to say as little as possible.

Charlee was taking in the opulence all over again. "I think I'll just go," she said softly, the hand holding the card falling back to her side. She backed up a step or two, the backpack flipping over her shoulder once more.

Ylva stood. "No, really, it's fine," she said. "You can trust me, Charlee. I'll get the card to him."

Charlee gave her an effortful smile. "I told ya. It's stupid, anyway." She turned and headed for the door, and Ylva chewed her lip, trying to think of some way to keep the girl from bolting from the restaurant like a frightened (*intimidated*) animal.

The girl slowed as she passed the uncleared table, looking at it. Then she halted. After a moment of thought, she turned and looked at Ylva over her shoulder. Her red hair curled about her face, masking nearly all of it except for the one black eye looking at her. "Would anyone mind if I took the scraps?" She pointed at the remains of the steak dinner on the plate. There were a couple of inches of what had been a twelve-ounce steak sitting in congealed mushroom gravy.

Horror touched Ylva. "You're hungry?" she asked softly, stepping toward her.

Charlee smiled quickly. "Nah. I got a dog. *She's* always hungry."

Her relief was so great Ylva felt shaky. For just a moment, she had relived the lean, hungry years of her childhood, when entire families had perished because they could not grow crops. The year of no summer, they had called it. The blight year, the year god had cursed them all as sinners. It had taken many years after that for food to become plentiful once more and by then, she had no longer been human.

Her relief let her move around the bar to dig out one of the plastic bags the peanuts were kept in. She dumped the small amount of remaining peanuts into the dish they were served in and carried the bag over to the table where Charlee stood. She scraped the meat into the bag and twisted it closed. She held it out to Charlee. "We've always got scraps to spare, if you ever need them."

The same brightness lit up her face and her eyes. "Really? Thanks!" She tucked the bag away.

"Are you sure you don't want to give me the card for Asher?" Ylva asked once more. "*I* don't think it's stupid to thank someone for being helpful."

"It's just a dumb piece of paper," Charlee said. "I don't have money for a real card." But she was pulling the card out, anyway. Slowly she held it out.

There was a recognizable dog on the cover, with its tongue hanging out. The "thank you" in rough block letters arched over the top. "This is your dog?" Ylva asked.

"Yeah. That's Chocolate."

"It's a great name." She pushed a finger inside the card and looked at Charlee. "May I?"

"Sure." Charlee shrugged, but it was an embarrassed movement.

Ylva opened the card.

To Asher. From Charlee and Chocolate. It was very neat writing. Care and attention had been put into it. A small tree had been drawn next to Asher's name. An ash tree, she realized. It had the characteristic thick trunk and massive, top-heavy foliage of an ash.

"You didn't put a symbol next to your name or Chocolate's," Ylva pointed out.

Charlee shifted on her feet again. "He knows what my name means." Her cheeks flamed a red that matched her hair.

Ylva gave her a smile. "It's a very nice card," she assured her. "I promise I will give it to him."

"'kay." Charlee hitched the backpack over her shoulder, settling it into place. "Thanks. I gotta get home before supper."

"Will you make it in time?" Ylva asked, thinking about the subway at this time of day, and the long ride to the Bronx from here.

"There's a 4:20 express and the subway is just around the corner." She backed up a few steps. "Thanks for the meat." Then she turned and walked toward the door.

Ylva watched her legs swing. She was going to grow up into a long, leggy woman, she calculated.

As Charlee stepped out, the sun caught in her hair, lighting it up just like her smile had.

And she is going to break hearts, Ylva added to herself.

Chapter Four

Torger
Gender: Masculine
Usage: Norwegian
Meaning and History: Varient of *Torgeir*
(from the <u>Old Norse</u> name *Þórgeirr*,
which meant "Thor's spear" from the
name of the Norse god *Þórr* (see <u>THOR</u>)
combined with *geirr* "spear".)
Related Names: *Variants*: <u>Torgeir</u>, <u>Terje</u>
Other Languages: <u>Þórgeirr</u> (Ancient
Scandinavian)
From *BehindTheName.com*

"Ylva, do you think boys are stupid?" Charlee asked, after swallowing a mouthful of the delicious pancakes.

Ylva reached out to test the heat of the teapot against her hand. It was a very ladylike gesture. Everything about Ylva was ladylike. Charlee wanted to grow up to be just like her. Well, her hair was never gonna be the same as Ylva's but she could be the same, move the same as her.

"You know, there are more leftover pancakes in the kitchen. You don't have to eat quite so fast. And yes, I think boys are very silly, very often. Why do you ask?"

"You have a lot of leftover pancakes for such a fancy restaurant," Charlee observed.

Pierre came up to the table, his chef's whites pristine and crinkling. He grinned at Charlee.

"Hey, Pierre!" she greeted him. "These are really good, you know." She held up her fork. "I don't get why people don't want to eat them."

"They are good because I make them," Pierre told her. He bent from the waist. It almost seemed like he was bowing. Ylva had explained he was very old-fashioned like that. It didn't bother Charlee at all.

"But I 'ave 'ere, for your doggie. Look." Pierre placed the plastic bag on the table. It was full of meat scraps and had been sealed off properly.

"You're the best, Pierre," Charlee told him.

Pierre brushed at his mustache with quick little movements. "It is nothing," he assured her and walked back to his kitchen.

Ylva watched him go, with a smile of her own.

"He really isn't cranky like you told me he was," Charlee said.

"I think he likes you," Ylva told her. She touched the bag with the scraps in it. "And he makes pancakes just like you like them." Her gaze lifted up from the teacup in front of her. She looked at Charlee quickly, like she had said something she shouldn't.

Charlee lowered her fork. "He makes these *for me*? I thought...but you said they was leftovers, like the scraps for Chocolate!" She felt queasy. She didn't have the money to pay for real food.

"They *are*, Charlee," Ylva said. She patted her hand. "Tell me why you think boys are stupid?"

The tiny door chime sounded softly and Ylva looked up. Charlee looked around, too. It was barely four in the afternoon and she had learned over the last couple of months that customers rarely came in that late...or that early.

Asher was shaking off raindrops from his coat and hair, looking down at the plush carpet as he ran his fingers through the almost white locks. Then he looked up and Charlee felt a jolt of pleasure course through her. She had forgotten how tall he was and how big across his shoulders were.

His hands were just as big as she remembered them, only she remembered them curled around the hilt of his sword (*that no one must know about*).

She grinned. "Asher!"

He didn't smile back. He looked at Ylva, who remained seated at the little table they were using, close to the bar.

"You remember Charlee, don't you?" Ylva said softly.

"You got my card, didn't you?" Charlee added.

He took off the raincoat and threw it over the back of the nearest sofa. He wore a suit underneath, but the tie was loosened (*like it was when he—*).

Charlee got to her feet, chopping off the thought. His lack of a smile scared her. "You're mad at me."

Asher looked at her. His eyes were very blue. She hadn't really seen them properly in the dark, but now she could.

"I'm not mad at you," he said. "I'm just surprised to see you."

Charlee touched the table, where Ylva still sat. "Ylva and Pierre give me scraps for Chocolate. You...you don't mind, do you?"

He came closer. His gaze roamed over the table where they sat. Ylva had her teapot and the tiny, fancy teacup with the little curly handle that was hers alone. Everyone else had to use the squat white cups for tea and coffee. There was a plate with the other half of a croissant on it that she never finished. Charlee often ate that, too. Then there was the big round plate Charlee was using to eat Pierre's pancakes.

"They're leftovers," Charlee said quickly. "No one likes Pierre's pancakes, but I do. They're great." She wasn't sure why she said it, especially like that, like she was in trouble. But while Ylva wouldn't talk much about Asher and neither would Pierre, she had built up an impression that Asher wasn't just a manager. He was more than that. And here she was, eating his food and taking it for Chocolate.

Asher and Ylva exchanged one of those adult glances that seemed to say a lot without words. Charlee was getting better at reading them, but this one sailed by her and remained a mystery.

Ylva pulled out one of the other chairs at the table and patted the cushion. "Sit and have some tea with us, Asher."

He looked at his watch, then seemed to decide that he did have enough time. He pulled the chair up to the table and picked up the remaining half of Ylva's croissant and bit into it like he was very hungry. Ylva pulled a cup and saucer off the next table, and poured tea into it. She seemed smug about something.

Then Charlee looked at Asher again, taking in details about him that she had forgotten, or hadn't noticed, that first night. He was her first real hero. It was important that she get all the details right in her mind. There was still a lot she had to learn about him. But that was her secret to keep (*just like their secret was a real, grown-up secret*).

Asher chewed and swallowed. "Good," he said and reached for the teacup Ylva offered him. "My thanks."

She nodded her head at him. It wasn't so much a nod, but she rolled it forward, like they did in historical movies. Charlee stared at her. It had been such a...a *royal* thing to do.

"So. Charlee," Asher said, drawing her attention back. "How is Chocolate doing?" He was staring at her in an odd way, the same way he had been looking at her that first night. *(Our secret! Remember!)*

"She's doin'—*doing*—really good. Do you work at a bank, too?"

Asher blinked. Then his puzzlement cleared. "The card," he said, rolling his eyes. "That's how you found me. You starred the number."

"But it's taken weeks and weeks to find you, though. Ylva said you would be along eventually. You're a very strange manager, for a manager. Ylva's a manager and she's *always* here, almost every single day when I stop by, but you're not."

"I'm a different sort of manager," Asher agreed.

"You got my card?" She was reluctant to ask again, because the card had been such a pathetic thing. But she had wanted to do *something* to mark the difference he had made in her life, and a card was the least dangerous thing she could think of. She had composed the message for the inside with the greatest care. Anyone but Asher who might read it wouldn't have understood what it said, but *he* would.

Asher smiled and this time it wasn't an adult smile. It was a nice smile that reached his eyes. "I did get your card. Thank you. You haven't had any more trouble, I'm guessing. You didn't call."

Charlee wrinkled her nose. "They're still there, but they don't bother me." The Lightning Lords had gone right back to lolling against fences, picking on passers-by, and maintaining their turf. Charlee had started to use different routes to and from school, going out of her way by three or four blocks, to minimize the chance of running into them again.

Then, two weeks after she had met Asher, she *had* run into them. The new leader was bigger, taller and looked stronger than the late and unremarked Lonzo. He had stepped in front of her, barring her path, and looked her up and down. There was a heat in his eyes that scared her, because she had a nebulous idea about what he was thinking. It had to do with the giggling, disgusting stuff the girls at school often talked about when no adult could possibly overhear them.

Boys and what they did to girls.

Fright curled through Charlee. Chocolate, by her side as she always was now, growled quietly in the back of her throat. Chocolate's fearlessness helped Charlee stand tall. She spoke quickly. "You don't wanna mess with me."

The new leader looked her up and down, amused. "Says you."

"Ricky," one of the gang against the fence said quietly.

Charlee glanced at him and recognized him. "Ask him," she said, nodding at him.

Ricky looked over his shoulder. "Listen to the brave chicky."

"Ricky," the skinny one on the end insisted. "That's *her*."

"You better listen to him," Charlee added. "You do anything to me, I'll get him back here right this moment, just like he did in the alley. You touch me or my dog, he'll appear just like he did then. He don't like you messin' with me. I don't like it, neither."

Ricky looked like he was about to burst out laughing, then he seemed to really see her face properly. His laughter faded. He looked at the skinny one again, and the skinny guy shook his head. He wasn't anywhere near laughing.

"Any of you, all of you. Don't ever come near me again," Charlee added. She didn't understand it fully, but she knew in her gut that the balance of power was shifting to her. She would use it for as long as she had it. "Don't come near me, my family, or my dog. Or I'll call him down on you. He can be here just like his weapon appeared." She looked at the skinny guy. "Just like *that*," she added and clicked her fingers.

The skinny guy flinched. He remembered.

Charlee looked up at Ricky, who wasn't smiling anymore. "Get out of my way," she said. She was shaking inside, but she knew it was very important that he step aside for her, rather than she walk around him.

Ricky glanced at his friends, then back at her. She could tell he wanted to pull the power back, that he was looking for something that would let him. But the longer he stood not saying anything, the weaker he looked.

Finally, his expression thundery, he stepped aside. "Get the fuck out of here and don't come back along this way, or I'll change my mind about you not being worth the trouble." It was sheer bravado. She had won and he was trying to save face. She knew that, but it took all her courage to step past him and expose her back to him.

Chocolate walked behind her, growling softly and continuously, until they were fifteen yards on. Then she stepped up beside Charlee once more and grinned up at her. Charlee held herself down to a walk until she had rounded the corner and was out of their sight. Then she broke into a panicky, frightened run and sprinted all the way home, her breath pushing out of her in shaky pants.

She had spotted the gang multiple times since then, but they had acted like she was invisible. They didn't speak to her, or even look at her, but Charlee still crossed the street when she saw them ahead.

"I haven't had any trouble," Charlee told Asher, picking her words carefully. "Thanks to you."

Ylva was smiling as she watched Asher, who stared down at his teacup, his big hands making it look tiny. He looked almost uncomfortable.

"I'm not supposed to say thank you?" Charlee asked.

"Asher isn't used to people saying thank you," Ylva explained.

"'splains why he's blushing," Charlee observed. "You should help people more," she told him. "Then you'd be used to it."

Ylva laughed.

Asher stood up. "I'll see you onto your train."

"I'm fine. It's just around the corner."

"It's raining. I have a big umbrella. Do you?"

Defeated, Charlee shook her head and picked up her backpack reluctantly. "I guess I'll see you, Ylva. Thank you for the pancakes and the food for Chocolate." She slipped the sealed bag into her backpack.

"You're more than welcome, Charlee." Ylva stood up and began to clear the plates on the table with professional efficiency.

"I'll be back in ten minutes," Asher told her, and Ylva nodded.

* * * * *

"If you have such a large umbrella, why didn't you use it when you walked to the restaurant just now?" Charlee asked.

"I like the rain," Asher said. He was holding the black umbrella mostly over her and she wasn't getting a drop on her as a result. "How have you been, Charlee? Are you truly okay?"

"I really am. So is Chocolate. She meets me at the train each night, when I get back home, because she knows I'll have food for her. I feed her and then I go home. The gang is scared spitless of you. I remind them whenever I have to."

Asher's mouth pulled up into a smile and she got the impression that he really didn't want to smile, but was smiling anyway.

"Ylva said I should go to the restaurant for scraps. Whenever I wanted to," Charlee added.

"You can," Asher confirmed. "And you can eat all the pancakes Pierre cooks, if you like."

"Do you...does the restaurant belong to you?"

Asher glanced at her. There was something troubling in his eyes.

"Truth for truth," she added. "Deal, remember?"

"Yes, I own the restaurant."

"And you work at a bank. Or do you own that, too?"

"That's a bit more complicated."

"You don't work there."

"Not exactly."

"It's called Strand Manhattan Trust. Your last name is Strand. Is it your bank?"

Asher sighed. "In the way you mean, yes, it's mine."

"And you have a magic sword that you use when no one is looking."

Asher looked over his shoulder.

"It's okay. No one is close enough to hear," she told him. "And the rain is loud, too. I think I've figured you out."

Asher looked both surprised and amused. "You have?"

She nodded. "You're a superhero. But not exactly like Superman. You look out for the little guys. Like me. And you keep it a secret from everyone."

Asher laughed. It was a rich sound that matched his voice. "Truth, Charlee?" he said when he finally had himself back under control.

"That's the deal," she agreed.

"I'm so far away from a real superhero, you'd be disappointed if you saw what I'm really like."

"I don't believe that. You saved Chocolate. And me. You didn't do that because you're mean or bad."

He paused at the top of the steps leading down into the subway, then shrugged. "I'll take you to the platform," he said and started to walk down the steps beside her, folding away the umbrella. "I helped Chocolate because I had to," he said. "I should have walked on and minded my own business. It's...well, it's dangerous for me to get involved like that. It makes it risky. People could find out about me. So I should have walked on, but then I heard Chocolate cry out, and...." He pulled a big breath into his lungs, glancing at her.

"You couldn't walk on after that," Charlee finished. "That makes you a good guy."

"I'm not, Charlee. I'm really not."

"You are to me."

He pushed his big hand through his hair. "Hell's bells," he muttered. "Look, Charlee, you can't go and get some harebrained idea into your head that I'm some angel or something. I'm not a superhero. I don't go around saving people. I'm just a...a man."

"I know that."

"You do?" He seemed surprised.

"You..." She looked around for listeners, as it was more crowded in here. "You did that thing to Lonzo," she said cryptically. "Superheroes, the ones like Superman in the movie, they don't k.... They don't do that to people, no matter how bad they've been."

"And that makes me human?" Asher was back to being puzzled and amused at the same time.

The express pulled in with a hiss and clank of wheels and the doors whooshed open. Charlee took a step toward the train, then looked back at him. "I know you're human, because you seem sad. And angry. Superheroes, the ones in the stories, they don't have bad feelings. But the superheroes that are human, they do. They always feel bad. Haven't you noticed?"

He was staring at her. "No, I didn't notice," he said slowly.

Charlee ran for the train and at the door, once it was closed, she waved at him, for he was still standing by the bottom of the steps.

Asher lifted his big hand in farewell and she saw once more in her mind's eye his fingers curled around the hilt of the big sword.

She hugged herself, keeping her secret inside, where it warmed her.

* * * * *

"Whenever you get back, Charlee," Darwin prompted her softly.

Charlee blinked and refocused on him. "Jeez. Sorry," she said, straightening up and squaring up the notebook in front of her.

Darwin closed the textbook, keeping his finger on the page they were up to. "That's the third time you've zoned out on me. Do you want to quit for today?" he asked her, not unkindly. Charlee was the sort of student most teachers dreamed about—self-directed, disciplined, with a crystal-sharp mind. But it was a lazy, warm Saturday afternoon. The sound of kids playing out on the street, where a fire hydrant had popped its cap, the rushing sound of the water and the soft tinkle of Anna-Marie's wind chimes in the open living room window were distractions of their own. He had a beer chilling in the fridge to drink after Charlee's lesson, and his throat contracted at the thought of the cool liquid hitting the back of it.

"It's a hot day. We can always pick this up again next week," he told her.

"No, I'd like to finish, if that's okay?" She gave him a smile. "I won't zone out again. I promise."

He opened the book again. "Something wrong, Charlee?" God knows, with her family, anything could be wrong. Maybe her drunken mother had fallen down the stairs. Her father was losing weight the way a wilted flower sheds petals, and looked just as dried out, too. The way Lucas was filling out around the shoulders and shooting up toward the ceiling, he would be creating his own mischief sooner rather than later.

"Nah, it's nothing," Charlee said. "Just a book I'm reading."

"They give you interesting books at school?" He often rolled his eyes at the education system's idea of appropriate reading material for school kids.

"I got it from a friend. It's a history book. Pliny the Younger. It's sort of about that volcano. Pompeii."

"Vesuvius is the name of the volcano," Darwin corrected her absently, while he considered the matter. "Pompeii is one of the cities it destroyed. You're reading Pliny? Who gave that to you?"

"A friend."

"Who likes history?"

"He knows a lot of history," she replied. "But he doesn't think much of history books. He says that everyone who ever wrote a book about 'real' events is a flat-out liar."

Darwin grinned. "He might be right. Did he say why?"

She nodded and reached for another cookie. He always laid out six of them, but she would only ever take three. "He said that people who were writing about events that they saw happen are all mixed up about it. They could be writing about it because they were slaves and didn't like what happened to slaves, so whatever they write will make slaves look good and slave owners look bad, which isn't the way it really happened, but who knows the truth if they're the only ones who wrote about it? And if they didn't actually go through the events, then they're using someone else's opinion about what happened and that's even worse."

It was a simplistic model of the subjectivity of historical records, but it was workable and it had struck the right note with Charlee. She was thinking about the veracity of what she read, now. Darwin felt a grudging respect for this friend of hers.

"If he dislikes historical books so much, why did he give you one to read?" Darwin asked curiously.

She munched, then shrugged. "He says everyone should know history. Because if you know what happened in the past, then you won't go and do the same stupid sh... stuff again."

Darwin recognized Edmund Burke's philosophy. *Those who don't know history are destined to repeat it.* He nodded. "He sounds like a smart boy, this friend of yours."

Charlee hesitated, then she nodded. "He is." She finished the cookie and wiped her fingers of crumbs. "Can we finish?" she asked, touching the geometry book.

Darwin picked up where they had left off, with the very basic history of Euclid and his measurements, and realized what had prompted her trip down memory lane. And while they finished the lesson, he wondered who her friend was, who knew history was usually a pack of lies but also the most valuable information in the world? That didn't sound like any ten year old Darwin had ever met.

* * * * *

Charlee slipped into the kitchen via the back door and dropped her backpack to the floor.

Pierre was yelling at one of the kitchen hands. Well, not yelling. He didn't yell, but he started to speak very fast, and use more and more French as he forgot the right English words. His hands would speed up their frantic waving, keeping time with his tongue.

Charlee waved to the kitchen hand from behind Pierre. He grinned and waved back, then blinked and looked at Pierre, wiping the smile from his face. Pierre turned around, exasperated, then beamed at her. "'ello, Charlee, my fiery beauty!" He hugged her, then she brushed the flour off her shirt.

"Hi, Pierre. You be nice."

He looked puzzled. "I am always nice. Very nice." He turned back to the kitchen hand and began to speak rapidly again.

Charlee helped herself to a plastic bag from the dispenser and picked through the scraps bucket they kept just for Chocolate, selecting the best pieces, while the scolding continued. She sealed the bag and dropped it into her backpack, then went through to the front of the restaurant and dropped into the chair opposite Ylva, who put down her newspaper and picked up her teacup.

"Hi Ylva. Where's Asher?"

Ylva lowered her cup to the saucer carefully. "He didn't come here today."

Charlee wrinkled her nose. "Bugger."

Ylva looked shocked. "That's not a word you should use on a day-to-day basis."

"Asher does."

Ylva rolled her eyes. "Nor should you scrunch up your face in that way. It's not very attractive."

"It's not?" Charlee bit her lip. "Damn," she said softly.

Ylva sighed.

Charlee considered Asher's absence. It wasn't the first time he hadn't turned up at the restaurant, but it was unusual. He was here nearly every single day when she arrived, either sitting at the bar or at the table with Ylva and holding a teacup that was dwarfed by his hand. Often he had a book for her to read, or some other item that they might have been discussing the day before. Once, he had brought his dog, Torger, for her to meet. That had been late in the summer, because he'd had to leave Torger outside, tied up to the fence, because Pierre would have burst into tears over a dog being in his kitchen. That's what Asher had said, although Charlee privately thought he didn't want Ylva to get mad at him and start yelling about inspectors.

Torger was a multicolored mutt. Charlee loved that Asher had rescued him and raised him to be one of the best-behaved dogs she had ever met. He held his paw out to shake hands with her when he was introduced, and sat up and waved goodbye when she left. But Asher wouldn't let her feed him, not even a treat. Food was something Torger had to work for. He was a type of guard dog and very good at his job, Asher explained.

Charlee looked out the window at the snow drifting across the road as the wind pushed it along. She was glad the subway entrance was just around the corner. It meant she didn't have to stay outside for too long. Her coat wasn't very thick and the wind always seemed to cut right through it. It was last year's coat and the sleeves were too short—her gloves didn't reach all the way up, leaving an inch of skin around her wrist exposed.

"It's cold out, isn't it?" Ylva said, drawing her attention back to the table.

"Uh-huh."

"*Yes,*" Ylva corrected.

"Yes. Sorry. Yes, it's cold out." Charlee put her hand against the pot, checking the temperature. "Would you like me to pour you a cup?" she asked Ylva.

"Thank you, yes."

"Is he seeing anyone, Ylva?" Charlee asked as she poured. "Is that where he is?"

Ylva shook her head. "He's just busy."

"It's not good," Charlee said. She had been thinking about it. "He doesn't see anyone. He works. He goes home at night. Well, I assume he goes home at night. He could be sleeping on park benches for all I know."

"Asher has a home," Ylva said gently. "And between you and me, I don't think he lacks companionship when he wants it." She smiled and Charlee noticed, not for the first time, that the wrinkles around her eyes were getting deeper and more pronounced. Jerry, Ylva's husband, was much older than she looked, which made Charlee wonder how old Ylva really was.

"He's angry all the time," Charlee said, getting the last of it off her chest. She looked at Ylva. "He is nice to me and to you, but I know he's angry. It sits at the bottom of his thoughts, like the tea leaves in a pot, making him stew."

Ylva put her cup down slowly. "You may be right."

Charlee twined her fingers together. "Please don't tell me it's complicated and that I won't understand. I *want* to understand."

Ylva gave her one of her understanding smiles. "It *is* complicated, but I would tell you if I could. I'm not entirely sure I understand myself."

"*Please*," Charlee begged. "You two know more about me than my own brother. I don't know anything about you except you run Asher's businesses, and I know just as little about Asher."

Ylva shook her head. "I can't. To begin with, Asher's story is his to tell. And I cannot tell you mine."

Charlee sighed. "Is he...is his anger something to do with me?"

Ylva didn't hesitate. "Absolutely not," she said gently. She leaned forward. "Have you ever had to keep a secret, Charlee?"

"Yes," Charlee replied flatly.

"Did you ever want to get rid of that secret? Did you want to tell anyone—*everyone*—what the secret was, so it didn't sit in your mind all the time?"

Charlee shook her head. "It's my secret. There isn't anyone I want to tell it to."

"Not even Lucas?"

Charlee hesitated. Especially lately when she and Lucas were talking, the things she and Asher spoke about—some of the wildly odd and strangely different things—would sit in the middle of her mind, just like Ylva had described. Then, she would have trouble concentrating on what Lucas was saying. "I think about things Asher said that are different to what Lucas says. Then I want to tell Lucas about the way Asher said it...but I can't. Is that what you mean?"

"In a way," Ylva agreed. "That pressure to tell people, if you hold onto it for a very long time, becomes immense. It can become the only thing you can hear in your mind. Secrets grow. They build weight. They can gnaw at you."

"Asher prefers to tell the truth," Charlee said, thinking about their first deal, about how he had laughed whenever they were truth-telling. He always seemed somehow lighter when they were talking truth. But they hadn't spoken truths for a long, long time.

"Yes, he does prefer the truth," Ylva agreed.

"Then it *is* my fault," Charlee murmured unhappily.

Chapter Five

Earl

An **earl** (UK /ɜrl/ [1]) is a member of the nobility. The title is Anglo-Saxon, akin to the Scandinavian form **jarl**, and meant "chieftain", particularly a chieftain set to rule a territory in a king's stead.

from *Wikipedia*

Asher gazed fiercely at the clock on the wall, making the hands come into focus one at a time. Then he put together what their positions meant in his mind. It took a moment to make sense of it. Then he had it. It was a quarter to five.

He sat on the sofa, opposite the clock, which was under the TV. He'd been sitting there for what seemed like only five minutes, but when he thought it through, the time stretched out even longer. He had been sitting there for a very long time. It only *seemed* like he had just sat down.

He looked at the clock again. Why had he been trying to figure out the time? Was it important?

The wind moaned around the window frames, pulling his attention to the glass. The bottom half of the outside pane was frosted, with starred flake shapes patterning the glass. Was that why he was sitting here? Too cold to go out? But it wasn't *that* cold, not really. He could remember cold winter mornings when he was a child and it had been much colder. He'd also been farther north, and the building he had called home didn't come with central heating and double-glazed windows. Oh no.

But that was then and this was now, and—

He stared owlishly at the clock again, trying to remember what the time had been when he had figured it out, instead of reconstructing the time in his pickled brain once more. He would have to add half-an-hour (*five minutes?*) to that time to get the correct time.

The hands came into focus. Four-forty-seven. Time was just flying by. Why was he sitting here? He looked around, noticing the frost on the windows. There was glass in front of him, too. His glass.

Wine. There was wine in the glass. Not much, only dregs at the bottom. There wasn't enough of the wine to make it look dark. Instead, it was a pale, washed out red.

The wine was loosening its hold on him. Thoughts began to connect in longer sequences, letting him put together more complex reasoning.

Why was he sitting on his sofa at five in the afternoon, ripped out of his skull on expensive red? And why was he doing it alone?

How long had he been sitting here, drinking by himself like a pathetic bum?

More distant thoughts swam back into the range of his focus. *The council meeting*. That had been…when? He remembered it happening. He had been there. For some reason, it seemed important that he recall what had happened.

He frowned down at his hands, struggling to recall the meeting. But nothing would come. Is that why he had started drinking? To forget about the meeting? He'd done a bang-up job, then.

He looked at the window again. That seemed to be significant.

Time. It was all around him. Prodding him. Rushing by frantically while barely moving. And what happy horseshit was he thinking about time, anyway?

The window. He studied it. Nothing there.

He had been at the council meeting. When was that? What was today? He closed his fingers, turning his hands into fists, and squeezed hard, *making* himself sort it out.

It was nearly five o'clock in the afternoon. Already the light outside was failing. But despite the way time was zipping (*crawling*) past him, he was sure that a whole night had not passed. That made it Thursday. Still.

Which meant he had gone to the council meeting this morning. Something relaxed inside him with a silent sigh as he put this together. It was still Thursday. He hadn't dived into a bottle so deep the world had turned on its axis while he wasn't paying attention. It had only been a few hours.

He shook his head, trying to clear it even further. What had happened that made him think getting drunk as a skunk would fix things?

Think! he commanded himself, squeezing his fists even tighter. *When did you get there?* He had been late, which was usual, and almost everyone was there already, standing around waiting for the stragglers. Eira and Stefan were…

* * * * *

…standing at the top of the long table, for this month's meeting was being held at the big hall, so they were the hosts.

The portals had been busy, which slowed some of the attendees' travel, but New York had the advantage of being directly connected to Oslo so Asher arrived as the bulk of travelers did, and his lateness became a non-issue.

The council room was a large, airy chamber with tall walls punctuated by thick marble columns and a ceiling that had been painted to resemble the early morning sky, with wisps of cloud floating overhead. Like most of the mountain hall at Tryvannshøyden, the council chamber was a grand reception room designed to intimidate those who dared to step inside.

There had never been any attempt to copy older, more traditional styles of halls. Stefan and those who had come before him had deliberately aimed for the unique. The remarkable. It was impossible to cross over to Tryvannshøyden and mistake it for somewhere else. When you stepped through the portal to the main hall, you *knew* you were in the home of the Regin and Annarr of the Kine, and it was hard not to be impressed.

But Asher had visited so many times that the scale and beauty of the halls and passages failed to impact upon him as he hurried through them to the council chamber. The meeting had been called for nine in the morning New York time, which was mid-afternoon in Oslo. The high western windows that punched through to the great circular central hall were beaming bright winter sunlight down onto the shining marble floors, warming them in big rectangular patches, and dazzling anyone who walked through them.

The council chamber had no external windows, so the light was kinder. Asher slipped in through the twenty-foot-high carved teak door that stood ajar in welcome. The murmur of those who had already assembled greeted him.

He spotted Roar halfway down the length of the long table and moved around to that side, angling for the chair next to Roar. Every earl and his stallari were expected to attend these councils, along with miscellaneous other Kine, including Sindri, the little dark man who was an unacknowledged expert in the manipulation of auras here on Midgard. There were others who acted as consultants in aspects of Kine life who were regularly invited to the meetings.

Roar gave him a stiff smile as Asher sat down. "Good to see you here," he said in a tone designed not to carry too far.

"I haven't missed a meeting in six months," Asher pointed out, stung.

"Considering how often you bothered attending before last summer, I still feel relief when you arrive."

Asher tried to dismiss the implied criticism as the meeting started. He was used to Roar's constant prodding. It was a big-brother thing, and most of the time he deserved it. But now he was getting flak for something that had happened more than six months ago.

It soured his outlook, which had been precarious to start with. He was not fond of the council meetings, which meandered on for far too many hours, covering little of direct interest to the New York hall. Roar got more out of the endless discussions and wrangling than Asher did.

He found his mind wandering. Why *had* he started attending these things without fail? It wasn't as if he'd had a sudden wake-up call last summer, turned over a new leaf and mended his ways. He'd just…started attending. He could even count the exact number of meetings he had come to (*six*), because somewhere in the darker recesses of his mind he had been keeping count. Noticing.

What had changed? He couldn't think of anything…well, that wasn't true. Since Jessica had broken up with him, he hadn't had a single relationship that had lasted beyond a first date. Even the first dates had slowed to a trickle. That was different.

He roamed over the landscape of his life, taking a tally. He wasn't drinking as much—not that he had been drinking huge amounts to start with. Well, maybe the odd indulgence or two (*every night, you mean*). But there were some Kine for whom drinking was their major pastime. Roar liked his scotch, too. Then there were the endless barrels of mead supplied for any official event. Getting sloppy was a Kine tradition.

But he'd just…stopped. He had a glass of wine in the evenings when he was home, but he was rarely at home. The bank and the restaurant seemed to be chewing up more of his time than ever before, and the new franchise he'd started in New Mexico was booming, too.

He was busy. When had life become so damned busy? Last solstice, he'd stood at the windows to his apartment, watching a Christmas parade go by—not the big Manhattan affair, but a smaller community one put on by the Lions Club or somesuch—and considered how barren and empty his life was compared to the average human, who had family and friends and commitments and responsibilities. Well, that had changed, too.

Asher had grown up on the equivalent of what humans now called farms. It had been a very large establishment and as the second son of a king, he had responsibilities quite a bit different from the average villager and farmhand. But because he had spent his childhood in rural farming country, he was very familiar with the annual cycle of summer growth and winter fallow, spring blooming and autumn endings. He still tended to think in countrified metaphors and it occurred to him as he sat in the council meeting and brooded about the shifts in his life that he had entered a change of season, one that had come unlooked for and slipped in the door with the quietness of a late autumn, when leaves suddenly turned overnight.

It had been a very long time since such a shift had happened. The novelty of it kept him preoccupied for the rest of the meeting.

When the council was adjourned, Sindri, the little dark man, came up to Asher. He was barely five and a half feet tall, and Asher had never met anyone quite like him, either Kine or human. There were all sorts of races and breeds within the Kine, for battles had been fought all over the world and all of them had heroes, but Sindri did not seem to match any of the races of man. He was quite bald and his head was high domed. He had taken advantage of his baldness to tattoo across his head and face markings that no one but Sindri recognized. They might have been tribal markings, or some ancient runes that had long been forgotten. Some speculated that the markings were to do with Sindri's interest in magic, that the markings themselves had power that no one on Midgard understood.

It gave him an odd appearance among so many of the Kine, who tried to blend in with their human surroundings. There were just as many pairs of jeans and business suits at the meeting as there were traditional robes and gowns. Sindri, however, always wore a plain black robe, completely devoid of any identifying cut or design. Asher couldn't recall seeing him outside a Kine hall. He didn't seem to have any connection with humans; he lived and worked among the halls. Stefan and Eira used him as a consultant and he seemed content with the uneventful life to be found among the Kine.

He approached Asher now, the long and wide sleeves of his robe swinging as he hurried. "Freyr Askr," he said. The formal greeting.

"Freyr Sindri," Asher acknowledged.

"You're leaving so soon?" Sindri asked, as Asher pushed his chair in.

"I have business back in New York. It's a busy day for me."

"That's a pity. I thought I might be able to coax you into an evening of quiet enjoyment, here." Sindri gave him a stiff smile. "I will walk you to the portals and talk on the way. It will not slow your departure." He stepped aside.

Asher couldn't find anything in the man's words that he could use as a reason to refuse, even though he wanted to. Sindri was being courteous and reasonable, but Asher had never got around to liking him. He had not spent enough time in his company and nothing the man did in public had given him reason to seek him out or for the both of them to spend time together where he might get to know Sindri better.

It would be churlish to brush him off, just because he didn't know him well enough, so Asher waved his hand, silently indicating that Sindri should accompany him.

Sindri turned and paced alongside him as Asher threaded his way between the thinning council members, heading for the door. The portals were in the big central hall, just beyond the council room.

"You seemed somewhat distracted during the meeting," Sindri ventured. "Not that it was obvious to everyone at the table, I assure you.

But I did sense that your mind was elsewhere."

"And that is why you seek me out?" Asher asked curiously.

"Boredom at council meetings is an interesting emotion to detect."

"I have things on my mind. It wasn't boredom," Asher corrected him.

Sindri smiled. "Last year at the feast of the equinox, I heard you talking with your brother, the earl. Do you remember the occasion?"

"Remind me."

"You were discussing the rules of *laun*."

Asher recalled the conversation with a jolt. "You heard that?"

"You were speaking quite loudly."

Asher stepped around the door and Sindri slipped between others and caught up with him, while Asher considered him more carefully. "So I was talking about *laun*. So what?"

"You have a very interesting perspective on the matter."

"I'm not the only one who thinks it should be discarded."

"Dilettantes, all of them," Sindri replied. "You feel rather more strongly about it than any of its other detractors."

Asher halted and turned to face him. "It was a private conversation at the end of a long night and everyone had been drinking." He glanced around the huge rotunda, looking to see if anyone was taking an interest in their conversation now. "Talking about breaking *laun* is not a smart move. Not in any hall, but especially not here."

"And most especially your brother's hall," Sindri added. He held out his hands in a gesture of acceptance. It made the sleeves of his robe swing, almost like wings. "I have a salon here, just off this hall. I entertain friends there. It would please me if you would stop by."

"I cannot," Asher replied. "I did say I had a busy day back home."

"Home. What an interesting name for it." Sindri gave him a short smile that thinned his lips. "You are welcome in my salon whenever you wish to visit. The door is always unlocked for you."

It was an odd way of phrasing it. *Who is the door locked against?* Asher wondered. But he gave the same polite smile that Sindri had used. "You are a considerate host. I appreciate the invitation." The words were automatic.

Sindri stepped back, clearly disengaging. "Do bear my offer in mind. I suspect you will find more of a home in my salon than ever your empty hall has provided."

"I will consider your offer," Asher lied with flat sincerity. "Thank you."

Sindri turned and walked away and Asher hurried with even more urgency across the hall to the alcove where the portals were located. He wanted to be home—yes, *home*, damn it—as quickly as possible.

But when he stepped through to the hall, it rang with echoes, hollow and empty. There was a soft shuffle of feet and murmurs at the entrance where Kine were stepping between the two portals that flanked the stairs. Most of them were acknowledging the guards at the head of the stairs, or talking to each other as they walked through in pairs. But the rest of the hall was bereft even of Amica. It was neat and clean.

Asher hurried down the steps and headed for the street. Forty minutes later, he was home. It had taken nearly forty times longer to travel the length of Manhattan as it had to step around the globe from Norway to the United States.

Such was his fractured life.

He had uncorked the wine bottle straight after shutting the door and dropping his keys onto the desk next to it….

* * * * *

….and he couldn't remember so much as loosening his tie before gulping down half of the first glass.

He looked around the apartment now. There were two bottles, empty, on the coffee table in front of him. Another on the dining table over in the corner by the big windows. Were there more in the kitchen? He didn't have the energy to get up off his ass and look.

He fell back against the sofa and looked up at the ceiling, blowing out a heavy breath. He remembered it all now. There were some parts, when he had been swimming at the bottom of the wine, that he couldn't pull together except in hazy snatches of impressions, but everything leading up to that first mouthful of wine was clear.

And he still didn't know why he had taken that first mouthful. It was like someone or something had goosed him into it. He had reacted to an invisible stimulus…what the hell had triggered him?

He tried to summarize the day in headlines. The meeting, Sindri…and that was it.

Sindri. Was it something to do with him? But he had been hurrying to get away from the meeting before Sindri had got close enough to open his mouth. Yet…and yet…he had been hurrying even more after their conversation, which had left him with an unsettled feeling.

Guilt, it's guilt, you daft bugger.

Sindri had stirred up feelings of guilt.

Yet he had been sitting in the meeting feeling a small sense of pride because of the way his life seemed to be settling down (*dismay, asshole. That was dismay*).

Really?

Asher straightened up and leaned forward, resting his arms on his knees and threading his fingers together. *Think!* he commanded himself. It was an old exercise, this self-demand for clear thinking. Confessors and insightful friends were scant in the life of the Kine. They had to think for themselves because talking through their problems wasn't possible.

You were ready to bolt at the end of the meeting because your buttons had already been pushed. Sindri just nudged you over the edge.

Why?

He frowned. His head was starting to throb now, with the heavy bass beat of a drum. He was going to pay mightily for this day of hiding away from the truth.

Pushed…pushing…people pushing him around.

Charlee. The thought came to him suddenly, from nowhere. And that made the thing he had been trying to dredge up from his sodden consciousness rise to the surface and make itself felt again.

He glanced at the window, where the frost was starring the glass in a graceful reversed bell curve, remembering.

It had been early fall, when the leaves were turning but not yet falling. Ylva had someone sweep the sidewalk in front of the restaurant every day so silly customers didn't slide on a leaf and sue them for negligence. Asher liked fall and winter, because it reminded him of when he was young. He always felt happier when the leaves turned.

Charlee had stopped by after school, as always, and her red hair had been a match for the maples out the front of the store and went well with the darker browns and maroons that Ylva used for napkins and tablecloths in winter. She seemed to glow with energy, with happiness, with life.

They had been talking about….they had been talking about….

* * * * *

"What do you mean, it doesn't matter?" Charlee asked, as she carefully lined up the seams of the napkin she was folding, concentrating on getting it just right. "Of course it matters!"

"You're never going to get it perfect," Asher pointed out. "There's no such thing."

"I don't want it perfect." She didn't lift her head or shift her gaze away from the napkin. The overhead light was making a halo around the top of her head. "I just want it to be the very best I can do."

"The customer isn't going to care."

She put the carefully folded napkin in front of him. "But I care and I'll know if I don't do it properly."

"So?"

Ylva just smiled as she sipped her tea, although he had a feeling that she was laughing at him. But she wouldn't come right out and laugh in front of Charlee. She had too much class to make him look small, even in front of a child who was more than smart enough to figure such things out for herself.

Charlee crossed her arms. "So, because," she replied. Then she leaned on her arms, sliding them across the tablecloth so she was looking directly at him from a foot closer. "Have you ever not done something, or done something bad because it was easier than doing the good or right thing?"

Asher rolled his eyes. "Do you want a list? We could be here a while."

"Really?" Her interest was piqued. She straightened up. "Like what things?" she asked, avidly curious.

"Things," Asher said flatly. "Most of them things that a ten year old shouldn't know about."

"I'm eleven."

"When you're eighteen, come ask me."

"You'll tell me then?" Her eyes lit up.

"Probably not, but by then you'll know why I won't."

Charlee pouted.

"Let's assume he did something bad, for the sake of your argument," Ylva said.

Charlee glanced at him and Asher knew exactly what she was thinking about. Lonzo.

"Not just something bad," Charlee said quickly, "because people do bad things for really good reasons, sometimes. I mean doing something bad because it's easier than doing good, or not doing something good because it's easier not to."

"Let's say I've done both of those," Asher said. He shifted on his chair, feeling a sudden discomfort. If he had really analyzed his uneasiness then, he would have recognized that what Charlee was describing was pretty much his entire life now, but denial is a powerful thing. He pushed the recognition away and closed a mental door on it.

"Then, if you have, then you know the prickly gruellies you get when you do it?"

"The what?" Asher asked as Ylva laughed, this time out loud.

Charlee rolled her eyes. "The prickly gruellies. That's that I call them. I don't know if they've got a real name. You know, when your tummy gets all knotty, and you get hot and sticky, especially under the arms. You feel sick, but you're not really sick, but if you get 'em bad enough, you really *could* be sick. And your heart goes a million miles an hour."

"Are you talking about a guilty conscience?" Ylva asked. "Because guilt does all that to a person."

"Yeah, it could be guilt. See, I told you it probably had a name. But the thing is, you get the pricklies, you get guilty, even when you don't do something or you do something bad and you get clean away with it. You might not get 'em so bad you want to up-chuck—"

"Vomit, Charlee. If you must talk about it at all, use the right word," Ylva said softly.

"Okay, vomit," Charlee amended easily. She rubbed her fingers through her hair, causing the mass to wave and toss before letting it fall back over her shoulders.

"You don't up-chuck," Asher said, shooting Ylva an amused glance, "but you get the prickly gruellies anyway. Sitting in the back of your mind. Making you sweat, even just a little bit."

"*Yes,*" Charlee agreed, her hand pressing flat on the tabletop for emphasis. Then she pulled the next napkin over in front of her. "*That's* why I do things as good as I can, even if no one is watching. I hate the pricklies. They're horrible."

"Me, too," Asher said with feeling.

* * * * *

The light had nearly disappeared from the window while he had been trying to remember. The last of the sunlight struck the pane and glistened as it reflected off the thousand surfaces of the frost.

"Prickly gruellies," he whispered wonderingly.

Hadn't he spent the last few months trying to avoid the many, many prickly gruellies in his life? He'd turned up to meetings, made appointments, looked after business. He'd virtually stopped drinking and the barnyard dance of first dates had soured in his mouth because of the hypocrisy inherent in wooing a woman who was looking for a relationship that he could never provide.

All because a ten (*eleven*)-year-old girl had prodded his guilt.

That was why he had tried to dive back down the rabbit hole as soon as the meeting had finished. That's why Sindri's talk of bucking the system had sat so ill with him. Not because Charlee was right, but because he *didn't like it.*

He covered his face with his hands. Prickly gruellies. It was such a good name for them.

Then all the cascading thoughts swirled together and finally he understood why the window had kept drawing his attention. Calling silently to him. It was five o'clock and freezing outside. He'd let Charlee walk to the subway alone, in the cold.

Some superhero you are. The voice was his, but he could imagine Charlee saying it.

63

Chapter Six

Sindri
Origins unknown. Possibly one of the
last Valravn and leader of the Brennus
(Latinized form of a Celtic name or title
that possibly meant either "king, prince"
or "raven".) See *Brennus* for more.
Sindri is not considered a traitor,
although his actions…
From *The Complete Kine Encyclopedia,* by
Darwin Baxter, PhD. 2019 Edition

Sindri had been watching the riots in England with sharp interest for weeks. Brixton, Birmingham, Leeds…the poorest of the poor in major cities around England were taking on the police and venting their frustrations.

Like most rioters, they would end up losing. But what caught Sindri's attention were not the riots, but the reasons for them. He absorbed all the many news reports with a growing sense of excitement, for it was clear that these people were not protesting over an ideology, but pouring out their fears and anger upon the authorities for the deprivations they suffered daily, they and their children.

The poorest of the poor were nearly all children and their lack of a promising future was driving the rioters' fury.

Fury. Violence. Fear.

It was perfect.

Sindri made his arrangements. He sent several of the Brennus to England, to keep a watch over critical areas in that country while he completed a few preparations of his own.

Then, two weeks later, as summer was bursting into being, the word came and along with it a location: Manchester.

Sindri hurried to the London hall and caught one of the human trains from Euston station. Three hours later, he stepped out of the Piccadilly station in Manchester and waved down a taxi. The taxi driver glanced at him sharply, but accepted the fare. Sindri had not bothered overly much with costume or disguise. He wore human street clothes, but his head was bare as always. In England, for these strange times, he would not stand out terribly much, and virtually not at all once he had reached Bradford.

His Brennus contact had been right. The taxi came to a halt a quarter of a mile away from the stadium, unable to proceed, for a mob had formed in the middle of Ashton New Road, blocking off any traffic in either direction.

"Gotta drop yer 'ere," the taxi driver told him. "I ain't gone ter go near that mob. Yer right daft if yer thinkin' yer will."

"My thanks." Sindri pushed a fifty-pound note through the window.

"You betta wotch yerself!" the driver called as he tucked the note away and pulled the taxi around in a tight circle.

Sindri studied the mob ahead, taking note of the low buildings on the side opposite the stadium. There was more green space here than he had been expecting. The stadium itself was protected by a barrier of hip-high concrete walls. He studied the stadium. It was more than sufficiently tall, but there would be security.

He weighed the risks, then crossed the road, slipped over the concrete and with a pinch more effort, over the fence that surrounded the building. He strode toward the stadium entrance, already whispering the incantations he would need, letting them roil and build power inside him.

Inside, he struck remarkably little trouble. Only one guard challenged him. Sindri dealt with him easily, leaving him bundled in an electrical cupboard. He would wake in six hours, none the worse for his confinement and clueless about how he had arrived there.

The lack of security bothered Sindri, until he realized that most of the guards would be watching the mob building out on the road, assessing it for any danger to their stadium. He could hear the mob's low murmur leaking through the walls as he climbed the stairs.

He made his way to the back row on the top tier, where windows gave him a view of the road and the mob. He had to stand on the back of a seat to reach the glassed-in section of the wall, but his view was unobstructed and he would be unobserved, as he was tucked in behind the edge of the scoreboard.

The police were confronting the mob now, dressed in full riot gear, Plexiglas shields held at the ready like a modern-day version of the wall of shields the Romans once used to mow down their enemy. Nothing ever really changed, Sindri thought dryly.

He examined the top of the wall beneath the window area. It was wide enough to stand upon. He just had to get up there. He looked around once more for observers. He couldn't use a cloaking spell. They used up far too much energy and he would need every skerrick of his power for what was to come. Lifting and hovering didn't draw nearly as much because he was so practiced at it. He just didn't want anyone to see him do it.

The stadium was utterly empty. There was not even a bird sitting on the edge of the roof, soaking up the bright sunlight.

Sindri lifted himself up, until his toes were level with the top of the concrete wall. Then he stepped onto the wall and spread his feet, adjusting his balance. The glass was bare inches from his chest, making balancing a challenge, but the heavy-duty plastic gave him an unobstructed and undistorted view of the crowd below. He could see many heads down there, while the police lines were dotted with black helmets that glinted in the strong sunlight.

He settled his feet more soundly and spread his arms. The light raincoat he wore billowed out behind him at the movement.

He could feel the crowd, feel their anger. Good. It rose into the air like warm currents that only he could feel. He sank into the miasmic stench/feel of emotions roiling through and above the mob, sampling it. There was power there, but not enough, yet.

Summoning the words he needed made his body throb. This was going to take an enormous effort, but the potential payback was worth it.

Sindri gathered the power within him and sent it out to mix with the mob, to soak them with its fallout.

The mob almost flinched with the impact. The volume of their chanting and cries leapt upwards as they moved forward almost in unison, in the cohesive and fascinating gestalt in which mobs seemed to work. This time, though, their union was real. The power Sindri was feeding them was also uniting them in an intangible but very real way.

Their combined emotions rose like a heat haze over their heads, visible to someone like Sindri. Visible and arousing. He responded, his power swelling and feeding back to them.

The mob pulsed forward again and the police stirred. Batons were raised, the Plexiglas shields grounded more firmly. Now Sindri could feel *their* fear. It mingled with the emotions of the mob and added to the feedback loop. The mob responded by pushing forward yet again.

Then the first rock was thrown. It smashed against the Plexiglas with a solid, unexciting 'thunk'. But that was all it took. The police stepped closer and so did the mob.

Violence. Sindri closed his eyes and breathed in the unique bouquet. It added to the hysteria like yeast, lifting it higher and higher. The riot had been birthed and was squalling with hunger. Sindri didn't have to feed it anymore. It was breathing independently.

Instead, he switched polarities, drawing *in* instead of feeding. It took conscious effort to draw because the mob-being was hungry, sucking in every little heartbeat and anxiety anywhere near.

Sindri could feel its power, now. It was a growing thing. A *huge* thing.

He closed his eyes once more and concentrated on syphoning the pure, raw power from the crowd. The crucible was ready, waiting to accept the white-hot and pulsing power. It began to glow warmly against his flesh, throbbing with the energy it was absorbing. He had prepared the crucible well. It had almost infinite capacity to take power into itself.

The police were shouting. The mob was screaming. Batons rose and fell. Individuals staggered away from the fraying edges, blood streaming from cracked heads, nursing broken arms. But still the mob persisted, pushing and harassing the police. The noise was simply amazing.

But then, when the crucible had received all the power it could pull from the crowd, the mob for the first time paused. It staggered and became a collection of individuals once more. The power that had been driving them was gone, locked within Sindri's crucible.

The police were well trained. They moved forward to disperse the crowd despite no longer being driven by the combined energies swirling around them. Now their job was much easier. People were looking around, taking in their surroundings. Some were surprised, others puzzled. The power had gone, letting them think once more.

In the space of a few heartbeats, what might have been one of the worst of the English riots had dissipated and blown away like so much pollen in a breeze, all their fury and violence and fear evaporated.

The police would congratulate themselves for dispersing the crowd so efficiently and it was possible even the media would give them a small line or two of applause. None of them would ever come close to realizing the truth, Sindri thought as he lowered himself down to the level of the seats. He closed the raincoat over the crucible and became once more just an odd-looking human with some remarkable tattoos.

One or two sensitive humans in the crowd might wonder at the sudden turn of the event. They might tell their friends about how the stuffing got sucked out of the rioters (*"fucking cowards!"* they would declare), but no human could possibly guess the truth because in their world, magic didn't exist and power was something that ran their lights and microwaves.

Which suited Sindri just fine. "All the more for me," he murmured and climbed down the steps, human-fashion.

* * * * *

Lucas tapped on the front door of the house two up from theirs. Subconsciously, he noticed that the white paint was fresh and so was the green trim around the door. There was a pot of some pretty red flowers on the stoop, nodding in the early summer light. He didn't know what the flowers were (betcha Einie would), but the effect of neatness and homeliness was not lost on him.

The comparison started up the old itchy, uncomfortable feeling deep in his gut, the one he got whenever he thought about his home in comparison to someone else's. So he deliberately turned and looked out into the street, where kids were bouncing a basketball across the road, one sidewalk to the other, in between passing cars. Their throws were heroic, making them grunt with effort to get the ball all the way across in one bounce and making the kid on the opposite side jump high to catch it.

The door opened, pulling Lucas' attention back around. Darwin Baxter stood in the open doorway, his head almost brushing the top part of the doorframe. There was grey in his hair and his beard, but the rest of it was as black as he was. "You're Charlee's brother, aren't you?" he said.

"Yes, sir. Mr. Baxter, did Charlee come visit you for her lesson today?"

Darwin looked at him sharply. "She isn't at home? I've been worrying for about an hour now."

"Then she didn't come," Lucas said, something tightening up inside. It wasn't the same as thinking about home. It was a very specific worry. "She's in her bedroom," he told Darwin. "At least, I think she is. She hasn't come out of it for three days."

"Not even to eat?" Darwin asked.

"Charlee, well, she likes you teachin' her, so I figured she might have come here like usual and then you might have asked her what was wrong."

"What *is* wrong?" Darwin asked sharply.

"I dunno." Lucas shook his head.

Darwin stepped back. "Come in."

Lucas stepped into the very neat, tiny front room and Darwin shut the door behind him. There was a clock ticking away the time somewhere, but what caught his eye were the books. Shelves and shelves of them, wherever there was a wall with space to put up a few inches of MDF. It was so much *not* like home, so different, that the usual tight itchiness didn't rise in his belly. Instead, Lucas looked around curiously. Tentatively, he decided he liked all the books. It didn't feel like a dusty, must-stay-quiet library, which was the only place he had seen more books than this gathered in one place.

He could see why Charlee kept coming here. It was peaceful. There wasn't even a TV in the corner.

"So tell me about Charlee," Darwin said. He picked up a book that had been lying open and face-down on the easy chair, slid a bookmark into it and closed it properly. "Did she go to school the last three days? You said she's been staying in her bedroom."

"I *thought* she went to school. She left like always, but I think she snuck back home. Her bedroom door is closed when I get back and I always get home long before she does. Charlee barely makes it back for supper, most evenings."

Darwin's brow lifted. He sat on the footstool in front of the easy chair, sinking down onto it like he was barely aware of what he was doing. Lucas got the impression he was thinking hard.

"She didn't come down for supper Thursday night or last night. She yelled through the door that she wasn't hungry. I haven't seen her since Wednesday," Lucas added.

"You didn't go into her room to check on her?" Darwin asked.

Lucas could feel his cheeks heating in response. Not because it was a prurient question, but because he understood the assumption behind the question. Darwin hadn't asked if his parents had checked on her. He was asking if Lucas had. How much did he know about home, anyway? How much had Charlee told him?

"She locked the door," he replied. "I think she's sneaking out at night when everyone's sleeping, and using the bathroom and stuff, but she won't talk to anyone." He couldn't help adding, "Not even me." Because at the bottom of his concern, he was hurt—just a bit—that Charlee didn't trust him enough to come to him with whatever the problem was. What could be so dire in an eleven year old's life that he couldn't fix it for her, after all that he *had* mended?

Darwin was looking at him again with the same penetrating stare as before.

"I figured she might come talk to you, though," Lucas finished. "She likes you."

Darwin blinked. The corner of his mouth ticked upwards. Then he sobered. "What about that friend of hers? Did you ask him?"

"What friend?" Lucas stretched his memory, searching for a clue about who Darwin was talking about. Charlee didn't have friends. In the merciless hierarchy that was the school caste system, Charlee was a freak. She wasn't pretty by normal standards, and she waltzed through classes and scored top marks with what appeared to be little effort. That would be enough to ostracize most kids, but to add insult to injury, her family was... *a drunk. Her mother is a drunk.*

No one ever said anything to their faces, and neither Charlee nor Lucas ever invited anyone into the house to visit, where they would see the facts for themselves, but somehow, people knew. Maybe their parents talked too much over dinner, maybe someone in the neighborhood had noticed all the beer bottles. It didn't matter. In the mysterious, deadly swift communication channels that kids used, word had passed. The Montgomery family had a drunk mother and were the poorest of poor. It marked both of them indelibly. Lucas got around it by being damned good at any team sport they picked him for. It won him an acceptance that was denied Charlee.

All of this went through his mind at lightning speed, barely registering in coherent terms, but the itch started in his belly, crawled up to his chest and squeezed. "Charlee doesn't have a lot of friends," he said.

"The one that likes books and history," Darwin clarified.

"That's you."

He shook his head. "There's a boy. He's smart. He's been lending books to her."

"Mr. Baxter, you gotta understand. No one hangs with my sister. She goes to school, she comes home. She visits you on weekends." Even as he was saying it, Lucas heard the still voice in his head add, *but where does she go between school and home, huh?*

Her school, PS 157, got out just after three. She didn't walk in the door until supper time, which was supposed to be five-thirty, but was usually closer to six by the time their mother got herself sorted out. She would slide in through the front door and hurry up to her bedroom, dump her bag and come back down to sit at the table even as the plates were being handed out.

Mom never noticed and even Dad, who might have commented once, didn't seem to care. The medicines that littered the table next to his recliner seemed to take away any interest in the world beyond his knees.

Lucas had noticed, but he had deliberately not questioned Charlee. Everyone was entitled to their secrets (*like the second-hand copies of* Hustler *under your bed, right?*). Charlee always came in looking refreshed and happy. Whatever she was doing, it was essentially harmless and seemed to be good for her, so Lucas had kept his mouth shut.

Now he regretted it. If she had a friend of the male persuasion who she was hiding from him, what did she and her friend get up to that made her look so damned happy?

She's only eleven, he reminded himself. But was he going to have to sit her down and give her the same lecture his father had given him four years ago? Were his parents so deep into their own concerns that they hadn't noticed how tall she was getting?

The tightness in his chest increased and Lucas looked at Darwin unhappily. "I don't know about any friend." *But you do. You did know, but you didn't care enough to find out what she does after school.*

Darwin sighed. "Then something happened on Wednesday. Something that has upset her. Charlee doesn't dump her problems on anyone without encouragement. She's holding it in and working it out for herself. What happened Wednesday that you can remember? Anything significant?"

Lucas thought that Darwin had got closer to the essence of Charlee than anyone had ever bothered to try. She did figure things out herself. She was so fiercely independent that sometimes Lucas thought she *preferred* to be by herself, to do it herself. It wasn't anything he could understand. He liked hanging out with friends, talking shit over and hearing how they'd resolved problems. It made everything seem lighter that way.

"Wednesday night, she didn't eat dinner. She sat at the table for about sixty seconds, then dumped her plate—" He stopped suddenly, surprised at his own observations.

"What?" Darwin prompted.

"She dumped it in the sink. She didn't scrape it. She always scrapes her plate. Ours, too. But she dropped it in the sink. Then she went upstairs and that's the last I saw of her."

"Was she upset?"

"Quiet. But that's usual." Lucas frowned. Why hadn't he taken better notice? He had wolfed down his own dinner—he was always hungry these days—with half an eye on the TV playing in the corner. He couldn't say now whether she had been normal, or if she had been holding something in. "I shoulda looked harder."

"Kid, this isn't on you," Darwin said kindly. "Don't take this on, too."

Lucas could feel his face burning again. How much had Charlee really told this man? But she wouldn't have told him anything. That was something Charlee seemed to just know, agreeing silently with him without the need for discussion. Any details about their home life stayed at home. Friends, neighbors, the kids at school, and especially the teachers, who were the front end of a chain of authority figures that could destroy their lives—nothing ever got shared with them.

Lucas shifted on his feet. "What do I do?"

Darwin sighed. "You're going to have to talk to her."

"You mean, force in her door?" The idea horrified him. Charlee had very little. She didn't have nice clothes, a big boom box, friends, or even a life that he would ever care to have himself. But the privacy of her room and abiding by the declaration made by her locked door was something he could give her. He'd be pissed as hell if she forced her way past his closed door.

"Lucas…" Darwin began. "Can I call you that?"

Lucas nodded.

"Sometimes, Lucas, people just don't know what's good for themselves. They get so worked up inside they don't see things straight. Adults *and* kids. Did it occur to you that she's kept the door locked for three days because she doesn't know how else to yell for help?"

Lucas felt his heart physically lurch in his chest. "No," he breathed, feeling sick. Had Charlee really wanted him to bust down her door, after all?

"You're the only one at home that would notice the door had been shut so long," Darwin added. "It seems to me that she's reaching out to you in particular."

The urge to run home—*sprint* home—gripped him. Lucas licked his lips. "I gotta go," he muttered, turning.

"Do me a favor, kid?" Darwin asked.

He looked over his shoulder.

"Let me know what the problem is, when you find out? Charlee hasn't missed a lesson in nearly two years. It has to be something dire to keep her away."

* * * * *

Ylva came out of the kitchen with her fresh pot of tea, just in time to see Asher standing at the coat rack, swapping out his suit jacket for the more casual leather bomber he kept there.

"Where do you think you're going?" she asked, her tone sharper than she usually liked to let it get.

He glanced at her as he transferred his wallet and keys, all the human accoutrements, from his suit jacket. "She hasn't shown up for two days, Ylva." In the late afternoon sunlight streaming through the big plate glass windows, his hair was dazzlingly bright. He wasn't handsome in the modern sense of the word, but his confidence in his ability to defend himself and the square, sure way he carried himself gave him a bone-deep sexiness that Ylva had been watching women fall foul of for a very long time. She steeled her heart, tucking away the fact of their friendship so that she could do what she needed to do. "You can't go to her, Asher." She put iron into her voice. Once, that authoritative tone had always been there.

"Nearly a year, and she doesn't miss a single day," he replied. "Something has to be wrong for her to not come by for two whole days." He wasn't listening to her.

"Asher!" she snapped.

Finally, he looked at her. *Really* looked at her.

She shook her head. "You can't go there. It's Saturday. Her family will be there. You can't just turn up at her house and demand to see her and to know what's wrong."

"I know where she lives…." He processed her words and frowned. "Why can't I go there? I just want to know that she's okay."

"She's *eleven years old*, Asher! Think of how it will look. A grown man comes calling on a young girl."

His jaw clamped and rippled. His eyes narrowed. "What are you saying?" he asked, his voice hard.

"I'm not saying anything. I'm telling you how it will *look*! I know what the facts are. I know what this really is. I've sat here for a year drinking tea with her, too. I'm worried, of *course* I'm worried. But you can't just turn up at her house. They'll report you, or worse."

His jaw wasn't loosening up at all. There was a hot light in his eyes. "I'm supposed to just sit here and wait for her to show up again?"

"As hard as it seems, yes, that's exactly what you get to do."

"What if she's in trouble? *Real* trouble, I mean."

Ylva knew exactly what he meant by "real" trouble. The sort of trouble that one of the Kine, one with a sword, could resolve but that no normal human could fix.

"I could help her," Asher insisted. "I'm *supposed* to help her."

Ylva smiled a little. "I know the doctrine as well as you…." The expression in his face halted her. "You're not talking about just service to humanity, are you? You're talking about *helping* her. Charlee, specifically. Is that how…is that why you met her? What does she know about you, Asher?"

"Nothing," he said flatly. "She knows not to ask, and she never did." He shoved his hands in the front pockets of the jacket. "I'll get a cab. It'll be quicker."

"You're risking exposure," she countered. It was a last desperate bid to keep him here, but it was a genuine concern, too.

His answer was to head for the door.

"Let me know what happens!" Ylva called after him, then she grimaced at her own hypocrisy. She wanted to know what had happened to Charlee as badly as Asher did. Who was she fooling with her talk of duty and *laun*? She watched through the front window as Asher climbed into the back of a cab. She clearly hadn't fooled Asher. If she had, he wouldn't have left.

What had happened to Charlee? Please let it be nothing serious. Ylva glanced up to the ceiling as she sent up her silent prayer, then carried the pot back to the kitchen. There was no one left to share it with, out here.

* * * * *

Lucas kept up his tapping on the door, even though Charlee didn't answer. He couldn't bang on the door the way he really wanted to. The fear was careening around inside him now, a runaway train that was building up speed with every passing minute. He kept seeing things in his imagination, scenarios of disaster all of them. Rape. Gang rape. Extortion. A newly acquired drug habit. Police brutality. They weren't just ideas ripped from the headlines, either. Lucas knew kids who had been through all of it and worse. There wasn't anything about his and Charlee's lives that would protect Charlee from some of the nightmare situations that a kid growing up in the Bronx could face. All those possibilities formed in his mind, making him sick, making his heart thud hard and making him want to ram down the door like it was a tackle dummy, bust in there and demand to know what was wrong with her, at the top of his lungs.

But banging, shouting, anything loud or unexpected would raise his parents' attention, downstairs. Mom wouldn't come to see, but his father might, if the noises were alarming enough.

So Lucas forced himself to tap quietly, but persistently. He put his mouth close to the door frame. "Charlee, if you don't let me in, I'm going to stand here and scratch at your door until you do. I'll drive you fucking crazy. I wanna know what's wrong, so open the goddamn door!"

Nothing.

He started tapping again. Now that Darwin Baxter had clued him in, he would stand here for a month, if that was what it took to wear her down. But he would find out. He…would…find…out. He tapped in time to his thoughts. Tap…tap…tap…tap!

It took twenty minutes. By that time, Lucas had swapped hands a dozen times over and had resorted to holding his forearm with the other hand to support it. But he didn't stop tapping.

The door unlocked with a soft 'snick' sound as the bolt was drawn back. That was the only sign that he had won. Lucas stepped back, staring at the chipped dark brown paint on the door, at Charlee's hand-lettered poster declaring it was *Charlee's room, stay out!* The door didn't move, but he hadn't imagined that quick click of the bolt.

His heart in his throat, making his mouth dry, Lucas curled his hand around the doorknob and turned it. The door gave way and his heart leapt even higher. He pushed the door open, wondering what he would see. *Pregnant. Raped. Beaten up. Black eye. Stitches. Bruises across her whole body.*

Charlee sat on her bed.

The bed was perfectly made. The bedside lamp wasn't on because it was still mid-afternoon and the sun was high overhead.

Lucas found he was examining Charlee from kinky head to bare toes. No stitches. No baby. No bruises.

Then what is wrong with her?

He shut the door. "What's wrong, Einie? What's happened? What happened on Tuesday?"

She flinched. He saw what looked like bruises under her eyes that he hadn't seen with his first swift scan. She had lost weight (*she hasn't been eating, you dork!*), which made her look even more gawky and long. For the first time, he noticed that the hem of her jeans stopped short of her ankles by a bit more than the fashionable length. She was growing. Again.

"Charlee?" he coaxed softly.

She just sat, mute. But something, some emotion, was flowing off her like a heat wave. He couldn't figure out what it was. Sorrow? Anger? Both?

"Charlee, please," he added, when she didn't speak. "You're scaring the shit out of me."

Her eyes grew bigger and he saw surprise there.

The front doorbell buzzed like an angry wasp, yanking his attention away from Charlee. He swore, because Dad wasn't home. He'd caught a rare overtime shift on the docks where he worked. Only Mom was home and she wouldn't—

"Lucas!" she called from the kitchen, her voice wavering up to them. "Someone's at the door." There wasn't too much slur in her words yet, but the game was on. By the end of the fourth quarter....

"I gotta get the door," Lucas told Charlee. "Promise me you'll tell me what's wrong when I get back. Promise?"

She considered him. Then she nodded, her head moving by a fraction of an inch. But it was a promise.

Grimly pleased, Lucas rushed downstairs, taking them three and four at a time, gripping the bannister to keep balance. He glanced through to the kitchen. His mother was out of sight of the front door. So were any beer bottles. The relief he felt was almost subliminal.

He yanked the door open.

There was a giant standing on their stoop. That was his first impression. The guy was huge. He wasn't just tall; his shoulders were like a professional football player's. He was wearing a leather jacket, one of the trendy ones that looked like Indiana Jones' jacket, but it was black. He studied Lucas for a moment.

Fuck, are his eyes really that blue? Lucas wondered inanely. Or did he do something to them to make them look that way?

"Lucas?" the man asked.

Lucas drew in a sharp breath, shocked. "Who wants to know?" he retorted automatically. Defensively.

"You don't know me," the guy said, then his gaze flickered over Lucas' shoulder, and up. "Charlee," he breathed, sounding just as surprised as Lucas was.

Lucas whirled. Charlee was standing at the top of the stairs, gripping the bannister like it might fall down…or she might. Her eyes were huge, the bruises under them making them seem even bigger.

"Hell's hounds, Charlee," the man said roughly. "What's happened?"

Lucas watched her, amazed that she had emerged from her room. Fear leapt in him as tears sparkled in her eyes and slid down her cheeks. Her chin quivered as she looked not at him, but at the man.

"They killed Chocolate," she said, and began to cry in soft, heart-wrenching sobs.

The man slipped past Lucas and climbed the stairs in four big strides. He wrapped his arms around Charlee and sat right there on the step, holding her against him.

Lucas didn't know what to do. He didn't know the man who was (*hugging her, he's hugging Charlee*) sitting on the stairs, but Charlee did. And who the hell was Chocolate? Her mystery book-loving friend?

Charlee wrapped her arms around the man's neck and tucked her face into his chest. She wept in big, almost silent heaves, her shoulders shaking.

Lucas couldn't help it. He glanced through to the kitchen again, checking. But the game was clearly going well, for the volume had been turned up. Mom wouldn't move from the table until it was all over, now.

Lucas climbed up to where the man's feet were propped on the step five below the one he sat on. He wore shoes that looked expensive and a long way away from what a professional footballer would wear, or even Indiana Jones, come to that. The pants above them were that dull shiny material that really good suits were made out of.

He got as close to them as he could on the narrow stairs. "Who the fuck are you?" he demanded in a low voice.

The man looked at him. "Asher Strand," he said and miraculously, his voice was just as low as Lucas'. Charlee's arms tightened around his neck, and his hand soothed her shoulder. Lucas wasn't sure he liked that much. But this dude had unlocked the dam inside Charlee just by showing up, when he, Lucas, hadn't been able to get her to even unlock her door for three days.

"No offense," Lucas said, "but your name doesn't tell me dick. Who *are* you?"

"A friend," Asher Strand said. "Look, Lucas, Charlee and I have to head out into the neighborhood for a while. I need to take care of something for her. You can stay here, or if it makes you more comfortable, come with us."

"You ain't moving anywhere with my sister," Lucas shot back, his anger boiling.

"Then you're coming with us," Asher concluded. He stood up and helped Charlee gently back onto her feet. Her sobs had diminished to sniffles and hiccups.

"What the hell is going on here?" Lucas demanded, baffled and uneasy.

"Come with us and find out," Asher replied, then looked at Charlee.

It was the sadness in his expression that talked Lucas into agreeing.

* * * * *

Once they were outside and beyond the view of the house, Asher Strand didn't wave down a cab or head for a car, as Lucas expected. Instead, he looked at Charlee. "Where is she?" he asked.

Charlee drew in a shuddering breath. "This way," she murmured, and hurried down the street.

They followed her around the corner and over to Trinity, then across 162nd, then 161st, running to catch the lights and breaks in traffic. Once they were on the other side, Asher stretched out his stride and drew level with Charlee. "Is she in the alley?"

Charlee nodded, looking down at her feet. Then she looked up at Asher. "That's how I know it was them."

Lucas wanted to demand explanations, for none of this was making sense. Was there really a body in an alley, somewhere ahead? A person called Chocolate, who Charlee had been grieving over for two fucking days without telling anyone? And who was "them"? The dire range of possible answers to his unvoiced questions kept him silent. He would rather wait for the truth.

The alley was one of the crooked ones that bent around the outside of a building. This one was on the corner of 160th, a big ten-story apartment block. He hurried after the odd pair ahead of him, the skinny red-headed girl who was his sister and the giant mystery man who seemed to know more about Charlee than he did.

Charlee stepped around the bend in the alley and up to the wooden paling that separated the alley from the back yards of the houses on the next block. There was a collection of rusty and dented trashcans and the miscellaneous garbage that always collected around them: big, flattened cardboard cartons, unwanted and junky furniture with the stuffing hanging out, old tricycles and toys that had faded from lying in the sun.

Charlee lifted one of the bigger cartons away from its lean against the fence. She stood there with her head down, her eyes closed. "See," she whispered.

Lucas hurried over to see for himself, his heart thundering.

The dog had been dead for three days, but even so, it was horribly easy to see what had killed it. While Lucas' mind jerked to a halt in surprise, then hurried to put things together in light of this most obvious (*in hindsight*! his mind whispered defensively) possibility. Chocolate was a dog and from the look of it—her—she had been a stray.

But homelessness hadn't killed her. Charlee was right. Someone had cut her throat. Right here by the look of it, because it—she—was lying in a pool of dried blood. The smell must have been ferocious for a few days, but the worst of it had faded. Now, flies buzzed around the carcass. In a few days (*so glad you didn't get to see that, Einie!*), there would be maggots crawling out of every orifice.

Then, secondary details registered. There was a long piece of twine tied around the dog's neck in a rough-and-ready leash. The dog had been led here to her death.

Anger roiled in him. Who could do this to a mutt? *Why* would they do it and put his sister through hell and back?

Charlee looked up at the man. Her eyes were swimming again. "They did it to get at me."

He sighed. "I'm afraid so, Charlee," he said softly. "They must have found her roaming the streets."

Lucas stared at them, astonishment warring with his still bubbling anger. Someone had done this deliberately. Someone had done this *precisely* to put his sister through hell. "Who are they?" he demanded. "I'll fucking kill them."

Asher shook his head. "You won't do anything at all. You're going to leave this to me."

Lucas' breath pushed out in a rush. "*You*? Who the fuck are you? Why should I leave this to you? It's my sister these fuckers came after."

Strand turned away from his study of the dog to round on Lucas. His eyes were chilly, his jaw set. "Do you want to go back to high school next year, Lucas? Do you want to be breathing when September rolls around?"

Lucas scrambled to assimilate his meaning. "Who *are* they?" he asked, his voice lower, his anger cooled.

"Someone I thought I had dealt with once before," Asher said, sounding mildly annoyed.

"Lightning Lords," Charlee added.

"What the hell are you doing fucking around with a gang?" Lucas cried, his voice rising again. "Jesus H. Christ on a pony, Charlee! The Lords don't pull their punches. Not with anybody."

"You know them, then," Asher said, with what sounded like a degree of satisfaction. "Good."

"*Good*?" He was aware that his voice was even higher now.

Charlee pulled the carton that had been leaning over the dog to one side and stood it up so that it was resting on the open end.

"Tell me about them," Asher said, his voice a shitload softer than Lucas' was right now. Soft, but with an edge to it.

Lucas stared at him. The man was well over six feet tall, because that was Lucas' height and this guy topped him by a few inches at least. As for his shoulders… But it was his eyes that Lucas kept coming back to. His eyes, so blue that it didn't look real, except for the coldness in them. It wasn't for him, that coldness, or for Charlee. The chill was absent when he looked at her. But he was letting Lucas see it.

Anyone who crossed him or got in his way, that's what they would see. That would be the last thing they would see for a while, anyway, Lucas thought. Arctic coldness backed up by absolute assurance that he could do with them whatever the hell he wanted.

Lucas thought about Asher confronting the Lords, perhaps in some lonely alley like this one. He thought about who would get to walk out of that alley afterward and realized that he would probably put his money on this guy, despite knowing what the Lords were capable of.

"They've got a new capo," he said. "I heard the guy is whacked in the head. Crazier than a loon. He had them take over the Angels' territory a week after he took over the gang."

"When was that?" Asher asked.

"I don't know. I just heard it at school. Maybe two months ago."

Asher glanced at Charlee, where she was interleaving the bottom flaps of the carton, rebuilding it. "That explains a lot," he said. "Do you know where I would find them, generally?"

"We're right in the middle of their turf, right here," Lucas said. He was glad to hear his voice was back to normal. Calmer. "There's a bodega on Cauldwell, right by the park next to Charlee's school. They hang out there, sometimes, especially when it's hot, like now."

"Is that why you haven't been to school or anywhere else, Charlee?" Asher asked her.

Charlee looked up from the carton, her eyes big. She nodded slowly. "That…and I just didn't want to go anywhere. Not for a while."

"What *are* you doing, anyway?" Lucas asked, as she flipped the carton over.

"We're going to bury Chocolate," she told him. "While Asher deals with the gang."

No fucking way am I touching that thing, Lucas thought and held his lips together tightly.

Chapter Seven

Asher Strand
b432 AD — Norway, as Askr, son of
Brynjar, a.k.a Asher Brynjarson, Asher
Strand, Dr. Andrew Beach. Made
Einherjar circa 470AD. Various human
roles and locations after the Descent. As
one of the Kine, is principally known for
his role as Stallari of the New York hall,
and for his outspoken political stance
against *laun*....
From *The Complete Kine Encyclopedia*, by
Darwin Baxter, PhD. 2019 Edition

They buried what was left of Chocolate under a tree in Ayton playground, behind the enclosed basketball courts. It was shady and cool, and by the time they were done, the sun had set. Lucas couldn't believe that some adult hadn't come up to them and demanded to know why they were digging up the soil in a public park, but the whole afternoon had been one surreal event after another. It seemed perfectly in sync that they should dig a grave and hold funeral rites for a mutt and have absolutely no one protest or call the police. It was just that sort of a day.

Charlee remained silent while they dug and Lucas left her alone, not asking any of the hundred questions he had. When the grave was deep enough, he opened the carton and reached in to pick up the dog's hindquarter, which was the way he had got her in there. Charlee didn't protest over what she might consider to be a cruel way to handle the carcass. She was dry-eyed and astonishingly calm.

He laid the dog in the bottom of the hole, carefully curling her up in a rounded curve so she fit in the hole, trying not to touch too much of the decaying flesh. He glanced up at Charlee, resting back on his feet. His T-shirt was sticking to him, but the very slight breeze felt great against his sweaty skin. "Want to say something, Einie?" he asked.

Charlee looked down at the dog. "She never hurt anyone," she said softly and looked up at Lucas and nodded.

As an epitaph, it was a fine one. There were too few humans about whom the same could be said. "Amen," Lucas added and started shoveling the soil back in over the top of the dog with his hands.

The backfilling went far more quickly, but the light was failing by the time they patted the sods back into place. Lucas folded up the carton and stuffed it into the nearest trash can while Charlee washed her hands in the drink fountain.

They turned and headed for home.

They had crossed 162nd before either of them spoke again. "What do you think he's doing?" Lucas asked, as if Asher had been on both of their minds while they were walking and he was just picking up the ends of the silent conversation.

"I don't know," Charlee said softly. "It's better that we don't."

It was a disquietingly adult observation.

"But I wouldn't want to be one of the Lightning Lords tonight," she added.

Amen, Lucas thought.

* * * * *

The gang had belonged to Sergio since early April, when Ricky had up and disappeared without leaving behind so much as a smelly fart to explain where he had gone. Most of the gang figured Ricky had skipped town two steps ahead of the police and was living it up in Tijuana or Acapulco, high on the good life.

Benny would never say it to anyone, but he didn't think Ricky had skipped at all. He didn't know for sure what had happened, but in his slow-moving brain he had put together two possibilities.

Either the girl and her dog had brought the wrath of the blue-eyed man down upon Ricky for some imagined transgression, or Sergio had quietly dealt with him in the dark of the night, clearing the way for Sergio to step in and take over the gang.

Benny had waffled between favoring one or the other possibility. Each had seemed likely in his tiny mind. But the deciding factor was Ricky himself. The dude had lost face with the gang, especially after he'd let the girl strut on by that day. As a result, the stuffing had dropped right out of Ricky. He had been barely hanging onto the gang's respect and even though Benny wasn't particularly smart, he knew in a gut instinct way that Ricky didn't have the balls to do anything that might bring the big guy down on him.

Because Ricky's grip on the gang had been crumbling, it had only been a matter of time before the issue was dealt with one way or another. Sergio had been the one to deal with him, Benny felt sure in his bones.

But every time one of them wondered aloud about what Ricky was doing down in ol' Me-hick-koh, he would dutifully laugh right along with them. He didn't want Sergio to look at him in that steady way he had, wondering why Benny didn't find the idea of Ricky sunbathing on an

Acapulco beach funny.

Benny didn't want Sergio looking at him at all. He hadn't yet got around to the full realization that Sergio was crazy in a sociopathic, burn-down-the-mission way, because the concept was a complicated one. But he was getting there.

He was also entertaining vague notions of sliding out of town himself, wetbacking across the border and finding that beach they kept talking about. It wasn't fully set in his mind, just like Sergio's madness had not fully penetrated.

So for tonight he hung with the gang like always, pretending he was as carefree as the rest of them pretended to be. Sergio was the only one who seemed to be genuinely relaxed, with not a care on his mind.

Benny hadn't slept well since Sergio had done the dog in. His dreams had been shot with dark silhouettes of giants with swords. He would wake in the middle of the night, his body coated with sweat and the sound the dog had made, the frightened whimper that had suddenly cut off, echoing in his mind.

Sergio had giggled when the deed was done. He had looked down at the dog's twitching body and the laugh that had emerged from his mouth was that of a little boy who had kicked over a trashcan and was delighted by the mess and the smell and the sheer audacity he had displayed.

They were wandering up Cauldwell Avenue now, aimlessly quartering their neighborhood. The idea hadn't been said aloud, but Benny knew Sergio was looking for trouble. He was itching again. The delight over the dog hadn't lasted long at all.

It was another hot night. June was being a real bitch this year. Flowers wilted in their pots and the grass in the parks was a tired, bleached yellow. It was nights like this Benny thought about knocking over a fire hydrant and playing in the water just like the little kids did. But Sergio would think it a stupid idea, so he said nothing.

They turned into 161st and headed for Trinity and Benny got jumpy, looking around and over his shoulder.

"Got ants in your pants, man?" Sergio asked, grinning.

"We shouldn't a come down this way," Benny muttered. He was too uneasy to care that Sergio had been setting the direction, that this was Sergio's idea.

"We go where the fuck I like," Sergio replied, the happy grin not shifting an inch.

Benny shut up, but he hunched his shoulders, trying to ease the tight skin between them. They crossed Trinity, and Benny realized Sergio was heading for the park. It was a dark patch in among the lights, just ahead. The park didn't have floodlights. It was too small for the city to bother with security or policing. The pocket of blackness in among the traffic and the housing had served the gang admirably on more than one occasion. This time, though, Benny didn't want to step into its shadows. Nuh-uh. No way.

His breath started to whistle in and out faster than usual. Barely noticed, the dark, overwhelming imagery from his dreams skittered through his mind, but his heart picked up speed. He started to sweat harder. His silk shirt stuck to him because his tank was wet through. But he was a good, unimaginative soldier, so he kept right on trucking with the rest.

Sergio jogged into the thick blackness that enveloped the park, giving out a great shout, throwing it up toward the high-rises that surrounded them. It was a defiant sound, without words but full of energy.

The others, six of them tonight, trod dutifully after him, Benny included, but his throat had closed down to a pinhole and breathing was painful. He looked around wildly, his eyes wide as he tried to penetrate the black and see what lay in wait, but the dark hid everything.

Sergio paused at the drinking fountain and took in big mouthfuls. Then he whipped his hand through the catch tray beneath, spraying those closest to him with the tepid water. The concrete at the foot of the fountain was damp with the overrun, making Sergio's thousand-dollar shit-kickers squish as they moved through the muddy grit. It sounded loud in the silence and Benny tamped down the urge to shush Sergio. Noise wasn't good. Noise drew attention.

"What d'fuck was that, man?" Jesus muttered, spinning around to look behind him, into the dark. "D'ya hear that?"

"'s nothing, ya pussy," Sergio growled. He held his silk shirt open and flapped it, letting in cooler air around his body.

Benny backed up, away from Sergio. He could hear his own heartbeat, slamming inside his head. "Not good...not good," he whispered to himself.

There was a little light, spilling across the dark playground from the apartments and the street lights, and now his eyes had adjusted. Benny could make out the shapes of the swings and slides on the south side, and the scraggly bushes on the west. That's where the shadow emerged from, and Benny happened to be looking right at it. He saw the shadow and he heard the sound he had only heard once before, in an alley he was trying hard to forget. The sound was metallic, but there was something layered over the top of it, like the metal was bubbling away in a pot.

Benny remembered the sound with perfect clarity, far better than he could recall the chores his mother had given him that morning. When he heard it, his bladder let go, wetting the front of his jeans in a hot cascade, but he wouldn't notice until it was all over.

The shadow loomed up behind Sergio. A forearm that looked as big as a tree trunk to Benny in his panicky state looped around Sergio's throat and tightened up. Then Benny saw the sword. It seemed to almost glow in the dark. So did the guy.

But it was the sword Benny couldn't take his eyes off. He had seen what the sword could do. And the guy, the dude, he had the tip of the sword pressed up underneath Sergio's chin (*just like Lonzo!*).

"Holy fuck!" one of the others cried as they all fell back a few steps in sheer surprise. All except Sergio, whose eyes were bugging out as he scrabbled at the arm around his neck.

"If you don't keep still," the guy said, "I'll tighten my arm, and you'll black out from lack of oxygen. Then I can do what I want to you."

He would, too. Benny knew that as surely as he knew Sergio wouldn't let that happen. Sure enough, Sergio stopped struggling. "Fucker," he muttered, his voice indistinct.

"You want to be very careful what you do and say in the next two minutes," the guy said. "I can push this blade up through your jaw and into the base of your brain with very little effort. It would take about fifteen pounds of pressure, and I've got two pounds on it already, pushing it up against your chin."

Sergio was scowling. He didn't like that.

The others were hovering in a rough semicircle around them, standing anywhere from ten to fifteen feet away. They looked scared. Benny was scared, too, but an unholy fascination kept his feet planted where they were. This was the embodiment of his nightmares. He was helpless to do anything but let it play out.

"Thing is," the man continued, "I've had a lot of practice with this. I've used it so many times I've lost count. I blooded this blade when I was sixteen and I was taught by the best swordsmen in the world. I want you to appreciate that history. I want you to understand that I wouldn't just jam the blade into your skull, because that would be crude and it wouldn't be nearly enough to make up for all you've done."

"I haven't done nothing!" Sergio protested, the words fuzzy because he couldn't move his jaw much. The angled point of the sword was pressing against the skin there, and Benny thought he could see blood.

"You and I both know that is a lie," the man said softly, "so shut up and listen. I have a profound understanding of how your brain works. I know the areas that keep your heart ticking, the parts that let you move when you want. When I push this blade into your head, I'm going to move it around. I'm going to aim for all the interesting sections. You won't die straight away. But you will feel pain, because I'll make sure I hit the thalamus, and that's the pain-processing center. Then I'll make you squirm like a kid that needs to go to the washroom and can't. You'll dance a jig like you've never danced one before." He was crooning all this into Sergio's ear, sounding like he would love every second of it.

Benny couldn't look away. He wanted to be sick. A vision of Sergio dancing, his arms and legs flailing like a bug on a pin, was stuck in his brain.

Sergio's face was shiny with sweat…and Benny wondered if they were tears he could see glistening under his eyes. But Sergio also looked mad. Furious, like if he got even the smallest chance, he was going to turn this around and cream the guy into so much paste.

"I can make you smell and taste things you've never eaten before," the man continued. "Want to know what it's like to eat your own shit? Then, as an encore, I can make you vomit until your eyes cloud over red from the strain, and your throat rips out, burned out by the bile you choke up…and you'll keep on doing it until I move the blade to a new location. I can make you do anything I want you to do, just with the tip of this sword. Do you believe me?"

Say yes! Benny pleaded silently. He didn't want this to continue. He was sold.

Sergio looked like he could do the guy in just by staring at him. But his head moved fractionally, up and down.

"Good," the man said. He glanced up at the rest of them, who stood in the rough semicircle, watching this all go down with the same fascination they would have watched a lynching, or a car accident, or a tenement burn down with people still inside. The man's eyes seemed to glitter in the dark as he looked at them all, one by one.

He's remembering us, Benny thought. *Holy fuck, he's taking names!*

When the man's gaze came to Benny, his eyes narrowed. But his gaze moved and Benny felt a touch of relief.

Then the dude looked down at Sergio and gave him a little shake. It made Sergio's head move from side to side, while the sword stayed still. The point dug a furrow into Sergio's chin and this time there was no mistaking the blood dripping from the cut.

Sergio bared his teeth, a hiss of pain whistling past them.

"When I let you go, you should talk to your friend over there, the fat one with the long hair. Ask him about Lonzo, and make sure you get all the details."

Benny could see that Sergio had focused in on the first bit the man had said, and hadn't heard the rest.

When I let you go.

Sergio's fear diminished. Now there was just wordless fury in his eyes.

The man shook him again, making him hiss. "Are you listening?"

"*Yes*," Sergio muttered through his teeth.

"In case you haven't figured out why I'm here, I'm going to make it very plain and simple for you. Your predecessor understood. Now I'm giving you a chance to abide by the rules, too. You stay away from the redhead, Charlee Montgomery. You stay away from her, her brother, and her family and anyone she appears to be friends with. You don't bother her. You don't talk to her. If I hear of any one of your gang even so much as whispering to her or making her life uncomfortable in any way, even indirectly, I will hold you personally responsible. I will find you and this sword is going to make you quack like a duck in front of all your friends. Do you understand me?"

Benny held his breath until Sergio nodded, and it took fifteen very long seconds before his head shifted up and down.

"Say it," the man demanded.

"I understand. Prick."

"You're a smart man," the guy said. "I'm going to leave now and I suggest you do the same. There are some very bad people heading in this direction. They will make you think I am an angel in comparison." He let Sergio go and pushed him away with a heavy shove.

Sergio staggered forward, coughing, then spun around to look at the guy. Benny looked, too.

He was gone.

Benny was never sure what prompted him to move right at that moment. He didn't even think it through. Sergio wasn't looking at him right then, and neither were any of the others. They were all gawking at the place where the dude with the sword had been. So he stepped backwards. One quiet pace. Then another. A third, then he turned and started running like the blue-eyed guy was coming for him. For all he knew, he *was* coming for him. He recalled the man's words: *There are some very bad people heading in this direction.* It gave him speed he didn't know he possessed.

By ten o'clock the next morning he was on a Greyhound, heading for San Diego, spitting distance from the Mexican border. Considering what happened to most of the others in the park that night, where they lingered to talk over what had happened to Sergio, who had also slipped away into the night, Benny proved to be the smartest one of them all.

* * * * *

The restaurant, when Darwin found it, was a surprise. Rather than being the hole-in-the-wall he had been expecting, he discovered that The Ash

Tree was a large store-front establishment on Angel Street, with new, dark green awnings over the glass windows, traditional brass curtain rods holding café curtains across the bottom half of the windows, and tubs of flowers on either side of the doors, cascading multi-hued petals down to the sidewalk. More flowers dripped from hanging pots on either end of the awnings. It was a low-key, attractive place and it looked like it had been there for a long time. Years.

He pushed his way inside. There was a discreet chime somewhere toward the back of the restaurant.

It was just after three-thirty in the afternoon. He had taken a few hours of personal time in order to come down here and still be home at a reasonable hour. He had also wanted to arrive here more or less at the same time Charlee had been visiting.

It had been nine days since Lucas had shown up on his doorstep and eight days since the boy had sat at his kitchen table and laid out the whole story, while Darwin had listened, stunned at times and concerned at others.

Darwin preferred to think things over before he did anything. Time had a way of tempering the strongest situations and a good, long contemplation gave his instincts a chance to sniff things out and come to a decision. Just like any commander in history that he'd ever studied, he preferred to look at the whole view before making up his mind.

He had already suspected he would be making this call even before Lucas hurried home again to check on Charlee, but he had bided his time. It was a rare day when thinking things through didn't provide some of the information he needed, but this time around, Darwin had a lot of questions and not too many answers.

He still would have waited, but Charlee's situation had hurried him and made it imperative that he stop by today, Monday.

Inside, the restaurant was as neat and charming as the outside. There was a couple of elderly ladies sitting at one of the tables by the window, where the afternoon sun fell on them. They were gossiping softly, heads together over a pot of coffee and cakes. One of them cackled with laughter as Darwin stepped in the door and it was a merry sound that made him smile.

There was a small bar at the back of the room, on the right-hand side. In front of the bar was a collection of low tables and big easy chairs, four to each table, their arms butting up against each other. There was a sofa, too.

Half a dozen leather padded stools were lined up in a regimented row in front of the bar itself, all except one. There was a man sitting on the second last from the curved end of the bar. He had a coffee mug in front of him, and a sheaf of paperwork spread across the bar. He was a big, blond man and when he looked up at Darwin's entrance, Darwin could see he had very blue eyes.

A woman stepped out around a flat panel that was clearly hiding the kitchen entrance, for Darwin could just see a sliver of a door behind the panel, slowly swinging back and forth behind her. She walked over to Darwin, her legs swinging with the easy gait of a woman who liked her height (*and she's pretty damned tall*). She was dark haired, and Darwin calculated that she was in her late forties.

She held his gaze as she approached, a small smile building at the corners of her lips. She was wearing one of those rayon dresses that the fashion magazines kept blathering about and seeing it on her, Darwin finally understood the hysteria. It wrapped. It clung and made the most of her figure, which was a curvy mature woman's shape.

By the time she stood in front of him, Darwin was feeling the impact of her appearance with an elevated heart rate and the stirring of urges that had been dormant for years.

Up close, he could see fine lines at her eyes and that her hair had been carefully colored. He took in the tiny hint of soft, pale skin around her jaw, the kind that old people get when their flesh loses the elasticity they'd taken for granted the last five or six decades. He was well acquainted with the sensation and because he had become so preternaturally aware of the signs of aging in his own body, he recognized them in her. Mentally, he pushed her age up into the late fifties or early sixties, but *damn*, she was a fine-looking woman.

She smiled at him, her full lips with their soft coral lipstick revealing even white teeth. "Well, hello," she said. Her voice was exactly right for her, a mellow contralto.

"Hi," Darwin offered.

"I do hope you're here to enjoy our hospitality." She raised a brow. "You've not dined with us before, have you?"

The impact of her presence was thrumming through him. It wasn't sexual. It wasn't *just* sexual. There was a vitality about her that stirred his blood. It was like the day, the week, his *life* had taken on energy that had long been missing. He pushed out a breath, riding it out. "Actually," he said regretfully, "I'm pretty sure I'm here to see that man." He pointed to the blond man at the bar.

She glanced back over her shoulder toward the bar. "Your regret is mutual," she told him, looking back at him. "Perhaps I can talk you into sharing a coffee and patisserie once you have finished your business."

"You could probably talk me into anything you wanted," Darwin said, then grimaced. What sort of a jerk-off high school thing to say was that?

But she merely smiled again, a very knowing, understanding smile. "Let's start with coffee." She waved him toward the bar, with a gesture that told him he should go ahead, then turned and walked back into the kitchen. Her rear view was as enticing as the front. He loved that her hair hung past her shoulder blades in silky waves. After fifty, most women seemed to think it was the law that they chop off their hair to somewhere around their ears, which he thought was a crying shame. Men had had it good in Victorian times, which was probably the last time a woman kept her hair at waist length for her entire life.

He walked over to the bar. Strand, if it was Asher Strand, sat watching him, his pen resting on top of the paperwork. He had guessed that Darwin was here for him and was waiting for him. He held the coffee mug now and it looked like a miniature in his big hand.

Darwin walked right up to him. "You're Asher Strand, I guess."

Strand swapped the mug over to the other hand and held out his right one. "You have the advantage of me."

It was an oddly old-fashioned thing to say, Darwin reflected as he automatically stuck out his hand, gripped Strand's and shook. There was strength in the man's grip, but he wasn't trying to impress anyone. The grip remained firm and that was all. "Darwin Baxter," he told him.

Strand's brow lifted. "Ah…" he said, and pointed to the stool behind Darwin.

Darwin sat on it and kept his feet on the floor, his legs stretched out. He was tall, but not nearly as tall as Strand and now he was standing next to him, he could see that Lucas hadn't exaggerated the shoulders. He realized he was keeping his legs stretched out to make himself look taller. It was the old male instinct to show up the competition and he mentally sighed at himself for letting the man intimidate him.

But damn it, he was as fine a specimen in his way as the lovely hostess had been, only quite a bit younger. And while he was immune to it, Darwin could still feel the same vitality and aliveness in the man that the hostess had radiated with such impact.

"You know my name," Darwin said. "Someone has been talking about me."

Strand nodded. "Charlee. Given what happened last week, I imagine you're here to talk about that and about her. I must admit, I was expecting one of her parents to appear. Her father, most likely."

"He's sick," Darwin said shortly. "Charlee hasn't figured that out yet, but it's serious. I'm surprised he has the energy to complete a shift. He's got a job on the docks and that's back-breaking work even for a healthy young guy like yourself." He stopped himself from saying anything else, like his suspicions that Montgomery was not just sick but dying, and the only thing keeping him heading off to work each day was the fact that in that family of four, he was the only one bringing in any sort of income. Darwin also didn't speak of his worry about what would happen to those two kids when Montgomery got too sick to work.

Strand nodded. "I had my suspicions, from what Charlee has said about life at home. Is he dying?" he asked, the blue eyes holding Darwin's gaze steadily.

Darwin pulled in a breath, riding out his surprise. "I think so," he admitted reluctantly.

Strand absorbed that with a thoughtful, sober nod. "So…Darwin Baxter. Charlee has told me quite a bit about you. I envy you your profession, by the way."

Darwin rolled his eyes as the truth dawned on him. "You're the history nut," he said, feeling slightly stupid. He hadn't put it together until this very moment. "She let me think you were a kid at school."

"Charlee does know how to be discreet," Strand agreed. "But I'm sure that now you know who I am, you have a lot of questions." He hesitated. "Is Charlee alright? I haven't seen her for over a week and she used to stop by every afternoon after school, like clockwork."

"She stopped here?" Darwin asked, looking around.

Strand nodded. "She would collect leftovers from our chef, for her pet stray. A dog she called Chocolate. That was how we met. The local gang leader hurt the dog and I stepped in and chatted with them."

The 'local gang' he was talking about were the Lords. Lucas had filled Darwin in on the Lords and their reputation, and Darwin had heard plenty about them himself. Strand spoke very casually about dealing with them, but Darwin suspected it hadn't been simply a matter of chatting with them at all.

"Did you 'talk' with them last week, too?" Darwin asked curiously.

"I did. They have a new leader, one who didn't understand the rules I laid out last year. I think he's got it straight now."

"Rules?" Darwin prompted. Strand's quiet assurance was almost unnerving. Darwin would have hesitated to tell that pack of hyenas the time of day, but he spoke of laying down rules like it was a chess match.

"One rule, really." Strand shrugged. "They're to stay away from Charlee and her family. And her friends." He smiled briefly, then looked toward the kitchen door. "Ylva, are you there?" he called, raising his voice a little.

After a few seconds, Darwin heard the kitchen door swing. Ylva appeared once more and Darwin stared unabashedly as she walked in that loose, easy swinging way toward them. "Asher," she acknowledged.

"Would you like more coffee?"

"Always," he told her. "I want you to meet Darwin Baxter. He's been tutoring Charlee for a few years."

"Darwin, yes of course," Ylva said and held out her hand. Darwin was still getting used to the idea of shaking women's hands, but he didn't have any trouble shaking hers. She made it seem quite natural. Her grip was surprisingly firm. Lots of women didn't understand how to shake hands properly, but she did. Then her soft hand slid out of his. "Charlee has spoken about you many times," she added.

"To you, too?"

"Ylva is my business manager," Strand said.

"Charlee visited every day after school," Ylva explained. She nodded toward the table. "She would stop by for scraps for Chocolate each day and sit and have tea with us. Usually around this time, too. I have just poured a fresh pot of tea, as it happens. The habit has become ingrained now. Would you join us?"

"I guess...yes. Thanks." He didn't like tea all that much, but sitting and talking to Ylva would make up for it. Plus he could grill Strand more.

Ylva smiled, like his agreement had overjoyed her. "I'll go and get the tea," she said and hurried away.

Strand stood up. "We usually sit at that table there." He nodded toward a small round table on the edge of the sea of white tablecloths.

"You do own this place, then," Darwin observed, standing up. "Charlee didn't seem to know, exactly."

"I don't like talking about myself all that much." He shuffled the papers together and left them in a nearly-neat pile, then walked over to the table. He waited until Darwin had caught up before sitting down.

"You seem to be making an exception for me," Darwin said, pulling out a chair.

"You came here for answers, didn't you?"

"I was expecting to have to drag them out of you," Darwin admitted.

Asher smiled. "You were braced for what? Some sort of monster?"

Darwin couldn't find a decent answer to that, because even though he hadn't quite categorized it that bluntly, he *had* built a picture in his mind of some sleazy asshole who (*go on, admit it, even if it's just to yourself*) liked children a bit too much. He had heard stories about such men before, always whispered and alluded to.

"How on earth did you meet Charlee?" Darwin asked, steering the conversation away. How they met was the key to it all. It would explain a lot.

"I have an apartment in the Bronx," Asher said, surprising the hell out of Darwin.

all the way downtown every weekday without fail just to get food for her. I think she scraped dinner plates at home to give her breakfast on the way to school and on weekends, too. From what Charlee told us about herself and all the things she didn't say, I know how lonely she is. It doesn't surprise me that she's not bouncing back." He put his cup down. "But I've had an idea." He lifted his chin in a way that made Darwin look out the window behind him. He stared at the buildings opposite, trying to figure out what Asher was talking about. Then he saw the sign and it all came together.

He looked back at Asher. "What are you thinking?"

"I know the manager," Asher said. "I think I can convince her she needs more help for the summer."

"A place like that couldn't afford summer help. They live on donations."

"Voluntary help," Asher qualified. "Charlee will like the idea that she's providing a genuine service."

Darwin went back to sipping his tea, hiding his admiration. This Asher had Charlee's character nailed down good and proper. She *would* like the idea of helping, especially there. "How soon can you arrange it?" he asked.

Chapter Eight

Laun
Old Norse; "secrecy." The rule of
secrecy that shaped the division
between Herleifr and humans.
Contributed to political policy, laws and
social structure after the Descent. Major
proponents of *laun* included…
From *The Complete Kine Encyclopedia*, by
Darwin Baxter, PhD. 2019 Edition

Charlee hung back, overwhelmed and just a little bit afraid. The big room was full of dogs. Everywhere. Tumbling over each other, rolling on the ground, bouncing up to catch balls. Big, short, fat, skinny, long sausage dogs, even mutts.

"What is this?" she whispered. The sound the dogs were making was astounding. They were yipping, barking and panting happily. None of them were fighting, which was the most astonishing thing of all.

"It's a doggie playground," Asher said. "I think," he added.

"That's a pretty good description," the white-haired lady standing next to him said with a smile. She had twinkling brown eyes and had asked Charlee to call her Carole. "It's a very new idea in animal care that we're trying and it does seem to be working. Did you know, Charlee, that the dogs can get sad and sick if they're kept locked up in cages without human contact or contact with other dogs?"

Charlee nodded. "I read about it," she said. "Canine depression. They can die if they're left alone."

"Charlee's pretty smart," Asher told Carole.

"So I see," Carole said with another smile. "Of course, you wouldn't have to spend all your time supervising the playground. There's a lot more to the rescue center. We have a medical section, staffed by volunteer vets. That can be a busy place. People bring in animals all the time, and they very nearly always need some sort of medical care. But we wouldn't ask you to work in there until you had basic training in medical assistance. That's something you could work up to, if you're interested."

Charlee nodded. She would study for a year, if that's what it took.

"There's a very large cat home on the other side of the building, too," Carole added.

"Cats?" Charlee breathed.

"Then there's the avian area," Carole finished.

"Birds, too?" Charlee pressed her hands together. "Can I see it?"

"Of course you can," Carole said. "This way."

* * * * *

They were back in the office once more, with Charlee's head reeling with facts, figures and pure delight, when she realized for the first time that Asher was no longer with them.

"I believe Mr. Strand went back to the restaurant, just after we left the playground," Carole said, picking up the reading glasses that hung around her neck on a chain and sliding them onto her nose. "He said you should stop by when you were done here and tell him how it went." She pulled a sheet of paper out of a drawer in her desk and placed it in front of Charlee. "This is a volunteer profile. Mainly, it is contact information so we know where we can reach you if we need to. What hours can you give us, Charlee?"

"Right now, all the hours in the day," Charlee said. "School's out for the summer."

"Yes, it is, isn't it? Which school do you go to?"

"I start junior high in September."

"I think you might be one of our youngest volunteers. But we take anyone who wants to help us, so don't worry." Carole smiled at her. "It's important that you work the hours you say you'll be here. We schedule paid staff around volunteer work schedules. We'll be counting on you, Charlee. Volunteers are what keeps us out of the red—well, mostly."

"When can I start?" Charlee asked.

Carole considered her. "How about now?"

Happiness burst through her. "Yes."

* * * * *

Ylva looked up from the cash register as another customer came through the door, and smiled when she saw Charlee standing uncertainly just inside the door. The restaurant was busy, for the lunch rush was in full swing. She waved Charlee over.

The girl hurried over.

"They took you, then?" Ylva asked, and counted back change to the diner whose bill she was settling.

"Ylva, it's perfect! There's all sorts of animals. I've been cleaning cages, and talking to them, and...." She shrugged, but Ylva could see the happiness in her eyes and the energy crackling from her every movement. "I'm on a lunch break. Is Asher here? I wanted to thank him."

"He had some things to take care of." Ylva considered her. "Have you eaten?"

"I...uh...no, I guess not. I didn't know I would be working all day." She smiled.

Ylva turned her and pointed at one of the few empty tables. "Go and sit down. A customer just sent a chicken dinner back because it had gravy on it. I'll get the sous chef to reheat it for you."

"Really? That would be wonderful. I didn't know how hungry I was until just now."

Charlee sat at the small table. It was one of the two-people-only tables that were popular in the evening. Because office lunches usually needed seats for three or more, the two-people tables often sat empty.

She was nearly through the small portion of the roast chicken dinner when Asher arrived. He spotted her in among the diners and came and sat down. "You're still here?" he asked.

"I am a volunteer at the SPCA," she said proudly.

"They have you working already?" He seemed amused.

"I wanted to."

He nodded. "What time do you finish?"

"Four."

"So you'll be catching the 4:20 as usual." He seemed to be saying it to himself.

Charlee rolled her eyes at him. "You're doing it again."

"Doing what?"

"Thinking hard and only speaking a third of it aloud. It's difficult to understand when you leapfrog like that."

His grin broadened. "You're smart. Can't you keep up?"

"Mostly, I do. But you're thinking about me. That makes it harder."

Asher sat back. "You should stop by for lunch each day."

It was a complete change of subjects. Charlee frowned. "Are you checking up on me?" Then she stared at him as his comments pulled into a cohesive pattern. He hadn't been changing subjects at all. "You *are* checking up on me. What's going to be at the other end of the 4:20, Asher?"

He hesitated for a long moment, his big fingers playing with the neatly folded napkin on that side of the table. "Either Darwin or Lucas will meet your train, each day. They're going to walk you home."

Charlee put her fork down. "I'm nearly twelve years old. I can walk home by myself. I've been doing it for months."

"Things have changed. You know why." He looked at her steadily, reminding her without words about what had happened to Chocolate.

Charlee pressed her lips together. "Okay," she said with a sigh. "But just for a while. Just until we know if he's gonna come back at you."

"It's not me he'll come at," Asher said quietly. "He dealt with Chocolate. There's Lucas and Darwin, but he'll look at them and figure they're too much trouble. But you're not. If my warning wasn't enough to deter him, if he's as crazy as Lucas says, then he'll come after you next."

Charlee pushed her plate aside. Her appetite had fled. She felt a little sick, her heart lurching in her chest.

Asher sat forward again. "I'm sorry to scare you. But you need to know this," he said gently. "The problem is, I don't know how long it will take him to decide that getting even with you will be worth the risk of having me come after him. He might be just sensible enough to decide you're not worth the trouble, either. But he might not." He frowned. "He didn't give way at all when I was talking to him. He didn't back down mentally even when I had him…when he was cornered."

Charlee swallowed. She had deliberately not wondered about what Asher had done the night they had buried Chocolate. But now she was getting a possible glimpse of it. She wasn't sure she liked it.

It also didn't seem very real right now, with Asher sitting across the table from her, looking very normal in his business suit and tie. He'd already loosened it, but that didn't take away from the urbane impression he gave. Even his hair was short, unlike a lot of men these days who grew their hair down past their collars. Even the Wall Street types sported mullets and long locks.

In some ways, Asher was almost, well, square. Charlee didn't like to admit that even just in her mind. But it was true. He had short hair, he wore suits. He didn't seem to drink or go dancing at discos, or have dates, which Charlee figured most men did if they weren't already married. He just seemed to work all the time.

….isn't that what superheroes do? The question popped into her mind and she recalled almost with surprise that she used to think of Asher as a superhero, like Superman. When had that changed? Because it must have changed in her mind at some time if she was looking at him now and having trouble thinking of him doing heroic things.

"What's wrong?" he asked. "You've gone all quiet."

She shook her head. "It's nothing. Just thinking about Chocolate," she lied.

Was she growing up and moving on from nonsense like superheroes? It worried her. She remembered every moment in that alley like it had happened yesterday. She would never forget it, nor would she forget what Asher had done for her and Chocolate. But she had known Asher in his daytime disguise a lot longer than she had seen him being heroic. The daytime mask overlaid everything.

Besides, it was secret. Never to be spoken of, just as Asher had changed what he had been about to say a moment ago.

Asher leaned forward again. "Hey," he said quietly. "Chocolate was lucky. You loved her and took care of her for a long while. There are some animals out there that never get to be loved by anyone at all. They have the most terrible lives."

"I know," Charlee agreed, thinking of some of the poor creatures she had been caring for that morning. "But now I can help as many as I can." She tried to smile, to reassure Asher. "You...you'll be careful, won't you?" It blurted out of her, pushed out past the old secrecy injunction.

His brow lifted and she could tell he knew she was talking about his superhero stuff. "I'm always careful," he said. But there was a flicker in the back of his eyes that seemed to refute him.

It made her say firmly, "I'm going to stop by here every day during my lunch break. I want to make sure you're...being careful."

Asher started to smile and she could tell that he was going to laugh, too.

"I mean it," she added.

His smile faded.

"If you're going to insist that someone walk me home, I'm going to insist on this," she said. "Deal?"

Asher considered her for another long moment. "Deal," he said.

* * * * *

Asher kept up his end of the deal. Every day when she arrived at the station from her job (and she felt very grown up about having "a job", although she would never tell anyone that), Lucas or Darwin would be waiting at the bottom of the stairs to the platform. It was Darwin more often than Lucas, for the train he usually caught home at the end of the day arrived at the station at nearly the same time she did. But when he was late, or couldn't make it for other reasons, Lucas was always there.

One day, it had been Asher himself. He had straightened up from his lean against the bottom of the stairs and dropped his arms down to his sides. "Lucas is at the training camp and Darwin is working late." He said it in a way that made Charlee think he was apologizing.

She grinned at him. "So you walk me home instead. That's great."

He seemed troubled by her answer. As they headed across the road and out into the strong early July sunshine, he glanced at her. "Charlee..."

"What?"

"You know that some people, including your folks...they wouldn't like the idea of you and I being alone together."

Charlee bit back her protest, as vague hints and conversations at school rose to mind. While standing at her locker, Charlee had heard Amy Green, who had transferred in only two months before the end of the year, talking to the big circle of girls who had instantly gravitated in her direction because of how pretty she was. Amy had been talking in a loud whisper about a girl at her old school and the rumors about her and a male teacher. The teacher had quit mysteriously, but not before the girl had transferred out. Amy had been pulled out of the school by her parents, suddenly and without explanation. Her mother had been upset for three days and hadn't relaxed until Amy was settled at PS 157. Even then, someone picked her up from school every single day.

"What did he do to her?" one of the other girls had asked, her eyes big. That had been Noreen Tartt, who liked to tell everyone she was going to live up to her name. Charlee guessed it was a way for Noreen to jump ahead of the teasing she would have got otherwise.

"Who cares?" Amy had replied shortly. "He got me kicked out of the best school ever."

Charlee had nearly finished at her locker. She slowed down her movements, wanting to hear more.

"Do y'think he did things to her?" one of the others asked in a hushed voice.

"Prob'ly," Amy replied, with a disinterested tone, fiddling with her hair and tossing it over her shoulder. She was watching Chuck Benson walk by with his football teammates.

Charlee had given up on the conversation then and hurried to the subway station to go downtown. Amy had only been interested in why she had been forced to come to PS 157, which was a perfectly good school in Charlee's estimation. Charlee didn't think any of the male teachers "did" things, for a start. That was the point she kept returning to. What did 'doing things' involve?

Was it…was it sex?

Charlee had known about sex for a few years. Books were freely available that had given her an intellectual understanding of reproduction and human biology, but the knowledge had only lodged in her memory at a superficial level, a set of facts that seemed slightly disgusting (*a man really does that to a woman?*) but explained a great deal of odd adult behavior she had observed that had once been inexplicable.

She had sat on the train, not reading but instead thinking through what Amy had implied about her old school. Had the teacher done something to the student, something sexual? *Could* a grown man do that? She supposed they could. But why would they *want* to? She had a hard enough time imagining a man actually liking sex with an adult woman, who supposedly wanted sex just like he did. A girl the same age as Charlee wouldn't want sex. So how could a man want to do sexual things to a girl? It defied understanding, but she had to suppose that anyone could be sexually drawn to anyone. There were gays and transsexuals, and she guessed there were probably even stranger combinations and pairings, stuff that adults kept well hidden from kids.

Charlee had left off her ruminating at that point. It just didn't interest her enough to keep her wondering.

But now she looked at Asher, startled. She hadn't considered that people might look at Asher and her in the same way as the teacher and the student at Amy Green's last school. "But you're not like that!" she said.

Asher smiled. She liked his smile, when he smiled like he was doing now. It made his eyes twinkle and made her feel nice, just by looking at it. "Thank you for that, Charlee. I'm not like that at all. You and I know that, but it doesn't look good on the surface, which is the only place most people look. Do you remember the deal we made back in…" His eyes widened. "Hell's bells, that was nearly a year ago. When you found Chocolate?"

"When you saved her," Charlee amended. "But I remember the deal. I don't tell anyone about you. I don't even get to tell them how you saved Chocolate."

"*Especially* about how I saved Chocolate," he amended. "This—us being alone together—if someone didn't like it, they might start looking for more information about me and my life. The reason for our deal, for keeping things secret…that's not something I can afford to have come out as public knowledge. Do you understand?"

"Sure," Charlee told him. "If they started digging, they'd dig right past your daytime disguise and they'd find out you're a superhero underneath."

Asher had stopped protesting over the superhero classification a long time ago. Now, she saw his eyes roll a little bit, but he was smiling, too. "Okay," he agreed heavily. "They'd find out I'm a superhero. Let's go with that, then. My…what did you call it? The disguise?"

"Your daytime disguise. Like Superman. You're a mild-mannered businessman during the day. But at other times, you save people and no one recognizes you as the businessman." She considered. "But you're not mild-mannered, even in the daytime."

"Are you calling me rude?" he asked curiously.

"I mean, your daytime disguise is kinda square. I guess that's another way of saying mild-mannered. Except Clark Kent was scared of his own shadow and you're not that way even in your suit."

"*Square?*" he repeated disbelievingly.

"Sure. You work. You sleep. You work again. I've never seen you get into any of the trouble that single guys are supposed to."

"What sort of trouble?"

She shrugged. "You name it. Booze. Ladies. Drugs. Staying out all night. My dad says that Lucas is going to go to hell in a handcart because he got my mo—" She stopped and pressed her lips together, realizing what she had been about to say.

Asher kept on walking, as if she hadn't shut up mid-sentence.

Charlee could feel the heat rising, making her throat and cheeks warm.

"That's your secret, isn't it?" Asher asked gently.

She drew in a breath. "Yeah."

Asher stopped and turned to face her, right there in the middle of the sidewalk. His expression was a kind one. "You know that I've probably guessed a lot of it, don't you?"

That was worse than telling him. If Asher had guessed, how many other people knew? Charlee could feel a tight knot sitting in the middle of her chest, making it hard to breathe. "Did you tell anyone else?" she asked.

Asher looked at her for a good long while. She could hear her heart thudding in her ears. Why wouldn't he just say "no" and put her out of her misery? Instead, he drew in a long breath. Was he feeling upset, too? But he spoke simply enough, with no heat or anger. "I've been keeping secrets for a very long time. When you do that for long enough, it becomes a part of you. You automatically don't tell people everything, even if you could. I know you know what I mean by that."

She nodded. Not talking about herself and her family was just the way it was. Always and forever. Just like not talking about Asher.

"Because I'm like that, I knew that you were like that," Asher added. "It worked that way for you, too. You knew, when we first met, that I had secrets because you were keeping your own. You probably didn't think about it that way. You just knew I was like you. That's why we could make a deal."

Charlee had spent a lot of time thinking about Asher and what he had done that night. She had long ago decided that they were kindred spirits, like Anne in the *Anne of Green Gables* book used to describe old friends who had just met each other.

"What your actual secret was…well, I figured that out because of our deal. The first deal."

"We don't lie to each other," Charlee supplied.

"And we don't," Asher agreed. "But neither of us tells each other everything. You have secrets. I have secrets. But I guessed what yours were because what you *do* tell me is the truth and you told me enough of it for me to fill in the blanks."

"Oh." She breathed in, her chest loosening. "I don't mind you knowing," she added. "You won't tell anyone else."

His eyes seemed very blue as he looked at her, and his hair almost white in the dazzling light of the day. "I haven't told anyone else and I won't," he said, "only if you promise me something."

Her heart caught again. "Another deal?"

"No, not a deal. Because there's nothing I can promise for my side of…" He stopped. "You know what? There is. Very well, a deal. You promise me that if anything ever happens at home, if you're scared or just uncertain about what's happening, if anything happens to your parents…if anything happens at all that you know isn't right or is dangerous—and I know you're more than smart enough to figure out when something wrong is happening—then I want you to promise that you'll come to me for help."

"And what do you promise?" she asked, almost breathlessly.

He wouldn't stop looking at her in that direct way of his. "I promise that if you ever ask for my help, I'll help. No matter what it is, Charlee, I'll help you."

Charlee felt a little sick because she also felt giddy. Dizzy with…something. It was relief, she realized. A lifting of a weight she hadn't known she was carrying. All the little fears she wouldn't even let herself think about, all the things she and Lucas didn't discuss that sat between them like mute, glowing neon—the way Dad constantly coughed, the medicine bottles lined up like soldiers on the table next to his easy chair, the empty beer bottles ranked along the kitchen window, and the cartons of empties next to the garbage can outside. The fact that Lucas was starting to cook dinner for the family more and more often, sometimes giving up football practice and basketball training to do it. All the little things they didn't talk about that added up to scary, big grown-up problems that, if they kept going as they were, would put her and Lucas in a position where they wouldn't be able to hide things anymore. They wouldn't be smart enough or old enough to fix things.

But now, Asher was there. If the worst came, whatever that might be (and she wouldn't think about what that might be, not now), then it wouldn't be the end of their world because Asher would help, and he was a superhero. He could fix it.

Charlee blinked rapidly as her eyes stung. She hated crying. *Hated* it.

Asher turned and started walking again. "You don't have to say anything," he said.

She couldn't have said anything right then, not even to save her life, because her throat was so tight with tears it hurt. She stumbled along the sidewalk next to him, the concrete a blur in front of her feet.

"So, tell me about your day," Asher prompted her. "Did that Irish Setter knock you off your feet again?"

When she thought she could speak without blubbering like a baby, she told him about her day, her wonderful job and the beautiful creatures she got to play with and love each day.

And that was the last time they ever spoke about that particular deal. But Charlee remembered it, always, for it made her feel warm and oddly safe, even though she knew there were authorities and agencies and even the police who could step into her life at any time and tear it apart, separating her from Lucas. But Asher could fix anything and he had promised.

That was one of the best summers of Charlee's life. The minimizing of her chronic, low-level fear let her enjoy the simple pleasures of her life in a way she had never experienced before. Now, the dawning of each day brought her a peaceful contentedness. She could spring out of bed and dash to catch the train to work, looking forward to mastering the complex world of animal care.

She borrowed books from the community library, upgrading to the adult non-fiction section, putting herself through a crash course in basic zoology that focused on domestic animals and birds.

On the weekends, she had more lessons with Darwin, and he lent her even more complex books on everything from animal husbandry to veterinary science, to biographies of Charles Darwin and treatises on his theory of evolution. It was heady stuff and she rolled around in the fount of knowledge like a puppy in a puddle.

Then she got to apply some of what she had learned, on the job. It was pure bliss, with nary a shadow to spoil it.

Until Lucas walked her home one night late in August. The anniversary of the day she and Asher had met had come and gone. They walked home in companionable silence, and Charlee reflected that while Lucas was clearly getting taller, she had done some of her own growing somewhere over the last few weeks, for he didn't tower over her as much as he used to. She'd never catch up with him because their parents were both tall -- Dad was well over six feet and her mother was five eleven—and Lucas had got the best of their genes in that respect. He was going to be very tall, possibly close to Asher's height. But perhaps she was going to be tall, too. She wasn't sure how she felt about that. Not yet. Ylva was tall, and she made it seem like a good thing. But the girls at school called taller ones like Evvy Paetro, who had shot up two feet in almost as many months, lots of nasty names like "stork" and "freak."

"So…school starts in a week," Lucas said, interrupting her thoughts. "Junior high. Excited?"

She shrugged. "I suppose. School's okay. I'd rather keep working at the SPCA, but Carole says I should get a science degree. Then I can work for some private company and get a ton of money."

"That sounds like a smart idea to me."

"Money sounds good," Charlee agreed. "But I want to work with animals."

"You can't do both?"

"Do you know any millionaire veterinarians?"

He didn't reply. That meant she'd won that round.

They'd covered another half block before he spoke again. "You still doin' lunch at that place across the road from the SPCA?"

"You mean Asher's place?" She'd figured out a while ago that Asher owned the restaurant. He was too relaxed and casual when he was there to be an employee. Besides, his suits were too expensive. She was able to tell the difference now. The Wall Street area was filled with suits to study. "I go there most days." It was a mild understatement. She went there every single weekday to check up on him. That was the deal. Deal number three. But she made it sound more casual and hit-or-miss than it was because she knew that the truth would provoke more questions from Lucas that she couldn't—*wouldn't*—answer.

Lucas walked on for a bit before he replied. "Do you think you should trust him so much, Einie?"

"Give me one reason why I shouldn't," she demanded, anger roiling up inside her like a geyser, ready to spew scalding heat all over Lucas.

He lifted his hands in a placating gesture. "I'm just asking. I'm not saying you shouldn't. I'm asking why you do."

"None of your business," she shot back.

"Yeah, it is," he snapped. "I coulda asked Darwin or Dad about it, but I didn't. I'm asking you. He phones Darwin and next thing I know, Darwin and I have marching orders about walking you home. He gets you a job right across the road from him. It's…it's not natural, Charlee."

She was still angry. She could feel the ugly tension inside her. But the heat had turned to a cold block, letting her think properly. "You were there when he went after the gang a second time," she said. Her voice came out heavier than she had ever heard herself speak. Heavier and more grown up. "The gang hasn't been back. You really have to ask if he can be trusted?"

Lucas was looking at her like she had grown two heads, his expression one of amazement. Then he shook his head. "That's not what I meant, exactly."

The coldness in her allowed her to speak the words without flinching, without embarrassment. "You want to know if he is a pervert. If he interferes with children."

Lucas blushed right up to his hairline. He looked at her sideways, his gaze skittering.

Bingo, Charlee thought. She struggled to find a way to phrase her answer so that Lucas would really understand. He did deserve an answer, even though the question was offensive to both her and Asher. But how could she phrase it so that Lucas would *really* get it? Then she had it.

"Remember when you started with the high school basketball team last April?" she asked him. He wasn't even a senior, yet, but he had been placed on the starting lineup of his high school's team. Charlee hadn't been nearly as surprised as Dad had been; she knew exactly how hard Lucas had worked at perfecting his shots and handling the ball, night after night, out in the back yard, which had been covered in concrete by some previous owner of the house. "Remember when you told me about passing blind?"

"What about it?"

"You said that when someone called for the ball, you didn't look up at them because it would slow down your pass. If they called, you threw the ball to where their voice was. You had to trust that they were clear and could catch it. You had to trust them. And, you said that it was really hard at first, because you didn't know anyone on the team. But after the first tryout, even though you didn't know any of them any better, you could trust them to know what they were doing. You trusted them enough to pass blind."

"I remember," Lucas said, a little impatiently.

"I trust Asher enough to pass blind to him," she said. "I trust him enough that if he said 'jump from the third floor, now,' I would do it instantly and I wouldn't look, because I know he would be there to catch me. I trust him because he knows what he's doing. We're alike, Asher and I. Just like you trust your teammates because you know you're the same, even though you didn't know everything about them."

Lucas blew out his breath doubtfully. "How can you know that?" he demanded. "He's so much older than you, Charlee. It's a little creepy that he's even a friend."

"He's not a friend."

"Then what is he?"

"He's just a part of my life. Because we're alike. And we *are* alike. How old he is doesn't matter."

"You mean, you're both super brainy?"

Charlee didn't know if Asher was super-smart. She didn't care. But she lied with a straight face. "Yes, that's how we're alike."

"Darwin did say he was lending you books," Lucas muttered, staring ahead. He shrugged. "Okay, Einie. If you say you trust him, then I'll take your word for it. But I don't have to like him."

"I'm not asking you to like him," she said flatly. She had the shakes. She had never flat out lied to Lucas before and because she hadn't, he had accepted her lie without a quiver. It made her tremble, because she knew that something had shifted between them. Things would never be exactly the same as they once were. Lucas may not realize that, because he didn't know she had lied to him. But she would know.

It was only later that night, when she was lying in bed waiting for sleep to take her, that she realized what she had done. She had lied to protect Asher. She had put Asher ahead of her brother.

Chapter Nine

Mead

(/ˈmiːd/; archaic and dialectal "medd";
from Old English "meodu"[11]) is an
alcoholic beverage created by
fermenting honey with water, and
frequently fruits, spices, grains or
hops.[2][3][4] (Hops act as a preservative
and produce a bitter, beer-like flavor.)
The alcoholic content of mead may
range from about 8% ABV[5] to more
than 20%. The defining characteristic of
mead is that the majority of the
beverage's fermentable sugar is derived
from honey.[6] It may be still, carbonated
or naturally sparkling, and it may be
dry, semi-sweet or sweet.[7]
from *Wikipedia*

There were very few mourners at Jerry Mallery's funeral. Asher looked around the parlor at the handful of people sitting on the odd collection of chairs and stools that Ylva had found. Most of the mourners were very old. Undoubtedly human, he catalogued. It meant that he was the only one of the Kine in attendance, which made sense under the circumstances.

He watched Ylva move around the room, speaking to each of the attendees. She wore a black silk dress that made the most of her figure in a subtly sexy way. Ylva had always had incredibly good taste.

After a while, she made her way to him and he held out his arm. Ylva stepped into the hug and held him tightly. When she stepped back and looked up at him, her eyes were sparkling with tears. But she spoke evenly and softly. "He was ninety-seven."

"You made him happy for most of those ninety-seven years. It wasn't the wrong decision," Asher reminded her.

"But I must go on alone...and for how much longer?" Now her sadness was visible.

"No one knows," Asher replied. No one did know. The last Eldre had died long ago, at the advanced age of one hundred and forty-nine human years. But there had been others who had died very shortly after their human spouses had passed on. Just like humans, the Eldre found life without their life-mate intolerable.

Ylva might live for only another few years…or she might find pleasure or purpose in life in some way. It would all depend on her. Asher looked for a way to tell her that, a way that wouldn't sound bleak and indifferent. "You have to assume you've got a long life ahead of you," he told her. "You have to decide what you want to do with it."

Ylva tilted her head. "You're a very sweet man."

"Don't tell anyone that."

"You've stood by me despite everything. I won't forget that. Ever."

Asher shifted uneasily on his feet.

Ylva gave him a glimmer of a smile. "You also got me into the worst sort of trouble. Remember when we got drunk and raided that Rus encampment on the borders of Finland? You could barely stay on your horse."

Asher laughed softly. "You *couldn't* stay on your horse." She had fallen off her horse's back when the mare had taken a small jump. Then she had lain on ground that was mushy with melted snow, laughing fit to bust.

When the Rus had fallen upon them, though, she had fought as well as a man, a smile still on her lips. They had sobered up quickly, standing back to back, until Asher had been able to call his horse to them. They had clambered upon Fiskr's back, still fighting off the horde, and galloped across two valleys in the moonlight until they figured they were safe enough to wait out the rest of the night.

That had been part of the time when Ylva had been young and supple, and Asher had been called *Askr*, his birthname. It was a part of time long before Ylva had chosen to give up her life as one of the Kine. "A long time ago," Asher murmured, studying the fine lines at her eyes and her carefully colored hair. She hadn't aged as fast as her husband. That was the dilemma of those who chose the way of the Eldre.

Ylva tucked her hand under Asher's elbow. "I'll walk you to the door," she said.

Asher nodded and let her lead him through the fanciful parlor where they had gathered after the funeral. He needed to get back to the store. Charlee worked at the SPCA three days a week after school, and she often stopped at the restaurant on her way to the shelter or on her way home. It was a very cold winter and it helped ease his mind if he saw her at least once a day to ensure her life was as untroubled as he could make it, and maybe walk her to the subway entrance.

"Asher," Ylva murmured, bringing his attention back to her.

"Mmm?"

"I've already decided what I'm going to do with my life." She said it in a way that alerted him.

"You're leaving the restaurant. Leaving me."

"Yes, Asher. I'm leaving. It's time." She gave his arm a little shake. "I've been running your life for you for forty-three years. You don't need me anymore."

"Bullshit," he said violently, anger stirring. "No one knows the restaurant better than you."

"You can afford to hire the best manager in the city. They will run the restaurant better than I ever did." Her gentle response told him that her decision had been made. He knew from hard experience that no argument he could muster would change her mind now.

With a vexed sigh, he let it go. It was the only choice he had. "What are you going to do?" he asked, feeling a little numb. The shock, he suspected, would set in later. Ylva had been a part of the fabric of his life for a very long time, both as one of the Kine and as an Eldre.

"I'm going to buy a house across from Central Park. I know exactly the one I want. Then I'm going to start my own business."

"What sort of business?"

"A school. A sort-of school."

"Children?" he asked, surprised.

"Women," she amended. "Young and young at heart, and those willing to learn."

"Human women? What will you be teaching them?"

"Amica," Ylva corrected him. They had reached the front door and she opened the tall brass and glass door for him. With her hand on the long handle, she smiled at him. "I'll teach them everything I know."

"*Amica?*" he repeated, astounded. "Why on earth would you want to do that?"

"Because there are none of us left to teach. Those of the Kine," she amended, "have learned all there is to know. There will be no more of us, so the knowledge must be passed on. We cannot give the knowledge to humans. The Amica are the natural successors."

"Stefan will not like that," Asher said, thinking of Stefan's almost blind adherence to *laun*. Ylva's plan ran perilously close to breaking *laun*.

"You forget," Ylva told him. "I am no longer one of the Kine. I owe no allegiance to Stefan, or whoever sits upon his seat next. I do it for the women, Asher. Eira would understand perfectly."

"But you will not tell her, will you?" Asher guessed.

"It quite possibly will slip my mind. It has been so long since I spoke to her." Ylva's smile was cheeky, reminding Asher of many more occasions in the past when she had worn that smile, besides the time in northern Russia.

Asher laughed and stepped past her, pushing on the storm door that protected the vintage one that Ylva held open. Ylva stopped him with her hand on his arm again. "Askr," she said gently.

He looked down at her.

"About Charlee…"

His gut tightened. "What about her?"

Ylva's fingers gripped the sleeve of his jacket, tightening slowly. "I've never said anything. I wouldn't have, except that today seems to be a good day to say it. I'm entitled to say it, because today is my husband's funeral."

Asher stared at her. His heart had picked up speed. "Say what?" he asked. His lips felt rubbery, like they didn't really belong to him.

"Let her go, Asher," Ylva said softly. "Let Charlee go and let her live her life."

The shock of her words seemed to jolt his entire spine. Asher cast about for something to say. Anything. What emerged was a weak protest. "I'm not holding her. Gods, Ylva, do you really think that—"

She shook his arm, silencing him. It was more the look on her face that stopped his words than her shaking him.

"Jerry was eighteen when I met him," Ylva said urgently. "*Eighteen*. It took me nearly ten years to work up the courage to pick him over the Kine and I don't regret my choice, but you would, Asher. The Kine are everything to you and you would grow to hate her—"

"She's a little girl, Ylva. You can't assume—"

"I *know* what time does," Ylva flung back. "I see her looking at you. She's young, but she's a woman and in a few years she's going to know what she wants and you can't give her what she wants. You'll destroy her because of what you are, and I don't want that for either of you."

Asher swallowed, his throat abruptly dry, as he stared down at her.

"Think about it," Ylva said. "Promise me."

Promises. He'd made promises before. "I'll think about it," he said hoarsely.

Ylva let his arm go and stepped away.

Asher pushed his way out of the house, almost startled by the chill of the day and the low, mournful light. All the houses along the street had colored lights tacked around their windows and doors and threaded through balcony railings and it reminded him it was Christmas for humans. The winter solstice for the Kine.

The reminder made him angrier, although he wasn't sure why (*everyone else knows who they belong with*) it should do so.

He flagged down a cab as it passed and gave directions for the restaurant. The driver had music playing softly, but Asher could hear the melody. Jimmy Buffett was warbling about how he had everything but snow.

"Could you turn that off?" Asher growled.

The startled driver met his eyes in the rear-view mirror, then clicked the music off with a stab of his finger.

Asher grew more restless the closer the cab got to the restaurant. He fidgeted. He shifted on the seat. He pushed his hands through his hair. There was a tight band around his chest and butterflies were rousing in his stomach.

After twelve minutes by the digital clock on the driver's dashboard, Asher gripped the wire mesh barrier. "Can you pull over?" he asked. His voice was thick.

The driver must have thought he was going to puke, for he swerved to the curb with a suddenness that made the hood of the cab dip and the tires squeal. Another taxi behind them blared its horn, an aural middle finger, as it scooted by.

Asher was thrown against the door. He splayed his hand flat against the glass. It was cool against his fingers. The chill always made him think of the white, cold winters of home, the long part of the year when everyone stayed inside around the fire as much as possible. Men repaired harnesses, made tools, sharpened blades and more. The women sewed and wove cloth, cooked and cleaned. Children were allowed to play once they had completed the household tasks that had been assigned to them, for everyone worked to support the family. But they had been warm times. They had been comforting.

"Four-fifty," the cab driver said, prompting him to get out.

Asher sat up. "Head for Wall Street," he said. "I've changed my mind."

He hadn't really changed his mind. He just knew he couldn't go to the restaurant (*can't face Charlee, you mean*). He needed time. Breathing room.

As the cab pulled away from the curb once more, something related to relief touched him and that made him angry, too.

* * * * *

The cab dropped him off on Pearl, as directed, and Asher took the elevator, too impatient to climb the stairs.

Roar was sitting at the table, a pile of paperwork in front of him. He looked up as Asher walked in, then turned himself on the chair, propping one elbow on top of the files and the other on the back of the chair. The modern pen and calculator on the table and the jeans he wore were jarring notes against the traditional embroidered open robe he wore over his jeans. "You look like you lost a battle," he said. "Who was she?"

Asher moved straight to the cupboard where Roar kept his scotch.

"Do you mind?"

"As I'm out, not at all."

Asher glanced into the cupboard. No scotch. There was crème de menthe and daiquiri mix. He wasn't so desperate for a drink that he'd touch either of them. The scotch would have been a concession as it was. "No mead?" Asher asked hopefully.

"Too long since the last feast," Roar replied. He only brought mead into the hall for special occasions, as it didn't keep well.

"It's the solstice," Asher pointed out.

"Solstice is eight days away."

Asher shut the cupboard, irritated. He *did* want to drink, after all. Mead was the exact thing he wanted. It wasn't his favorite, but he could almost feel the touch of the thin, cool liquid against the back of his throat, and the slightly bitter after-taste of the honey and spices. Why he would abruptly thirst for mead he didn't stop to analyze (*feasts, family, happy times*), but he did know where he could get some, almost guaranteed. He straightened up. "Gotta go," he told Roar.

"That's okay," Roar replied. "Monthly rosters are going to be better company than you tonight, I'm guessing."

Asher waved away Roar's comment with an impatient gesture, heading for the door.

"Be careful!" Roar called after him.

* * * * *

Asher stared at the heavy wood and iron door, his heart thudding unevenly. Why was he here?

There'll be mead.

Was he really so weak that criticism from a trusted friend would send him running to find a barrel of mead to drown himself in?

Despite the thought, he lifted his hand to pick up the iron knocker and paused. A clear, cold, sober voice whispered silently. *Go back home. This isn't for you.*

Why was he here?

The selfish, whiny part of him rose up, protesting. *I just want a drink, for Odin's sake. Why am I dithering like a four year old? It's just a drink.*

When Ylva had said her piece at the front door, a series of quick images had flittered across his mind. Charlee, some years ahead of now, sitting at a window seat (*what seat would that be? He didn't have one. He was pretty sure she didn't. But there had been one in the house he'd lived in, in Amsterdam, nearly three hundred years ago….*). She had been bowed over, her face in her hands, hiding the older version of herself from his inner eye. She had the same radiant hair, spilling over her shoulder in red waves and curls. He couldn't see her face, but he could see well enough that she was bent over with grief, and he was the reason why. He had done this.

You can't give her what she wants.

It was the self-loathing that was rising like the tide inside him with each repetition of that image that finally made him reach for the knocker for a second time.

The door opened before he could touch it. The man who opened it fell back a step in surprise. Asher searched for his name. Øystein, who had been brought to the First Hall a long time after Asher had. He was based out of New Delhi now, or had been the last time Asher had spoken to him.

"Askr Brynjarson!" Øystein said.

"It's Asher Strand at the moment," Asher told him.

Øystein actually rolled his eyes. *Rolled* them. The reaction jolted Asher. He had never seen anyone treat *laun* so casually, especially inside the Second Hall itself.

"You're coming inside?" Øystein asked, stepping back and bringing the heavy door with him.

The open door drew Asher's attention to the noise and light beyond. It had registered subliminally, but now he noticed consciously that it was dim inside, and the light flickered like that of candles, lamps or a fire. The sounds coming from the room were more than familiar to him. Because the Second Hall was beneath Tryvannshøyden, the *lingua franca* of the hall was Norwegian. There was a babble of voices and much laughter flowing over him, all spoken in the language of his childhood.

It was a reminder of evenings around the supper table, while his family and his father's men and their women entertained themselves after a long day in the fields, or a long day of fighting. Both peppered Asher's childhood memories. There would be singing and dancing, drinking games, and music, but what Asher remembered most clearly was the laughter that punctuated it all. Here it was again.

"Sindri is at the fireside. Come and say hello," Øystein urged him, waving him in with his hand and stepping back so Asher could enter. Asher found himself moving into the room, drawn by the sounds. There was even music, played quietly enough so it was a sub-layer to the conversation, lending its joy and beat to the mingling happening over the top of it.

He could see that the mead was plentiful, too. There was short mead, sack mead and long mead, at least. His throat contracted dryly at the sight, but this was Sindri's salon. It was polite to speak to him first, before he accepted a cup of the man's hospitality.

Øystein led him through the room, which was a large, stone-lined chamber without windows, like most in the Second Hall were. There was the huge fireplace at the end, also stone, but carved into elegant scrollwork, with two lions' heads on either side of the stone mantel. It was taller than most of the men standing near it and was burning fiercely, throwing off light and heat.

Sindri stood on the left of the fireplace with a bronze cup in his hand. He alone in the room wore traditional robes. Actually, the robes he always wore, the unrelieved black. Everyone else wore modern clothing. Some of it was *very* modern, and alternative in taste. Asher did a quick tally and figured he was the only one wearing a suit. There were jeans, leather pants and jackets, skinhead clothing with its rips and tears, safety pins and studs, bohemian artist casual, a few kilts, and a lot more leather. Most of its seemed to be dark in color, which made Asher—with his hair and his silver-grey suit—stand out like a beacon. He was definitely turning heads.

He knew everyone in the room by name, or knew them well enough to recognize even though he might not have spoken to them before. It wasn't that the Kine were few in number, although their numbers diminished each year. It was simply that they had all been here on Midgard for so long that Asher had got to know most of his fellow Kine over time.

There were no women in the room, not even Amica pouring drinks. That was an oddity he would explore later. For now, he needed to pay his respects to his host.

Øystein presented him. "Lord Sindri. You know Stallari Asher Strand, of the New York hall."

"Stallari to the earl Hroar Brynjarson, and brother besides." Sindri inclined his head in a short bow. "Yes, Asher and I are acquainted, thank you, Øystein. Would you please pour the man a drink?" His Norwegian was flawless, as had been his English when Asher had spoken to him last year. In part, that was why the mystery of Sindri's origins remained unresolved. He spoke all languages equally well, with no accent to betray his roots. "Short or long, Asher?" he asked.

"Long, please." He liked the beery taste of hops they included in "long" mead, which the mead was called simply to differentiate it from short mead. The spices and bubbles of short mead tasted too much like sweet champagne with curry powder or pepper in it, a taste he had never grown accustomed to, although the ladies liked it a great deal.

Øystein went away to get the drink. Asher studied the short man in front of him. For the moment, they were alone, for the pair Sindri had been speaking to had melted away as Øystein brought him closer. "You call yourself 'Lord'?" Asher asked curiously.

"I do not. But here in my salon, my guests do."

"The English title? It's an odd choice."

"*Freyr* is such an *old* word," Sindri said, with a small smile. "In here, we do not cling to tradition as much as our beloved Annarr and Regin would prefer."

Asher looked around the room with an exaggerated swivel of his head. "Then you fooled me."

"Ah, I do see why you might be confused. The solaces of homes we all remember are not the same as traditions that obligate us unnecessarily. In here, you are free to relax, Asher Strand, in any way that you find the least binding."

A large cup with a smooth bowl and elegantly curved stem was thrust into Asher's hand. Øystein intruded on the conversation only enough to pass the cup to him, then withdrew.

Asher curled his fingers around the cup but did not drink. Not yet.

"Please, do not wait upon my welcome to take your first sip," Sindri told him. "Go ahead and drink. I know you want to. As I said, here you can do anything you want, *be* anything you want."

Asher lifted the cup slightly toward him. "My thanks." He took a long swallow. The mead was excellent, as it always was in the Second Hall.

But Sindri had not finished his declaration. "If you would rather pretend you are human, why, we can accommodate that."

Asher lowered his cup, looking at him. "Excuse me?"

Sindri laughed, showing very white teeth. His black eyes glittered. "Did you think I had forgotten our long-ago conversation about the values of *laun* and the role of the Heirleifr on this very modern Midgard we find ourselves shipwrecked upon?"

Asher considered him. Sindri had used the full and proper name for the Kine. He didn't recall anyone else using the name for a very long time, except for formal records in the halls. Sindri was an odd mix of old and modern ideas. Did the ancient attitudes come from studying the old records as much as it was rumored he did? And if so, where did he get his modern ideas? For he certainly wouldn't have come by them here in the longhouse, with Stefan at the helm. Yet it was said he never left the hall.

Asher shoved all his questions aside. He really didn't care. The mead was flowing and for right now, he didn't have to remember what he could or couldn't say.

He deliberately up-ended the cup in a slow arc, draining it. He wiped his lips with the back of his hand and threw the cup to the floor. A cheer went up from those around him and a patter of applause.

Sindri smiled with satisfaction. "There is plenty more where that came from, my friend."

"Good," Asher told him and took off his jacket.

* * * * *

Charlee opened the screen door slowly, so it wouldn't squeak, and leaned inside. The kitchen was the same organized hysteria it always was, but she had learned from Patrick, one of the sous chefs, and from things Pierre had referred to, that a busy kitchen always looked chaotic, but if it was a good kitchen, there was an order and control to the activity. It was just emotional chefs and harried staff venting their stress by swearing, or throwing up their hands or something that made the kitchen look like it was on the brink of imploding. But dishes rattled and oil popped, which added to the racket, as Patrick said with a cheerful grin. He was the most unflappable man Charlee had ever met. Only someone as calm as he could have coped with Pierre for a boss.

Patrick was casting an eye over three plates about to be served, as the server loaded them onto her tray. He saw Charlee and gave her a short nod, to let her know she had been seen.

Charlee stepped back out and leaned against the wall to wait. She pulled her coat tighter around her. It was March, but it was one of those days when winter was winning the fight against spring, which had gone back to bed to recover. Everything looked grey, wet and slushy. The trees looked bare and forlorn, and the grass that had been uncovered by the snow was brittle and ochre-colored. The snow had gone and so had the really cold temperatures, but nothing had sprouted. Green buds would have at least said that this would be one of the last days of winter and that spring was on the way.

Patrick slammed open the screen door nearly ten minutes later and banged his way outside, his kitchen whites a bright contrast to the overcast day. He might be calm in manner, but he was clumsy in movement. His size thirteen boots were always thudding up against cupboards and corners, catching on chairs and table legs.

He was carrying a soup bowl with a spoon in it, a towel underneath to protect his fingers from the heat. "Here, it's a new recipe. Tell me what you think," he told her, thrusting the bowl toward her.

Charlee took it curiously, sliding her fingers beneath the same way he had been carrying it. "It smells divine," she told him. Rich, brothy scent, spices she would never be able to name, all in a thick stew of what looked like simple old cauliflower and a meat of some kind. Possibly chicken. She took a careful mouthful and let her brows lift to show surprise. "Delicious!" she declared, once she had swallowed. "Is that chicken?"

"Shrimp," Patrick told her. He leaned back against the wall as she had been and lit up a cigarette. "How you doin', kid?"

"I'm doin' fine. Just fine," she told him, between mouthfuls of the beautiful soup. Stew. Whatever it was. "Did you have a good week off?"

"The best," Patrick said, with a sigh.

"Lord Tight-Pants still on your case?"

The manager Asher had hired when Ylva left had been running one of the restaurants in the Waldorf Astoria. Anthony Brigand, which was his real name, was the best of the best, Pierre had told Charlee. Asher had gone for quality and got it. But while Anthony shined as a manager, he made up for it with a complete lack of people skills when it came to the staff.

He was a martinet who made the kitchen staff's lives a misery when Pierre was not there, and the front of house staff miserable *all* the time.

He always wore skin-tight suit pants and jackets with huge lapels and shoulders, in garish pinstripes. Everyone was wearing suits like that now, but what fascinated Charlee was the strained fabric of his trousers. It pressed against his crotch, showing almost everything. She had looked away, dismayed, the first time she had realized that what she was looking at was his thing and now she avoided letting her gaze get anywhere near his general hip area.

Patrick blew out another breath, expelling a heavy cloud of smoke at the same time. "Anthony is an asshole, but he really knows his stuff."

It was because of Anthony that she no longer used the front door of the restaurant. He did not allow her to sit at the tables the paying customers used. He frowned upon her visits, but in a moment of unusual sensitivity, had suggested that if she *must* visit, she arrive via the kitchen entrance, where all her friends were.

"Pierre tipped him off that you're a friend of Asher's," Patrick had told her confidentially. "He's got just enough sense of self-preservation that he didn't kick you out and tell you to never come back. Although I bet he wanted to. If he knew you were eating out of the kitchen and cutting into his profits, he'd have a cow."

"I eat leftovers," Charlee pointed out.

Patrick had grinned. "Sometimes they're not that left over," he told her. "If Lord Tight-Pants has pissed all over someone, they'll get up a plate for you, just to spite him."

She didn't mind using the kitchen entrance, anyway. It was true; she had friends in the kitchen and now, no one at the front of the house to say hello to. Which brought her back to why she was here. Charlee tipped the bowl to get at the dregs, enjoying every last drop enormously, then made herself ask the question. "Is Asher here today?" She was pleased when it came out sounding very casual and offhand.

Patrick didn't move from his tired lean against the wall, his big boot pressed up against the wall behind him for added stability. "I haven't seen him since I got back." He pulled out another cigarette and lit it with the butt of the first. "Sandy said he hadn't seen him for a while, when he handed off." Sandy was one of the other three sous chefs the restaurant rotated through.

Charlee bit her lip. That made it official. Ninety days exactly since she had last seen Asher. Ylva had left (and that was another blow), he'd hired Anthony to run the show and disappeared himself.

Where was he?

Patrick straightened up and screwed the butt of his cigarette into the ground with his food-splattered boot. "See ya tomorrow?" he asked.

She had made a deal, she told herself. She would check up on Asher every single day, just to make sure he was being careful. Just because he wasn't here (*didn't want to be here*) when she was, didn't mean she got to bail on her half of the deal. She would not feel right (*prickly gruellies!*) if she didn't.

And she really wanted to know where Asher had been. She was going to kill him herself when he did finally show, and he would. Sooner or later, he'd turn up again. This was his restaurant. The place where he could almost be himself. He'd turn up again because there probably weren't that many places where he *could* be himself, where the superhero could just sit and relax.

He's found another place. A better place. The thought surfaced as it always did whenever she reasoned out that he would reappear someday, which she did frequently. She was only thirteen, but she was old enough to know that even though they were alike in some ways (*secrets! Lies!*), her company wasn't nearly as distracting as other attractions would be to a man like Asher. New York crawled with them, some legal and some not.

And that was where her heart would sink and her fear rise. What if Ylva's leaving and Asher's disappearance were somehow connected? What if he had given up on life in general? What if he was shooting up, or blowing his brains out on crack? Sick with some disease he'd picked up from a whore? What if he had AIDS?

Damn it, where are you?

But…she had made a deal. Charlee sighed. "I'll be here tomorrow," she told Patrick.

"Good deal," he said and she looked at him, startled, until she realized he was using the new street lingo, not commenting on her promise (*which was secret*).

Charlee handed him her empty bowl then walked back out onto the street, to cross over to the SPCA. It was the Easter break, when school was out for two weeks, and she was more than happy to spend her vacation at the animal shelter (*closer to Asher*). Toward the end of last summer, Carole had offered her a tiny cash wage for her time, as she was their best assistant. Carole had also started her training the volunteers when they began. Charlee had been assisting in the hospital for nearly a year already.

It was highly satisfying work and had completely cemented her plans to find a profession that let her work with animals full time. She had chosen every science-based option available at school, to pave the way for college, although how she was going to pay for college was a giant, nebulous problem she put off thinking about whenever the question arose. There was time yet.

Carole had already promised her a proper, wage-paying job as soon as she turned fourteen and could be legally employed.

Charlee glanced at the front door of the restaurant as she passed it and sighed again.

Where are you, Asher Strand? Are you being safe?

Chapter Ten

Guillory, Unnur
Guillory; French surname, derived from
a Germanic name, composed of the
elements wil, meaning "will", and ric,
meaning "powerful". Unnur Guillory
became one of…
From *The Complete Kine Encyclopedia*, by
Darwin Baxter, PhD. 2019 Edition

Unnur Guillory unlocked her tiny storefront shop at 7:47 a.m. just like she had been doing for the last eleven years. That was going to change soon, and she already knew in broad sweeping outline how that change was going to happen. She also knew that there was nothing she could do to redirect her fate.

Her routine was unvarying, for reasons of health and sanity as much as because she had been following this routine for over a decade. She rose at six every morning, including Sundays, slowly drank her breakfast of juiced wheat grass and apples, and then read for an hour before showering and dressing for the day.

Sometimes she read fiction, but most often she reached for well-thumbed books about her personal heroes and their work: Edgar Cayce, Jean Dixon, Sylvia Browne. Sometimes she would range across the work of "lesser" souls like Jane Roberts and Ingo Swann, but only when she wanted something light and not too taxing. That usually happened on hot, humid mornings, when the national weather service radio reported the potential for thunderstorms in the afternoon.

On those days, Unnur had to force herself out of the little apartment above her store and down the narrow and open wooden stairs. She had replaced the iron stairs within a week of moving into the apartment. The conductive qualities of steel had made her tremble every time she had used them and she had been completely unable to touch the steel bannister. She would stand and hug herself and wait for her balance to return, risking a fall backwards down the stairs, instead of gripping the bannister and anchoring herself that way.

She pushed aside the folding cage door that protected the whole front of her store, window included, and unlocked the glass door behind it. She didn't see her reflection in the glass. She had long ago stopped looking in mirrors. She was thirty-seven years of age, and she had come to know nearly twenty years ago that the red tracks and scarring on her face, radiating out from her right cheekbone like the roots of a particularly obnoxious weed or the bad blood of infection and disease, would never fade like it did for most victims.

She had been marked.

The brace she wore on her right leg, to compensate for the wasted muscle below her knee, clicked as she swung forward through the door and flipped the sign hanging on the inside of it from "Closed" to "Welcome! Come on in."

The one plate glass window on the right of the door she had set up with a wide shelf in front of it to display products that could catch the eye of passers-by. There were pretty collections of scented candles, which she personally did not have much truck with. If she was going to use candles (and they had their uses, no argument), then plain household candles did the job. It was the candle's flame that held the power, not the wax holding it up or the aroma it gave off. But people seemed to like them.

There were glass and crystal paperweights, glittering globes in a range of sizes, each with something intriguing in their centres: flowers, a small globe of the world, or colored shapes that rebounded light back at you in a thousand different colors. They sold quite well.

Then there were the plain crystal balls. Unnur displayed them on their own individual stands. The stands themselves were enticing, she admitted. She had found a wood-turner who was handy at turning a lump of kindling into a beautiful stand of intricate curves and valleys. She bought them from him for fifteen dollars apiece, then sanded and painted them herself at night. She could get fifty dollars for the stand alone. A nice stand with one of the bigger crystal balls on them she could sell for over ninety dollars. If she draped a hemmed piece of silk over the ball, and handled it with a degree of wariness that looked a lot like awe, she could ask a hundred and fifty, and it was rare they didn't take out their pocketbook without demur.

The store was longer than it was wide so in the front section, where tourists and the merely curious browsed, Unnur had put stands of what she tended to think of as gewgaws. Cystals, more candles, scents and essential oils, cards, books on horoscopes ("*What does YOUR future hold?*"), Chinese sun signs, jewelry, magazines and more. There was a waist-high, V-shaped stand that held big posters inside plastic sleeves, including fantasy scenes, movie posters and occult calendars. The sale of all the paraphernalia was where she made most of her rent.

It wasn't that she thought most customers were gullible, or that the products she peddled for revenue as quackery, but she did think of them as essentially harmless trinkets.

The *real* stuff, where the true power lay, was at the back of the store. Here, she had spent weeks stripping back decades of indifferent paint colors, right down to the cement floor and cinderblock walls. Then she had painstakingly resealed and repainted everything. The floor was unapologetic black, sealed over so feet didn't scuff it, although she had refinished it a few times since the original application. The walls from curtain height through to the ceiling and the ceiling itself were a matte black, and in among the pot lights and spot lights, she had added little fairy lights, the ones that adorned Christmas trees. She had stripped off the decorative crystal-shaped tips and left just the bare light to gleam like the stars she had wanted them to represent.

On the walls on either side, she had spent nearly three weeks drawing by hand and then painting two long fantasy murals. She had copied them out of a fantasy art book that she had bought as starting stock for the store but never got around to actually putting on a shelf for sale. It had been a draw-by-numbers exercise, for she knew her mind wouldn't be able to hold the image for long. She would forget bits of it and others would rub themselves clean out of her memory. So she had drawn a grid over the images and scaled up a larger replica grid on the walls and she slowly drew in the elements with constant reference to the originals. Painting them had been the same dot-to-dot duplication, and she had pushed herself to finish them, working late into the night, until her one good leg throbbed from carrying her weight for so long without cease and her headaches had threatened to call in on her.

The result was two landscapes that looked, so customers said, like you could step through the wall and roll around in the purple grass and play with the baby dragon. Unnur always looked and saw the mistakes she had made. But it pleased the customers.

The murals drew the more-than-curious customers deeper into the store and it was there that Unnur's real work happened.

On both sides of the store, on low, stand-alone shelving units that didn't block the view of the landscapes, were the Tarot.

There was every type of Tarot deck available, including some of the gimmicky ones that featured sea creatures, or elves, or other nonsense that Unnur didn't truck with, but the Tarot was the Tarot: Its power came through no matter what the card carried on its face. She preferred the standard Waite-Rider-Smith deck, herself, and that was the one she used for personal and pay-for readings.

There were also books, and it was in this section that she kept big and small posters of the Minor and Major Arcana.

Her reading table was at the back of the store and in between customers, she would handle the deck, shuffling it and pouring her warm regard over it. Sometimes, she would do readings for herself, asking questions as they occurred to her: *What will this week bring the world? What will come to this little corner of Florida?* A favorite was, *What will the weather be today?*

But the question that brought the most interesting answers wasn't a question at all. She would hold the pack in her hands, cradling it softly, and when she was relaxed and ready, she would whisper to the ether: *Tell me.*

Then she would lay a six-month special spread out upon the silk and see what it was she was to hear.

Unnur had stumbled upon The Question, as she had begun to think of it, almost eight years ago to the day. She had been between customers. Back in those days, customers had been rare. On that day, she had just had a visit from the princeling who ran the company that owned her building. She was behind in her rent, didn't she know? Well, of course she knew. Her rent covered both her business and her home. She was preternaturally aware of each due date and (usually) the yawning gap between what she owed and how much she had. Her little occult store was ailing. It seemed there wasn't much call for divination in Lakeland. But Unnur didn't know how to do anything else. She *couldn't* do most other things that a body might do to pay for their daily gumbo. Her weak right leg wouldn't let her do manual work at the pace they would want her to, and her marked face meant that jobs like selling pretty smelly stuff in the local Walgreens or trading stamps door-to-door were just as out of reach.

But she could read the cards, better than most. She had been marked, and this was the other side of that marking. Ever since the day she had got her mark, she had sometimes just known things: things that had happened in places far away, things that were about to happen.

Her mother had called people like her gifted, but what she had really meant was that they were cursed, for she would have no dealings with anything that held a hint of heresy. She was a good Catholic woman and God was her guide, as He should be for everyone. Unnur had been old enough when she was marked to know that revealing her new gift to her mother would end with her cast out of the family. Her acceptance as a good girl by her mother was already in jeopardy because of the mark. Her mother hadn't quite made up her mind if the mark was a sign from God or if the other fella had singled her out.

Unnur had her own opinion on who had done the marking and wisely kept it to herself, along with her ability to sometimes see things before they happened or just know things that she didn't have any right knowing. She knew her daddy was seeing the waitress at the diner where he ate lunch every weekday. She also knew her mother wouldn't live another two years because the growth in her belly had already grown an inch across and was sucking the life out of her body, even though no one, including her mother, had any idea that she was anything other than perfectly healthy.

When her mother had died almost exactly two years later, her father had already been absent for nearly a year; so had the waitress. Unnur had worked a series of jobs trying to support herself. The most successful of them had been hard labor as a dishwasher in the big kitchen at the Richmond Hotel on Main Street, where she could keep her back to most everybody most of the time. But the slave wages hadn't covered her few bills, so she had added a second job as kitchen hand in another hotel, but that hadn't worked out so well with her gammy leg and they had let her go.

She had learned about Tarot cards from one of the kitchen hands at the Richmond. He had been a short, pure-blood Shawnee Indian, whose real name, Tenskwatawa, no one could pronounce, so everyone called him Tenska. Tenska had a Tarot deck that he kept in a silk sleeve in his back pocket and whenever he had a spare moment, he would shuffle the cards. He would use them to answer even simple questions, like whether he wanted to take a smoke break outside. Unnur had no idea what the cards told him, but it was the images on them that fascinated her.

On her lunch break two days after Tenska had started, he sat down on the opposite side of the tiny table she always used, at the far corner of the little closed-in yard the staff were permitted to relax in. He had studied her closely. His whites were grease-splattered and there was a burn on the corner of his apron. But his eyes were clear and very young, while he looked old, like he had seen all of history and was wearied by it. It was the first time she had ever looked at them closely.

"It's time for you t'learn," he said. His voice was astonishingly deep for a man so small. He was shorter than her.

"Learn?" she asked.

Then he did something so totally unexpected that it left Unnur frozen and speechless. He reached out with one long finger and very gently touched the center of her mark, high up on her cheekbone. "You're the one."

Then he had started laying out the cards, face upwards, talking softly with his deep voice, telling her the story of each one.

"Don't you have your own gods, who tell you these things?" she had asked. It was an impertinent question, but she felt like he owed her for touching her mark.

"My gods, your gods...they're all the same god," he said, with a smile. "Just like these cards. The cards are just a way for them to talk to you and me. Others use different ways. My neegah, she looked into the water and that's how they talked to her."

A week later, he didn't show for work and was never seen again. It was as if he had arrived in time to show her the power of the Tarot, then left. She was more sure of that when she discovered his name meant "open door". He had opened a door for her that would never be closed again.

She hadn't learned everything in those few days. The learning, the heavy study, would be a lifetime's work. But Tenska had shown her the way.

Unnur realized she was shuffling the cards in her hands, staring without seeing at the silk cloth laid over the velvet cover that draped over the whole table, right down to the floor. She often did this when she was about to ask The Question. She would come to and realize she had spent long minutes wandering through memories or thinking about something. She accepted that this was her way of preparing herself for the reading.

The cards themselves had guided her to The Question. She was not the most powerful medium in the world. She knew that very well. Her sight was weak and intermittent, but she was a willing student, prepared to work hard to maximize what little power she had.

She had bought her first Tarot deck the day after Tenska disappeared, and borrowed every book about Tarot available from the library. Her mother was sick by then and spent most of her time in bed, so Unnur could spend her evenings reading, in between morphine shots. Reading, and laying out spreads and studying them.

Because her memory had been fried at the same time as her leg had suffered, Unnur wrote down every single spread she laid, along with her interpretation and the date. She developed her own notation system for the cards, which made understanding them easier, too. Each card was related to other cards, not just those in their own suite. The Major Arcana fed their power into the minor cards. The royal cards built upon the number cards. They were life itself, tangled, interwoven and persistent as hell.

Unnur did her first reading for someone else nearly a year later. Her mother had been transferred to a hospital for more dedicated care than Unnur and her crooked leg could manage, and her father still hadn't reappeared. The reading had happened casually, quite by accident, which was the only way it could have happened for her. Because of her mark and her brace, she was timid about talking to complete strangers, but this one had stopped by her corner of the big table at the library, where she was reading an in-house-only volume and laying out cards experimentally as she read.

"Do you do readings?" the well-coiffed woman asked.

"I…" Tongue-tied, Unnur looked down at the tabletop. Her glance had fallen upon the Strength card: the woman in white, taming a lion not with physical strength but with her will and her courage.

It was silent encouragement.

Unnur lifted her head to look at the woman again. "I do readings," she said.

Seven months later, she opened her store.

* * * * *

Tell me.

Once Unnur had learned to listen instead of asking, the cards had begun to speak. Sometimes, she needed to clarify their message with follow-up questions, but usually the meaning was very clear. In hindsight, she realized she had been gumming up the channel with her misguided questions.

She didn't know if it was gods or God who spoke to her. She thought of them/it as the Earth reaching out to her, as she was one of the few who could hear. She called it Gaia when she really needed a name for it.

After the first time she had thrown her mental hands up into the air with a plea for guidance, things had begun to change. Customers increased. Not a flood, not all at once, but foot traffic through the door picked up slowly and surely.

The cards told her where to advertise and where not to advertise, when she had not thought of paying for advertising at all before that moment. Soon, she had a monthly mail-out newsletter service with over five thousand paying subscribers. She got calls from all over Florida and the eastern seaboard, asking about readings and products she had advertised.

She did readings over the phone, and three years ago she had taken her first go-to appointment. He was an extremely successful entrepreneur here in Lakeland, and he had stressed—and paid for—an extraordinary level of discretion. Unnur understood why he was concerned about appearances. The cards told her to take the appointment and abide by his restrictions (he had appeared as the Two of Wands), and soon enough, he had referred her to another businessman, this one in Tampa. The Tampa mogul had arranged for a car to drive her there and back and she had charged two hundred and fifty dollars for the reading and her time. That had paid for new product stands for the front end of the store and a fancy new window display stand, covered in crushed purple velvet.

Daily, she consulted the cards to hear what she should do next. Sometimes the messages were minor, or she thought they were. The cards had told her to skip an occult conference in Miami. Later, she found out the flight she had been booked on had crashed, three miles out from Miami. No one had survived.

Two years ago, the King and Queen of Wands had appeared for the first time. Unnur had traced back through all her recorded readings to check. For general readings, for answering questions and for commercial readings, they had appeared. But they had not appeared in any of her communications with Gaia. *Not once.*

The two court cards most definitely represented actual people in her spreads. Who, she didn't know. The cards would tell her in time. Court cards could indicate people, or they could sometimes represent ideas and concepts. Abstract meanings. But this time, from the cards surrounding them, Unnur knew that two people, a man and a woman, had been brought to her attention.

Patiently, she kept on working, obediently following her guides and increment by increment, her business improved and life became a smidgen more comfortable. She knew that she would have made faster progress if she were more powerful, but she had been touched with only a small dose of the Sight and the cards were limited by her inabilities. They could be shouting their messages at her via the world's largest sound system and even though she stood with her ear pressed against the speaker, she could only hear the messages in fits and starts.

But she was content with what her little talent provided. She had a roof over her head, she ate when she needed to and she had the privilege of being paid to do something she loved. Who'd've thought little Unnur Syeda Guillory, who had been struck on the face by lightning when she was sixteen years old and had been pronounced officially dead for five minutes, would ever have amounted to this much?

The King and Queen of Wands kept appearing after that. Not in every spread, but always together. Unnur gradually built a picture of the pair. He was a leader, bold, forceful and charismatic. She was creative, working to accept the position life had thrust upon her. Unnur began to like them and look forward to their appearance.

As she shuffled her cards, she wondered if she would see them today. It had been a few weeks since they had come back to visit. Wondering so might skew the reading, so she cleared her mind once again, holding the cards.

Tell me.

Slowly, she laid the spread upon the table, her fingers dexterously manipulating the cards with the mastery of long practice, while she held herself in a mental breath-holding position. She meditated her way through the laying out, so that her thoughts and expectations did not affect the spread in any way. She made herself a pure conduit.

Only once the last card had been laid and she had reverently placed the remainder of the pack at the top of the table did she study the cards.

There they were, together as always. *Well, hello!* Unnur smiled and moved on, looking at the cards around them.

The Devil. The Lord of Sorrows, with his three swords piercing the heart and dripping life's blood. The Lord of Ruin—right next to the Queen. Unnur stared at the ten blades thrust into his back, her heart screaming along in her chest.

Violence. By the blade.

Unnur sent out her thoughts to the King and Queen, wherever they were. *Be wary!*

She stroked the side of the Queen's card, where the bloom was. *Especially you,* she added, for the danger surrounded her on every side except the one where the King lay.

* * * * *

Sergio was very happy. He was twitching with it. Positively fuckin' wired to the max.

Oh, it was going to be a *beee-you-tiful* night, filled with righteous fuckin' comeback. The monkey that had been on his back for two dark years was about to get his. Oh, yes he was, in every way Sergio could think of. He had spent every night for the last two years fantasizing about what he would do if this *exact* situation ever came to pass, so now he didn't have anything left to plan. He knew exactly what he was going to do.

He sat in the back booth in Green's deli, where they sold excellent milkshakes that tasted even better when he was high. He was waiting for the others to report in and it gave him some spare time. He let himself savor the upcoming payback.

He didn't know how many people there were in New York. Fuckin' millions, he guessed. The chances of accidentally spotting someone you really wanted to see, to see them bop along by, completely unaware that you had seen them, why, those chances were so thin that you could practically see your hand through them.

But someone was dealing out lucky breaks and his number had come up.

Ruffy, one of only three of his soldiers who had made it out of the park alive that night, had come hurrying into the deli three weeks ago, his hood up over his head, not wearing his colors and sniffing away his need for a fix. It was only just past noon, too early to start dishing out crap about not wearing his colors.

He'd slid onto the bench opposite Sergio, his hands still deep in the pockets on the front of his hoodie, slouched down on the seat until his chin was bare inches above the table. His leg instantly started to bounce up and down under the table, his sneaker doing a soft tap on the lino beneath.

"What't fuck d'you want?" Sergio demanded. He was enjoying his buzz. Being disturbed ruined it.

Ruffy sniffed and brought out a hand to wipe at his nose with the back of it. "I saw him, man."

Sergio stared at him. He couldn't even be bothered asking who. He just plain didn't give a fuck.

Ruffy leaned forward earnestly. "*Him*," he whispered.

Sergio didn't need to be told more. *Him* could only mean one dude: the fucker who had choked him off in the park. The one who had thought he could get away with threatening him. The one who had stood over the red-haired dog-loving freak and her puny brother like an invisible shield for two fucking years.

Sergio snatched at Ruffy's hoodie and dragged him across the table. His milkshake spilled and the glass rolled up against the wall, slopping green milk across the Formica. "You better not be fuckin' wit me."

"Honest to god," Ruffy said. "I saw him real good that night. An' I just saw him now. Walkin' into a buildin' on Wall Street, cool as a cucumber."

"What'choo doin' down there?"

"Delivery," Ruffy said, sounding scared. "You said to give the stuff to that guy. Remember?"

"Right." He had to check. Sometimes the shits decided they were gonna do their own thing and had to be reprimanded. It wasn't *his* memory that was slipping. He remembered just fine. "Which building?"

* * * * *

Ruffy took him back to the building. It was a fuckin' bank, but that figured—it was Wall Street. Sergio had stood across the street, just out of the line of suits hurrying along the sidewalk and settled in to wait. The guy would eventually leave the building again. If he'd already left, then he'd be back. Sooner or later.

After four hours, Ruffy got the fidgets bad enough he was drawing attention, so Sergio sent him home with a growled command. But Sergio stayed in place, steady as a rock, his gaze on the street entrance of the Strand Manhattan Trust building, scanning every tall man who stepped out through the glass doors.

Sooner or later, he kept telling himself. He was filled with energy. Pumping with it. He knew he could stand here for a century if that's what it took.

Sooner or later.

It took four days.

Sergio used the payphone ten paces away to call up his soldiers, while still keeping an eye on the glass doors. Once his men arrived, he sent them for food and used them for washroom relief as he needed it. He got rid of the patrolling cops by telling them he was loitering because he was waiting for his brother, the vice-president of the bank over there. They were going to do lunch/dinner/whatever meal was closest, but his stuck-up brother didn't want him seen by his stuffy co-workers. It had just enough of a ring of authenticity that the cops left him alone to wait, watching the doors over the road. They had no fuckin' idea.

Sergio slept in Central Park. There was no one who would dare fuck with him even there. He returned to his post early each morning and so it was that he was in position close to eight in the morning, Wall Street already firing on all cylinders, when he saw from the corner of his eye a tall suit striding toward the bank.

His eyes narrowed. His heart revved up.

It *looked* like the fucker. He was tall enough and the shoulders were big enough. The prissy blond hair, though…he hadn't guessed the guy was a faggot. No one had hair like that for real. It came out of a salon where all the queer boys got up each other. Had Ruffy got it right? The fucker that had shoved a goddamn sword up under his chin and locked him into that iron-hard arm lock was…a suit?

It was an expensive suit. Not that Sergio knew anything about suits, but it just *looked* expensive. The faggot had pulled his hair back into a goddamn for-real pony tail. Shit on a stick.

His surprise kept Sergio completely still for twenty vital seconds. Then he took off like a startled rabbit, diving between cars and cabs, until he jumped onto the opposite sidewalk and slowed to a walk as hurried as everyone else's. He pulled off his shirt and turned his cap around, so he looked like any one of the dozens of maintenance dudes and grunts coming in and out.

He came up behind the fucker and got his first true measure of the guy's height, which matched his memories. Then there was a jam at the door, a woman coming out with a walker trying to pull it open ahead of her kiddy, which caused the four people trying to get in the door to bunch up in front of it. The front one held the door open for her. Which put Sergio right behind the fucker and then he *knew*.

The smell was right.

It wasn't often Sergio took conscious note of smells, but the fucker had held him up against his chest, his arm wrapped around his throat, Sergio's ear jammed into his armpit. He might not have been able to describe that scent but as soon as he smelled it, he recognized it. It made him flash back to the night two years ago in the park: the pain of the sword digging into his chin, the iron band around his throat, the fear crawling low down in his belly, writhing and wanting to leap right up into his throat. The flashback and the start it gave him convinced him more than anything else he had the right guy.

He faded away, back into the crowd, before the fucker could even twitch that he'd been there.

Sergio spent the next three days carefully finding out more about the dude. He started with one of the security guards at the bank, slipping him a package of the good stuff. Sergio's description made the guy raise his brows. "*Him?*" he whispered, looking around, suddenly scared. He flipped open a binder filled with plastic sleeves and tapped the page. "Him?" he questioned.

Sergio looked. Blue eyes, prissy white hair shorter than it was now. "That's him," he confirmed. He glanced down at the bottom of the page. These were mug shots that the guards used to identify key personnel in the building and this one had a neat description underneath. *Asher Strand, President, Strand Manhattan Trust.*

"He owns the fucking bank?" Sergio asked in disbelief. A bank president was the guy who had tried to fuck him over?

"He's the president. It don't work like that on Wall Street," the guard said.

"Too fucking bizarre," Sergio said.

The guard had got edgy after that, refusing to give up anything else. "They'll know it's me," he said, shaking his head. Sergio took back the coke. One of his men would have to visit the prick one night soon. Explain the facts of life to him.

The next step was an unprecedented one for Sergio, but he was sorta in the area. He climbed up the steps to the New York Central Library, staring at the freaky lions with amusement. Who'd've ever thought he'd find himself here?

He could feel himself shrinking back to elementary school size as he stepped inside. Grade nine was about the last time he'd been in one of these, but the single fact he remembered about libraries from school had brought him here: librarians knew everything and if they didn't, they knew how to look it up.

He walked right up to the first librarian he could find and asked his question. The librarian, a grey-hair with one of those grandfather cardigans with pockets on the hips, considered for a minute then beckoned silently with his finger.

Twenty minutes later, Sergio had his answer.

He looked down at the address he had scribbled on scrap paper using the librarian's pen. "Got you, you fucker. Now I know where you live."

* * * * *

Since then, Sergio had been dreaming up his vengeance. The fucker, this Strand faggot, was just a guy. Even though Sergio's cranky memory and imagination had played and replayed the few moments in the park until the fucker had taken on the proportions of a giant with super-human strength—no wonder he, Sergio, had been overwhelmed!—he was human. If he was just a guy, then Sergio could deal with him. A guy, any guy, had weaknesses. Vulnerabilities. While there wasn't much Sergio was good at, he did have a keen animal instinct for sniffing out weaknesses in his enemies.

He laid his plans.

Now he sat in his favorite booth at Gold's, waiting for someone to report back to him. Every time the bell dinged over the door, he let his gaze flicker over to the new arrival.

Then Julio stepped in. Like a good soldier, he was wearing his colors, and his swagger told everyone he was carrying. Julio liked to brag, but that was okay. It was good to have confidence, even if he was new to the family. Sergio had been keeping an eye on him, watching to see if Julio was going to let it go to his head. He'd have to bring him back into line if it did. But that's what a good leader had to do: purging and herding.

Julio spotted him and bebopped over to the table. He placed both hands flat on it. "Found her, boss," he said quietly, his grin huge.

Chapter Eleven

Annarr
(Old Norse; Annarr – "second").
Herleifr title that indirectly refers to
Odin's position as the leader of Valhalla
and general of the Einherjar army. The
Annarr ('Second to Odin') is the most
senior Einherjar and custodian of the
Kine (joint responsibility shared with
the Regin – see *Regin*). Title and role
created shortly after the Descent.
From *The Complete Kine Encyclopedia*, by
Darwin Baxter, PhD. 2019 Edition

Asher was halfway across the rotunda when he heard his name being called. He sighed, vexed, and turned to see who wanted him now.

Stefan stood on the far side, near the big double doors that led to the main hall. He had his squat little clerk with him, but the clerk was turning to leave. Stefan lifted his hand and beckoned.

What was it, Asher wondered, about all leaders that gave them that complete confidence that their will would be done? The flicker of the fingers, the command that was to be unquestionably acted upon; they all seemed to acquire the attitude sooner or later.

Stefan's dark eyes flickered over him as Asher got closer.

"Annarr," Asher acknowledged, bowing his head shortly.

"Asher," Stefan returned. "You're looking...casual."

Asher looked down at his jeans. They were the first thing he'd grabbed when he'd got home, stripping off his suit almost before he got in the door. Suits were constricting but necessary to complete some business. He'd found, though, that it was easier to wear comfortable clothing. It let him think better. More often than not, he grabbed jeans. The shirt was the one he'd worn with the suit, but it was black and it was half hidden, anyway. Winter still gripped Oslo, so he'd thrown his long coat on just in case Øystein and the others wanted to head out somewhere.

"You're wearing your hair longer," Stefan added.

Asher remembered loosening the thong that he had tied it back with this morning, but he'd left the thing sitting on the bathroom counter. Oh well. "Just keeping up with human fashion," he told Stefan.

"I don't recall meeting a bank president that looked quite as you do," Stefan said. "I have appreciated your input in council meetings lately."

It seemed like a shift in subjects, but Asher remained wary. Stefan was like a terrier, coming back time and time again to nip and wear down his victim. "Thank you," he said. It was a neutral response.

"I've also heard that you have been seen in the company of the Brennus, more and more."

The Brennus was the name that had seemed to evolve in the last few months, used to describe Sindri and his friends. It wasn't until Asher had got to know most of them better that he realized how extended Sindri's circle of friends was. "The Brennus..." Asher repeated. "It's a silly name for a group of people who like to drink together."

Stefan tilted his head. "I have always thought of you as a smart man, Askr Brynjarson."

"You think the Brennus are political?" Asher gave a short laugh. "Since when did drinking become political?"

"It is not the mead I refer to. It is the words spoken over it that concerns me," Stefan replied, a finger running over his closely cropped beard, the big ring with the orange stone winking at Asher as the last of the daylight touched it. "I was not the only one who heard you speak in the last council about better integration with humans."

Asher blinked. In truth, he regretted saying what he did. It had been spoken in heat and without thought, something that Roar was always on his case about. But there had been no response to his bitter comments, which had surprised him. He had been braced for a lecture from Roar at least.

Was this the lecture, now? Had Stefan decided it should come from the Annarr himself?

Asher chose his words carefully. "The council meeting was over a week ago, my lord."

"I am not your lord," Stefan shot back.

"Freyr," Asher amended, mentally kicking himself. So much for speaking carefully. "You seek me out now to speak about a comment I made in haste in a closed-door council meeting?"

"You and I were not the only ones in that meeting," Stefan replied evenly. "What you said was heard by all. You may not like it, Asher, but everything you do and say is political. For one like you, trying to ignore the influence you wield is akin to trying to shed your skin because you do not like the way it chafes."

"Influence?" Asher swallowed the laugh that rose once more. "I think you overestimate my value, with all due respect, Annarr."

Stefan just smiled. "I'm quite sure I have not," he replied. "Nor has Sindri overlooked the influence you hold over the younger Kine. You are Roar's brother, and the strongest stallari we have. Because of the relationships that have developed between the halls, there are others who believe you have the ear of the most powerful among us."

It was the closest anyone had ever come to saying out loud what had only been apparent by observation: that Eira, Stefan's Regin, was silently in love with Roar.

Asher swallowed, as the implications of what Stefan was not saying became clear. Because Eira favored Roar, for whatever reason, Asher was in a position to use that favor. Use it for what, though? He hated politics, and Stefan's view that he was a political figure whether he liked it or not was almost repulsive.

Stefan was nodding, as if he could see Asher work through the implications. "You have always been open in your contempt for *laun*," he added, "and you well know my views."

Asher did know where Stefan stood on the matter of *laun*. Stefan was one of the most insistent defenders of the laws and principles of secrecy. It structured their world and determined most of the details of their day-to-day lives. In nearly every way, Stefan was conservative and traditional, and upholding *laun* was a part of that.

He wanted the Kine to live quietly. He wanted his own rule to be a peaceful one. He had been born to rule as a human king during one of the most chaotic periods in English history and his kingship had been a period of turmoil and bloodshed. He had died on the battlefield, as had they all, but was one of the few Kine who felt their human life had been wasted. Stefan believed the slaughter and near annihilation of his people was because he had not been strong enough, even though he had been one of the last men standing, holding the final defense line against the enemy. Now he was determined to do right, to lead the Kine and maintain a peace he had failed to find as a king. He always chose the safe path, the route that guaranteed the fewest number of noses would be bent and the least number of people would protest.

As a result, Stefan usually looked beaten-down and tired. Leading the Kine with their hero-warriors and stronger women, most of them leaders, fighters, the most courageous of the brave and fallen...it must be like riding an unbroken stallion, Asher thought. It didn't help that he wore clothing that was not traditional but was always several decades out of date. It was as if he was clinging to the past in every way he could. At the moment he wore what one could most kindly call a robe, but that Asher recognized as something his friends had been wearing when Vietnam protesting was at its height.

The thought slipped into Asher's mind from left field. *And Charlee thinks I am square?*

He shut down the thought and the memory/image of red hair and black eyes, barely before it registered, for that was an area of his life he had put under wraps, like so many areas and people and centuries gone by. He was usually very good at compartmentalizing his serial and parallel roles, but that one continued to break through every now and again, usually when he was not braced for it.

He didn't let Stefan's old-fashioned appearance fool him, though. Stefan wanted peace at any cost, and he was a good enough leader that he had got his way for nearly three hundred years.

Stefan dropped his hand away from his beard, which had not changed since Asher had first met him. "Those who *do* like their politics will have noticed that we disagree on the matter of *laun*. If they thought you felt strongly enough about it, they would find you a useful lightning rod for others who have grievances."

Asher frowned, trying to anticipate where Stefan was taking this and failing.

Then Stefan stepped back and held his hand out to one side, as if he was waving Asher past him. "Enjoy your mead and your company, Asher. I am glad you can find good cheer in my hall."

"Annarr," Asher murmured. He bowed and turned back to face the big open rotunda. He was halfway across the echoing chamber, heading for Sindri's salon and anticipating his first mug of mead, when Stefan's true meaning fell together with an impact that caused him to slow his walk, as his heart leapt.

Enjoy your mead and the company, he had said. What he had *not* said was the real message: Enjoy the mead and the company, but don't mess with the politics that comes with them.

Don't become a lightning rod. Not in my hall.

Asher picked up his pace again, not wanting to look addled, standing in one place with his mouth open. He didn't look back because he knew that Stefan would not be there. The man had buried his barb with more expertise than Asher had given him credit for.

* * * * *

Lucas took his time walking home from practice. He ached with the good pains that came from a great workout, and hunger was starting to kick in now the adrenaline from training was disappearing. He considered what was in the fridge and the pantry, recalling the items from memory as he walked. If dinner wasn't ready when he got home, there were a few different things he could put together in about twenty minutes, which meant he wouldn't be sick and shaking from hunger by the time it was ready. He was leaning toward fish sticks and fries, because they were fast and they filled him up better than something like scrambled eggs would. Besides, Charlee loved fish sticks.

It was a golden day, one when spring was definitely in the air. It was still warm, despite the setting sun. Very warm after putting up with a long, cold winter. A light windbreaker was all he needed.

Tonight the coach had given him the thumbs up after their scratch match, second string against starting lineup, and patted his shoulder. "I've got my eye on you, Montgomery," was all he'd said, but it meant a lot, for Coach Sanders had more than one contact in the NFL. Now, that would be the thing. Even a contract as second string for a bottom-of-the-ladder team would take care of all his worries about what to do about things at home after he graduated in June.

The idea had given him hope he hadn't known he was looking for.

But for this fine April day, even that concern was far away. The sunset, something he rarely bothered to admire, was really something, with the reds and golds bathing the high-rises as it sank down behind them.

Then the knife pushed up against his back.

A short Latino wearing oversized sneakers and a silk shirt stepped up alongside him. "You wanna do what we say, see. Coz we got something of yours."

His first immediate thought was a panic-filled one. *Charlee.* Hard on the heels of that was cold reason. *They wouldn't dare, not after Asher Strand dealt with them.*

But Asher had been gone for months now. Charlee hadn't said much about it, but his disappearance had upset her in the same lonely and silent way that the dog's death had. The only thing that had stopped her retreating all the way into her room and shutting out the world was her job at the SPCA. It made Lucas want to kick Asher's nuts off, if he ever got the chance.

He'd never stopped to think that Strand flaking on Charlee meant that all bets were off with the Lords.

Oh fuck, oh shit... he whispered mentally. Sweat popped out on his temples as he kept walking just to stop the knife from sliding between his ribs, which he knew it would do if he stopped.

The Lord next to him grinned, showing very white teeth. "Now yoo got it," he crooned. "Just a little walk around the corner here'ya."

What could he do? How was he supposed to get both him and Charlee out of this? Unlike football or basketball, there were no rules and no boundaries. In sports, he could read the upcoming movements in games and take advantage of what players were *about* to do, but he acknowledged the bitter truth that in *this* game, he was completely out of his depth.

Hot sourness filled his mouth as they turned the corner into 161st.

He eyed the cars idling at the lights, three feet away from him.

"You don't wanta call out," the Lord said next to him. "Your sister don't wantcha calling out, dig?"

Lucas swallowed and nodded.

They led him along 161st, then across Trinity. He knew then where they were taking him. He also knew that no one was going to come to his rescue. They were risking this in broad daylight. The sun was barely touching the horizon. To be so open about it meant they had their backs covered somehow. They weren't afraid of Asher Strand; that was for sure.

For a long, aching moment, Lucas wished that Strand would magically appear and do whatever it was that he did when he 'talked' to the gang. Lucas didn't care if he carved them up with a chain saw. He just wanted him to come *now*. He wanted Strand to know by divine intervention that he was desperately needed. But that wasn't going to happen. The Lords had seen to it, somehow.

The park they were heading for was just up ahead. It was a tiny thing, tucked in among all the apartment towers that dotted this block like sentinels, overlooking the yards and roofs of the houses across the street and far below. One of Lucas' teammates, Greg Peterson, lived on the top floor of the southern-most tower. When he visited, Lucas had looked down at his neighborhood, fascinated by the ant-like size of the buildings he walked past every day.

There was no hope Greg would look out and see what was going down. His tower was on the far side of the park and his apartment on the other side of the tower, facing Manhattan. Besides, from up there, the two Lords who were escorting him and Lucas himself would be too small to make out any detail.

Lucas was still casting about frantically, trying to dream up ideas, solutions, something, *anything* he could do to get out of this, when they turned into the park and pushed him around one of the big bushes that clogged up the corner and created a great shield against passers-by.

Charlee was there, but she wasn't alone.

Lucas' heart lurched in his chest, then hurried on at a pace that made his chest hurt. He felt hot, sick and angry all at once.

They had taped her mouth with what looked like duct tape, running the stuff right around her head, layer over layer. It was way more than was necessary. They had caught hanks of her hair under it, while others hung freely, falling over her eyes. Her eyes were huge, over the top of the tape.

She had her arms behind her, and Lucas knew with another sick, sinking sensation that they'd taped her arms back, probably with the same wild abandon as they had done with her mouth.

There was more tape around her ankles, which had pulled

indifferently at her tights, tearing great holes in them. Just beneath the hem of her pretty pleated skirt, Lucas could see that her legs were trembling. She was shaking with fear.

The realization calmed him and blew away the sickness. The world became muffled, the way it often did when he was on the field or the court. Everything unimportant faded away from his attention, while the thing he was focusing on became crystal clear. His heart slowed down. His thoughts calmed. The movements of the gang around him slowed down, while every sound they made he heard, from the susurration of their clothes as they shifted, the quick rush of sour air through their mouths as they breathed heavily and unevenly.

Lucas stopped on the spot of grass where one of them pointed and looked at Charlee. "It'll be okay," he told her. He didn't know one way or the other how this was going to go down, but Charlee needed to hear it, so he said it.

Then he looked at the man standing next to her. The man was only an inch taller than Charlee, with a fine, pointed chin that at any other time Lucas might have considered weak. His eyes were close-set. He was smiling with a chilling sort of glee, showing rows of ragged, blackened and ruined teeth. The same impish joy glowed in his eyes.

He was waving around a knife with a strange handle with holes in it and a double blade that looked like it split in the middle. Lucas had never seen one before, but he coupled up the split blade with chatter at school and wondered if this was what the street kids called a butterfly knife. It was long and looked very sharp.

"You must be Sergio," Lucas said.

"You don't get to talk, fucker," Sergio told him.

"You must be one of the stupidest idiots on the globe," Lucas told him. "You've been told what would happen to you if you ever bother my sister. But that's okay. If you quit now, if you let us go, then I can maybe stop what will happen to you next. But only if you let us go now."

Sergio had a grip on the knife that made his knuckles whiten. He waved it around so that it swung in front of Charlee's stomach with each circle of his arm. "I took care of that faggot banker man," Sergio said. "I got him what they call neutralized. It's just you and me and skinny cunt-face here."

Lucas glanced at Charlee. Her huge eyes were watching him, but as he looked, her attention was caught by something over her shoulder. She looked back at him and her eyes widened even further, which was not something he thought was possible. Warning him?

There was a soft sound that Lucas recognized. It was a police radio crackling, the sound turned down low. The sound made his guts loosen with hot relief, but he kept still, trying to hold on to the calm pocket that was letting him think and keeping the fear at bay.

"Shit, fucking cops!" one of the gang whispered. Lucas hadn't looked at the others, for he had their locations mapped in his mind in relation to where he was standing and that was all he needed to know, but he heard them now as they shifted restlessly, looking around wildly.

A dark cloud passed over Sergio's face. He didn't move, even though the others clearly wanted to leave.

From just behind them, probably on the other side of the bushes screening them, came the same electronic crackle. "Yeah, just checking out that ten-ten that was called in. Gimme a few."

Lucas felt rather than saw the gang members melting away, because they did it silently and swiftly and he didn't watch them go. He kept his gaze on Sergio, who was still swinging the knife, but in smaller circles now. Sergio had a look on his face that Lucas recognized with a twist of fear. He looked like a little kid who had just been told he had to come into the house, play time was over. Sergio looked like he was ready for a full-on tantrum.

His knife was still too close to Charlee for Lucas to try anything, even though Sergio's back-up had all fled. What Lucas did know was that the moment the cop spotted either Sergio with his knife or Charlee who looked exactly like the hostage she was, it would trigger…he didn't know what.

All the silvered calmness that had let him think disappeared. Lucas was back to being scared again.

* * * * *

Asher shut the apartment door and looked around the dim room, feeling an odd weariness in his bones. It was only six in the evening, but he had already put in a long night. While they didn't get jet lag from the portals, there was a disconnect and disorientation that developed if you used the portals too much. It came from having to deal physically and psychologically with successive changes of time zones, climates, times of year and more. He had definitely been using them a lot.

More and more, he was starting to understand why most of the Kine found accommodations as close to the hall as possible. It made life considerably more simple if you only had to step across the road or walk a block to get home from the hall. He had to think hard to recall why he had settled in the Bronx, (*families, neighborhoods, homes*) and remember the satisfaction he'd felt when he'd found this place, which had been so far *away* from the hall.

141

He tossed his keys and the long coat onto the sofa and scrubbed at his hair, yawning. He couldn't go to bed yet, even though he wanted to. He needed to stay up a few more hours so he was sleeping through more or less a normal night.

There was a "1" glowing on the answering machine.

Curious, he headed over to the machine. Everyone he knew usually waited to see him to pass on news. They were all Kine and used to communicating in person. If humans needed him, they tended to call him at the restaurant or the bank, as the only humans that might want to talk to him were associated with his businesses. It was rare to get a phone call at home; most of them were survey companies or people trying to sell something, and they didn't leave messages.

He pressed the playback button and stared out the window at the street below, which was going through the early evening routine. Supper, TV, bath and bed, for most of the houses he could see down there.

The machine beeped as the tape stopped rewinding, then clicked into play mode.

"I got the girl, you faggot motherfucker."

Asher whirled to stare at the machine. All the mead he'd drunk in the last few hours seemed to swirl in his gut. He knew the voice. He didn't even have to guess. He just knew.

Charlee. They've got Charlee.

But the voice kept going, speaking of things Asher hadn't put together fully yet, laying it out in grisly detail. "I know where you live, faggot. I know where you work. I know about the bank and your little restaurant. I know all about you, fucker. So now you know how this goes. If you come after me or touch any of my men, if you bother us in any way at all, I'll come looking for you and yours."

But he has Charlee. The thought stayed front and center.

The tape was still rolling. "I get the redhead. Then, faggot, we're done. We're square and you can stay in your hole. But I get the skinny bitch and no interference. That evens the score."

The tape stopped and the machine clicked and rewound itself neatly while Asher stared at it. His mind worked slowly, for it was bogged down in horror.

He flipped open the address book on the table and looked up the number for Darwin Baxter and dialed. The phone rang and rang at the other end. No one home.

The ringing sound went on, muted, as he put the phone back on the base, thinking it through. He couldn't call the SPCA to get her number. They were closed. He didn't have a single phone book in the apartment, either. He knew all the numbers he needed.

Darwin Baxter had been his one shot. He didn't know how to reach Charlee in any other way. She had always been there, for lunch or after school. She was just there. He'd never had to contact her the human way.

He sank down onto the sofa. His keys dug sharply into his hip, but he barely noticed it. A more painful truth was making itself known: he had to wait. He had to wait and hope that Charlee would call him.

You haven't bothered talking to her for months, you asshole. Why would she reach out now?

He hung his head and closed his eyes, dealing with the stark reality. She might call because of their deal and she needed his help now. But she probably wouldn't call...because he had made sure she wouldn't want to.

Chapter Twelve

Beyond the Skáli
Literal translation from Old Norse;
"beyond the hall." A Kine form of
expression indicating something, or
someone, outside the Herleifr system.
From *Darwin's Dictionary*, 2017 Edition

Charlee woke to pain. It seemed to be blanketing her entire body, like a mist with tendrils that worked their way inside through every pore. She came swimming up from (it's all black, where have I been) somewhere, to an awareness of herself and how all of her seemed to throb with the pain.

For a while, she had no idea how long, she floated in that state. As she pulled more of her consciousness together, she felt glad about the pain. She didn't know why she should feel that way, but she did.

Then sounds drew her attention. She was hearing sounds around her now. Soft sounds. She wanted to stay in the misty place where pain was the only thought, but the sounds were pulling her up toward the surface, making her focus.

She listened, not analyzing. Stayed small and mute. Far away, there were happy sounds. Music. Even though she didn't want to, she could identify it. That was a television.

Noticing the television helped the other sounds make sense. Beeping, steady and slow. She had never heard it in real life, but she knew what it was: a heart monitor. Then she heard the soft squeak of rubber on linoleum, the shuffle of someone rearranging themselves in a chair and she knew where she was.

The pain seemed to gather and leap in intensity and now it had a focal point. Her face, the left side of her face, was a white-hot mass of shrieking agony. She groaned as she opened her eyes.

Her groan brought attention. Her father rose from the chair by her side to lean over her and stroke her forehead. "Hi, sweetie," he breathed. He was unshaved and his eyes were red. The whiskers that were growing in were reddish brown. Their color had explained to Charlee her own red hair, once she had learned about genes. The loose skin under her father's chin wobbled as he leaned. The bulgy bit that used to be there had gone. *When had that happened?* Charlee wondered groggily. *How did I miss that?*

He kissed her forehead and she smelled his aftershave, but stronger than that was a minty smell. Like mouthwash. His whiskers tickled her forehead.

"Hurts," Charlee whispered...or tried to. The agony in her face wouldn't let her move that side of it. The word came out slurry. "*Hursss.*"

"I know, honey," Dad said gently. "They said you might hurt when you woke. I can get the nurse to give you some more painkillers, if you want."

"Wait," she said, working to form the word properly. There were questions she wanted answered, first. She refocused beyond her father, beyond the end of the bed. There was another plastic chair there and her mother was curled up in it, her head on her arm. She was asleep. That explained why her father had whispered.

"Time?" she asked.

"It's nearly two in the morning," he told her.

She was remembering now. She didn't want to, but it was coming back on its own. The park. Sergio. The knife....

"Lucas?" she asked.

Dad nodded. "He's here, too. He's just across the passage, there. They say he's going to be out until morning. He was in surgery until a couple of hours ago."

Charlee closed her eyes. She remembered it all now, the last few minutes before the blackness. The cop stepping around the bush, walking like he was bored out of his brain, his gaze scanning the trees. He'd seen them and his eyes had widened and his hand jerked down toward his gun as he realized what he had walked into.

Sergio stood in front of Charlee, between her and Lucas. He had grinned at the cop, the big knife waving unceasingly as it had since he had dragged her off the sidewalk an hour before.

The cop pulled the gun.

Sergio's grin seemed to widen. Then he moved, so fast that Charlee didn't really see it. He seemed to throw out his hand toward her, the one with the knife. There was a tearing sound—she remembered it, would remember it forever—and her brain was just starting to say, with some surprise, *why, that sounds like it's coming from inside me*, when the pain hit. It was hot and cold at the same time, across her cheek. There was incredible heat on her chin, moving down her neck.

Her eye on that side seemed to lose focus. Her leg buckled and she realized she was falling to the ground. But her mind, her curious mind, kept recording things. The cop's gun firing. The way Sergio spun around that made her think with fierce satisfaction that the bullet had got him. But that wasn't it at all. He was spinning, whirling with the ferocious energy of a kid's toy top, the kind they didn't make anymore but that she remembered playing with when she was smaller. The knife was whirling, too. Whizzing fast, making a whistling sound and that was a sound she would remember forever, too.

The blade slid into Lucas' thigh, on the side, almost exactly halfway between his knee and his hip. It punched in like a hot knife would slide into butter, right up to the top of the blade. There was a muffled, wet sound that reminded Charlee of cracking wet branches over her knee.

For a moment they froze in their positions and it looked grotesquely like Sergio was just resting the side of his fist against Lucas' leg, the way buddies did it, but usually against each other's arms or shoulders.

Lucas started falling sideways.

That makes two of us on the ground, Charlee thought and followed it up with an idea that shocked her even as it formed in her mind. *Now the cop has a clear shot. I hope he takes it.*

But the shot didn't come. Not that Charlee heard; the mist that was blurring her vision in her left eye crossed over to the right and became dark instead of light.

Charlee blinked, coupling up those last moments with these new ones: hospital, surgery, pain. She could see through the door of the tiny ward. There were only three other beds in the ward and they all had their curtains drawn around them. Through the door and on the other side of the wide passageway, there was another open door similar to this one. A cop sat on a chair reading a magazine, next to the door. He looked bored.

How they had both arrived here, she would find out eventually. Probably the cop had called an ambulance. The more disturbing question was created by the cop outside Lucas' ward. If there was a cop guarding him, she guessed there was one guarding her, which meant that Sergio had got away. Where was he?

"Is Lucas going to be okay?" she asked her father. The full sentence, with six whole words, made her face blaze with agony.

He stopped fussing over straightening the sheet and covers over her, but didn't meet her eye. "They had to put a steel pin in his thigh. The bone was...it was pretty bad, honey."

"But he's okay?" What she wanted to ask was if he would live, if he would survive this. *Is he dying?* But actually saying those bald words out loud felt like she might invoke that very fate for him. So she edged around it.

"They'll know more when he wakes up. The surgeon...he thought it went well."

It's not like he'd say he'd screwed up. The thought, like the hope that the cop would shoot Sergio, seemed to come from an inner place she hadn't been aware of before. They were adult, uneasy thoughts, and even as she had them, even while she was busy being shocked, the same inner place was nodding, agreeing with their pragmatic realism.

But Lucas would wake. It sounded like his leg was badly broken, but people always recovered from broken legs. She spared a thought for his football ambitions. He had confided to her only a week ago that he thought he might be up for selection. Straight out of high school, it would be a dream shot, but there had been comments and praise and he had been introduced to some very interesting people lately.

All that was gone, at least for now, and Charlee tried to feel sad for him but she didn't. She was just fiercely glad that he was still alive. It was the same gladness that had embraced the pain when she had been coming to, thrilled that she could feel any pain at all.

Her father tucked her sheet neatly around her middle. "There's someone waiting to see you. Do you feel up to having a visitor?"

"At two in the morning?" she asked, wondering who on earth was out there.

"This is the ER, honey. They can wait in the waiting room all night if they want. He said he wouldn't go home until he talked to you."

"Sure," she said, running through the very short list of possible males that might want to talk to her. There was her teacher, Mr. Osman, and maybe Darwin. Darryl from the clinic, but how would he have found out?

Her father headed for the door.

"Daddy, could you ask the nurse if I can have that painkiller?" Charlee asked. Talking was killing her. She had to stop with the long sentences.

"Sure thing." He disappeared around the corner, a medium-height man with a medium build and a face he called 'forgettable', but she loved him all the same. It was a love that sometimes hurt, but it was there and undeniable.

A few minutes later he came back and Darwin was right behind him, his head nearly brushing the top of the door. His hair was wild and kinky and shot with grey. He had red eyes and he was wearing no socks. His shirt was rumpled, with the ironed-in wrinkles that came from having worn the shirt too long.

Charlee was very glad to see him. Her eyes watered, although the left one seemed drier than the right. She blinked rapidly. She hated crying in front of people.

Darwin rested both hands on the rail that ran along her bed and she saw him tighten his grip. "I just had to say hello before I went home," he told her. "I wanted to find out what happened and make sure you're...well...." It was the first time she had ever seen him trip over his words. Darwin knew every word in the world and how to use it. She learned most of her new words from him.

And now he couldn't find any. His eyes looked suspiciously watery, too.

"Daddy, could I talk to Darwin alone for a minute?" she asked.

Her dad glanced at Darwin, surprised. But Darwin looked as harmless as he really was. He was a sixty-year-old sort-of librarian who looked like he had been sleeping upright in a chair and couldn't even remember to put socks on. Her father worked on the docks (and he taught her more new words, although most of his were for smashed-my-thumb occasions) and saw all kinds of tough and dangerous people. She saw him assess Darwin in one quick glance. He already knew Darwin had been teaching her for a few years, although he'd never really discussed it with her. Now he nodded his agreement. He stepped out into the passage, moved down to Lucas' door and went inside.

Darwin's eyes narrowed. "It was the gang, wasn't it?" he asked.

"You can't go home," she said urgently, cutting right to the chase. Trying to lead up to it, trying to explain things, would take too much talking and she was nearly out of words. The pain was building now. It was a high singing in her mind, trying to steal her attention and make her focus on it and nothing else.

He straightened up, like she had surprised him. "I'm not safe?" he asked carefully.

She shook her head. "Not now."

Darwin drew in a breath, his gaze unfocused. He was thinking. "Because Asher isn't here?" he asked softly.

The reminder made her heart hitch a little, then hurry on. She shook her head. "That was the start," she said, struggling to make her words clear. But the pain was winning. Her words sounded slurred and hard to make out, even to her. She gripped the railing next to Darwin's fingers and waited for the sharp wave to pass. Then she held up her hand and wrote in the air with an invisible pen.

Darwin pulled out the little notepad he always kept in his shirt pocket and a pen from his pocket, flipped the notebook open and handed both of them to her. Charlee held the pad over to her right, where her right eye could focus better, and scribbled quickly.

sergio didnt get his fun the way he wanted
he'll look for someone else to hurt
he knows about you

Darwin read what she had written and his chest rose and fell with a deep sigh. "I'll call in sick tomorrow," he said and looked up at her and smiled sourly. "I was going to, anyway. Tonight hasn't been restful."

She took back the notebook. *Don't go home*, she wrote, and underlined it.

"Figured I'd stay here and wait for Lucas to wake, anyway." He shrugged. "I like the coffee you get out of that machine thing."

She smiled, but the pain rippled through her face and she stopped. Instead, she nodded. *See you for breakfast?* she wrote. *Tell me when Lucas wakes?*

Darwin put the notebook and pen on the bed next to her hip and patted them. "Yes to both."

He was nearly out the door when he put a hand on the thick steel plating that protected the corners and looked back at her. "While you're lollygagging on the mattress there, I have a marine biology book I found on a shelf at work. You could get some time in on that, if you like."

Charlee rolled her eyes at him.

He smiled and headed across the corridor. She watched him go into Lucas' room as the nurse came with one of the kidney-shaped bowls in her hand. Her painkiller had arrived.

Thank god.

* * * * *

Lucas turned the scrap of paper around and around in his fingers, watching the digits written on it twirl. They had been written on the margins of one of the sheets of paper that were attached to the clipboard hanging off the end of his bed, then the corner had been torn off, so there was pale green printing and a square border on part of the triangle. The thick, firmly formed numbers had been written in the clear space on the edges.

The sun was shining almost directly onto him through the window next to his bed, making the paper a dazzling white. Hypnotic.

He was drifting in and out of sleep, still coming to full consciousness, but in his lucid moments he had been thinking with the same sort of calm clarity that had gripped him in the park.

His leg was hoisted up into the air, a sling under it and a small factory's worth of crane apparatus overhead. The bed had been lifted up at the head and he was now folded into almost a V shape, his back forming one side and his leg the other. The good leg rested under the sheet.

He had been in the same position when he had first woken. Thinking about it now, he figured they were pumping him full of something powerful to mask any pain, for he didn't feel anything but sleepy confusion until he had seen Darwin sitting silently on the chair next to the door. Then thought fragments pulled together in one leap. "Darwin," he whispered. "Charlee warned you?"

"She has now," Darwin told him, getting up slowly and cautiously. It hadn't been completely dark in the room, then, but the light coming in had been low. Darwin was just a black shape in the gloom as he moved closer. "What happened? Your sister isn't in a state to do much talking."

The knife flashing. The slicing sound. Then the red mark on her cheek, from high up near her eye, down to her mouth, cutting through the duct tape like it hadn't been there. It had turned red and the blood had started to run immediately, like the Niagara, pouring over her jaw and onto her neck in a wide red sheet.

Lucas sucked in air. "Sergio," he breathed. "I'm gonna kill him."

Darwin shook his head. "You aren't moving out of this bed for a while."

"I'll get crutches. I'll find him."

Darwin was still shaking his head.

"I *will*."

"Lucas, you just woke up after three hours of surgery. They had to pin your femur, by the look of it. Not only are you going to be here for a while, but they're probably going to have to teach you how to walk all over again when you do get out. Leave Sergio for the cops. You've got better things to think about."

Lucas shut his mouth but the desire, the *yearning*, to have his hands around Sergio's neck was like a hunger, gnawing at him.

He blinked as his eyes tried to close. He was going to sleep again. It was pulling at him, tugging him back to the land of Nod. He gripped the rail of his bed, fighting back. "Give me his number," he told Darwin. "I know you've got it."

"Whose number?" Darwin asked, genuinely puzzled.

The sleep was washing over him, pulling him down. It was then that Lucas wondered if the saline drip next to his bed was plugging more than salt water into his arm. "Asher," he ground out. Even the feel of the cold rail under his fingers was drifting away. "If I can't, he...."

He what? Who?

The vagueness was the last he remembered before waking up once more, still lying in the same position, his mouth open, the corner damp with drool. Sunlight blazed through the window and Darwin had gone. But there was a triangle of torn paper next to his hand. He had picked it up and blinked at it until his sight pulled together enough to make sense of the numbers. Seven of them.

Asher Strand's phone number.

He turned his head on the pillow. There was a phone jack in the wall, but no phone. He would have to wait for the nurse to come. So he turned the paper over and over in his hands, thinking of Charlee, thinking of vengeance, thinking of nothing else, and waiting.

* * * * *

Asher got up stiffly from the barstool. It was a comfortable enough chair, even if you sat in it for a few hours. He knew that because customers often remarked on it. They had picked the chairs deliberately, Ylva and he, to encourage diners to stay where they were and have one more drink, then another. Inebriated customers tended to eat hugely, with less regard for the price than sober ones.

But after nearly eighteen hours on one of the stools, including five hours of drifting in and out of sleep with his head pillowed on his arm on the bar, the stool had come to feel like one of Torquemada's torture devices.

He picked up the coffee pot and cup that had been sitting in front of him, right next to the phone, and made his way back to the kitchen. He needed more black juice. He was flagging. There were more than enough staff in the building now, prepping for the lunch rush that would start any time now, that stepping away from the phone for a moment would be okay.

He nodded at the sous chef (*Patrick, his name is Patrick, Charlee likes him*) who was testing the soup and walked over to the hot beverage counter and began setting up the machine to brew another pot. He had done it a few times already last night and this morning and it was a familiar task now.

He had arrived here last night just as Anthony was shutting down for the evening. Anthony and one waiter were the only ones left. The waiter had been upending chairs on tables while Anthony counted the money from the registers in his tiny office. Anthony had shot to his feet when Asher stepped into the office, shocked.

Asher had told him to go home as usual.

"Can I get you something before I leave?" Anthony asked.

"I just need coffee and I can take care of that myself."

"It's no bother. I can set up the machine for you." Anthony hesitated. "Is there something wrong, Mr. Strand? It's an odd hour to visit."

Visit. Asher focused on the word, tasting it mentally. Anthony was right. He was a visitor. The last time he had been here was just after Ylva had left, shortly after Anthony had taken over management. He had been uncomfortable even then. The clock had held some mystical power to keep drawing his gaze and it wasn't until he had escaped, walking fast and heading for Wall Street, that he had realized that the closer to noon (*Charlee's lunch break*) it had got, the jumpier he had grown. If he couldn't be bothered attending to his own business concerns, then the staff had a right to think of him as a visitor.

"I'm waiting for a phone call," Asher said truthfully. He had remembered barely an hour ago, after sweating out four hours on his couch while the phone hadn't rung, that the number he had given Darwin Baxter had been the restaurant's number. It had galvanized him into a flurry of action: throwing on a change of clothes, tying back his hair, grabbing his keys and wallet and heading out the door to flag down the first cab he could find, all in a tornado of impatience because he couldn't just step through a portal and be at the restaurant right *now*.

"There haven't been any calls for me tonight, have there?" Asher asked. He almost didn't want to know the answer. If Darwin had called, there was trouble. If Darwin had called, then he had missed the call and still did not know what he could do to help, or where to do it. If he hadn't called, then he was just as screwed.

Anthony shook his head regretfully.

"I'm going to wait up," Asher said.

"Hence the caffeine," Anthony said, putting it together. "You might want to help yourself to food, too. It will help you stay awake. There is a pot of the house jambalaya in the pantry."

"Thanks," Asher told him and headed back to the kitchen.

He hadn't felt like eating, in the end. The coffee had been warm, although after three-quarters of the first pot, he no longer appreciated its flavor. It was just hot liquid and the act of sipping gave him something to do.

Sleep had battled to take over a few times. That was when Asher had pulled the phone behind the bar over to where he was sitting, parking it right in front of him. If he did fall asleep, he reasoned, then he would surely wake if the phone rang right next to his ear.

But the phone stayed silent while he watched the street empty and the passing cars slow to one every few minutes. He watched the light of dawn emerge a degree at a time while he thought he was only imagining the increasing light, until it was no longer possible to say that dawn wasn't here. Then the sunlight had jumped from the tips of the buildings, one to the next.

He had stayed sitting, waiting, until the sous chef had rattled the back door as he unlocked it. Then he had gone through to the kitchen to ask Patrick, as it turned out, to please make him a quick breakfast, nothing elaborate, before he began the murderously heavy load that was a sous chef's daily lot. Asher had hurried back to the bar to watch the restaurant stir around him as staff arrived and began to take care of things.

The floor under the tables had been vacuumed and the chairs put down. The tables had been set. Good cooking smells had emerged from the kitchen, making his stomach growl. He was hungry, after all. His breakfast had arrived and Asher fell on it, devouring it in a few massive mouthfuls.

He had used the bathroom to wash his face and neck, after that, to wake himself up and look a little less like he had spent the night sitting at the bar, then he had gone back to sitting and waiting.

Once the need to sleep had backed off, he had nothing more to do than think. Thinking, though, was not a fun exercise. He kept circling around the same boggy ground. He kept hearing Sergio's voice, the vicious delight in it and the edge of madness shading and shaping his words. Remembering the call would jerk Asher's heart into overdrive, making his body tense and his fists curl up tight. He kept finding himself reaching for his hilt and having to abort the movement, especially once customers started to arrive.

I'm going crazy, he realized, glaring at the phone. If he didn't shift his mind off the subject, he was going to go silently nuts here on this stool.

As he stood waiting for the latest pot of coffee in a long line of such pots to finish brewing, Asher dug his finger and thumb into the corners of his eyes, rubbing away sleep. He had to find something to do. He couldn't keep just sitting at the bar, waiting for the phone to ring.

Then again, why couldn't he? He could sit there until the wind changed. He wasn't hurting anyone. This was his place.

What if no one calls? Ever? The thought struck him as he was cleaning up the filter and putting away the coffee and he stood with the coffee cone paused over the garbage can, absorbing the possibility with something like horror curling through him with cold fingers.

Finally, he tipped the used filter into the can, and turned back to finish cleaning up, moving slowly, trying to think around the stiff shock the idea had generated.

Had he really alienated her so much that she wouldn't reach out even for something like this? Had he really fucked up that badly?

You're a prince. A real asshole. How in hell did you think she was going to react? You've spent months teaching her you're not a superhero at all, that you're the ass end of a superhero. She can't rely on her family and now you've explained in neon letters that she can't rely on you, either.

Well done, asshole.

The phone rang.

* * * * *

153

Asher almost dropped the full pot of coffee when the phone buzzed next to him. There was an extension here in the kitchen as well as the one on the bar, so if the hostess was busy, the staff behind the bar or in the kitchen could take the call.

Asher fumbled the coffee pot, burned his fingers on the sides of it and dropped it two inches onto the counter with a hiss of pain. He rounded the big stainless steel table and lunged for the phone hanging on the wall.

It fell silent just as he got his hand on it.

He hurried out to the bar, to take the phone from whoever had picked it up, but the phone was sitting on its base where he had left it. He turned to look at the hostess's podium, but there was no one there.

Anthony. He hurried back into the kitchen, then down the corridor past the pantry and cold room to the little back office area. Anthony was standing at his desk, his raincoat hanging over his arm, a briefcase on the desktop, talking into the phone. "Next week would work better," he said after a thoughtful silence. "It will be a slow week and we can manage without the freezer while you work on it." He turned and looked over his shoulder at Asher, giving him a rueful smile and shaking his head.

Asher went back to the kitchen, his heart slowing.

She's not going to call, he told himself. *You're just going to have to go there. Walk right into the middle of whatever the trouble is and try to sort it out on the go. She hates you and it won't change her mind about you, but you're not going to like yourself* (prickly gruellies) *if you don't.*

He dumped the coffee in the big sink, and put the pot on the drainer, his energy rising. Going in there without knowing the score was a rank beginner's error, but he felt better, anyway. It was action. It was doing something.

The phone rang as he was finishing and this time he picked it up casually, already occupied with planning out his next move, and trying to guess the unknowable shape of the problem and what he might face. "The Ash Tree," he said.

"Is that Asher?" The voice was soft and he could *hear* the pain in it, even through the phone line.

Asher turned his back to the kitchen. His heart was back to jumping again. "Lucas?" he asked, for the voice was nearly unrecognizable. "What's happened? Is Charlee okay? Are you?"

Silence. Just for the space of a heartbeat, but it might have been a year while Asher waited to hear the answer.

"She's...it's not good."

He closed his eyes. *Your fault. This is your fault.* He reached out with his hand and propped himself up against the wall, his fingers splayed out next to the phone. "Where are you?" His own voice was soft, now.

"We're at Mercy General."

The answer dropped his heart right down to his toes. "I'll be there as soon as I can," Asher told him.

* * * * *

He looks worse than I do. That was Lucas' first thought when Asher finally walked into the room. The last time—and the only time—he had met Asher in person, he had been wearing a suit. His hair had been a lot shorter and his eyes had blazed with life and energy, the blue almost fizzing with it.

Now the suit had gone, replaced by jeans that looked wrinkled and worn. Lucas could see a simple, cheap T-shirt, in some nondescript brown color under the black leather jacket. Black sneakers. *Sneakers,* Lucas repeated to himself. He didn't know much about this guy, but he knew enough to know that sneakers were a low point for a man who ran a bank, owned a restaurant and was so full of self-confidence that keeping a whole gang in line was reduced to "chatting" with them when he bothered mentioning it at all.

"Where is she?" Asher asked. His eyes were red around the blue, and the beginnings of shadows and dark rings were forming on the flesh around them. He had been seriously sleep deprived lately, Lucas guessed. "You said she was in the room across from you. It's empty."

Lucas clenched the sheets as the dull fury returned. "They're sending her home."

"*Home?*" Asher repeated, sounding as appalled as Lucas felt. He shoved his hands into the deep pockets of the leather coat and moved his shoulders, like he was shifting a heavy weight around on them. "Is it insurance?" he asked Lucas, his tone gentle.

The low-grade anger caught at Lucas' throat and made him choke. He nodded instead, but even that took effort. "I think they'd toss me, except I can't even walk. They're putting me in a general ward sometime this morning."

"So where is Charlee now?" Asher asked.

"Out in the ER waiting area, waiting for someone to pick her up." Lucas made himself look squarely at Asher. "They took the guard off my door this morning. I don't think there's anyone with her, either."

Asher considered him for a moment. "Who is going to pick her up?" he asked bluntly.

Lucas drew in a breath, quelling his embarrassment. He forced himself to speak about things that he *never* spoke aloud. He had called Asher here, he reminded himself. "Dad's working...or he's too sick to work. Darwin was here all night, but the nurse that came on this morning kicked him out because he's not family. He said he was going to go to his office at the library, lock the door and sleep. I don't have his office number. Mom, well, I don't know if she would even understand the call from the hospital, if she took it. It would depend on...on...how many...."

He couldn't finish the rest and just looked at Asher, hating his uselessness.

Asher must have sensed some of what he felt, for his pulled his hands out of his pockets and came closer. "You did the right thing, calling me," he said. "It might not look like it right now, but I can and will take care of this."

Lucas believed him. The air of doubt had evaporated from around him. The vitality that he remembered from before could be glimpsed in his worn features. "Charlee might not want you to," he told him.

Asher nodded, as if this wasn't a surprise to him. "Do you?" he asked.

The fury swelled up again. "*Yes*," Lucas muttered, his teeth clenched.

Asher gripped his arm reassuringly. "Sleep. You look like hell."

"So do you."

"I'll look a lot better in a few hours." He headed for the door.

"Asher!" Lucas called.

He looked back.

"I didn't call you for Charlee's sake."

His fingers tapped along the steel strip protecting the corner of the doorway, as he considered his answer. "It'll all work out the same way for Sergio," he replied and left.

Lucas would never tell anyone how truly satisfying Asher's reply was.

Chapter Thirteen

Lightning Lords
A small but powerful street gang that operated in the Bronx, NYC, circa 1983-1988. At least ten murders have been attributed to the gang in the years they operated, although both leadership and membership changed frequently, making assignation of responsibility for the murders difficult. No formal charges were ever laid. The connection between the Kine, specifically Asher Strand (see *Asher Strand*), and the demise of the gang is purely speculative...
From *The Complete Kine Encyclopedia,* by Darwin Baxter, PhD. 2019 Edition

Whatever industrial strength painkiller they had given her last night was still in her system. She had fallen asleep barely ten minutes after the shot last night, crashing like she hadn't slept for a week, and she had barely been able to keep her eyes open since, but it had stopped the pain like a dam wall.

Now she sat in the big chair, waiting for someone to come pick her up, while the duty nurse kept a careful eye on her. *Maybe she's afraid I'll fall right out of this chair.*

In truth, she did feel like a boneless pile of goo. The temptation to slide into sleep (and slide off the chair) was strong. But she knew she had to think. Lucas was stuck in a bed. She had been allowed to speak to him for a few minutes before they had wheeled her out to the waiting room and put her in this chair, right in front of the nurses' desk. Darwin had gone to the library to hide out and sleep. Her parents were not involved in this and she wouldn't speak of it to them. Her mother thought it was simply a random act of violence, that the gang had picked on her because she was passing by and Lucas had tried to help (and he had!).

Charlee hadn't seen any police officers guarding their doors when she had left with Dad around six this morning. Dad had to go to work. It was an unspoken understanding that he had to take as many shifts as he could physically withstand. The drugs he used now were more expensive than ever, and there was her mother's drug of choice, too.

"Charlee." Asher dropped down to a crouch in front of her chair and flipped her hair out of her eyes. "Oh, Charlee."

She took in the lines around his eyes, his unshaved cheeks. He looked like he had been wearing himself out. And his clothes....

Bright, hot hardness gripped her throat and burned in her eyes. "You haven't been careful," she said, and burst into tears.

* * * * *

Asher held her against him, her unwounded cheek resting on his shoulder, as Charlee cried and hiccupped her way through her tears, wetting his neck and the band of his T-shirt. She hadn't screamed at him to go away and obtusely, that made him feel worse. If she had turned away from him, or even yelled at him, it would have been right. It was what he deserved.

You haven't been careful. Her first thought, her *very* first thought when she saw him was about him. Their stupid deal. *Deals.* She was holding to the deals. Jesus Christ and Odin himself...how relentless (*loyal*) could a person be?

He felt small. Tiny. Completely inadequate and unworthy of her friendship. He knew, just from her reaction, that she had spent the last few months checking in to see if he was there, every single day, just like she had promised. It would have troubled her, his non-appearance, but she wouldn't have told anyone because that was the deal. He'd left her to carry her troubles all alone.

He was starting to understand how the rabid Christian extremists thought flaying themselves was such a good idea. Skewering himself right now, twisting the knife around in his gut...yeah, that would help wipe out his sins. Charlee wasn't going to accuse him, or blame him, or say anything (*we're alike. We both have secrets we don't tell each other*), and that made it worse. He couldn't skewer himself, but he would go a long, long way to make up for what he had put her through.

He picked her up, scooping her out of the chair and up into his arms. "I'm going to take you somewhere safe and warm. Then I'm going to take care of something else."

Charlee's arms tightened around his neck. "Thank you." It was soft, and heart-felt.

And that burned in his conscience, too.

* * * * *

Charlee slept on the way to wherever Asher was taking her, her head against his shoulder in the back of the cab. Sleep had claimed her, a truly deep and restful sleep. She could let down her guard and sleep properly, now he was here. Later, there would be questions, but for now, everything was as it should be.

He shook her awake some time later, and she blinked, looking around. *Why, that was Central Park*, she thought, looking out the driver's side. This had to be Fifth Avenue, or else they had turned around somewhere, or else the sun was all wrong, which was just stupid, so this was Fifth Avenue. Wow.

She looked around curiously as Asher paid the driver, then he slid out and turned around to reach for her.

"I think I can walk," she told him.

"Let's not risk it." He picked her up like she weighed nothing at all and carried her up the steps of the house they had stopped in front of. Charlee had always considered herself a sophisticated New Yorker, just because she had grown up here, but she had never been on this side of the park before.

She had known such houses existed in Manhattan, but the idea of gaining access to one had never occurred to her. The type of people who could afford to live in that type of housing not only didn't mix with Charlee, they weren't even her customers. Their grooms and secretaries, bellboys and doormen brought their pets to the clinic, and their secretaries and assistants chose pets for their children, after consulting with Carole, while Charlee helped ordinary people off the street.

Even the front entrance of the house was grand, with sweeping stone steps and a thick stone balustrade that curved in on itself to hug the steps and the big double doors of lead-lined glass that made up the entrance. Potted miniature fir trees stood like sentries on either side of the doors.

The house, Charlee estimated, rose for at least three floors, but she couldn't see any more of it without craning past Asher's chin and she was suddenly shy.

Asher didn't get a chance to press the doorbell. The door was suddenly flung open. "Oh my great heavens! Charlee! What happened?"

It was Ylva.

Charlee didn't realize she was crying again until Ylva wiped first her own cheeks and then Charlee's as she drew them inside and shut the door.

Ylva took them up a long flight of stone steps, then into a thickly carpeted corridor and a room that opened off that. Charlee was overwhelmed by the lush opulence. There were too many details to take in all at once and too many questions crowding in for her to concentrate on her surroundings.

"Put her down there," Ylva said softly, but firmly.

Asher lowered her onto a bed that she sank in to. There was something incredibly soft under her back, and the pillow was even softer.

"I'm going to take the pillow away and then look at your wound," Ylva said. "May I, Charlee?"

Charlee struggled to find a coherent answer among the many that occurred to her. If Ylva wanted to, of course she could look, although Charlee wasn't sure why she wanted to. But she was also aware of Asher standing at the foot of the bed, watching her and shyness touched her again. It was a different shyness this time. She didn't want Ylva to take the covering off her face. She didn't want Asher to see the wound.

Her gaze flickered in his direction. *Oh, he looked so tired!*

Ylva stepped back. "Asher, would you leave us?" she asked, her voice the same gentle but firm tone.

Asher drew in a breath, making his shoulders lift. "I have something to do, anyway." He glanced at Charlee.

Sergio. She licked her lips.

"I'll be back around sunset," he told Ylva. "I'll have to take her home then."

"Sunset?" Ylva seemed horrified. "That's not nearly long enough."

"That's all the time I can give you," Asher said. "I don't want her parents to wonder or worry."

"They don't know where she is?"

Asher threw another glance in Charlee's direction and this time she thought she saw an apology in it. "I don't think they even know she has been discharged from the hospital." He patted Ylva's shoulder. "Do the best you can. I'll be back, Charlee, I promise."

"Be careful," she told him.

He smiled the way he used to smile, before. "I will."

The door shut softly behind him.

Ylva leaned over her again and touched her temple, above the tape that held the dressing against her face. "May I?"

Charlee nodded.

Ylva peeled away the dressing carefully. Her face was quite still while she looked at the wound. "Knife wound," she said, as if she was cataloguing it. "But I've never run across one quite like this. What sort of knife was it, Charlee?"

"I think...butterfly." She didn't want to talk. Talking made the wound move, and made her conscious of it. And if it made her conscious of it, then talking would draw Ylva's eyes toward it. Besides, Charlee really didn't want it to start hurting again.

"Is there much pain?" Ylva asked, almost like she had read Charlee's mind.

"A bit. More if I talk."

Ylva made a silent "oooh," sound with her mouth. "Then I'll just have to read your mind, won't I?" She smiled and straightened up. "I'm going to go and get some things. I'll be right back. Are you comfortable enough?"

"Very," Charlee confessed. She had never felt a bed that was so soft before. She was sinking into nothingness. "Are you a doctor, too?" she asked.

Ylva smiled at her. "My family taught me very old ways of healing and caring for wounds. That's why I know it was a knife that did that. I've seen hundreds of them before. You're quite safe. In fact, it's possible I can do a better job than the doctors." Her smile turned into a slow wink.

She walked toward the door. Charlee saw that she was wearing trousers in some soft material that seemed to float around her legs. She had never seen Ylva in pants before. Her hair was longer, too. And was it possible she looked younger? Her face looked the same as before, yet she seemed younger.

Ylva closed the door softly behind her, leaving Charlee alone.

For the first time since she had met her, Charlee wondered who Ylva really was.

* * * * *

Ylva came back about fifteen minutes later, carrying two heavy boxes that looked a lot like a handyman's toolboxes. There was a young woman with her carrying a pile of white cloth. The cloth turned out to be squares of some soft material that Ylva used instead of the cotton wadding that the hospitals always used.

The boxes also turned out to be toolboxes. The girl, who didn't look much older than Charlee, put the cloth on the bed by Charlee's feet, and pulled a low, backless chair over to the side of the bed. Ylva put both toolboxes on the chair and opened them up. They each expanded into two stepped tiers of trays.

Bet there's no wrenches in there, Charlee thought, almost giggling.

Ylva pulled a glass jar out of the bottom of one of the boxes. "I'm going to get you to breathe in the air over this pot, Charlee. It's going to make you sleepy. You should sleep if you can. What I'm going to do might be a bit uncomfortable for you."

Charlee nodded.

The girl climbed onto the bed and smiled at her. "Hi, there. My name's Mary Sue." Her accent was pure south. "I'm going to lift you up."

"I can sit up," Charlee protested, struggling to rise out of the depths of feathers and mattress.

"You just relax, honey. We've got this covered." Mary Sue lifted her shoulders, propping her up in a sitting position with astonishing strength and dexterity.

Ylva took the lid off the pot, being careful hold it away from herself. "It's very strong, but it's a pretty scent," she told Charlee, bringing the pot under her nose.

Charlee sniffed, then breathed in the aroma.

It is pretty....

* * * * *

Mary Sue handed tools to Ylva as her mentor murmured, asking for them. Ylva bent over the skinny girl on the bed, her brows pushed almost together as she worked on the wound. It was an ugly one. Mary Sue had seen more than a few wounds in the few short weeks she had been in the house, and this one was one of the worst. Not because it was a complicated or jagged wound. The blade had cut clean. But it had cut deep.

Once Ylva had loosened and removed the stitches and they could see better, she sighed. "Almost completely through the cheek," she said softly. "Her cheekbone saved the eye. But there's muscle damage..." She pulled at her fingers, cracking the knuckles, and glanced at the clock sitting under the dome on the mantel over the fireplace. "No time to dither," she added and turned back to the box. "Thread, Mary Sue. We'll need lots of it. The finest I have. I'll reconstruct on the way out, and treat at the same time." She blew out her breath and smiled at Mary Sue. "Layer by layer. Step by step."

She bent back over Charlee once more.

Mary Sue passed the jar with the poppy smoke back and forth under Charlee's nose, careful not to breathe it in herself. Then she prepped the thread and the herb mixes Ylva would need.

"If you don't mind my asking...?" she ventured, handing over the curved needle and the thread. There was no need to wear gloves. Both of them had sterilized their hands and the toolboxes were kept in a sterile state at all times. Sterile by Ylva's standards was something that doctors could only dream about, as Mary Sue had learned swiftly. Her first weeks in the house had been spent learning what sterile *really* meant.

"It's your job to ask," Ylva said absently.

"Is this girl...is she Amica?" Mary Sue had thought she knew all the Amica, even the newest ones. A new recruit was a rare event, and news about it spread swiftly through the ranks. She had never heard of one being recruited so young. The girl looked maybe fourteen years old, although she was tall.

"No, she's not Amica." Ylva reached back for more of the unguent that Mary Sue had learned fought off infection in all but the most dire of cases. One day, she would be trained in the art of preparing all the creams and gels that the toolboxes held. There were concoctions that restricted blood vessels, to stop bleeding. There were others, more than one, for infections. There were creams that increased healing. Then there was the vast pharmacological range of preparations that promoted general health, boosting the metabolism, healing the gut, and more.

There was a whole host of creams and preparations that were purely for vanity: skin care and enhancements that did more for a woman's beauty that a whole boatload of French fancy stuff could have managed.

It had only taken Mary Sue a week to know she had made the right decision, accepting this apprenticeship. She had learned more in the last couple of months than twelve years of schooling had ever imparted.

She glanced at the interior of the box, then at the fragile-looking pale skin of the human on the bed. "Do you think...I wonder...that skin-firming gel you made last week. Would it work on the muscles? Keep them tight and firm, so her face doesn't sag on that side?"

Everything Ylva made was natural. It could be used inside the body and out, although the stink and taste of some of the preparations would ensure that no one ever voluntarily swallowed them.

Ylva considered. "Good idea," she said softly and stretched sideways and backwards, flexing her spine. She kept her hands in the air, not touching anything. "Could you get the jar for me? Sterilize the outside of it and also your hands, again."

Mary Sue hurried away to get the jar. So, if the girl was human, who was she? She would have to ask. It was her job to ask. But she would ask later. She already knew that the patient's needs came first, above and beyond anything else.

* * * * *

Sergio roused from sleep, slowly. He smiled to himself, not sure why he was smiling, except that it was a beautiful night. It was damn near perfect.

He scratched his crotch and rolled over, reaching for the warmth of the girl. He couldn't remember her name. But she had been small and smelled good, and her flesh had been hot against his.

The bed was empty.

That made him crack his eye open just a little bit. Where was the fucking bitch? Running off in the middle of the night wouldn't make her any friends, if that was what the cunt had done.

The yellowed sheets, which had started out life a pale green, were rumpled and soiled, but Sergio barely noticed them. He was usually drunk, often stoned and sometimes both when he fell into bed. The state of the sheets was of barely passing interest.

Last night he had celebrated with the gang, once he had caught up with the fuckers. They had hovered a block away from the park, keeping an eye out for the cops and listening to the ambulance sirens. The sirens had sounded like a very personal and particularly poignant music to Sergio. He had laughed and laughed and my, it had felt good.

Then he had wolfed down a whole pizza himself, hungry after a good night's work. They had toked, shot up, burned and drank themselves into a very happy oblivion. Sergio vaguely remembered pulling the girl into his bedroom. She hadn't been willing at first, but she had soon come round to his way of thinking. He was good at talking girls around.

His orgasm had been the topper on the night and sleep had grabbed him almost straight after that.

Sergio blinked. The late afternoon sunlight was his alarm clock. It always fell almost directly on the bed, waking him up with the heat and brightness. It wasn't quite to the edge of the bed yet, making it around four, he guessed. Too early to wake him, so what the fuck had? If that little whore had banged something around out there, he'd have to explain it to her all over again.

He rolled onto his stomach and contemplated the pack of cigarettes on the bedside table. He couldn't be bothered lifting his arm to pick them up. Too much effort.

There was a very soft sound of breathing. So soft he might have missed it if he hadn't been lying so still, watching the dust motes dancing in the sunlight.

A breath. An unsteady breath.

"Lilla?" he asked. If that slutty bitch was sitting watching him, just sitting on her ass, not even bothering to do something constructive like make coffee, he'd tan her ass. He rolled back onto one hip and forced his eyes open, blinking.

Ruffy was staring back at him.

Wh'fuck?

Sergio stared back at Ruffy, trying to figure out what he was doing in his bedroom, and lying on the carpet like that, too. And Julio, lying on top with his eyes closed. *Queer for each other?* Sergio's badly shocked mind pondered slowly.

Then he saw the blood on Julio's mouth and the truth began to filter through. He sat up, still not getting it completely, but he would in fewer than sixty seconds.

He scratched at the hair on his chest lazily, staring at Ruffy and Julio, lying on top of each other. Lying very still....

Understanding blazed in his mind like a Hollywood spotlight and he scrambled out of bed, whirling to face the door. His heart was pumping too hard, his abused and weakened pulmonary system stressed by the massive shock.

Lilla stood there, naked as a jay. She was looking at him, both eyes filled with something that Sergio thought might be hate, or glee, or some animal emotion he didn't get. Even the eye that was dark and almost swollen shut glittered with it. Who the fuck understood women, anyway? Except she was naked; no weapons. And she was a cunt, a split-tail. No way would she be able to do Ruffy and Julio in. No way would she have the guts to stand there and wait for him to find them.

Sergio turned toward the corner where the closet spilled its contents onto the floor like it had spewed them all forth in a violent eruption of fabric.

He was there.

Sergio clutched at his chest as massive pain ripped through it. "You."

The fucker stood there calmly, like he had been waiting just for this moment. He had both hands resting on...*on a fucking sword*. It stood point down, the tip pushing a furrow into the wooden floor. The bottom two feet of the blade were red with blood, which had pooled around the point.

"I know where you live, Sergio," the fucker said.

Pain gripped Sergio's arm in a vice-grip. Oh man, he'd never felt such pain before. He groaned.

The fucker turned his head toward the girl. "Go."

She lifted her chin and shook her head.

"Very well." The fucker lifted the sword, spinning it in a way that told Sergio he was an expert with it. Then he fell on him and Sergio learned the *real* meaning of pain.

* * * * *

Asher climbed out of the cab and looked around. It was peak hour, no time to hold up a cab on the side of the road. Where was he?

Darwin stepped out of the early evening shadows pooling around the base of the lion and crossed the sidewalk to where Asher stood. He looked into the cab. Charlee was curled up in the far corner, wrapped up in a blanket. Her wounded cheek was hidden by a fold of the blanket. She stirred sleepily.

Darwin turned back to Asher. He looked like he'd had a tough time of it lately. Maybe even have lost weight, but the shoulders were still those of a bear. "Your phone call was a surprise, Mr. Strand."

Asher winced. "We're back to last names." He sighed and stepped away from the side of the cab. "The driver has been paid to take you both home. You can tell her parents you brought her back from the hospital."

"Charlee thought it wasn't safe for me to go home."

Asher shrugged. "It's safe now."

Without warning, a cold finger rippled its way down his spine, making Darwin shiver. "Is that so?" he asked.

"This time, I'm absolutely sure of it."

Another echo of a shudder ran through him. "What do I tell Charlee?" he asked.

Asher smiled. "Tell her that when she's ready, when she's well, I'll see her after school, at the restaurant."

Darwin looked at Charlee again, at the dressing on her face that was visible now. It was like no other dressing he had ever seen, and it wasn't the one she'd had when he'd been at the hospital. "Will she be well again?" he asked.

"She will," Asher said with complete confidence. He pushed his hands into the long coat he was wearing, which struck Darwin as odd for the end of April. It wasn't light enough to be a raincoat. He pulled out a hand and held out a jar, a pretty thing made of green glass, squat and bulging. The lid was ceramic. "Tell her to leave the dressing in place for two days, then leave the wound open to the air and put this on it twice a day." He pushed his hand closer to Darwin.

Darwin picked up the pot curiously. "What is it?"

"It'll help with scarring."

Scarring. It was Darwin's turn to sigh. "That poor girl," he muttered. "As if life wasn't hard enough for her."

"Well, that's something I will remedy the best I can." Asher pushed his hand back into the coat.

"Hey, I'm waiting!" the cab driver yelled.

"Keep it down," Darwin told him. "You'll wake her." He turned back to have a last word with Asher.

The sidewalk was empty.

Chapter Fourteen

Fyand
Herleifr name for an enemy. Specific to
someone pursued because of
transgressions against the rule of *laun*,
before the strictures of *laun* were
formally abandoned. Usually applied to
Herleifr, but was also used to describe
humans who unwittingly learned of the
existence of the Herleifr. From
Fjándmaðr - "enemy" in old Norse.
From *The Complete Kine Encyclopedia*, by
Darwin Baxter, PhD. 2019 Edition

Full battle formation, Asher thought, letting his gaze move across the faces of those assembled as he walked the length of the great hall.

Stefan stood in front of his big chair, and Eira in front of her only slightly smaller one. Roar was to Stefan's right. There were a handful of other earls. Not all of them, for they would not have been able to assemble so quickly. The portals were instantaneous, but the far-flung halls still had to cope with time differences, sleep cycles, and simple things like finding the earl at the other end and bringing him to the nearest portal. Mere human transportation took time.

There were no stallari present, which told Asher exactly how seriously they were taking this.

But Sindri was hovering just behind Eira's shoulder, watching Asher approach the dais with his black, beady eyes. Had Sindri always been slightly repugnant to look at? Had the scales finally dropped from his eyes? He thought that perhaps, yes, they had.

He stopped ten paces from the dais, a position close enough to speak easily, but not too close. He didn't have to lift his chin to look at them from here.

No one sat down.

Asher nodded to Stefan and bowed low to Eira. "I came as soon as I got your message."

"You know why we are here," Stefan said. "Is it true, about the girl? You brought her to one of our halls and had her treated?"

So, it wasn't to be quite what he had been braced for. "The matter of three human bodies does not stress you, but the saving of a wounded girl does?"

"You broke *laun*! Willfully!" Stefan cried.

Roar stirred, shifting on his feet. Asher spared a moment to feel sorry for him. He was between a rock and a hard place right now. He believed in *laun* as avidly as Stefan did, but family ties were also strong. He would be feeling stress because it was his brother standing before the quorum, who handed down summary justice on matters of *laun*. It had been nearly a century since the last Kine had been sentenced by the quorum instead of his case being heard by the general council and discussed and decided upon. Roar's face was a rock, hiding everything.

"I did not break *laun*," Asher replied. "The girl—her name is Charlee—was taken to the private home of one of the Eldre. She had no idea where she was except that she was in the home of a human friend. She still has no idea of the truth."

"Is it true that she was treated for wounds?" Eira asked. "Ylva treated her, yes?"

Asher flashed on Ylva's quick comments over the top of Charlee's sleepy head resting on his shoulder, as he'd picked her up to take her home. "I am one of the Eldre now, Asher. My skills are not what they once were."

"A woman who was one of us a long time ago treated her wounds as best she could," Asher replied.

"She used Valkyrie skills," Eira pressed.

"She used her considerable medical expertise," Asher replied, his irritation stirring. "Ylva has not been one of yours for over eighty years."

Eira drew in a breath, as if she would respond, but then she subsided. Ylva's history still roused tempers and put them on the defensive. But then, they'd tried to ignore her all these years because it was more comfortable to pretend she didn't exist anymore. Now they were getting their noses rubbed in it.

Asher was suddenly sick of the side-stepping. "There is nothing to be afraid of," he said. "Charlee knows nothing and never will, not from me. There is no threat, and *laun* has not been broken."

"Is it true," Hamish, the earl of the hall in Baghdad, asked, "that you've known this human girl, this Charlee, for some years?"

Asher glanced at Sindri, anger touching him. So much for the confidentiality of Sindri's salon. He didn't remember speaking of Charlee in any specific detail, but the little man was superb at reading between the lines.

"I've known her for some years, yes," Asher agreed.

"Forgive me for the personal question," Roar asked, "but in what capacity have you known her?" He sounded genuinely curious.

"Charlee is a friend," Asher replied flatly.

Torville, earl of Madrid, snorted. Asher held in his reaction. Torville *would* leap to the worst and, in this case, the wrong conclusion. But then, it was unspoken knowledge that Torville kept a harem of men in his hall whose ages would qualify them better as "boys". He would naturally distrust any claims of a simple friendship.

"You're friends with a girl. A human," Roar clarified.

"Yes."

"*Why?*" Roar asked.

"I like her."

"And you have managed to maintain a friendship with this young human for many years without her suspecting anything at all?"

"Yes." There was no need to get into details, and the more he explained, the more guilty he would look.

The assembled quorum looked at each other, a puzzled expression passing from one to the other.

Sindri cleared his throat. "Perhaps we could simply accept that such an unlikely friendship is possible and move on?"

Asher scowled. The man's support would do him no favors with Stefan.

"Do you intend to keep seeing the human?" Stefan asked.

"Charlee comes to check up on me each day at the restaurant. I don't think I have a choice in the matter," Asher told him.

"Check up on *you*?"

"She likes to know that I am keeping safe."

Silence.

"Does that mean, then," Eira asked, "that she might have reason for thinking you could be unsafe? How did you meet?"

"I saved her pet mongrel from a gang that were going to kick it to death," Asher told her. "Charlee decided I was her personal superhero after that."

Eira began to smile.

"This would be the gang we had to...clean up, then?" Stefan asked.

"There were only three of them," Eira murmured. That told Asher that she was now on his side. Roar was still a question mark. As for Stefan.... A year ago, Asher would have bet that Eira's switch to his defense would sway Stefan, but he couldn't say that with any certainty now, not after Stefan had fired that shot across his bows last week.

"We still had to clean up a mess that could have been a disaster," Hamish pointed out. "You used your sword on them."

"I made sure they were all quite dead before I left," Asher pointed out. "I didn't leave anyone behind to tell tales." It was a lie, but he felt quite comfortable speaking it. The girl Lilla had been filled with the sort of silent fury that only a woman could carry. Afterward, as he had put her on the bus for L.A., she had been almost glowing with victorious satisfaction. She had kissed his cheek and muttered in Spanish, her one good eye staring at him. No, she would never speak a word of what she had seen. Ever.

Stefan stepped down onto the intermediate step, just before the floor level, where Asher stood. "We well know your feelings about *laun*, Asher. You must see this as we do. Help us to understand that we have not been exposed."

"My word is not enough?" Asher asked. "It always has been, until now."

"Your behavior has been alarming lately," Roar said. "We would like to take you at your word, but you are not the man whose word we could so easily trust, anymore."

Asher nodded. "Fair comment," he agreed. He didn't look at Sindri while he spoke. "I've been distracted lately. That's why Charlee was hurt in the first place. That's why I'm going to stay involved in her life and that's why you can trust my word now."

Eira tilted her head. "Would you explain that, Asher? I would like to hear the story."

Asher began to speak. It took a while to tell the full story, and he carefully omitted the one fact that would condemn both him and Charlee; he did not tell them she had seen his sword. But everything else was innocent, and he had no need to lie. He told them everything up to and including his visit to Sergio's apartment yesterday afternoon, and the results of that, including the reasons why he had left such a mess for the Kine to clean up.

"They would have kept hunting down Charlee and her family. It had turned into an obsession. It was time to stop it from progressing. I cauterized the situation."

"You certainly did that," Roar agreed. He looked at Stefan. "I do not see where *laun* has been broken. There's no threat here."

"You are not the best person to judge that, surely?" Sindri asked. "Someone with a more neutral perspective would be easier to agree with, and I, for one, would like to see agreement reached on this matter. One human child has already taken up far too much of our time."

Sindri was trying to minimize the problem and make everyone see it as a trivial thing, but Asher resented his interference. He had done enough damage. Asher wasn't certain that Sindri didn't know exactly what his contribution to this "situation" had been.

Was it possible that Sindri was a better schemer than everyone in this room? Better than the most powerful of the Kine?

Or was it just that he moved in the background, mainly unnoticed?

Asher stared at him openly, not smiling. *I have noticed you now.*

Stefan crossed his arms, considering. He still stood on the step below everyone else, but it also put him out in front of everyone. "My concern is the risks that this friendship of yours could pose in the future. We already walk such a tightly held line. We must protect them, we must mingle with them and pretend to be human, just like them, but human relationships come with such great dangers that to do more than merely pretend to be human brings perils we cannot ignore."

Asher's heart squeezed. Was that to be the price for his sins? They would make Charlee *verboten*, off-limits, and enforce it?

He held up his hand and he wasn't surprised to see it was trembling, but none of them standing on the dais facing him were close enough to see it. "I can allay your fears," he said. "There is a simple solution."

"Something we've missed?" Roar asked, genuinely curious again.

Asher let his hand fall. "Let Charlee live her human life for now. When she is old enough, she can be recruited into the Amica."

Silence. Again. Asher knew he had astonished nearly everyone in the great hall.

Eira was the first to speak. "You would let your friend...you would have her chosen by another?"

Asher shrugged. "She might be selected for domestic duties. It doesn't matter, does it? If she is one of the Amica, *laun* is preserved. Where she ends up within their ranks is irrelevant."

Stefan was smiling. "I believe that I, all of us, have underestimated you, Asher." He turned to face the quorum. "Is this an acceptable solution to the matter? Raise your hand if you feel it is not."

Silence. For the last time.

Asher let out a heavy breath, hiding it from those watching him.

"Very well," Stefan said, turning to face him once more. "Once the girl Charlee is old enough, she will be recruited into the Amica. I thank you for your frankness, Asher. You have made it easier for us to reach a peaceable solution."

Asher bowed his head and the quorum began to break up. One or two of the earls from halls on the other side of the world yawned and stretched. They hurried away, heading for the portals and their halls, to catch up on sleep.

Eira stepped down onto the floor of the great hall and swept over to Asher's side. She was wearing a dress in pulsing, vibrant red, which went well with her dark hair and olive skin. "It is a pity I cannot meet your Charlee just now," she said. "She sounds like someone I might like."

"You would," Asher agreed truthfully.

"Perhaps when she has joined the Amica, you would introduce me?"

"I'm sure that can be arranged," Asher replied.

Eira turned him away from the dais, her hand on his arm gently insistent. "There is something about this matter that you have not shared with us," she said. "You would not so easily sell your friend to the Amica, not when you have stood here defending a right you do not have to stay friends with her."

Asher stayed silent, schooling his face to stillness so he would not give anything away. Eira was watching him carefully, reading his reaction. She watched enemies over the edge of her sword in just the same way. Eira was the strategist. She saw patterns before anyone else and had led armies to victory because of it.

Then she smiled. "Defending that right and winning, too. I am glad you are not yet an earl, or I would be worried about Stefan's longevity as Annarr."

Stefan and Roar stepped up on either side of her. "You are heading back to New York?" Roar asked.

"To sleep for a week, if I can," Asher said in agreement.

"Walk with me," Stefan said, moving past him toward the big doors at the end of the hall.

Asher turned and kept pace with him and Roar fell in on the other side of Stefan.

"You were eloquent in your defense of friendship with a human," Stefan said.

"I simply spoke the truth as I see it."

"That is what surprises me," Stefan said. "You are full of contradictions, Askr Brynjarson. Your own brother learned one of the hardest lessons we of the Kine have ever had to face."

Asher glanced at Roar. He was walking with his gaze ahead, his expression fixed. Even now, he could not speak of it.

"It is your brother's tragedy that has formed the principles of *laun* more than any other single experience, yet you choose to ignore all that and embrace the dangers of a human dalliance, instead."

"I am not dallying with her," Asher shot back.

Stefan lifted his hand. *Peace.* "Any relationship with a human carries the same perils. I can already see the signs in you, Asher. You have vigorously defended your human here tonight. That is not something you would have done with such zealousness if you didn't care for her. From such simple beginnings, all things grow."

"Then tell me not to see her again," Asher said. "I know you wanted to."

"Would you obey, if I say you must cut her out of your life?"

Asher hesitated. "If I don't protect her, if I don't watch out for her, she will...." He blew out his breath, rubbing at the back of his neck where the hair used to be. It would take a few days to get used to having short hair again.

Stefan smiled and rested his hand on Asher's arm. "You see?" he asked simply. "I would rather keep you safe within my hall, where we can protect you when we need to, than have you defy everyone and be left exposed when you are most vulnerable."

Asher stared at him. "She's just a friend," he said weakly.

"A friend that makes you feel like a superhero. Yes, I understand," Stefan replied.

"Lord Asher," Sindri called, hurrying up.

"I hope your sleep is a peaceful one, Asher," Stefan said and pulled Roar away, back toward the dais, talking softly.

It left Asher standing alone. Sindri stepped in front of him. "Sleep is such a waste of time," he said. "My salon is open tonight. Can I talk you into sharing a cup with me before you leave for home?"

"I'm tired," Asher said. "Not tonight."

He turned to leave, and Sindri moved to his side, following him. "I have a barrel of the Romanian mead coming in tomorrow night. I know you are particularly fond of it."

Asher turned to face him. "Actually, I don't like mead much at all."

Sindri licked his lips. "Then it is the company you prefer?" he said.

"I have my own company," Asher said flatly.

"Your human?" Sindri asked, and this time, his contempt was visible.

Be safe, Asher. You haven't been keeping safe. Her voice was a silent whisper.

"Her name is Charlee," Asher told him. "Goodbye, Sindri." He deliberately and pointedly stepped around him and strode to the giant doors. They were perfectly balanced so that a single man could move them on his own, but it still took muscle to get one of them swinging slowly open or closed. He stepped around the silently opening door and saw Sindri standing where he had left him, scowling, both hands buried deep inside the wide sleeves of his robe.

Stefan and Roar were both watching him from their place near the dais. As Asher's glance fell on him, Stefan inclined his head.

173

Chapter Fifteen

It is fair to say that Lucas Montgomery's
influence and guidance during his
sister's most impressionable years is
vastly underestimated by historians.
This history will attempt to show a
clearer picture of Lucas Montgomery's
life...
The House of Wands by Unurr Guillory

There was a new girl in school. The gossip grapevine in high school is just as efficient as any newspaper at digging up the facts and passing them along, and far more casual about the truth. By lunchtime of that Monday, Charlee had already overheard that the girl's name was Elizabeth Brinkmeyer, and she was a junior, like Charlee. Everything else she heard seemed unlikely: that she had been expelled from every high school in the Bronx, that her father was richer than Warren Buffett, that her family owned half the neighborhood or maybe all of it. They said Elizabeth had been delivered to school in one of those long limousines (Charlee wanted to see one take a corner. She didn't know how they could possibly turn without bending in the middle).

It was a miserable February day, when the wind sang with high, bitter notes, slicing through every layer she wore and imprinting her flesh with cold fingers. Charlee couldn't stay warm, and she was merely waiting for the end of the day when she could go home and curl up under a quilt.

But it was still lunchtime, and she had a few hours to get through first. She found a table at the far corner of the canteen where the sun shone through the high windows. It was warmer in that corner, and by the end of the lunch break it would be cozy with all the warm bodies around her.

Charlee shook her hair over her face, propped one of her books up in front of her, leaning on all the rest, and laid her sandwich out in front of her. She had taken a bite and finished off two pages of *A Tale of Two Cities* when she heard, "Can I sit here with you?"

She turned her page and kept reading.

A hand came down over her page. The fingernails, Charlee saw, were beautifully manicured. Long, with the white stuff they put under the nails. A million miles away from Charlee's jagged, raw nails. She looked up.

The new girl, Elizabeth, was standing over her table.

Wow, she's so pretty! was Charlee's first thought.

"I said, can I sit here?" Elizabeth said. "Do you mind, or is the book really that good?"

Charlee stared at her. She wondered if this was a joke. Had someone put the new girl up to it? "You don't want to sit here," Charlee assured her. She glanced over at the big tables in the center, where all the cool kids hung out. Chrissie and Suzy and Daphne were all watching this go down. Suzy was smiling, like it really was a joke, but Chrissie, to whom all at that table tended to look, was glaring. "That table there," Charlee said, nodding. "There's a seat there."

Elizabeth sat on the chair in front of Charlee. "I can't sit with them," she confessed. She smiled, and it was a beautiful smile. "Don't make it obvious that you're looking, but see the blonde girl at the end of the table with the blue sweater?"

"Marcy Graham?" Charlee clarified, too curious to protest that Elizabeth had sat at her table without specifically being invited.

"Marcy, yes. She's going out with my brother, and he's trying to dump her." Elizabeth rolled her eyes. They were big, green eyes with thick black lashes. Charlee couldn't stop looking at them. They really were that gorgeous. "Marcy is so stupid, she hasn't figured out he doesn't want to see her. So, it would be really awkward to sit at that table."

There were over a hundred tables in the big cafeteria, all of them bursting with kids. But there were spare chairs all over the place. "If you sit somewhere else," Charlee said slowly, "you won't get half the flak you will if you stay here."

"Because you're the freaky redhead?" Elizabeth asked curiously, putting her smart leather handbag on the table in front of her, pushing it up against Charlee's pile of books.

Charlee had no response for that. She stared at Elizabeth, who smiled again. This time there was a hint of mischief. "I've started a new school every year for the last four years and this year, this is my second school. In every single school, there's a group that is the popular group. In every single school, there about five kids that everyone thinks of as freaks or just plain weird."

"I'm one of the five," Charlee agreed. Elizabeth wasn't saying it in a way that made it sound like a bad thing. She said it as if this was just a fact of life, like spring following winter, which followed fall.

"Yes, but you're *smart* freaky. That makes you a different sort of freak. They told me you get one hundred percent nearly all the time, and you take all the heavy courses."

"That's why you sat with me?" Charlee asked, astonished.

Elizabeth threaded her fingers together and rested them on her bag, leaning forward. "I'm trying to break the run. Five schools in four years…my dad was so angry about the Academy last week that he did what he threatened. I'm in public school, now."

"You got kicked out of private schools?" Charlee asked, astonished.

Elizabeth rolled her eyes again. "I'm not so hot with books and stuff. Classes are boring, and in private school they take all that stuff soooo seriously. I honestly couldn't be bothered. My dad is rich as anything and I got my mom's looks, so they're probably going to get me married off as soon as they find someone suitable, so who needs it?"

Charlee was speechless again. Not because she had nothing to say, like last time, but because there was just so much she *could* say about Elizabeth's out-there question that she didn't know what to say first. "Well, I need it," she said at last.

"Need what? Classes?" She seemed genuinely curious.

"I need to graduate as well as possible. It's the only way I'll get to college. I'm not rich, like you."

"I know." Elizabeth smiled. "That's another reason I sat here. You're totally *not* the kind of person I would talk to. If I do everything different and opposite this time, then maybe something different will happen, don't you think?"

Charlee nodded slowly.

"Public school is the *total* opposite of private schools, so I figured I should stay with the theme. It'll be fun finding out what happens, anyway."

"So I'm an experiment?" Charlee asked.

"God, I hope you're not. You walk and talk just like a human, and they haven't invented robots yet, so I figure you're normal."

Charlee shut her book. "My grades aren't the only reason they call me a freak," she said carefully. "Did they tell you the other reason?" She didn't move her hair out of the way to reveal it. If she did, the rest of the cafeteria would see it.

"Something about a scar." Elizabeth shrugged. "I can't see it, so I don't know what the fuss is all about. Who cares anyway, right? You're the freak genius. A little scar can't stop you, unless…." Elizabeth tilted her head. "Are you a freak genius *because* of the scar?"

Charlee took a breath, trying to catch up with the whirlwind changes of direction Elizabeth was bouncing in. "The grades came before the scar," she said slowly.

"So the scar is nothing, then," Elizabeth said.

Charlee stared at her, absorbing her prettiness and the fact that she was sitting there, at her table, and also that the scar that had had such a profound effect on Charlee's life had been dismissed inside sixty seconds as irrelevant. It was almost a relief to have it treated in such a cavalier fashion instead of being stared at and treated like she was diseased and infectious.

"Do you really read all through lunch?" Elizabeth asked.

"I really do."

"How do you not get bored? I would be."

"How do you not get bored talking about clothes?" Charlee asked, genuinely curious.

"Because it's clothes!" Elizabeth leaned forward, excited. "There's *so* much about fashion and it's changing all the time. In last week's *Glamour*, they had leopard print leggings…." She stopped. "That's why you don't get bored with books, right? Same thing?"

Charlee nodded.

"Hey, that was clever. You explained it to me so I got it." Elizabeth picked up her bag. "This is a Louis Vuitton bag. It's called the Alma."

"It's expensive," Charlee guessed.

"Very, but mostly because it's Vuitton and the style only came out this year, not because of what it's made of." Elizabeth grinned. "The blonde girl sitting opposite Marcy has a Louis Vuitton, too, but she probably doesn't know that *I* know it's two years old."

Charlee blinked. "That's bad?"

"If it was *twenty* years old, I'd have more respect. Even if it was ten years old. But two just means she's out of date." Elizabeth crossed her arms, her beautiful nails resting against the velvet of her jacket, which was a deep green that played nicely against her eyes. "And that is all you need to know about fashion. Everything else is just details." Then she laughed. "Now I've explained something to you."

Charlee took a bite of her sandwich. She had almost forgotten it was there. "You have to be rich to keep up with fashion," she surmised.

"Rich, or smart," Elizabeth said. "There's this whole vintage thing, though—you only wear vintage designer wear, but you spend your *life* in the consignment stores trying to find the good stuff and I don't have that sort of patience. Then there's this gypsy romantic thing. You wear cast-offs and hand-mades. Sort of a shabby chic thing. There's lots of possibilities, even if you're dead broke."

It was like having a door thrown open upon a whole room of knowledge that she had not been aware of until that moment. "But wouldn't wearing vintage or…or…shabby chic… wouldn't that be not being in fashion?"

"That's called making your own fashion statement," Elizabeth corrected. "Only the most iconic and stylish women make their own fashion statements."

Charlee stared, absorbing this. "Like who?" she asked, certain that

Elizabeth would be able to name such women.

"Audrey Hepburn," Elizabeth said instantly. "Grace Kelly. Rita Hayworth."

"So, you have to be a really old movie star to be iconic?"

Elizabeth rolled her eyes. "Madonna."

"Rock star," Charlee classified.

"Cindy Crawford. Naomi Campbell."

"Supermodels."

Elizabeth stuck her tongue out at Charlee. "They're *famous*. That's the point. If I said that Marjorie Prescott is an iconic dresser, it wouldn't tell you anything."

"Who's Marjorie Prescott?"

They looked at each other for a moment, then burst out laughing, startling the sophomores at the table next to them, who sent them dirty looks that both of them ignored.

* * * * *

When Lucas stopped by during the afternoon lull, Asher was at first surprised, then pleased.

The boy had finished filling out over the last year. Life on the docks was just physical enough to keep him in shape. He'd finished growing vertically, too. He didn't look like he was much shorter than Asher. His hair was black and his skin fine and pale and clear, with a touch of color in his cheeks from the early March chill. With his dark eyes, identical to Charlee's, he had the sort of black Irish good looks that tended to turn women's heads. If there had been any women sitting at any of the tables, they would probably be checking him out as he stood at the hostess podium looking around, his hands thrust deep into his jacket pockets.

Then Lucas spotted Asher at the bar and lifted a hand in greeting.

Asher waved him over. "Welcome to my office."

"I've never been here before," Lucas said, looking around. "It's nice."

"It does pretty well," Asher told him. He had just finished reviewing the accounts that Anthony had prepared for last month's take, and they were doing very well indeed, which was astonishing considering the economic downturn all the newspapers were blaring about. "People have to eat, and Wall Street types think it's not cool to bring their lunch in a brown bag." He pulled out the barstool next to him and patted it. "So why the honor of a visit now?"

Lucas hitched one hip onto the stool. His legs were long enough that he didn't have to lift himself up to do it. His hands were back in his jacket. "I wanted to talk to you about something."

Asher nodded, letting Lucas spit it out at his own speed. The lunch

178

rush had just finished. He wasn't needed at the bank. There was time.

There was always time.

Lucas hunched his shoulders, like he was trying to relieve pressure. "You never said so, but I figured…I thought…I guessed you were in the military once."

Asher knew why he had come to that conclusion. "Intimidating a few punks into toeing the line doesn't take military skills. Mostly it's basic human psychology."

"You knew what to do. Physically. I…I didn't."

"How is the leg?"

Lucas' hands tightened into fists, the knuckles lifting the thin fabric of his jacket. "I think I'm going to join up."

Asher considered him. The statement wasn't the surprise it might have been before he'd mentioned Asher's military background. "What's happened?" Something must have tripped Lucas into facing this decision.

Lucas' gaze dropped to his thighs. "Dad's sick."

Asher waited. Their father had been sick for years. Lucas had more or less taken over his father's job at the docks because he couldn't make the shifts. That decision had been a pragmatic one although Asher hadn't been thrilled about it, as there were plenty of better opportunities for a boy like Lucas. But it kept Charlee's family functioning and for that, Asher had admired the kid. But this, joining up, seemed to be coming out of nowhere. There had to be more to it than Lucas spontaneously deciding it might be a good idea.

"Charlee and I…we can't look after him anymore. He needs help with just about everything. He fell out of bed a couple of days ago, when I wasn't home. Charlee didn't have the strength to lift him back up, so he just…he just laid there until I got home."

Asher didn't ask where their mother was when this happened. He had a pretty good idea why she hadn't helped and it didn't matter anyway. "Are you thinking he should be in a hospital?"

"There's a hospice. Not far away…." Lucas sat there looking miserable.

Asher sighed. "You're going to have to lay it out for me. I don't see why your dad going to hospital means you have to sign your life away."

Lucas looked up then. "You don't think I should."

"I don't know why you want to. Explain that to me, then I'll tell you what I think."

Lucas kicked at the leg of the chair with the heel of his sneaker, watching his shoelaces bounce at the movement. Then he looked up again. "The navy will pay more than I can get on the docks. It'll cover the bills."

"Not much more than you're getting now, not for a fresh recruit."

Lucas went back to looking at his shoes.

Asher studied him. "Why the navy?"

Silence.

"Lucas?"

He glanced up again, and Asher saw that his face was infused with red, darker than when he had come in. He couldn't keep his gaze up. It fell back to his toes. "SEALs," he said flatly.

Asher would have shrugged that one off. Every kid thought about becoming a SEAL, for at least thirty seconds. It was a standard boyhood fantasy these days.

"Well, you'll probably get paid more as a SEAL, if you get selected for it and if you survive the training," Asher said carefully. "But you'll never be home. Have you thought about that?"

"I can send money home."

"You could get a job here on Wall Street, trading commodities. Shorter training and better pay, even these days. You'd be home every night."

Lucas shook his head and the short, controlled, tight little movement told Asher that it wasn't embarrassment staining the kid's cheeks. It was anger.

"It's not just the money, is it?"

Lucas shook his head again.

"You're going to have to spit it out," Asher told him, "because I can't see it from here."

Lucas' nervous tic with his foot stopped. He grew still. "I don't ever want to not know what to do again." He said it so quietly Asher had to cock his head to hear it properly.

Asher sat back. *Ahh...* he breathed mentally as it all fell into place. He picked up the coffee cup and swirled the lukewarm dregs around the bottom of it, giving himself a moment to think. "You'll know what to do if you become a SEAL, that's for sure. You'd be able to take on three Sergios at once and not break a sweat. But you won't be *here*. You'll be in Papua New Guinea or the Middle East, sitting on a steel ship waiting for orders."

"There's Sergios there, too," Lucas muttered.

"But your sister won't be."

Lucas flinched.

So, he'd thought about that, too. Asher sighed. "It's a one-way ticket, Lucas. You sign up, you'll never go back to normal again. Even if you quit and get out, it stays with you, in your head."

"Good."

Asher didn't just sigh this time. He blew out his breath. "You don't have to do it. You shouldn't do it, not for that reason. If you're going to join up it should be for positive reasons. Because you want a challenge. Because you want to serve your country. Because it's a better opportunity for you. Not because you got caught up in a crappy, once in a lifetime situation where you were helpless and didn't like it. Normal people *don't* know what to do in moments like that, and that's the way it's supposed to be."

"Charlee and me, we're not normal. Not anymore." Lucas lifted his chin once more, but he was still having trouble meeting Asher's gaze. "We're...what it is at home...it's not normal."

"You think there isn't a single other family out there that isn't dead broke, with a drunk who is drinking away the money and someone who is sick?" Asher asked gently. "There's probably a dozen families that look like yours, just in the Bronx alone."

Lucas flinched again at the word "drunk". Then he squared his shoulders and met Asher's gaze. The worst had been said. It was out in the open now. "If dad doesn't go to the hospital, Charlee would have to quit school to look after him full time. One of us should get to go to college, and it's not me."

"Don't do it for her. She'll hate you changing your life around just for her."

"It's not just her." Lucas pressed his lips together. "It's been nearly three years. I still lie awake at night. Wondering what I should have done. Wishing I had done...almost anything. It makes me sick. It makes me sweat." He shrugged. "I don't want to do that anymore."

His ego was tied up in knots over it. Asher sighed again, this time in his head. "I'm not sure why you're asking me what I think. You've made up your mind."

"Charlee." Lucas grimaced. "I don't know who else to ask. Someone has to watch out for her."

I've been watching her all along.

"I don't know you much, but I trust you," Lucas added.

"Thanks." He meant it. "If you have to do this, then I'll make sure Charlee is okay while you're gone."

Lucas relaxed. His shoulders fell back into place. "Okay. Good. Thank you."

Asher thrust out his hand. "Good luck, Lucas. Although I don't think you'll need it."

Lucas grabbed his hand. Asher picked up the kid's palm and pulled it along the inside of his forearm and curled his own fingers around Lucas' arm. Lucas got it quickly, although he gave a short laugh as he gripped

Asher's arm like Asher was doing to his. "Weird."

"Old," Asher corrected. "It's how warriors used to measure the strength of their enemy before the battle, before it turned into just a type of handshake."

"Cool."

"Not really." Asher let his arm go. "But you'll be a warrior soon enough."

"I don't even know for sure they'll take me."

Asher ran his gaze over him, assessing. "They will."

* * * * *

Charlee hurried home. It was nearly dark and therefore very late, and it made her hurry. She should have gone home straight after school, but Elizabeth had invited her to her house, and Charlee had grown to love visiting Elizabeth's place.

Elizabeth might have cared less about schooling, but unlike every kid Charlee had ever heard talking about their home life, Elizabeth got along with her mom and dad. Actually, she loved them, quite openly. They clearly loved and approved of their daughter. Her lack of academic ambition wasn't a barrier to their love. They teased her about it and Elizabeth teased right back. Besides, Elizabeth was *trying*. She was really working her ass off to make it in school, because she didn't want to disappoint her father again.

Charlee barely noticed the size of the house when she was there. It was big and it was more luxurious in comparison to any home Charlee had ever seen, except on television, where the houses were beyond ridiculous. But Charlee's attention was always caught by the harmonics that resonated in Elizabeth's house. Everyone liked each other. Everyone spoke to each other nicely. Caringly. The atmosphere was free of tension and worry. It was a relaxing and enticing place to spend time.

So she had lingered far later than she could really afford to, then sprinted for the train. The train had been almost empty because it was so late and that had made her feel even worse.

Now she was hurrying down the street, only a few houses from home and running through her mind what needed to be done as soon as she got in. Her father would need the sheets on his bed changed, for sure. There was some of the casserole that Lucas had made yesterday still in the fridge. That would be their supper. She could feed him first, then eat hers in her bedroom while she tackled her homework. It was late. By the time she was done with her father, it would be almost time for bed.

When she passed Darwin's house, she was hailed softly. She looked over the fence, noticing only now that Lucas sat on the front step there.

182

Darwin was sitting next to him.

It had been a warm day, one of the first warm days this year, but now the sun had set, the chill had settled back in. "Why are you sitting outside?" she asked, resting her hand on the top of the gate. She didn't want to go into Darwin's yard and get involved in a conversation. She needed to get home as quickly as possible.

"Waiting for you," Lucas said. "I've seen to Dad, so don't worry."

Charlee relaxed. "You have? Thank you. I got caught up—"

"Lucas has something to tell you," Darwin said. "Want to step in here so he doesn't have to tell the whole neighborhood at the same time?"

Charlee pushed past the gate and hitched her book bag to get it settled back on her shoulder properly as she walked down the concrete slabs that made up Darwin's front path. The soil had been weeded and raked on either side of the path and new annuals dotted the dark loam. In a couple of weeks, Darwin would have pansies exploding all over the beds. Pansies had been his wife's favorite flowers, so he planted them every year.

She stopped in front of them. "What's up?"

Lucas held up some folded sheets of paper in his hand. The white paper seemed to almost glow in the gathering dark. "I joined the navy, Einie. They took me in."

For a moment, her surprise was so great that no thoughts came to her at all. Lucas had never spoken about the military before. He had been more interested in sports. She couldn't even recall him watching a war movie. "Why would you go and do that?"

Lucas looked surprised, then puzzled. He frowned, looking down at the ground at his feet. "Lots of reasons," he muttered.

"You should be proud of him, Charlee," Darwin said. "Proud that he wanted to and proud that he was accepted."

"I guess, yeah, I am. About both of them. It's just, well, it's a surprise," she confessed.

"Once I'm in, there'll be money for the hospital we looked at," Lucas added.

"Oh." Now she understood. "You didn't do it just for Dad, did you?"

Lucas frowned. "You sound just like Asher."

This day was handing out more surprises than the last three months combined. Charlee stared at her brother. "You spoke to Asher? You went and saw him?"

Lucas shrugged as if it were no big thing. But he had made his feelings about Asher and their friendship more than plain, years ago. For him to seek Asher out voluntarily seemed...peculiar. And significant.

"This is going to change things, Einie," Lucas said, patently steering the conversation away from Asher.

"You figure?" she asked dryly. As soon as he'd said he'd joined up, she had seen the difference it would make almost immediately. "I'll be home alone." Then she added, "With mom."

"No, *not* alone," Lucas said quickly, with a force that made her step back mentally.

"I'll be keeping an eye on you," Darwin said.

"You graduate in just under two years." Lucas was moving the folded sheets of paper between his hands, flipping the little rectangle over and over. "Then you'll be eighteen and no one will give a damn what you do. But for the next two years, Darwin and Asher will be there if you need help."

"You arranged this," Charlee said, indignation stirring. "You talked to both of them before talking to me."

The paper stopped moving.

Darwin studied Lucas, too, as if he wanted to know the answer just as badly as she did.

Lucas looked up at her and she saw how uneasy he was. "You would've said no. You would have talked me out of it."

She opened her mouth to protest that he was lying, but couldn't speak. Because it was true. "You're doing this for everyone but yourself," she pointed out.

Lucas took in a deep breath. "The *biggest* reason I'm doing it is one hundred percent, purely for me."

Darwin rested his hand on Lucas' shoulder. "As it should be."

Charlee looked from Darwin to Lucas and back. Darwin understood something that she did not. It was uncomfortable, not understanding what was happening and she realized that it had been a long while since she had felt this confused sensation, as she clutched at anything that might offer a clue that would unravel her confusion. She had grown up trying to understand adult behavior and all the implications and assumed knowledge that informed their speech. Gradually, she had acquired the necessary experience, so gradually that only now she realized how long it had been since a grown-up had made her feel naïve.

She didn't like it much, especially now because it was Lucas who was making her feel hot and squirming with embarrassment because she didn't understand.

"Well, okay," she said, with a sigh. "I don't get it. But I guess that doesn't matter, especially now." It hit her from nowhere. Her eyes stung with hot and sudden tears. "But I'm going to miss you," she whispered.

Lucas surged to his feet and hugged her. "God, me, too." His voice was rough. "More than you know."

Chapter Sixteen

Stallari
The highest officer of the *hirð* was the
stallari (literally "marshall") who served
as the king's champion and also as a sort
of general of the *comitatus* forces.
from *Viking Answer Lady*

Nigeria was in the northern hemisphere, but only just. Because of how close it was to the equator, "winter" was only different from summer by a few degrees, and the midnight air was warm and scented by the thousands of plants and trees nearby. Even this high above sea level in the southern mountains, it was still pleasant, and Sindri went about his work in a good mood, completely undisturbed by locals or tourists, or even the native wildlife.

The Alok Ikom Monoliths had the virtue of being unknown anywhere else in the world except for a tight radius of locals who stayed away in fear of the gods that haunted them. Even the brave and faithless would shun the area on this night, for it was the winter solstice. They might not believe in their gods, but they lived in close harmony with the earth and the sun, the movement of the moon, and the crops the fertile soil provided. The power of the solstice was as real to them as the dawning of the sun and so they stayed away.

For this reason, Sindri had picked the Nigerian monoliths. Those in Europe and Britain were too well known and too popular. The solstices always brought out the heathens and neo-pagans to prance around the stones in the belief that they were communing with imaginary entities that they called "gods." Their antics were harmless and seemed to bring them pleasure, but their presence at the stones year after year had begun to hamper Sindri's collection process.

Last year, he had barely managed to avoid detection and had sworn that this year, he would find another focal point to use.

Nigeria was also considerably warmer than the French standing stones, while the Giant's Dance at Amesbury was a complete misery at this time of year.

Sindri didn't need to consult a watch to know when the solstice approached. He could feel the stones almost vibrating with the coming moment, gathering their power, bringing it all into a gestalt moment that the locals were wise to hide from.

Sindri stood among them, right in the center, and raised his arms. The crucible was ready. It was already warm against his skin and he touched it with his thoughts, sending warm regard over it. The crucible was growing more and more potent. With each collection of power, its strength built. It wasn't ready, not yet. But Sindri could feel that the time was near.

Tonight would add considerably to the crucible's power. Unlike the other winter solstices when he was forced to gather the current from some safe distance, tonight he stood in the very heart of the gestalt. It would be…enormous.

He began the incantations. The power swelled, beating at him in silent waves. He closed his eyes, feeling it throb around him. The solstice was approaching at stellar speed. He must take the power at its very zenith….

Now.

He drew the power into himself, and through him, it fed the crucible. It was a jolt of white energy, a powerful zap of pleasure that coursed through his body, which responded with an almost instantaneous orgasm that added its tiny dollop to the stream.

And just as suddenly, the moment was gone. The sun had moved on, past its zenith. The alignment with the Earth altered and the power diminished.

Sindri lowered his arms, panting. The crucible was glowing against his chest. His flesh beneath the metal was burning. Blistering. He only noticed the pain now. Carefully, he removed the crucible and returned it to the velvet-lined box that carried it, moving stiffly now that the power had gone.

But he was very pleased. This had been a most successful reaping.

Soon, he told himself. Very soon, the time would be here to share what he had achieved.

She would be so proud of him.

* * * * *

Unnur's store had seen an uptick in customers that had kept her busy for months. These were genuine, paying customers, not merely people curious about the macabre little place on the wrong side of west Main Street, tucked away behind the main street stores.

It wasn't just serving the long, almost continuous stream of customers that kept her busy. The increase in business meant an increase in *everything;* she found herself restocking shelves at night and

186

coordinating stock orders so she wouldn't run out of anything. Even trying to anticipate how much of any one item to bring in took longer because now she had to reconsider such basic decisions all over again. Simple things like her daily sales journal entries took three times longer, just because there were so many more sales.

Some nights, she didn't fall into bed until after midnight, her eyes bleary and her body aching from shifting heavy boxes around. Her lifeless foot was even more useless when it came to lifting things, and she had done more heavy lifting in the last few months than the previous year combined. Her hands sometimes throbbed in the mornings, her fingers swollen from the effort of gripping and twisting, dragging and tearing open cardboard, to the point where she had trouble closing her fingers.

Handling the cards was a problem on days like that, but in a way, that was a relief. So was the steady stream of customers. Everything that kept her at the front of the store by the cash register, or in the back stock room, was a blessing in disguise, because it meant that she didn't have time to sit at the round table and read the cards.

Reading the cards had become…uncomfortable.

Unnur could hear the tale that the cards told more easily than the average Joe on the street, but that just meant she had a bit more talent than the rest of them. To her, the messages in the cards were muddy and distorted, or she didn't have the skill to read them properly, although she had been working diligently for over a decade to become better at that and had become very good at interpreting them. No, the problem was her as the medium. Perhaps it was because her talent had arrived by a freak accident instead of her being born with it. The lightning strike that had scarred her face and turned her right foot into a shrivelled, lifeless lump of meat where the current from the bolt had left her body and been absorbed into the earth…well, it had scrambled her brains, too.

She had trouble remembering things. Her memory was bad enough that she was careful to write down everything. Her notebook went everywhere with her. She was plagued by headaches. Not every day, not even every month, but once she got one, it would settle in for a good long visit, resistant to every headache nostrum known to man. Sometimes the headaches were so bad, she was forced to shut up the store and lie in bed in the dark, her eyes closed, afraid to move lest her movement set off another series of sharp, throbbing waves of pain that made her feel sick and giddy.

Neither the headaches nor the memory problems had been part of her life before the lightning strike. She had been blissfully unaware of what the future held. It had been as much of a mystery to her as it was to everyone else, which had made life very simple.

So while the gods had been scrambling her brain and taking away her memory and leaving behind a reminder of their visit on her face, they had also added something. Compensation. Or perhaps the headaches and the shoddy recall were payment for their gift of foresight. The gods, Tenska had once said in those short three days she had known him, always asked for payment in advance. You knew when you had made full payment, for then you received your reward.

She had paid and was still paying. Hers was not a strong talent and no matter how skilled she grew at reading the cards, their messages would always be muted and garbled.

But what came through was enough. She had been grateful that the cards spoke to her at all, until lately.

The overall message in the cards had grown darker. Forbidding. The King and Queen of Wands had come to visit more and more frequently. Now, they were in almost every single spread, but they were accompanied by warnings of doom and destruction.

The Magician was appearing more frequently. Unnur suspected that he was a person the cards were referring to. Possibly, he was someone known to the King of Wands, for he was nearly always on the King's side of the lay.

It was possible the more general interpretation could apply: new beginnings, the start of a new phase. Eternity. But the Magician was also a channel between the human world and other worlds. Unnur had always instinctively understood his bridging abilities, for they aligned with what she did as a medium. He stood with his staff raised to the air and his other hand pointing to the earth. In an odd way, he made her think of lightning rods and how they channelled power, too.

The Magician would have been her personal card, except that the Magician always represented a man. At first, Unnur had assumed that the Page of Cups was hers, for the Page rarely appeared in her personal readings -- which were never about her—and the Page was either a young man or a maiden woman, whose intuition was gradually emerging.

Over the years of the readings, though, she had come to hope that Strength might be her card. Strength was the combination of intuition and personal power. The intuition was hers thanks to a lightning strike. Her personal power had been gradually building to match the talent she had been gifted. Strength did not appear in the readings very often, either.

Lately, the Magician and the King and Queen of Wands had been surrounded by toil and trouble. The Death card did not particularly worry Unnur, for she understood far better than her customers that Death was a symbol for endings. Closure. Death could be a hopeful card.

The Tower had been appearing frequently, along with many of the

Major Arcana. Lots of Major Arcana cards always meant movement, big events. Drama. The pseudo Chinese curse about interesting times always occurred to Unnur when she saw a spread with many trump cards.

Death, the Tower, and the Chariot, over and over again. The Chariot mixed up with the Tower and Death meant that someone was about to face a deeply emotional crisis, and all her lays seemed to focus on the King and Queen of Wands.

It was a relief to have an excuse not to read the cards. Being busy kept her mind off their garbled messages and her own inability to hear them more clearly. It was frustrating. Their messages were frightening and she thought that if she had a greater gift, if she could hear more clearly, then she would understand what they were trying to tell her.

The vague warnings she received lingered and she would find herself puzzling over them when she had a spare moment, nuzzling the mysteries the cards hadn't revealed.

The cards weren't telling her what to do anymore. They were warning her and she knew that if her gift from the gods had been greater, then she would have heard their warning as clear as a trumpet call, or a fire siren, and known what to do. Instead, all she could do was wait and watch when she could for more answers. Her ignorance increased her worry, rather than keeping her dumb and unconcerned.

So she found herself avoiding the cards and their constant cries of coming disaster, but her sleep grew more disturbed, troubled by dreams. When she woke in the middle of the night, her thoughts would turn to the unknown King and Queen, and all her worries would gather around her.

Today, just behind her eyes, she could feel the growing pressure that heralded another headache, but she was busy enough with customers that she could ignore it even though she knew that it would not go away now.

Finally, when the shop emptied, she rested her elbows on the counter and palmed her face in both hands, closing her eyes.

Not looking at the cards was worse than listening to them. They would torture her with nightmares and migraines until she agreed to hear them out. With a sigh, she straightened up and went back to the round table (*step, drag…step, drag…*), sat and picked up the deck. She shuffled it while she gathered her courage.

"Tell me," she whispered and began to lay the cards.

The King of Wands

The Queen of Wands

The Tower.

Unnur's hands began to shake and her headache stepped through the door, arriving with a bolt of pain that echoed on and on like thunder rolling in the distance.

She turned the next card, almost dropping the entire pile because of her shuddering fingers.

The Chariot.

Completely unnerved, she put the pack down, face down, and pressed her hands flat against the silk to stop their trembling.

This was …the cards were *shouting* at her. Could there be any more direct a message than these four cards, one after another?

After a long moment, while Unnur rode out the pain banging and careening around inside her head, she picked up the balance of the pack again. "What do I do?" she whispered, for talking took effort and even the sound of her voice started the throbbing up once more. "I've heard. Command me."

She turned a card. The Lord of Despair. The Nine of Swords. The bringer of nightmares.

Nightmares.

She stared at the card. How many dreams had she had in the last month? How many a *night?* She had ignored them all, assuming in her foolishness that they were the price she paid for her gift with the cards. Never in a single moment had she considered that the dreams themselves were the bearers of the messages she had been looking for.

Unnur put the pack down once more, this time placing them on the silk softly and with reverence. She rested her fingers on top of the pack while she stared at the King and Queen. "Dreams. *My* dreams. I understand. Thank you."

Then, even though her head felt like a vise-grip was trying to squeeze her temples together, she got up and greeted the next customer through the door with a dazzling smile.

Tomorrow, she would begin her new quest for answers.

In between customers, she sent her thoughts out to the King and Queen, wherever they may be, for they were about to face a very personal challenge. She sent them her warmest wishes, the kind of wishes a best friend might bestow. She did not think it was inappropriate, for she knew them as well as a best friend might. The cards, over the years, had told her much about them. They were friends, even if they never met.

It didn't occur to her to wonder if they would ever meet. Plain, maiden Unnur Guillory, with her mark and her useless foot, and her little talent, wasn't the type of person who got to meet such wonderful people.

It just wasn't in the cards.

* * * * *

Charlee was in her advanced chemistry class, concentrating on getting the glass still working properly, when she was called down to the front office. Principal York, who everyone called Principal Pudding behind his back, took her into his office and shut the door, then told her that her father had died forty minutes ago.

Charlee nodded, feeling the superficial calm surround her and freeze her reactions. The calm part of her observed that this was almost the same kind of thinking/non-feeling sensation she had felt when she had met Asher, or when the gang had taken her.

Shock. It's shock, she told herself. Nearly seven years of continuous education in the sciences had taught her that much. *You're going to break through the calm in a minute and then it will hurt like hell.*

But was it shock? It wasn't like she hadn't known this was coming. Her father had been sliding toward death for a few weeks now. He had been moved to the palliative care ward two weeks ago. Renee, the shift nurse who was most often on duty when Charlee got to the hospital each evening, had sat her down in a quiet corridor to explain what the move meant. She had been gentle, but frank, using terms like "the end" and "preparation." But she hadn't said weeks. She had said days.

Dad had hung on for at least twice as long as they had thought he would. Every day, Charlee had expected this news, and every day it had failed to arrive. Until today.

She looked up at Principal York (*pudding*), and noticed clinically that his shirt didn't quite meet over his belly. The buttons were strained, and his white T-shirt peeped out between them. She said, "Could I...would you mind if I used your phone? I need to make a few calls."

He had been talking about arranging a cab for her, and someone to collect her things from her locker, but now he broke off, surprised.

"I need to call my brother," she added. She didn't mention that it would be an international call.

"Can't you...can your mother call him from home?" He tried to say it nicely, but he was clearly flummoxed by her request.

"We don't have a phone at home." She gave him a stiff smile. "My mom is at the hospital. She won't be thinking straight," she lied, injecting as much humble pathos into her expression and tone as she thought she could get away with.

"Oh. Of course. Yes." He picked up the black mobile phone sitting next to his desk phone, unplugged the lead from the base and closed it up. The rubber antenna caught on the edge of the desk and nearly yanked the long plastic oblong out of his hand. He slapped his other hand around the top of it and gave her an apologetic smile. "I'll just..." He waved toward the door.

"Thank you."

She waited until he had shut the door, then picked up the phone and dialed. Asher answered almost immediately. *His* cellphone was one of the smaller, silver things that folded up and fit into a pocket. "Charlee, what's wrong?"

Charlee clutched the phone, her tears spilling hot and fast down her cheeks. *Oh good, I am normal after all*, the calm part of her mind whispered. "Asher…" It was all she could choke out.

"Is it your dad?" His voice was gentle.

She nodded. But that wasn't going to work; Asher wouldn't see it. She cleared her throat. "Forty-five minutes ago." Her voice sounded strange even to her. High and childish, not the usual low, graceful tone she had tried to cultivate so that she would sound like Ylva.

"Where are you?" he asked. "I'll come and pick you up."

"No, that's not—"

"*Yes*, it is. Damn it, your father is dead, Charlee. The world can go screw itself for two days while you say goodbye to him any way you need to. If that means I'm seen with you, I don't give a fuck. Where are you?"

Knowing that she had wanted this all along, that she had reached out to him first, even before Lucas, with the unvocalized hope that he would take care of this (*her, take care of her*), she sniffed and told him where she was.

Twenty minutes later, she slid into the back of the cab, into his arms, and cried her eyes out. It was the only time she let herself cry in front of anyone for the next four days and with Asher, it didn't count.

His arms were warm, and even though he had never hugged her and only once had held her against him, and even then she had been high on painkillers, his arms were familiar and dear. It was like coming home.

* * * * *

The four of them sat in Darwin's tiny kitchen around the peach-colored Formica table, which was patterned with the outline of boomerangs, over and over. The Formica was chipped here and there and the steel legs were wobbly, but Charlee had sat at this table so often she didn't notice it any more.

She crossed her legs and pulled down the hem of her black dress, which Elizabeth had helped her pick out, while Darwin poured four glasses of wine from the bottle he had opened. He handed her a glass first, then one for Lucas and Asher and finally picked up the last one and held it up.

"To Brentwood Montgomery." He took a breath. "A man who hung in there with sheer relentlessness far longer than any man would have been expected to, and he did it only because of his kids, something I will remember for the rest of my days."

"Dad," Charlee murmured, and sipped her wine.

"Fucking A," Lucas agreed, and knocked back nearly half his glass. He wore his Class A uniform, and even though it had very few ribbons (*so far*, she added) on the breast, she thought he looked very fine indeed. Her gaze kept going back to his hair, though, which was shorn almost completely, except for a thatch of black sprouts on top. She hadn't seen it so short before.

Lucas was tanned and leaner than before he had left, but he moved with energy and there was a faraway look in his eyes that she had never seen before, like he was dealing with a whole lot of thoughts he wouldn't or couldn't share. Secrets, she realized. Was that faraway look something she wore? It was a startling idea she would have to consider, later.

Lucas grimaced and hissed through his teeth as the wine went down. "Well, it's not beer, is it?" He put the glass down.

Darwin leaned back on his chair and cracked open the fridge door. He tossed a can of Coors to Lucas. "Philistine," he added.

"Damn right." Lucas cracked the seal with relish and slurped up the froth that emerged.

Asher reached over and hooked Lucas' half-full glass. "Waste not," he said and poured it into his own glass, topping it off. Then he drained what was left and wiped drops from his jacket. His suit was dark charcoal, the closest to black she had ever seen him wear. The tie was black, the shirt a silvery grey. His shoulders seemed even wider under the padded shoulders of the jacket. Darwin's tiny kitchen seemed even smaller, almost claustrophobic, with Asher in it.

Darwin had his chair tilted on the back legs still, like a kid in grade school. His long legs rested on the steel chair legs. He looked very comfortable and also looked about twelve years old, despite the grey at his temples. Charlee hadn't realized that Darwin was the shortest of the three of them until this moment, but he was only missing an inch.

She looked around the table as she drank more of the sweet wine. Her sadness hovered like a grey mist at the bottom of her soul, but despite that chronic foundation, soaring over the top of it was an undemonstrative happiness. Three of her favorite people in the whole world were sitting right here, right now. There wasn't anyone else she would have wanted here, except maybe for Elizabeth, but Elizabeth wasn't a part of this group. She wouldn't have fit. No, these three were the core of her life right now, and they were all here. Even Lucas, who had been on the other side of the world forty-eight hours ago. Her happiness didn't make her feel like smiling, but it warmed her in a quiet way.

Darwin lowered his chair back to the floor with a soft thud. "So. We should probably figure this out, before we get too ripped to think straight."

"Speak for yourself, old man," Asher growled and knocked back a large mouthful of the wine.

"I could drink you under the table," Darwin shot back.

"It's such a little table, after all," Asher observed, a smile tugging at the corner of his mouth.

Darwin rolled his eyes.

"Figure what out?" Charlee said.

Lucas had grown very still. He was watching Darwin and suddenly, she knew.

Darwin gave her a smile, one she hadn't seen for a long while. She remembered the smile from when she had been much younger. It was, why, it was almost patronizing. Except that Darwin had never spoken down to her, not even once.

"We have to figure out what happens to you now," Darwin said. "How long do you think it will take for someone to figure out your mom isn't around anymore?"

Even though Lucas' wariness had warned her, it was still a cold shock to hear the words spoken aloud. "How did *you* know?" she asked, putting her glass down.

Darwin tapped his temple. "I'm not as smart as you, Miss Einstein, but I've still got a few marbles left, rolling around up here. I figure she's been gone, oh, about six weeks now."

"How did you know?" she demanded. Fear was pushing at her. If Darwin had figured it out, how many other people had?

"It's been about six weeks since the empty beer bottles stopped piling up next to your garbage can."

Charlee couldn't help it. She shot a glance toward Lucas. He rolled his eyes. "We forgot about the empties," he said, sounding vexed.

"You've been hiding it, making out that everything is normal," Darwin said, "so I didn't say anything. You've always been about six years older than your birth certificate says, Charlee, so I wasn't worried. Well, not much."

"But he did tell me," Asher added. He glanced at Lucas. "There's been a private security firm watching the house since I found out."

Lucas drew in a breath and let it out. "Thanks. I think."

"And no one said anything to me? The three of you did this little conspiracy dance around me instead? What *is* it with men?" Charlee picked up her wine again and swallowed the rest of it with a jerk of her wrist. The wine burned on the way down, bringing tears to her eyes, but she had been tearing up all day and most of her makeup was gone, so she didn't worry about it. She blinked furiously to clear her vision. "So why tell me now? What's changed?"

"Your father's passing, Charlee," Asher said. "There will be lots of state and federal processes that get kicked into action now, and they'll be looking for your mom to complete some of them. She's most likely your father's beneficiary, just to begin. They'll need her to sign documents and provide information, and I'm guessing they won't find her."

Charlee shook her head. "I don't know where she is. I woke up one day and she just wasn't there anymore."

"Had her drinking got worse?" Darwin asked.

"Yes," she and Lucas said together.

Charlee bit her lip. "I'm so close to graduating," she said. "It's not like I can't look after myself, with Lucas sending half his check. I already have." With her mom gone, the utility bills had dropped down to next to nothing. With only herself to feed, and the rent to cover, Lucas' money stretched a long way. Elizabeth had been as useful a source on *not* spending money as she was on shopping.

"They're not going to see it that way," Asher said quietly. "You're still not a legal adult yet."

"What will happen to her?" Lucas asked. He sounded resigned, which roused her indignation. After conspiring with her for six weeks, he was abruptly caving, as soon as Asher spoke. Why was he giving way so easily? Didn't he dislike Asher? Didn't he object to Asher even talking to her?

But now that she was thinking about it, she realized that there hadn't been one strained word between the two of them all day. She and Lucas had been busy, maintaining the fantasy that their mother was back home, sedated and too overwhelmed to attend her husband's own funeral. Lucas (*the legal adult*, she thought dryly) had dealt with the funeral parlor manager.

And now she remembered that Asher had hovered by Lucas' shoulder, while Charlee had been thanking everyone who had attended. There had been a surprisingly large group of attendees. Quite a number of people from the docks who had worked with Brent; Darwin and Asher; Mr. and Mrs. Clancy, the Irish family that lived behind them; even Principal York, which had been her biggest surprise. He had let his gaze flicker once from her feet to her hairline, then shook her hand quickly and moved on.

It had been a strain to speak to everyone. Talking to relative strangers always was, these days. Especially today, when she couldn't let her hair drape around her face, not with the dress she was wearing, nor for the reason she was wearing it. She had suffered through the strained conversations about her father, while they did everything they could not to look at her face. Some had openly stared. But Principal York's reaction had been the strangest one.

And now Lucas was bailing on her, after all their efforts. Handing her over for the authorities to do whatever they did in these cases.

"Foster parents, probably," Darwin said softly, in answer to Lucas' question.

Charlee bit back her protest. It would be selfish to complain about changing schools so late in the year. She bit her lip again and stared at the boomerangs on the table.

"Which is why I think you'd better move in with me, Charlee," Darwin added.

Charlee couldn't help it. She glanced at Darwin, surprised, then at Asher, to see what he thought of the idea. Asher sat on his chair, his arms crossed. His face gave away nothing, like it often did. But his blue-eyed gaze was on Darwin. He didn't even seem surprised, damn it.

"Will they let you do that?" Lucas asked doubtfully.

"I'll talk to them," Asher said, dropping his arms. "I'll get it smoothed over."

Darwin studied him. Then he grinned. "I hope you're not going to talk to them like you talked to those punk kids that cut up Charlee and Lucas."

For the first time, Asher was startled. Then he grinned and shook his head. "I'll just have a chat," he said. "I know a few people. It will be worked out." Then he looked directly at Charlee. "That is, if it suits you?"

Confusion clouded her pleasure at being consulted. How *did* she feel about leaving the only home she'd ever known?

"You'll be able to finish school," Lucas said. "And after June, you'll be eighteen and can decide where you want to live for yourself."

Charlee saw that Darwin was watching her anxiously. He gave a small shrug. "My kids are long gone, but I still remember what it's like to have one in the house. I'm sure you and I can get along well enough until your birthday. If you misbehave, I'll just make you read more books."

Charlee grinned. "Can you cook mulligatawny soup?"

Darwin's face fell. "No, but I can read a recipe."

"That's alright. I cook it even better than Lucas used to. I pay my half of the expenses, though, okay?"

Darwin opened his mouth to protest.

"She doesn't agree to this if you don't let us pay her way," Lucas said, his tone firm.

Darwin lifted a brow. "Okay, then. I guess I'm outvoted."

Charlee held out her hand and Darwin leaned over the table and shook it solemnly. She glanced at Asher and saw that he was studying her, his arms crossed again.

The expression on his face was a weird echo of Principal York's.

Chapter Seventeen

Freyr or Freyja
(Old Norse *freyr*, feminine Old Norse
freyja) is a Common Germanic honorific
meaning "lord", "lady", especially of
deities.
From *Wikipedia*

For a low-income librarian, Darwin knew his wines, Asher reflected as he picked up the latest bottle and refilled both their glasses. Darwin was busy cooking something. Whatever it was, it smelled pretty damned good, making Asher realize that underneath the light buzz he had from the wine, he was really hungry.

Lucas and Charlee had gone back to the house to pack essentials for Charlee and start what would be a long and painful process of deciding what to do with the contents of the house. Darwin had stood and stripped off his tie and rolled up his sleeves, announcing that he was going to cook dinner for everyone. He had refilled Asher's glass along with his own, and started working at the counter.

Asher countered with the thought that it was time for him to get back to the restaurant, which Darwin had quashed forcefully, holding up the kitchen knife to emphasize his point. "You're not going anywhere. We have some talking to do, so drink and shut up."

Asher had eyed the black man as he moved around the little kitchen. He was tall, but if he weighed two hundred pounds, Asher would be shocked. Even his knees looked knobbly, pocking the fabric of his black suit trousers. The implied threat, that he would be kept in his seat even if he didn't want to stay there, was an empty one, but Asher stayed seated.

They hadn't got around to talking until they had done eating. The stew was a hodgepodge of leftovers, with rice added in, but it was surprisingly good. Stone stew, Darwin called it. "My wife used to make something she called stone soup, using up all the leftovers, but I ain't got the patience to grow a soup stock the way she would. So I make stone stew instead. It's amazing what a can of tomato puree and a heavy dose of spices do to left-over chuck steak."

It was a pity they couldn't serve stone stew in the restaurant, Asher reflected, thinking of the huge amount of perfectly good "leftovers" that got tossed from the kitchen.

After, Darwin cleared the table, telling Asher to sit down again. "You'll just get in my way," he said. He poured the last of the bottle of wine into their glasses and handed Asher a new bottle to open. Then he produced two bowls and dug a carton of caramel and chocolate chip ice cream out of the freezer.

"Ice cream with *wine*?" Asher said.

"I happen to like ice cream, though my doctor keeps nagging me about giving it up. Today is a day for ice cream." Darwin pushed one of the bowls in front of Asher and held out a spoon. "If your delicate palate objects, I'll eat yours, too." He put the rest of the ice cream away and sat down, pulling his bowl over in front of him.

Asher shrugged. It would be impolite not to at least try to eat it. He took a mouthful and sampled the flavor combined with the wine residue on his tongue. It wasn't too terrible. He took another spoonful and let the flavors settle. No, not too bad at all.

He eyed Darwin. "Now you've softened me up with food and wine, shall we talk?"

Darwin gave him a half smile. "Not until I'm done with my ice cream. I don't want to spoil it."

"Whenever you're ready," Asher told him, hiding the sinking sensation he felt in his belly. This didn't sound good.

They ate in silence, although the silence wasn't strained. Asher realized he was enjoying the ice cream much more than he had thought he might. When Darwin scraped the bottom of his bowl and licked the spoon, Asher got up and took the bowl from him. "I know how to drop dirty dishes into a sink of water," he said, and slid them into the bowlful of suds Darwin had run. Darwin had steadily washed dishes as he had used them. The cooking-and-cleaning was a smooth routine that he had clearly developed from living alone for so long.

Asher sat down again and found his wine glass full once more. He picked it up. "My thanks for your hospitality. You have been very generous."

Darwin studied him for a long moment with an odd look in his eyes. "Very gracious of you to say so."

Wariness touched him. Had what he said been too odd? Too *old*? Damn, he had started to relax and let down his guard. So he straightened up and pushed his glass as far away from him as his arm would reach. "What did you want to talk about?"

Darwin scratched under his chin. "I don't like to dig up the past so much, but I heard something, oh, about three weeks ago. I've been pondering whether to tell you or not, but stirring you up over what amounts to second-hand gossip seemed like too much effort at the time.

But you're here now, so I figure…."

"What did you hear?"

"You have to bear in mind where this comes from," Darwin said. "The brother of the father of a kid who got mixed up with the gangs for a while a couple of summers ago. That means it's passed through three mouths that aren't close to objective about it."

Asher waited, curbing his impatience.

Darwin sipped the last quarter inch in his glass, lowering it by a fraction. "I never did ask how you planned to talk to the asshole Lightning Lords, after that thing with Charlee and Lucas. I didn't want to know. I live smack in the middle of their turf, and I used to watch them strut on by, scaring the neighbors and generally stirring up trouble. There was always talk about bigger things, more serious things. They looked like kids dressed up for a party, most of the time, with that jewelry and the silk shirts, but I heard enough to know it wasn't a good idea to make them angry."

He took another sip. He had slid into a rhythm of telling a story that Asher recognized from the hundreds of bards and story-tellers he had listened to. Darwin was setting up the background before getting to the meat of it.

"I always saw them hanging around," Darwin said. "Every day or so I'd get a glimpse of them, most usually down by the market on the corner of sixty-one. I had the leader pegged. That was one sick boy." He tapped his temple. "I could see that in him even before he decided he'd rather have you pissed at him than miss the chance of fucking with Charlee and Lucas."

Asher pushed aside the ancient habit of keeping his mouth shut and said, "He found out who I was and where I lived. He figured that me knowing he could reach me whenever he wanted took me out of the equation." He shrugged and didn't elaborate. It had been hard enough to say that much of the truth, but Darwin deserved even a partial explanation in exchange for the fear and upset it had caused.

Darwin nodded. "I didn't know that, but I did know that something had changed for them to come at Charlee the way they did. Then, after that, I didn't see the gang again. Not even once. They dried up and blew away like so much leaf litter." His gaze lifted to meet Asher's, square and confrontational.

How much had he guessed? Asher didn't underestimate his reasoning abilities. He might be a simple archivist, but he was extremely well-read. The spines of the many books in the house that Asher had glimpsed as he passed by told him that Darwin roamed all the historical eras, philosophy and much more. The most interesting theme among the many books was that of war. There had been a single shelf devoted to the writings of some of history's most capable generals, all the way from Julius Caesar to McCarthy. Well-read people were generally clear thinkers, and Darwin had soaked up strategy and human psychology from every critical battle and war that had shaped modern history.

So Asher stayed silent in the face of Darwin's mute question. He had to tread very carefully, now.

Darwin gave it thirty seconds, then he shrugged again. "I'm better off not knowing the details," he agreed, as if Asher had spoken. "I've gone this long not knowing, so my curiosity can stand the mystery a bit longer. Thing is…" He sipped again. He was getting to the point, now, and pausing before the big moment in his story. "This kid, the son of the brother of the man who told me the story…this kid got hooked into the Comanches for a bit, down in lower Manhattan. Gangs don't like to let go of a brother, so the father figured the only way to fix it was to move the whole damned family out of Manhattan. They moved up here and lived with the kid's uncle for a bit, until they got their footing and found a house. Point is, the kid had stories to tell, and one of them was about a captain from a heavy-duty Bronx gang who had arranged to trespass on their territory for a few days while they dealt with an enemy."

Asher fought not to react and to wait for Darwin to reach his point, which was close now.

Darwin shrugged. "It would have been of zero interest for me, except that the kid even had a name for the guy they were hunting." This time his gaze drilled into him.

"Strand," Asher said softly.

"Strand," Darwin confirmed. "You're known to the gangs," he added. "The Comanches have known about you for over three years and even though they tend to shoot first when another gang member strolls onto their turf, word still manages to pass among them. They would also know the Lords have up and disappeared, too, and they'll make the same connection I did."

"Perhaps that's why they haven't come calling," Asher said.

"There's no profit in it for them, right now," Darwin agreed. "But they would have watched you. You're on their interest list, now."

Asher smiled. "I'm a very cautious man."

"And these guys make the Lords look like ballerinas. Well, I've told you." Darwin sat back.

"How is it you know so much about the gangs, anyway? It's not the usual area of interest for an archivist."

Darwin snorted. "Because of you. I've been listening and watching and talking to interesting people for a few years now. Gangs aren't like they used to be in the fifties and sixties. They're organized. Structured. There's money behind them. They're considered revenue generators for the money men and they're the sort of money men that settle financial disputes in a way that needs body bags, not legal battles." Darwin pushed his lips out, a rueful expression that seemed to sum up everything he'd gleaned about New York gangs.

Then he straightened up and stretched hard and put his hands back on the table. "Gangs aren't all I've been reading up about."

Asher reached for his glass of wine again. Screw it. He wanted the rest, after all. And it gave him an excuse not to look Darwin in the eye.

"I'm damned good at my job," Darwin said. "It helps that I like what I do, but that's beside the point. The point is, I can usually find any information I want. If it's out there in the world somewhere, I can track it down, because I know where and how it's all stored and how to access it."

"I'm quite sure you are *very* good," Asher said sincerely. He looked at his watch. "You know, I really should—"

"I can't find anything on you," Darwin said flatly. "Twenty years back, in the early nineteen seventies…every trace of you disappears. "

Asher stared down at the ruby liquid. His heart galloped.

"You're young, yet, but you're more than twenty years old," Darwin said flatly. "Then there's the odd things you say and the way you say them, like that thing about my hospitality."

Asher winced mentally.

"Then there's your name. Names are one of the most revealing things, did you know? Even the fake ones. There's always a reason someone picked the name and if you noodle it around for a while…." He trailed off as Asher shook his head.

"Don't," Asher said gently, his heart slamming now.

Darwin grew wary. "Don't …what?" he asked, just as quietly.

"Don't pursue this. Don't dig into records. Don't ask questions, especially about me."

Darwin licked his lips, watching Asher, working it out. "Charlee…" His voice was strained.

Asher gave a soft exhalation. "Christ, Darwin, after what I've done to protect her, do you really think I would let her walk into danger because of *me*?"

Darwin was fast. He got it almost straight away and he seemed to slump. "Then there *is* danger. Around you, because of you." His voice sounded far away.

Asher shook his head. "Not because of me. Because of what I am." Nausea washed through him and cold sweat broke out all over. This was incredibly close to breaking *laun*. It was flirting with overwhelming danger. "If you ask, if you try to dig up stuff," (*the truth, dammit*), "then the wrong people will learn of what you're doing."

Darwin swallowed. He looked completely unnerved. Asher wanted to take that look away, but he couldn't.

* * * * *

Standing in front of the impressive black oak and brass door, waiting for his buzz to be answered, Darwin brushed down his jacket nervously and looked around at Fifth Avenue. Even though he worked in the general area, the lifestyles of the residents here existed upon a different plane that ol' Darwin Baxter would never be able to reach.

The girl who answered the door looked like she was barely eighteen, but she was stunning in a dewy rosebud way. Darwin cleared his throat. "I'm looking for Ylva...um...Peterson." At the last second, he recalled the surname.

"Is she expecting you?" the girl asked.

"Uh, no. Can you see if she would speak to me for a few minutes? It's very important. Tell her we've met before, several years ago."

The girl gave him a polite smile. "And your name?"

He told her.

She shut the door on him and Darwin was back to being nervous again. Why hadn't he worn a tie?

When the door opened again, Darwin fully expected the girl would either tell him to go away, or he might be escorted into the interior of the mansion to speak to Ylva for the few short minutes he had requested.

Ylva herself stood there, in classically stylish pants and a crewneck sweater in some material that seemed to glow softly, like her hair, which was longer than he remembered.

She smiled at him. "Darwin, this is a surprise."

Completely floored, Darwin just stared at her. He had forgotten the power of her voice. The low contralto. How it curled around you....

Ylva's smile faded. "Is something wrong with Charlee?" she asked.

"Yes. I mean, no, there's nothing wrong with her. Charlee is fine." He grimaced. "I *think* she's fine. That's why I'm here. Asher gave me your address." He pulled in a calming breath. "I need a woman's perspective," he said frankly.

"Oh." She pressed her lips together briefly, like she was trying to prevent a smile. "There are not dozens of women in your life that you could have consulted, instead of schlepping all the way down here to see me?"

He wouldn't have called visiting a house on Fifth Avenue schlepping, not in his wildest dreams. He shrugged self-consciously. "Every woman I know has that blue-rinse hair thing going on or wears support hose. One of 'em told me to make Charlee drink boiled prune juice every night because that would fix her right up." He shook his head. "I need a sophisticated woman. You're the only one I know."

Ylva smiled, her smile making her eyes dance. "Well, thank you. You'd better come in." She stepped aside, and Darwin glanced up at the winding stone staircase and the cage thing that was in the middle. Then he saw there was an honest to goodness crow sitting on the stand in the middle, pecking at a tray of seeds. It *was* a birdcage. But…crows? He blinked and followed Ylva upstairs, his gaze shifting back to the crow with every couple of steps. The crow considered him right back, its head tilting to follow his movements.

They moved into a room at the top of the stairs, one filled with antiques that Darwin just knew hadn't been picked up at the local op shop. The impression in the room was one of graceful, aged comfort and a preference for fine things, which were revered for their function as much as for their beauty. It wasn't an overwhelming room, but Darwin still felt like he'd stepped into that other plane that he had thought about while waiting for the door to be answered.

Ylva sat down on a striped sofa that looked like something he'd seen in illustrations of life in the French court in the seventeenth century. Then she surprised him by easing off her high heels and tucking her feet up on the cushion next to her. She grinned at his expression. "I prefer to be comfortable in my own home," she said. "Please, sit down. I asked for coffee to be brought and it should be here very shortly."

He sat in the armchair next to the sofa. It didn't match the sofa, but it was wonderfully comfortable and soft.

"You're well, Darwin?" she asked.

"Very well, thanks," Darwin said truthfully. "I don't know if Asher told you or not, but Charlee moved in with me after her father died last year. I gotta tell you, having someone else, especially a young someone else, around the place really makes a difference."

"I know exactly what you mean," Ylva said. "I have several young people kicking about this place at any one time. I find it invigorating."

"Exactly. Invigorating," Darwin said. He fidgeted, pulling the edges of his collar together (*should have worn a tie*) and tapping on the arm of the chair, until he realized what he was doing and dropped his hand back to his knee. Ylva was the sort of woman who wouldn't settle down to business until the pleasantries were done and coffee was served.

"Perhaps you'd better tell me what's on your mind. You look like a man on the horns of a dilemma." She smiled to take away any insult in the observation.

He jumped a bit. "Being here isn't helping," he confessed.

"You don't like my home?" she asked, sounding curious rather than affronted.

"I love it," he said quickly. "But Charlee doesn't know I'm here. She doesn't know I'm up against a wall on this one and talking to other people about her. She'd be mad as hell if she knew, but she doesn't like to talk things out like most women do. She keeps things very close."

Ylva nodded. "I do remember that about her. What is the problem, Darwin? What do you *think* is the problem?"

"I just don't know," he said flatly.

Ylva didn't laugh. She didn't smile, either, and he felt relief. There, he'd betrayed his ignorance and the world hadn't collapsed around him. Now maybe he could fix this.

The door to the room opened—lounge room? Parlor? Private retreat? It was hard to tell because there wasn't a dining table, or a sideboard or even a television, nothing to say what the room's function was supposed to be. The young girl who had first answered the door came in, kicking the door shut behind her. She was carrying a huge tray loaded with cups and a coffee pot, and a basket with cookies in it, napkins and other serving items. She carried it like it weighed nothing but before Darwin could get up to help, Ylva jumped up and pulled a small side table over between her sofa and Darwin's knees.

Then the girl left and Ylva poured coffee. "Would you like a raisin oatmeal cookie?" she asked, and looked at him from under her brow as she poured. "I believe they're your favorite."

Charlee.

Darwin mentally sighed, accepted the cup Ylva handed him and took two cookies. He'd been outed, so why not? The coffee was delicious in a way he couldn't get a handle on and he decided it was more of the same; a preference for quality and care taken with the making of it, which turned out coffee like this instead of the swill the deli on the corner made and left on the hotplate for hours on end.

Ylva settled back on her sofa with a graceful swing of hips and limbs that culminated in her being seated with her feet back on the cushions. Not a drop of coffee spilled as she did it. Darwin marveled at her flexibility. He would have dumped the entire cup *and* the cookies if he'd tried something as athletic as that.

She sipped and put the cup and saucer down on the tray in front of her. "Forgive me for prying, Darwin, but you are a parent of your own children, aren't you?"

"Two boys, ma'am. Long gone."

"They live in other cities?"

"They both went to Vietnam." He grimaced. "They didn't come back."

"I'm so sorry," she said softly. "I didn't mean to stir up sad memories."

He shook his head. "It was a long time ago. World's a different place now. But maybe knowing that will help you understand. I didn't get to raise a girl. Just boys, and they're different from girls as night is from day. And Charlee…well, she's not properly a girl anymore, either. But something is eating her, and I can't for the life of me figure out what. It's like when that mutt of hers was killed, years ago. She just went inside herself. Only this time, she's not hiding out in her room, which makes it next to impossible to figure out. She's polite. She even smiles. But her eyes are blank, like she's going through the motions."

"She's trying not to worry you," Ylva said.

Darwin blinked. "I hadn't thought of that. I thought she was trying to hide it, so no one would know anything was wrong."

"She *is* trying to hide it, from the people she cares about and doesn't want to worry."

Darwin pointed at her. "See? I knew you were the right one to ask. Prune juice…." He screwed up his nose.

Ylva laughed and sat forward, her hands clasped together in a way that made the most of her long, elegant fingers. "What has happened in her life lately? When did you notice her change?"

Darwin went through the last couple of weeks slowly, thinking it through carefully and itemizing anything unusual or different for Ylva to consider. There wasn't much. Both he and Charlee were very set in their quiet little routine. Breakfast, then work for him and school for her, then home for supper, and after the dishes they both settled at the table, him to read and her to do homework, until they were ready to fall into bed. On Saturdays, it had started out with Charlee helping him clean the house, but now, it was Charlee who cleaned and he got on with taking care of things that had been neglected for years because of lack of time, like digging new flower beds, and cleaning gutters, fixing siding and more. The weekends were down time when they both pottered around the house.

It was a comfortable life that he wouldn't admit to anyone was much better than the life he'd led alone. Alone didn't look so hot now. Charlee suited him down to the ground, and he was beginning to hate the swiftly coming time when she would move out and take up her own life.

"But doesn't she go out with friends? Dates?" Ylva asked curiously. "She is nearly eighteen. She should be rebelling and climbing out her bedroom window to go drinking and dancing, like any modern teenager should."

"Her exams are close," Darwin said weakly, for this had bothered him, too. Charlee just didn't seem to be like other teenagers in that regard. His own boys had been hell on wheels at times. If only they had studied enough to earn a scholarship for college, they'd still be alive now and raising their own kids, because the war had ended only weeks after they had died. But that was wishing for a different life, and this was the one he had and Charlee needed him. "She's determined to go to college in September."

"Has she had any offers?" Ylva asked. "It's April and I know they start selecting even this early."

"I think she could take her pick," Darwin said slowly. "Even Harvard would welcome her if only she was a paying customer."

Ylva's face shadowed. "Oh. Oh, dear, that is unfortunate. Even with all her talent, there are no scholarships for her?"

"She's applied for them all. Every single one she learns about. It's almost a full-time preoccupation right now. She hasn't heard back from any of them." He sighed. "But that's not it, because she talks to me about that." Charlee's withering comments about the ridiculous amount of red tape involved in grant and funding applications had privately delighted him. She had a very adult perspective on the process. "Well, she talked to me about it before. But she hasn't talked to me much about anything for a bit."

They reconsidered everything once again, but this time even Ylva was puzzled. "I just can't see it," she said. "Short of sitting Charlee down and asking her point blank, I don't think we're going to be able to figure it out. Besides, it might be more respectful to Charlee to simply ask her, don't you think?"

Darwin sighed. "It probably would, but...." He didn't know what came next. He just knew that asking her would be *something* unpleasant. Deep reluctance seized him every time he considered this very sensible solution.

"You don't want her to know you're not omnipotent, do you?" Ylva asked.

Somewhere in the house, beyond the door, Darwin heard a phone ring softly. After a few rings, the sound stopped.

Darwin glanced at Ylva to see if she was laughing at him, but she wasn't. He could feel his cheeks heating anyway. "Damn it, I'm supposed to be taking care of her. And I can't figure out this little thing? It's embarrassing."

Ylva gave him a sympathetic smile. "As you said, you didn't get to raise any girls. Now you've got a full grown woman on your hands. I suspect it would be a tough adjustment for anyone to make."

A knock sounded on the door and the sweet little rosebud stepped into the room. She handed Ylva a folded piece of paper, which Ylva unfolded and read, then handed back. "Not now," she said gently.

The girl traipsed back out and shut the door.

"The phone…" Darwin said slowly, straining to recall whatever it was that suddenly felt significant. Then he had it. "I don't know if this has got anything to do with it. It's such a stupid thing."

Ylva folded her hands again and looked at him with polite curiosity.

"About, yes, about the right time, too, I think. Charlee's friend Elizabeth phoned. When she came back to the kitchen table, she was kinda quiet."

"Then it was something that Elizabeth said?" Ylva asked.

"But Charlee told me what they talked about. Elizabeth was over the moon because some boy at school had finally asked her to the prom."

Ylva grew very still. Her eyes seemed to focus on nothing. Then they shifted back to him. "What did you say when she told you that?" She said it in a pent-up way that made Darwin nervous.

"I don't remember. Something about…." He frowned, trying to pull back the memory. "But she wasn't upset!" he protested. "She was so happy for her friend. And I said…" He shrugged. "I don't really remember. I joked about it."

Ylva's eyes seemed to be staring through him. "Can you remember what you joked about?" she asked.

Scared now, knowing that this was somehow his fault, but unable to grasp what it could possibly be, he pummelled his memory, backtracking through the evening: the phone call, Charlee settling back down at the table and picking up her pen. His casual inquiry about the call, which had left a smile lingering on her face. Her grin as she told him Elizabeth was beside herself because Tommy Hancock had asked her to go to the prom with him and she had been holding back on a dozen other requests, just waiting for him to call and he had…and Darwin had said….he'd said to Charlee…

"And who's the lucky guy that gets to take *you* to the prom?" Darwin repeated the words, imitating the same teasing tone he'd used that night, but wretched sickness was pumping through him now.

Ylva looked horrified.

"But she laughed!" Darwin said. "She even said something about wouldn't I like to know."

"Of course she would joke with you," Ylva said, very gently. "Charlee wouldn't have wanted you to know that your joke had hurt her."

"*Hurt* her?" Now he was flat out horrified. "I figured she'd like the idea of guys drooling after her. Don't all girls want that?"

Ylva reached out and rested her hand over his. It was a soothing gesture. She was offering comfort. "Charlee isn't like other girls. We've both agreed on that."

"But, she's beautiful!" Darwin said, honestly bewildered.

Ylva gave him the same sympathetic smile. "Charlee doesn't think she is, and for that reason she won't be asked to the prom."

Darwin could feel his jaw dropping. "Won't be asked? But that's…it's friggin' ridiculous, excuse my French. Any boy, any man with an inch of taste would trip over themselves to ask her out." He drew in a breath. "What is it I don't get?"

Ylva folded her hands together once more. "She has a scar on her face."

"But that's…but it's *just a scar*!" Anger was starting to stir in him. "You mean, they, the kids at school, they're, what, teasing her about it?" The anger was building swiftly. He suddenly wanted to flay the hides of some of those snot-nosed boys he saw walking home from school each day. If they had been doing this to his Charlee….

Ylva waited until he was paying full attention again. "I'm sure the teasing has diminished after all these years, but Charlee is an ace student, I believe, yes?"

Darwin nodded.

Ylva held up a finger. "She's smart." She touched the next finger as she raised it. "Her father died." Another finger. "She lives with an elderly man who used to be her neighbor." Another finger. "She got a scar from a gang fight." The thumb this time. "She has never had a lot of money to spend on the latest fashions and accessories, so the pretty, popular girls wearing Prada and Guess would look down on her for that."

Ylva lifted her other hand and held up her thumb. "She has extraordinary looks. She isn't blonde and blue-eyed in the conventionally pretty way. She is an exotic lily among pretty daisies, and most high school boys aren't discriminating enough to notice."

Darwin nodded, because that was *exactly* what Charlee was.

Ylva dropped her hands. "In the years when conforming to everything is so incredibly important, when being as much like everyone around you earns social brownie points, Charlee is as different from the average senior as it is possible to be. I am quite sure that no boy would care to be seen with such an oddity, even if he privately thinks she *is* pretty."

Darwin fumed. "Damn it, *I'll* take her."

Ylva shook her head. "Please don't be offended, but to people Charlee's age, you're very old. Taking her to the prom would just make her look even more strange."

He sat stewing in his fury. How could kids be so goddamn mean to each other? It defied comprehension.

"Don't you remember your own high school days, Darwin? That would have been sometime during or just after the second world war, yes?" Ylva asked softly.

"*Everyone* was odd, then. There were no clothes, no food, not much of anything. Making fun of kids because they had funny clothes was pointless, because everyone was dressed funny."

"What about your prom?" Ylva asked. "Were there girls every boy knew it would be fatal to ask out?"

"Sure, there was Maureen Taggart, but that was because her parents were divorced, which in those days was practically the same as being a commie…." He trailed off. "Or black," he finished softly. "Or having a scar, or red hair." He blew out his breath. "*Shit* damn," he said with feeling.

Ylva smiled. "Agreed in triplicate."

He scrubbed at his hair. Proms were important. They were a rite of passage that every kid in America should go through. The idea of Charlee sitting at home at the kitchen table with him while her class was whooping it up in the gym…it made him feel sick all over again. "What am I supposed to do, bribe some kid to take her?"

Ylva pursed her lips. Even she didn't bother responding to such a stupid idea. Then she pressed one manicured fingertip against her pouting lips. "I have an idea."

Chapter Eighteen

Eldre
Out-flung former Herleifr who have
given up the pure life, and found their
own niche within human society. They
have accepted mortality and returned to
a nearly human state. This is the most
common form of depletion amongst the
Herleifr. Analysis of...
from *The Complete Kine Encyclopedia,* by
Darwin Baxter, PhD. 2019 Edition

Three days later, Charlee was waiting in the kitchen for Darwin when he got home. Her eyes were shining. She held up the cable sheet in her hand. "Lucas has shore leave! He'll be home in a week…and Darwin, he wants to take me to the prom!"

Darwin managed to look surprised. His pleasure was completely genuine, though. "That's great, Charlee. He looked pretty impressive in his Class A's, too." Then he added the question that would never have occurred to him to ask without Ylva's coaching. "What are you going to wear?"

Charlee's eyes widened. "Oh my god!" she said. "A dress! I'm going to need a dress, and my hair, and…." She started to look horrified. Terror wasn't far off.

He held up a hand. "Prom dresses and old men don't mix. I couldn't help you out with fripperies like that even if I was forty years younger. But I just thought of someone who might."

"Who?"

"Ylva, the lady from the restaurant."

Charlee crumpled the cable in her hand as she gripped her hands together. "Darwin, you're brilliant." She reached up and kissed his cheek. "I'll stop by to see her tomorrow."

* * * * *

Once they were both settled, a cup of tea in front of each of them, Ylva looked Charlee over. "I'm so pleased to see you, Charlee."

Charlee bit her lip. "I didn't know if I should come back. I could barely remember being here, that last time. I wasn't even sure I had the right house." She realized she was touching her scar and put her hand back in her lap. "It all seemed so…well, secret."

"But you would have been very welcome," Ylva told her. "There's nothing wrong with a friend stopping by, and we did become friends when I was working at the Ash Tree."

Charlee looked at the teacups and the squat pot of tea. There was a small stack of pancakes on a plate close to her knee, and the sight of them had made her smile. "Just like old times," she said.

"I was hoping you'd feel it was," Ylva said, sounded very pleased with herself. "I'm quite sure my pancakes are nowhere near as good as Pierre's, though." She put down her cup. "How can I help you, Charlee?"

Charlee felt suddenly bashful. "Darwin said you would know… I mean, you could help…." She stopped and blew out her breath. "Oh, Ylva, I'm going to the prom next week and I haven't got anything to wear, and Lucas will have his Class As and I didn't even *think* about a dress, even when Elizabeth was trying hers on weeks and weeks ago. I didn't think I would ever be going, but now I am and it's only a *week* and I need shoes and stuff I probably haven't thought of yet—"

Ylva was smiling.

"What?" Charlee asked, feeling silly.

"You're asking me to help you with your prom dress," Ylva said. "I'm so *pleased*."

Charlee blinked. "You are?"

Ylva nodded. "I've never had a daughter I could help dress up for her prom."

"Oh." She hadn't thought about it that way. "Really? You'll help?"

Ylva stood up. "I'd like to do more than help, if you'll let me. I'd like to buy your dress for you, as a graduation present."

Charlee pressed her fingers to her lips, to stop them trembling. But she couldn't do anything about the tears in her eyes. She blinked furiously. "If you're sure," she said, her voice wobbling.

"I'm very sure. Come along."

"Where are we going?" Charlee asked, putting her cup aside.

"To buy your dress."

"*Now?*"

"Why not?"

* * * * *

Charlee ran up the stone stairs, calling Ylva's name. Already, the house was familiar to her and she already knew the first name of most of the women who lived and worked there.

Ylva stepped out of the room she called her day room, one hand on the doorframe. "The shoes didn't fit?" she asked, sounding worried.

Charlee stopped in front of her and realized with something of a start that they were the same height. She had always had to lift her chin to look at Ylva before. "No, the shoes are perfect. It's just…" She could feel her cheeks heating.

Ylva waited with the graceful patience that was so much a part of her.

"I can't wear my hair down with that dress," Charlee said, forcing it out.

"I agree. Wearing your hair down would ruin the style." Ylva tilted her head a little to one side.

Charlee raised her hand to her cheek.

"Of course," Ylva said and took her arm. "Come with me."

* * * * *

Charlee stepped in front of the mirror once more and turned her head, studying her scar.

Ylva stood beside her, looking in the mirror as well. She held the little pot of whatever it was in her hand and a cloth in the other one. "I don't think you can completely hide it, Charlee, because it's raised above the skin around it. But we can cover the redness, and if you make sure the makeup you use is completely and absolutely matte, it won't pick up the light. That means in photos it will recede rather than draw attention to itself."

"Photos…." Charlee let out a shaking breath. "I hadn't thought about photos." She bit her lip. "Perhaps I should just leave my hair down, after all."

"If you do, I'll take back the dress," Ylva said quickly.

Charlee looked at her, startled.

Ylva smiled at her. "You know that you're the only one who cares about the scar, don't you? You're the only one who notices it."

"Strangers notice. They stare at me all the time."

"But the people you know, they don't even see it. You're going to be with Lucas and Darwin, and people like your friend Elizabeth."

Charlee blew out another breath. "Okay…." she said uncertainly.

Ylva gave her a hug, then stood with her arm about her shoulders as they both looked in the mirror. "Stars above, your legs do go on forever, Charlee. You should wear hot pants to the prom. No one would notice your scar then."

They both laughed at the idea.

* * * * *

212

Charlee was at the hairdresser's when Lucas called. Darwin took the call, the tea towel in his other hand, for he had been chopping onions for the early dinner he was making. He remembered how much alcohol had been consumed at his own prom, and he wanted Charlee to have a full stomach when she went out the door. "Baxter house."

"Darwin, it's Lucas."

Darwin gripped the towel harder, his heart sinking. "Tell me you're in New York and about to catch a cab," Darwin pleaded.

"I'm in fucking L.A.," Lucas replied. "The transport got diverted. They're giving me a commercial flight to New York, and it leaves in fifteen minutes, but then I have to get from the airport to your place. And my dress uniform is in the suitbag back in Manila. *Fuck*."

The distress in his voice came through clearly, and contrarily that calmed Darwin, letting him think it through. "Just get here as fast as you can. I'll pull out my suit, you can wear that. I'll even meet you at the airport with it and you can go straight to the prom and meet Charlee there."

"But—"

"No buts, not tonight," Darwin said firmly. "I won't allow it."

* * * * *

The front of the school's big gym was flooded with light, making the open area right next to the long series of glass swinging doors that led into the gym bright as daylight. The concrete slabs that made up the open area between the gym and the road looked almost white in the harsh lights, but no one noticed that except Charlee.

She stood close to the brick walls that flanked the gym, holding back terraces of grass and low-lying bushes. There, she wasn't in anyone's way and no one noticed her. She pulled her wrap closer around her, scanning the road and the steady line of private cars and rented limousines and cabs that were dropping off kids and their escorts and sometimes their parents.

Thickly clustered about the concrete slabs were four hundred and twenty-three seniors, dressed up in their very best finery. The boys were sober, darkly suited punctuation to the astonishing array of dresses dotted between them. If she wasn't feeling so ill, Charlee would have been happy just to stand here for the rest of the night, watching the endlessly fascinating dresses go by. There were big, full, hooped ball gowns and short, tight, shimmery dresses. And there was everything in between, in every color possible.

But Charlee was too worried to enjoy the pageantry. She had stopped being nervous thirty-five minutes ago. Now, a sick, sinking certainty was filling her, convincing her that Lucas wouldn't make it here in time. It was already seven-forty, and the prom was supposed to start at seventy-thirty. Any second now, Principal York would get up on the stage and announce the start of the evening, and Charlee would be left standing here, patently without an escort, clearly friendless and alone. Elizabeth had sailed by on Tommy's arm, incandescent with happiness and almost oblivious to Charlee's dress or the fact that she was standing by herself.

She shouldn't have come. She *wouldn't* have come, except that Darwin had almost forced her into the cab and pushed a fifty-dollar note at the driver, before grabbing his own cab to the airport, his suit folded over the other arm.

"He'll *be* there," Darwin had assured her. "Just wait out front where he'll be able to spot you when he gets there."

But waiting out front also meant drawing attention to herself, so she had chosen this shadowed spot by the wall where she would be out of the way. She could scan the arrivals and would see Lucas when he arrived. Then she could step out where the floodlights were brightest.

As the minutes ticked on, she became more and more certain that Lucas was not coming. Her cheeks heated and her gut roiled. She was being stood up. Stood up by the poorest date possible, her own big brother. How stupid was she to even think this was a good idea?

It was Elizabeth's fault. If she hadn't spent so many weeks dreaming out loud about her dress to Charlee, then Charlee would never have started to think how wonderful it would be to dress up in a long evening gown. Now she was here, alone.

The worst of it was that she wasn't completely out of sight. Heads kept turning. Their gazes would light upon her and take in her solitary state. Then they would bend back to whisper to each other. Then there would be a second glance as they *all* looked at her. Who? It didn't matter. It was kids she knew and kids she only knew by sight. But they knew her, oh yes. She was the freak who had turned up at the prom, waiting for a date who couldn't be bothered to show up.

The stream of cars out front was starting to slow down. Music fired up inside the gym. After a few seconds, she recognized Janet Jackson's "Because of Love." That would get everyone on the dance floor. Everyone who was already inside.

Charlee knew it was time to leave. She eyed the arriving cars. There was a cab pulling up to the end of the queue. She could grab that when the passengers got out, and go home. She could escape this humiliation and spend the rest of the weekend wondering how she was going to keep her head up at school on Monday.

She settled the wrap around her once more, picked up the skirt of the dress so she wouldn't trip on it, and headed for the spot where she estimated the cab would stop. She timed it almost exactly, for she was only a few steps away when it came to a jerky halt and the back door was flung open almost instantly.

Asher stepped out and straightened up. He was sliding his other arm into a black tuxedo jacket and paying the driver all at once, his blond hair in the floodlights looking pale and thick.

Charlee halted. Her legs, her face…her entire body went numb. She couldn't move. Breathing was hard. Was he really here, or was she just projecting one of the private fantasies she had been having for the last week, ever since she had brought her new dress home?

Asher turned, scanning the crowd the same way she had been.

"Asher," she said and was surprised when her voice came out at all. It sounded different, not her own.

He turned his head at her call, then saw her. He smiled, and it was one of his warm, private smiles. "Surprise," he said.

She nodded. "Yes, it is." Her throat was closing up, but she was *not* going to cry, even if she had to step on her toes with her own stilettos to halt the tears. She worked her throat hard, pulling them back, getting control of herself.

Asher threw his hands up. "Damn the gods, I nearly forgot—" He turned back to the cab, which was starting to leave. He thumped on the roof, and when the driver jerked it to another stop Asher opened the back door. He leaned in, then re-emerged.

This time, he was carrying a single, long-stemmed flower. A lily. It looked a lot like one of Ylva's purple calla lilies. Asher brought it over to her and held it out. "Ylva insisted that I bring this, not a wrist corsage. Now I see you, I can see that she was right. A corsage would have been pretty, but it wouldn't have matched you."

Charlee reached out for the stem and took it. "Thank you."

Asher offered his elbow. "Shall we go in?"

"Are you sure?" she whispered.

"Now I've seen you, I'm sure. Do you care to know what happened to Lucas and why I'm here instead?"

She shook her head. It didn't matter. Lucas had been delayed and someone—Lucas or Darwin or perhaps even Ylva, who was apparently mixed up in this, too—had yelled for Asher to step in, and he had arrived still throwing on his tux. But he was here.

As they wended their way around the clusters of belles and their escorts, she saw that heads were turning again. Their eyes were even more rounded than before as they took in Asher, beside her.

Charlee gripped Asher's arm even more tightly. "I would have asked you," she said. "I wanted to. Of everyone I know, I wanted you to take me to the prom, but…"

"But now I'm here." He gave her a small smile. "Enjoy the night, Charlee. You deserve to."

She didn't walk into the gym. She floated.

* * * * *

In the foyer, there were kids everywhere, laughing, screaming, shouting at each other, swirling multicolors everywhere. It was loud, and Asher could see heads turning and elbows nudging as one by one, they noticed Charlee.

Charlee seemed to shrink into herself. He could see her shoulders hunch under the wrap. So he stepped up behind her. "Look them in the eye, Charlee. You're with me. Do you have any doubt I won't beat the snot out of anyone who even *thinks* about giving you a hard time?"

She smiled up at him. "They'll arrest you."

He held up his finger. "One finger. That's all I need."

Her smile became a laugh. "I think I would actually like to see you do that. There's some creeps here who would be better people if their egos took a beating."

Asher leaned down so he could drop his voice. "Don't look now, but I think you're already crushing some egos. There's some girls over by the doors there that look ready to kill you." Then he straightened. "Give me your wrap. I'll check it, then we can go in and find a table."

Charlee hesitated. Then her shoulders lifted as she drew in a breath and took off the wrap and held it out to him.

Asher took the offered wrap, moving purely on automatic. His gaze, all of his attention had been riveted to Charlee and whatever it was she was wearing. It was a dress, he knew. Ylva had mentioned it was some designer or another, but he'd paid no notice. He still didn't care, except that the difference between this dress and every other dress he'd spotted since the cab had pulled up was as vast as the Pacific.

Creakily, his mind restored itself to normal order. He made a small fuss of folding the wrap over his arm while he gave himself a moment to clear his head and get his reaction under control.

Every other girl here looked like exactly what she was: a seventeen-year-old high school student in a pretty dress. Charlee looked like a woman.

He glanced at her once, quickly, as she stood tall and slender, her chin up, a small, black evening clutch in her hand. Then he forced himself to move over to the coat check counter and deal with the kids behind the counter, while his mind raced.

The dress was some velvety black material and it *clung*. To everything. When had Charlee grown so tall? When had she filled out like that? She had *curves*. Everywhere.

There was a white band at the top of the dress. He didn't have the skills or knowledge to know what it was called, but it wrapped around her shoulders and met in the middle with a bow. There was nothing else holding up the dress.

He glanced back at her while he was waiting for the ticket. She had done something with her hair. It was piled up on the back of her head, but then it tumbled down her back in a series of waves and curls, brushing the curve at the back of her waist. The red was lustrous, gleaming like silk, making him want to run his fingers through it.

Odin help me. He took a deep breath, becoming abruptly conscious of the covert attention he was drawing. That he *and Charlee* were drawing.

He moved back to her side and held out his arm. "Let's go in."

She nodded. Her deep black eyes were bordered by long, thick lashes, making them seem larger than ever. "Thank you for this," she said, her voice low.

Her thanks centered his focus. It made him remember why all three of them, Darwin, Lucas and Ylva, had been so ferociously insistent that he drop everything immediately and sprint for the gym to find her. "I'm glad I'm here," he told her truthfully.

He led her into the gym, and even though he wasn't looking directly at her, he could sense the way her hips were moving as she walked, and the elegant curve of her chin and jaw.

Focus! he reminded himself.

* * * * *

Everything went dreamily perfect, until the photographer arrived. Charlee had basked selfishly and without regret in the attention Asher was drawing, almost fiercely proud of the fact that he was with her. She knew he was raising questions she would have to deal with on Monday. His height and his build made him stand out. Also, even though Asher seemed young, no one would ever mistake him for a high-school-aged boy.

Even Elizabeth had sent her a startled, raised-brow look and that one had pleased Charlee more than any of the others. But for now, Charlee was more than happy to let the mystery around Asher go unexplained.

Even Principal York had seemed startled. He had been involved in a conversation with two other supervising teachers, close to their table. He had been perspiring heavily, and the white material of his jacket had darkened and was stained with sweat rings under his arms. When the conversation broke up, he had seen her watching him and gave her a smile. "It's a warm evening, isn't it? We have some iced punch out in the caretaker's office if you'd like something stronger." Then he peered at her and his jaw had actually dropped. "Good god, Charlee! I mean…dear Lord, I didn't recognize you. I thought you were one of the parents."

"Clearly," Charlee replied. "You wouldn't push alcohol onto a minor."

He looked even more horrified. "Now, there's no need to go and repeat that anywhere. It was an honest mistake."

"Of course."

He glanced at Asher and then did another almost comical double-take. Charlee hid her smile, absorbing Principal York's astonishment with relish.

"This is my friend, Asher Strand," she told him. "Asher, this is Brian York, the principal of the school."

York stuck his hand out, and Asher stood up and shook it. York looked up at him, blinking. It really had been too perfectly funny.

Charlee danced whenever Asher asked. The music that had been playing when they first sat down was another current dance hit and Asher had frowned, studying the kids gyrating on the dance floor. The girls looked a little odd, bouncing and jumping with their full skirts twisting around them.

"I'll ask you to dance when the *real* dancing starts," Asher told her.

"I don't dance," Charlee said, alarmed, looking out at the full dance floor.

"That's not dancing," Asher said flatly.

Twenty minutes later, the music had geared down and the lights lowered on the dance floor, so the mirrored balls hanging above them glittered and shimmered over everything.

There was a collective groan and the dance floor emptied.

Asher picked up Charlee's hand. "*Now* let's dance," he said.

They were the first onto the floor. It would have been alarming to be the *only* focus of so many gazes like that, except that all Charlee's attention snapped inward as Asher swept his arm around her back and pulled her up against him.

He began to move in time with the music and Charlee found herself following his steps automatically, while she dealt with the fact that he was holding her against him.

It didn't feel odd, and she knew it should have. This was the first time she had been held by anyone like this, boy or man. It should have made her blush or giggle like a girl. Or stumble awkwardly about. But she was…well, she was *dancing*. Her feet were moving in graceful steps. It didn't feel odd, it felt natural. His arm around her was natural. The warmth of his hand around hers was right. He even smelled right.

It made her aware of her body in a way she had never before felt. Her hips, brushing lightly against his jacket. How heavy his arm was, against her back. The heat of him, right in front of her.

By the time he took her back to the table, she could feel that she was flushed and was thankful for the low light that hid her reaction. She sat recovering and wondering what she would say if he asked her to dance again.

But the next time the music slowed and Asher stood and held out his hand, she got to her feet and slid her hand into his without even considering it.

Charlee had begun to think of the evening as a smashing victory, until the photographer stepped up to their table and raised his camera.

Alarm crashed through her. "No," she managed to say before the flash dazzled her. As the light flashed, Asher threw up his arm, shielding his face. She saw it only because she had quickly turned her own face away, hiding her left cheek.

"Damn, I'll have to do another one," the dumb kid said, winding the film on.

Asher stood up. "How many have you taken with that roll?"

"What?" The kid had a rash of pimples on his forehead and protruding front teeth. Bucky, Charlee remembered. They called him Bucky, and he was as much of a freak at school as she was. He was also as dumb as a box of rocks, or so she had heard.

"I said, do you remember who you've taken a photo of, on that roll?" Asher asked, tapping the camera.

Bucky considered. "Sure," he said. "I've only taken two others."

"Great. Can I see that?" Asher took the camera from Bucky's hands and opened up the back.

"Hey! You'll ruin the film!"

Asher pulled out the roll and grabbed the end of the film and unreeled it from the canister, exposing it. "I'll buy you another roll of film," he said, looking steadily at the boy. "So you can retake the other two photos you just took. But you don't take any photos of Charlee. She objects to it. Do we understand each other?"

"Hey, man, there's no need to get so mad!" Bucky snatched back his camera as Asher closed the back of it. "Jeez…."

Asher patted Bucky's shoulder as he pocketed the exposed film. "You need to ask before you take photographs. Not everyone likes it."

"Sure." Bucky moved away, glaring at Asher over his shoulder.

Asher sat down again and glanced at her. Charlee gave him a stiff smile. She hadn't wanted her photo taken because of the scar. She had been caught off-guard and not given time to compose herself, to brace herself for the inevitable. But Asher had thrown up *his* arm even as she had reacted. He hadn't wanted his photo taken any more than she had.

She sat quietly, sipping her almost lukewarm pop, reacquainting herself with facts that felt like ancient history.

He's a superhero, she reminded herself and realized that it had been a very long time, *years*, since she had thought of Asher's real identity in any sort of terms at all. The superhero label seemed childish now, but there was nothing else to take its place. They didn't talk about it. She didn't know what to call him. She didn't know what he was, except that he wasn't normal.

For the first time, she wondered if he was even human.

The fast electronic bebop tune ended, and the lights dropped to their lazy flicker as Peter Frampton started singing "Baby, I love Your Way." Asher picked up her hand, and she let herself be led out onto the dance floor.

She had got over the shock of being in his arms. Sort of. But this time she barely noticed. Her thoughts were keeping her attention fixed firmly upon those things they had never spoken of. The mysteries that surrounded him.

Who is Asher? Really?

"You've gone very quiet," he said. "Are you not having fun anymore?"

"I don't know what tonight is, but it's not what I define as fun," she said truthfully.

"Retribution?" he suggested, his brow lifting. He was watching her with frank interest, waiting for her answer.

She shook her head. "It's more like turning my back on them. All of them."

He frowned.

"A symbolic walking away," she added. "In four weeks' time, I will literally walk away. I don't know why adults look back at high school like it was some magical time of their life. Most of the kids I know have hated it. Me, too."

"I think most adults look back at the lack of responsibility and the freedom from cares and concerns they have now, and think of it as a pleasant time in comparison to current life."

He hadn't referred to his own experience. She pushed a little harder. "Is that how you remember high school?"

His gaze was direct. "I don't think about high school at all," he said flatly, and she knew it was the truth. But what did it mean?

He brought her around in a big circle, and she saw with distant interest that Chrissy and Daphne and Marcy Graham were watching her with hawk-like interest from their joined tables, where their boyfriends were yukking it up together at one end, ignoring their girls. Chrissy was not smiling.

Charlee hadn't cared much what Chrissy thought of her. At least that was what Charlee had told herself for the last three years. But right now she *really* didn't care. Chrissy and her mean way of making sure the freaks of the school were kept in their place was so trivial in the grand scheme things, Chrissy could have been an ant waving her fist at the express train about to pass her by. Chrissy was nothing.

Magic was real. Superheroes existed. The world was a lot stranger than Chrissy and her snotty friends realized. But Charlee knew. Out of everyone in the gym, she was the one to know.

Know what, exactly?

She looked up at Asher, leaning back a little so that she could see him properly. "I never did thank you for saving Chocolate, did I?"

He looked surprised. Then amused. "*Now* you're getting around to it?" His tone was teasing.

"I don't think I really understood what you did, that day. Not then. I was too young. Now I can see it a little better. Especially the Lords. The risks you took."

His teasing smile faded. "Don't mention it." And she knew he really meant "*Do NOT mention it.*"

"That's your life, isn't it?" Her anger seemed to come from nowhere. "Secrets. All of it is just one secret after another." Why on earth was she becoming angry? But it was there, writhing in her chest, stealing her breath and making her feel warmer than even dancing with him made her feel.

"Charlee..." he began with a reasonable tone, as if he was going to soothe her down like some upset kid. She glared at him, daring him to try, to once more smooth this out and paper over the lies. His eyes met hers and he didn't finish the sentence. Instead he drew a breath that made his chest lift. He shook his head. Just a little. "I *can't*," he said flatly. Softly. So softly she barely heard it even over the subdued music.

"Bullshit," she said hotly. "You just *like* being a superhero. But you stopped being Superman for me a long time ago. You're just...you're just...." She couldn't finish it because the truth slammed into her, whole and complete. But that was something that couldn't be said either.

She wrenched herself out of his arms and hurried to the ladies' room to hide in one of the cubicles and let the heat flushing through her dissipate in the cooler air in there.

She couldn't love him. It wasn't the way it was supposed to work. He was so much older than her. She was seventeen, for heaven's sake. She was supposed to have crushes on boys like Tommy Hancock, and it was true that she and Elizabeth had discovered how cute he was about the same time at the beginning of their senior year. But that wasn't the same thing at all.

She had looked at Asher and *felt* her love, like a thick, syrupy layer over her thoughts and feelings. It colored everything. It was simply there.

After ten minutes, she forced herself to step out of the stall and wash her hands at the basin. She wanted to splash water on her face, but that would ruin the carefully applied makeup hiding her scar—well, diminishing it to a fine line, anyway. Instead, she wetted down a paper towel and dabbed it to the back of her neck and her shoulders, letting natural evaporation cool her instead.

The girls standing gossiping in the corners and around the other basins took no notice of her, but she could hear that their talking was slower and more sporadic until she opened the door and stepped out, and then it fired up to machine gun level.

Asher was pacing by the front doors, his tie unravelled and lying on his shirt. "Charlee, for heaven's sake!" He came striding over to meet her. "Don't ever run off like that," he told her. "Especially to the goddamn ladies' room. I can't protect you there."

"Is that what I am?" she asked curiously. "Someone you have to protect at all costs?"

He straightened up, like she had slapped him. Shock skittered over his face.

"Never mind," she said tiredly. "Forget I said that. It wasn't fair."

"Why not?" he asked, his shock gone. Genuine curiosity had replaced it.

She rubbed her arms with her hands. "Could we go?" she asked. "I've had enough of getting even, if you don't mind."

"Of course. I'll get your wrap." He turned toward the coat check counter, digging into his pocket for the ticket.

Charlee watched him go, trying to see him the way the rest of the world would see him. A tall man with big shoulders, very pale hair and the blue eyes that seemed to be what women focused upon first. A successful businessman who didn't seem to have a life outside of his restaurant and occasional visits to the bank that carried his name.

But she couldn't see him like that. She might not have consciously thought of him as a superhero for a very long time, but the secret was firmly entrenched in her psyche. It colored every dealing she had with him. Every exchange. It had brought them step by step, month by month, to this moment. The secrets in his life had more power than the surface reality.

Asher dropped her wrap around her shoulders and opened the door for her. They stepped out into air that felt delightfully cool in comparison to the crowded gym. Behind them, muted by walls and doors and bodies, Sheryl Crow was crooning that all she wanted to do was have some fun.

That had never been Charlee's ambition. Getting to college, like Lucas and Darwin kept coaxing her to do, had filled her days and nights for years now.

There were already cabs waiting at the curb, and Asher opened the back door of one for her. She slid onto the seat and Asher gave the driver her address. Silence settled back around them.

Charlee watched the view slide past. So ordinary. So mundane.

If Asher was different, and the few facts that she had confirmed that yes, he was very different from the average person, then how different was he? Were there even more differences hiding behind the shield of secrets? Would she be shocked? Terrified? But she didn't believe that; the little that Asher let the world and her see of him, the small amount she really knew, told her that he was kind and considerate. He cared. Those weren't the characteristics of a monster. He wouldn't change his entire personality once he took off the mask. She had to believe he was essentially the same man, regardless of what hid behind the mask.

If he was very different, or even if he was just a little bit different, wouldn't that mean the rules the normal world followed didn't apply to him? Well, yes, she already knew that. The image flickered in her mind, barely registering, of his sword and the way it had just appeared and then disappeared. *Magic*.

She shivered and pulled the wrap even more closely around her. As a coat, it sucked, but it was all she had.

Asher wasn't normal. She didn't even know if he was human, although he seemed *very* human to her. But if he wasn't normal, then maybe the rules about falling in love with someone like him didn't apply either.

It's just a crush, she told herself firmly, as hope swelled in her chest almost painfully. *In two weeks, you'll have forgotten all about this.*

But she knew it was more than a crush. Just like Asher, she wasn't normal. Not anymore. Not since he had come into her life. She had bypassed normal teenage crushes.

The cab slowed and came to a halt at the house before Darwin's. Close enough.

"Hey," Asher said as she reached for the door. She felt his hand on her shoulder and looked over it at him.

He wasn't smiling.

"Thank you for taking me to the prom," she told him.

"You're still angry."

She turned on the seat to face him properly. "No. Not anymore."

"You're not happy. Tonight was supposed to make you happy."

She sighed. "Tonight was perfect," she told him. "It was better than I dared hope it would be, thanks to you."

Asher relaxed, and his smile tugged at one corner of his mouth. "Good. I'm glad."

He had been worried that he had spoiled it for her. The insight let her smile at him. "I can take it from here," she said, reaching for the door handle once more. She knew without discussion that he wouldn't walk her to the door. It was too powerful a symbol.

"Let me." He reached across her and pulled up the lock, the reason she hadn't been able to get the door open in the first place.

He had been closer to her when they had been dancing, but that had been in a cavernous gym, among five hundred other people. In the close confines of the backseat of the cab, his closeness was intimate. Private. His scent washed over her, and her nerve endings all shot awake, sizzling. Charlee drew in a breath that seemed to pull into her lungs in a hot, miasmic soup.

The door opened, washing them both with air that seemed frigid, as Asher drew back. Their eyes met as he straightened up. They met and locked.

It was a moment of perfect understanding. Charlee often wondered what Asher was thinking, but not right now. She *knew*, and she knew that he knew what was in her mind. The kiss hung between them, a throbbing, unspoken and unfulfilled wish.

She just had to lean forward. She knew that if she did, he would complete the action. He would take her head in his hands and his lips would meet hers. All she had to do was lean. Her lips were already parted; it was the only way she could breathe.

"That'll be ten and a quarter," the cab driver said.

But that didn't shatter the moment the way it would have in a movie or a book. The tension between them wasn't a delicate thing. It was alive and growing with each passing second.

Asher's hand, where it rested on the back of the front seat, curled into a fist, his knuckles whitening. "Go," he breathed.

Before it's too late. She understood what he had not said as clearly as if he had spoken the words.

"It's already too late." She slid out of the cab, but not before she saw his eyes widen.

Deliberately, she turned and walked to the front door, pulling out her keys, her back to the cab, which didn't move. She made herself step inside and shut the door without looking back, but once the door was safely closed, she let herself sink down onto the little stool Darwin used when he was putting on his shoes to go out.

She was shaking, and it wasn't a good feeling. It made her feel sick. All the moments she had shared with Asher were flickering across her mind like a movie, or one of those sentimental look-backs they did for the Oscars, all the long-gone but great moments playing out while soppy music ran.

"Hey, you're back!" Darwin said, coming down the stairs. He was already in his dressing gown and slippers, his skinny ankles showing below the hem of the tartan gown.

Charlee looked up at him, her reaction fading and the one fact her quick jolt through the past had given her at the forefront of her mind. "He hasn't aged," she told Darwin.

He came to a halt in front of her, puzzled. "Asher?"

"No grey hair. No wrinkles. He still looks exactly the same as the day we met."

Darwin considered her with an expression that held no surprise. He nodded, like she was confirming something he had already known.

They looked at each other. It was a night for clear communications, Charlee thought, for she knew exactly what Darwin was thinking, too.

What hid behind the mask called Asher Strand?

Chapter Nineteen

"The role of the Eldre was originally shaped by the strictures laid down by *laun*, which is to say, exclusion and a life lived as humanly possible. Perhaps because of their isolation, the Eldre have emerged as a force for knowledge, learning and above all, *change*."

Ylva Fedya Baxter, "An Interview With Ylva Fedya Baxter," *New York Times* Sunday Supplement, February 2016

Asher slipped into the darkened room and stood at the back, listening as the graduates' names were called. "Rick Lemora," was the next one called. So they were still to come to the Ms. He hadn't missed her walking across the stage.

He looked around the very full auditorium. There were parents standing at the back and along the sides, just like he was. He looked for Darwin, who would be easy to spot because of his height, working systematically from the front row to the back, and finally found him standing on the right side, a camera in his hands. He was watching Asher and as Asher spotted him, he nodded and turned his attention back to the stage.

So did Asher. There was a sinuous line of kids in caps and gowns, from the far right of the stage, snaking back to the wings and on into the dark. Charlee's graduating class had over four hundred kids in it. It would take a while for them to all cross the stage, take their diplomas and shake the principal's hand. But Asher could already see Charlee in the lineup. She was taller than anyone next to her and stood like a slender sapling, watching the others walk the stage rather than talking to anyone. Her hair had been looped up into some sort of elegant knot at the back of her head, beneath the brim of the mortar board cap. Even capped and gowned in identical fashion to everyone else, she still stood out like neon.

Finally, her name was called. She walked across the stage, her long legs swinging easily under the gown, and shook York's hand with a small nod of her head. It was as if she were choosing to accept the diploma.

Asher found he was clapping harder than anyone around him, the heat and tension in his chest catching him by surprise. *I'm just proud of her*, he told himself. And he was. But the degree and fierceness of his pride puzzled him.

Once Charlee had climbed down the steps and was seated with the other graduates, Darwin worked his way past the other standing parents until he reached Asher's side. "Step out for a minute," he said shortly.

They pushed passed waiting parents and went out into the foyer. There were more people out here, too. Darwin went over to the seat in the lounge area. The bar itself was closed, the metal grill rolled down and padlocked, the area behind it dark.

Darwin threw himself into one of the chairs and waved to the other.

"Something you couldn't discuss over the phone?" Asher asked, sitting down.

"I don't trust those cellphone things," Darwin said. "Who's to stop people from listening in?"

"It doesn't work like a CB radio."

"I wanted to see your face when I told you, anyway," Darwin said.

"Tell me what?"

"She's not going to college." Darwin scowled.

"Why the hell not?" Asher demanded. "She's been dreaming, working toward it for years! What happened?"

"You tell me, hero."

Asher caught his breath. "What?"

"What?" Darwin asked, puzzled.

"What did you just call me?"

"A polite form of asshole. This has something to do with you."

"Her not going to college? I haven't spoken to her for weeks." Not since the prom. Not since he had nearly kissed her. Even now, just thinking about it made his heart start thudding and not in a good way. He savagely shoved the memory away and looked at Darwin expectantly. He certainly had not talked her out of college. Of course she had to go.

"She says she's going to live with Ylva. Some sort of apprenticeship. I can't even get my head around it." Darwin's distress was showing in his voice. For him to not understand something must be a rare thing.

But Asher understood now. He looked right though Darwin, putting it together. Ylva and Charlee had kept in touch since she had left the restaurant. That was to be expected. They had been close. But what had Ylva told Charlee? What had the power to make Charlee want to give up on college and work at Ylva's? The apprenticeships Ylva put the newly recruited Amica through were tough, both physically and mentally. The compensation Ylva would have had to have dangled to convince Charlee life in Ylva's house was better than a degree and a career must have been powerful indeed.

"I'll kill her," Asher muttered.

"Charlee?" Darwin asked, concerned.

"Ylva. She talked her out of college somehow."

"Then you didn't?"

Asher rolled his eyes. "Of course I didn't. College is the best place for Charlee to be now." *Best and safest, for it was far away from him.* He stood up. "I'll talk to her."

"Charlee?" Darwin asked again.

"Ylva."

"Isn't it Charlee who is making the decision here?"

"Have you ever had any success talking Charlee out of something once her mind was made up?" Asher asked.

Darwin sucked at his teeth with his tongue. "Nope," he admitted easily.

"I want to find out what Ylva told her. I might be able to do something, once I know what Charlee thinks she'll get out of living there." He pulled out his cellphone and dialed Ylva's number.

Darwin's face scrunched up. "I don't know which one I'd least like to talk to about this," he said. "Seems to me that Ylva might get just as stroppy as Charlee over it."

Asher looked at Darwin and saw they were both thinking the same thing.

Women.

* * * * *

Ylva tucked her feet up next to her. "Charlee asked me, Asher. I thought she was heading for Harvard in September, too."

Asher sank down onto the arm of the lounge chair sitting next to her sofa, most of his anger evaporated by surprise. "She talked to you? Do you know why she won't go to college, then? Is it a matter of money?" Money could be found. There was always a way around money.

"She was offered a full scholarship to Harvard. All she would have had to find would be living expenses, and I would have paid those in a heartbeat," Ylva said. "It's not money. She wants to stay in New York."

"There are colleges here."

"I don't think they'll teach her what she wants to learn," Ylva said placidly.

Cold fingers walked their way up his spine. "You can't teach her that! There's *laun*, she's not Amica. They'll kill you both."

"I am not beholden to the Kine anymore, remember?"

"You know that makes no difference when it comes to *laun*. She's not Amica." Fresh horror gripped him. "She's not being recruited? Please say she isn't."

Ylva tipped her head to one side. "Isn't that exactly what you promised Stefan and the seniors, a few years ago? When Charlee came of age, you told them you would have her recruited into the Amica to preserve *laun*."

"Yes, but how did you know that?" he demanded.

"You are not the only Kine who continues to speak to me," Ylva replied.

Asher stood up, unable to stay still. "You're recruiting her?"

Ylva considered him for a long, silent moment, while his heart tried to rip itself out of his chest.

"No," she said at last. "It isn't my place to recruit the Amica for you. I merely train those who have already volunteered. If Charlee wants to become one, later on, I won't stop her. It will be her decision, and I will ensure it is an informed one." She lifted her hand. "Do not ask me again about whether I intend to break *laun*, Asher. You do not need to know that."

Fear was a runaway train in his chest, making his heart work like an overheated piston. "You'll put her in danger. You know the penalties as well as I do. Better than I do."

"Charlee will be quite safe with me," Ylva said serenely. "Safer than she would be with you."

"With me?"

"Charlee is irrevocably a part of our world now, Asher. She knows that and she has convinced me of it. You may not have intended to do so, but your protection has brought her into our shadow. Secrecy will no longer serve her. Knowledge will protect her and give her choices. She might yet enjoy a semblance of a life that she would not otherwise have." Ylva seemed sad. "She no longer can have a human life. That is impossible now."

Asher pushed his hands through his hair. "How can she know that? How can *you*? If I leave, if we step right out of her life, it isn't too late."

"Could you really do that, Asher?" Ylva asked gently. "Could you leave, move somewhere she would never find you, and pretend you never met her? Let her wonder and worry about you for the rest of her life?"

"I'd...I'd say goodbye first," he said weakly. "Make it clean," he added. But he was lying. He couldn't do that to Charlee.

"She wouldn't let you," Ylva said. "Charlee worries about you. She worries about the parts of you she doesn't know, as much as the parts you've let her see."

Asher walked toward the window but found he was walking in a tight circle. He stopped and reached for calm. "What did Charlee tell you, to talk you into thinking this was a good idea?" he asked. That was the final piece of the puzzle. That was what he had come here to learn, although he had thought it was something that Ylva had told Charlee.

Ylva simply studied him, a sad smile on her face.

Asher closed his eyes. "No." He shook his head, trying to deny the swirl of pain circling through him. "Not Charlee," he said hoarsely. Helplessly.

"Do you see, now, why she must learn it all? She must learn everything, so that she understands as well as you do," Ylva replied.

Her logic was irrefutable.

* * * * *

Charlee slipped off her high heels and rubbed her toes. They were beautiful shoes, but they killed her feet, and she had been on them for hours. "He didn't want to stay and see me?" she asked.

Darwin pushed her gown aside. She had dropped it onto the table, her cap on top, then sat down and immediately got rid of the shoes. He slid the cap and gown off the end of the table so they dropped onto the seat of the chair, put the big mug of hot chocolate in front of her and sat opposite, his own smaller mug between his hands.

"I think he was too upset to want to speak to you." He grinned.

"Did it work? Did upsetting him make him slip up? Did he give away anything?"

Darwin sipped. "You were right about the 'hero' thing. He would have spit up his dinner if he'd been eating." Then his smile faded. "But digging up the facts about Asher Strand is kind of redundant, now, isn't it? You're off to Ylva's to get the dirt wholesale."

Charlee squeezed his arm. "I'll still come home to visit when I can. It'll be exactly the same as if I had gone to Boston."

Darwin shook his head. "No, it won't," he said gently. "You said Asher had changed you. Well, if we're even half right about what we think Asher is, and the secrets behind the mask, then this is going to change you even more. You might come back to visit once in a while, but this won't be home for you."

"I'll still love you," she told him softly.

"Get on with you," he said, and rolled his eyes.

She grinned and stuck her tongue out at him, then drank her hot chocolate.

It was a moment she would remember clearly and sadly for the rest of her life, for they hadn't been close to right, and what they had guessed had been only a tiny corner of a reality they couldn't possibly have suspected was there.

It was also one of the last moments of her youth.

"Are you sure about this, Charlee?" Darwin asked. "There's still time.

You could still talk to Harvard."

She gave Darwin the same answer she had given Asher in the cab, after her prom. "It's too late." Then she tried to explain, because Darwin deserved it and he was upset. "I think it became too late eight years ago, when I saw his sword and he swore me to secrecy. I think that locked it in. I was never going to be normal after that."

A week later, she took up residence in Ylva's house.

NEW WORLD

Chapter Twenty

"The Amica train harder than Navy
SEALs. Anyone who says they are
ornamental should take a year of basic
Amica training…if they last the year."
Anonymous comment.
"And that makes them different from
the average soccer mom how?"
Anonymous response.
"They get paid."
Anonymous reply.

Huffington Post, "Who Are the Amica, Really?",
June 2016.

The next six years didn't just fly by for Charlee. They slipped away unnoticed, exiting stage left while the focus of her attention was on center stage.

"You'll work harder than you've ever worked in your life," Ylva had warned Charlee the first few days she had moved in to the tiny room in the basement of the house, where there were at least a dozen other similar rooms, all occupied. "You'll become a virtual slave to the older Amica, and—"

"What are the Amica?"

"That's something you'll learn eventually. You're starting very much behind the other women. They come to the program with a solid understanding of our world, and they are already committed to becoming one of the Amica. You don't even know what our world is. You will have to catch up by yourself. I will expect you to carry your full share of responsibilities and keep up with your studies to an acceptable level of accomplishment. The gaps in your knowledge you will have to fill in your spare time, and there will not be a lot of it." She smiled a little more kindly. "If I do not hold you to the same standards as the others, Charlee, they will resent you."

But she had been resented, anyway, even though it felt like she was working twice as hard as any of them, just to keep up. She was not a full Amica recruit. She was merely a human to whom Ylva had offered the full benefits of her training.

It took years for Charlee to even begin to understand what Ylva's full training encompassed and why being privy to such training would cause such resentment.

Ylva had not exaggerated about the amount of work each day presented. Her house was a large three-story on Fifth Avenue, but the human world and its petty concerns stopped at the black oak door and the world of the Kine, the Herleifr, took over.

The house was very nearly self-sufficient. It drew a little water, gas and electricity from the mains, enough to keep authorities satisfied that all was as it should be. But Ylva had installed banks of solar power panels on the other side of the roof garden when she had moved in, and most of the house's power came from these panels, and all of its heating.

It was the job of the newest recruit to clean the panels daily, regardless of the weather, and in winter when the snow fell it was a miserable and thankless task that Charlee struggled through, sweating under her parka, while her fingers turned red with the cold and she lost feeling in the tips.

It was also the newest recruit's responsibility to see to the kitchen fires. Charlee had been astonished to find that most of the first floor of the house was given over to a large kitchen workroom that featured a blazing fire in the middle of the floor. There were also two big, black iron ranges that the cook needed burning at all times. Charlee had to learn how to manage the ranges by the feeding of wood and the controlling of the vents, so that they were able to leap from fresh flames to the hot, glowing coals that produced the steadiest and hottest ovens for the cook.

In between stoking the ovens, Charlee's duties in the kitchen also involved scrubbing dishes, for Ylva's kitchen did not feature anything like a dishwasher or an electric or even a gas oven. Charlee also scrubbed the floor and walls and kept the big wooden work tables cleaner and more sterile than an operating theater, all while listening to and watching the Amica trainees working at the other big tables on the other side of the kitchen, through the arch.

When the cook, whose name was Skuld, deemed that Charlee had sufficiently grasped the fundamentals of keeping a kitchen clean and orderly, she had moved her to the beginner's table on the other side of the kitchen.

Another Amica was given responsibility for the ovens, although Charlee continued to clean the solar panels. Once she had come inside each morning, she would present herself at her table and Skuld would tell her what she wanted from her for the day.

Charlee's starting responsibilities included peeling and preparing vegetables, something she had considered she was already adept at doing, as she had been prepping vegetables at home for years. She learned very quickly that she barely understood the first thing about such a lowly task.

The vegetables had to be cleaned properly. This usually involved soaking in a solution of vinegar and water. The vinegar was made here in this big kitchen, but that was an advanced skill Skuld would pass on to only the most gifted Amica. As most of the vegetables came directly from the roof garden, picked carefully by a pair of Amica for the ideal degree of ripeness, they usually required scrubbing as well as soaking.

Charlee wondered if the top layer of the skin on her hands would flake away as she had them constantly immersed in the acidic solution, but Skuld had given her a little glass pot of ointment with no label and told her to rub it in each night before bed. The ointment, which smelled like nothing she had ever sniffed, kept her skin soft despite the vinegar.

Skuld was a martinet about vegetable preparation and would stand over Charlee's table, lecturing about the proper way to hold a knife, the proper way to slice carrots, wash lettuce, and more. But Charlee was not the only one Skuld would shriek at. One of the other tables was reserved exclusively for the preparation of meats, and that table was scoured and sterilized obsessively. One of the big tables was used mostly for the preservation of things: bottling vegetables, pickling everything, drying and curing. In late summer and into the fall, the work on that table spilled over to the others as the produce from the garden on the roof and produce bought from the fresh organic food market at wholesale prices was prepped and preserved and the long rows of bottles and cans, barrels and bags were stored in the root cellar. The produce in the root cellar would feed the entire household for the coming winter.

Charlee's afternoons were filled with cleaning. The entire house was cleaned from top to bottom by the more junior Amica. There was a year-long schedule that was consulted daily. *Clean* by Amica standards was a standard that Charlee had never even dreamed was possible. The cleaning schedule included seasonal maintenance, and Charlee's education leapt upwards when each Amica armed herself with toolkits that included hammers, saws, pry-bars and more, and took to installing storm windows, repairing wiring, cleaning gutters, fixing hot air ducts and more. There were no men in Ylva's house, but it was a better maintained and working house than any Charlee had ever known.

After a year, Charlee was moved out of the kitchen and into the one other workroom on the main floor, long before Skuld was even close to being pleased with her skills enough to move her onto one of the other tables.

The other workroom was simply called 'the store' by the Amica. It took Charlee a few days to realize that they meant "store" in the sense that the room was a storage facility and a place where things could be acquired. What things?

Charlee's earliest tasks in the store were once again cleaning and maintenance, and she learned that yet another level of clean existed. The need for cleanliness and sterility were even more necessary in the store, for it was here that, for example, the ointment she had used on her hands to prevent drying from the vinegar solution was prepared.

There were dozens and dozens of ointments, salves, lotions and preparations made in the store, and Charlee was quite certain that she was seeing only a small portion of the range of possible products. They encompassed simple beauty treatments, such as skin cleansers, toners, tighteners and moisturizers, and even makeup, to household cleansers, to preparations for washing laundry and people. Charlee's first solo project was to make more of the pretty-smelling soap they used, and she completely ruined the mixture, resulting in a foul pot of oozing fat. The carbolic mixture had reddened her hands beyond the help of moisturizers. A week later, her skin had peeled. But by then, she had produced another batch of soap that had passed inspection.

The store also made products that were medicinal in nature, but Charlee learned this only by listening in to the Amica working at the other benches over fresh blueberries and their leaves and stems, and realized that what they were making was a painkiller that far surpassed anything Tylenol could claim to ease. Her attention was caught, for she was reminded sharply of the big bed in the quiet room, and Ylva's soft command to relax and sleep while she worked at Charlee's wounded face. The whatever-it-was they had made her sniff had knocked her out as efficiently as any operating room injection.

After the soap incident, Charlee was shown how to make a simple kohl preparation that nearly everyone in the house used as eye liner. In its more liquid form, by adjusting the amount of wax and oil, and other ingredients, it became mascara.

Other more complex projects were given to her by Silia, who supervised the store. Charlee began to realize that the formal training she had been waiting to begin had started the day she stepped into the house with her single duffel bag. There was no such thing as formal training here. There were no classrooms. The teachers were Amica who knew more than she did, and everyone learned by doing. It was a highly practical apprenticeship.

After that, Charlee found her arduous duties a little easier to bear. She began to ask questions about everything she did, as that was how she would learn not just what she was to do, but *why*.

In her third year, Charlee was still working in the store, but she had advanced through beauty products and household products, on to very basic medicinals and health preparations. It was there that Charlee realized her learning would be sharpest, for in order to properly understand how the preparations worked, she needed to know advanced anatomy and biology, plus a good grounding in chemistry and hands-on medicine. She realized she was learning by practice what a good country doctor would have known in the nineteenth century.

But she did no book-learning. Everything was explained to her as she did the work. Silia or one of the more senior Amica would walk her through the first repetition, telling her about the preparation, what it was used for, secondary uses that it might be useful for, plus side effects. There were no serious side effects, unless the patient had a severe allergy to the common ingredients they used, as the preparations were non-toxic and depended more upon the mysterious powers of plants and herbs to do their curing than the stringent and harsh power of chemicals.

Shortly into her third year in the house, Ylva sent for Charlee.

Charlee brushed off her hands and then washed them carefully, for she had been making a coagulant and it could tighten the surface of her skin up painfully if she let it dry there. Then she peered in the mirror to ensure her appearance was suitable and made her way up to Ylva's office on the second floor.

Charlee passed through the front sitting room into the office itself. Ylva was reading one of the big, ancient tomes that were kept on the shelves in here and accessed by no one without her permission.

Ylva took off her glasses and smiled at her. "Charlee, it's been a while since I saw you. You're looking well."

"They said you went away," Charlee said.

"Up to the north of the state for a few days, visiting an old friend." Ylva smiled. "Are you happy, Charlee?"

Charlee considered the question. "Yes," she said, surprised. "Very." And she was. She was learning so much, and endless questions were welcomed. Where else could she have got to dabble in dozens of pools of knowledge, feeding her curiosity with an endless supply of things she didn't know, that she hadn't dreamed existed.

"Are the older Amica still running you off your feet?"

When she had first begun here, the more senior Amica *had* resented her, just as Ylva had predicted. As the more senior of them supervised the younger Amica, they took their resentment out upon her by giving Charlee the worst, the dirtiest and the hardest duties. She had been a slave to their every wish.

"Not anymore," Charlee told Ylva. "I think they quit because I wouldn't complain."

"Good for you. Silia and Skuld report very favorably about you." She picked up her glasses and wrote on the paper in front of her, next to the big book, and tore the sheet off. "I want you to run an errand for me.

The address is on the outside of the note. Deliver the note to the address."

Charlee looked at the address. "I can walk from here."

"Yes, it's a pleasant twenty minutes from here. Ask for Anja. Take your coat. It's brisk out today."

It *was* brisk, and very nice to be out in the fresh air. Some of the Amica were responsible for the rooftop garden and spent most of their summer mornings weeding and planting. It seemed to be very pleasant work. Charlee wondered when and even if that duty would become hers. She didn't fret about it, though. Ylva's house and the schedules and routines and even the structure of one's apprenticeship were organic and cyclic. Sooner or later, Charlee would be ready to learn the lessons imparted from the responsibility of feeding the household.

She didn't get out of the house very often. There was no restriction upon leaving the house. It was simply that her duties were long and hard and she didn't have the energy to socialize or even go shopping after that. She had money, if she needed it. On top of the room and board that Ylva provided, she paid a small stipend to each Amica for the work they did to keep the household running. But Charlee didn't need to buy anything, for everything she could possibly need could be found right there in the house. It was made, or there was no need for it.

So she enjoyed being out of the house for the change it brought, but the hurried and harried pedestrians looked sour, and the sound of the traffic along Fifth Avenue was louder than she ever remembered it being.

When she reached the address she was looking for, she found it was a big, boxy building with few windows on the ground floor. It was made of red brick and was an ugly, squat thing with three floors. Weeds grew out of the cracks in the sidewalk.

Tentatively, she knocked on the iron door that seemed to be the main door. There was no buzzer. After a few minutes of steady knocking, the door opened and a girl who couldn't have been much older than Charlee looked out. "Hi."

Charlee checked the name on the folded note. "I'm looking for Anja."

The girl stepped back and opened the door so Charlee could come through. "You shoulda come round the back. Back's always open," she said, her Bronx thicker than Charlee's had ever been.

Charlee looked at her again. "Are you...?" Then she halted. She had no idea where she was, or where this building fit into Ylva's world. She had to be cautious until she understood more.

"I'm Bree," the girl said and gave her a quick smile. Bree was wearing a pair of pants and a tailored shirt that looked incredibly expensive and completely out of place in this old building. "C'mon, I'll take you to Anja." She led Charlee through a short, dim passageway and pushed open another door. The door gave onto a factory-sized room that rose right through all three floors. The windows in the second and third floors spilled natural light onto the room. There were dozens of women here, all working over gigantic tables.

And everywhere, there was fabric. There were rolls of the stuff, lying on racks that reached up dozens of feet high. Many more lay on the tables, unrolled enough to spill the fabric across the surface.

Other tables held machinery: sewing machines, cutting machines, and even more machinery whose functions Charlee couldn't even begin to guess at. Then there were racks of finished garments at one end of the room. Charlee couldn't see all of them from the doorway, but the little she could see looked odd.

"Over here," Bree said and walked in between the tables and their operators, waving here and there. She took Charlee over to a woman who had the pure white hair of a very old woman, but her hair hung down to her waist and curled softly. The woman looked up as Charlee approached and Bree waved to her. "This is Anja," Bree said.

Anja seemed to be very young, despite the hair. She looked at Charlee with her brows raised. "Hello," she said cautiously.

Charlee held out the folded note. "It's from Ylva. She asked me to deliver this to you."

Anja unfolded the note and read it quickly. Then she folded it again, and looked Charlee over. "What *are* you wearing?" she asked.

Charlee pulled self-consciously at the sweat pants and T-shirt she wore under the peacoat. "I guess they're house clothes. I work a lot. Physically."

Bree grinned, like she had said something funny.

Anja crossed her arms. "So do I work a lot. Physically. Am I wearing what you're wearing?"

Charlee took in Anja's nicely fitting skirt and the jacket she wore over it. The jacket had three-quarter sleeves, which wouldn't get in the way as she worked. There was a blouse underneath that looked like it might be silk. Charlee could feel herself blushing. "I guess, no. You're not," she replied to Anja.

Anja snorted. "I should think not," she said and twirled her finger in the air. "Turn around."

"Excuse me?"

"Spin. Like a top. I want to see your shape."

"But I should be getting back."

"Ylva has a dozen or more apprentices. She can do without you for now. Turn, I say."

Helplessly, Charlee turned.

"A nice figure," Anja said. "A bit tall and a bit skinny, but workable. Bree, get her working at the beginner's loom."

Bree jerked her head in an unmistakeable 'follow me' movement.

Charlee bit her lip as Anja put her hands on her hips, daring Charlee to refute her order.

Charlee followed Bree instead, who took her over to one of the big, tall, spidery machines that held hundreds of thin threads running up and down the frame. It confirmed what she had suspected. "You actually *weave* cloth here?" she asked Bree.

"Some cloth, for special occasions, but mostly what we get out of beginners like you is cloth for washrooms and test garments." She patted the wide, hard stool. "Have a seat and I'll walk you through it."

Charlee sat. The sun was going down when she stood once more, while Anja inspected the yardage she had created that day. "It's fair to middling," Anja decreed, her nose wrinkling. "I'll show you some tricks tomorrow that'll make it smoother and tighter."

"Tomorrow?"

"Seven sharp," Anja added and walked away.

Charlee apprenticed in Anja's factory for the next year. Anja didn't just make clothing from cloth she and her workers wove. They also spun wool and cotton to make the threads to weave and knit. But they used commercially created fabric, too, for demand for their work was too high to meet otherwise.

As Charlee learned in her year there, Anja's factory also worked with leathers, creating close-fitting, shaped garments in a stiff leather that reminded her strangely of the breastplates and armor that the Romans had worn. When she had asked about this, she had received a short nod from the Amica who was teaching her to cure the hides. "The stiffer the leather, the better it turns knives and spears. We hope that the Einherjar who wears these has sufficient skill to turn a sword with his own sword blade. Still, he would not be an Einherjar if he was not a warrior." She shrugged and moved on with the lesson.

Einherjar was a term Charlee had heard before, but she was still waiting for the opportunity to ask what it meant, for every Amica she met seemed to know. This was one of the areas of insufficient knowledge that Ylva had warned her she would come across.

But there were assumptions she could make without asking. She had only ever heard the Einherjar referred to as "he", so it was a fraternity. A group of men who used swords, spears and knives. Was Asher one?

She had not seen Asher since the prom and in a way, it was a relief.

She was learning too much and had too many pressing questions. It wasn't time for her to see him yet. She had not yet seen fully behind his mask. But she missed him. She missed their weekday check-ins, and the way his smile warmed whenever he saw her walking through the door.

But she was often too busy to miss him. Anja kept Charlee running as fast Ylva ever had. Each morning she would arrive at seven and be put to work, either completing a current project or learning the skills to move onto the next one. For the first half of her year, she had learned how to design, cut and sew garments, including the critically important and complex elements of fit. "Fit is everything," Anja had said during one of the three breaks everyone took during the day. "A perfectly tailored garment that does not fit well will look like garbage and make the wearer look fat and old and ugly. A simple garment, made with perfect fit, will make the wearer look like a princess." Charlee was not the only one to absorb this lesson. The Amica in Anja's factory were all sensitive to not just proper fit, but their appearance overall. Charlee learned that the flawless appearance Bree had presented the day they met was a standard all of them aspired to.

Over the next year, Charlee made herself a large wardrobe of clothes, designed to meet any occasion, to fit her perfectly and to flatter her appearance. The design of the garments and the cloth they were made of was not left to her sole discretion. Each item of clothing was discussed *en group*. The virtues of the design and its practicality and beauty were debated and the design adjusted until it was considered as close to perfect as a mere Amica could get.

For the last three months of the year, she learned more about the making of armor, which was a fascinating study.

It was fall once more when Charlee met Ylva on her way down to the front door to head for Anja's factory. Ylva was standing inside the birdcage and called Charlee's name softly.

Charlee halted at the bottom of the stone staircase, her breath catching, for there was a falcon sitting on Ylva's outstretched arm.

Charlee crept toward the bars. "Oh, he's beautiful!"

"Step into the cage," Ylva told her. "Help me feed him."

"But I'm late for—" She shook her head. It didn't matter. She wouldn't pass up this opportunity to feed a real, live falcon. She draped her coat over the balustrade and stepped slowly into the cage and shut the door. The falcon flapped his wings, but Ylva crooned to him and he settled down again.

"Should I put on a glove?" Charlee asked.

"Do you feel you need to?"

But Charlee couldn't take her eyes away from the proud head of the falcon, the big hooked beak and the barrel chest, spotted with black and white feathers. She realized she was picking up the food only when the coolness of the raw meat registered on her fingers.

She made a fist around the meat, so that it poked from the top of her fist like a posy of flowers and held it out toward the falcon. He looked at her, assessing, then bent and tore at the meat.

Charlee realized she was grinning like a little kid.

"He's been visiting for about a week now," Ylva said quietly. "I think he's looking for somewhere to nest for the winter. I would like you to step into the cage each day and see that he's fed. Skuld will give you meat and seed for the others."

As the falcon took another bite at the meat, Charlee tilted her head back and looked up at the top of the cage. In all but the very worst weather, the skylight that opened the cage up to the fresh air was kept open. In winter, all but one pane was closed, and the pane that was left open had a flap that spun open and shut like a spindle. The wild birds that knew about the cage knew how to dive through the flap, hitting it with their beaks so that it would turn and let them through. It let them access the cage all year round.

"You want me to feed the birds?"

"Yes, please," Ylva said. She still hadn't moved her arm. The falcon gripped her wrist through the leather guard she was wearing, at ease with both of them. "And while I have your attention, Charlee, Lucas is home."

Quick delight filled her. "At Darwin's?"

"He had a week's leave. I told him when he phoned this morning that I would send you home to visit."

"Will it be alright for me to go?"

Ylva was watching the falcon and didn't turn her head. "You've made good progress, Charlee, despite your lack of grounding in the subjects you've been exposed to. I think a few days off won't hurt."

"I can't feed the birds while I'm gone."

"They'll be here when you come back." Ylva looked at her then, and smiled. "You will be back."

It didn't sound like a question, but Charlee answered it that way. "You know I will. Nothing would make me stay away, now."

Chapter Twenty-One

Einherjar
In Norse mythology, the **einherjar** (Old Norse "single (or once) fighters"[1]) are those that have died in battle and are brought to Valhalla by valkyries.
Wikipedia.

"God, look at you!" Lucas exclaimed. He stepped back from hugging her and looked her over from head to toe. "You look amazing. Whatever Ylva is teaching you, I'd say it's agreeing with you."

He looked very good himself. He had filled out around the chest and shoulders, and especially through the neck. He was tanned and looked fit and... Charlee reached for just the right word and found it. He looked *hard*. Seasoned. It was his second year in the SEALs. "I'd say life is agreeing with you, too," she said.

"Ah, you know, jumping from twenty thousand feet every month tends to keep you appreciating the small stuff. Like being home for a visit. Have you seen how grey Darwin is? He must miss you."

Darwin grinned. He stood behind Lucas. "I don't miss her hogging the popcorn in the slightest. Coffee is on, Charlee. Come and sit down and tell us all about it. I've been trying to explain to Lucas and not doing too well."

Charlee caught Darwin's eye as they walked into the kitchen, and he shook his head. Then Asher's secrets were safe. He hadn't passed them on to Lucas.

The Amica in Ylva's house had a standard cover story for curious humans that Charlee borrowed shamelessly. As they settled at the battered table and while Darwin poured coffee for them all, Charlee explained about the home economics and domestic science apprenticeship she was completing, including all the non-mysterious hard work, the drudgery, the teasing of the older students and the study.

"Hell, it sounds like high school all over again," Lucas said, sitting back, slightly baffled. "I thought you would have wanted to leave all that behind."

"I *like* it now," Charlee said flatly. "I like what I'm learning. I like the people. And the teasing is never cruel." She realized she was touching her scar and put her hand down.

"Well, I can't argue with the results. I don't think I've ever seen you quite so...." He shrugged.

"Content," Darwin supplied.

Lucas nodded. "She's glowing, almost." He crossed his arms over his chest, still leaning back. "Seen Asher lately?" he asked.

Charlee almost jumped. Almost. She had been expecting a question about Asher, but her heart still leapt. "Not since the prom," she said. "Too busy."

"I thought you two were glued at the hip or something."

Darwin stood up. "I'll get lunch going. There some chili in the freezer and I've got buns."

"Ah, hell, let's go out somewhere nice," Lucas said. "Not that your home-cooking isn't just like home-cooking, Darwin. But I've been dreaming about the chicken dinner at Scachi's since I got my leave approved."

Charlee jumped up. "That sounds great. Let me get changed and we can go straight away."

Lucas didn't seem to notice the shift in subject, and Asher wasn't mentioned again.

After a long lunch, on the way home, Lucas started yawning heavily. "I'm still on London time," he confessed. "Do either of you mind if I hit the sack?"

"You should maybe try to stay up later, and go to bed at a normal time," Darwin said.

Lucas shook his head. "Nah. I learned a long time ago that sleeping through to the next morning is the best way to do it."

"That's over twelve hours," Charlee pointed out.

"If I get up at five, it'll be nearly thirteen." Lucas grinned. "I'll sleep like a log. You could let off bazookas downstairs. I won't hear them, but when I get up in the morning, I'll be adjusted to local time and rarin' to go."

When they got home, Lucas headed upstairs and shut the door on Charlee's old room, leaving them alone.

Darwin rested his hand on her shoulder. "Finally, a chance to talk."

They took the wine bottle out into the tiny back yard, to the little table and chairs there. Wrapped up in their coats, they basked in the last of the sunlight and drank. Darwin rested his long legs out along the concrete, his ankles crossed. "So, how has it been?"

"Marvelous. Interesting. Absorbing." She shrugged. "Every day is different. I don't know what I'll be doing from one day to the next."

"Still nothing resembling a curriculum or books?" This point had bothered him from an academic perspective. During her last flying visit, a

246

few months before, he had circled back to it just as he was now. "Still no books," Charlee confirmed. "Everything they teach you, they do one-on-one. Demonstrations and explanations. No notes."

The lack of books and notes was one of the reasons Charlee was slow at discovering more about Asher's real world. The only way she could find out was to ask one of the other Amica and usually, she was too overwhelmed learning whatever she was learning to push a conversation around to what would amount to idle gossip for the Amica she worked with. They all knew the mysteries she was trying to unravel one slow clue at a time.

"Any new words?" Darwin asked.

She nodded. "But I might get it wrong again." None of the words and names Charlee had brought back for Darwin to mull over had meant anything to him, and they had decided that she might be mispronouncing them or just plain getting them wrong.

"Hit me," Darwin said.

"Eye-n-here-yar," she said slowly.

Darwin sat bolt upright, shock making his eyes widen and his mouth open. He spilled the glass of wine he was holding, and it was his favorite. He didn't seem to notice the wetness on his hand or his knee as he leaned forward. "Einherjar?" he repeated, sounding stunned.

She nodded. "Yes, that sounds just like Victoria said it."

Darwin spelled it out for her. "If that really is the right name," he said slowly. His expression was distant. The wheels were spinning. "It can't be right," he said. "But now everything else makes sense. Well, sort of." He frowned.

"Magic is real, remember?" Charlee said. "If magic is real, then anything is possible."

Darwin nodded, his eyes still far away. Then he stood up. "I'll be right back." He disappeared into the house and she watched him reappear in his office, the tiny room at the back of the kitchen. He reached for one of the books that were kept high up near the ceiling. He opened it and started flipping through it even as he returned to the back door.

As he got closer to her, he spun the book in his hands, then laid it gently on her knee and sat down.

Charlee looked at the page he had opened the book to. There was a full-color picture on the left of a massive tree. Around the tree, nine planets were arranged. The one at the top left was labeled "Asgard" and in smaller letters beneath it was "Valhalla".

She looked up at Darwin, startled. "Vikings?" she breathed.

He shook his head. "The gods of the Vikings." He was almost whispering, too. "Thor. Odin. Feyr. They had dozens of them." He considered what he had said. "They *have* dozens of them." Then he scratched at his head. "Jesus Christ on a pony. It all makes sense now."

"It doesn't to me." She closed the book. "Asher isn't a god."

"No, he's not," Darwin agreed. "I'm pretty sure he's one of the Einherjar, though."

"And they are?"

Darwin leaned forward. "Didn't you learn any of this at school?"

"Any of what? The closest thing to ancient history that we got was the founding of America. Everything else was modern history. Anything that happened before the Renaissance I learned from you." She tilted her head. "You didn't teach me about Vikings."

"That's because this stuff is their mythology, not their history. Well, it was mythology until about five minutes ago." He blew out his breath. "Let me match it up with what you've learned."

"Yes please."

"Valhalla was the hall where Odin ruled. He was one of the major gods." He grimaced. "I keep speaking in the past tense."

"Never mind. Tell me the myths. We'll sort the facts out as we go."

"Okay. Valhalla was on Asgard, one of the nine worlds. I won't go into the rest of the worlds right now. You can read about them yourself. I don't think it's relevant right now. I think we're just dealing with Valhalla."

"Which is supposed to be on Asgard."

"That's just it. I don't think it is." Darwin pointed toward the ground. "This here, Earth, is Midgard. Then there's Asgard, where Valhalla was supposed to be, but I think Valhalla is here, on Midgard. Or something *like* Valhalla is here." He leaned forward again and tapped the book on her knee. "All this stuff, all the stories about their gods, it was all written down in medieval times by writers who had heard the stories from other people. The stories in the Poetic Edda and the Prose Edda were already centuries old when those books were written, and they're two of only a handful of recognized authorities on Norse mythology. The Norse didn't write anything down themselves. They didn't have a written language, not until medieval times, so all the stories about their gods were spoken, passed down one generation to the next."

Charlee shivered. "That would have been how they taught the new generation essential knowledge, wouldn't it? They would have shown them. Told them. No books. No notes."

Darwin nodded vigorously. "And you know what else fits?"

She just looked at him, a little amused by the almost tangible excitement emanating from him.

"The words and names you've bought home. I thought it was some modern language, and I've been working my way through every translation program I could find, plugging them in to see what hit. But if they are using Old Norse as their common language, and if the names they use are from Old Norse, then it's no wonder I couldn't find anything to match."

"Does *anyone* speak Old Norse anymore?" Charlee asked. "I thought it was a dead language, like Latin, or Old English."

"They use it. I bet your bottom dollar. If they're still calling themselves Einherjar and Valkyrie, then they're still using Old Norse."

"Valkyrie…" Charlee could feel her eyes opening wider. "Really? Could Asher be one of those?"

"The Einherjar are men," Darwin said flatly. "There was no such thing as equal rights back then. The men were the warriors, the women kept the homefires burning." He grinned. "But Norse women were known for their fierceness and their ability with weapons. They had to defend their farms while their men were in the longships, pirating their guts out all over Europe. Even the Americas."

Charlee grinned "That sounds better." Then a thought struck her. "Is Ylva a Valkyrie, then?"

Darwin frowned. "I don't know. I'm still wrapping my head around the idea that Odin and Valhalla and the Einherjar are real and living in New York City. That all by itself is a mouthful. *Why* they're here and what are they doing while they're here, that's a whole other mystery."

Charlee rested her hands on the book. "Amica. Valkyrie. Einherjar…" She stumbled over the word only a little. "Lawn. That's the other word I heard. It seems to be some sort of secret. You never found that one, either."

"Give me a day with my computer at the office and I'll find it now," Darwin assured her.

Charlee started leafing through the book, picking up words and phrases. *Ragnarok. Loki. Jötunn. The Æsir.* There were images, many of them, and most were violent, showing gods and men and fantasy creatures locked in battle. She closed it again, quickly. "If Asher doesn't age, and we're pretty sure he doesn't, then that would mean he has lived a long time, wouldn't it?"

"That would follow," Darwin said.

"How *long* has he lived, then? And where did he come from? The real Valhalla?"

"Maybe they've been here all along," Darwin said slowly. "Maybe Valhalla was always here. The concept of it being on Asgard, that might have been the ancient way of saying it was "another world" like we talk about remote or beautiful or alien locations being another world, like the Grand Canyon or the Ellora Caves, or the cemeteries in New Orleans. Or

New Orleans itself, if you're talking about midnight on Bourbon Street."

Charlee laughed.

"One thing I'm pretty sure of is that Asher started out life as human as you and me."

"Why do you say that?"

"Because of what the Einherjar are," Darwin said. "The Valkyrie had one particular job, Charlee. When a battle was done, they would ride among the dead and gather up the strongest and most courageous from the fallen and take them to Valhalla. In Valhalla, the fallen warriors became the Einherjar, and it was their job to prepare for the final war, when they were to protect humans. If Asher is Einherjar, then once upon a time, he fought and died on the battlefield, and I guarantee he wasn't wearing khaki when he did."

Charlee's heart was hurting. She pressed her hand against her chest to ease it. "His sword..."

"His magic sword," Darwin said in agreement.

They both looked at each other. Charlee wondered if her expression was as strained as Darwin's was. "Are we talking ourselves into this?" she whispered. "It's all so fantastic."

Darwin blew out his breath, his cheeks billowing. "I wish. But consider: you saw his sword disappear. Both of us have noticed that he isn't aging. And the guy has secrets. We've both run into the iron shield he has over *something* in his life. Then, he takes you to Ylva when you're cut up by another blade, almost like she could do better than the doctors."

"She did," Charlee said, touching her cheek. "But Ylva is, well, she's old. If they have been here forever and they don't age, why is she old?"

"I guess that goes onto your list," Darwin replied.

"My list?"

"The things you have to find out." He grinned. "And when you do find out, you report back to me on the double."

* * * * *

When Charlee returned to the big house on Fifth Avenue, she was assigned a table in the Store and after feeding the birds, including the falcon who had returned, she was put to work making a simple analgesic, using turmeric and ginger, and oil from a fresh batch of peppermint. It was absorbing work, but that wasn't the only reason she was pleased with her new assignment.

Working on medicinals meant that her earlier work on the other tables had been satisfactory. She had been promoted.

It also put her next to the table where Victoria was working. Victoria was the Amica who had first mentioned Einherjar to Charlee, sometime before she had heard it again in Anja's garment workshop, when she had been learning to mold the heavy leather armor. Now Charlee had more context for *that* skill. For whatever reason, Asher's people still maintained a war-footing. Darwin had said the Einherjar were expected to prepare for a final battle. That would include keeping armor ready and weapons prepared, but actually making the armor would be considered a woman's task. So the Amica or the Valkyrie—Charlee had yet to sort out if those terms were interchangeable—built armor from leather, rather than the plate armor the medieval knights had used. That gave Charlee a glimpse into the age of their culture, just as the lack of books and a written language had earmarked them as ancient.

Victoria was a short, happy Amica with a bubbly personality and long, straight blonde hair that swung around her hips when she let it loose. Mostly she wore it in a ponytail, with four leather thongs tied at intervals along its length. Hair was very dirty in medical terms, and Silia was a tyrant about keeping stray hairs under control.

Victoria seemed to be semi-competent with her work. It was her second stint in the store, but mostly she seemed to like singing and music. Once Charlee had picked up on this fact, she used it to prompt Victoria into talking about her studies, about the people she had met and about the Kine, simply by asking questions that barely seemed nosy. Victoria liked to talk as much as she liked to sing, Charlee swiftly discovered, and Charlee's knowledge of the Kine exploded.

The Kine was the short name the Herleifr used for themselves. Herleifr was the proper name for the Einherjar and Valkyrie collectively. Darwin had looked into the name, now he knew the etymological roots, and let Charlee know via text on the cellphone he had bought her that "Herleifr" loosely translated as "the army."

Darwin had grown almost obsessed with figuring out the intricate details of Kine life. He figured that "Kine" was their word for "kin", the English word for family. Little etymological discoveries like that seemed to delight him.

But Charlee was more interested in the structure of the Kine, and how everyone fit into that structure. That was a picture that was slower to grow because even Victoria was not privy to all of it.

But one thing was clear from Victoria's cheerful gossip: the Valkyrie and the Amica were not the same. They weren't even close to being the same, for the Amica were human.

Victoria had been born the year before Charlee, in Iowa. Her mother had been one of the Amica, as had her grandmother and her grandmother's mother. Victoria was a fourth-generation Amica and had known almost from grade school that she would become one.

"They don't let just anyone become Amica," Victoria explained. "A new recruit, someone who hasn't grown up in their world, is a huge risk."

"Someone like me?" Charlee asked.

Victoria had nodded quickly. "You're not even Amica yet. You haven't been formally recruited or had the basic training for Amica. You are very different from us. I don't know how you managed it. You must be very clever."

Charlee didn't think there was any cleverness involved. She'd had the good fortune to meet Ylva when she was young and to stay in contact with her through the years. What was clever about that?

But it had given her much to think about.

Victoria babbled whenever they had a moment when concentration wasn't needed, but unfortunately, those moments didn't happen often and were usually cut short by one or the other of them having to bend back to their task. So questions and answers were sometimes days apart, and a conversation about a single aspect of Kine life could take a week or more and never be completed to Charlee's satisfaction, for the subject would get forgotten or go off on a tangent.

It would have been easier to interrogate Victoria and insist she stay on topic, but that would never happen and even if it did, it would alert the Amica and any Valkyrie in the house that she was digging for information. Charlee had learned that that wouldn't be a good thing.

One of the themes that seemed to recur in Victoria's ambling narrative, over and over again, was that of secrecy. The Kine's presence here on Earth was a closely guarded secret that the Kine worked to keep. The Amica were the only humans permitted to know about them, and the Amica were very carefully chosen and recruited.

How closely guarded was the secret? Charlee texted Darwin the question. His answer was pithy and to the point.

have they killed to keep the secret?

Yep guaranteed

She folded her phone closed and put it back in her pocket, a great wash of uneasiness spilling through her. Old memories resurfaced, of Asher standing in front of her that first night. He had seemed to be bigger than a mountain, then. He had stood in front of her and watched her with what she now realized had been a hyper-cautious wariness. *You seeing my sword puts you in a different sort of trouble, Charlee. You and me, both.* That had been what had forged their very first deal. A conspiracy of silence over what she had seen.

Darwin's text message replayed in her mind: *Have they killed to keep the secret? Yep, guaranteed.*

Asher had been protecting her from the start, working to keep the

Kine from knowing she had seen the sword. He had probably saved her life, when all this time she had believed Chocolate's life was the only one saved that night.

The Lightning Lords! she remembered with an audible gasp. After they had cut her and Lucas up, after that long, long night, the Lords had disappeared. Was that Asher's doing? Or had the Kine swept in after him to clean things up, including all human witnesses? Had he used his sword and left a mess behind for them to deal with?

The Valkyrie ride through the battlefield, picking up fallen warriors. What if that was not all they did? What if they now rode through a battlefield and cleaned up…everything? That would keep them hidden. That would keep their secret.

If they did that, then they would have to know when and where a battle took place.

And again, that first night she had met Asher replayed through her head. The way he had hustled her out of the alley. The birds lining up on the fence behind them, that Charlee had glimpsed from the corner of her eye as Asher led her back to the street.

Birds.

Charlee thought of the birdcage in the foyer and of Ylva standing with a wild falcon on her arm and shivered.

If they would kill to keep their secret, if they had remained hidden for the centuries that Darwin was estimating, then Charlee had to be even more careful about what she found out.

Why had Ylva ever agreed to let her live here in the first place?

* * * * *

Even though Charlee knew what Asher was now, she still put off seeing him. She had his cellphone number, the numbers for the restaurant and his office at the bank. But she didn't use them. As the days and months and years rolled on, she became even more reluctant to call. If he was pretending to be human, then his life had moved on from that silly prom night moment. She hadn't seen him since. He would assume she had no intention of seeing him again. The more time she let slip by, the more likely it was that he would write off their friendship as something that had ended.

But he still lingered in her thoughts and even haunted her dreams. She missed him, much more than she missed Lucas, who at least showed up every now and again to give her a hug and tell her how pretty she was.

Asher had disappeared. Perhaps he didn't want to speak to her again, either. Maybe *he* wanted their friendship to end. It was that possibility that made her reluctant to call him, much more than her own stupid

253

justifications. For the same reason, she knew she must wait for Asher to reach out to her. But never once since she had known him had Asher inserted himself into her life. He had only ever appeared when she had called him, or when she had stopped by the restaurant. His friendship had been passive. He had not initiated anything.

She knew why, now. She knew that Asher had been walking a tightrope with the wrath of the Kine on one side and the condemnation of humans on the other, humans who would only see a grown man befriending a young girl.

For the same reasons, he would not call or visit or seek her out even now. He had set the limits of their friendship, and he was abiding by them. *If he wants to see me at all*, she thought dismally.

Charlee would counter the bleak thoughts with work. There was always more to do and she threw herself into her work, learning all that she could and practicing. And so the days rolled on.

She loved feeding the birds. She had taken the task over almost completely, happy to stand in the middle of the cage and coax whatever birds were stopping by onto her hands and arms and shoulders, and sometimes even her head. During the winter, blackbirds and sparrows and robins would throng the cage. In the summer, every day was a surprise; tits and swallows, and the bigger birds, including ravens and once, a beautiful owl that had spent a week hiding on a branch at the back of the cage, peering out from between the big leaves, before venturing out to the end of the branch to accept the meat Charlee offered him. Toward the fall, the babies would come with their parents.

Often Ylva would stand on the outside of the cage and tell Charlee about the birds she was feeding: what they liked to eat, their feeding, how they raised their young. Sometimes, Ylva would talk about how the wild birds could help hikers find their way home, if they knew what to look for, and other telling habits.

Charlee got used to one or more of the Amica stopping outside the cage to watch the feeding. Since Charlee had taken over the task, more and more birds seemed to flock down the long cage at feeding time, to call and twitter and coo around her. It was noisy, happy and interesting work, and the Amica seemed to find it endlessly entertaining, especially when the babies came to visit.

It was December in the new millennium, and only a few days before the solstice, which was celebrated instead of Christmas in Ylva's house. Charlee crept down to the birdcage early; the birds would be hungry, as the snow had been falling for two days and food would be hard to find.

She picked up the platter of seeds and peered through the leaves to see if any birds were already in the cage and waiting for her. Delighted, she saw that the owl was back, his winter feathers fluffing him up into a snowy, white ball with big eyes. "Well, hello," she murmured to him and reached back for the meat she kept in a separate container, just in case some of the carnivores visited.

"Hello, yourself." Human words. Spoken behind her. Male voice.

She whirled, her fright tearing up through her throat and emerging in a little, soundless gasp. The seeds scattered from the platter in her hand.

Asher stood on the other side of the bars.

She ran her gaze over him, hungrily absorbing details she had forgotten, or remembered so often they had distorted. The blue of his eyes. The width of his shoulders under the heavy, dark coat he wore. The size of his hands and the strength of his wrists (*all the better to hold his sword with*). His height, which didn't seem to be quite so towering anymore. He was just a tall man.

"And she doesn't say hello," Asher said softly. He sounded worried.

"I'm too astonished that you're here to even think of saying hello." She stepped closer to the bars. "Do you know how long it's been since I last saw you?"

"I know to the day."

She shivered. "You stayed away."

He nodded.

"Because of…?"

His gaze dropped. It was answer enough.

Her heart was slamming madly, the sound of its frantic beating throbbing in her ears, in a rushing sound. "Then why come back?" she asked.

He stepped close to the cage. Close to her, but the wide-spaced iron bars were still between them. "You didn't kiss me."

Charlee stared at him, the birds, the seed platter, all of it forgotten. "That's why you're here? Because I didn't kiss you?"

He lifted his gaze to meet her eyes. "You could have. We both know you could have. I would have let you. It was yours to take, but you didn't. I want to know why."

Her delight at seeing him began to congeal into a lower, harder emotion. "You know why."

His gaze wasn't letting her go. "What I am—" he began. Then he stopped and she could see him swallow. "Who I am, that has never been between us."

"Have you spent the last, what is it? Four years? More? You've spent all that time wondering why I didn't kiss you?"

"I saw you on Bleecker Street. Last week."

She had gone to lower Manhattan to run an errand for Ylva,

dropping a box of salves off at an apartment there. The woman who had accepted them had been tall, young and incredibly beautiful, her long, dark hair tumbling about her shoulders. She had thanked Charlee in faintly accented English. *Valkyrie or senior Amica*, Charlee had figured.

The whole journey had taken barely an hour and she had hurried along, the cold seeping into her bones, her head down, keen to get to the train and inside once more.

"You've got taller, I think," Asher said.

"A bit," she conceded, puzzled. She put the platter down, stepped out of the cage and brushed bird seed from her dress. "Why are we talking about my height?"

His answer took a long while to emerge, so long that she thought she would scream. "You've changed. I don't know what to say, anymore."

"Truth for truth, Asher. That's the deal, remember?"

He let out a breath, heavily. "I remember." And he smiled. It was his old smile.

"You asshole!" she railed at him. "Four freaking years!" She pummelled his shoulder with both fists, suddenly furious.

Asher laughed and gathered her up in his arms and hugged her. It felt heavenly. Warmth and safety and good feelings all at once. She smelled snow and cold and his unique scent that she would never forget.

Chapter Twenty-Two

How many of our diverse cultural
influences are not only global, but reach
back further into our past than any of us
realize? The Kine moved among us for
centuries, quietly recreating a world
they knew with all the comforts of
home, including their longhouses and
inns. Humans were exposed to Kine
culture long before we even knew they
existed. We have yet to know if that
influence was useful in the events that
followed…

_____

*Kine Culture, A Study of Herleifr Life after
the Descent.* Darwin Baxter.

Asher spoke to Ylva, and Charlee was relieved of her duties for the day
so that Asher could take her out. Where? She didn't care. It wasn't
unusual for one of the Amica to have a visitor and be excused for the day
and routines were robust enough that their absence was covered almost
automatically, so Charlee didn't feel guilty about stepping out with her
own visitor.

Asher piled her into a cab and gave the address, and Charlee pressed
her gloved hands to her lips. "The Ashtree," she murmured. "That's
perfect."

"That's what I thought, too. Pierre will have hysterics when he sees
you." He grinned.

Charlee studied him carefully.

"What is it?" he asked.

"You haven't changed. Not at all."

He shrugged. "Clean living and no vices."

She let it pass. He wouldn't admit he hadn't aged, not even if he
suspected she knew. Instead she turned the conversation, asking him
about his life and catching up on the last four years.

Pierre did have hysterics when he saw her, but that was later in the
afternoon. First, Asher sat her at the bar, his *de facto* office, sat down
beside her and ordered lunch and a bottle of champagne.

"I should warn you that trying to get me drunk won't do you a bit of
good," she said. "Ylva has wine served at both lunch and dinner. I've

grown immune to the effects."

"Champagne just tickles your nose, anyway." He poured her a glass and pushed it in front of her.

"I've heard that mead is like champagne. Some types of mead, anyway." She picked up the glass. "I wouldn't mind trying that, one day."

Asher froze. He kept his gaze on the glass he was filling and didn't move for several heartbeats. Then he carefully and slowly returned the bottle to the ice bucket and dropped the napkin over it. Finally, he picked up the glass and held it toward her. "To old friends, friends once more."

"Absolutely yes," she said and tapped her glass to his and drank.

He was studying her. Wondering, possibly, what she would say next. So Charlee smiled at him. "Are you dating anyone, Asher?"

He shook his head. "I barely have the time to check in on Torger."

"Oh, Torger! How is he?" She felt a genuine delight. Torger had been such a cute dog and so obedient.

"Still in love with animals, then." He seemed pleased. "Perhaps I should take you to see him."

"Won't he be working?"

"Not once I walk in the door. He knows he's off duty and can relax."

"So you would take me to your apartment?"

Asher's gaze caught hers. "That's where Torger is."

"Then I would like to see your apartment."

He straightened up and picked up his glass. "So, tell me about life at Ylva's."

Charlee spun him a tale that was half fiction and half fact. She did not lie about the hard work and her growing love for the strange world she found herself in. But she carefully minimized her knowledge of the Kine. If she was right about their rules of secrecy, Ylva could be in trouble for allowing Charlee to learn as much as she had. If she let Asher know how much she knew, then he would become entangled in her lies.

Their truth-for-truth deal had always been very literal; they would tell each other the truth when they revealed anything, but they did not reveal everything. Asher never had revealed everything. There was a whole world of secret people he had kept from her. In turn, he had carefully not dug into the details of her own odd life with a drunk mother and a dying father, and a brother who had been forced to grow up too fast. Instead he had let her pretend she was a normal kid enjoying a simple life.

It was ironic, really. Neither of them was close to being normal. But they had both pretended to be.

So now she gave him a pretty picture of her life with Ylva. How much of it did he believe? Did it matter?

They were finishing lunch when Pierre burst through the kitchen door and flung his arms out to her, babbling incoherently in French.

"You're early!" Charlee cried and hurried over to hug him. He held her tightly and with a jolt, she realized that she was taller than him now.

"Mister Anthony called, told me you were here. I did not believe him, but I hurry down to see for myself. Ah, Charlee, you are beautiful! A brilliant butterfly, hatched from her cocoon! If I were younger, I would flirt with you and make eyes at you."

"You're making eyes anyway," Asher pointed out.

"I do, but it is only because such beauty deserves applause," Pierre said with dignity. "I will make you my best dessert, to go with your lunch and your champagne."

"No, Pierre, really—" Charlee began, but he had gone back into the kitchen. They listened to him bawling at the sous chef at the top of his lungs. Charlee winced. "Well, at least all the customers have gone."

"He's shouting so you will hear him and be impressed." Asher was smiling.

Fifteen minutes later, Pierre appeared with a plate in his hands, a silver cover over it. "*Voilà!*" He whipped the lid off.

It was a stack of pancakes. Charlee burst into laughter and let him present the plate, placing it in front of her with a flourish. "It will soak up the champagne," he said, "and the syrup, it is not that sump oil Americans like so much. It is much, much better." He blew her a kiss and went back to his kitchen.

Charlee took a small bite. The sauce was strawberry-based and delicious, and Pierre was right, it went with the champagne perfectly.

The sous chef, someone Charlee didn't know, appeared with a tray bearing coffee and cups a few minutes later, then disappeared just as discreetly, but he kept looking at Charlee as he set out the tray, his gaze flickering over her. Then he would look at Asher and away quickly.

"Am I creating gossip about you, being here?" she asked Asher after he was gone.

His mouth turned up. "Probably. You know how much I give a damn about gossip, though."

"You used to care what people thought about you—and me—very much."

"Not for the reasons you think."

"Ah, but you have no idea what I'm thinking."

Asher gave a small laugh. "Not anymore, I don't."

* * * * *

"You don't live in the Bronx anymore?" Charlee asked when the cab dropped them off in Soho.

"You knew I lived there?" he asked, startled.

She smiled. "I couldn't figure out why you would be in my neighborhood, just passing by in time to rescue Chocolate, unless you lived there."

"I bought this apartment about four years ago," he said. "I got sick of the commute."

That would have been around the time she moved to Ylva's. Charlee didn't say it out loud. Instead, she looked up at Asher's new home as he led her inside.

The building was one of the classical New York brownstones, but from the look of the foyer and the number of mailboxes on the wall there, it was one of the ones that had been gutted to make bigger studio apartments, with only two or three apartments per floor.

After so many years, money would accumulate, she realized. That was why Ylva lived in a big house on Fifth Avenue and Asher could afford what had to be a multi-million dollar apartment in Soho.

Which must mean that Ylva had lived for a long time, too. But her age! Her age meant she couldn't be a Valkyrie.

What if she used *to be one?* The question popped into her head mixed up with a "d'uh" sensation. A *former* Valkyrie? Could there be such a thing? Did they just give it up, somehow?

Asher's apartment was on the third floor. There were only two doors leading off from the elevator foyer and as he unlocked the door, she braced herself for large-scale sumptuousness.

He pushed the door open. "I'll go in first, so Torger doesn't mow you down."

Already, Charlee could hear the click of toenails on flooring, heading toward them. Asher stepped through, and she caught a glimpse of big sash windows and sunlight. He swung the door until it was almost shut and she heard him through the door. "Good boy," he murmured. "Very good boy. We've got a guest, so put on your best manners, yes? No drooling on her pretty dress."

Charlee held back her laughter as the door opened once more. Asher beckoned her inside.

Torger was sitting five paces inside the door, his tongue hanging out as he panted. His pushed-in nose was turned up toward her eagerly and his tail moved, brushing across the floor.

Charlee bent down toward him. "Torger, you ugly thing you. You're as beautiful as ever."

Thump, thump. Torger's tail hit the floor solidly. His back hips wriggled. But he didn't move. His eyes slid over to where Asher was standing, watching them.

"Yes, boy. You can say hello," Asher told him.

Torger seemed to laugh. His mouth opened, revealing more of his pink tongue, as he jumped up and tried to lick Charlee's face. She reared back, only just managing to keep her balance, and he jumped again, his paws landing just above her knees. He gave a soft bark and she scratched behind his ears. "*Good* dog. Good Torger. You remember me, don't you?"

He chumped his jaws together as if he were agreeing and panted happily, his eyes rolling, as she scratched and patted.

"Of course he remembers you," Asher said. "Who could ever forget you?"

Charlee looked up at him and rolled her eyes. "I'm lucky if Lucas remembers my birthday."

Asher shook his head. "I guarantee he remembers. But his life isn't…."

"Normal?" Charlee asked.

"Not normal in the sense that he gets weekends off to mow the lawn, no."

Charlee gave Torger one last pat and stood up, looking around. She had focused on Torger as soon as she had stepped inside, and nothing had registered beyond the big windows and the warm sunlight spilling through them. Now she looked about curiously.

The first impression was that there were books everywhere. And bookshelves. The big room wasn't quite a studio. There was a door through the wall at the other end, and she could see a bed through the doorway. It was unmade, the cover tossed back to the point where it was threatening to slide off the end of the bed. Charlee could just about see Asher throwing it aside as he rose from the bed.

Quickly she turned back to the main room, not allowing herself to follow that line of thought. The kitchen and living area were all one room. On the wall opposite the windows, bookshelves rose from floor to ceiling and from wall to wall. There were even shelves above the apartment door. The kitchen area took up the wall to her right, with a breakfast bar separating it from the rest of the room.

Most of the bookshelves held books. There were more books on the coffee table, some of them open and resting face down. There was a French press on the kitchen counter, half-filled with cold coffee, and a mug and empty plate next to it. The remains of breakfast, she presumed. She could hear Skuld's voice in her head, lecturing about the dirty dishes and how food scraps invited germs. She could also hear Silia, murmuring about the waste of coffee, the properties of caffeine, and how it could be used for a variety of ailments, if it was prepared properly.

There was a wine glass on the coffee table, the dregs of red wine at the bottom. The cushions scattered across the sofa were squashed and folded, from being sat upon and leaned against.

It was a lived-in apartment and despite its size, it felt warm and comfortable. Charlee looked around, starting to like it. "I had no idea you owned so many books."

"I didn't have room for them in the Bronx apartment, so I've had them in storage. It's good to have them accessible again."

"I imagine some of them are impossible to replace, too." She moved toward the nearest shelves, to read the spines and from the corner of her eye, she saw Asher settle on the arm of the sofa, his arms crossed, watching her.

It ruined her concentration. She pretended to look at the spines, but she barely absorbed what she was reading. Finally, when her heart was hurrying along like she had sprinted a hundred yards, she straightened and turned to face him. "You're watching me."

"You're the only thing moving in the room," he said reasonably. Torger was sprawled on the floor at Asher's feet, his eyes closed.

"That's a neat evasion. I'll have to remember it."

Asher didn't move. He was still looking at her.

"Truth for truth, Asher," she said. "Why did you haul me here to your apartment?"

"Why did you let me bring you here?" he shot back. "Truth for truth."

She took a deep breath, for courage. "I want to know more about you. The real you. You've been holding out on me for years. This seemed like a good way."

"Didn't Ylva teach you that stepping into a man's apartment comes with certain implications?"

"I've known that for years. But you're not just any man."

He seemed to grow wary and still, again. "Then what am I?"

"Someone I trust absolutely."

Asher's mouth quirked. "Thank you."

"And why did you bring me here?"

His little smile faded. "I want to know why you didn't kiss me. We can't be interrupted here. No one will overhear you. So tell me."

She stared at him. "Your ego is not so delicate that a woman holding out on you would crush it, so why do you want to know so badly?"

He stood up. "I know you wanted to. You're one of the most stubborn people I know. If you want something, you take it, but you didn't take your kiss. *Something* stopped you, and it wasn't the moral right and wrong of the situation. Something in you made you not take what you wanted."

"You wouldn't have let me, anyway," she shot back.

"No, but you didn't try to take it. What stopped you?"

Charlee considered him curiously. He was quite serious about this. He wanted to know, and it had nothing to do with his male pride.

"Truth, Charlee," he prompted her and she realized that he was a lot closer now. He had been taking small steps toward her while they spoke. Now she had to tilt her head back to look him in the eye.

"I don't know," she told him.

"You do. You just don't want to think about it. *Think*," he urged her. "What made you stop?"

Charlee tried. She recalled those tense, short moments in the back of the cab, after the prom. They were hazy now (*liar!*). But the air between them, the way it had thickened and grew warmer, the sudden heaviness of her body and sluggish thoughts, those things she remembered.

Her heart began to thud just like it had that night. "You were so much older…" she whispered.

"*Were?*" He shook his head, dismissing it. "Try another excuse."

Charlee swallowed. "Why do you care, anyway? You said you would have stopped me, so what does it matter?"

"I would have stopped you for reasons that have nothing to do with you personally. But you stopped for reasons that were *very* personal to you." His eyes seemed to be holding her gaze, like a magnet. "Tell me what it was. I want you to see it."

Horror touched her. "You know why?"

Asher nodded. "It took me a long time to figure it out. But I think I know, now."

Charlee realized her hand was cradling her cheek only when Asher's gaze shifted to her fingers. She tried to drop her hand, but couldn't.

He was staring at it. "And now I know for certain." His gaze shifted back to her eyes.

"I was seventeen," she said defensively. "Of course I thought I didn't deserve to kiss you."

"You still don't, because of a little scar." He reached out and grabbed her wrist, and lowered her hand away from her face.

"It's not little!"

"I've seen far worse."

"You see beautiful women every single day! You're surrounded by them! I don't think I've met a single ugly Amica. Not one! They're all stunning."

Asher froze again, staring at her. It was the same as when she had mentioned mead. She had surprised him. Shocked him to the point where he didn't know how to respond. No, he was *afraid* to respond. He was controlling his reaction with the equivalent of an iron fist.

"You know what the Amica are?" he said. His tone was cautious.

"Not exactly." The truth was a good enough answer this time. "I'm still sorting out who in Ylva's house is Amica and who isn't." At the last split second, she chose the indirect reference. She had a feeling that speaking words like Valkyrie and Einherjar aloud would scare Asher even more. Perhaps scare him into a reaction that his Kine had been using to keep their secret for centuries. She didn't know enough yet, so she said that, too. "There's so much to learn. Each day I learn a bit more and that tells me how much more there is to learn."

"You're learning?" It was the same wary tone.

Afterwards, Charlee was never certain what had prompted her to say it. But she looked him in the eye. "Your secret is safe, Asher. Ylva hasn't told me. No one has." She had figured out much of it merely by observing, and from Darwin's obsessive researching. But it was still true: his secret was utterly safe in her hands.

His hand around her wrist dropped. Shock, or dismay? His expression was the same neutral, assessing one. "Let's change the subject."

"Truth for truth," she said flatly. "You don't mind *keeping* secrets, but acknowledging you even have one is out of bounds?"

"Truth, Charlee?" He had crossed his arms again, but this time she knew it was because she was pushing him, stirring things. He was in defensive mode, perhaps the first time she had ever seen him that way with her. "Even acknowledging that there are things that must stay unspoken—that's how talking begins. That's how truth is revealed, a small slip at a time."

"You risked that much when you saved Chocolate. You spoke about your secret then."

"Yes, and look where we are now. Look at your life. Look where it took you." His gaze fell upon her cheek.

"I wouldn't change any of it. Not a moment."

His eyes met hers. "Really? You prefer being a woman who thinks she's not worth a single kiss that she wants?"

She swallowed. Now *she* was on the defensive. She could feel the empty denials rising up. She wanted to say he was wrong, but she couldn't.

Asher stepped back. Away from her. He reached for the buttons on his shirt. "Don't get the wrong idea, alright?"

She laughed. It was supposed to be a dry, sophisticated sound, but it *did* come out sounding nervous. "You're unbuttoning your shirt. What *am* I supposed to think?"

He pulled the tails of his shirt out of his pants. "I want you to see something."

"Well, that's a twist on asking me to see your etchings."

He rolled his eyes. "No, I want you to see this." He pulled the shirt open.

She looked. Of course she had to look. He was naked beneath the shirt, but she had always known he never wore a T-shirt or undershirt. His flesh was quite pale, but the scars were not. They slashed and writhed, at least four of them, across the flat plane of his stomach and over his chest. Charlee couldn't tear her gaze away from them. She held back the question she most wanted to ask.

Which of these was the one that killed you?

There was a rounded scar, just under his pectoral muscle, on the left side, and suddenly she knew that was the one. That was what had killed him. Sword, or spear—or a tree stump, it didn't matter.

She didn't realize that she was staring at them until Asher spoke once more. "You're not the only one with scars, Charlee. Yours is visible to the world when you step out your front door, but that's the only difference." He closed his shirt again, and buttoned it.

Charlee blinked. "Do the Amica have scars like that?"

"No."

"Do other women you know?" It was a roundabout way of asking if the Valkyrie had scars like her.

Asher tilted his head to study her. "You're the only woman I know who is marked just like a lot of men I know."

Her heart lurched. Startled, she stared at him. *All* the Einherjar had scars? Well, of course they would. They were all warriors. They had all died in battle. But she hadn't.

"Scars like yours are honorable war wounds," Asher added.

This time her laugh was genuine. "I wasn't in a battle."

"You clashed with an enemy." Asher wasn't laughing.

"I didn't have a weapon."

"Warriors fight without weapons at times."

"I didn't *do* anything!"

"You survived."

Asher hadn't survived. Well, not in human terms. "Is that what defines a warrior? Survival?" she asked curiously.

"Warriors are those caught up in wars, whether they are soldiers or just survivors. You were not a soldier, you were a survivor. You did the job you were supposed to do."

"I lived?"

"Exactly." It was odd the way his blue eyes were drilling in to her, holding her gaze.

She spoke the very first thing that came to her. "I want my kiss, now."

The moment before he responded seemed to last forever. His gaze didn't let her go. "The reasons for saying no still stand." But his voice was deeper. Rougher. And she knew that he wanted her to kiss him. He wouldn't take one for himself, but he would let her have her kiss, if she insisted.

It gave Charlee the courage to step close to him and rest her hand on his chest, over the scar there, that she could feel under her fingers through the fine cotton of his shirt. "I want my warrior's reward," she told him.

He drew in a breath. "Charlee…." It was a warning.

She kissed him.

She was wearing stilettos that made her four inches taller, but she still had to lift herself up onto her toes to reach his mouth. His lips were unexpectedly soft. His scent enveloped her and made something in her belly roll over. Her body felt heavy and drugged, but where it pressed against Asher, her flesh seemed scalded.

But he was not responding. Disappointment touched her. Of course he wouldn't respond. It was just her. Not a magnificent Valkyrie, or one of the models he sometimes dated. She was human. Just Charlee.

She let him go, but before their lips barely separated, his hand caught the back of her head, holding her there, and his lips pressed against hers.

Heat consumed her, racing along her limbs, throwing her heart into a stuttering, racing confusion. *He was kissing her.* It was a sweet victory and a sultry reward, all at once. And it was good. So good.

Asher pulled away from her, almost *tearing* himself away. He drew in a deep breath, his eyes closing and grew still, half turned away from her so that she could see the thickness of his shoulder.

Finally he breathed again. "That was not a good idea," he said very quietly.

Charlee agreed. Her heart was hurting and her legs were shaky. She felt a bit sick with the tidal forces of physical need surging through her. "It won't happen again," she said flatly.

He looked at her over his shoulder. "Never promise absolutes," he said bleakly.

She picked up her clutch purse from the back of the sofa where she had rested it. "Like promising to never speak a secret?" she asked. She didn't wait for his answer. His eyes widening were answer enough.

She let herself out of the apartment.

* * * * *

Asher had dressed and was almost out of the apartment, when he realized that what was driving him was an old habit. He had been about to step out the door and head for Oslo. For Sindri's dark salon and the depthless mugs of mead to be found there.

He stood with his hand on the door, while Torger sat panting, watching him curiously. He spun his keys on his finger, looking down at Torger. "I'm a fool," he told the dog. Torger slurped and brought his jaws together with a snap, as if he was in full agreement.

Asher turned and leaned against the door, dropping his keys onto the desk next to it, and made himself deal with bald facts instead of operating on auto-pilot. He'd been doing way too much of that lately.

(*Since Charlee had kissed him.*)

Charlee had gone back to her life at Ylva's, he assumed. He hadn't heard from her. Which was the way it was supposed to be. He had his life—his secret life, that Charlee couldn't be part of. She had her odd life that she was building for herself, that didn't make sense to him, to Darwin or even Lucas. But she was happy.

Leave her alone, he told himself. Let her have that life.

I'm just thinking about stopping by. Is she happy? I should make sure.

Asher pressed his fingers to his temple. "Stop it! You're trying to justify yourself."

I'm the one that upset her.

"She's not upset." He said it to the air. Defiantly.

But the idea had got hold of his brain now and wouldn't let go. What if she was brooding over what she thought of as a rejection? She was fragile.

Charlee is made of teak, he argued to himself, while Torger sat panting, the drool almost reaching the floor, his small black eyes watching Asher for a command, a prompt so that he would know if he was on duty or not.

Charlee has lived through much more than a kiss gone wrong.

But it *hadn't* gone wrong. Not at all.

Asher shut his eyes and jammed the heels of his hands into his sockets, trying to rid himself of the pervasive images. The reaction she had provoked in him. This was why he had been heading for Sindri's. Enough mead and the memory and the fantasies would go away.

She's just a girl. A young girl!

But it hadn't felt like that at the time. Charlee had sat there with him over lunch, and he had forgotten her actual age. She had seemed at times to be older than the gods. Her responses had been, as always, unexpected and original. Charlee could think for herself. But wrapped up in the woman she had become, it was a lethal combination.

So when she had kissed him, it had seemed like the most natural thing in the world. He had fought not to react, to not take control in any way, but he had given in just for one sweet moment.

"Aaagh, damn it all to hell!" he raged.

Torger jerked, almost flinching away from him.

"Sorry," he said, holding out his hand. "Sorry, my friend."

Torger sat back down, but his eyes were wary.

"I'm going to stay home and watch television like humans do, alright?"

Torger almost stood up, but realized he hadn't been dismissed, so he sat down again.

"Yes, television and a glass of wine," Asher said, trying to sound like it was a delightful prospect.

Instead, he reached out his hand, picked up his keys and opened the door.

Fool! he raged to himself as he hurried down the stairs. But calling himself names didn't quell the happy expectation rising in him.

* * * * *

Charlee stepped into Ylva's day room and shut the door. It was past eight in the evening, but Ylva used the room to greet guests and conduct business. Her office, which was the inner room accessed from this one, was a workman-like place that outsiders rarely saw. Even the Amica were granted entry only under limited circumstances.

"Ylva, you asked to see—" She didn't finish the rest of the sentence, for Asher was standing there, his hands in the pockets of his leather jacket, watching her.

So was Ylva, who got to her feet. "This is ill-advised, Asher. She is not Amica."

Asher didn't speak. His gaze was on Charlee.

"May I know the nature of the disagreement, as it seems to be about me?" she asked.

"Asher wants to take you out for the evening," Ylva said shortly.

"And you don't think it is a good idea because I am not one of the Amica?"

"No." Ylva said it flatly. She was angry and even though she was far too gracious to take that anger out on anyone, it did tend to make her speak with more bluntness that usual.

"Asher is a friend," Charlee said, using the same flat tone Ylva was. "Why would being one of the Amica make any difference?"

"Thank you," Asher said softly.

Charlee didn't look at him. She kept her gaze on Ylva.

"The details do not affect this discussion," Ylva said.

"If it is something you choose not to disclose, then it cannot be considered in the discussion at all," Charlee said. "Therefore, as I am well over eighteen and legally an adult, I'm free to choose to go out with Asher." She gave Ylva a moment to respond.

Ylva looked surprised. Then concerned.

"Do you now want to expand on why being one of the Amica would make a difference?" Charlee asked.

After a moment, she shook her head.

Charlee looked at Asher for the first time. "Give me five minutes to change?"

He nodded.

"I'll meet you by the birdcage."

Ylva sighed.

* * * * *

Asher took her to a pub on Fulton, within spitting distance of Broadway. It was tucked away on the second floor of the building, accessed by a narrow set of wooden steps that were unadorned, but scuffed smooth by many feet. At the top of the stairs was a wooden sign that had been hand-painted, declaring that this was Heidrun.

Heidrun looked like something out of a medieval movie, but the details weren't exactly right. There were benches and stout tables, and massive fake beams across the ceiling that were dark with age. Beer was served in mugs and the waitresses wore dresses with straps over their shoulders and white collarless shirts beneath.

It was crowded and noisy, and the air was rich with the smell of beer and wine and a lot of bodies crammed into the small space. The lighting was a low, golden yellow and there was a huge fireplace at the far end of the room, flickering with low flames even though it was a mild evening.

Asher nodded to one or two people who waved at him, including some of the waitresses.

Charlee looked at the decorations curiously. There were paintings of Viking ships at sea, round shields with axes strapped to them. "What is this place?" she asked as Asher pulled out one of the wooden bar stools for her and patted it.

"A bar."

"No, really. What does Heidrun mean?" She knew he would know.

His mouth lifted at the corner. "The Viking Place."

She nodded, absorbing the noise, the atmosphere, and the details. She didn't need confirmation to know that many of the people here were probably Kine, just like Asher. There were humans, undoubtedly, for this was a public bar. But the Kine would use this place, too, because it was homey. This is what they were used to.

"I like it," she declared. And she did. It would be very easy to relax here.

The barman put a glass of wine in front of both of them.

"No mead?" Charlee asked.

Asher raised a brow. "Have you ever tried mead?"

She shook her head. "It's not something you can get easily."

"Probably just as well." He picked up his glass. "The home brewed stuff can knock you around if you're not used to it. Wait for a special occasion, Charlee, and I'll get you some to try."

"Okay." She picked up her own wine glass. "What shall we drink to?"

He looked her in the eye. "To friends."

She took a deep breath and let it out. Relief. He was going to ignore the kiss. They were back to normal. They were back to being friends.

Thank the gods, she mentally whispered and touched his glass with her own. "Friends," she agreed wholeheartedly.

Chapter Twenty-Three

"I know what the scientists say, Anderson. But does prophecy really destroy free-will? Generally, I've found that once a human is told their future, they become highly determined to choose their own fate."

——
Unnur Guillory, on AC 360

Asher didn't take her out every night, or even every week. He would appear abruptly, without warning and at any time of the day, sometimes even for breakfast. He would whisk her out to somewhere novel, to do something interesting. One breakfast had been a champagne picnic in Central Park. There were meals at some of the fanciest restaurants in New York and other meals in the dingiest little dives, where the food was excellent, even if they did have to eat it with their fingers.

There was skating at Lincoln Center. Strolls through the West Village. Picnics in Central Park. Shopping in Soho. Hiking High Line Park. Ice creams on Coney Island. Asher seemed to have an encyclopedic knowledge of the city, every little nook and cranny and hidden treat, and he took her to all the interesting ones.

They had fun. She grew to look forward to their outings. Even in her own mind she refused to call them dates, for Asher was the friend he had declared himself to be. They laughed a lot. They talked a lot, but always about general things. The hidden side of both their lives had returned once more to the realm of the unspoken.

But things were different from the years when Charlee had been dropping in to see Asher and Ylva at the restaurant each day. Back then, their friendship had been simpler. Now there was an awareness, bubbling below the surface of all their interactions. She would sometimes catch Asher studying her with a watchful gaze that would evaporate the moment she saw it. Sometimes their conversation would stumble to a halt, as the awareness rose to the surface and rippled the peace. There would be a look. Or a touch that left invisible electric print-marks in her flesh, making her shudder.

But most of the time, Asher was scrupulous in avoiding physical contact. It worked, most of the time. It worked well enough for Charlee to continue to go out with him and to look forward to each occasion, even if she did lie awake in her narrow bed at night, sleep far away and her body tight with need.

It was not all good times. The bubbling tension below the surface sometimes seemed to be unbearable, and it was usually during those times that Charlee found her restraint sliding. One of the more memorable occasions was at the opera. She had never been to the opera, and the little opera music she had ever listened to seemed to be incomprehensible, but Asher had insisted she try at least one opera, and he had tickets to the opening night for the season at the Met. It was one of the few occasions when he had given her advance warning.

The gown she had worn was a strapless velvet that reminded her vaguely of the black velvet prom dress she had worn many years ago. But this dress was a deep, dark green and it clung to every inch of her between her breasts and her knees, then flared out to drag behind her by an inch or two. The dress was finished off with satin gloves that ended above her elbows. Opera-length gloves, Ylva had called them.

Charlee had felt over-dressed and uneasy, until they had arrived at the opera house and she saw that on the contrary, she was most suitably dressed. She should have trusted Ylva, who had never been wrong about appropriate degrees of dress the entire time Charlee had known her. So she had tried to relax as much as the dress would let her.

Asher had looked exceptional in his formal tuxedo, with a white tie at his neck, and there had been a light in his eye as he looked her over that made Charlee catch her breath. But he had said nothing other than his usual offhand comment. "You look beautiful as always."

Charlee had long ago figured out that he said it as a way of reassuring her, to compensate for her scar. She hadn't forgotten their one kiss and the conversation that had preceded it. But one kiss was all that he would allow in order to prop up her confidence.

Asher had another surprise: their seats were in a private box on the second tier. Feeling pampered and extravagant, Charlee had slid onto the chair behind the balcony rail. She couldn't stop smiling.

The opera was in sung in Italian, even though it was set in nineteenth-century Paris. That was because the composer, Giacomo Puccini, had written the lyrics in his native language. The story, Asher assured her, would speak to her despite the language barrier. Music was universal.

La bohème was a tragic love story, and as soon as Charlee realized that the two principal singers were doomed lovers, her happiness dissipated like smoke before a breeze. She clutched the balcony rail, squeezing with all her might. *What is wrong with you?* she railed at herself. *Get it together! Asher will notice.*

When Mimi died, with Rodolfo bent over her, Charlee felt like she had been stabbed in the chest. Her heart actually hurt and she clutched at it, trying to ease the pain. As Rodolfo cried out his misery, Charlee could stand it no longer. She lunged to her feet, almost tripping over the hem of her dress as it tangled with the tiny feet of her chair.

"Charlee, what's wrong?" Asher asked, softly so he wouldn't disturb anyone else.

Charlee shook her head. She wouldn't look at him. She didn't want him to see the tears cascading down her cheeks, probably ruining her makeup. She stumbled to the box exit and down the carpeted corridor to the elevator. She needed fresh air. She need privacy. Above all, she needed to be alone in her misery because what she really wanted was to throw herself against Asher and weep her heart out while he soothed her, but he wouldn't allow it.

Sadness struck her afresh, and she pushed out through the doors and into the night air, just barely holding back her sobs.

She found a dark corner away from the spotlights lighting the big square in front of the grand opera house, especially around the big fountain in the middle. The comparison to standing outside on her prom night was not lost upon her, and that made her feel even sadder and even more miserable. She turned her back on the world and battled to keep the sobs silent so she wouldn't draw attention to herself.

"Charlee." His hand came down upon her shoulder, warm and big.

She shrugged it off. If she could not have his comfort, she would take nothing from him at all, not even a token touch. She propped herself up against the wall, hiding her face.

"Charlee, for heaven's sake…" He didn't touch her again. Of course he wouldn't. "Tell me what's wrong."

She got her sobs under control by breathing deep and slowly. "Was that supposed to be a message? Some sort of object lesson for the particularly dense Charlotte Montgomery?"

"You and I both know you're anything but stupid." She heard him sigh. "It was just a night out. I thought you would like dressing up. I know I liked the idea."

"Why did you think I would like such a story? It was horrible!"

His hand came down on her shoulder once more, this time firmly enough that she knew he wouldn't let her shrug it off. He turned her so she was looking at him. "Not everything I do is a metaphor, Charlee."

"You've never said anything in your life that wasn't layered or a downright riddle!"

His freshly shaved jaw flexed. "You and I both know—"

"No! Don't give me the big secret thing again. I'm so *sick* of it I

273

could scream. I'm sick of not talking about it, I'm sick of only getting to share the leftovers of your life." Her tears were running again, hot across her cheeks, but this time they had nothing to do with doomed Parisian lovers.

His hands were clenched. She saw it in a dim way, but didn't process it. "The *leftovers*," he repeated grimly, "are a perfectly normal life."

"You're not normal."

"I'm as human as you."

"You're not human at all!" she cried.

He didn't freeze like he normally did whenever she got too close to the truth. His expression darkened. "Charlee, if you have the sense of self-preservation of a gnat, for god's sake, shut up now."

"Why? So you can just shovel it all behind the curtain again?"

He looked around, over his shoulder. The opera was over. People were leaving in thick streams now. Some were looking at them curiously, Charlee with her ruined makeup and Asher with his fisted hands and taut posture.

Lovers' quarrel, they'll be thinking. It made Charlee abruptly sad and resigned. Her anger left like water draining from a sieve. "Could you find a cab?" she asked him. "I want to go home."

"I'll take you home." They had come in the private limousine that Asher often hired.

"No. I want to go home alone."

Asher looked at her for a long moment. "Very well," he said flatly. Finally. He turned and walked away, heading for the road where he could hail a cab for her, without another word.

* * * * *

Asher wasn't sober, but he wasn't nearly close to drunk enough to suit his mood.

The barman whom everyone, even the human customers, called Eric the Red, was a black Nigerian, one of the very tall, lean and lanky types that so often did well in track and field. He kept a barrel of mead behind the bar for special occasions, and Asher was probably a quarter of the way through the barrel. It was a special enough occasion in his estimation, and Eric hadn't argued with him.

It was getting late. Later than late. He had yanked out a chair at one of the few small tables not long after ten, waved his hand at Eric, whose real name was Aliko Azikiwe, and pulled at the ends of his tie with an impatient tug. Aliko had placed the mug of mead in front of him less than two minutes later.

"The enemy that slew you did me an untold favor," Asher told him.

"The enemy that slew me died for his troubles three heartbeats later, or so my ancestors remember." Aliko answered in pure, fluent Norse. He grinned. "Have a care with that vintage, my friend. It was a particularly potent brew, that one."

"Good," Asher said with feeling, picking up the mug.

That had been...how many mugs ago? He didn't know and he didn't care. He took no notice of anyone around him, except to glare if anyone looked like even thinking about talking to him. He was left alone, the table to himself, as the customers thinned and time marched on.

A hand rested on his shoulder, heavy and hard, and squeezed.

Asher made himself look up, blinking at the harsh overhead light as it stabbed at his eyes with silvered splinters. Roar stood beside his table, in jeans and a suede jacket, his honey-blond hair falling over his face and casting a shadow over his eyes. "You look like you're in the wrong mood to be drinking alone, brother." He was using English.

Asher leaned back in his chair and pushed the one opposite him out with his foot and waved to it. "Did Eric call for reinforcements?"

"Because you decided the bottom of the mead barrel looked enticing?" Roar stepped over the seat of the chair and lowered himself into it. "That isn't nearly unusual enough to call out the troops."

He was a big man. Half an inch taller than Asher. Roar often drew attention when he was out in public. There were three young women in one of the booths against the wall eyeing him up now and whispering to each other.

But there was also a table of Einherjar by the fire, and they were also leaning in and talking while shooting glances at Roar. His brother had been recognized. It was one of the reasons why Roar rarely left the hall. Wherever he went, he tended to stir waves of consternation and interest in a way that would make humans curious about who he was, especially here in New York, where fame was nearly as much a city-wide pastime as in Los Angeles.

Aliko placed a shot glass in front of Roar and filled it in front of him.

"You are a kind and considerate host, Aliko. My thanks," Roar told him. "How much has my brother had?"

"That mug in front of him is the eighth." Aliko grinned at Asher. "I expected him to pass out two mugs ago."

Asher shrugged.

"He has a hard head." Roar picked up the glass, his big fingers making it look miniscule. "Runs in the family." He hefted the glass in an informal salute and knocked it back with a grimace. "The good stuff. One more, please, Aliko."

Aliko filled the glass once more and went back to his bar.

Asher watched Roar. "Come to take me home?"

"I imagine I will be pouring you into a bed somewhere tonight, yes. But that's not why I'm here." He was running his finger up and down the short length of the shot glass. "I expected you to have company. From what you're wearing, I'm guessing you were out somewhere earlier, probably with the same company."

Asher snorted and drank some more. He was starting to lose his taste for the stuff, a good sign he'd had enough for the night. But it wasn't shutting down his thoughts the way it usually did. "Good to know your spy system is working efficiently."

"I've heard from several different people that you've been here a lot over the last year or so. Usually in the company of a redhead, and they describe *her* in endless detail." Roar grinned. "I'd be jealous of my brother and this world-stopping beauty he's been seen with, except that she's not here now and you look like you always do when you're into the deep end of your 'I hate the world' phase."

"Is that what you think this is?" Asher asked. "The mood of the season?"

"The redhead. Is she the girl you helped ten, twelve years ago? She would be a grown woman now."

"If you're going to keep talking about her, use her name."

"I don't remember her name."

"Charlee." Asher gripped his mug tighter. "Charlotte Montgomery."

Roar's blue eyes, the midnight blue, drilled into him. "Did she spit in your eye, Askr? Is that why you're here?"

"What, are you here to help me mend my broken heart?" Asher laughed.

"Is it broken?" Roar asked curiously. But his gaze wouldn't let Asher go.

Asher had always had trouble lying to him. Damn it. He looked down into the contents of his mug. Half-empty. Half-full, he corrected himself. And who gave a damn, anyway? He sat up straight, jerking himself upright, aware that he was sprawling across the table. He looked Roar in the eye. "I'm fine." He said the words carefully, without slurring them.

Roar shook his head. "No, I don't think you are."

"Doctor Big Brother." He laughed again, but it didn't sound funny even to him. "Why *are* you here, anyway?"

"You already asked me that."

"What was your answer?"

Roar leaned forward and dropped his voice. "Tell me you haven't lost your head over her, Askr. Tell me you haven't fallen in love with a human."

Asher sat up again. In between mouthfuls he had fallen back into his sprawl. "I am not in love with her." He enunciated it perfectly. Then he clutched the table, as the room shifted around him. Roar was the only thing that was staying still. Asher focused on him fiercely, fighting to keep it together. Roar was doing that watching thing again, and he wasn't smiling. "I won't make your mistake," Asher added. "I'm not that shoo…stupid."

Roar's expression shadowed briefly. His jaw moved. "Yes, you are," he said softly with something that sounded a lot like pity, except that couldn't be it, because Roar was usually angry at him and sometimes amused. But he didn't pity him. Pity would make Asher…what? Pathetic?

Roar stood and came around the table and picked up Asher's arm. "Come on, little brother. Time for you to lie down."

"I'm fine."

"Yes, you're fine. You're also so drunk you can't stand on your own. C'mon." He tugged on his arm again.

"Can, too." Asher pushed himself to his feet, which took a degree of effort that surprised him. He stood up and looked Roar in the eye. Then the floor swayed like the deck of a ship and he reached out blindly for support.

Roar grabbed his arms and held him upright. "Yes, you absolutely can," he agreed dryly.

"Don't love her," Asher muttered. It seemed important he make this point, that Roar understand it completely. It was important because…why? He couldn't remember.

Roar nodded. "Sure. Let's just get you home."

* * * * *

After their first argument, which Charlee figured had been a long time coming, Asher stopped making his abrupt appearances. By the time the winter solstice approached, when Ylva's entire household was thrown deep into the meticulous and extended preparations for the feast day, which Ylva celebrated instead of Christmas, Charlee's stout assurances to herself that he would eventually show up again were starting to wear down, like a pestle ground against a mortar for too long.

She had apologized almost the next day, sending the apology by text, hoping it would bring him to the house. Then she could sit him down and talk it over. Above all, she wanted to talk it out. It was all sitting inside her chest, a hard mass of feelings and emotions.

But mostly, she wanted to assure herself that she hadn't damaged their odd relationship. As the weeks rolled on without Asher, though, her confidence weakened and doubts began to gnaw. Her sleep grew sporadic, and worst, she began to make mistakes with her work.

She had graduated to the top tables in the store and was now also the sole keeper of the wild birds that visited, seeing that they were fed and if any of them were hurt, caring for them until they were healed. Any other animals in the household tended to be brought to her when they were in need, too, so she often found herself nursing kittens and puppies, dog and cats, rabbits, chickens, and the household goat that lived in a pen on the roof.

In addition, she had been given gardening privileges, a role she took nearly as much delight in as caring for the birds. Some of her most peaceful hours were spent tending the big rooftop raised garden beds, learning how to shepherd plants along to fruition and harvesting them. It gave her a vested interest in finding out what happened to the produce after harvest, and she volunteered for canning and pickling and all the other preservation techniques used to store the food long term.

As a result, she was always busy and with Asher gone, she found it easier to bury herself in her work, learning everything she could.

Grimmer was the household guard dog, a lumbering cross-breed that was part Great Dane and a lot of Husky, for he had the barrel chest of that breed but was exceptionally tall and light on his feet. He was as well-trained as Torger but easier to fool. Charlee liked to take him for walks in Central Park to get him out of the house, which sometimes seemed to be too small to contain him.

Early in December, she snapped on Grimmer's lead and he danced around her in delight as she led him across the road and into the park itself. His energy and enthusiasm made her feel guilty. It had been too long since she had stretched his legs.

The sky was iron grey and it felt cold enough for snow, but there wasn't the crisp coldness in the air that usually came with it. Charlee enjoyed the coolness and the way it cleared out the park. Besides, a lot of people were out Christmas shopping.

Grimmer pulled on the lead, eager to sniff trees and benches and that twig over there, and wait, is that a *squirrel*? He led her deeper along the path toward the pond, and all Charlee's attention was on keeping him on the path and hauling on the lead so he wouldn't take off. He was usually well-behaved and totally obedient, but this was his vacation time and he took full advantage of it. It made Charlee laugh to see how much puppy was still inside such a large dog.

When he spotted the smaller dog ahead, sniffing one of the green garbage containers, he stiffened and Charlee hurried to catch up with him.

"Grimmer, behind me," she said with a snap in her voice. She waited until Grimmer obeyed, then checked to see what the other dog was doing.

It was Torger.

Her heart dropping in a weightless nosedive, Charlee looked to Torger's owner at the other end of the lead.

It was a blonde woman, petite and dressed in a fur coat and designer sunglasses. Her boots were leather with spiked heels and she had a leather clutch in her other hand, the hand not holding Torger's lead.

Charlee's heart lurched sickly. She stared at the woman, not understanding. Not able to put it together.

The woman stared right back. Then her gaze dropped to Charlee's own sensibly heeled boots. "Does he know you?" she asked in a haughty voice.

Torger was jumping around her feet, trying to scrabble at her knees, whining loudly. Grimmer was growling deep in his throat, but staying obediently behind her. She blessed him, for two dogs trying to take each other on right now would be the least of her problems.

"Torger, sit," she told him.

Torger sat, his tongue wagging.

"Good boy," Charlee told him.

"I've never seen anyone able to do that with him. The thing is a beast," the blonde said and stepped closer, rolling up the leash. "I don't believe we've met."

"No, we haven't." Charlee could barely speak the words. "Why do you have Torger? Where is Asher?"

There was a crunch of dried leaves, inside the trees that lined the path and hung over them with bare branches. The blonde looked that way. "There," she said simply.

Asher stepped out onto the path, lifting up the green tennis ball that Torger liked to chase. "It rolled a long way—" His gaze fell on Charlee.

Charlee could barely breathe as the truth started to finally jell in her mind. The two of them together. A beautiful blonde. *Another* beautiful blonde.

"I guess you've moved on from being mad at me, then." Her voice came out shaky. *Not good,* she told herself. *Not good at all, crying in front of him.*

So she turned and ran out of the park and away from Asher.

Grimmer thought it was great fun.

* * * * *

The garden beds were fallow, ready for winter. Nevertheless, Charlee picked at the soil, removing tiny weeds and working it over with a trowel, just to give her hands something to do and to give her an excuse to keep her head down and not talk to anyone, including Billy in his enclosure, who stood watching her as he slowly chewed mouthfuls of straw, his little goatee flapping contentedly.

That was where Asher found her. He slammed the door to the roof shut and halted, his hand still flat against it. The long leather coat swung around his knees, hanging open. Of course, he didn't think this kind of weather was cold. "For Odin's sake, didn't you hear me calling you?"

Charlee kept her head down. "You don't owe me an explanation."

"It's not what you think."

"It doesn't matter what I think."

"Damn it to hell, Charlee, of *course* it matters!" He was suddenly there, his hand around her elbow, hauling her to her feet.

She looked up at him, glad that her tears had dried. "It would have mattered if it was the day after I texted you. It would have mattered a week after that. Even a month. But not now. Your silence was eloquent. I understood."

She tried to turn back to the garden, but he held her still. "No. You listen to me, Charlee—"

"Let me go!"

"Not until you hear me out."

"You don't deserve a hearing!" she screamed, her fury suddenly huge and all-enveloping. She was hot with it, pulsing with it. She wanted to hurt him, even a little bit, for the last three months of misery and wondering, while he had been out enjoying himself to the hilt.

Asher's mouth dropped open and he let her go, just like that.

She staggered, found her balance and straightened up.

"You're still pissed at me?" he asked, sounding bewildered.

"I'm pissed at you all over again! I beggared myself, Asher! I apologized for being a bitch that night, and you didn't even acknowledge it. Two words! That's all it would have taken to let me know the score. Dear Charlee, it's over. But you couldn't even do *that*!"

"Goddamn it, Charlee, I was pissed at you, too!" He threw out his hands. "What do you want from me? I screwed up. I couldn't figure out how to face you after I packed you off in the cab."

Charlee stared at him. "You don't make mistakes," she said slowly, feeling her heart in her throat, hearing it in her ears. "You're a superhero."

Asher threw back his head, looked up at the sky and swore, long and hard. Then he looked at her once more. "I make just as many mistakes as any other man," he said flatly. "More, even."

"The blonde in the Barneys fur. Was she your next mistake?"

His jaw rippled. "She's the wife of one of my bank board members. I was walking her through the park so her husband could pick her up on Eighth Avenue." He gave her a small smile. "You didn't see the wedding ring on her finger while you were critiquing her clothes?"

"She was wearing gloves." Charlee tried to breathe. She was feeling suddenly weightless.

"So she was. I barely noticed." He took a step toward her. "I'm sorry Charlee."

"About today?"

"About all of it. The whole last three months. Can we…would you agree to just forgetting about them? Pretend this didn't happen?"

"Only if you forgive *me*."

"For what?" He shook his head. "It didn't happen. We just agreed on it."

Charlee threw her arms around his neck and held him tightly. Her breath caught as his arms came around her and she was squeezed back. Ah! His scent tickled her senses and she sighed.

* * * * *

They stayed on the roof for another two hours, sitting on the concrete cinder blocks that made up the edge of the raised beds. Charlee was cold, all except for the side of her leg and her shoulder, which were next to Asher, but she would slit her own throat before saying anything out loud, for Asher was talking. Really talking.

He sat with his hands on his thighs, the big fingers loosely curled and relaxed, and told her about the last three months. How he had got drunk and how his brother had hauled him out of Heidrun and dumped him on his sofa with a bucket next to him and zero sympathy for his self-induced state.

"What's your brother's name?" Charlee had asked, holding back her amazement that he had a brother in the first place. He had never spoken of him before. Not once. And now, an older brother.

Asher hesitated. It was the first and last time in those few hours when he did. "I can't tell you everything. After all this time, you understand that, yes?"

"Whatever you want to tell me is fine," she assured him.

His gaze caught hers. "Are you sure?" And there seemed to be a warning in that look.

She really did understand. She knew that this was a point where they could turn back and remain superficial friends. Or she could go forward into a future that was still unknown to her, although after her time in Ylva's house, she was beginning to see the raw shape of it.

"Tell me about your brother," she urged Asher.

Asher sighed. And for a long moment he said nothing, but simply stared down at his hands. Then he began to speak. She learned about his brother, Roar. "It's really Hroar," Asher told her, then spelled it out, "but without exception, everyone trips over either the spelling or how to pronounce it if they see it written down. Roar figured dropping the 'h' would make life a lot simpler."

He told her about the last three months spent working like a slave, which kept him occupied and to a degree, contained any thoughts about anything else in his life.

Me, Charlee realized. *He didn't want to think about me.*

"I felt like such a fool after the opera," he confessed, staring down at his toes. "I can't remember the last time I felt so stupid. When I was a child, I think. A long time ago."

Charlee leaned forward so that she could see his face, for it was turned from her. "Are you feeling foolish right now?" she asked.

"Why?"

"You've stopped looking at me. You're staring at the ground."

His gaze flickered toward her and he drew a deep breath. "I'm not used to talking." He said it like it was a highly embarrassing confession.

Charlee frowned. "But…"

"Not like this," he amended. "Not personal details."

"Not *ever*?" she asked, appalled. "But you've had girlfriends and dates and relationships that lasted longer than a week. I know you have, I watched you. What did you talk about with them, if you didn't give them personal details?"

His fingers threaded together and squeezed. "I listened," he said simply.

"Oh." That explained a great deal about his life, right there. If he never allowed himself to become intimate, then no wonder all his relationships had crashed and burned. He would have been the ultimately unavailable man. The perfect date, but beyond reach of anything meaningful. Every woman who had even the slightest involvement with him wouldn't have understood *why* he wasn't there for them in spirit as well as physically. "You must get lonely a lot."

He looked at her squarely. "Not lately," he said. Then, as her breath caught, he grimaced. "Except for the last three months, that is."

Charlee laughed. "A compliment, then a reminder of guilt. You really know how to boost a woman's ego, Asher."

"I thought we had agreed to forget that whole thing?" he demanded.

"We did," Charlee agreed easily, but she knew that she would never forget, for that ugly night had brought her to this sweet moment. He was talking to her. *Really* talking. There were things he couldn't speak of and she accepted that happily, as the cost of getting to know Asher better than she ever had.

The early sunset was threatening when Asher stirred and looked around. "Shouldn't you be working?"

"I should," Charlee agreed. "But I can catch up. I was ahead anyway. I worked late last night so I could take Grimmer to the park."

"Are you enjoying yourself, Charlee? Here in this house?" he asked, with a touch of awkwardness.

"Are you asking if I'm happy?"

"Yes."

"I'm happy."

He nodded, then got to his feet and brushed the grit from the cinder blocks from his coat. "I should let you finish your work."

Reluctantly, she stood. "When will you come by again?" she asked, and now *she* felt awkward. She made herself look him in the eyes. "I hope it won't be another three months this time?"

"It should be," he said flatly. "If you had the sense of a guinea pig, you'd tell me to go away and never come back."

Charlee wrapped her arms around herself and shivered, with more than the cold. "Have you heard that saying people have, about the road not taken?"

He frowned. "Something about no regrets. Is that what you mean?"

"I spent most of my childhood expecting I would go to college and become a doctor or a scientist, or something grand like that. I had no idea how I was going to pay for it, but that wasn't going to stop me. Instead, I'm here, apprenticing with Ylva. This is my road that by rights I shouldn't have taken, but I did. So there's no reason for me to regret or wonder what might have happened, because it *is* happening."

"You have no idea where the road leads." His tone was soft.

"And if I'd gone to college I could have been run over by a truck in my sophomore year. No one knows, Asher. Not even you."

His eyes, that seemed so incredibly blue in the soft winter light, held her gaze for a moment. "You're right," he said slowly, like he was tasting the truth for its flavor and finding it unexpectedly interesting. "Yes, you are right." He straightened up. "Come to dinner with me at the Ash Tree next week. Pierre would love to cook for you."

"Like he really does any of the cooking." She smiled. "It sounds lovely."

"Tuesday night?"

"Tuesday," she agreed.

Chapter Twenty-Four

Once a soldier, always a soldier. --
Unknown

After the apology, Asher never stopped talking. Charlee realized quickly that there was no one else in his life that he could speak with in quite the same frank way he spoke with Charlee. If Asher and Roar were typical brothers, Asher wouldn't be able to tell Roar the things he shared with her. She didn't know yet how it worked in his world, but clearly, talking over problems with friends wasn't possible for Asher.

But now he told her everything that was trivial in his life. The big things like the structure of his world, the name of things and many people, anything that might reveal more of his life than what was in his heart and mind, he held back. Instead, Charlee applauded his little triumphs and success. She listened to the human drama of his days, dealing with the bank's board, diners at the restaurant, staff in the kitchen, customers at the bank. Which pair of shoes Torger had chewed up this month. His search for the perfect sound system. His plans for the apartment, which never seemed to shift into first gear. And she commiserated while he complained and vented his frustrations. It was all small things he told her, but he *was* sharing and she couldn't ask for more.

Of all the tales he told, the most precious to Charlee were stories from his childhood. He carefully omitted specific details that might tell her where and when he was raised, but slowly, Charlee drew a picture in her mind of his early years. He had lived on an estate that was mostly one big farm, with more farms around it. His father was a leader in the community. Asher described him as "a sort of country mayor", which Charlee translated as being a sort of nobleman. The Norse equivalent of a baron, perhaps.

When she checked with Darwin, he had looked thoughtful. "He probably was an earl. They migrated the title to England when the Anglo-Saxons took over. There are still earls around today, but they're pretty low on the totem pole. But in Scandinavia, they were the local power holders. Next step up was the king. There were plenty of those, too, once upon a time."

Asher's raising had been one of almost complete freedom, once the chores of the day were done. But the chores were heavy, gruelling work, the sort of work and responsibilities that would make kids of today scream abuse. Even though he and Roar had been children, they were expected to do their part in the running of the estate, while also keeping up with their education. "Such education as there was," Asher added dryly. "Most people considered getting the crop harvested far more important that learning Latin conjugates, and that included my father. Most of my formal education I caught up with years later."

But Asher clearly remembered his boyhood with fondness and with a deep regard for his parents. His mother died when he was young, barely sixteen, and his father had taken another wife quickly, but she figured little in Asher's stories. "She was almost as young as me. I'm not sure if my father was marrying a wife or a nurse."

"Both, perhaps? He must have been lonely," Charlee said.

"Perhaps," Asher agreed slowly. "She kept to herself most of the time. I never really did get to know her well."

After the argument, Asher stopped abruptly appearing without warning. Instead, he would call her or text her and suggest they have dinner, or see a movie or play, or do more wonderfully different and interesting things. Even something as simple as walking Grimmer and Torger in Central Park was turned into an occasion. The two dogs learned to tolerate each other and after a while, even to like each other. But Torger had too much common sense and attitude, while Grimmer like to bound around like the puppy he no longer was, cheerfully causing chaos with his lead and his big feet and long legs. He apologized with damp nuzzles, which rarely helped, while Torger looked on with an expression that seemed to be both bored and condescending at once.

Asher helped Charlee straighten out Grimmer's worst habits and he became obedient and a very useful working dog, to the point where she and anyone else in the house could walk alone at night, if Grimmer was by their side. If a stranger got too close that he didn't like the smell of, he would stand in front of whomever he was guarding and growl warningly until the stranger moved on. When he was on duty, he was highly selective about whom he would allow near his protectee.

They celebrated their birthdays and both solstice and Christmas, and any other event that seemed like a worthy excuse. Then there was Darwin's birthday and Ylva's birthday, and every time Lucas was granted shore leave Darwin threw a party, from massive welcome-home events involving most of the neighborhood to the four of them sitting around his backyard with a beer each and a bonfire.

It was at one of those beer and bonfire nights that Asher and Lucas disappeared for nearly an hour. When they returned, Charlee sniffed the air and found no tension and no hostilities. And after that night, whenever Lucas was in town, he would phone and invite both Charlee and Asher out, but Charlee never found out what they had talked about that night.

* * * * *

Asher had gone along with Lucas' suggestion they head down to the corner bodega more easily that Lucas had expected and they walked down the sidewalk, their strides matching. It was a mild April evening, but Lucas found it cold and damp after so long in Afghanistan and left his jacket on.

Asher was wearing a button-up shirt, with the sleeves rolled up. It was the closest Lucas had ever seen him come to laid back clothing. "Man, do you ever just chill out and wear a basic T-shirt?"

"Sometimes. But not when I'm with Charlee." Asher glanced at him. "Is that why we're talking, Lucas? You want to do the 'what are your intentions' thing?"

Just like that, they were in the middle of it. Lucas drew in a short breath that seemed to be overheated. "That and something else."

Asher halted and turned to face him. "Should we find somewhere more amenable to conversation? I don't like talking where I don't know who could be listening."

Fifteen minutes later they found themselves sitting on a bench in the same park where Sergio had taken them, all those years ago. Since then, a community league had raised money for renovations. The big bushes that had provided such great cover for the gang were all gone. The park had new turf, a whole new playground, and trees had been planted in one corner. It would take them a few more years to be useful shade-givers, but now with the moon high overhead and the swings empty, the bench was as private as they would be able to find anywhere outside.

Asher raised a brow, encouraging Lucas to speak his mind, but he couldn't find the words. He rubbed his hands together, looking for a way to say it.

"Relax," Asher told him. "Tell me when you're ready. Is that recent?" He nodded toward Lucas' forearm. His jacket sleeve had slid back, revealing the ugly, pink, raised weal that Lucas had spent all night hiding from them.

Lucas hissed his annoyance. "Yeah. I dropped my guard. Thought she was just a woman. Turns out she was the wife of one of the Taliban jerks we'd been chasing for a month."

Asher's mouth lifted at the corner. It wasn't quite a smile. "So you're still figuring out what to do in tight corners, then?"

Lucas sighed. Suddenly, the words were right there and gratefully, he spilled them. "It's not what I thought it would be. You know? I thought,

286

once I had it down, nothing would ever make me feel…" He swallowed. "Helpless," he finished. "All this training, all these years, and I still got caught flat-footed and blinking, wondering what the fuck I'm supposed to do next."

"What *did* you do next?" Asher asked.

"I didn't kill her."

"Good." Asher fell silent, waiting.

"I knocked her out." He curled his hand into a fist and watched the scar writhe on his flesh. "Right to the temple. She dropped like a bag of rocks. Then I threw her into the back of the Humvee, and we dropped her off at the local detention center for them to sort out. They probably interrogated her and let her loose. I didn't ask."

Asher straightened up. "Then you *did* know what to do. You figured it out."

"Figured out what?" Lucas asked, honestly bewildered. "There's no training, nothing covers the shit we face over there. How do you deal with the uncertainty? Not knowing who is really an enemy and which ones are the civilians? Who's going to reach under their dishdasha and press the button on ten pounds of C4? Which of the hysterical women is carrying a PK machine gun under her burqa? It's got so I can't relax. *Everything* has the potential to blow up on me. How do you deal with that?"

Asher was quiet for a long time. "I think you're dealing with it as best you can."

"Was it like that for you?" Lucas asked.

Again, the long, contemplative silence. "War was a lot more personal when I was in it."

It was the first time Asher had ever openly admitted he had been in the military—*any* military. Lucas blew out his breath. "You knew who the enemy was."

"It was pretty clear who the enemy was. It was usually the guy trying to kill you, and the one after that and the one after that."

"The Gulf War?" Lucas asked. "Somewhere in Europe? Serbia?" Except Asher had been right here in New York when the Bosnian War had been going on, so it would have had to have been a war or battle before they'd met, at least. Vietnam?

Fleetingly, Lucas wondered how old Asher really was. He always seemed just slightly older than Lucas, but he didn't look any different from the last time Lucas had seen him.

Asher leaned forward, resting his forearms on his knees, looking at the ground. "Fighting is much more impersonal now. It's nebulous. With drones and long-range rockets and snipers that can reach out across half a mile and snuff out a life, all the killing is done at a distance."

"SEALs aren't at a distance," Lucas pointed out.

"But you're just a tiny cog in a big, sprawling machine. You get your orders to go in and take out a building, or find a general, or whatever your mission is today, but you don't know how that fits in with the overall offensive, do you?"

Lucas shook his head. "It's not a good idea to ask for that sort of information. You usually get told it's above your pay-grade."

Asher nodded. "So you're cut off, with no idea why you're doing what you're doing. You just have to trust that someone, somewhere, has a reason for it and it really does advance the war."

Lucas fell back against the bench. "Yep," he said. "That's about it."

Asher looked over his shoulder at Lucas. He grimaced. "There's not much chance anyone at all would feel like they know what they're doing, or that they have much control, in that situation. Including me."

Something loosened in his gut. Lucas let out a breath that was shaky. "You figure it out as you go along?"

"Sometimes, I barely work it out." Asher straightened up. "I end up going with my gut far too often. It gets me into corners as tight as yours." His finger lifted toward Lucas' arm.

"But you *do* end up knowing what to do."

Asher turned on the bench. "I fuck up all the time," he said flatly. Lucas had the eerie feeling that Asher wasn't just talking about tight situations, or war. "But there are some times, some situations, where everything just clicks into place. They call it being in flow, now. You've heard of it?"

"Not in connection with fighting."

"It works with any skill, any action that you're good at, that you've practiced over and over again. Fighting is in that category. For both of us."

Lucas nodded. It made sense to him, put that way. "Is that what happened here? With Sergio?"

Asher didn't answer.

"Charlee said there were things—subjects—that were off limits with you. Is that one of them?"

Asher looked back at the ground. "Is that what she said about me?"

"Man, she doesn't say much at all, when it comes to you. 'None of your freakin' business' is about the extent of it. Along with 'stay away from touchy subjects'. And that wasn't the language she used."

Asher grinned. "You must have got her temper roused, to make her swear."

"I've been trying to figure out how it is between you two for years. She won't say."

Asher dropped back into the same contemplative silence. Then he said softly, "Honestly, Lucas, I don't know, either."

It was the last thing Lucas expected him to say. "Fuck…!" he breathed, the retort pushed out of him.

"I know she's part of my life, now," Asher added. "There's no going back on that one."

"You tried, then."

"I told you I've fucked up more than once or twice."

Lucas grinned. "She didn't like it."

"Mild understatement." Asher paused again. "I do know one thing. You might take some comfort from it." He sat up again and stretched out his feet, like he was relaxing, but Lucas knew when a man was sizing up the territory in a covert way, and Asher was doing it now.

"There's no one here, man," Lucas assured him. Keeping tabs on who was in the vicinity was just second nature now. "Not for half a block or more."

"There's sightlines, but the tree will cover me enough, I think." He reached into his pocket and pulled out—

"Holy fuck," Lucas breathed, for the sword was suddenly just *there*.

No one was that fast on the draw. Where had he been hiding it? The questions started coming faster and faster as Lucas took in the silvered blade, the workmanlike hilt and the rounded pommel. Was this what he had used on Sergio? Had Charlee seen it? He was almost certain she had. The sword stood point upwards, an extension of Asher's hands, for he held it in both. He held it in a way that told Lucas he knew what he was doing with it.

Then he flipped it and rested it carefully, point down on the soil between his feet and looked at Lucas. "People who see this sword tend to disappear, Lucas. It's the way of things. So once we've finished with this conversation, you should forget all about it."

Lucas swallowed. The questions were still there. Who *was* he? Had the sword really just appeared? And if it did, what was it? Even in the depth of his confusion he rejected the word (*magic*) that floated up from his subconscious.

Asher hefted the sword, lifting it a fraction of an inch. "I've used this twice to protect Charlee. Both times, everything was clear. I was in flow. I knew exactly what I was doing. I've had times like that before, too. Do you know what the difference is between those time and all the others?"

Only later did Lucas wonder just how many 'others' there had been. He shook his head.

"It wasn't my life I was fighting for."

And just like that, it all clicked into place for Lucas. He understood.

It's not about me at all. Then he remembered the night when he had been facing Sergio, when all the circuits had been cleared and everything had been slow and calm, and lit by almost incandescent light, even though it had been pitch black. He had been in flow then, but he hadn't been thinking about himself at all. He had been thinking about Charlee.

He blew out his breath as peace entered his soul. It all made sense.

Asher was still contemplating the sword, which seemed to glow in the low light. "You have Charlee and Darwin, too. One day, there might be someone else. There's your father and everything he did for you. All your friends, everything that makes life worthwhile. Every one of them is in jeopardy, every time you suit up. If you keep them in mind when you're on point, I guarantee you won't choke."

"I won't," Lucas agreed. He knew it in his bones, now, just as he understood without being told the strength of the bond between Asher and Charlee, and that little would break it.

Asher sat up again, spinning the sword with a cock of his wrist. As the point reached the apex of the swing, it disappeared. It didn't dissolve or slide away. One moment it was there, then it was gone. Asher straightened and pushed something into his pants pocket. The hilt?

He stood up. In the dark, he was just a larger silhouette, outlined by the sodium arc light far away in the parking area between the apartment towers, behind the park. "You need to fight for Charlee, and anyone else you hold dear, but at the same time, you have to know that nothing will ever harm her, not while she lets me stay in her life. I'll do everything in my power to ensure that nothing ever troubles her, either."

"Don't promise absolutes," Lucas said, and his voice was a little hoarse. Who had told him that? Probably Charlee.

"It isn't a promise, it's a guarantee," Asher said flatly. "And it isn't an absolute."

"What is it, then?"

"Certainty," he said flatly.

Chapter Twenty-Five

In Norse mythology, a **valkyrie** (from
Old Norse *valkyrja* "chooser of the slain")
is one of a host of female figures who
choose those who may die in battle and
those who may live. Selecting among
half of those who die in battle…the
valkyries bring their chosen to the
afterlife hall of the slain, Valhalla, ruled
over by the god Odin. There, the
deceased warriors become einherjar.

Wikipedia

Charlee would always remember the date when the world shifted, for it happened the day after Elizabeth's second wedding, which in a way triggered it all.

Charlee had gone stag to the wedding, only because Asher had one of his mysterious out-of-country errands that he often did, and because he insisted that she go and that she take someone with her whose company she would enjoy. Darwin was also busy and Lucas was on active status. Charlee couldn't think of a single other person to ask. Ylva was good company, but she was also her boss and it just didn't seem right. So Charlee went on her own. She knew that Asher would be mildly annoyed over that.

Elizabeth caught up with Charlee after the simple ceremony, trailing ribbons and lace and netting, and dragged her into the ladies' washroom and over to the little bench opposite the bank of mirrors. They sat in absorbed silence for a moment, looking at each other. Elizabeth looked older. Her eyes were the same beautiful green with the thick lashes and brows framing them, but there were fine lines at the corners. Her skin was still porcelain pure and smooth, but her makeup was very carefully applied.

"I can't believe it's your *second* wedding," Charlee said at last.

Elizabeth rolled her eyes. "That's not why I wanted to talk to you. It's been so long, Charlee. Can you believe how long ago high school was?"

Charlee shook her head.

"You look like a million dollars, honey. I can't believe you couldn't find a date to bring with you, not looking like that."

Charlee smoothed down the silk of her dress. "Like it?"

"Love it. I can't figure out the designer, either." Elizabeth pouted.

"Me."

"No!" Elizabeth's eyes widened. "You *make* clothes now?"

"I make a lot of things." Charlee smiled at her. "You'll see some of what I can make in your wedding present."

Elizabeth pressed a finger to her lips. "I'll make sure I put your gift to one side and open it myself."

Charlee squeezed her other hand. "How are you? Really?"

"I'm married!" She held up her left hand with the gold ring, her smile impish.

"I mean, it was so fast, Elizabeth. You only got divorced…." Charlee paused. "Oh, wow, that was nearly two years ago, wasn't it? I take it back." She hesitated. "Does he make you happy?"

Elizabeth rolled her eyes. "The first time around I married Chuck because my parents thought it was such a good idea, but I think they were more in love with the idea of Chuck's mom and dad becoming a part of the family. Dad and Charles used to go fishing together, long before Chuck asked me out. So I married him." She shrugged. "You know how you're supposed to look at the bright side of anything? I think Chuck was a trial run, a way for me to figure out what marriage was all about. Peter…" She sighed. "I got to pick Peter out myself."

Charlee didn't point out that she hadn't answered her question. "Have you really figured marriage out?" she asked curiously.

"Who knows?" Elizabeth laughed. "What about you, though? Anyone special in your life?"

"Perhaps." Charlee gave her a small smile. "It's complicated."

"It always is," Elizabeth assured her.

Charlee kept her smile in place. There was nothing she could say to that.

Elizabeth's expression sobered. "I sometimes think you had it right all along."

"Had what right?"

"You were always talking about making something of yourself. Your own career. Your own life. I don't think you had a single boyfriend the entire time we were in high school together, and it didn't seem to bother you because you were so busy studying and figuring out what you were going to do with your life. I thought you were crazy, being so obsessed with success and whatever it was you kept daydreaming about."

"I guess I must still be crazy," Charlee murmured.

"No, I think you knew, even back then."

Charlee just looked at her, puzzled.

Elizabeth sighed and pushed back the edge of her veil. "I know I'm going to wake up sometime tonight, and look over at Peter and think 'Is this it? Is this all there is to life?"'

Charlee stared at her, appalled. "Oh, Elizabeth," she breathed.

Elizabeth carefully dabbed at the corner of her eye with her fingertip, collecting the tears that had gathered there. "I can't see ahead the way you seem to be able to. I can't figure out what I want."

"So you got married?"

Elizabeth pressed her full lips together. "What else was there to do?"

Charlee had spent the next twenty minutes trying to shift Elizabeth's mood, to make her laugh once more, so that she would walk out of the washroom with a smile on her face, as any bride should on their wedding day.

But her friend's mood stayed with Charlee and her words lingered. *Is this all there is*? Charlee wanted to know the answer to that herself. Her apprenticeship with Ylva was satisfying in an intellectual way and every day was work-filled and absorbing, but where did it lead to?

What comes next?

It was a question that Charlee had begun to ask herself lately, about everything in her life. Elizabeth had clarified and focused her thinking.

What now?

* * * * *

The day after the wedding, Charlee made her way to the store after taking care of the current pets and domestic animals, including a brushing for Grimmer, and was delighted to find Victoria working at the next table.

After they had hugged and exclaimed over how long Victoria had been away from the house, they settled back into their work, standing on the far side of their own tables so they could look up and see each other. The work went faster that way and talking was easier.

But Elizabeth's question was tapping on the corners of her thoughts, like a crow tapping at a window. The question wouldn't go away, and Charlee knew she couldn't even begin to formulate a response without more information.

"But where have you *been*?" The question burst out of her, interrupting Victoria's commentary about how much she missed the store.

Victoria looked puzzled. "What do you mean?"

"All of you, you all go away on mysterious trips and errands. A day, a night, a week, a year, then you come back again. Sometimes. But no one says where they've gone!" She thumped the marble mortar she was holding on the table, not heavily, but the marble made a heavy thud against the wood, anyway.

Victoria's big, grey eyes were very large now. She frowned, a line puckering between her brows. "But you do, too. You were away for nearly a year."

Charlee shook her head vigorously. "That was learning, at Anja's shop."

"There are other shops besides Anja's," Victoria said gently. "And you do, too, go away for more than learning. I've seen you with Asher Strand."

Charlee blinked. "You know who he is?"

"*Everyone* knows who he is."

Charlee looked down at her bowl. "*I* don't."

"But…" Victoria bit her lip. "Never mind." She began mixing again.

"But what?" Charlee pressed.

She shook her head.

"*Please*, Victoria. I'm so tired of not knowing what everyone else knows."

Victoria glanced around the big workroom. She dropped her voice. "Of course you don't understand. You're not Amica. And *laun* means I can't tell you."

"Screw *laun*. I know how to keep my mouth shut. I need to know. I need to start making decisions."

"Are you going to join the Amica, then?" Victoria asked.

Charlee blinked. "Is that even an option for me?"

Victorian picked up her spoon and began stirring again. "I wouldn't know," she said blandly. "But you live in this house. I'm sure Ylva would arrange it if you wanted it. She likes you."

You live in this house. "Okay, here's a really dumb question, then. What *is* this house? An Amica house?"

Victoria rolled her eyes. "Hardly. This is Ylva's home."

"Yes, and…?" Charlee coaxed.

Victoria shook her head. "Ylva is not Amica," she said.

Charlee gripped her pestle, controlling her reaction. The next answer would step into territory that she had never reached before. Territory that was hidden behind *laun*, the mysterious wall of silence that everyone—Asher, Ylva, and anyone connected with them—seemed to understand. It was a stony conspiracy that everyone maintained with rigorous discipline. Was this at last a chink? Could she hammer her way inside now?

She made herself work the pestle with casual movements. "Of course Ylva isn't Amica," she said, as if this had been long known to her. "She's a Valkyrie." She held her breath, waiting for Victoria's response.

"Well, not anymore, of course," the woman responded and picked up the jar of olive oil and poured a few careful drops. "But yes, that's what I mean."

Charlee kept her hands moving, watching them while her mind raced and her heart thudded sickly. Ylva was, or used to be, a Valkyrie. It was all true, everything she and Darwin had extrapolated and conjectured. The Einherjar, the Valkyrie, here on Earth.

She carefully formulated her next question. "So you went visiting another Valkyrie house?"

Victoria laughed. "Hardly. Ylva knows Eira, of course. Eira wanted an Amica to fill in for one of her own, who had accepted a short-term contract with an Einherjar in another hall. I was actually working right there in the Second Hall." She said it with pride, the capital letters implied by a subtle emphasis.

Charlee had to work to keep her breathing steady and not in any way let Victoria know that all of this was new to her. All the assumptions in Victoria's answer and what they implied made her pulse boom in heavy waves. She didn't know who Eira was, but from the context, she had to assume that Eira was a Valkyrie. Amica worked *for* the Valkyrie, in ways she had yet to figure, but from all the learning she had done in this household, it seemed safe to assume that the duties were domestic. Cleaning and maintaining a "hall", perhaps. If Victoria had worked at the "Second" Hall, then there was more than one. Where was the Second Hall? Here in the city, somewhere?

Forcing herself to physical stillness, while her mind reeled and the questions came faster and faster, Charlee tested the mixture in her bowl and sniffed it carefully. "The Second Hall itself? Of course they would pick you for that. You're so good at everything."

Victoria's cheeks turned pink. "I don't think I was picked for my singing. It was the *Second Hall*, Charlee." She leaned forward conspiratorially. "I think I might have caught the eye of one. He asked me to keep him company the last night I was there." She blew out a sigh. "If I'd had a little more time, I might have had the chance to make a permanent arrangement, or even a short-term contract."

Charlee stared down at the wooden tabletop blindly, as understanding slammed through her. Her awareness shifted and new patterns formed. The training she had received here; the emphasis on appearance, clothing and presentation; the constant trial-and-error search for the potential in all of them, developing skills that would serve whomever they were assigned to. Then there was the sheer beauty of every Amica Charlee had ever met.

The Amica were *companions* for the Kine. Housemaids for the Valkyrie and partners for the Einherjar. They were trained as paramours, their natural talents enhanced, their loveliness showcased, their training every bit as nuanced and detailed as that of a geisha's.

Her heart was swinging around in her chest, hurting in its frantic beat. Charlee let out a shaky breath. Her head felt thick and hot with pressure. "Was he handsome?" she asked Victoria and her voice sounded far off and hazy to her. "Your Einherjar?"

Victoria smiled. "Who cares? He's *Einherjar.*" She carefully stirred the contents of her bowl. "They were saying in the Second Hall that there's too many Amica now. Of course, they need a lot because the Valkyrie are diminishing and the Einherjar outnumbered them to start with. But…" She leaned forward again. "Can you imagine not being chosen? How humiliating it would be, to have to fall back to being a cleaner or a cook or something boring like that."

Charlee almost gasped. The facts were flowing over her now, each a revelation of its own. "You wouldn't want to just *be* in the Second Hall?" she asked, trying to sort through all of it and not give Victoria any hint that she was holding up her end of the conversation with sheer bluff, feeling her way ahead with the information Victoria was feeding her with every answer. "Would it matter what you were assigned to, if you could just be there?"

"Well, I suppose," Victoria said slowly and doubtfully. Then she brightened. "Of course if you're *there*, then even if you're just serving the tables, you could still catch the eye of an Einherjar. Like Kate and Salomon."

Charlee could feel tremors starting up in her knees and her belly. She was going to have to take a risk now, or Victoria would shut down on her completely. She shook her head a little, looking thoughtful. "I don't think I've heard that story. Kate and Salomon, I mean." Victoria had said the two names in a way that made her think of story titles and book names. *Tristan and Isolde. Antony and Cleopatra. Kate and Salomon.*

Victoria waved her fingers, wriggling them with excitement. "You *haven't?* It's such a great story. He's Einherjar, but there was a human woman he was in love with, but he wouldn't leave the Kine for her because he was a stallari and his earl needed him. It was back centuries ago, when they actually got to use their swords out in the open, like humans were still doing. Salomon was told by the Council he had to pick an Amica and forget about the human woman. He saw Kate tending the firepit in his hall, and he chose her, the first Amica he saw. He didn't care, he was heartbroken over his human lover. But Kate was very, very smart. She wouldn't sleep with him at first. She told him she would be a friend and never try to take the place of his lover. And she was.

"For years, she took care of him and didn't ask for a single thing in return. She kept assuring him that his lost love was important to him, and he should remember and honor her. And bit by bit, he forgot about his human and fell in love with Kate. They lived together until Kate died of old age, and then Salomon mourned *her* as the greatest love of his life." Victoria smiled dreamily. "I would love to meet him one day. I heard he is with the hall in Thailand now and they don't mix with the others as much, but they do come to Council, so if I was with the Second Hall, I might see…. Charlee, what's wrong?"

Charlee gripped the table hard, trying to clear the dizziness in her head. She heard Victoria's quick, concerned question, but couldn't answer. She could barely draw breath.

"Silia!" Victoria called. "Quickly, something's wrong with Charlee!"

Charlee shook her head in denial, or thought she did. White noise was booming in her head, making sounds around her ebb and fade in waves. Strong hands were on her arms, lifting her, keeping her on her feet. People were talking, but she couldn't hear them.

Finally, she closed her eyes and gave up.

* * * * *

"If it wasn't a faint, it was something just as alarming," Ylva said, folding her hands over her crossed knees. "Sudden traumatic emotional upheaval can look very much like fainting."

Charlee tried to lift herself up higher on the chaise longue, but didn't have the strength. She felt so tired. "I'm fine," she said once more. "Really. I just need to find my phone. I dropped it somewhere."

"It's probably still in the store. Why do you want it?"

Charlee rolled her eyes. "I want to make a call."

"Clearly. I would like to know who you need to call so desperately immediately after you just collapsed with shock."

"It wasn't—I didn't collapse. I'm just tired, Ylva. It was a late night last night. Maybe I ate something at the wedding that doesn't agree with me."

Ylva gave her a small smile. "I've known you since you were ten years old. Do you think I didn't figure out long ago what your tell is? You can't lie to me."

Charlee couldn't meet Ylva's gaze. "Just a friend. I just want to call a friend."

"Asher?" Ylva asked, and her voice was very gentle.

Charlee swung her legs off the lounge and faced Ylva. "You loved your husband very much, didn't you?"

Ylva drew in a breath. Slowly. "Yes, Charlee, I did."

Charlee watched her face carefully. "He wasn't Einherjar, was he?"

Ylva grew still. Statue still. It was an echo of the same way Asher responded whenever she said too much.

"Did he know what you are?" Charlee asked, almost whispering it.

Amazingly, Ylva's eyes filled with tears, which spilled down her cheeks. "Oh, Charlee," she breathed.

"Did he know?" Charlee pressed. It was important she know the answer to that.

Ylva wiped her cheeks. "I didn't want him to know," she said, her voice strained. "I thought it was kinder for him to think I was as human as he was." She pressed her fingers to her lips. "Charlee," she said through them. "I'm so sorry it came to this."

Charlee stood up. Carefully. "I have to speak to Asher."

Ylva jumped to her feet, too. "Charlee, please, please, be *very* careful what you say to him. Asher is…he's…"

"He's still Einherjar," Charlee said. "And I'm just human," she finished bitterly.

* * * * *

Charlee barely noticed the sumptuous décor. She could only just process the names of people as they introduced themselves and almost immediately forgot them as soon as they turned away.

This last one, the woman she was following, was Margery. From her classic skirt suit and the sensible heels, Charlee tagged her as a senior secretary of some sort. Margery walked right up to a set of double doors, made of wood with brass fittings. She tapped lightly on one of the doors, then turned the handle and pushed it open. "Go right on in," she said, with a smile.

"Thank you," Charlee told her, but couldn't summon up a smile. It just wouldn't form.

"Would you like some water, dear?" Margery asked, her voice lowering. "You're very pale."

Charlee shook her head and Margery stepped aside, letting her go through. Charlee heard the door shut behind her, but that was something else that barely registered.

Asher was standing in front of a big executive desk and for the first time, his pristine suit matched his surroundings. "Is this the mountain coming to Mohammed?" he asked, smiling. "I am finally graced with a visit here."

He was coming toward her. Charlee's heart squeezed and her pulse zoomed. The noise was starting to come back. She held out her hand, silently begging him to stop. "I know," she said. Her voice broke.

"Know…?"

Charlee swallowed. "I know everything I need to know. I know you can't say anything. I even know why, now. But it doesn't matter because I found out anyway."

"Charlee…." He was coming toward her again, his expression concerned.

"I know what you are, Asher."

Shock slithered across his face. He halted, just as she had wanted him to. "Who told you? Ylva?"

"It doesn't matter. I know you're Einherjar. I know Ylva was once a Valkyrie. I know that *laun* has kept you silent all these years. I know the story of Kate and Salomon now."

Asher closed his eyes and turned away. He walked slowly over to the big window, his feet wandering, until he was standing at the glass.

Charlee made herself breathe, shallow and fast, but enough so that the screaming white noise receded a little. "What I don't know, what I can't figure out is, why you didn't cut me out of your life years ago, when it still wasn't too late."

He dropped his head.

"Asher?"

"I tried."

"What?"

"I said, *I tried*." He turned to face her. "I couldn't do it."

"We're *forbidden* to be together! You knew that, but you kept me dangling, all these years." She sucked in a breath. She was shaking now. "You could have found some excuse. *Anything*. You were moving to Timbuktu. You had a wife and three kids in New Jersey. I'm too ugly with this damned scar—"

"Charlee!" He was shocked.

"*One* kiss!" she railed at him. "Did you have fun watching me trail after you like some dumb dog that is hoping for her next treat?"

"Stop it, Charlee. I mean it."

"You can't stop me," she shot back. "I'm single, white and female. And I'm *human*."

"You're upset."

"Damned right, I'm *upset*!" she screamed. "Do you know how much I wanted you? Dreamed about you? About us together? If you had only said something, *years* ago, I could have…I would have…." *Done nothing different. You would have done exactly what you did. You took the other road, because that's where Asher was.*

She buried her face in her hands, the cold truth chilling her and stealing away the temper she had been trying hard to build all the way downtown. She felt cold, used, and exhausted and desperately wanted to be held and comforted, but that was never going to happen. Not now. Not ever. It had never even been a possibility, except in her own starved imagination.

His arms came around her, hot and comforting. "I'm sorry, Charlee," he whispered. "I was selfish. I wanted you in my life any way I could get. I told myself I wouldn't let you get hurt and that let me do it."

Charlee blindly wrapped her arms around his neck, her cheek against his shoulder. "I hate you."

"I know." He pushed her hair away from her cheek. Slowly he drew his finger along the scar. "Hate me as much as you need to, Charlee. I deserve all of it."

She sighed. "I can't. I tried once, but I just can't. You're my superhero."

Asher groaned. "That stupid, *idiotic* fantasy of yours. Hasn't this, right here, proved I'm just as weak as the next man?"

She lifted her head from his shoulder, to look at him properly. "But you're not a man, are you? I can't decide which way it worked. Compared to the Amica, I'm a scarred, mere mortal so your self-restraint all these years could be explained that way, but—"

"Hel's hounds, Charlee," he whispered. "Don't do this."

"—but my ego, it seems, would prefer to think that you have been writhing in agonized dilemma and that's why you won't touch me."

"Damn, but you will *never* leave well enough alone, will you?" His eyes were blazing with something that seemed like fury.

"It's a simple ques—"

His lips stole the rest of her words, pressing against hers with a hard, demanding pressure that snatched away her breath. His hand was in her hair, holding her head so that he could kiss her harder. His tongue thrust into her, and Charlee closed her eyes as her body seemed to ignite and burn in white-hot flames. She couldn't get close enough to him, even with his arm holding her pressed against him.

Asher groaned and lifted her off her feet and carried her three short steps until her back was against the wall. He put her back on her feet and his lips pressed against the flesh between her breasts, revealed by the V-neck of her dress. Moist heat bathed her flesh, making her moan in desperate need. She clutched at his head as his mouth trailed up the length of her throat, sending ripples of pleasure down her body. He reached her mouth and kissed her again.

There was a soft ruffling noise and something brushed her feet. His jacket. He had dropped it heedlessly to the floor. He pulled at the ties of her dress. "You can halt this any time you want. But I won't. Not now."

Something primal and feminine leapt inside her. "Don't stop." Her voice was husky.

He closed his eyes briefly, his chest rising. Then he tugged on the ties, unravelling them, and her dress parted. His gaze almost burned with intensity as he took in her body. His hands trembled as he fitted them around her waist. "So small." His voice was as hoarse as her own. His thumbs brushed down her flesh, making her shudder.

The urge to hurry was building. Charlee reached for the belt on his pants and slipped it undone. Trembling, she slid down the zipper, feeling the heat against her knuckles, and sought for the opening.

Asher's fingers curled around her wrist, halting her. He lifted her hand up, and up, until he had her wrist pinned against the wall, next to her head. He looked into her eyes and shook his head. It was a tiny movement. "I can't."

She swallowed. "I'm not enough."

"You're more than enough." His jaw rippled. "I want you. I've wanted you for years and you *know* that. But you also know what I am." He stood up, and gently closed her dress.

Charlee stared at him, breathing hard. "You dated all those women. *Human* women. They had no idea about you and the Kine. I do know. It should make it easier, not harder."

He fastened and straightened up his clothing, moving slowly. "What is it that you want, Charlee?"

"You."

"Are you sure?"

Charlee laughed. With shaking fingers, she tied her dress closed once more.

Asher sat on the front edge of his desk, his arms crossed. She suspected he was trying to look composed, but the joints of his fingers were white with the pressure he was exerting. "If it's just me you want, you can have me. I'll commit to you, body and soul."

Her heart leapt.

Asher lifted a hand in warning, even though she had made no attempt to speak. His hand trembled and he returned it quickly to grip his arm once more. "But that's all you can have, Charlee. Just me. The rest of it, the rest of my life…you can't be a part of it."

Her elation evaporated. "Not even to *talk* about it?"

"If they even suspect how much you know already…. Charlee, I've spent nearly all your life trying to protect you and not just from the Lightning Lords of the world. I *can't* talk about it. There are laws."

"*Laun*," she concluded bitterly.

He drew in a breath. "Yes," he said flatly. "But that's not all. If you want this, if you want…me…." He hesitated. "I can't give you anything else. Do you understand?"

Charlee was back to trembling again. She shook her head. It was too

301

hard to think, too painful to try and anticipate what he meant.

"The house in the suburbs. The picket fence," he ground out. "Children…."

Charlee sighed. *Of course*. The final piece of the puzzle.

Asher watched her, waiting for her reaction.

She fumbled for the handle of the door, next to her hip. "I must think about this."

This time, Asher sighed. "Yes, you must."

* * * * *

Darwin couldn't understand why retirees bitched about retirement. He'd been retired for nearly six months already and every day was a joy to wake up to. He'd make himself a modest breakfast and head out for a long walk around the neighborhood. There were more interesting things to see and people to chat with than he'd ever suspected in his forty years living here. Now that he had the time and freedom to explore, the world around his house was opening up to him.

After his walk, depending on how he felt, he would tidy up the house. But that didn't always happen because it barely got untidy anymore. More often he'd go back to his office and settle in to catch up on email. Lucas was very good at writing, and even Ylva sent the odd polite and delightful note or two. Charlee hadn't got around to getting her own computer yet, so she sent text messages, but he was working on converting her, any day soon. Then there were professors and librarians and scholars from around the world that kept up a running commentary on aspects of information retrieval, history and just plain ol' interesting stuff, that kept him busy chatting. He loved the world-shrinking qualities of the Internet and email.

After that he worked on what he liked to think of as his Projects. He had a long list of research subjects that over the years he'd always wanted to delve into deeper. In the back of his mind was the slowly forming idea of writing a book, but there was no hurry yet.

Sometimes he'd work on his projects late into the night. That was one of the beauties of retirement: there was no one to answer to anymore. He could sleep all day and work all night if he wanted to.

He walked down Trinity, admiring the leafy fullness of the trees and the way they bowed over the road, almost meeting in the middle, creating puddles of cool shade along the pavement. He reflected on how good life was.

That was when the cab pulled up beside him and Charlee flung open the door and scrambled out of the back seat.

Alarm crashed through his peace and joy as she hurried over to where he stood by the fence. Her face was white and pinched, and her eyes big and bewildered, reminding him of a little girl about to burst into tears.

"What's he gone and done now?" he demanded and opened up his arms.

Charlee press her face against his chest and cried.

Chapter Twenty-Six

Eira
Senior Valkyrie and Regin from 1801
until the end of the First Alfar War.
Born to a plebian Roman family, circa
85AD. Earned a position within the
Roman Legions and was rapidly
promoted…
From *The Complete Kine Encyclopedia*, by
Darwin Baxter, PhD. 2019 Edition

Darwin put the second bowl of mint chocolate chip ice cream in front of her. "I'm told it helps," he said. "Personally I think it's just a good excuse to snarffle down ice cream, but give it a try."

Charlee smiled wanly at him and picked up the spoon.

He settled at the table with his own bowl, for this was the perfect excuse to eat ice cream at ten o'clock in the morning. He had to keep Charlee company, after all. He caught Charlee looking at him.

"Whenever you're ready. Or not," he told her. "Even if it's just a big version of how prick-like men can be. I'm listening."

He was rewarded with another small smile. "*Some* men," she qualified.

"Is Asher part of that fraction today?" Darwin asked, keeping his tone light and casual. He became alarmed all over again when her eyes filled with tears that trembled on the brink of spilling over. "Oh, hey, c'mon, Charlee. Please. I don't know what to do with a crying lady. Ice cream is the best I've got."

She sniffed mightily. "You do just fine, Darwin." Her voice was hoarse.

Uncomfortable, he poked his spoon into his ice cream. He liked it stirred and creamy, until it was about running off the spoon. Not that he gave a damn right at this moment, but it was better than looking at her red eyes and the hurt look in them. "What'd he do?" he asked, damping down his anger all over again. If the bastard had been mean, or mistreated her in any way, he'd be right back in that restaurant to have a piece of him, oh yes.

Charlee sighed. "He's Einherjar, Darwin. It's all true. Ylva was a Valkyrie, but she's not anymore, because she chose to be with a human. But Asher can't be with me. Not in any way that has any real meaning."

Darwin felt like half his brain had leaked out his ears. He scrambled to absorb what she was saying, hooking it up with all the speculations and theories they had bandied about for years. Finally he sat back, his ice cream forgotten. "You're *shitting* me," he breathed.

* * * * *

Darwin poured the last of the bottle of wine into her glass, and Charlee sighed. He had been giving her the lion's share of the wine all night, and she knew he was trying in his gentle way to smother some of her pain under an alcoholic haze. It might have worked, except that her tolerance for liquor was so much greater than he remembered, now.

She watched him fondly as he settled back into his customary chair, behind the stack of books spread out across the table. They had sat into the night like this many times in the past.

"Drink up," he told her, as he flipped one of the books that lay open back up so the page was facing him and tapped it. "She said 'stallari,' right?"

Charlee nodded. "It's not the first time I've heard it. I think Asher is one. It's something to do with earls. The stallari report to them."

Darwin nodded. "That would make sense. 'Stallari' is Old Norse. It means captain, or lieutenant. A fighting man. The leader of the earl's fighting forces, perhaps?"

"Would earls be in charge of the halls that Victoria kept talking about?"

Darwin pursed his lips, considering it. "It's hard to imagine that every hall would be run by a king. Too inefficient. But earls would make sense. What I want to know is who is running the show."

"Excuse me?"

Darwin touched the books. "Someone has to be in charge. The mythology that humans recorded we've agreed is probably wildly inaccurate, but it's all we've got for right now, and *that* mythology said that the Einherjar and the Valkyrie lived in Valhalla, and Odin was their leader. Odin is one of the major gods of the Norse pantheon. So where is he? And if he's not around, who is the leader now?"

Charlee wrinkled her brow, thinking through every hint, every intimation, every offhand comment that had ever been made within her hearing. "Why wouldn't Odin still be around?" she asked. "He's a god. If the Kine are immortal, then he most certainly would be. Why wouldn't he still be here?"

Darwin raised his brows. "You haven't been keeping up with the reading list I gave you, have you?"

"I'm too busy being Mata Hari and digging up cool factoids for you to drool over," she shot back. "You're the researcher, Darwin. You tell me why Odin isn't here on Midgard."

Darwin blew out his cheeks. "Where to start? Okay, to begin, the Norse didn't have just one god. They had dozens and dozens of them. Major and minor deities."

"Like the Greeks and Romans did," Charlee said.

"Yes, exactly. But the Greek gods and the Roman gods have strong parallels. The Greeks called their version of Cupid Eros, Mercury was Hermes, Neptune was Poseidon, Mars was Ares and so on down the line. The Norse didn't have anything like the same sort of gods. *Their* gods were…well, here's an example. Odin was known as the Furious One. He fathered sons by a dozen other gods and humans, too. Most of the Norse royalty—human royalty, I mean—counted ancestors in their family line who were the offspring of Odin." He grinned. "And he gouged out his own eye."

"*Ugh*." Charlee grimaced. "Why?"

"He wanted the knowledge and wisdom that would be his if he drank from Mimir's well, but she told him the price for a drink was one eye. So he plucked it out and dropped it into the well."

"For *knowledge*?" Charlee shook her head.

"He slept with the daughter of the god of poetry and stole her father's blood, which he then spat all over Asgard. The dribbles that missed the pots the Asgardians laid out to catch the blood fell upon Midgard, and that's why humans are blessed with poetry today." Darwin wrinkled his nose. "That is, if you want to call it 'blessed'. I read some of that modern stuff they call poetry and have to wonder about that."

Charlee gave a short giggle. "Oh my…."

"Thor was into cross-dressing," Darwin added.

Charlee's giggle became a full-scale laugh. "*Cross*-dressing?"

Darwin nodded sagely. "A giant stole his hammer—"

"The actual hammer of Thor?"

"The *actual* hammer. The only way the giant would give it back was if he could marry Freyr, a woman in Thor's family. Freyr seemed like one of the few sensible gods I've read about so far. Guess what her answer was?"

Charlee smiled. "I'm guessing it wasn't a resounding yes."

"One of the versions I read said that the halls of Asgard shook with the power of her fury." Darwin lifted a brow.

"So Thor dressed like Freyr to get his hammer back? Really? Why didn't he just steal the damned thing?"

"Oh, it gets even weirder than that. There's adultery, bastard children, betrayed brothers, chest thumping, rending of garments and all sorts of hysterics." Darwin sighed. "It's some of the best melodrama I've seen outside of a pro wrestling series. Very entertaining, if you can stop from laughing your head off. But that's the point, Charlee. If the humans that wrote down all this stuff, such as the *Poetic* and the *Prose Edda* and the other fragments that have survived, even if they exaggerated the crap out of what they did know about the gods, once you deflate the hysteria and try to give it a more realistic spin, the gods still end up looking like wayward two year olds in need of a good spanking."

Charlee pressed her fingertips to her lips, holding back more laughter.

Darwin tapped the book again. "Don't you think that if Odin were still around, we dumb ol' humans would have noticed? A man-like figure with one eye and supernatural powers, raping human women and making babies all over the place—he would have hit the headlines sooner or later."

Charlee's smile faded. "Perhaps he's mended his ways since then. It was a long time ago, and the Kine have spent centuries hiding from us. Odin might have applied some self-discipline, and curbed his more extreme habits."

"Unlikely, but mildly possible, once you agree that the Kine are really, actually here and not in Valhalla anymore." Darwin patted the thick leather and brass bound book of Norse mythology under his hand. "Except that if Odin is here, that means the rest of the gods would be here, too, and I don't for a moment believe they *all* have managed to behave themselves since they got here. Besides, they're not all human-shaped. There's wolves and horses and giants, shape-shifters and serpents…and that's just the gods. Once you descend to the citizens of the nine worlds, it gets even more bizarre. I think we would have noticed if the gods or the population of the nine worlds were all living here on Earth."

"Nine Worlds." Charlee muttered, frowning. "I've heard that before."

"If you've done any reading at all from my list, then you would have seen it there."

"No, someone said something. I can't remember right now." She let it go. "I'll remember it later, and let you know. So who do you think is the leader of the Kine, if it's not Odin?"

Darwin shrugged. "It has to be one of their own. An Einherjar most likely. The Norse were patriarchal down to their toes, and the Einherjar all came from times when women were property at the very least—"

"Why do you say that?" Charlee asked sharply.

"Why they wouldn't have a woman as a leader? I'm not being sexist, honey-chile. That's just the way it was. Is. Probably."

"No, I mean about *all* the Einherjar coming from times long ago. That's a presumption you can't make. You don't know that they're all that

307

old. The Valkyrie pull fallen heroes from battlefields and they become Einherjar. There have been battles right up until yesterday, all over the world. There's probably one happening right now."

"Yes, but where do the Valkyrie come from?" Darwin asked patiently. "You said that your friend at the house—Victoria—she said that there wasn't as many Valkyrie as there were Einherjar, and there are fewer every year, or something like that. The Valkyrie numbers are diminishing. If Ylva is a good example, then some of them have given up their Valkyrie status for love and a human life. Others might have died from accidents, or suicide. My bet is on suicide. After thousands of years, life would become a major drag."

Charlee's eyes widened. "Suicide. Or perhaps they distract themselves by diving into drink for a month or two. Or take up with a human that doesn't know what they are, just to feel normal for a while."

"You can't think you're just a distraction for him," Darwin said gently.

Charlee shook her head. "I might have been, to start with. It's moved on from there. Too far on." She smiled sourly and sat up straighter. "So the Valkyrie are diminishing."

"Not just the Valkyrie. All of them." As gently as he could, he said, "No children."

Charlee drew in a breath and let it out in a long sigh.

"They're immortal beings who are slowly dying despite their immortality, hiding out from humans and with no way to return to Valhalla, or they would have gone back long ago," Darwin summarized. "Their gods are gone, their powers diminished—"

"Diminished?"

Darwin shrugged. "The Valkyrie can't create Einherjar if they can't get back to Valhalla. I have no idea how Valkyrie are created, but it's clearly not possible for them to procreate anymore, so the loss of Valhalla is part of that, too." He pursed his lips, considering. "Life can't be happy for them, Charlee. They're dying, powerless and homeless, living in a world that would be extremely hostile to them if they were discovered. They've lived on the knife-edge of imminent discovery for centuries, and you have to admire them for maintaining their secrecy for that long, even if some of the ways they've pulled that off were bloody and ruthless." He looked at her. "It's not a pretty picture, is it?"

Charlee pulled her melting bowl of ice cream toward her and picked up the spoon. "No," she said flatly.

"The Amica, these human women that serve as paramours and housekeepers—you said that all of them that you've met, they're proud to be Amica?"

"Not just proud," Charlee said, and licked the bottom of her spoon. "They all feel special, that they've been chosen for a prestigious and glamorous career."

"Indoctrination from childhood would help that along," Darwin muttered. "You said most of them were born into it?"

"Their mothers and grandmothers and more were also Amica. For most of them, it's a family thing." She grimaced. "A family secret. They inherit their role from their mothers."

Darwin nodded. "They would have grown up hearing the stories and absorbing the glamour and glory of it all. The Kine would prefer to use the offspring of those already granted access to their world, for the traditions and secrecy would be ingrained."

"That's a cold way of looking at it," Charlee protested.

"I was just summarizing. But here's the thing. Given the grimness of their world, and faced with a long, slow extinction, the Kine must have found the Amica a relief. With them they can let themselves feel human again." Darwin sat back. "I don't think the glamour and prestige is purely imaginary, Charlee. I think that for the Kine, the Amica are…well, a godsend. I think they might just revere them as much as they do their old gods."

"Now I think *you're* exaggerating."

"I had the pleasure and privilege of living with Anna-Marie for sixteen years. There's not a day goes by that I don't miss her, and it'll be twenty-nine years this spring since she died. She was the engine in my life and she's still shaping it. I don't plant petunias every spring because I like them, you know."

Charlee smiled softly at him. "Or clean the sink after you've done the dishes."

"Or drop the lid on the toilet once I'm done." Darwin grinned. "But that's just the petty stuff. She was the one who insisted I go back to school and get my degree, and then worked her butt off for years so I could do my Master's. I'd still be working in a grocery store, stacking shelves with Chinese noodles, if it hadn't been for her."

"I wish I'd met her," Charlee said wistfully.

"So do I," Darwin told her. "She'd have liked you. A lot. It's just not the way it worked out. But I think I know how the Einherjar might feel about their Amica, Charlee. They're not just the…what did you call them? The human whores? That's part of it and it's an important part, but it's not just sex, or they would have invented for themselves a whorehouse of prostitutes instead of these gorgeous, highly skilled Amica. Or they'd just slip down to the local red-light district whenever the itch strikes them. But they didn't. They formed the Amica and I think most of the design came about because the Amica, in a very practical way, saved their sanity. You can't help but revere a person or an entity that keeps you sane and happy."

* * * * *

Charlee carefully closed the door to the kitchen before she turned on the light. It was three in the morning and Darwin was snoring peacefully in his room. She didn't want to wake him. Her own sleep had been fractured enough to drive her into an uncharacteristic kitchen run. Darwin's ice cream beckoned. Somewhere in the back of the freezer there would be a bucket of salted caramel fudge flavor, which was so rich that both of them could only eat a few mouthfuls at a time.

But when she flipped on the light, she saw her reflection in the window and halted, examining it.

She was wearing one of her old robes from when she had been living here. It was an inch or so too short for her, made of a pale green polyester that had been designed to look and feel like silk. It had been all that was in the closet and she had brought nothing with her. She had come straight from Wall Street to Darwin's house, her mind a tumble of pain and the pressure to make a decision.

What did she want?

That was the question she had begun the day wanting to answer. *What now?* She had wondered, with no idea what the rest of the day would bring.

I'll commit to you. Body and soul.

Was that what she wanted? She would get Asher, yes, but none of his life or the things that gave it meaning for him. He would be a shell. A body and mind, but the soul he wanted to give her would be closed off. Unavailable.

What else was there for her?

It still wasn't too late for her to resurrect her childhood dreams. An advanced degree and a career in one of the sciences.

Or perhaps…history. The past had intruded into her present, and she had a perspective on ancient history now that would make the study of it enticing. But it might be a reminder of what she left behind, too.

She looked at the reflection in the window once more, cataloguing the changes that had happened since she had last caught a glimpse of herself in this window. Her hair rested coiled on her shoulders in big, loose curls, gleaming in the kitchen light. Ylva had finally managed to tame her wild locks and taught Charlee how to keep them contained and ladylike.

Was her face thinner? The chin more pointed? Her shoulders more square? She was definitely taller, but her hips looked broader and more rounded, even though her waist was as small as it had been in high school. (*His fingers sliding around her waist, branding her flesh with his heat.*)

Charlee drew in a sharp breath and headed for the fridge and the ice cream with an impatient sound. She settled at the table with the bucket and a spoon, and her mind slid back into the same weary channel.

There was no way to have Asher in her life except as a shallow relationship. But if she didn't agree to those terms, then what?

The door to the kitchen squeaked as it opened and Darwin shuffled in, rubbing his fingers back and forth through his iron-grey hair. "I guessed it was you. It's a night for contemplation, isn't it?" He squeezed her shoulder gently as he moved past the back of her chair and sat in his. He belted the robe more firmly around his middle, then propped his head up with his hand, his elbow on the table. His eyes were still half-filled with sleep.

"I woke you. I'm sorry."

"Sleep gets a little bit more sparse as I get older. Don't worry about it. I can always snooze my day away on the sofa to catch up." He tilted the ice cream bucket toward him and inspected the inside of it, then wrinkled his nose and stood it back upright. "Trying to figure out what to do?"

Charlee sighed. "I can't seem to move beyond the basic fact, Darwin. I grew up knowing in my bones that Asher was the man I'd be with forever. It was in the back of my mind, always. A fact, just like the fact that I'm right-handed, and can roll my tongue and that math is easy for me. That's how sure I was about it. I knew that I was red-headed and I knew that Asher was mine. When the other girls at school would talk about dating, or one day getting married and if they wanted kids, I didn't have to wonder about who I would end up with. I just knew it would be Asher. And I never had to worry about dating, because Asher was there. I can't imagine him not being in my life, Darwin. But now I can't have *all* of him in my life, and I don't know if I can accept the little bit he can give me."

Darwin blinked sleepily. "You love all of him," he said. "The human side and the hidden side. Makes sense you don't want to give half of that up."

Charlee looked at him, startled. "Yes," she said slowly, putting down her spoon. "I'm in too deep now."

"Doesn't mean you can't back out. There's always a way."

"Could you cut off your leg, Darwin? Just to move on to a new life?"

His gaze was steady. "I guess if I had to, I'd do it."

"Would you give up your memories of Anna-Marie, if you were told that's the only way to live another ten years?"

"Honey, I'm an old man. I've had my time. You've got your whole

311

life ahead of you. It's different."

"You'd say no, wouldn't you?"

"Yeah, I'd say no." He grimaced. "Even if it gave me immortality, I'd still say no."

Charlee got up and put the ice cream back in the freezer.

"You've decided, haven't you?" Darwin asked.

"Yes, I know now what's next."

* * * * *

Ylva got up from behind her desk and walked over to the window, where climbing hollyhocks were in full bloom on either side of the frame. She liked them around the window because they enticed hummingbirds, she had said once. But now she was looking through the glass and Charlee knew she wasn't seeing the flowers at all.

"Isn't that something you thought might happen when I came here?" Charlee asked reasonably.

"It's one of the reasons I let you come, yes," Ylva said, keeping her back to her. "I wanted you to be able to make an informed choice. But this isn't what I intended."

"You wanted me to learn all about the Kine, so I could choose to forget about them?" Charlee asked, puzzled. "Go off and have a normal, human life as if I didn't know they existed?"

Ylva turned and rested her rear on the sideboard under the window. Her hands gripped the edges, beside her hips. "I thought that if you chose to join the Amica it would be a positive thing. But you're using them to hide."

"I don't think there's ever been an Amica who could hide," Charlee said frankly. "They all tend to turn heads when they walk into a room."

"But you think you won't do that. You think you'll disappear into their ranks, still a part of Asher's world, but unnoticed. Because of your scar and because you think you're unremarkable and ordinary."

Surprise jolted Charlee into sitting upright. "I do not think that."

Ylva smiled grimly. "You refer to the Amica in the third person. As 'them' not 'us', despite living among them for so many years. You don't think of yourself as ever being able to match them. You don't think you'll ever really be one of them. But you want to use the Amica as an entry key to the Kine."

"Yes," Charlee said flatly. "I want to be a part of this world. Joining the Amica is the only way for me."

"But do you really understand what it means?" Ylva asked.

"Sexual partners?" Charlee said calmly. "Yes, I understand."

Ylva studied her. "But you think you won't be chosen. That you won't draw the eye of any of them."

Charlee couldn't meet her gaze. Ylva had spoken aloud the belief she had formed when thinking through this decision. "They're all so beautiful. Stunning."

Ylva shook her head. "And what about Asher?"

Charlee looked down at her hands again. "I…may see him in the halls."

"Charlee, look at me."

Charlee reluctantly obeyed.

Ylva leaned forward a little. "There is no way to guarantee your assignment. You understand that, don't you? Of all the many halls, you may serve in Europe or Asia or South America. There are halls on every continent, in every country. It will be up to Eira to decide your posting and I have to warn you, Charlee. Eira already knows who you are and your association with Asher. For that reason, she may decide that having you in the same hall with him would distract you from your assignment. You would be there to serve. With Asher nearby, you would be distracted from your work. It's quite likely that Eira will find you an assignment a long way from New York."

Charlee's heart hurried along. "I guessed that might be how it worked. I understand."

"You would give up any hope of a relationship with him, Charlee," Ylva added.

The words were hard to form. "I know," she whispered.

"Oh, Charlee. I thought you loved him," Ylva said softly.

"He won't…he can't be with me. Not properly. But I love this world, Ylva. I love this part of him, too much to give it up altogether. If I can't be with him, *properly* with him, then I think I can be happy living in his world. I know I will be happier than if I have to give up both him *and* the Kine."

Ylva studied her for a long moment. "Charlee, you know about me. You know why I am no longer part of the Kine. That is an option for any of the Kine. It is a difficult choice, but even Asher could—"

Charlee shook her head. "No."

"Then you've thought about it," Ylva said.

"Of course I have! But I won't ask that of him. I won't let him do it. This is the only way, Ylva."

"If you were to ask him, I believe Asher would consider it. For you, he would give it all up."

"No."

"But—"

"No, Ylva. Your husband never knew what you were and you

thought that was doing him a kindness, but if he had known, I think he would have fought to make you stay with the Kine. If he loved you, he would have insisted you stay."

Ylva blinked. "It was my decision," she said, her voice thick.

"To die for him?" Charlee asked, as gently as she could.

Ylva quickly wiped at her eyes. "I have never regretted my decision. Not even now."

"Then let me give you the human perspective. Your husband's perspective, if he had known. I will not ask Asher to give up the work and the life that defines him, that makes him who he is. I *love* that part of him, just as much as I love his quick temper and his dry sense of humor and his suits and Torger and his apartment in Soho, all the things he does as a human. If he left the Kine, he would become someone different. He would grow to hate the half-life left to him, and he would grow to hate me for bringing him to such an end. I won't do it."

"You don't know that," Ylva replied. "Asher is a strong man. If he left, it would be because he wanted to. He would make the decision and live with it."

"But he wouldn't live forever." Charlee shook her head. "I've thought about nothing else for three days. This is the only way."

* * * * *

Unnur looked down at the three cards she had drawn. It was supposed to have been a three-card weather spread. But from the way the hairs on the back of her neck were standing up, making her shudder, she knew the cards were talking to her directly.

It had been months since they had spoken. Her dreams had become the medium for instruction, and in truth, the success of her business and the never-ending flow of customers and orders via the Internet, and all the endless details of keeping her flourishing business flowing meant that she hadn't dealt a spread for herself in a very long time.

She had employed her first assistant nearly two years ago, and when business pushed beyond her assistant's abilities, Unnur had finally hired a store manager to take over some of the more complex ordering and administrative tasks.

Unnur's private reading sessions for some of the most influential businessmen in the southern states had boomed. She began to fly from state to state, city to city, to consult with leaders and entrepreneurs, to read for them and discuss their concerns.

It was all as her dreams had predicted.

She had come back to Lakeland to check in on the store and see that Bridget was managing well enough without her and to take a small vacation—one day of working in the store and sleeping in her own bed. It was the best sort of relaxation she could think of.

And so she had laid out the weather spread, as it was late summer and stiflingly hot outside. It was good thunderstorm weather, which always made her nervous.

Unnur looked down at the three cards, her heart thudding erratically. "Oh dear," she murmured and let her fingertip slide along the side of the Queen of Wands. She sat on the left, but the King was not next to her. For the first time ever, he was separated. He sat on the right and he was reversed. *Impulsive, ruthless. Demanding.*

"What happened?" Unnur cried.

For sitting between them, keeping them apart, was The Lovers…also upside down.

* * * * *

Asher stepped back from the open door in confusion, for Eira stood in his apartment doorway, wrapped in a fur-lined shawl and wearing heavy sunglasses. "Regin," he said formally, bowing his head. "This is…unexpected."

"I'm here as a friend, Asher. Please let me in."

He stood aside and she strode into the room, looking around. "Very comfortable," she remarked and took off the sunglasses. "Do you have anything to drink?"

Asher shut the door. "There's some Johnny Walker from the last time Roar visited." Eira didn't like wine or light mead or any of the drinks she called frou-frou fripperies. She took her alcohol neat and harsh.

He pulled the bottle out of the cupboard on the front of the kitchen island and searched for clean glasses and put them next to the bottle.

Eira had shrugged off the shawl. She wore, as always when in civilian clothing, boots with heels, pants that clung to her powerful thighs, and a silk shirt in a color that flattered her dark brown eyes and dark hair. There was a pendant visible between the open fronts of the shirt and as she moved, Asher saw that it was a black iron triquetra. Humans thought it was a Celtic symbol, but Odin had claimed it as his long before the Celts existed.

"Let me," Eira said, picking up the bottle before he could.

Asher demurred. As the Valkyrie in the room, it was her choice to serve the drinks if she wanted to. As his Regin and his guest, she would have been perfectly correct to let him pour the drinks. But she was not here as Regin. That worried him, but he let none of it show.

"You are well, Eira?" he asked, keeping to the pleasantries.

"Well enough, thank you. Oslo is very pleasant in summer."

"But you still wear furs despite the pleasantness." He grinned. "And you wonder why Roar chose New York."

"The opera house, I believe, had something to do with it."

"That wasn't built when we first arrived."

"Then I was misinformed." She picked up a glass and held it out to him. "Einherjar," she murmured formally.

"My thanks." He took it and waited for her to pick up her own. That was one human custom he had been happy to adopt. It had always felt rude to him to guzzle his drink while a woman stood by watching empty-handed.

Drunks love company. He could hear Roar's voice dryly countering his reasoning.

They drank the stiff shots she had poured and Asher winced. No, he was never going to love whiskey.

Eira picked up the bottle again and poured until Asher's glass was nearly half full. Four or five shots, at least. Then she pushed the glass toward him.

"Why are you here?" Asher asked. The formalities were done with.

Eira put the bottle down and her gaze caught his. "You'll hear about this in the halls soon enough, but I thought I would tell you directly. I recruited a new Amica today. One that has no family connection to the Amica or any history with us."

"Why are you—" *telling me this*, he began to say, but the truth was obvious.

"Red hair, an intriguing scar on her cheek, and a direct way of dealing with the world," Eira said. "She will be popular among the ranks."

Horror spread cold fingers through him. "No, no, no, no. You *can't*. Eira, take it back. Tell her you changed your mind. Refuse her a place."

"Ylva and Charlee both spoke very eloquently in petition to have me take her on." Eira picked up the glass and put it in his hand, curling his lifeless fingers around it. "The matter is done, Asher." More gently she added; "Drink."

He couldn't move. The agony was too great. It had claimed his nerves and his thoughts. "I did this," he whispered.

Eira picked up the bottle. "You did nothing that you did not promise the Council, years ago. Did you think I had forgotten, Asher?"

No, but he had. That stupid promise. It had got him out of a tight corner at the time, but he had forgotten as usual that time would catch up with him. Time always did. Eventually.

Eira played with the corner of the label, picking at it. "Now that I've met Charlee, I think I know now why you were so complacent about having her join the Amica. You thought her scar would be a drawback, that it would make her less attractive to the others."

He couldn't speak. Could barely unlock his chest enough to draw breath. He put the glass down as he curled over, hunching forward, trying to relieve the pain.

That's all I can give you. He had been so adamant. So inflexible. He had driven her to this.

"I don't believe her scarring will be any sort of deterrent at all," Eira said. "There is a life to the woman, a brightness that will have them flutter around her like moths at the flame."

Asher gasped, gripping the edge of the counter for balance, as his mind filled with images. Charlee at a feast, the men pawing her as she served their mead. Worse, some faceless, nameless Einherjar trapping her in a dark corner of a hall and forcing himself on her.

"There must be some way to reverse this," he pleaded, his voice strained.

Eira gave him a pity-filled smile. "Drink, Asher," she urged.

He picked up the glass again and drank deeply.

Chapter Twenty-Seven

A day in the halls is possibly the most
balanced and organically structured day
you could spend – better than a day at
the spa. The Kine know how to eat,
how to work, and how to play. Man, do
they ever!

—

AnnaJo Albert, former Amica, on Facebook

As the power of the solstice came to a peak, Sindri opened himself up, drawing it to him and channelling it to the crucible, which almost glowed with the energy pulsing in it. He had grown so practiced at these collections and so efficient, that he often thought he could detect a non-animate shock emanating from the power itself, as it was ripped away from the path it would naturally take, along ley lines and through to the core of the earth and was instead funnelled into the crucible.

The crucible itself had grown heavier with every collection. From the weight and power fields that pulsed around it, Sindri knew that the time was very near. His work was almost done. And then…and then he would be able to prove to her that he was worthy.

He gasped aloud his hope and joy as the last of the power rushed through him, and lowered his arms, panting. He looked around. There was child standing in among the vines, watching him with big eyes. Here in the depths of the Amazonian jungles, Sindri had not expected to be disturbed, but humans were persistent creatures, thriving in the most inhospitable corners of the world. They were like the cockroaches Sindri had grown to abhor.

He lifted his hand, fingers spread toward the child and muttered a word.

The child turned and sprinted back into the jungle, leaping over trunks and stones and other obstacles like a fleeing deer. It would not remember Sindri, and he was content.

He touched the crucible. This had been a great collection. Here on the equator, a solstice was neither summer nor winter. It just *was*. The slackening of the Coriolis forces here enhanced the power of the alignment, focusing it. The crucible was warm and almost comforting, except for the power fields still strumming around it. Reluctantly, he removed it and laid it carefully in its carrying case and closed the case.

Soon, he promised himself and her, even though she was thousands of miles away and couldn't hear him. But soon, she would. Soon, she would listen to every word he spoke.

Soon.

* * * * *

Eira walked through from the private section of the bedroom into the public area, and Charlee watched the sway of her hems critically.

"What do you think?" Eira asked.

"I think you would rather be wearing your trousers and your sword strapped to your side."

Eira smiled. "Or the latest Prada pantsuit. Or a tunic and mantle, which are the only civilized thing to wear to a feast. But they do insist on tradition, and so…" She spread the skirts of the apron dress, her fingers spreading across the fabric. "It's so *soft*," she murmured. "You've outdone yourself once more, Charlee."

"Thank you."

Eira studied her. "Are you nervous?"

"Is there a reason I should be?"

Eira smiled knowingly. "Your first full feast, with every hall in attendance."

Charlee laughed. "Nervous about that? No. But I'm still very grateful you chose me to attend you. Everyone assures me the sight of the halls in full assembly is breathtaking. This will be my first chance to see it for myself."

"It's not every single Herleifr," Eira said, as she turned away. "I don't think the entire Second Hall could hold all of us at once. But every hall will have two representatives there, and that is still nearly two thousand people." She picked up earrings and held them up.

"Not the green ones," Charlee told her. "The red ones there."

"Thank you." Eira looked at her in the mirror. "Asher will be there."

"He might be," Charlee agreed, squashing the flutter of her heart.

"He will be. I checked. His attendance is confirmed."

The flutter increased. Charlee shrugged as casually as she could. "In a hall with over two thousand people, the chances that I'll run into him are remote."

"When was the last time you saw him?" Eira asked.

"It's been over four years."

"A long time."

"Not to the Kine," Charlee said. "He's probably still angry." She had run into Asher in the round hall, five weeks after she had been taken on as the newest Amica recruit, and she hadn't been ready for it. She doubted she would have ever been braced for that meeting.

It had only taken days for Charlee to know her decision to stay among the Kine was the right one. Life among the Kine was a richly filled smorgasbord of cultures and people, all of them known to each other, all of them distant or close friends. Life was utterly different inside the halls, where they could drop their human roles and truly be themselves.

Eira had undertaken to train Charlee herself, and so Charlee had taken her first walk through the portals, from New York to Oslo, accompanied by an Einherjar from the Second Hall. He had explained the portals to her as his gaze flickered over her, but English was not a strong language for him, and Charlee was left to figure out most of it for herself.

"They're controlled worm holes?" she asked finally, when he brought her to stand in front of them. There were two portals, one on either side of the broad flight of steps that led down to the front door of the New York hall. Charlee would have liked to have stopped to look around the hall itself, but the Einherjar had seemed hurried.

"No. Not wormholes." He shook his head, frowning, as he sought for the right word. "*Magic.*" He lifted his finger and thumb, held closely together. "*Un poco.*"

Just a little.

"Little magic?" Charlee queried.

"All the magic that is left, except—" and he patted his sword hilt. His sword was fully extended, but she assumed that it would disappear just like Asher's did. The portals, then, and the swords was all the magic the Kine had left, if she followed him properly. That meant that at one time, there had been more. Where had it all gone?

The Einherjar held out his hand to her. "Must, to go through. Or you," and he hit his chest with the flat of his hand.

"I can't go through unless you're touching me?"

He beamed and nodded and held out his hand again. She took it and he stepped through the curtain of grey mist, pulling her after him. She stepped through nervously, and felt a slight tug, then his hand pulled her forward. She took another step and emerged into huge room, blinking.

Her first incoherent thought was *my jeans were so the wrong thing to wear!* For everywhere she looked, there were men and women in formal human clothing, long robes, even a full kilt. There were light summer linens, heavy winter outerwear, boots, sandals, and shoes of all types. Weaving among them were more men dressed similarly to the Einherjar who was escorting her. Swords, leather breastplates, and more leather armor covering their arms. Thick leather bands around their wrists. There was an astonishing array of weapons worn: knives thrust through belts, axes, and the big swords hanging at their hips. Charlee was looking at her first Einherjar in the closest thing to a uniform they had: battle gear.

There were a number of women wearing what Charlee recognized as apron dresses. She had made more than a few of them herself while apprenticing with Anja. The pattern was a simple one made of triangles and squares, using up every inch of a length of cloth. But there were endless variations on what one could do with the garment once it was cut. Embroidery, overskirts, under-dresses, looped up hems, lacings, jewelry, smocking...the design and construction could run from work wear to high formal gowns. The ones she was seeing here in this cavernous great hall were more workmanlike.

Amica, she guessed.

The Einherjar tugged her hand again, drawing her across the hall. It rose for endless feet up to a rounded roof. Pillars circled the hall ten feet inside its walls, holding up the roof. At the domed roofline, windows punched through the stone walls. Light spilled down from them onto the marble floor, leaving pools of bright sunlight that everyone walked through.

On opposite sides of the rounded room were more of the portals. Perhaps ten on each side. This, then, was a cross-road to other halls.

Charlee didn't know it then, but she would get to know the central hall very well. It was more than just a cross-road for the portals. Most of the major public rooms and galleries that gave access to them fed off the rotunda, including the great hall itself, the Second Hall. Tryvannshøyden, which everyone called the Second Hall, was the seat of power among the Kine.

Eira was their Regin, first among all Valkyrie, and leader of armies. The last had startled Charlee until she had seen Eira actually using a sword. Then she had no doubt that the stories she had already heard about Eira's human life as a sword-for-hire were not exaggerated.

Sword-wielding was not the domain of the Einherjar, or even just the Valkyrie. Charlee learned the very next morning after her arrival in the Second Hall that there was an aspect of Amica life that Ylva had overlooked in her apprenticeships. Everyone, Kine and Amica, was expected to prepare for war and fighting. A Kine's early morning was devoted to training their bodies and minds, maintaining physical discipline and mental strength. The Amica were not excluded from the expectation, and the main hall itself was given over to training for two hours before breakfast was served.

It was then that Ylva's parting gift to Charlee made sense. Ylva had handed Charlee the long parcel, wrapped in the marbled paper that Victoria liked to make, as Charlee had been leaving the house, a duffel bag her sole piece of luggage. "May they serve you well," Ylva told her. "They did me."

Inside were two short swords, or long knives. Charlee couldn't decide which. They had long handles that ran almost half their length, while the other half was wickedly sharp blade. They were light and easy to swish around with one hand. Charlee knew they had been made for Ylva, for her upper strength and height.

On the first morning of training in the big room, Charlee had been assessed for her overall fitness by a sharp-eyed Einherjar called Howard, while everyone around her was parrying, tackling, and going through balletic movements with swords and knives and more. It was a large-scale gym without any of the usual equipment found in human ones, and no padding. When they fell, they fell flat upon the marbled floor, with nothing to cushion their error.

Howard had not been impressed. "You must build your fitness first," he said. "Your wind, in particular. I will set a program for you and you must follow it. What is your weapon? Do you have one?"

"I...er...yes, I have one," she said, realizing then the practical nature of Ylva's gift.

"Bring it tomorrow. I will examine it for its usefulness." He had left her to complete the routine he had set for her, a series of deceptively simple exercises that left her heaving for breath and trembling with exhaustion.

The next morning, she brought her knife-swords with her. Howard had examined them critically, then nodded. "I have someone who can teach you how to use these. Begin your program. They will find you."

An Einherjar appeared ten minutes later, weaving his way through the crowded work-floor. Bahram looked young and forced Charlee to keep reminding herself that looking young, here, didn't necessarily mean young. His English was good, but accented. He examined the swords as Howard had done, his lips pushed into a doubtful purse. "Good for stabbing," he decided.

"Howard said you knew how to use them," Charlee pointed out.

Bahram grinned and stepped back from her. He was wearing gym pants and a T-shirt, and a sword belt around his hips. From the belt he slid two curved swords, which he began to spin like scissor blades, until with a lunge, he thrust one at her. It came to a stop mere fractions of an inch from her stomach. "I know how to use them," he agreed, his olive face amused.

And so she had begun her training with the swords. Eira had smiled when she saw them in Charlee's hands. "I remember those. They were Ylva's." She patted her own sword, strapped to her hips. "A long sword is still the ultimate weapon."

"I thought you would prefer a short sword," Charlee told her, for she had already learned that Eira had emerged from the Roman Empire and worked her way across Europe and into Scandinavia, long before Europe and Scandinavia even acquired those names.

"Short swords are only good if that is all the enemy has, too. A long sword has reach."

Not everyone trained within the great hall itself. The Kine who were attached to the Second Hall lived in Oslo, but only a small number of them actually lived in the hall. Still, some of the Kine chose to come to the hall each morning for their training, while many others trained at local gyms, by themselves, and only attended training in the hall when they wanted specific arms practice. At the hall, they could tap into the combined knowledge of centuries of warfare, pitting their skills against others and keeping them fresh.

Howard, Charlee discovered, was the hall's chief stallari, although for such a big hall, he had lieutenants and assistants to help complete his work. He supervised the training but was also responsible for weaponry, armor, and general battle-readiness.

"That is our primary role," Eira explained. "It was handed down from Odin himself that we prepare and always be ready to defend Midgard."

"Against what?"

"Against whatever aggressor appears."

"What about Man himself?" Charlee asked. "He seems to be doing a pretty good job of destroying himself, these days."

Eira had smiled. "Man has been fighting man since the first two men picked up rocks and threw them at each other. The weapons are more powerful now, but Man is still essentially weak. They will need us if ever..." She shrugged. "Who knows?" she said, her smile fading. "It has been a long time and Midgard continues to remain isolated and safe from the other worlds, but we prepare anyway."

Eternal preparation against an enemy they did not believe was a threat anymore. Charlee began to think that Darwin's theory about diminishing numbers through suicide and despair and plain disinterest might be right, but it was not something she would ever be able to ask. The loss of a single Kine was a tragedy for them, and they mourned each and every fallen and departed Kine endlessly, remembering them in conversations and referring to their deeds and achievements.

Ylva was among those numbers, and Charlee learned more about her dramatic and heart-wrenching decision to live as a human, along with her exploits and abilities as a Valkyrie. "Ylva might have become Regin," Eira pointed out offhandedly, "but for her emotional weakness."

Once a Kine chose to live as a human, they were cut off from the others and treated as if they had died, which eventually became true. Whatever the sustaining force that kept the Kine alive through the ages ceased to work on them once they had left the halls forever. Even though their lives as humans would be long, they would eventually age, wither and die, just like the humans they had chosen to live among.

Asher had been unusual in that he had refused to pretend that Ylva was dead. He had championed her decision to leave, which had not made him popular among the very traditional Kine. Once Ylva had left, he continued to see her, making her a manager of his various business affairs and keeping her a part of his human life. When Ylva had brought Charlee to Eira, to ask Eira to take her in as an Amica, it had been the first time they had seen each other since Ylva had left, decades before. At the time, Charlee had thought the air between them was strained. Now she understood better why Ylva had been treated so distantly by Eira.

Life in the Second Hall was just as busy as her time in Ylva's house. Charlee's apprenticeship there had prepared her very well for the life of an Amica. She was the first new recruit in several years and with Eira training her, it might have been difficult to adapt. But all the basic domestic skills were already ingrained, which left Eira with the task of educating her in the ways and history of the Kine.

As the newest recruit, Charlee received a great deal of scrutiny from every Kine she met, particularly the Einherjar. But it wasn't until the first formal dinner after her arrival at the hall that Charlee really understood the shape of her potential future. The dinner was not an official one, but Stefan and Eira wanted the Amica to serve the meal as women would have traditionally done. Charlee had been assigned to the task, along with six other Amica who were also a part of the hall.

She had dressed in the plain apron dress and underdress and reported to the kitchen that served the hall itself and glanced at the other Amica. They were all stunningly beautiful women and Charlee tugged at the layers of her dress, feeling uncomfortable and out of place.

The work of serving the meal was physically demanding. As the cooks doled out the meals in a controlled frenzy, the Amica carried plates four at a time out to the big tables that had been set up in the hall. There were four courses and beverages to see to, each course had to be cleared before the next was served, and while the diners ate, the Amica washed and dried the dishes of the previous course. Two of the Amica would circle the tables at all times, with pitchers of mead, to top up mugs and glasses.

When it was Charlee's turn with the pitcher, she took the pitcher with secret relief, for serving drinks seemed like an easier chore. But even as she was filling the first mug, she learned differently.

An Einherjar on the opposite side of the table from where Charlee was standing looked at her with a critical eye. "You're the new one, aren't you?"

All heads at the table turned to look at her.

"The new what?" she asked.

"The newest Amica. You've got a scar across your face. I heard about you."

They were all looking at her now.

"She's a pretty one, even with the scar," one of the others on her side of the table said. "I might have to steal more than just a drink from her."

Charlee's pulse leapt. The one who had spoken was unshaved, bleary eyed and carried extra weight, which was no small feat for an Einherjar who worked out for two hours every day.

One of the others hitched his hips, moving along the bench to clear a few inches, which he patted. "Come and have a seat, sweet one. Let's talk."

Charlee looked at him. He was ugly. There was no other word to describe his pinched features and lopsided nose. He was still patting the bench, his grin revealing missing teeth.

"We'll talk when you learn to speak intelligently," she said, then froze. Where had that come from? It had just dropped out of her mouth. The Kine expected respect at all times, especially from the Amica.

But the entire table had burst into loud guffaws of laughter. Some of them banged the tabletop with their fists. The sound made heads at neighboring tables turn to see what was happening.

"Oh, hark the lass!" the one with the bleary eyes said. "You're going to have to work to keep up with her, Denney."

One of the younger-looking ones grinned at her. "Come and sit by me," he said. "I guarantee you'll find the conversation stimulating."

"I could prick my fingers with a dagger and find that stimulating, too," she shot back, "but it doesn't mean I find it pleasant."

The whole table roared with laughter again, most of the men rocking back, throwing their heads back to guffaw loudly. They banged the table with their fists, making the plates and cups jump. All the diners at the tables around them were looking over now, too.

They like sass, Charlee realized, as she filled the last of the cups. They like being challenged. She drifted over toward the next table.

"Hey, don't leave us yet!" the bleary-eyed one called out.

"I left you behind a long time ago," Charlee shot back, picking up a mug from the next table.

The occupants of both tables laughed at that one, and the fellow next to bleary-eyes nudged him in the ribs.

"You have good taste," the Einherjar said as she placed his mug back in front of him. "We're much smarter at this table."

Charlee looked them over deliberately and carefully. "I don't see it," she said, shaking her head.

The laughter was even louder this time.

Her heart thumping, Charlee filled more mugs and moved on to the next table, where the men there also tried to cajole or wheedle her into joining them and she would throw back insults of her own.

Charlee spent the rest of the night pouring mead. None of the other Amica would trade with her. The oldest of them shook her head. "You're entertaining them. Whatever you're doing, it's spreading cheer. Keep doing it."

Eira had agreed, much later that night, as Charlee had helped her pull the pins from her hair and comb it out. "I don't think anyone has tried it before. A choosy Amica who is just a little bit unattainable will give them a novelty they've not had in a good long while. You might very well have them tripping over themselves next time to earn your approval."

Eira's guess was correct. She assigned Charlee to work at the very next formal occasion, and the joshing and heckling began almost before the opening formalities were completed. One of the Einherjar caught her around the waist as she tried to move away from the group she was serving—on this occasion, they were all standing and moving freely around the room—and Charlee had almost squeaked her shock aloud. The mead sloshed in the pitcher she was carrying.

He had pulled her up hard against him. "I heard about you," he said, and his hot breath fanned her face. "You'll find me more than agreeable to you, girl."

Charlee stamped on his foot with as much force as she could muster when she was being almost pulled off her feet. Like before, she wasn't sure where the instinctive response came from, except that the vaguest memory of historical romance heroines doing something similar tickled at the back of her mind.

The Einherjar howled in pain, for she had aimed not for his toes, but the arch of his foot. He dropped her and his mug, which was still empty. It gave a loud, hollow "bong!" sound. But both his howl and the clattering mug were drowned out by the laughter all around them.

"She bites!" came a delighted cry.

Charlee was trembling, but she looked at the man bent over and awkwardly balancing on one foot while he rubbed the other. "You dropped your mug," she told him as evenly as she could, then turned and moved away, her chin in the air.

Three days after the stomping incident, Charlee saw Asher in the round hall. She had been hurrying to clear the big boardroom before the full Council meeting began, and her arms were full of notepads, pens, and two empty glasses. By the time she had finished clearing the long table, Council members had already been arriving for the meeting, milling around the edges of the room and talking quietly, making her hurry.

She slipped out through the big doors, and cut across the round hall, toward the narrow doorway next to the grand entrance to the main hall. The doorway accessed the service passages behind and on either side of the hall, and provided short cuts to many of the function rooms, minor halls and meeting rooms on this level. She had been so intent on not dropping the glasses and juggling the handful of pens and notepads that she had taken no notice of anyone around her. Besides, the central hall was always full of strangers, many of them literally passing through, using the portals to reach another hall somewhere else. Even in three short weeks, she already knew enough people by name that if she acknowledged everyone she saw, which would encourage conversation, it would take her an hour to cross the hall. So she had kept her head down, watching the glasses and her footing.

A hand gripped her arm, bringing her to such a sudden stop that she almost lost her footing. Her momentum carried her around in a swinging arc and she clutched her burdens desperately as the glasses jogged in her arms, a breathless gasp pushing from her.

Asher looked down at her, his expression neutral. "Charlee."

Cold shock (*no, it's fear*) gripped her chest. What would he say? Do?

But he did nothing. He just stood there. Even his grip on her arm ceased, as he dropped his hand to his side. He was wearing black jeans and a white business shirt. It looked very human, she decided.

His gaze flickered over the length of her, much as hers had done with him. His eyes were bloodshot. And he hadn't shaved. His cheeks were bristly.

"How are you, Asher?" she asked.

"How very polite of you," he growled. "I'm already hearing stories about you. You toy with them. Deride them."

"You make it sound like I'm condescending."

"Aren't you?"

She wanted to say 'no', firmly. But hadn't there been just a tiny bit of superiority driving her flashy comebacks? Wasn't it that in the back of her mind she held the belief, deep in her subconscious, that she was smarter than them?

Asher's jaw rippled. "You think none of us are good enough for you."

It felt like a slap to the face. "That's not true," she denied hotly. "They *like* that I'm…unavailable." At the last second, she recalled the word Eira had used to describe what she was doing. Asher's words were all negative. They put the wrong spin on it. But were there others out there thinking as he did? Did they resent her?

It was also terrifying to hear Asher include himself in the body of Einherjar that he believed she was rejecting.

"Unavailable?" he repeated, with something like scorn in his tone. "But you're not unavailable, are you?"

There was nothing she could say to that. She was now an Amica. Her scar was of little protection, her intelligence less so. Sooner or later, she would draw the eye of an Einherjar, one who would drive through all her petty defenses and stake his claim on her. She had the right to refuse—they all did—but why refuse? She had become an Amica for that very reason, or so everyone believed.

Even Asher believed it.

"There's only one Einherjar I'm waiting for," Charlee said. It was flat, unvarnished truth.

Asher's jaw loosened. His lips parted. Surprise, as much as Asher ever showed surprise. He glanced from side to side and shifted so that he was standing closer to her. "Tell me," he growled. "Please tell me you didn't do this based on some misbegotten belief that I would rescue you?"

Fear circled through her, making her cold. Asher wasn't reacting the way she thought he would to her revelation. "Rescue?" she repeated. "No, not rescue."

He scowled. "Truth for truth," he said. "Why the Amica?"

Truth time. She tried to draw a full breath, but the fear was closing down her throat. Squeezing her chest. "I wanted to be a part of your world. *All* of it. Not just the paltry little human side of it you offered."

He considered her, his jaw hard. "So presented with a choice between everything I could give you and nothing, you chose nothing."

"It's not nothing," she said quickly. "This life, it's far from nothing."

"Oh, yes, it's very glamorous when every Einherjar in the hall is panting after you. But Eira controls your life now. You handed over control when you became an Amica, and Eira won't waste your potential on a lowly Einherjar like me. She'll wait until someone with real power takes a fancy to you and use their interest to tie them to her locus of control."

A fine trembling began in her legs and hands. She was cold, so cold. Words failed her. There was nothing, no argument she could use to dispute him. Even as he said it, Charlee's perspective shifted and the shape of the pattern reformed, letting her see motives and agendas, including Eira's, clearly.

"Why do you think Eira took on your training personally?" Asher asked, his voice dry. "She knows quality when she sees it."

It was true. He was right. Charlee stared at him, the first tendrils of horror growing in her gut.

Asher straightened. "But it's done now," he said flatly. Again, his gaze shifted sideways, as he checked for witnesses. Charlee looked around herself and more cold fright touched her when she saw that Eira was standing by the hall doors, watching them. How much had she seen?

But they had simply been standing here and talking. Outside observers wouldn't guess the degree of gut-wrenching emotions ripping through her. She had learned how to mask her true feelings from watching Eira control her reactions. Eira had explained the reasons why it was better politically to keep strong emotions hidden, because they were a weakness and made you vulnerable. They could be manipulated and used against you.

Asher took a step away from Charlee, moving backwards, like he was wary. (Or *retreating*.)

Charlee threw out her hand. "No, wait," she begged softly.

"I did wait. I waited over ten years." His jaw flexed. "I won't sit there and watch you get bartered off to the most influential bidder. I refuse."

"Asher...."

He shook his head. "Goodbye."

And before she could scrape together a protest, another denial, anything that would keep him there in front of her, he was gone. He turned and strode toward the portals and stepped into the New York one and disappeared.

Charlee had rushed to her room and shut the door and stayed there for hours. Eira had been silently understanding, not calling upon her until the evening preparations were needed. Charlee emerged at her summons and woodenly helped her with the evening work, her mind blank and frozen.

At the end of the evening, as Eira stripped the formal garments from her and thrust her long legs into jeans, she had glanced at Charlee where she stood waiting with the gown over her arm. "It's better this way," she said gently.

"Is it?" Charlee asked. She didn't bother asking if Eira was talking about Asher. Eira had seen them together. She had watched Asher walk away from her.

"You have the potential to make a powerful alliance, Charlee, if only

TRACY COOPER-POSEY

you play your cards right."

"And for what reason?" Charlee shot back. "To become the paramour of a powerful Kine? Why are the Kine even here? What is the point? What good is power if there's no love?"

"You tell me the meaning of life, Charlee, and I'll answer your questions." Eira gave her a small smile. "I don't know why we're here. We're here, just as humans are here. We gave up long ago trying to understand why we were thrust upon Midgard."

"And you think becoming more powerful is the answer?" Charlee asked. "What good is it struggling to climb a ladder, if the ladder is leaning against the wrong building?"

"It's better to climb, than to sit at the foot of the ladder and get squashed when it falls," Eira shot back. She sighed. "I know you're confused, Charlee. It probably doesn't help if I tell you that every Amica before you has reached a similar point in their lives, and questioned what they were doing. But you have unique opportunities. You must understand that."

"Better to be the companion of the most powerful Kine, if you can't be the most powerful Kine yourself?" Charlee asked bitterly.

Eira's expression shifted, as something came and went swiftly across her face. "Better to be the most powerful Valkyrie, if you cannot be a powerful Einherjar," she replied.

Charlee stared at her, her misery forgotten for a moment. She glanced at the long sword hanging on its pegs on the wall over Eira's bed, the pattern shifting a little bit more. Eira had been a warrior among men, her whole human life. "You were taken from the battlefield by the Valkyrie." Charlee murmured.

"And taken to Valhalla," Eira confirmed. "Only to learn that there are no women Einherjar. I became a Valkyrie, instead."

"Oh." How that must have rankled!

"And now I am the most powerful Valkyrie," Eira added, with one of her mischievous smiles that Charlee suspected very few people ever got to see. "Once you climb the ladder, you can see much farther than you can at the bottom. Power gives you options, opportunities that would never come your way as the lover of a stallari in a small hall in the States."

Charlee went thoughtfully back to work. She didn't see Asher again for over four years.

Chapter Twenty-Eight

Charlee had seen large assemblies of Kine before, but nothing like this. The central hall and the main grand hall were full of Einherjar and Valkyrie in their formal best. Only the Amica wore the traditional apron dresses, and they were scattered among the crowd in the round hall, serving the several different varieties of mead available. Tonight, unlike almost every other night and event held in the halls, every single Kine was given a serving of mead, poured into a glass, not the usual mugs.

The Kine wore human fashions, for the event was a reaffirmation of their service to humans and their oath to Odin to remain ready to defend Midgard.

"Tomorrow's High Council meeting is where the old clothes and the old traditions are trotted out," Eira had explained as they were getting ready.

The High Council meeting was held every five years and was when the terms for the Annarr and Regin were renewed…or a new Second and Council were elected, if the former pair had not served adequately.

"There won't be any challenges," Eira said complacently. "Stefan is one of the strongest and most able Seconds we've had, so they will put up with me for the sake of keeping Stefan."

It had taken Charlee a while to understand that even though Stefan and Eira were the equivalent of a ruling King and his Queen, they were not life partners or involved personally in any way. Eira respected Stefan, and if she thought he had any weaknesses, she did not speak of them to Charlee. But since the Descent, whenever a new Annarr was appointed, a new Regin was generally rotated into the big chair, too.

"Would Stefan resign if they tried to remove you?" Charlee asked curiously.

"He would threaten to," Eira told her. "He has in the past."

That not everyone liked Eira as Regin was a shock to Charlee.

"I have made changes in my two hundred years on the chair," Eira said frankly. "Change is hard for humans to handle. For the Kine, for whom time marches on endlessly, change can stir the strongest fear. The only reason I can make those changes is because Stefan maintains peace and prosperity, which everyone likes. We complement each other."

At Eira's suggestion, Charlee had taken five minutes to race to the gallery that lined the round hall, high up by the roofline, a soaring sixty feet above the assembled Kine, and looked down upon the sea of heads and shoulders.

There were far more Einherjar than Valkyrie, even though many of the earls had brought with them their mates and most of the earls' mates were full Valkyrie. For tomorrow's council meeting, they would bring their stallari and there would be no Valkyrie in the room except for Eira.

There were no tables and no benches. The hall would not hold everyone *and* the tables, too. It was taking a long time for the Kine to make their way through the big doors into the hall itself, even though the entire hall had been emptied to make room for them.

Eventually, though, the last of them stepped through and Charlee hurried back down to the hall level, to help close the doors and begin the ceremony of reaffirmation.

As Annarr and Regin, Stefan and Eira stood upon a small platform that was higher than the tallest of them in the room, so that even those at the back of the room could see and hear them.

Sindri, the little man with the strange tattoos and the black, medieval-looking robes, stepped to the front of the platform, facing everyone below. "We swear fealty to Odin—" he began, and everyone in the hall instantly followed after him, their voices rising to the beams far overhead;

"—the first among us, whose wisdom and strength is our guiding light. We swear to protect humanity, whose care was given into our hands. We will remain upon this path, forsaking all others, and forsaking our own humanity in order to provide the strength and valor that Odin has granted us. So say we all."

An almost total silence gripped the hall, as everyone raised their glasses and drank.

Then, every single one of them smashed their glasses to the floor. The compound sound of thousands of glasses breaking with a sodden tinkling sound was one that Charlee knew she would never hear anywhere else.

Then, almost at the same instant, everyone cheered. Many of them were turning to each other and hugging, slapping themselves on the arms and shoulders, and laughing.

Charlee looked at the other Amica ranged beside her along the edges of the hall. "Amazing," she murmured.

"Makes you wish humans did something like it, too," one of them said back. "It looks like fun."

Charlee didn't think it was fun, exactly. It looked superficial and showy, on the surface, but there was a deeper significance to the short ceremony.

"All of us, Einherjar and Valkyrie, are tied to each other," Eira had explained. "The reaffirmation renews that bond. We can choose to break it, as the Eldre do when they choose a mortal human life once more. Then they must retire from Herleifr affairs as Ylva did, to be with her human lover. The tie, the bond, is what lets the Valkyrie know an Einherjar has fallen on the battle field. It's what lets us know when trouble brews."

Since the Descent, the Valkyrie had been called to a battle to retrieve fallen warriors with sharply decreasing frequency. They had healed the chosen warriors, but the warriors had not risen as Einherjar, because the way to Valhalla had been lost.

"Closed. Lost. The bridges are gone," Eira declared. "How and why doesn't matter. We're lucky the bridges are not there, anyway. You think the Kine are bad, Charlee? You should meet some of the races from the other eight worlds."

Since 1815 and the Battle of Waterloo, the only call the Valkyrie had felt had been for one of their own. Modern battles, with their impersonal long-distance weapons and battle lines drawn far apart, failed to touch their bond or call the Valkyrie to them.

As a result, there had been no Einherjar or Valkyrie created since the sixth century, when the Kine had descended to Midgard and Valhalla had been lost to them. The longer they stayed on Earth, the more their numbers dwindled. Of the nearly one thousand halls around the world, over two hundred of them were empty and abandoned because there were simply not enough Kine to populate and maintain them.

"The longer we remain on Midgard, the weaker we become," Stefan had told Charlee once, on a rare occasion when he had visited Eira in her private chambers to discuss something between them, out of hearing range of other Kine. "If we were called upon to truly defend humans, now, I'm not sure we would have the necessary numbers or strength. But we do what we can," he added hastily.

"Reaffirmation helps," Eira had added.

"Not enough to overcome small numbers," Stefan responded.

"But defend humans against what?" Charlee asked. "I thought Ragnarok had already happened."

"Ragnarok is not the only threat," Stefan had said. "There are plenty of others. The Vanir gave us dozens of prophecies besides Ragnarok, and not all of them have happened yet."

"The Nine Worlds Prophecy," Eira had murmured.

"And that's a perfect example," Stefan had agreed, although neither of them had told Charlee was the prophecy was. The subject had shifted and soon after, Stefan had left for his own quarters.

Ragnarok had been the original war that Odin had been preparing for, long before the Descent, even further back into early human history. Darwin had defined it as the equivalent to the end of the world. "The Apocalypse," he had said. "Or Judgment Day, if you want a modern metaphor. There are prophecies forewarning them about the invasion of the nine worlds and the chaos to follow."

But Ragnarok had already happened, millennia before. Eira had explained it simply. "The Bible talks about a flood that wiped out everyone except Noah and his Ark of animals. They drew inspiration for that story from somewhere, Charlee. Ragnarok was quite real, and humans only barely survived it. Although I don't think the Christians' one true God started it."

Charlee watched the reaffirmation with a deep appreciation for the symbolism and meaning behind it. It wasn't really fun at all. It was a way for the Kine to remind themselves that there was a purpose for them, however vague and distant it might seem to them. There was a reason they were here on Midgard. They just had to be patient.

She could understand why the five-yearly reaffirmation helped strengthen their mutual bond. She could also understand why the reaffirmation was held the night before the High Council meeting: it would take a strengthened and renewed bond to keep the meeting from descending into a morass of negativity and doom-crying. Being freshly reminded of why they were here would give the participants a sense of vigor and direction.

Charlee gripped the handle of her broom. "Ready?" she asked the Amica ranged beside her.

They nodded and sailed out into the hall, thirty Amica pushing their brooms before them, to sweep and wipe up the remains of two thousand broken glasses and the dregs of the mead that had been in them, while the celebration went on around them.

Another forty Amica slipped between them, carrying mugs—not glasses, this time—and pitchers of mead. The formalities were over and the party had begun.

* * * * *

After four years, Charlee knew a great many of the Kine by name, and even more by sight. She liked nearly all of them and while an old-fashioned taint spoiled the attitudes of some of them, there wasn't a single Kine she could say she disliked. So moving through the great hall, greeting Kine by name and pouring them a drink was barely taxing work. She enjoyed it, most especially on this night of nights.

The knowledge that Asher was somewhere in the room slipped deeper in her subconscious, barely rousing her, so that when she *did* see him, it was almost a surprise.

He was part of a circle of five Einherjar standing and talking together, but he had obviously seen her first, for he was turned away from them and toward her, as if he had been watching her slow progress through the crowded room for some time.

Charlee came to an abrupt halt, the mead sloshing in the heavy pitcher. Her heart leapt high and hard, and her innards roiled. She had been heading directly for him. His group would have been next.

She hadn't noticed him at all, but that was perhaps understandable. He looked so different! Hungrily, she ran her gaze over him, absorbing the difference, the details. He had let his hair grow. It was down to his shoulder blades and tied back with a leather thong, but that might be because this was a formal occasion. And he had let his beard grow out. Unlike his pale blond hair, his beard was a darker honey shade.

And he was thinner than she remembered.

He was wearing a shirt with a black band instead of a tie, and a leather coat cut long that was a substitute for a formal tuxedo jacket. His trousers were dark. It was a barely passable attempt at formal wear.

What had happened to him? Was she responsible for his current state? But she denied that possibility quickly, before it could take hold and root itself in her mind.

Then she saw one of the others in the group peer around the shoulders and backs facing her. It was Sindri, straining to see over the tops of the taller men and spot her.

Charlee didn't like Sindri. He was the one exception within the Kine, for most often she barely thought of him as one. He did not seem physically intimidating. He wore the strange robes and the odd markings. He had never said anything rude to her, or shown by an inch that he considered her desirable or even just plain beddable. He gave her the shivers (*prickly gruellies*), the way he was always standing off to one side and watching. Constantly watching. What went on in that domed head of his? She could never see behind his eyes. Thoughts didn't reflect there. He just watched.

No one else seemed to think he was odd, not in this race of oddities, mixed cultures, ages and backgrounds, so Charlee had kept her feelings to herself.

But now, with Sindri staring at her, it made her turn and walk away. Away from Asher and all of them. Her heart was aching, her pulse thready and uneven. She slid between groups and pairs, slipping through openings with practiced ease. At the edge of the hall, she found one of the small tables that held empty and full pitchers and dropped hers onto it with a panicky thrust, the mead slopping out across the pitchers that were already there.

She didn't care. Her breath was coming in hard gasps now. She just wanted to get away from everyone. She dived through the swing door that gave access to the service corridors and hurried down its length.

The door crashed open behind her, making her jump hard, her breath emerging in a squeak.

"Charlee!" Asher roared.

She halted and waited, pressing her back against the dark-painted wall because she was shaking so badly. If he would pursue her into the service corridor, where the Einherjar normally didn't intrude, then he would follow her wherever she went. Better to get this over with now.

Asher strode up to her. He was breathing as hard as she was. "You're running away from me?" he demanded angrily.

She tried to claw together a semblance of control. "I have to," she confessed. Abruptly she felt like crying, because the knowledge was sitting right there in the front of her conscience, like a neon light. She still loved him. She still wanted him, more than ever. Her body was tingling with need, making her want to press against him, to kiss him. She wanted to feel his heavy body against hers. Her memories of the one time he had held her like that were tattered remnants now, and she ached to feel that good, hard pressure again.

Instead, she closed her eyes and turned her head away.

"Charlee," he said, more softly this time, making her open her eyes. A pair of Amica hurried along the corridor, sidling past them. Asher turned to give them room, and it brought him around so that he was facing her squarely. His blue eyes met hers. "What's wrong?" he asked, his voice even lower so the Amica wouldn't hear.

She could barely speak for the constriction in her throat. "Gods, Asher, I was so wrong and you were right. Right about everything."

His gaze seemed to be boring into her.

She bit her lip. "You haven't been taking care of yourself, have you?" she asked. "I can see it in your face."

His gaze skittered away from her face. "Don't," he said softly.

"I thought I'd got over you," she said. "I thought I was happy. Well, happy enough. But I was wrong."

"Don't do this," he ground out.

"I love you," Charlee whispered.

He hung his head. "Ah, *guds*, Charlee," he breathed and lifted his head to look at her once more. His hand came up and for a breathless, dizzy moment she thought he would touch her, perhaps even stroke her cheek. But he instead moved it and pressed the flat of his hand against the wall by her head. "It doesn't matter," he said, his tone bleak. "You're Amica now."

She nodded. Hot wretchedness pulled at her, making her body ache. There was nothing she could do to deny it. She was Amica, and Eira would never let them be together. The Regin was far more ambitious than either of them.

The swing door slammed open again, this time bouncing off the wall and slamming right back against it again as someone fumbled against it. The light from the hall was blocked by a big barrel shape.

Arsenios stepped through the doorway and stood swaying blearily just inside the door, which slowly swung shut again behind him. He blinked at them. Arsenios was the rotund Einherjar, the first to ever flirt with Charlee. She had got to know him as an uneducated, but well-intentioned and very lonely Einherjar. The Amica would have been developed for Einherjar just like him, until their use as political tools had been discovered. He had flirted with little hope with Charlee since she had met him, passing a few minutes each time with pleasant compliments and hopeful innuendo.

Now he put his hands on his chubby hips. "Is he bothering you, Charlee?"

Asher made an annoyed sound and straightened up. "Your admirers await you," he said dryly. "You should go and do your job."

"No, Asher, please...."

He cupped her cheek with his hand, and for one electrifying moment his gaze met hers. His touch was hot and she shivered.

Then his hand was removed. Asher turned and strode toward Arsenios. "Go get 'em, my Greek friend," he said and patted Arsenios on the shoulder.

Charlee forced her sluggish, shell-shocked mind into moving. Her body, too. She almost stumbled along the corridor, toward Arsenios. "Arsenios, this is a bad time," she said. "I have to serve mead."

He moved quickly, his arm snaking around her waist and pulling her up against him. The smell of hot mead fanned her face. His arm had all the strength of a vice and she remembered that as an Einherjar, he would have been selected from among the fallen warriors on the battlefield for his fighting prowess, strength and courage. She couldn't afford to underestimate him, no matter how lonely or pathetic he seemed to be.

"He said I should—" He burped. "—go for it," he finished. "You're such a pretty thing."

"Arsenios, you really have to let me go," Charlee told him as firmly as she could manage, wriggling inside the iron band of his arm.

"No, I don't. Just a kiss. Just one." He leaned over her, trying to kiss her and Charlee pulled her head out of the way, her neck straining.

At the same time, he jammed his other hand between her thighs. His fingers scrabbled, trying to push through the fabric of her dress, to reach deeper between her legs. The hem of her dress was climbing swiftly up her legs as he sought her flesh.

Charlee shrieked in shock and for a moment, she froze. Then instinct took over. She head-butted him, aiming the top of her forehead not for his head, but for his nose. She connected squarely, and she heard and felt the crack of bones. His big nose flattened itself against her flesh, sliding greasily.

Arsenios squealed. His arm dropped from around her waist.

She reached down for the wrist belonging to the hand between her clamped thighs. The calm, directing tones of dozens of trainers and instructors over the last few years blended in her mind into a single thread of thought. One always worked *against* a joint for maximum disabling power. So she yanked his hand from between her legs, lifted it, and brought her right arm swinging in a hard arc, her fingers lifted up, and drove the heel of her hand right up against the side of his elbow.

She heard the crack and felt his arm go limp, then she staggered away, trying to yank the dress back down, as Arsenios bent over almost double, his arm hanging uselessly, and his other hand clamped across his nose and mouth. He was making muffled squealing noises.

"What the devil is going on in here?" came a new voice.

Charlee tried to untuck the hems that were caught up between her knees, but she was shaking too much.

A hand on her shoulder turned her gently but firmly around. "Here, they're hooked up." Hands tugged on the panels and the dress dropped down to the ground again.

Charlee looked over at Arsenios. He was breathing heavily, even closer to crumpling to the floor than before. Then she looked up. Roar stood looking from her to Arsenios. Roar, Asher's brother. Had he come looking for him?

Then Charlee coupled up more facts, her mind starting to sluggishly turn. Roar was an earl. He had caught her almost red-handed, physically attacking an Einherjar, an act that came with dire consequences.

She brought a shaking hand up to her mouth. "Oh Hell's bells, what have I done?" she breathed, looking at Arsenios.

Roar looked at her sharply. Then he moved quickly and grabbed her arm. "Come with me. Quickly now." He said it kindly enough, but his voice was low and firm, demanding no protest.

She let him pull her out of the service corridor, around Arsenios and into the light in the hall, which seemed so much brighter than when she had been in the hall last, only a few short minutes ago.

Shock was making her thoughts buzz high and loud. Nothing registered. Instead, over and over again, she kept playing the moment when he had tried to kiss her. The shock of his hand against the junction of her thighs.

Roar caught an Amica's elbow in his hand and tugged her around. It was Gan-shu, the tiny pixie from China. "Quickly and quietly," Roar told her. "Find an earl. Find Georges if you can. Tell him there's been an incident I witnessed. One of the Einherjar assaulted an Amica, Charlee. He's to keep him in a lonely room until I get back. Then find a Valkyrie. Anyone will do. Tell her that Arsenios is in the service corridor and needs medical help. Finally, find Eira. Tell her all this and that I'm taking Charlee somewhere quiet to recover. Do you understand all that?"

Gan-shu nodded, a sharp movement. "I have it." Her gaze flickered over Charlee, then she hurried away through the crowd, her tiny hips swaying despite their diminutive size.

Roar walked Charlee through the hall, holding her elbow all the way. Unlike when Charlee tried to move through the throng, people made way for Roar. He had the shoulders and the height that made it hard to miss him as he approached. People just naturally melted back out of the way for him.

"Where are we going?" Charlee asked, and was surprised at the breathless and weak sound of her own voice.

"The closest quiet place I can think of," Roar told her.

They moved through the big doors, out into the round hall, and he picked up his pace. Out here, there were people still moving across the hall in day wear and street clothes, heading for portals on the other side of the hall from the ones they had just stepped through. Roar was drawing attention in his formal tuxedo, his hand still firmly around her arm.

He was heading for the portal that jumped to New York and she realized, her mind taking seconds to work it out, that stepping through a portal would instantly bring them to somewhere much more quiet and discreet than Tryvannshøyden. Of course it was closer than anywhere outside the longhouse.

Roar pulled her through the portal, not breaking the pace of his step for a second. She felt/saw the wash of intense, dead blackness, then was stepping out the other side. The hall she had only caught a glimpse of four years ago was empty of people, silent and sparsely lit.

Roar let her arm go and seemed to relax. He turned to face her. "Well, that has got you out of the lion's den for a moment or two." He studied her, and Charlee realized that the principal similarity between him and Asher was their eyes, which were the same shape and had the same direct stare. But Roar's were a paler blue than Asher's. Right now, Charlee couldn't decide which of them was the taller and didn't care.

"Thank you for your help, earl," she told him. "I can sit at one of the tables up there. It's out of the way—"

"Do you like scotch?"

"I've never tried it."

"I don't think you should be alone, not for a while. My apartment is just off the hall here, and there is a scotch bottle in the cupboard that needs finishing. A glass, to warm you, then I will head back to Oslo to clean up this mess."

It was a reminder that she had attacked an Einherjar. How could she have been so stupid?

"Hey," Roar said gently. "Stop worrying. This will all work out."

Charlee took a deep breath. "I'll try."

"Come and have that drink." He turned and walked the length of the hall, Charlee following him. His stride was just like Asher's.

* * * * *

Charlee roused from sleep, to realize that someone was shaking her shoulder. She swam up from the depths of the most profoundly solid sleep she had ever experienced, trying to put together where she was. For a while, she thought it was the big hall and that Eira was waking her, which she had never done.

"Charlee, wake up." It was a male voice. It seemed like a voice she knew, but at the same time, it wasn't familiar at all.

Then she remembered. Fitting it together, she sat up, trying to come to full alertness as quickly as possible.

Roar was sitting on the edge of the bed, his tuxedo jacket unbuttoned, the tie hanging loose on either side of his neck. A thick lock of his dark blond hair was falling over his eyes, shadowing them.

"You're back," she said, then looked down at the bed. "I hope you don't mind. The sofa was full." The sofa was half-covered in CD cases, loose silvery CDs and old vinyl records. She hadn't been courageous enough to move them, in case she messed up an order she didn't understand or, heaven help her, she scratched one of them.

"I fall asleep on the sofa most nights. I think the bed can use the exercise," Roar told her.

"Did they…are they mad at me?" Charlee asked.

Roar grinned. The quick grin was like Asher's, but his chin was broader, the jaw not as sharply defined. "Eira was as pissed as a bee in a bottle."

"Oh." She plucked at the bedcover she sat on.

"At Arsenios, not you," Roar clarified. "She wanted to fillet him for messing with one of her ladies. I talked her down."

Relief touched her. "And Stefan? The Council? Am I to face them?"

Roar looked puzzled. "Why would you?"

It was Charlee's turn to be puzzled. "Because I hurt Arsenios. I attacked him."

Roar nodded. "I saw his elbow before they started working on it. It looks to me like you've had some training with Tiny Woods."

Charlee nodded, her surprise increasing. "I have." Tiny Woods was one of Howard's senior trainers, and he had been very critical of her fighting abilities when he had first started her on his basic program. Toward the end of her six weeks with him, he had smiled in approval. Once.

Roar threaded his fingers together and wrapped them around one knee. "No offense, Charlee, but I walked in and saw your skirt hiked up around your hips and you about to pass out. It doesn't take a genius to figure out what happened, which is just as well, because I'm not one. Yes, it's frowned upon for the Amica to attack an Einherjar. We don't like *anyone* assaulting us, when it comes right down to it. There's so few of us to start with. But that doesn't mean a justified attack won't be given due consideration."

She realized she was still plucking at the bedcover and made herself stop.

"Arsenios was more worried, once he had sobered up, about whether you would ever talk to him again. I don't think he really processed much beyond that point. The rest of us are more concerned about how a slip of a girl bested an Einherjar. I just won the bet, by the way."

"Tiny Woods?" she asked. A smile tugged at her mouth.

"Tiny Woods," he confirmed, "and a woman that kept her head." He stood up. "Eira knows you're here. I'll take you back to Oslo as soon as you're ready, but I suggest you wait until it is late morning over there, and the effects of the mead have dissipated."

"I ruined your evening," Charlee said.

"It's the same evening I have every fifth year. You didn't ruin it at all." He smiled. "It was a nice change, actually. I haven't rescued a damsel in distress for a very long time."

Charlee could feel herself blushing. "I really made a mess of things. But I just reacted at the time."

"And training did the rest." He slipped the tie from around his neck and opened the top button of the shirt. "It's nearly dinner time here in New York. I haven't eaten since lunch, and I know how hard Eira works you ladies. Would you like a very late supper, Charlee?"

Her stomach growled and he grinned. "I'll take that as a yes. I'll order a pizza. Come out and sit at the table. I'll make coffee. I'm in need of it."

In the end, Charlee made coffee *and* dinner. It began with her washing out coffee cups and then helping him grind the beans, and then he happily sat at the counter at her suggestion, while she took over the coffee-making. Her search for cream in the fridge let her discover the food already there. She glanced at the contents. "There's ground beef here, and onions and more. I could make karbonader, if you would prefer that to pizza?"

Roar looked hopeful. "Really? That would be…." He shook his head wonderingly. "I haven't had meatballs for the longest time."

So Charlee cooked the simple meatball and onion gravy sauce dish she had learned in Ylva's kitchen, while Roar sat and watched. She sipped her coffee as she moved about the kitchen, and refilled his. There were some vegetables in the crisper, including a lettuce, that were not completely beyond use, so she made a very simple salad and added it to the plates beside the karbonader and put one in front of Roar.

He sat up, looking at it. "It smells delicious."

"Wait until you try it," she warned him. "I'm better at calculus than I am at cooking." She sat on the other barstool and picked up her fork.

Roar had already speared and eaten his first meatball. He considered for a moment as he chewed, then swallowed and nodded. "If your calculus is better than your cooking, then the world of science needs to brace itself."

She laughed. "Thank you."

"I'm beginning to understand what they mean about the charm and danger of redheads."

"They do? I mean, people don't like redheads?"

"It's a history thing," he said apologetically. "There are a lot of redheads in Norway, more than any other country except Scotland. There were songs and stories about them. A redheaded woman was considered to be both a blessing and a curse, and they warn about her hot temper and her sexual drive. So Norse men are both drawn to and wary of redheads." He grinned. "They are if they heed the warnings from the past."

"The Kine take prophecies very seriously," Charlee pointed out.

"They do," he agreed.

"Do I frighten you, then?"

Roar gave her an easy smile. "I'll let you know."

She realized that he was looking at her from the corner of his eye. Not at her eyes, but slightly lower down. Then he looked away.

"It's alright," she told him. "You can look at it. It's only a scar."

"Mmm. I've seen lots of them, but never on a woman's face before. I'm sorry. I wasn't staring because it's a scar. I'm staring because it's clearly a knife wound."

Charlee nodded. "Do you know the story of how I got it?"

"Yes." He gave a small grimace. "Asher was forced to tell the Council about you and your scar, many years ago. The facts have stayed with them, though. It isn't general knowledge. But that wasn't why I was looking, either. I was thinking that every Einherjar that meets you must look at your face, catalogue the scar as a knife scar and wonder what sort of an adventurous, interesting life you led before you joined the Amica."

"An interesting life is considered a curse," she pointed out.

"Not to the Einherjar. We thrive upon interesting. It helps pass the time, which we have an abundance of."

"Life has certainly been peaceful since I started working in the Second Hall," Charlee agreed.

"Despite fending off drooling Einherjar with your razor-sharp mind?" Roar asked.

"Is that what I do?" she asked curiously.

"You're keeping *me* on my toes." He pushed his plate away and patted his stomach. "I think I can safely say that is the best meal I have had in months."

"You exaggerate," Charlee told him. "Pierre in Asher's restaurant is a brilliant chef. You must have eaten at the Ash Tree more recently than months ago."

Roar raised his brow and his lips thinned.

Charlee stared at him. "You've *never* been?" she breathed.

"I never got an invitation," he said shortly.

Charlee rolled her eyes. "Siblings!" she sighed. "My big brother would say something almost exactly the same, I'm sure. Asher would be so pleased if you stopped by, because it would look like you came without need of an invitation, like you *wanted* to be there."

Roar rubbed an invisible spot off the edge of his plate with his big thumb. "You could be right," he said.

Charlee laughed. "You've both lived for centuries and you're still behaving like school kids." She climbed off her stool and cleared the counter of the plates and cups.

"Do you see your big brother often?" he asked.

"Whenever he is in town. Eira doesn't mind me taking a few hours off and crossing over, although I usually get hustled straight out of your hall and out to the street before I can look around properly." She smiled. "Tonight—today, I mean—is the first really good look I've got."

"I'd be happy to give you the nickel tour before you go back."

"Thank you. I would love to see more. Your hall seems to be much different from Tryvannshøyden."

"They deliberately cultivate grandeur, in Oslo, to remind everyone that is the seat of power for the Kine. We prefer things to feel homier here."

"So this hall is more like it used to be?"

"With a few modern conveniences, like running water." He grinned. "Homelike is good. Too much like home would be a real pain in the rear, especially for the Amica who serve here. I've noticed that a woman's work is the last to receive updating and efficiencies. Men prefer to improve their own lives and work first."

"Perhaps because men understand their own work better than a woman's work, especially women in the past."

"I don't think it's just the past," Roar returned. "Modern women are expected to do it all, maintain a home *and* work full time to cover family expenses, yet the burden of child-rearing, household maintenance, cooking, cleaning, even running the kids to soccer practice, that is still often the woman's sole responsibility." He smiled again. "Eira says that women's fight for equality was the worst idea in history. They voted themselves right into overload. They were better off in many ways when the roles of men and women were divided and respected."

"And do you agree with Eira?" Charlee asked.

"Sometimes, yes, I do. But there are a lot of freedoms for women that came with the right to vote and social acceptance of the idea of equality that I don't think women should be in a hurry to give back. Traveling alone. Living alone, if you choose to. Entry into any career you want, if you want it badly enough."

"I guess I didn't want a career badly enough."

"You don't consider the Amica a career, then? Most Amica do. They fight as hard to be accepted into the Amica as any woman has fought to win a corner office for herself in the corporate world."

Charlee shook her head. "I see the Amica as a lifestyle choice."

"Then you did see it as a choice?"

Charlee hesitated. "I saw it as a choice between becoming part of the

Kine world, which I had caught just the smallest glimpse of from the corner of my eye, or fighting for that corner office, which seemed quite meaningless in comparison."

"You didn't want to stretch your mind, Charlee? Find out where it could take you? There's a whole world of science out there, and the horizon on what they're discovering is broadening every day."

"The Kine keep my mind more than stretched, thank you," Charlee replied truthfully. "It may not be science, but I've learned that Kine politics is just as complex and challenging."

Roar laughed. "Then the human world's loss is our gain."

Chapter Twenty-Nine

Prophecy is a tool of statecraft.

———

*Stefan, Annarr and Einherjar, from his
personal journals.*

Darwin switched on the lights, and banks of neon flickered into life,
making Charlee jump. "Should you do that?" she asked. "The light will be
seen through the window."

"It's not like we broke in here," Darwin pointed out. "You heard my
conversation with Frankie. The guards know we're here."

"They let us in because you won the last poker night," Charlee
pointed out. "It's three in the morning. I just thought that someone might
take exception to anyone roaming the library at this time of night." She
looked around the big basement room. "What is this place?"

"Archives," Darwin said flatly. He moved between four big empty
counters over to the bookshelves and cupboards against the walls. As he
passed the last counter, he leaned down and plucked surgical gloves from
a box on the shelf beneath and began to work his hands into them. "Did
you notice the hiss the door made when we stepped in here?"

"Humidity control?" Charlee asked. Her skin had tightened as they
stepped in, indicating it was dryer than outside.

"And positive air pressure. Just a bit. Encourages dust to stay on that
side of the door." He opened the glass front of one of the cupboards.
"This isn't the true archival vault. It's just a working room. The stuff in
here is valuable, but not so valuable that no one can touch it. It's where all
the professors come to do their research. I keep telling them they should
charge by the hour. They'd make a fortune." He reached into the
cupboard and picked up a book that looked ancient to Charlee. It was
about eight inches thick, and the covers were stiff and dark with age. The
edges of the pages were very yellow.

"Spread that cloth there across the counter for me," Darwin told her,
pointing with one gloved finger, the others curled around the edges of
the book.

Charlee found the cloth, which felt like a soft sort of plastic to her,
and unfolded it and laid it on the counter.

Darwin put the book down on the plastic. "This is a fifteenth-
century English copy of the eighth-century original. As the original was
written in Old English, a more or less modern English translation would

be a lot closer to the correct meaning than, say, translating from a Greek or German one."

"There's Greek and German versions of this, too?" Charlee asked, studying the cover, which Darwin hadn't opened yet. There was nothing on the cover. It was a blank leather slate, scored with scratches and stains.

"If there is, no one knows about it. This is the only copy in existence. The original Old English version has never surfaced." He touched the cover reverently.

Charlee didn't attempt to do the same. She wasn't wearing gloves and Darwin had not indicated that she could. The gentle and careful way he was handling the book told her that he would be just a little bit freaked by a non-professional trying to turn the pages. So she leaned close and watched carefully.

"Remember that Nine Worlds prophecy you told me about?" Darwin asked.

"You found it?" she breathed, stunned.

"Think so, yeah." He still hadn't opened the book. "Researchers figured this book was a joke. The English equivalent of Nostradamus spouting his nonsense that someone faithfully wrote down."

"It's a book of predictions?"

"Not like Nostradamus. He restrained himself and just dealt with human affairs. That's why this book was dismissed as nonsense from an academic point of view. There's talk of giants and dwarves, light elves, dark elves…sound familiar?"

Charlee nodded.

Finally, Darwin opened the book. "Then I found this." He carefully turned the pages, which were full of dark, Gothic-styled copperplate writing, and the occasional diagram drawn in spidery lines. Charlee pulled back as a sour, overripe stench washed over her. It made Darwin chuckle. "And now you can guess where this was found."

She wrinkled her nose and leaned back over the page he had opened it to and tried to read the first line. The lines were indented and more or less centered, like a poem would be in a modern text. She frowned as the stylistic text made her work to understand the words.

Øuerþrowe þe sayntful kynge and mercyful queene

Þe rawyn kynge shell

To bringe withine þe kynge ou kynges wyþ þe markd blowan

To face þe raþ ou þe worldes.

"There's p's everywhere," she complained. "What is this, Anglo-Saxon?"

"Middle English," Darwin replied. "It's close enough to modern English that if you stare at it long enough, it comes together. And the p's aren't p's. They're thorns. You pronounce them the same way you would the t and h in 'the'."

Charlee rolled her eyes and looked at the text again. "U's are V's, too," she murmured as the first word shifted into something she recognized. "That's 'overthrow'."

"Very good," Darwin murmured. "Go on." He pulled a pad of paper and pen from under the counter. "Read it out."

Very slowly, Charlee read out the words. "Overthrow the saintful king and merciful queen, the raven king shell—"

"*Shall*," Darwin corrected, writing quickly.

"To bring within the king of king with the marked blowan." She raised her brow at him. "Blowan?"

"Blossom. Bloom."

Charlee turned back to the page and tackled the last line of the prophecy. "To face the...the wrath of the worlds."

Darwin turned the pad around to face her and tapped it. His writing was neat and small.

Overthrow the saintful king and merciful queen
The raven king shall
To bring within the king of kings with the marked blossom
To face the wrath of the worlds.

Charlee stepped back and straightened up from her lean over the book. "That's the Nine Worlds Prophecy?" she asked. "It just says 'worlds'. There's nothing about nine of them."

"Don't forget that this is a translation of a much older book that would have been written in Anglo-Saxon. Translation can be a bitch, when you're working five hundred years in the future. All the contemporary culture of the original book is long gone."

"You mean the translator was guessing?"

Darwin grinned. "In a way. Academics do the same sort of guessing now. They choose the best translation given everything they know about life and literature at the time the text they're translating was written. But sometimes even dating older texts is a guess, too." He tapped the page gently. "Notice anything else about it?"

"It's really bad poetry."

He rolled his eyes. Then he moved around the counter, back to the glassed-in shelves. Underneath the glass fronts were open shelves where more modern books sat. He picked one up and brought it back to the counter. It had a reddish-brown, scratched and stained cover, and the spine, which was a good three inches thick, had raised channels across it, every inch or so.

Darwin didn't put the book on the plastic. "This was published in the late seventeenth century," he said. "No one knows who wrote it. The title page is missing, and they sometimes forgot to include headers and footers back then."

Charlee moved around the counter to look at the pages as Darwin rifled through it. He was handling the book with much less care, and she could see that the pages were printed, not hand-written. He flipped back and forth, zeroing in on the page he wanted. She could see many stanzas on the pages. "What is this?"

"Someone went to the trouble of collecting prophecies and writing them down. He's got Nostradamus, Coinneach Odhar, Mother Shipton, even Virabrahmendra, from India, so the guy did his homework. Not too shabby for the eighteenth century, which is probably why someone thought it was worth setting out the type to print the book in the first place, even though the content would have been considered anti-Christian for then and there. That's where I found this."

He spun the book to face Charlee and pressed his finger against the open page.

Topple the saintly king and merciful queen,
The raven king shall.
To usher in the king of kings with the branded bloom,
To face the wrath of the worlds.
The Nine World Prophecy—auth. Unknown

Charlee pulled the pad over and compared them. "They're the same, more or less." She straightened up again. "But what does it mean?"

"That's the problem with old prophecies," Darwin said. "They usually don't make much sense until they come true. Then, hindsight lets you figure it out." He tapped the page again. "Norse mythology describes nine worlds. So this prophecy deals with some sort of conflict involving all nine worlds. But you say Ragnarok has already happened, back in pre-history, so is this a second Armageddon?" He shrugged.

"A saintly king," Charlee murmured. "There was a Saint Stephen."

"You're thinking of Stefan?" Darwin grinned. "From what you've told me, Eira is the last woman I'd call merciful. Marc Antony in a dress, is more her style."

"So long as the dress is a Donna Karan original, yes." Charlee sighed. "And they don't call them a king or queen, either."

"But the symbolism fits," Darwin replied. "The original text, remember, was probably Old English. The dude who translated it in the sixteenth century probably used king and queen because those were the names for the leaders of his time. It would make sense to people reading his book, back then."

"So we should substitute 'President', then?" She looked at the first line. "The raven President will kill the President and the First Lady."

Darwin looked at her. "Even less poetry-like, ain't it?

Charlee moved over to the original medieval text. "It's not poetry, but when you say it like that, it stops being cute."

"I don't think it was ever meant to be cute, Charlee. This is talking about the equivalent of all-out war. Every world, every creature in those worlds, all coming together to heap their anger on us."

Charlee looked at his thoughtful face as he stared down at the modern translation. "But it could happen somewhere far in the future," she said. "The Kine are immortal. It could be talking about something in the thirtieth century. They'll still be here then."

Darwin closed the book in front of him, and it shut with a heavy thumping sound. "Let's hope so. We know the Kine are real, that magic is real, that Valhalla was real. The Vanir, who gave them all the prophecies in the first place, I guess they're real, too. One of their prophecies made it into human records, at least, and you said that Stefan and Eira speak of the Vanir prophecies like they speak about the portals and their swords vanishing at will, and like I talk about making hot chocolate. It's a normal, accepted concept, like gravity or evolution."

"There's plenty of people that dispute evolution," Charlee pointed out.

"And there're probably plenty of Kine that think the prophecies are just cute stories from their past, too," Darwin replied. "My analogy still stands." He was still frowning, shifting uneasily.

"What's bugging you?" Charlee asked softly.

"Ah, it's probably nothing." He gathered up the medieval text and put it back into the glass cupboard.

"Tell me anyway," Charlee said.

Darwin sighed and pulled off his gloves. "I've been circling around this since I found the prophecy a few weeks ago. You said the Kine have been deliberately keeping to themselves since they got here, centuries ago. It's their laws."

"*Laun*," Charlee said in agreement. "Which I'm absolutely breaking every time I talk to you."

"And I understand the privileged position that puts me in," he returned. "If Anna-Maria were still alive, I wouldn't have breathed a word of this to her. Knowing puts one in an awkward position."

"It puts you in danger," Charlee said flatly.

"Yeah, that, too. But the older I get, the less I care." He shrugged again. "Here's the thing. The Kine have been behaving themselves, playing nicely with humans, *being* human, ever since they got here. Asher might disagree—"

"He does."

"—But I think it's one of their smarter moves, staying hidden. So, look at Norse mythology, what we know of it. The Einherjar and Valkyrie are real. Magic is real. The gods *were* real, but no one knows where they are, and we should probably all be grateful they're not around anymore, because I can't see them being content to stay in hiding century after century, while this One True God gets all the kudos and worship."

"Aren't you Catholic?" Charlee asked, trying to hide her smile.

"I grow less Catholic with every passing day," Darwin said flatly. "These portals you described, Charlee. I think they're part of Yggdrasil."

Charlee had been doing her own reading. "The one tree that connects the worlds?" she asked now, remembering the name.

"Symbolism, remember?" Darwin asked. "The tree connects the worlds, yes. What if these portals are the tree? They're connecting everything."

Charlee frowned. "But they only connect places on Earth. Hall to hall, to hall."

"So, they're the roots, which are buried in the earth. If they are, and if the tree really is a metaphor—"

"Then where do the branches go?" Charlee breathed, finishing his thought. She held out her hand. "Bridges," she said. "There was a bridge or something."

"Bivrost," Darwin supplied. "It was the bridge from Asgard to the other worlds, or just to Midgard, depending on who's talking about it."

"Portals—roots—running across the world itself, and bridges—the branches—connecting the world to all the other worlds. The tree really is the center of the universe, isn't it?"

Darwin nodded. "And we should cry with relief that the bridges aren't open anymore. If all the concepts from the mythology are true and so far, the more you learn about the Kine, the more we're seeing that the concepts were right, well, the...*things*...on those other eight worlds...." He picked up the book with the modern translation in it and held it up. "Prophecies—*real* prophecies –they have a way of coming true. This is one prophecy I'd rather not live to see."

"To those who remember those times, this hall reminds them of the longhouses from the days when they were human," Roar explained as they did a slow circuit around the hall.

By the time Charlee made it back to the hall on Pearl Street, it was close to dawn. Even though she still considered herself a native New Yorker, she abided by the Kine's protocol when visiting a hall that was not your home hearth. She asked to be escorted to Roar's apartment door, where she knocked and waited.

Roar himself answered the door. He was already dressed. "Did you enjoy your evening?"

"Yes, thank you. Although Darwin was petering out. He's very used to his retiree hours now. I tucked him into bed and came straight here."

"It's nearly noon in Oslo," Roar said. "Let me show you around my hall, then I'll take you back."

It was clear from the pride in his voice as he showed her around that Roar was very attached to this hall. "It's much bigger than the original longhouses, of course. It has to be to contain everyone who is beholden to the hall, when they are all assembled."

"When were those days, for you?" Charlee asked curiously. "When were you human?"

"They didn't date the years when I was still human." Roar gave a grimace. "Long ago, let's say. The Kine found themselves upon Midgard in five hundred and thirty-five, the year of no summer. Did you read of that year in your travels through the history books?"

"I sort of remember. Isn't that the year that they believe Krakatoa erupted? The smoke and dust stayed in the air and covered the globe, so the sun couldn't get through."

Roar nodded. "It was a very grim year. No harvest, no fresh food. Many died, including those of the Kine. The slaves' religion took solid root that year, as humans looked for reasons why their world was so blighted. That their god was punishing them for not believing in him was very easy to accept. They had been turning away from our gods for centuries, but that year they embraced the new religion with fervor."

Charlee realized he was speaking of Christianity. "I've heard Eira say that was the reason why you were ejected from Valhalla. Because humans had stopped believing in you and the gods."

"It's one theory," Roar said. "We may never find out. We haven't so far. That year we were too busy learning to survive ourselves, to wonder why we were thrust upon Midgard. Instead, we turned to our older, human ways because they worked. We built halls like this one, as central locations from where we could begin assimilating into human culture.

We've been doing it ever since."

"Except when humans stopped building halls, you kept building them. Just hidden."

"The old ways worked," Roar said. "And while we must change our human habits to continue to look human to those outside the hall, inside the hall we can be ourselves." He gave her a smile as they approached the flat, low dais where the big chair sat. "We do not like change and the human world changes at the speed of light, making us dizzy trying to keep up with it." He rested a foot on the dais. "Here, we do not have to change."

"But you do change," Charlee pointed out. "Maybe not at the pace humans do, but human change influences you, and you *do* change."

His smile broadened. "I assure you that under this civilized veneer, I am the same blood-taking warrior I have always been. It is the price of immortality. We merely ape progress, while our instincts and preferences stay fixed. We are creatures caught in amber."

Charlee shook her head. "I don't believe that."

He raised a brow. "You would if you saw me drunk, or angry."

"You, and every adult male upon Midgard," she said shortly. "But you think women should have rights, and you fought to have me exonerated, last night, despite the law that says attacking an Einherjar is punishable, no matter what the cause. I don't for a moment believe that was what you were brought up to believe when you were human."

Roar considered her. "No," he said at last. "I didn't believe that when I was human." He said it thoughtfully, as if his mind was far away.

"Something in you has changed, then," Charlee finished. "Human influence?" she suggested.

He took his boot off the dais and stood up. "One day, I will tell you about a woman called Meggy. Come. I will take you back to the Second Hall."

* * * * *

It was barely a week later when Charlee began to understand the true consequences of that night. Asher's rejection was the most painful outcome, the one that lingered like a throbbing wound.

But almost immediately after returning to the hall and her normal responsibilities, Charlee noticed that the other Amica were treating her more like the outsider she had been in Ylva's house. The foreigner. They remained friendly, but she could sense they had their guard up. They were measuring what they said to her.

The Einherjar treated her with a new respect. The flirting, the teasing, the slightly less than serious suggestions, they all continued on unabated, for it was the role of the Amica to provide that delightful air of pleasant banter and a sense of community.

But many of the men watched her now with more than a friendly gaze. She caught from the corner of her eye their thoughtful expressions as they stared, expressions that evaporated the moment she turned to look at them properly.

A week almost to the day, Charlee learned the other great consequence of daring to lay a hand on an Einherjar.

She had been assigned to medical duties, working alongside Eira in one corner of the big hall. As a Valkyrie, Eira possessed remarkable healing powers, as well as the sum of all healing knowledge gathered by the Kine. When fallen warriors were gathered from the battlefields by the Valkyrie, they were brought to Valhalla and healed of their wounds. The Valkyrie were the ones to heal them, and they were granted almost magical powers, which had been supplemented by a very practical, down to earth medicine. Ylva had lost her Valkyrie powers when she had become one of the Eldre, but her knowledge of medicine, healing and wellness was as vast as Eira's, and she had used that knowledge to help Charlee after the knife attack.

Eira used the same knowledge, combined with her powers as a Valkyrie, to address any health issues among those that called Tryvannshøyden home. It had been Eira who had healed Arsenios' broken arm.

Those Amica who were skilled at the preparation of the ointments and creams that a Valkyrie used were much in demand as assistants, and many of them would choose to specialize in the work, especially if they considered their chances of forming a long-term contract with an Einherjar to be slim.

Ylva had stressed Charlee's skills in the preparation of medicinals, and Eira had remembered and selected her as her personal assistant from time to time. "But not too often, Charlee. It would send out a certain signal to the Einherjar that you should not be ready to declare just yet."

Instead, Charlee had spent most of her time doing more menial chores that nevertheless kept her in frequent contact with Einherjar who belonged to the hall or were visiting.

The week after the reaffirmation ceremony, Eira asked her to assist for the morning. "Arsenios will return today for me to examine his arm. I think he would appreciate the opportunity to speak to you and learn that you bear him no ill will." She gave a small smile. "And I will be there to moderate, just in case your need to inflict more bodily damage reasserts itself."

Charlee had flushed, but not disputed her. The feeling she got from most of the Kine when they referred to the matter with Arsenios was one of amusement and she had carefully said as little as possible about it, happy to let them laugh about it. They could have taken a far stronger and dimmer view of the affair if they had wanted to.

Arsenios was still yet to appear in the hall, although Charlee couldn't see the entire hall in one glance. In deference to modern human practices, most Valkyrie treated their patients behind screens and kept waiting patients separate, maintaining a degree of discretion that didn't exist in the original halls.

"The women would stitch wounds next to the center fire," Eira explained. "They would cauterize wounds using the poker from the fire itself. Everyone was privy to the treatment and discussion of wounds and sickness. They were all exposed to any infections that she treated, too. It was a true community. There was no such thing as doctor-patient confidentiality. That is a modern idea that can be quite inconvenient at times, but the Einherjar like it. It lets them keep their illusion of masculinity and courage." And she had laughed.

Between each patient, Charlee would swiftly sterilize any instruments, and prepare for the next one while Eira called them in.

Toward noon, when the line of patients had begun to dwindle, the next one stepped around the screen without waiting for Eira to call him.

"Roar!" Eira said. She opened her mouth to speak, but nothing emerged.

"Are you unwell?" Charlee asked, puzzled. He was wearing a suit and tie, and wouldn't look out of place on Wall Street.

"No." He glanced from Eira to her and back again. "I hope you don't mind. I came..." He blew out a breath. "I came to see if I could steal Charlee for the day. I have back-to-back meetings, including a business lunch that needs a woman to dazzle them while I spin the deal."

Eira closed her mouth and glanced at Charlee. There was something in her glance that Charlee could not interpret, which was not unusual with Eira, but Charlee suspected that this time it was important she understand the currents that were suddenly swirling around her.

"Of course she would be pleased to help," Eira said stiffly. Again the direct, loaded glance. "Charlee?"

Charlee understood that it was her choice. "Yes, I would be very pleased indeed. Any excuse to visit New York will do, but this is a fine excuse."

Roar smiled, pleased.

Charlee spread the folds of the work-a-day apron dress she was wearing. "I need to change into business-wear."

"I can wait," Roar assured her. "It's barely six a.m. in New York. My first meeting is at eight."

Eira pressed her lips together and nodded at her. "Ask Manorama to step in for you, would you? There are still six more people to tend to."

"Should I help you with them, instead?" Charlee asked.

"No, no." Eira shook her head. "Just ask Manorama to drop whatever she is doing, as you cross the hall."

"I'll be in the round hall by the portal," Roar told Charlee.

She nodded and hurried back to her room to wash quickly and put on the skirt suit she had completed only a few weeks before. She had drawn the pattern based on a photo in *Vogue*, adjusting for her height and her hip and waist ratio, which was larger than the average model's.

Then she applied subtle makeup and piled her hair on the back of her head, pinning it quickly into a French twist.

"Very New York," Roar said when she found him at the portal. His tone was warm and approving.

It was a fun day, although for most of the morning, Charlee was at a loss to understand why she was there. Roar introduced her as his assistant, and she made herself useful bringing coffee and clearing up after the truly back-to-back meetings he was sitting through. They were all human meetings, stemming from his daytime role as an entrepreneur, which was just non-specific enough to cover many of the activities and business deals he had to make on behalf of the New York hall. The hall was Kine, but it sat upon human soil, in a city that collected taxes, in a country that demanded record-keeping, reports, and more taxes. Roar, and all the earls ruling halls around the world, took care of human expectations attached to their halls with a number of guises that let them deal as humans.

Roar operated a perfectly normal-looking office on the first floor of the building the hall was located in. He had commandeered the boardroom there for his meetings, although she had glimpsed a big office connected to the boardroom through a door at the far end.

The office suite had secretaries, a receptionist, and clerks. All of them, as far as Charlee could tell, were Amica or Einherjar, which left her even more puzzled about her role for the day.

In between the first and second meeting, which started at nine, Roar stretched hard, his hands pressed against the small of his back. "These things are so monotonous," he groused. "I always put them off and off, until I can't procrastinate another day. Then I get stuck with a whole day of them."

"You haven't learned, in two hundred years of dealing with New York's business community, to spread the meetings out?" Charlee asked.

"I didn't think I *could* learn new tricks, until recently." He glanced at her from under his brow, then picked up the agenda on the table in front of him. "Who's next?"

The lunch meeting was at Aroma Borealis, the new and very trendy Italian restaurant right on Wall Street and just a block east of Pearl. They had walked there at a leisurely pace, weaving between office workers heading back to the office for the afternoon.

"The French are more civilized about their lunches," Roar said, as they were jostled by suits hurrying past. "Everyone gets two hours to enjoy a properly prepared meal. None of this gobbling food straight out of a paper bag while you run around doing errands."

"Is that why the lunch meeting is at one instead of noon?" Charlee asked.

"I couldn't squeeze anything more out of the morning," Roar confessed. "One is as early as I could manage it. Ah, well, it's been a productive morning, thanks to you."

"I did very little."

"Your presence does most of the work." He nodded toward the glass and brass restaurant ahead. "Keep them on their toes for me, Charlee. I need them distracted."

"I'll do my best, but really, you should have asked for someone like Donna Elizabeth if you want men truly dazzled." Donna Elizabeth was a svelte Swedish brunette, with large breasts and a waist that seemed impossibly small. She made the most of her natural bounty, making many Einherjar stutter and stop in their tracks, and earning her the nickname 'the brunette Marilyn'.

"I know Donna quite well," Roar told her. "I need someone who can hold up their end of a conversation and give it right back. Donna is lovely, but her English is less than adequate."

The Aroma Borealis was busy, but the host who greeted them at the door beamed when he saw Roar. "Your guests are already at the table."

They were led through the packed restaurant, where the aromas truly were star-like in their intensity and delight, through to a section that was curtained off from the main body of the restaurant. The host held the curtain aside and they stepped in to a private section that held just one table.

Charlee nearly tripped over her own stilettos, as she recognized the man rising from the table. Mayor Michael Bloomberg held out his hand and shook Roar's firmly. "*Heil og sæl*...did I get it right?"

"You did very well." Roar drew Charlee forward. "Mayor Bloomberg found out about my Norse ancestors and has been trying to get the greeting right ever since. Michael, this is a friend of mine, Charlee Montgomery. She counts generations of her New York ancestors on both hands, I believe."

"A native of the island. You're a rarity, Ms. Montgomery." The Mayor shook her hand.

"In all ways, your honor," Charlee told him.

He got a sparkle in his eyes. "Call me Michael, please."

Charlee wasn't sure if the lunch was a success in Roar's estimation, for there seemed to be very little business discussed. There was a lot of joking and laughter and the food was wonderful. So was the champagne. The Mayor's companion at the table was, as far as she could tell, one of his senior executive assistants. The man spent a lot of time thumbing out texts on his BlackBerry, although he was polite and jovial when he wasn't staring at the device.

Ninety minutes after they arrived, the Mayor got to his feet and shook Roar's hand again. He pressed his other hand against Charlee's when he shook hers. "It has been a pleasure, Charlee."

They let the curtain drop down behind them, leaving Charlee and Roar at the table alone.

"Did that go well?" Charlee asked, honestly puzzled.

Roar sat back with a sigh. "You did beautifully," he said.

The waiter stepped through the curtain and Roar held up one finger, then two together.

The waiter nodded and let the curtain drop once more.

"But there wasn't any business discussed at all," Charlee pointed out.

"Exactly. Michael wanted to nail me down on some complex agreements over the land our hall sits on. We've managed to supress taxes on it for decades, but it's starting to come to a head and the city pulled the Mayor into the matter just to throw some weight around."

"Then the deal you wanted to do was not deal at all?"

"Not yet," Roar agreed with a smile. "I just need to put the city off for twenty more days. Then a grandfather clause kicks in, and we get another ten years at the old rate. Only, he knows that too, so the pressure is on. Today, he thought he would be able to grind me down into dealing, with this private room and a fancy lunch. So I brought you along. He's a touch old-fashioned in places."

"He won't talk business with a woman present?"

"He won't do business when someone he doesn't know is in the room," Roar amended. "So I softened it by bringing a very beautiful stranger, instead of one of my assistants." He laughed. "Next time it will be a summons to the Mayor's office and we'll do business over the boardroom table instead of lunch. He won't make that mistake again."

The waiter stepped around the curtain once more. He placed a bowl of ice cream in front of Roar and lined up a spoon on either side of it, then nodded and left.

"One bowl, two spoons," Charlee murmured, remembering the signal. She leaned to look at the bowl. "Chocolate chip?" she asked, trying to hide her smile.

"My one indulgence." Roar picked up one of the spoons and held it out to her. "If you tell anyone, I'll kill you."

"Because it's such a profound secret to have."

"It is," Roar said gravely. "Cities might fall if it were to become common knowledge." He scooped up a mouthful and ate it with zest.

Charlee stole a scoop from his bowl, but let him eat most of it, which Roar had no trouble doing.

"I'm surprised, if you like ice cream so much, you don't smoosh it into paste and stir it smooth. My brother says that's the only decent way to eat ice cream."

Roar looked startled, then gave her a rueful grin. "I *do* that, but only when no one is looking."

Charlee laughed. "I wonder if I could get a coffee, instead?" she asked, putting down her spoon.

"For you, anything." He pressed the button at the edge of the table that called the waiter to them, and after consulting with her, ordered an espresso. Then he sat back. "Thank you for your help today."

"I'm not sure how I've helped, but it's good to know I made a positive contribution."

"I think that's one of your better qualities," Roar said. "Your humility is quite genuine. It's very refreshing, especially here in New York."

Charlee could feel her cheeks burning. "I don't know what to say to that."

"It's a compliment. You're supposed to say thank you."

"Yes, of course. Thank you."

"Then you say 'yes, I will'."

"Why do I say that?"

"Because I would like you to accompany me to the solstice feast at the Second Hall, next week. Will you, Charlee?" His expression had lost all its merriment. His gaze, so much like Asher's but yet so different, pinned her to the spot.

Charlee was abruptly breathless. *The solstice feast!*

She understood what Roar was not saying. The implications behind his request were profound. If she walked into that hall by his side, Roar would be declaring to the Kine world that he had made an unspoken claim upon her that she had agreed to. Shortly after that public and silent declaration, a formal request would follow. Then...a contract. Short or long, and the terms of it would be open to negotiation.

But this invitation was the start of a process that ended with her becoming Roar's...

She couldn't finish the thought. The whispering in her mind, the one panicky thought repeating itself over and over was a nearly incoherent pleading. *Asher...please, please, tell me what to do now!* The need to consult with him, to tell him what was happening, and to have him fix things like he always had, was almost overwhelming. She shifted on her chair, fighting the impulse to jump up and run all the way to the Ash Tree, which was only three blocks away.

"You look shocked," Roar said. He tried to make it sound jovial, but the worried note slipped through.

"I..." She cleared her throat. "I never thought anyone would ask me." The last was a whisper.

"Because of your scar, or because of Asher?" he asked gently.

Something grabbed at her chest. "Yes," she breathed. It was all she could manage.

"I like the scar," Roar said flatly. "It ties you to us in a way that reminds me every time I see it. Asher..." He let out his breath. "Asher isn't here. I am, and I am the one who is asking."

Charlee gripped her knees beneath the table, to stop them shaking. "May I...could I think about it? Could I give you an answer in a day or two?"

He considered. "That seems only fair," he decided. "But know this, Charlee. You kicked me in the heart last week, when you pointed out how much I have changed since the Descent. I have been thinking hard all week, and I've decided that you are right. I *have* changed, even though I have fought tooth and nail to stay as I was. But it's a good change and I want to keep on changing. I think you would be *such* a catalyst, the world will look quite different with you in it."

"You're equating me with common hydrogen peroxide?" Charlee asked, for that was one of the most common catalysts in the world.

He tilted his head. "No, I'm equating you with rare earth."

Charlee blinked, surprised.

The corners of Roar's mouth lifted. "You didn't think I'd know about chemical catalysts, did you? It's nice to know I can surprise you."

"You've done that more than once," she assured him.

"Think about it, Charlee," he urged her. "Mine is not the biggest or grandest hall in our world, but it has a degree of influence, nevertheless. I can't offer..." He swallowed. "I won't insult you by professing deep love, but that might come. I have a feeling that life with you in it will be more than sufficiently interesting and always changing. Who knows where we will end up?"

Coldness gripped her. "You're...you speak like you are looking years ahead." Her lips felt numb.

"I am," Roar said evenly. "I would not insult you twice by offering a paltry few years of my time and then tossing you aside like so much refuse." He hesitated. "Or, if you would prefer that, we can come to a shorter arrangement. I want to be fair, Charlee."

Fair. He offered fairness. Years of it.

Oh, gods, Asher! Where are you?

* * * * *

Eira was sitting at the long, narrow table she used for meetings. There was a large pitcher of mead on the table, and from the sharp smell, Charlee guessed it was sack mead, which had a higher alcohol content than any of the others. The pitcher was nearly empty. So was the glass in front of Eira, who sat with her head turned to study the painting on the wall in reaction to Charlee's news.

"I have to say no, of course," Charlee said, speaking as calmly as she could.

"Why would you do that?" Eira asked, her head still turned. "Do you not consider the earl of New York to be a sufficiently powerful conquest for an Amica like you?"

Charlee hesitated. There was something in Eira's tone. "I don't...that's not why I think I should refuse."

"Why refuse at all?" Eira asked. For a single moment her gaze met Charlee's face, then skittered away. She looked at her hands, lying motionless on her knees. "You've moved the earl of New York to the point where he wants to negotiate a long-term contract, a man who has never once in all his long years even so much as looked sideways at an Amica. You come along and in a week, you snare him. If you accept his contract, your fame as an Amica is assured. You will be remembered among the Kine forever. Why would you refuse such an opportunity? Is that not what the Amica are for?"

Charlee couldn't dispute her. This was the reason the Amica were given access to the highly protected inner halls of the Kine, why they were trained to within an inch of their lives to entice and enfold a man in womanly snares.

"It isn't why *I* joined the Amica," Charlee said, her voice weak after Eira's ringing tones.

"It is your *purpose*!" Eira shouted. With a scream that would freeze battleground enemies, she swept the glass and the pitcher off the table. She got to her feet, her chest heaving. "You will not refuse him!" Her eyes were glittering with fury.

With a hot rush of fear, Charlee put it together. It wasn't anger that was making Eira's eyes glisten. It was tears.

Eira loved Roar, but for reasons Charlee didn't fully understand, but knew would be political in nature, Eira had done nothing about it. She had been secure in the knowledge that Roar was not interested in the Amica or the companionship they offered.

And now he had changed his mind.

You would be such a catalyst, Charlee....

She stepped forward, closer to Eira. "Go to him," she urged. "Tell him. Now."

Eira laughed bitterly. "He's made his choice." She closed her eyes and turned away. "Finally, he has made a choice."

"I can still refuse."

"You would be a fool if you do. No man, no Einherjar, would make another offer if you turn down Roar. Your effectiveness as an Amica would be at an end."

"There are other roles. Medicine. The kitchen."

"You would end any chance of happiness in a man's arms, Charlee. You would lose not just Roar, but everything that counts in this world."

Including Asher.

But Asher was already lost to her. He had told her to do her job. This was doing her job.

Eira put her face in her hands for one long moment. Her whole body shook. Then she lowered her hands and squared her shoulders and looked Charlee in the eye. "As your Regin, I could not arrange a more advantageous match, Charlee. Take this opportunity. Roar is a good man. You will not suffer as his companion."

Charlee swallowed. "I don't want him." It was the weakest argument she could muster. But it was the truth.

Eira nodded. "Then we have that in common, don't we? We both must give up what we really want." Her smile was bitter.

Chapter Thirty

Hroar Brynjarson, who remained as earl
of the New York hall for nearly three
centuries, is generally considered to be
the stabilizing glue that held the Kine
leadership together despite its volatile
and disparate personalities. It discounts,
however, his personal tragedy, many
centuries before, that shaped Kine life
on Midgard. Hroar's impact on the
Kine tends to be overshadowed by his
brother…

———

The House of Wands by Unurr Guillory

Charlee stood off to one side of the round hall, watching gorgeously dressed couples head into the main hall through the towering double doors. She was wearing her best, and waiting for a man.

The parallel to the long forty minutes she had waited in front of another hall in the past was not lost on her. Only, Asher had come to her rescue that night.

He wouldn't rescue her tonight, for she knew he was already in the hall. She had watched him enter—alone—fifteen minutes ago, from the gallery high above. Only after he had gone in had she had the courage to step out into the round hall to meet Roar, as arranged.

She brushed at the skirt of her dress nervously. The dark green stretch velvet clung to her, all the way down to just above her knees, where it flared into a full-skirted hem that pulled along the ground behind her as she walked. The long sleeves extended over her hands, coming to a point just above the knuckles. The back of the dress dipped down below her waist, also coming to a point. There was nothing modest about the dress at all, even though it covered almost every inch of her.

She was getting glances from Kine as they passed her, heading for the doors and the bright light spilling out into the dimly lit round hall. The noise from inside was climbing in volume.

Charlee felt cold and gripped her hands together tightly.

(*…he's not coming. Not tonight. Tonight you get to live with your choice….*)

The sense of time running out, of gates starting to close, was strong.

Roar stepped through the New York portal, looked around and spotted her.

(...and the gate just closed.)

He came straight over to her, smiling. "You look stunning," he told her, picking up her hand. Then he studied her more closely. "You're shaking."

Her voice shook. "I...I'm scared." Then she pressed her lips together, dismayed as well. Why had she said something so stupid? Just because it was the truth, didn't mean she could just blurt it out like that.

But Asher would have understood, the devil's advocate in her mind whispered. *He would have joked, and made you laugh and made you know everything would be fine.*

Roar didn't do any of that. He just held her hand, looking at her. "Seventy years after we arrived on Midgard, I set up a hall in England. I met a Saxon girl who lived in the village that built up around the hall. Meggy, her name was."

One day I will tell you about a woman called Meggy.

"You loved her," Charlee breathed.

"Like the sun loves the moon, and the stars dance in the sky to proclaim it. I loved her with every fiber of my soul." Roar's blue eyes were narrowed, as if the memory was painful. "She was human, but I told her what I was, because I couldn't imagine loving someone that much and not having her love me for what I really was. And she did, Charlee. She loved me anyway." A fine line etched itself between his brows. "There were no children, of course." He lifted his gaze to the ceiling for an aching moment. "If only there had been, she might have been saved. But the village laid the blame upon Meggy."

Charlee caught her breath. "What happened?"

"They called for me to shun her. To turn her out. If I did, they would run her out of the village, for nothing was as useless to a village as a woman who could not breed warriors and wives for those warriors. They would cast her out, rather than share their food with her. So I told them what I was, to save her."

"You...*told* them?" Stunned, Charlee looked at him. "Did they believe you?"

"They were simpler times, when magic was used to explain much they didn't understand. They believed me." He sighed. "So they stoned Meggy to death for sleeping with a god and rising above her station."

Charlee let out her breath. "Oh, Roar...."

Roar dropped his gaze to the floor. "We learned from Meggy's death that we could not tell humans about ourselves. The principles of *laun* were laid down that same year, and they have not fundamentally changed since then." He brought his gaze back to hers. "I have not changed, either, or so I thought. I have not loved another woman since Meggy,

Charlee. I have not shared myself in any way."

No Amica. No Valkyrie. No one at all. "That was...fifteen centuries ago," she breathed.

Roar nodded. He lifted her fingers, caught in his. "I'm afraid, too, Charlee. This here...it has been a very long time."

She compulsively gripped his hand. "Don't let go, then. We can help each other up if we trip."

He licked his lips. "I hope to the gods we don't. You understand, Charlee, they will all be watching, the moment we step inside?"

She swallowed and nodded. "I guessed." Then she deliberately rolled her eyes. "That's a hell of a way to stop me being afraid."

Roar's mouth quirked upwards. "I wanted to share the panic. Isn't it supposed to be cut in half if you do?"

"I think that's a trouble shared that you're talking about."

He turned and led her toward the door. They were already drawing attention. From the corner of her eyes, she could see heads turning. People whispering.

"Trouble, yes," Roar murmured as they approached the doors, the light, the noise. "I knew you would make life interesting." His hand gripped tighter.

* * * * *

It was the spreading pool of silence with murmurs rippling over it that caused Asher to turn and look.

Roar stood just inside the big doors.

And Charlee.

Her hand was in Roar's.

Something invisible, large and powerful slammed into his chest. Asher sank onto the bench, the pressure so tight he couldn't draw breath. He hung his head, fighting to breathe and to make sense of what he had just seen.

You know what it means. You just don't want to let it be true. She's with him. She's with your brother. He had the guts to reach out for what you could not.

His chest unlocked and he could breathe, but the air he pulled into his lungs was dripping with acid pain that ate into him, spreading its noxious fumes, making him moan softly. He curled his hand into a fist, fighting it...and losing.

For a moment, even his vision faded. All that was left of his senses was a lingering memory of her scent, the taste of her against his lips.

"Holy cow bells," someone at the next table said. "That's New York isn't it? With that Amica, what's her name? The spitfire."

"Charlee," came the answer.

"She's delicious. Easy to see why he climbed off his high horse and took that one for himself."

Asher kept his head down. He would not watch them pass by. He wanted to erase the sight that was now etched onto the back of his eyes and was burning an afterimage into his brain. He couldn't leave until the feasting was done. It would be considered an insult of the highest order. He had nearly two hours of torture to get through before he could leave and deal with this in a dark room, alone and unobserved.

"Would you mind?" came a quiet voice behind him.

The bench he was sitting on shifted under him as the men shuffled along its length, making room.

A fourth man settled down next to him. "Could you pass that pitcher?"

The sound of mead being poured.

Then someone uncurled the fingers of his fist and a cool metal mug was pressed against his palm. "Drink, friend," came the quiet whisper. "When this is all done, I will see you home."

Asher clutched the mug in his hand and looked up. Sindri sat next to him, in the same black robes he always wore. He was watching Asher with sympathy in his black eyes.

"You know?" Asher whispered. How many knew? How many suspected?

"I recognized the pain in your face." Something shifted behind his eyes. For a fraction of a moment, Asher saw pain flash there, then it was gone and the same bland light filled them that was all Sindri ever held. "I know it well." His cold fingers touched Asher's wrist. "Drink."

* * * * *

Roar held the door aside. "I'm surprised it took you this long," he said. "It's been three days. I was expecting you to come banging on my door the next morning."

Asher pushed his hands into his pockets. "Had something to do." His voice was still raw from the mead and there had been singing and shouting, but he couldn't quite pull together a coherent memory of that.

"Is that this year's euphemism?" Roar asked dryly. "Come in. There's no need to force everyone else in the hall to listen to your yelling."

Asher stepped inside. The apartment was as neat as a pin. Even the dishes were done, and drying neatly on the rack. "What, you've got her keeping house for you already?"

Roar settled on one of the barstools. "I know how to clean when I have to."

"You didn't get one of your Amica to do it? Charlee really has you wrapped around her finger, doesn't she?"

Roar crossed his arms. "You know her better than I do. You know very well she would never keep company with a man who would let her do that. She has too much self-respect."

Asher tightened his fists inside the coat. "But you're going to change all that, aren't you?" The words came out tight and hard. "I suppose I should congratulate you. You're going to get to know Charlee very well indeed. It's quite a coup. She wouldn't look at another Einherjar, except to stick her nose in the air and tell him he wasn't good enough."

Roar just looked at him, with the same patient, understanding expression.

"Goddamn it, *why didn't you tell me?*" He could feel his throat straining with the effort to speak.

"Look at yourself. There's your answer," Roar said softly.

Asher spun and strode to the window. From where he was standing, he was just a black silhouette outlined in the glass. A blank negative space surrounded by the reflected apartment and Roar sitting calmly on the stool.

Asher held his jaws together tightly until the urge to yell or pull his sword had passed. Then he spoke as evenly as he could. "I care about her."

Roar shook his head. "You're forgetting a basic tenet," he growled. "We don't get involved."

"It's our job to take care of them. How can we not care?"

"We care for them collectively, as they are the weakest race, but we do not care about them individually." There was a deep furrow between his brows. Remembered pain. "We can't afford to," he finished bleakly.

Asher leaned his head against the glass. It was cool against his hot forehead. "Is that what this is? An object lesson? I care too much, so you will step in and make sure I learn the lesson you did?"

"You know it isn't."

"Then, why?"

"I have my reasons, but I don't think you're ready to hear them."

Asher closed his eyes. "You *do* like her."

"She's good for me." Roar cleared his throat. "She won't ever regret this. I won't let her."

Asher opened his eyes again and looked at the blank space that was him in the glass. He couldn't talk about her this way, not with Roar already speaking of a future with her. It would be giving up. "What is there for us, beside this pathetic gesture of a life?" he asked. "Are we supposed to just grasp at being human? Forever? Pretend to be humans, but never really *be* human?" He drew a breath that shuddered. "There's not even love left for us."

"We can love," Roar said softly.

"If we pay the price." He straightened up from the glass. "I wanted to hurt you."

"I know."

Asher shook his head. "Are you ever going to stop pretending to be the wiser brother?"

"I'll stop, if you stop pretending you don't give a damn."

"About Charlee?"

"About everything *but* Charlee. You've been riding the edge of this dilemma for centuries, Askr."

Asher stared at him.

"Time to choose, little brother."

"As you did?" he asked, the image of the pair of them at the feast, sitting with Stefan and Eira, playing out in his mind.

Roar stood up. "Time to be human, or not. You want meaning in your life? Make a choice. You can't have it both ways. Not forever."

"Any reason I had to be human walked into the great hall with you, three nights ago," Asher said, the bitterness biting so deeply, it hurt.

"Then I guess your decision has been made for you, hasn't it?"

The truth of that scalded, just like it had the first three thousand times he had faced it. Time had run out, which, as an immortal, he would have found ironically funny if his soul wasn't writhing as layers were flayed from it piece by piece.

* * * * *

Eira shivered inside the thick layers of fur and thermal insulation wrapped around her. Even the view available from the top of Tryvannshøyden, overlooking the city, wasn't enough to compensate for the bitter cold at the top of the mountain. It was nearly midnight, and freezing. "I've indulged you long enough, Sindri. What are you doing, anyway?"

Sindri didn't seem to feel the cold. He wore the same ancient robes as always, and his head and hands were bare. He had his head tilted up, looking at the night sky directly overhead. "It's nearly time," he murmured. "Just a few more minutes, that is all I ask."

"What happens in a few more minutes?" Eira asked.

"Something wonderful." He lifted his arms out from his sides. "It's coming," he whispered, but the whisper floated across to her on the crisp, still air.

"*What* is coming? Gods' teeth, Sindri. I'm tired. I'm cold, and I want a hot coffee so badly, I could slay every Einherjar between me and the coffeepot with my bare teeth. That includes you."

Sindri turned to face her. He was smiling. "I'm not an Einherjar."

"What?"

He pulled the front of his robe open, peeling aside the layers, from the waist up, exposing pale white flesh...and something around his neck.

Eira stepped closer. "I had a torc like that. Years ago. It disappeared."

Years ago.

"It was yours, but I have made it so much more than just a torc, now." His smile was gentle, almost blissful. His arms extended again. It was almost like he was offering himself up. But the lift of his shoulders told her he was not offering himself, but the necklace. He was exposing it.

"What are you doing?" she demanded, but it came out as a whisper.

"Almost time...." He was straining, lifting himself up toward the stars. "The solstice is almost here."

Solstice? Eira started, her mind whirling. The solstice was the moment of supreme power among the stars, or so they said. And he was reaching—for the stars.

"What are you doing?" she repeated, as unformed wariness curled through her.

Sindri grunted, as if he had been punched. He opened his eyes, looking right at her. "For you," he whispered.

The torc began to glow, then pulse with an unearthly light. Eira threw up her arm against the blazing light that blasted out from it, protecting her eyes. She backed off.

"Do not fear! They will not hurt you, queen of the Chosen Ones!" Sindri cried.

They?

The light leapt up toward the sky, a bright path that went on and on, reaching out to the stars.

Understanding slammed through her. "No! Sindri, no! Shut it down!" She leapt forward, reaching under her coat for the knife she always carried in her boot. "Sindri! Close the portal!" She moved around behind him and grabbed the back of his neck, and pushed the knife blade up against the side of his throat. "Shut it down. Now!"

The last of the light erupted from the torc, leaving a blazing trail across the inky black sky. The light in the torc faded.

"Too late," Sindri whispered.

"You *fool!* Do you know what you have done?"

"I opened the bivrost for you. I found you the way home, just as you have always wanted."

Eira threw her head back and cried out a formless, inarticulate protest. "You have exposed us all! Anyone can use the bivrost! Any of them can reach Midgard now!"

For the first time Sindri's confidence faltered. He did not seem to notice that the point of her knife was digging into his neck, causing blood to run that looked black in the dim light. "But you wanted this!"

"Not when we do not know how to reach Valhalla!" she cried. "We're weak without Valhalla, we have been weakening for centuries. We shut it down to protect ourselves! You fool! You stupid fool! Do you have any idea what you have done?"

Sindri had his head twisted back in her cruel grip, but didn't seem to mind that either. He just looked at her from the corner of his eyes. "I did it for you," he whispered.

"Why?" she demanded, shaking him like a terrier might shake a rat.

"So that you would see me properly. So that you might like me."

Eira took a better grip on her knife, ready to plunge it deep and tear it across his throat. Then she saw the look in his eyes and hesitated.

He knew what he had done. He had accepted his death. Now he simply watched her. There was sadness there. And love.

For her.

We both must give up what we really want.

Eira tossed him aside. "You have killed us all," she told him. "You can meet your fate with the rest of us."

* * * * *

Charlee hurried out onto Pearl Street, wrapping the heavy coat more firmly around her. The sidewalk was covered in soft snow, and more big, fat flakes were drifting down through the late afternoon air. It was already close to sunset. On the temperature gauge, it wasn't nearly as cold here in New York as it was in Oslo, but she had learned that cold was subjective. Twenty degrees here felt just as cool as sub-zero in Norway.

She glanced up the street, looking for a cab. Of course, in this weather, there would be none immediately available. No one was silly enough to walk far.

"Charlee."

She whirled and almost lost her footing on the slippery sidewalk.

Asher stepped away from the side of the building. His hands were shoved deep in his pockets. He wore his leather coat as usual. He never felt the cold. Never felt the need to huddle close to a fireplace, or enfold himself in warmth.

"Asher." She wrapped her arms around her middle. "Have you been waiting there?"

"Yes." He halted right in front of her. Close enough that she was acquainted once more with how truly tall he was, and how wide his

370

shoulders were. She always felt petite when she was near him, and she was taller than most women she knew. Eira and Ylva were taller, but only just.

"You've been waiting for me?" she asked. It was probably a self-evident question, but she was having trouble thinking. Standing before him like this…it was too suggestive. She struggled to banish the rush of memories it produced. The corridor where she had beggared herself with the truth, his office where he had pressed her up against the wall. The kiss she had nearly taken, so many years ago. There were not many days since when she failed to regret letting that moment go by.

"I've been waiting for you," Asher confirmed.

"Have you been waiting long?" There were snowflakes on his shoulders and hair, but now he had stepped out to the edge of the sidewalk, the tiny breeze was blowing them away.

He pulled his hands from his coat and cupped her face. "I would wait forever for you."

Charlee's breath caught. "Asher…" she began, barely above a whisper. She had no idea what to say next. Hope flared hot and hard in her chest, stealing her breath and making her heart race. He was watching her. His eyes were so blue!

He kissed her, his lips soft and she sighed into his mouth. The kiss lengthened and grew heated, and Charlee let it grow. There had been so few kisses, so she grasped this one eagerly. His arm came around her and she realized she had slid her own arms up around his neck. Even in her heels, she had to stretch to kiss him, but that was right, that was perfect.

The heat grew between them and Charlee moaned. Her body ached and throbbed. The depth of her need for him was a little bit frightening. She gripped his jacket, steadying herself.

Asher brushed her hair back from her face. "Will you come with me?" he asked. His voice was rough.

"Yes," she said, knowing exactly what he was asking and where he would take her.

* * * * *

They barely stepped through the apartment door before they came together once more. She heard keys dropping and Torger's happy panting, but Asher was kissing her again, and this time, the softness was swamped by urgency. Wanting. Driving need.

Unlike the few brief occasions in the past, this time Charlee knew that the Asher kissing her was the real one, stripped bare and exposed. He had come to her with all his shields down.

She wasn't aware that she was crying until he wiped her tears away. "Don't," he whispered. "Not now. You can cry and yell and call me every sort of fool under the sun. But later. This is just you and me for now. Forget the rest."

She forgot. It was easy, in his arms, to let the rest of the world and all her cares and worries float away.

She felt softness beneath her. Somehow they had made their way to the bed. Then the warmth of skin against her and Asher's weight over her.

When he slid into her, he hesitated as he felt the resistance, then cautiously eased his way in. "No one, Charlee?" he asked, his voice hoarse. "No one at all?"

"I didn't want anyone else."

He kissed her, his lips hard and demanding, telling her wordlessly that he didn't mind, that he was even a little bit pleased at her virgin state. It would appeal to his ancient psyche.

Then she forgot even that petty concern as the rhythm of pleasure picked her up and carried her along.

She didn't climax that time, nor the next, but she learned quickly and soon she was crying out her own sweet release, while the world shifted around them, forgotten and ignored.

* * * * *

Asher's fingers were trailing along her spine, keeping her just on the edge of sleep. She groaned. "Don't you ever sleep?" She turned her head on the pillow to look at him.

"With you in my bed?" He shook his head. "Sleep is just not going to happen."

"You're, what....? Two thousand years old or something. Elderly people need their sleep."

He laughed and his fingers drifted up to her cheek. "You're on Oslo time. It's three in the afternoon there. Of course you want to sleep."

"Because I've spent all of my last night and most of my current day having hot sex is why I need sleep. It's nine in the morning here. Even you should be passing out by now."

"I have all the time in the world to sleep. Later."

Charlee studied him, sobering. "Is this your way of saying goodbye, Asher?"

The corners of his jaw flexed. His gaze shifted away from her and his hand stopped moving. "It was supposed to be. I think."

"You *think*?"

"I haven't been thinking very clearly for a few days now." His gaze came back to her. "Mostly, I have been working on instinct. It has always served me well enough."

"On the battlefield, you mean?"

Asher blew out his breath. "I'm not used to speaking plainly. Yes. On the battlefield, I work on instinct."

Charlee sat up. "You've never had a relationship with one of the Kine? Amica? Not even Ylva?"

Asher leaned his head back against the headboard. "Only human," he muttered.

"Human women you couldn't talk to, not properly. Women you couldn't be yourself with."

He turned his head to look at her. "This is where you get to call me an idiot."

Charlee shook her head. "I was thinking about how lonely it must have been."

His lips parted, as if she had surprised him. He sat up and faced her properly, bending his knee and bringing it up to his chest and wrapping his arm around it. "If it was loneliness, then I suppose I have always been alone. Even among the Kine."

"You don't talk to Roar, either?"

Asher gave her a small smile. "Brothers, when we were human, were not like human brothers now. He was the heir to my father's kingdom. I was just the younger son. A place was found for me in my father's army."

Charlee picked up his hand. "Then you've always been alone," she summarized.

Asher stared at her. Through her. She had the sensation that his mind was working hard. Then he climbed from the bed and went to the window, which was frosted over almost completely. Charlee wondered if he was aware of how often he sought out the cold when he wanted to think. The icier the better.

She sat still, letting him work it out.

Finally, he turned to face her. His eyes were dark with stormy emotion. "I don't want to be alone anymore."

Charlee's heart lurched. "But...Roar...." She hated having to speak his name, especially now, but there were commitments she had implied she would make with him.

"There's a way around that," Asher said quietly.

The band across her chest tightened even more. "I don't understand," she whispered, but she *did* understand. She just didn't want to be right.

Asher crossed his arms and his knuckles whitened as he gripped hard. "I could...leave."

"Leave the Kine?" Everything inside her felt suspended, even her breath and her heart, as she waited for his response.

"Yes," he said at last.

"No, Asher. *No.* Not for me!"

"If not for you, then who else?" He came and sat beside her. "I can't think of a better reason."

"But you'll die!" she cried.

"Long after you have gone," he agreed softly. "But I will have a life with you before then." He held her face. "I want this, Charlee. I want to be with you. If leaving them is the only way, then I will leave."

"I can't ask that of you."

"*I'm* making the choice," he said flatly. "So tell me what you want, Charlee. What *you* want, not what you think is best for me. Be selfish for once in your life. If ever there was a moment to take what you want, it is now."

She swallowed. "I want you."

"With no conditions?" he asked gently.

"There have been criteria surrounding you being in my life since I met you. If you can throw it all overboard, I can. No conditions, Asher. I will accept you in any way you want to be a part of my life. No more fighting my instincts."

Asher closed his eyes for a moment. "So be it," he said and opened them. He smiled at her. "I am yours, Charlee. Lock, stock and rusty barrel."

She threw herself against him and locked her arms around his neck. "Only if Torger comes with you."

"So much for no conditions," he muttered and kissed her.

* * * * *

"Can I move in here?" Charlee asked, as she poured the coffee. "I don't have anywhere else to live, and Eira will drop kick me across the Pacific when she finds out."

Asher paused in the act of lowering bagels into the toaster. "Wouldn't you rather get a bigger apartment, somewhere nice? Up near the park? Or a house, even—but we'd have to move away from Manhattan."

Charlee pushed his mug toward him. "You really mean it?"

He kissed her nose. "I really mean it. The whole nine yards, Charlee. White wedding, the works."

Her breath whooshed out of her. "Wedding," she repeated, stunned.

"White picket fence, and Torger guarding the gate." He smiled.

Charlee carefully didn't voice the other half of that domestic cliché, but her heart shifted, sadness touching her.

Asher picked her up off the stool, his arms large and comforting.

"And children, Charlee. I can't give you mine, but there are hundreds of babies out there looking for people to love them."

She looked up at him. "Did I give myself away?"

"You didn't have to." He stroked her face, following the scar. "I want it all. I want all of it with you. I want children."

She pressed her face against his neck, closing out the light. "Me, too," she whispered, her lips brushing his neck. Happiness spilled through her. Had she ever been this happy? She didn't think it was possible.

Chapter Thirty-One

Doesn't everyone remember their first sight of an Alfar? When you see them you know the fantasy novels got it all wrong...and horribly right, too.

———
Comment on Everything Kine Bulletin Board.

Harry Jones had been delivering Her Majesty's mail for twenty-seven years, and even though his current route was through some of the worst areas of Fulham, he also got to walk past the Fulham Football Club every weekday, and even the BBC, although he didn't get to deliver their mail because they had their own direct truck delivery.

Fulham wasn't sexy like some other parts of London. Notting Hill and Soho were far more trendy, but Harry liked his route just the same. There wasn't nearly the same number of tourists and potential trouble. So he set out on Friday morning, thinking about the dart game that night and trying to decide which of the pub's two best dinners he could get. He was leaning toward the bangers and mash. That was another thing about his job: because of all the walking, he could pretty much eat whatever he liked. He turned into New King's Road and started to whistle. He really liked this section of his route. The houses were just lovely.

There was a very tall man just ahead, wearing what looked like a short dressing gown, in some silvery grey color, although it was hard to tell because he had his back toward Harry. He was standing on the footpath, his feet spread. He was wearing some sort of boots that hugged his lower legs, but they didn't have heels or anything like that.

Harry slowed his pace a little. He considered stepping off the footpath and onto the road to go around the chap. He generally didn't look for trouble, and the bastard looked dodgy. He made up his mind that he was going to cross the road altogether, then cross back when he was safely past him. Parson's Green was ahead a wee bit. He could see the trees just over the giant's right shoulder.

Harry spotted a break in the traffic and hurried across the busy street, heading for the pub on the south side. That was when he heard the screams from behind him. From the Green. He stepped onto the center strip and looked over his shoulder. The giant was still standing on the footpath, but now Harry could see through the trees that edged the green.

There were more of the giants. Many more. And they were…were they doing what he thought they were doing?

Harry bent at the knees to look underneath the fulsome foliage of the trees. He could see more through the trunks. He peered, then he clapped his hand to his mouth in horror.

The giants were rounding up people. They were scooping them into a pen of some sort, made of solid material that Harry couldn't begin to name. It was nearly midday, and there were usually a lot of people who took their lunch into the green and made a picnic of it. They were running in all directions, screaming and yelling warnings and as Harry watched, one of the giants stepped forward and swung a long knife—a knife so long it was almost a sword, like the little short ones the Romans had used, only edged on one side. The knife was attached to a handle that was almost as long as the knife itself. The giant swung the knife in a big underhand swing.

Harry moaned. He didn't see what the blade did to the back of the woman running away from the giant, but her feet stopped moving and she stopped screaming. Then she fell flat on her face onto the lawn. Harry would remember that sight for the rest of his life, which he didn't know then would only last a few more minutes.

Some of the people who weren't being picked up by their arms and tossed into the pen had reached the edges of the green. They bolted through the trees, and that was when the giant who had been standing motionless on the footpath moved. Harry realized the giant, the *thing*—for he had already begun to wonder if the tall human-looking giants were in fact human at all—the giant he had first spotted had been a sentry. Now he was moving into action, to hold back the people streaming through the trees and spilling onto New King's Road.

Traffic was squealing, drivers laying on their horns. The panic moved beyond the green, and for the first time Harry thought it would be a good idea to get off the road and move to somewhere safe. He thought of the pub and turned to cross the other half of the road.

People were jumping onto the island in the middle with him, but they weren't even trying to find a break in the traffic. Panic was driving them. They ran right onto the road, and cars whose drivers weren't already slowing to see what the hysteria was all about slammed into them.

Harry winced as a man in ragged jeans and a Chelsea T-shirt was tossed into the air by the bonnet of a Vauxhall Corsa, then dodged around the car himself, his mailbag bouncing against his hip. Behind him, he heard the car behind the Vauxhall slam into the back of the little car with the odd crumpling sound that modern cars made.

The screams seemed to be coming closer and Harry put on a burst of speed.

He ran down the footpath toward the pub's white door and that was when he realized his mistake. He should have kept running down Coniger Road, or dodged into one of the front gardens of the houses there and ducked out of sight. By turning and running down the footpath, he brought himself closer to the sentry giant, who was striding across the road, his knife-thing swinging in full circles, over and under, the under stroke slicing through anything and anyone.

The giant took another stride and Harry gave out a gasping, helpless cry, reaching out toward the pub door he could see just ahead. The blade sliced into his midriff and up through his ribcage and for a moment it didn't hurt, even though Harry knew he had been injured.

Then his feet stopped working, even though he was desperate to keep running. He fell to his knees, then toppled over onto his side and watched the giant turn and walk along the footpath in long strides, his knife swinging. He passed the pub door and kept going.

Harry died not knowing that he was one of the first people in human history to die at the hands of an alien species.

* * * * *

"Asher! Come quickly!"

Charlee's voice was full of something that sounded a lot like fear. There was a panicky quality he had never heard in her voice, ever. It was enough to shove him into bolting across the bedroom, and into the living room, where she stood in front of the TV, the remote in her hands. He was still holding the hand towel.

She pointed with the remote, wordlessly, at the TV. Her face was white, her eyes enormous.

Asher looked and his guts clamped coldly. He sank down onto the sofa, all thoughts about shaving to save her tender skin scattered to the four winds.

The news bulletin showed one of the regular anchors and behind her, on a smaller inset screen, was an image of England: the London Eye and the Tower of London, the Thames winding between them. Superimposed over top of that was a hastily cut-out image of something that he had never thought he would see again. The tall, slender figure had dark brown skin and pitch black hair tied at one shoulder over the leather body armor. The long knife was held above his head, his normally large and elongated eyes squinting as he took the measure of whatever enemy he thought he faced.

"...and for more, we go to Jane Edgecombe, on the ground in

London. Jane?"

The image shifted to show Piccadilly Circus, the statue of Trafalgar in the middle, but it wasn't the usual tourist photo opportunity. Everywhere, roiling across the screen, were Myrakar and Blakar, fully armed, thousands of them, fighting London's police, who wore full riot gear and carried batons.

"They're so outgunned," he whispered, appalled, as he watched police keeling over, clutching their stomachs and throats, the stumps of lost arms and legs. Blood ran over the concrete as the Myrakar spun their long knives like giant food processor blades, mowing down anyone in their way.

Civilians were screaming and running down the street behind the police, who were doing their best to hold a defense line.

A blonde woman holding a microphone was flinching and kept looking over her shoulder as she shouted at the camera. "This is Jane Edgecombe, reporting for ABC live and as you can see, war has come to London. It is a war that no one ever expected. You are seeing the first live footage of a war with an interplanetary species. Yes, this is not a movie. This is Earth's first contact with another intelligent species, but diplomatic dialogue has already proved to be impossible. These beings appeared in London's streets only a few short hours ago. They immediately began to round up people, herding them into what can only be described as alien vehicles of some kind. The police were called to full alert, and I have been told by a senior government representative that the British armed forces, all of them, are mobilizing."

"She's trying to invent a whole new vocabulary out of thin air," Charlee whispered. "Even as she's describing it."

"No one will have the vocabulary for this," Asher replied. He felt sick and his mind was sluggish. "The ones with the dark skin, the shorter ones. We call them Blakar. They're Blakalfar, the workers. What humans used to call cannon fodder." He grimaced. "The taller ones with the black hair and tanned skin, they're the Myrakar—the Myrakalfar. They're the officers. The ground strategists. They drive the Blakar."

"Drive?"

"Inspire. Direct. Crack the whip." He licked his lips. "This is really happening, isn't it?"

She held out the remote and clicked the channel selector. Quickly, she rotated through all the channels. All of them were playing either the same footage as the ABC, or similar, or they were simply off the air. The picture that built up from all the feeds was scary. Most of Britain was under attack.

Charlee paused when she reached one of the foreign language

channels. "That's Hong Kong," she said. The frantic Chinese voiceover accompanied nighttime pictures of a city on fire, with screams, sirens, gunfire and more. The images were grainy and whoever was holding the camera was barely holding it steady, making the images slant and jump in jerky, panicky movements.

Asher didn't have to see details. He understood only too well what was happening. "They're being slaughtered."

"Someone opened the bivrost," Charlee said, staring at the screen.

Asher looked at her, startled. But there wasn't time to question her on how she knew that. Then she met his glance, her eyes wide. "That's who they are, right? They're from the other eight worlds."

It took sheer willpower to say the words out loud, to overcome the conditioning of centuries of secrecy. Slowly, he said, "They're the Alfar. They're from Alfheim."

"They look like elves, except for their skin." She said it remotely, watching the screen again. Shock was setting in.

"They *are* what humans call elves," Asher said gruffly. "But there is nothing gentle about them. They're arrogant, powerful and believe they are the heirs to the universe. War is their life, and conquering all that stands before them is their *only* mission. And these are just the fighters. The Lajosalfar…they're the real bad guys."

She was clicking through the channels again, almost mindlessly, absorbing the bloody images. "China. Britain. France. Thailand. India." She whispered the names of the countries as the corresponding images appeared on the screen. Then she switched off the TV, put the remote down on the coffee table and turned to face him. "They're here to conquer us, aren't they?"

Asher nodded.

She thrust her hands together, the fingers twining. Her eyes were huge. Bewildered. "You have to go back."

There was nothing he could say in response, because she was right and he wasn't sure he could speak, anyway. He nodded again, the movement feeling like rusty chains running over unoiled gears.

* * * * *

Asher emerged from the bedroom twenty minutes after he had walked stiffly and slowly into it and shut the door. Charlee perched on the back of the sofa, waiting. She felt as inflexible as Asher had looked.

Shock, she self-diagnosed. But knowing that didn't fix it. All the classic treatments for mild shock—warmth, sleep, food and water—were useless to her right now. She could no more sleep than fly, and food was equally as uninteresting. The cold had settled into her bones.

Once he had closed the door, the silence had grown thick and frightening, so she turned the TV back on, lowering the volume until it was a frantic murmur of doom and disaster, an accompaniment for her ricocheting thoughts.

When Asher stepped out into the main room once more, she switched off the TV. He was carrying a duffel bag that looked heavy, and it reminded Charlee sharply of Lucas. He always left the house at the end of shore leave holding a bag that looked just as heavy.

Why wouldn't they look the same? Asher is heading off to war, too.

The thought jolted her onto her feet.

Asher put the bag down by the front door and came back to her and took her into his arms.

Charlee let herself cling to him and kiss him in a way that expressed everything she would not say.

He rested his head against hers. "I don't know what will happen now. I don't know how this ends. I could—"

She quickly covered his mouth, silencing him. She shook her head. "Don't say it."

"Who can I say it to, if not you?"

She drew in her breath, reaching for calm, as she realized that this was as new to Asher as her. He had never left anyone behind before. "Say it, then," she told him.

"No, you're right." His thumb swept across her cheekbone. "It shouldn't be said."

"Only good things, huh?"

"I'm leaving everything good behind me."

She swallowed. "So am I."

Asher stepped back, appalled. "No! You're staying here, in New York. Where it's safe!"

"I'm Amica, Asher. You're Einherjar. We have jobs to do."

"They're all *over* Europe! No!"

"It's my job," she repeated. "This is what I am."

"But…" He stared at her, his mouth working.

"You're Einherjar. The worlds have descended upon Midgard. You must defend the Earth. That is your role, your responsibility. You knew that as soon as you saw the Alfar on TV."

"Ah, *Christ!*" He whirled away, the strength of his emotions driving him into movement. He came up against the dining table and leaned on his fists, breathing hard.

"Once you go out that door, Asher, you stop being human forever. The world is going to know about the Kine, if not today, then very soon, because you can't continue to hide. Not now. This time here, today, last night, that is all the time you get to be really human. To love like a human." Charlee made herself go on. "You go back to being Einherjar and I go back to being Amica, because the world needs you more than I do." It took sheer willpower to stop her voice from wobbling.

Asher was staring at the tabletop, his jaw working. Then he strode back to her, pulled her into his arms and kissed her once more. Charlee inhaled the kiss, trying to hold on to it, because she knew it would be the last.

Then he let her go and walked back to the door and picked up his pack. He fumbled with the lock, then wrenched it open and looked at her one last time. "I love you, Charlotte Rose."

The door shut behind him.

WORLDS COLLIDE

Chapter Thirty-Two

"This world is waking up and remembering what it is supposed to be." — Verlan Seeker

Renmar stared at the map of the upper continent of Midgard. After a year, the land masses had become familiar, but the Mannlingar insistence upon divisions within the land, what they called 'countries', still remained difficult to understand.

But it was of little importance and was even of some tactical advantage. The Lajos had learned that cooperation across those artificial borders, between armies and leaders, was often slow and clumsy, which they used to their advantage. An assault that crossed those borders would almost certainly thrust farther than one that remained within a single country. So Renmar studied the map and considered the power of the leaders of each of the little countries, compiling permutations and possible combinations. Where was the potential conflict? What could he leverage?

Pernon entered, his shoulders stiffly square and his gaze directly ahead. Renmar dismissed the map image and turned to wait for the news Pernon must be bringing. He lightened the room to that of a sunny day.

Pernon lifted his face to the light, a small smile touching his lips. "Ah, blessed light…." Then, his prayer sent, Pernon looked at Renmar and touched his hand to his own eyes reverently.

"Tell me," Renmar ordered.

Pernon hesitated. He was an able captain, but Renmar found his constant reference to the emotions of others and the consequences of actions upon those emotions tedious. Now Pernon was trying to measure the effect of his news upon Renmar himself.

"Delay makes me angry," Renmar rumbled.

Pernon touched his eyes again, quickly. "Ganxiao has been retaken, Lord."

Renmar surged to his feet. "Fools! We have held that hall since the day we arrived on Midgard! Who was the imbecile who let the Herleifr take it back?"

Pernon dropped to his knees and groveled. "It was a concerted attack, Lord! Humans used their armaments upon the outer walls, while the Kine attacked from within, using the portal against us!"

"Humans! The Kine!" Renmar fumed. "Why do you use those folksy names for them? They are not *kinfolk*. They are ragged leftovers of the Mannlingar species. They lost all valor generations ago." He curled down his lips. "The Herleifr were chosen from among the *fallen*, not the victors. They are weak. Yet they defeat us. What does that say of your captaincy, Pernon?"

"Lord, I am not worthy of rank." Pernon spoke to the floor. "Strip me of all recognition, and I will return to my home and restore honor the only way left to me."

Renmar kicked him. "Get up."

Pernon got to his feet, but kept his gaze downcast. The hem and knees of his robe were dusty now. Dust on the floor meant the keeper wardens were not maintaining a strong enough aura around the eyry. It bothered him. Just one more minor problem he would have to deal with that should properly be well beneath his notice.

"How many halls are still ours?" Renmar demanded of Pernon.

Pernon straightened. "Thirty-nine, Lord."

Renmar considered the number for a moment. The Myrakar had learned much about the Mannlingar. As the message carriers of the Alfar, they were the perfect channels of information about the enemy. They had learned some of the many human languages, although they could not explain to Renmar why the humans didn't have a common speech. They were able to move among the humans, unlike the Lajos or the Blakar, and it had been the Myrakar who had learned of Ganxiao, the hall in the mountains.

The Myrakar had also learned that many of the halls the Herliefr had built were empty. Their capture of those halls when they discovered them was uncontested. Thirty-nine halls they could name as theirs was not victory.

Neither the Myrakar nor Renmar's generals had been able to discover how many halls there were in total. Information about the Herliefr and their occupation of Midgard was lacking even among humans. The lack did not aid decisions.

Decisions, decisions. Renmar was surrounded by generals who did not like to make decisions, bringing problems endlessly to his eyry.

"Make sure the portals are guarded," Renmar ordered. "Is Rama any closer to finishing the map of the portals?" That was more information they did not have and were blocked from acquiring because of the nature of the portals themselves. To determine where a portal led, it was necessary to step through and look. The generals could order as many Blakar through the portals as they had to hand, but if they did not return to report, then the intelligence was as lacking as if they had not stepped through at all. It told them nothing.

Still, they sent scouts through every portal they found and assumed that failure to return meant the portal linked to a hall held by the Herliefr. Those portals were guarded ceaselessly.

At least the portals they had built within this eyry were secure. The more eyries were completed, the larger their domestic and reliable transport would grow.

Pernon lowered his gaze once more. "I regret, Lord. The map of portals remains unfinished."

Renmar waved him away, annoyed. Pernon marched away stiffly, pausing only to lower his head toward Renmarie. Renmar had quite forgotten she was there. Renmarie gave Pernon a gracious smile and did not speak, which was proper.

Pernon strode through the arch, hurrying to leave his Lord's presence, no doubt.

Renmarie stepped out of the dark fold of shadow where she had been standing. The hem of her gown trailed for the correct length behind her. It would extend for exactly the length from her knee to her heel.

"Why do you obsess about their halls?" she asked. "Our eyries are larger and stronger fortresses than anything they could build. They have not used the auras for any of their structures. They are Mannlingar hovels."

"I *liked* Ganxiao," Renmar said coldly.

His wife gave him one of her most gracious smiles. "There are other mountains. Other heights."

He sighed, for she had named exactly the thing he had liked most about the Herliefr hall they had been forced to live in for a time, until the London eyry had been ready for his command.

"*London*," Renmar said, forming the name carefully. "Even their names are pedestrian."

Renmarie smiled as a wife should.

* * * * *

Lucas gave his service khakis a tug and a quick brush-down before stepping through the door the non-com was holding open for him. He returned the salute absently, already looking ahead.

The room was dimly lit. Most of the light came from the big screens on all four walls. At the big oval table in the middle of the room, Lucas spotted Simmons, the officer he had been told to report to ASAP. Even though he didn't know Simmons, it was easy to pick him out because he was the only United States Rear Admiral at the table. Simmons was outranked by everyone else, regardless of the uniform they were wearing.

Lucas flicked his gaze around the table, summing up. There was a

British general, and an air marshal from the Hellenic Air Force. Two senior officers from China and a single Indian Army representative, who was unique at the table because his aid, standing behind him, was wearing a full, formal sari. The double-edged traditional Indian Khanda strapped to her hip did not look out of place and these days, it would be far from merely ceremonial.

There were two officers from the AIFA. Of course there would be two. The Arab Israeli Federal Army was united only so long as egalitarianism reigned. Where an Israeli went, so did an Arab. Lucas was still getting used to seeing the white uniforms. It had taken a common foe to bring together two of the bitterest enemies in the human world. *The enemy of my enemy is my friend.* Who had said that? The Arabs and the Israelis were putting it into practice in a way that had encouraged nearly every standing military force in the world to toss its hat into the war arena and join them.

Lucas bent over to speak into Simmons' ear. "Montgomery. Reporting in, sir."

"Took your time, didn't you?" Simmons murmured.

"I was in Izmir when the orders came, sir."

"Turkey?" Simmons calmed down. "Bad over there?"

"As bad as it looks everywhere else." Which was true. One advantage about this war was that the enemy hadn't clued into electronics yet. They were free to broadcast and network across the globe and didn't have to worry about the enemy listening in. Network coverage of the war was thorough and ran twenty-four-seven on the dozens of stations that had mushroomed overnight solely to provide war news. It sometimes felt like there was a TV screen running coverage in every room in the world. There had even been a bank of four screens in the Lockheed on which he had bummed a lift to Odessa, tuned into channels that between them covered most of the global conflict.

Simmons nodded. "Step back and listen in. You'll know when I need you."

Lucas stepped back and looked around the room again. There were various aides, petty officers and non-coms in the room, working the communications equipment that hugged the edges. Only four other officers at the table had personal aides or assistants standing by.

The British general at the head of the table slapped the wood surface gently, drawing attention to him. "Are we secure?" he asked.

"All personnel with clearance below B-Level, please leave the room now. Security, check passes and lock down." The order came from somewhere behind the general. There was a drift of people toward the doors, and Lucas leaned back over Simmons' shoulder. "Sir…"

"Your B-level security grade was approved this morning," Simmons told him. "Stand back, pin your ears back and observe."

"Sir." Lucas stepped back again, swallowing his questions. They had pushed through a B-grade clearance for him? What the hell? He had been a lowly D-level yesterday, only one step above "E", which the US military had dubbed the "everyone else" level.

The general at the head of the table had watched their short exchange. "You have a new assistant, Rear Admiral Simmons. Would you care to ease our security concerns with an introduction?"

Simmons nodded. "Thank you, general. Everyone, this is Commander Lucas Montgomery, with the Naval Special Warfare Group 1." That left it nicely anonymous, especially for anyone not familiar with the structure of the US forces.

"You have a full Commander holding your cap for you?" the general asked. "A tad bit of overkill, isn't it?"

"It demonstrates the high regard the US holds for its Admirals, sir," Simmons shot back. His smile was very sincere.

The general smiled too, but his gaze was sharp. "A SEAL unit leader at that. Is there something you haven't shared with us about American expectations of outbreaks?" Which proved the general had studied a US military organization chart recently.

Simmons sighed. Lucas doubted if anyone else in the room would notice, but he was standing right behind the man. "We are not expecting hostilities to break out in Minsk today, general. Nor are there any covert operations of which you are not aware. That is the real question you wanted to ask, isn't it? Commander Montgomery was assigned to me for this conclave because of his knowledge of the Einherjar. You can think of him as an advisor. I personally will not be handing him my cap to carry. I'd prefer to keep my fingers intact."

Lucas barely managed to keep his surprise off his face. How in hell had they learned about his connection to the Einherjar? That wasn't something he had felt like volunteering yet. Besides, the sum total of his "knowledge" was a dusty memory of a man who had shown him his sword, once.

But that wasn't strictly true. He recalled with an almost guilty start the all-night briefing Darwin and Charlee had put him through, three days after news about armies of invading elves had brought the whole world to a screeching halt. *Elves!* Sometimes he still found himself marveling over the surreal quality of that fact. It was easier to think of them by their Norse name, the Alfar.

He had just barely made it back onto US soil when the reports about armies of bat-shit crazy elves killing and rounding up humans had begun to break on every channel that mattered. The Internet had gone crazy, bringing down servers with the traffic spikes and stampedes to download footage and images. Facebook and Twitter had crashed because of traffic, a first in human history. Lucas had been barely able to raise cell service and Darwin had driven down to Washington to pick him up, as there were no seats left on any commercial flights and all the military ones were heading to international destinations.

They had spent the drive back to New York listening to the radio with growing amazement, as reports about the violent invading forces trickled in from not just London, but countries all across Europe, the Middle East and Asia.

Darwin had been silent and introspective for the next two days, but Lucas barely noticed. He had plenty to think about all on his lonesome. On the Sunday night, Charlee had appeared at the house and he was startled all over again, as he was every time he saw her, because she was such a good-looking woman. She had a style and grace he would never have predicted when she was ten and spindly, with long legs and frizzy hair. Once his surprise faded, his pride in her surfaced.

Charlee had produced a bottle that had no label and looked like it was sealed with wax. She cut the wax away from the top with practiced movements with a sharp knife, while Darwin produced three glasses.

"Coffee mugs would be better," Charlee suggested. "It's more traditional."

Darwin had shrugged and reached over Lucas' head for the mugs on the shelf there.

"What is it?" Lucas asked as Charlee poured the nearly colorless liquid into the mugs.

"Sack mead." Charlee pushed a mug toward him. "You're going to need it."

He sniffed and his nose twitched. "Strong," he observed. "Where did you get it? Did you make it or something?"

Charlee tossed back her slug with a ladylike swallow and reached for the bottle again. "I got it from the Viking who made it. He got cut up badly when the first wave of Alfar invaded their hall in China and I healed him, so he gave me the bottle as a favor."

Darwin grinned, watching her.

Lucas put his mug down. After thirty seconds of trying to make sense of what she had just said, he shook his head. There were words in there he had recognized, including *Alfar*, which had been repeated endlessly on the long trip up from Washington and even more on the TV the last two days, but it didn't come together in a way that explained anything. Viking? Hall? "*What?*" he said finally.

"Charlee has a lot to tell you," Darwin said. "You'd better have another drink and settle in for a while."

Charlee gave Darwin a small smile. "Tomorrow morning, the Herliefr, who have been living among humans for nearly fifteen hundred years, are going to reveal their existence with a coordinated series of media conferences in nearly every major city in the world."

Lucas stared at her. "Asher," he said finally. "You've known all the time, haven't you?" he accused her, not sure if he was pissed about that or not.

"That's part of the story," Charlee had replied, and then she had spent the rest of the night telling him about Chocolate, the Lightning Lords and the facts about her life since then, including most of what she knew about the Kine and their origins. Darwin had weighed in a lot on that stuff. "It's been a pet research project for a while now," he'd confessed.

So yeah, Lucas could be considered an expert in that regard. He knew more than the Kine had given the public yet, enough to know that their culture and history wasn't something humans were going to be able to digest in a few days. It was a year, almost, since they had stepped out and every day something new emerged about them. Their ways were as complex and convoluted as any human society Lucas had come across in his travels, and he'd put boot to soil on every continent except Antarctica since joining up.

The general at the end of the conference table—Lucas had yet to hear the man's name—nodded his satisfaction over Lucas' qualifications. "As the doors are now secure, let's get started." He lifted a finger in an elegant movement. It was a signal to someone. "We flew a reconnaissance mission over London eighteen hours ago, using Einherjar intelligence about the structure of these towers the Lajos are building. This is our first close-up view of one of them." The lights in the room lowered considerably.

"You got past the shield guarding it?" one of the officers at the table asked. From the accent, it sounded like the Arab or Israeli.

The general shifted uncomfortably. "We placed an Einherjar in every plane. *They* were the ones to open the shields. They call them auras, by the way. It's terminology we should probably get used to straight away because we're going to be hearing it and using it a lot from now on."

The video began playing on all the screens. At first, it was very ordinary-looking footage of miles of rolling suburbs. Lucas could have identified Britain from the endless streets of terrace housing, even if he hadn't known where the flight had been.

The view switched smoothly between perspectives, although the details on the screen didn't change much. Clearly, there had been cameras in at least two of the planes, and someone had edited the combined footage. It was a pretty slick and professional job, too. On this approach toward London, the planes must have been flying close together, so each camera had recorded pretty much the same thing.

"If you look at the horizon," the general said, "you'll catch the first glimpse of the tower."

Lucas looked. There was a dark, elongated vertical smudge on the horizon, as promised. He frowned, trying to make sense of it.

"How far out from central London is this?" someone asked.

The subaltern standing behind the general answered that. "The approach was made from south-central England. Ah, Royal Air Force base Weston-on-the-Green, in Oxfordshire, to be precise. They're moving in a west-south-westerly direction. The town they're passing over right now would be Maidenhead, or Slough. That line across the lower corner of the screen would be the Thames."

The towns and villages and a diminishing number of patches of countryside rolled on, while the dark smudge grew bigger and bigger.

"This footage has given us some data to analyze that will keep us busy for a wee while," the general added.

Lucas rolled his eyes at the typical British understatement. If they had got anywhere closer to the tower than the five mile radius the shields had been keeping all traffic, then the data would be overwhelming.

"We *can* confirm that the tower is straddling the Thames," the general continued. "It has three…I guess you would call them feet. One of those feet destroyed most of Parliament House. I'll let you see the rest for yourself."

Lucas watched the landscape slipping down beneath the bottom of the screen, calculating quickly. Usually, the fastest planes were used for reconnaissance. They wanted to get in and out as quickly as possible. The Brits had their Harriers, which could do better than 700 mph and if that was what they had used for this mission, then the land rolling across the camera's viewpoint was passing by too slowly. They had slowed the playback so that details weren't missed. Ahead, the smudge had evolved into a discernible tower.

"It looks rather fragile, doesn't it?" the general murmured.

Yeah, that was one way to put it. Lucas had seen the tower before, but only in still shots and ground-based footage, taken from two and a half miles away, which was as close as the shield—aura, he corrected himself—would let anyone come. Watching the tower enlarge as the planes drew closer was fascinating. The first time he had ever seen the tower, in pictures online, the thought that had struck him was *lace*. It looked delicate, like a tall, slender finger pointing to the sky, made up of filigree. Daylight peeped through the edges of it, although the center was more solid. Now he was seeing the tower with a completely different and changing perspective, something else struck him hard. The familiar city skyline of downtown London hadn't shown up yet, but the tower that was planted over top of it was already clear, although still some distance away, which hinted at a scale that made Lucas uneasy. How *big* was the thing?

The suburbs were shifting and changing now, as London drew closer. The jets dropped lower, masking their approach.

"There is some turbulence as they approach the aura," the general said. "Then we lost imagery for exactly fifteen seconds while the shield was breached."

The screen blanked, then flickered.

"Hold for a moment please," the general called.

The image froze. Dominating the screen was the tower itself. At two and a half miles' distance, the top of the tower was already cut out at the top of the frame. The feet were spread around the base of the tower evenly, the tower itself expanding at the base in a graceful curve to match the spread of the feet. Lucas stared at the rubble and buildings visible at the feet, trying to orient himself. Where was the Tower Bridge? Where was Buckingham Palace? Big Ben? There was a rivulet of water emerging from beneath the tower.

The general picked up a laser pointer and pointed at the screen behind Lucas. He turned to look.

The red dot was moving in tight little circles next to the trickle of water. "That, gentlemen, is the monstrosity known as the London Eye. That should give you an idea of the scale of this thing."

There was a murmur around the room, and uneasy movement. That was the most these highly trained people allowed themselves to show, but the revelation was staggering. Lucas stared at the small dot the general had been pointing at. What he had thought was a trickle of water was the wide, graceful curve of the Thames itself, running past the Embankment, the Houses of Parliament and the London Eye. The rubble wasn't rubble at all—well, some of it clearly was—but the little squares and oblongs on the ground that he had thought was building debris were actual buildings. The jump jets had been a lot higher than Lucas had assumed.

He stared at the tower again, beginning to understand the true size of the thing.

"I'm quite sure you are all asking yourselves right now how tall that blighter really is. I had a pair of structural engineers run some scale calculations. The base of each foot, which is roughly triangular, is just over four hundred metres from the apex to the base. The base is also four hundred metres across. They're perfect equilateral triangles."

Lucas did the conversion to Imperial almost automatically, his jaw unhinging once more. A quarter of a mile! Just one foot of the tower was a quarter mile long!

"The engineers tell me that the top of the tower is just under four thousand metres high. Everest, gentlemen, is eight and a half thousand metres high. Ben Nevis, the highest mountain in the British Isles, is four and a half thousand feet. I looked it up this morning."

More murmuring. Lucas shook his head. The tower was nearly two and a half miles high!

"The mission was ordered to fly by once only and as quickly as possible to avoid any undue risks, as every vehicle was flying with only one pilot."

"Where were their navigators?" the Indian officer asked.

"The navigators gave up their seats so the pilots could take an Einherjar along with them. The Einherjar assured us they could breach the aura surrounding the tower for a short time, enough to pass through, and we thought it worth the risk to try." The general lifted his finger again and the video began to roll once more. "The flyby happens very quickly, but we will be examining every frame for details."

The tower tilted on the frame as the planes rolled, banking away from the tower to skirt it. Then the tower moved out of the frame as they straightened up and flew on, heading south, judging by the direction of the sun.

The screen went blank again and the dim lights came back on.

Everyone stirred, bringing their attention back to the table.

That scared them, Lucas realized. It wasn't a difficult guess. He could feel his own heart banging around inside his chest and the sour taste of adrenaline in his mouth. The scale of the tower, once he'd grasped the true size of it, was shocking.

Simmons was the first one to speak. "Do we have any idea what they're doing with the folk caught inside the shield, general?"

The general grimaced. "No. No one gets in and no one gets out."

"Your pilots got in," Simmons replied.

"Through some wizardry the Einherjar understand and that I do not." The general straightened. "I brought along a technical expert of my own, this morning." He glanced at his aide, who straightened up smartly and walked over to the doors. He tapped on the glass and the MP on the other side opened one side of it, enough to let through another figure.

Asher Strand.

Chapter Thirty-Three

Mannlingarr
Alfar name for Man (humans).
From *Darwin's Dictionary*, 2017 Edition

Lucas swore under his breath, as the possible reason for him being hauled out of Turkey at two in the morning made itself clear.

Asher didn't look anything like the urbane businessman and banker Lucas had known for years. Like everyone else on Earth, this war had changed him. Lucas looked him over, cataloguing the differences.

He wore combat pants that were common in nearly every army Lucas knew of, but they were a plain, dark brown. His shirt was the same tough fabric as the pants, but a lighter brown. It was sleeveless and the edges of the armholes were ragged, telling Lucas he had ripped out the sleeves that had once been there. The shirt was stained and wrinkled, lying in accordion-like folds that said Asher had recently been wearing body armor over the shirt, long enough to iron in the wrinkles.

There were heavy wrist guards on each wrist and he wore his sword openly upon his hip, the naked blade thrust through a loop on the second belt he wore. There was a long knife on the other hip and one tucked into the top of his...Lucas didn't know what to call them. He had wound belts, or long pieces of leather, around the legs of his pants, from ankle to knee, crossing them over and holding the excess material of the pants tight against his legs and out of the way. The leg armor the SEALs wore did the same thing, but the thongs would be lighter and less cumbersome and suitable for any combat situation.

He had three or four or more days' worth of growth on his chin and his hair was shorn short in such a ragged fashion, Lucas suspected he'd done it himself, without the benefit of a mirror and probably with the knife on his belt.

There was nothing close to a uniform anywhere in his garments. No insignia, and no suggestion of rank. Everything he wore shouted of purpose, from the leggings to the unsheathed sword, to the wrist guards, to the roughly cut hair. He was dressed for war.

Only Asher's eyes hadn't changed. He looked around the room with the same assessing stare that Lucas remembered. Lucas suspected that the hard stare and the calculating attitude were the genuine thing. What Lucas had known before had been a mask. Asher hadn't changed like the rest of them. He had simply dropped away all the masks and roles and disguises.

This was the true Asher.

He came to a halt at the other end of the table from the general, well back from the officers sitting there. He took a spread-legged stance and crossed his arms. The big biceps flexed. "General," he acknowledged. Lucas wondered if he had picked the spot because it put him within reaching distance of where Lucas stood.

"This is Askr, Son of Brynjar, Stallari of the New York hall," the general told them.

Asher nodded.

"You're a long way from home," Simmons said.

Asher glanced at him. "We have a hall here, in the hills around Vajenny."

Silence greeted him, as the humans in the room acquainted themselves once more with the fact that the Kine could step from one side of the planet to the other through their portals. Lucas still didn't fully understand how they worked. Very few humans got to use them. The Kine had made it abundantly clear that it wasn't that they didn't want humans to use them. It was because they *couldn't* use them, not if a Kine was not with them, and the Kine were severely limited in numbers.

This matched up with what Charlee and Darwin had told him about the portals and the Kine population.

"Askr is being somewhat coy about his activities. He is based in New York," the general said, "but I believe he has come directly from China where the Kine and the People's Republic have just taken back the Ganxiao hall. Is that correct, Stallari?"

That explained the battle-worn look about him. Lucas was willing to bet hard currency that the armor that had left the wrinkles in his shirt was sitting outside the conference room doors, where he had shucked it just before stepping through.

"The Ganxiao hall is ours again, yes," Asher replied.

"Stallari, there has been a question about the aura that surrounds the eyry in London. Could you explain how your people could penetrate the shield? I lack the knowledge, myself."

"You're not the only one, general," Asher said. "Magic isn't something that humans are used to thinking of in practical ways."

"Magic?" The question came from down the table. "These auras are magic?" There was derision in the tone. "Will there be fairies, next?"

Asher sighed. Lucas could hear it. "Colonel, 'magic' is just a word-symbol for something you do not understand. Humans have been using electricity and electronics for generations now, but the Alfar don't understand that any better than you understand auras. To the Alfar, electrons are magic. But they use auras and the power they produce in the same way electrical engineers use circuits and computer engineers use circuit boards. Auras are a practical form of power that drives everything they do."

"Do you use auras for your portals?" Simmons asked.

"Auras are used to generate the portals, but once they are connected, they are self-sustaining. When we first came among humans, we made a decision to minimize the use of auras, so that we could blend in with humans better. Very little of what we do, now, is powered by auras but we have always had the knowledge."

"Which is how they knew what to do with the shield around the tower," the general summarized. "Thank you, Stallari. Could you remain here for the rest of the meeting? I'm sure there will be more tricky questions."

Asher nodded once more.

"Will you share the final report on the analysis of the tower footage, general?" Simmons asked.

"Of course," the general replied heavily.

"We have experts who could help," Simmons pointed out.

The general smiled. "By all means, send them over. We have no objections to tapping the United States' unlimited military budget." He shifted on his seat, and pushed a folder aside from the stack in front of him, mentally shifting gears. "The recapture of the Ganxiao hall secures portals that have been vulnerable for a year and gives the Kine direct access to more halls. It's a positive outcome, but it's not the reason for this meeting. As coordinators for your forces, I wanted you to be the first to know what the Kine learned during the Ganxiao offensive. As the stallari was there and has been gracious enough to remain here for questions, I will let him impart the news."

Asher's arms dropped. He straightened up, obviously surprised he was being called upon. Then he dug into a pocket on his thigh and produced a very ordinary and quite human-looking cellphone and lifted it up. "I have photos on this, if someone can put them on the big screen?"

A technician stepped over from the desks against the walls and held out her hand. Asher thumbed through several screens and then pointed to something on the screen. "Those two," he said quietly and dropped the phone onto her hand.

She walked back to the desks and plugged the phone into a USB jack, then swiped at the touchscreen built into her desk. With a tap of her finger, the two images jumped onto the big screens, repeated around the room.

It was clear the photos had been taken quickly, with no time to properly frame the subjects. They were mid-distance from the camera lens. The one on the right looked vaguely human. It had two legs, encased in boots that made its legs look as thick as tree trunks, or perhaps it simply had thick legs. Two arms and hands, but there wasn't enough resolution in the photo to determine more than that. There was a head on top of joints that served as shoulders for the arms, recognizable eyes that tilted at a sharp angle, and a mouth. The area between was flat, with holes where a human's nostrils would be. What it had for flesh looked mottled, like freckles that had grown rampant and huge.

The creature was holding something that was clearly a weapon, for it was using it to fend off a man wielding a sword. An Einherjar, Lucas presumed, as the Einherjar would have used the portals to step through into the inner halls of Ganxiao, while the Red Army would have attacked from outside, and the man in the photo was neither Asian nor outside. But it wasn't a weapon that Lucas could classify except to say that it had a sharp edge and two handles.

The one on the left was also human-like in that it had two arms, two legs, a head and a torso, but that was where similarities seemed to end. It crouched low to the ground and one of the arms was propping it up. It was about to leap upon an Einherjar, who was just turning to spot it. It carried no weapons.

There was another round-robin of murmurs and exclamations.

"They are not Alfar, unless there are more than three races of Alfar?" Simmons asked.

"The one on the right," Asher said, "is a Sinnar. The little one on the left is an Asmegar. It doesn't look like it, but the Asmegar are pacifists. They prefer to live and let live. But they will fight when called upon to do so. Only the Sinnar can make them fight."

"And the Sinnar are what, exactly?" the general asked.

"They are many things," Asher replied. "But their primary role, the one that will interest you the most, is as Hel's warriors."

Simmons threw down his pen. "Wonderful," he said dryly. "Not only are we getting our butts kicked by the Alfar, but now there's a *second* world that wants to pick on the little kid?"

"Hell?" Lucas questioned softly.

"Not the Christian idea of hell," Asher said. "Hel is one of the nine worlds, just as the Alfar's world of Alfheim is one and Asgard, which was our home, once. Hel is the melting pot where unwanted species found themselves. The Sinnar and the Asmegar are two of them." He pointed at the photo. "They were fighting for the Alfar. We have to presume the Alfar recruited them. The Sinnar would sell their own children if it meant they could get into a fight somewhere."

The general tugged at his khaki tie. "That means the bridge to a second world is open."

Asher shook his head. "*All* the bridges are open, general. We think the others are waiting to see how this plays out. That's why we haven't seen Jotnar. The Nare—all except the Sinnars—usually prefer to stay out of off-world fights. They have enough troubles of their own, with so many species trying to survive there."

"Nare?" someone queried.

"All the species on Hel are called, collectively, Nare," Asher explained.

"Does the name have a meaning?" Simmons asked. It was a good question, Lucas thought. Most of the names *did* mean something.

Asher grimaced. "It means *the damned*."

Pens were scribbling furiously around the table.

"What other species might we expect?" the general asked. "What other Nare are there?"

Asher held up his hand and checked off the names as he spoke. "Sinnar and Asmegar. Mayjar and Ravnar. Mayjar are the messengers of the underworld, and they would have been the ones to deal directly with Renmar and the other Alfar leaders. They are all female. The Ravnar are creatures of the Mayar and are under their control. They are bird-like creatures and they prey on liars, thieves, and the immoral. Then there are the Furies—what you call demons. They are the mates of the Mayjar. There are Dolgar, who are invisible, but when they rise during the night, they sow confusion and fear, they screw up communications and put people at cross-purposes. They feed on violence and high emotions, which is why they like to cause trouble."

"They sound like ghosts, or psychic vampires," someone muttered.

"Humans probably got the inspiration for that stuff from them," Asher agreed. He checked off another finger. "Despair Dragons—early humans didn't have to exaggerate much when they made up stories about them. They're as deadly as they sound, but there's not many of them left, thank Odin."

The officers at the table were stirring now, uneasy in the face of the shopping list of potential enemies that Asher was reeling off. He had moved onto his other hand two digits before. Now he held up the eighth finger. "The Uppregin. Hel's gods. They disappeared just like ours did. There are no gods left that we know of." He frowned. "I'm missing one…" he muttered, and counted off on his fingers again, his lips moving as he worked through the roster once more. Then he rolled his eyes. "I forgot." He held up all but one finger. "The Kraken. You all know that name."

Simmons stood up. "Kraken?" he said sharply. "The big, deep-sea monsters that Jules Verne wrote about, and that silly movie about pirates?"

Asher dropped his hands. "That would be them," he confirmed.

Simmons spread his fingers across the tabletop, looking down at them. Then he seemed to come to some decision, for he raised his chin and spoke directly to the general. "We're the only navy represented at this table, sir, but I talk to enough of them to know we're not the only navy afflicted. In the last four days, we have lost three nuclear submarines and a battle cruiser. The cruiser was running parallel with the USS *Vermont*, and the *Vermont* watched it go down. The junior officer on watch was put on report because he said that tentacles wrapped around it, broke its back and pulled it into the water. All hands were lost."

The room fell silent.

"There have been commercial shipping losses, too," Simmons added. "We don't know how many because they don't have a chain of command to report to that would notice their absence—not for a while, anyway. Some of the supertankers are at sea for six weeks, with no contact with land at all. The only way we'll know they've gone is when they fail to show up."

Hell's bells, Lucas thought to himself. If shipping came to a halt, it could put a giant crimp in the distribution of all sorts of essential products, including oil. Food was at the top of the list, too.

The general put down his pen, for he had been scribbling notes just like everyone else. "This is information that will need to go higher up the chain. I suggest you all report to your superiors and any other coordination pods you belong to. This meeting is at an end."

Asher glanced at Lucas and jerked his head toward the door.

Fucking-A, we're going to talk, Lucas agreed silently. He stepped up to Simmons' side. The Rear Admiral was still standing. "Sir?"

Simmons glanced at him. "You look ready to leave."

"The consultant, the Einherjar. He's a friend of mine."

"I figured you knew each other. Strand sold your virtues heavily."

"I haven't seen him for years, sir. Would you mind?"

Simmons narrowed his eyes thoughtfully. "It might be good to have someone on the inside with the Herleifr. Why don't you go ahead and catch up with him? See where you end up. Report back as and when. Got a smartphone with a good ISD plan, Montgomery?"

"Yes, sir."

Simmons pulled his own phone out of his pocket. "What's your number?"

Lucas gave it to him. Simmons programmed the number into his contacts, then sent a text message to Lucas. Lucas felt his phone vibrate. "Got it, sir."

Simmons shook his head as he put the phone away. "I never could understand why the Alfar couldn't figure out how to tap into our phones and computers, given that they wrap the globe and they're insecure as hell, but Strand nailed that one neatly. Their auras are just mystery and magic to us, too." He straightened up. "Enjoy your catch up and keep your antenna up, Commander. From what I hear, you're about to head into Wonderland."

"I wouldn't know, sir." But Lucas was only partly telling the truth. Charlee's stories, last year, when he had been sober enough to absorb them properly, had hinted at a world far different from the human one he knew.

Part of him was eager to find out.

* * * * *

Asher was fastening the last buckle on his leather armor when Lucas reached him. He looked around and gave Lucas a small smile. "I owe you a drink."

"At least," Lucas agreed. "What did you tell them about me?"

"The truth," Asher said shortly, wrapping the belt around his waist again. He took back his sword from the MP who was patiently holding it for him and nodded his thanks. The MP saluted him and Asher raised his brows, surprised.

"It's been officially decided that stallari is the equivalent to lieutenant, so you outrank him," Lucas pointed out.

"We don't salute," Asher said shortly.

"We know that, too." Lucas grinned. "You'll notice he didn't hold the salute until you returned it?"

Asher pushed the sword through the belt. Lucas could see that the loop that held the sword was reinforced with small metal plates, just like the breastplate he was wearing, which had rows of them stitched across the leather. "You guys haven't got around to using sheaths to carry your swords?"

Asher picked up a metal helm off the bench beside him and tucked it under his arm. "In battle, you never put your sword away. Why wear a sheath that will bang the knees and risk being tripped up?"

It was more of the same pared-down thinking the rest of his armor and clothing demonstrated.

Asher looked around. "There was a car that brought me from the hall. I don't suppose it waited."

"There are taxis," Lucas said. "We can get one at the base gates."

"Then let's get that drink."

* * * * *

The Vajenny hall was the first Kine hall Lucas had ever seen. It was hidden behind a church with onion towers painted green, and they walked through the nave to reach the entrance, which was through a narrow and unremarkable door that might have been mistaken for a closet door by unsuspecting people.

"Are all the halls hidden like this?" Lucas asked curiously as Asher shut the door behind them.

"They're all hidden, but in different ways. We used the local environment and went from there."

The room they were in was perfectly ordinary, but there were two Einherjar guarding the arch at the other end. "Ruben. Otto," Asher murmured and led Lucas through the arch.

"I guess you guys all know each other," Lucas said.

"I know most of the faces, but I don't know everyone by name. I just happen to know these two." He lifted his chin, looking across the room they were in. "I don't know those two."

The room was big. Gymnasium big. The floor was raw floorboards, wide and dark with age and use. Dust lifted around his boots as Asher crossed the boards and somewhere overhead, Lucas heard the flap of a bird's wings as they were ruffled. "This is one of the empty halls?"

Asher nodded at the two guards. They were standing on either side of a very ordinary-looking door, except that Lucas couldn't see through the door. There was light on the other side that, while it wasn't dazzling, masked whatever was there. "That's a portal?" he asked.

"That's a portal," Asher agreed. "Put your hand on my shoulder. You can't go through unless you're touching me."

Lucas raised his hand to Asher's shoulder. The metal plates attached to the leather armor shifted under his fingers. Asher patted his fingers. "Squeeze, and hold on."

He squeezed.

Asher stepped through the misty light, pulling Lucas with him. Lucas found he was holding his breath as he stepped through himself. There was a tugging sensation, brief and mild. Then, as if he had simply stepped through a doorway, Lucas found himself on the other side, finishing the step he had started somewhere else in the world.

He looked behind him. The same colorless, dense mist hid what was behind him. The doorframe was carved and decorated. There was another one right next to it, and a third beyond that. More guards were standing on either side.

Lucas spotted pale cream and brown marble on the floors, the walls and a roof that soared up...and up. Then Asher was greeting one of the guards, pulling his attention back to the portals.

"Frank!" Asher said. "*Ciao. E 'stato un po'!*" They gripped each other's wrists, and Lucas remembered with a start the way Asher had taught him to shake hands, long ago. The warriors' handshake, he'd called it. This was the same grip.

Frank said something back, too fast for Lucas to pick up, then stood to one side for Asher to pass through. Asher glanced at him and Lucas gripped his shoulder again, quickly, as Asher stepped through the door, pulling him through...

...and out the other side.

This hall was even bigger than the last one and there were people everywhere. It reminded Lucas of the original Penn Station in size and echoing feeling, and in how busy it was. There were even blazing streams of sunlight falling from the windows high, high up near the vaulted ceiling, dolloping dazzling pools of light on the floor. This hall was round.

"Where is this?" Lucas asked. "Where was the last one?"

"The last hall was Rome," Asher said, tugging at his armor and straightening his wrist guards. "This is the main foyer of the Second Hall."

"There's a First Hall?" Lucas asked, hearing the capital letters in the way Asher stressed the name.

"There was. Valhalla was lost to us."

"So this is the capital...hall?"

"That's a way of thinking of it," Asher agreed. "The Regin and Annarr live and work here."

They were two names Lucas remembered from Charlee's run down of the Kine world. "They're your king and queen, right?"

"More or less. But don't call them that. Those are human titles. Call them the Second and Council, if you can't remember the proper titles."

He was heading across the round hall, weaving between people, and Lucas hurried to follow. "So where is 'here'?" he asked. He twisted his head and looked around like a tourist. He didn't care what he looked like. The scale and beauty of the hall was taking up all of his attention. So were the people. Were they all Kine? No, some of them would be Amica, like Charlee. But which ones? The women all looked stunningly beautiful.

But there were also some people in the crowd that were clearly human, for their garments were human and looked odd in this place. Every person that Lucas identified as human also had a Kine companion.

On the other side of the round hall was another bank of portals, and people were stepping into and out of them like commuters passing through ticket barriers at the train station. There were guards posted at every portal, not standing to one side, but standing in front of them, checking everyone who came through.

"*Here* isn't something you need to know just now," Asher said. "It's a security thing. You understand, right?" He glanced over his shoulder at him.

Lucas nodded. "You're keeping your Whitehouse under wraps, just in case."

Asher grinned. "Good analogy."

Lucas could tell from the direction he was taking that he wasn't heading for the opposite portals. "Where are we going?"

"You'll see," Asher replied.

There were a pair of doors ahead. Huge things. There were people moving in and out through the one door that was open, and he estimated the height of the doors by the size of the people passing through and whistled silently. The doors were nearly eighty feet high! That meant they were each about twenty feet across, at least.

They passed through the doors into a room that Lucas sensed was the *actual* hall in this structure, the area where the Regin and Annarr would appear. He could spot between the heads of people in front of him a high dais with broad steps leading up to it at the other end of the room, which seemed to confirm his guess.

But the hall was not a royal reception area right now. Lucas took in the folding privacy panels, the chairs and beds he could see peeking past the ends, and the flow of people through and around the panels. There were women pushing steel trolleys, all wearing dresses that came down to their ankles, or even longer, with white collarless shirts underneath. They all seemed to have long hair, tied up in a variety of ways. There were men sitting in chairs that ran down the middle of the hall, back to back. Many of them were wounded, but not seriously enough, it seemed, to need a bed straight away. All of the wounded were holding white cloths or pads to their wounds. It reminded him sharply of any ER in any big hospital, but the scale of this one matched the size of the room. There were five rows of cubicles, running the length of the hall. "I'll be goddamned," he muttered. "I guess you guys bleed after all."

"We're treating humans, too," Asher said, again speaking over his shoulder. He was threading his way through the more slowly moving traffic in the hall, and Lucas kept up with him with effort. For such a big guy, he moved fast. He strode down the length of the waiting area past soldiers in uniforms that Lucas recognized. Humans, then. There were also more than a few Einherjar, recognizable because of the lack of a uniform and a heavy emphasis on leather armor and old-fashioned weapons.

The hall was filled with a steady, low hum that was the sum of murmurs, talking, even moans of pain. But there was no hysteria, or rush to deal with emergencies. The calmness and sense of control was quite different from an ER. The atmosphere of assurance was almost relaxing. Lucas felt like he had stepped into a placid, warm pool. He could feel the tension running out of his shoulders and chest. He was absurdly glad to be here.

Even the wounded seemed to be happy.

Asher's stride checked, then he halted and Lucas almost bowled him over. Asher lifted his chin, indicating one of the cubicles on the left.

The cubicles weren't cubes at all, Lucas realized. They were triangular, so that the row behind this one slotted into the space left by the pair on either side. The panel facing the outside was shorter than the other two, making an opening that served as the door. The bed inside was a fold-up, roll-away contraption sitting next to the internal wall. It meant that the head of the patient was visible through the opening, but nothing else. It also meant the patient could see out, too. In fact some of the soldiers waiting in the chairs were talking to others in cubicles along the rows. There was no segregation of wounded from healthy. They were all in it together.

There was a woman treating the patient on this bed. Lucas could just see her arm, tugging a sheet into place over the man's chest. Then she stepped fully in to view.

"Charlee!" His surprise pushed her name from his lips.

She turned, and her eyes widened and her lips parted. Then she held up her hand, a finger raised either in warning, or a request to give her moment. She bent over the patient and spoke to him, and he grinned and nodded.

Charlee stepped out of the 'room' and moved over to them. Her gaze moved to Asher, then came back to Lucas. She hugged him and Lucas held her tightly. He was stupidly glad to see her. "God, you look so great!" he said. "Even wearing that funny dress."

She smiled at him. Her hair was tied back in a simple plait that hung down the middle of her back. The dress swept the floor, but it hugged her waist and hips and Lucas, although he preferred a woman in a mini-skirt and high heels, thought she looked sexy in a way that he'd never considered before. He glanced at Asher, to see if he appreciated her appearance, then looked away quickly, for there was a naked, almost embarrassing hunger in his expression as he stared at her.

"How long is it since you two saw each other?" Lucas asked suspiciously.

Charlee pulled her gaze back to Lucas. "Over a year," she said quietly.

"What the fuck?" he muttered, distress making his heart thud. "I thought you…I thought you two…Fuck!" he added, angry at the swirl of disillusionment swirling through him. He *hated* this sort of hard emotional crap and the way it made him feel. "All this time, I figured you were together," he finished bluntly. He looked at Asher. "You said you would take care of her."

"I am," Asher said flatly.

"He does," Charlee confirmed.

"By not seeing you for a year?"

She lifted her hands, taking in the whole room. "I am safer here than anywhere else on Earth."

Lucas blew out his breath and deliberately sought to change the subject. "So, what are you? Some sort of doctor?"

"You're working on your own," Asher added. "Eira is too busy?"

She answered both of them. "I seem to have a knack for it. Eira waved me away one morning and told me to go find someone to take care of. I've been doing it ever since." Charlee gave a small smile. "For the badly injured, I call for a Valkyrie, but there are so many wounded and so few Valkyrie…." She shrugged. "I mostly do it myself."

Eira. That was another name Lucas remembered from his long night drinking sack mead. He couldn't remember exactly, but he thought she was someone high up. Possibly the Regin herself. And Charlee worked for her?

"You look tired," Asher told her, beating Lucas to it.

"I *am* tired," Charlee confessed. "The Ganxiao battle brought a wave of wounded here. We're just getting on top of the rush now."

Lucas looked around. "Rush" was the last word he would have used to describe the tranquil atmosphere. He saw that Asher was looking at him.

"They're very good at this," Asher said, with a small smile of his own.

"I'm picking that up." He looked around again. "I suspect there is a lot you could teach western medicine."

"We've stolen ideas from human medicine here and there. It would be nice to give back, one day," Charlee said. Her smile was impish. "It's so good to see you. Both of you. But I must keep going. There are still people waiting."

Asher nodded. "We were passing through. I thought you might like to see Lucas. Count his teeth, fingers and toes and assure yourself he's fine, before I pull him back to New York."

"And I appreciate it enormously." She picked up Lucas' hand. "I'm always here in the Second Hall," she told him. "Try to come back for a longer visit."

He squeezed her hand. "I will," he promised, although he had no idea how he would make that happen. "If someone walks me through the portals, I could come back the next time I'm off duty."

"Go to the nearest hall," Charlee told him. "Give them my name and location. They'll bring you through."

"What if the nearest hall is an empty one?" Lucas asked.

"*All* the portals are guarded, these days," Asher assured him. He glanced at Charlee. "It was good to see you," he said softly.

She smiled at him. "Yes, it was." But there was a note in her voice and a light in her eyes that disputed that.

Was it misery? Lucas clenched his fists at the thought. "Time for that drink," he declared.

"Yes, it is," Asher said flatly. But the same misery was reflected in his eyes.

Lucas kissed Charlee on the cheek. "Go back to work," he told her. "You're needed."

She hurried away, down the length of the chairs toward the big dais, calling out to another woman in a similar dress, who began to push one of the trolleys toward her.

"God, she's so…" Lucas began, hunting for a single word that would encompass the air of competency that surrounded her. It was like nothing would ever surprise her, as if she'd seen so much of the world and everything in it.

"Yes, she is," Asher agreed and began to walk in the other direction.

They were out into the circular hall before Lucas could formulate his next question in a way that wouldn't embarrass him to ask it, or that Asher would find too nosy. "What happened with you two? I never liked the idea of you and Charlee, but that's because it looked so inevitable."

Asher didn't answer straight away. He picked up Lucas' hand and slapped it onto his shoulder, the plates and their studs digging into Lucas' flesh, then stepped through one of the portals, pulling him through.

Lucas looked around at the wooden walls, the fire in the center of the floor, the gritty tiles underfoot. The scale of this hall was much smaller and more intimate. It even felt friendly. "Where is this?"

"Pearl Street," Asher said.

"New *York?*" Lucas shook his head. "I had no idea this place existed and I grew up here."

"That was the general idea," Asher told him. He was unbuckling his sword belt and tugging at the buckles on the sides of his armor. "I have an office here and a locker to park my gear. Give me five minutes, then there's a little bar just around the corner—you probably don't know about that place, either. I'll introduce you to the barman, Eric. And I'll introduce you to mead."

"Charlee made me drink a bottle of sack mead, last year," Lucas said. "I don't think I could ever touch it again."

"Sack mead is hooch compared to the good stuff. You'll like it. I personally guarantee it."

Chapter Thirty-Four

Lucas did like mead. Perhaps too much. It slid down the throat with a vaguely fruity taste but had the same bite as a really good brandy did. He was ripped out of his skull but didn't mind at all.

The little bar around the corner had all the signs of being a Kine bar. There were shields on the wall and the same rough wood on the floors that the hall had on the walls. They served mead by the glass, which was surely the biggest tip off.

Lucas held up his glass, which had mysteriously refilled itself and he hadn't noticed. "Huccum you look younger every time I see you? That a Kine thing?"

Asher held up his glass, too. His hand was completely steady, unlike Lucas'. "I don't look younger. I look just the same. *You* look older, because you are older. Twenty years' time, you'll think I'm a smart-ass kid."

"You speak from experience."

"Yeah." He said it heavily.

They drank.

The walls below the shields were the same rough wood as the floors, and everywhere there were posters and flyers, hand-lettered ads and more. The whole bar was a community notice board, but the flyer that kept catching Lucas' eye was one with a glowing sphere drawn on it and thick black lettering.

Discover your aura! Learn the Herleifr art of Divination!

Asher put his empty glass down with a soft thump, which told Lucas he wasn't as sober as he appeared. "Now I caught up with you," Lucas said.

"You're two drinks behind."

"Can't have that." Lucas looked for his glass and didn't find it.

"Where was I? Yeah, caught you. Now we're the sh…same age."

"Okay," Asher agreed easily.

"*Hated* you when I was a kid."

"I know." Asher was smiling.

"'Coz you *knew* everything."

"I know."

Lucas rolled his eyes. "Charlee is like you now. She looks like she knows everything."

Asher tapped the glass in front of Lucas with his own. "Drink."

Where had the glass come from? Lucas shrugged and picked it up. "Huccum you don't use a gun?" Where had *that* question come from? Oh well, it was out now.

"Gun isn't silent."

"Shit, no," Lucas agreed. "SEALs use blades, but they're supposed to be sneaky. Everyone knows about you, now. Bullets kill Alfar. So, why no gun? You good with the sword?"

"I'm good with the sword."

"Huccum? That a Kine thing?"

Asher shrugged. "I practice."

There was a flyer pinned to the wall with staples, except for one corner that kept lifting and drawing Lucas' gaze. *Tarot Readings. Reliable. Unnur Method trained medium. Call 202-555-6773.* The little tags at the bottom with the number repeated on them had all been removed except for one.

Then he felt himself being lifted and looked up. He wasn't aware that he had lowered his head but he had to look up anyway. Asher was hauling him to his feet. "You need a pillow," the big guy said.

"Can't go home. Passport's in Turkey."

"I'll get you back to Turkey tomorrow. You're not going anywhere tonight."

"Pillow here, then?" Lucas asked, feeling like it was a killer question. Considering how pickled he was, he thought it was a pretty witty comeback. They were crossing the floor toward the door. He wasn't aware of moving his feet, but apparently he was. Or Asher was carrying him. Either, or. "Where we going?"

"My place."

"You got a place?" He was amazed, although a corner of his mind was laughing at himself. How did he think Asher had passed as human for so long if he didn't behave like one? Besides, he wasn't a vampire. He had to eat, shit, shower and shave just like the rest of the grunts. Lucas hadn't spotted a take-out counter or a mess anywhere in the hoity-toity halls Asher had pulled him through.

The entire thought was complex enough to make his head hurt and he groaned. That was pretty much the last coherent thought he had that night.

* * * * *

Charlee begged a bowl of stew from the kitchen staff and sat at the counter to eat while they worked. She knew most of them well, and the chatter was free and easy. Andrea, the Amica running the big gas range, mulled a large glass of mead in a pot off to one side of the meal she was preparing, dropping in spices a bit at a time until the kitchen smelled heavenly. Then she poured the hot drink into a self-warming cup and gave it to Charlee. "Drink that before bed and you'll sleep through just about anything. You look exhausted, honey."

Charlee thanked her for the wine, then wove her way back through the lines of wounded to the rotunda, then up to the private quarters on the second floor, to her room. It was quiet and still, there, and she changed into yoga pants and a T-shirt, and settled in front of her laptop. It was four in the afternoon in New York. It was possible she would catch Darwin at his desk.

She opened up a chat window and shook her head at the advertisement at the top. *Develop your Kine magic skills. Real, learnable. Courses start at $99. Registered Instructor. Click here for more.*

She put the cursor inside the chat window and typed.

CHARLEE: knock, knock!

Then she sipped her mulled wine and winced at the heat.

DARWIN: Hey! You stopped working for thirty seconds! I'm impressed. :)

CHARLEE: ha ha.

Then she hesitated. Was that why she had wanted to talk to him? To get it off her chest? It had been sitting there, a hard mass, ever since Lucas had left. She pecked out the message quickly and hit send.

CHARLEE: i saw asher 2day

Darwin's status changed briefly to "writing" then shifted back to "reading". It sat there for a long while.

Yeah, I didn't know what to make of it either, Charlee thought.

Then his response popped up.

DARWIN: you okay?

Charlee sighed.

CHARLEE: dont know

Her cellphone buzzed, and she sighed again and picked up the apron dress she had been wearing and dug it out of the pocket. It took so long to get at the phone through all the folds and material, she didn't wait to

411

check the caller ID. She just answered it so it wouldn't go to voicemail.

"I figured you could stand a phone call. You can't type worth shit," Darwin said softly. "So the big guy showed up."

"It's not the first time I've seen him," she reminded Darwin. "He passes through here a lot and there's council meetings and strategy meetings and he's expected to turn up at all of them, but today…." *Today he sought me out specifically.* She remembered something. "Lucas was with him, Darwin. He probably took Lucas back to New York and they were going to go drinking, so it's remotely possible you'll have Lucas leaning on your doorbell in a few hours, too drunk to get the key in the latch. He has zero tolerance for mead."

"You've had more practice than him," Darwin said and she could hear that he was smiling. "I consider myself warned. Is that why Asher came to see you? Because Lucas was with him?"

"That's what he said."

"*That's* why you're suddenly chatty, then."

"Why?" She was genuinely curious.

"Because he didn't come looking for you himself. He only came to bring Lucas to you."

Charlee sighed. "I sent him away. He's abiding by that. The man has too much honor."

Darwin was silent.

"What?" she demanded, almost able to hear the wrinkle of his nose. "Too much information, Darwin?"

"Sometimes I'd like to crack your heads together. Both of you. Then sit you down and do the Dutch uncle thing. You're being a girl, Charlee."

"I am?" She didn't like that much.

"You love him because he's being honorable and doing what you ask, but what you really want is for him to ignore everything you said and come get you anyway. Even though the High Council would flip their lid, even though Eira would skin him alive, even though his brother the earl has first dibs on you, and the whole Kine social structure says he can't have you. But you want him to ignore all that and turn his back on the society that *you* pushed him back into."

"He had to go, Darwin. The Alfar invaded."

"Agreed," Darwin said gently. "And you know all that, too." He paused. "You sound tired, kiddo."

She swallowed, abruptly close to tears. "Maybe that's it."

"Why don't you sleep on it?" Darwin said reasonably. "Drink some warm milk and sleep in, if they'll let you. It's gotta be close to one in the morning there."

"About that," Charlee agreed. "I have the warm milk already." She glanced at the mug of mead, where steam still rose lazily from the lid.

"Then go and get into bed. Go on. I'll wait."

She smiled and crossed over to the bed, shucking off her clothes as she went. She slid beneath the thick feather quilt, and put the mug on the bedside chest and the phone to her ear once more. "I'm back. Tell me about your day, Darwin. Did your hip behave itself?"

"It's always better in summer. It's been a good day. Want to hear some trivia?"

"Sure." She realized she was smiling. Darwin hadn't given up on his favorite research project even when the Kine had become just another alien species here on Earth. If anything, now that he could be open about his area of interest, his obsession with the Kine and their ways had increased. He loved imparting anything unusual he uncovered.

"They just took back Ganxiao the other day," Darwin said.

"I know. I helped treat the wounded. But that's not what I'd call trivia."

"No, but what they found there is, kind of. The Alfar had control of that hall for nearly a year. It was the first one they took, I recall. After the hall was retaken, half the Red Army whipped out their phones and took photos of everything they saw. I guess it was their first look at the inside of a Kine hall. They don't have one in the populated areas of China."

"Too difficult to blend in without epicanthic folds," Charlee pointed out. "Especially in medieval times. China was isolationist for a very long time. Ganxiao is in the mountains, away from everyone." She sipped, and suddenly yawned hard.

"Exactly. Have you ever considered that the mountains and the isolation was why the Alfar hit there first?"

She blinked. "An Einherjar mentioned that, when the war first started. I can't remember who. Something about the thin air and the altitude."

"Right. Look at that great big tower over London. The air at the top of that thing would be pretty thin, just like a mountain top."

"That's the trivia?" she asked.

"I guess none of it is really trivia. But that's not why I'm telling you this. The dudes who took the photos dumped them all on the Internet. I've spent a day or so finding them all and going through them. Took me a while to find them because it's all in Chinese, but once I figured out Ganxiao in Chinese script it was like hitting pay dirt. Hundreds of them."

"You clever little researcher, you." She closed the lid on the cup and put it on the chest. Darwin would eventually get to the point. He always did and besides, the detours were usually worth the wait.

"The Ganxiao hall is out in the open. Right there on the side of the mountain," Darwin said. "It looks like an ancient monastery."

"That's probably deliberate," Charlee pointed out. She snuggled down into the bed, pulling the covers over her, and switched off the light. Her phone glowed blue, lighting the cave she had made with the covers.

"I'm damned sure it was deliberate, but that explains why the Alfar found it. There was something else in the photos."

He had arrived at his point. Charlee smiled to herself. "What?" she asked.

"There were trees all over the mountainside, way up about two hundred feet above the natural treeline. They're trees I've never seen before."

Charlee considered it. "Alfar trees?" she wondered aloud.

"Alfheim trees," Darwin agreed. "It's a good bet. There are pockets of the same trees lower down, among the sparse stuff that grows naturally there, which is to say, not much. The Alfheim trees are twice as high, twice as thick, and taking over the land. Plus there's something else."

She waited.

"There are caves and tunnels and whole rooms, dug out of the side of the mountains."

"That could have been there before," Charlee pointed out. "The Kine built Ganxiao before Genghis Khan was terrorizing central Asia. They could have expanded the holding any time after that."

"The Kine build," Darwin said. "They don't excavate."

Charlee thought of where she was lying. The Second Hall had been scooped out of the inside of a mountain. But she couldn't say that. The exact location of the Second Hall wasn't something that was generally discussed. "They don't always build," she replied. "They'll take advantage of local conditions and local setups." She hesitated. "But you don't think that's what happened at Ganxiao."

"I think it's one of the Alfar races," he said. "One of them planted a forest for themselves. One of the others dug out a home inside the mountain."

"Why do that?" she asked. "They're quite capable of building what they want. Look at the tower."

"A tower that lifts them up where the air is thin and cool. I think they were terraforming."

Although terraforming was something that only humans could do to an alien landscape, she grasped his meaning right away. "Turning Ganxiao into another Alfheim?"

"Exactly."

She considered that for a moment. "You think that's trivial, Darwin?" she asked, finally.

"You don't think the Kine that were there saw all that for themselves and knew exactly what the Alfar were doing, straight off the bat?"

"Maybe, but I don't think I want to take that for granted. Would you send me the links for the photos?"

"Sure."

She yawned again.

"I heard that," Darwin said. "Turn off the phone and snuggle your pillow. Time for your beauty sleep."

She would have argued with him, except that she could feel sleep sliding over her, stealing her thoughts. "Night," she said, or thought she said.

Only a few seconds of blissful peace passed, then someone started hammering on the old, thick oak door, making it tremble against the frame. Charlee struggled awake and sat up, staring at the door blearily. She glanced at her phone, which sat next to her on the mattress. She hadn't put it aside before sleep had taken her.

Then she picked it up and looked at the screen saver more carefully. It was eleven in the morning. She had slept the rest of the night and well into the next day, the sort of sleep that passes in a heartbeat, solid and undisturbed by dreams.

The door shuddered again. Well, it didn't shudder. It was a normal knock, but because of the thickness of the door, most people had to bang heavily on it to be heard.

"Coming!" Charlee cried. She climbed out of bed and pulled her dressing gown off the hook on the back of the door and threw it on. She held it closed around her and cracked open the door an inch or two.

O'Malley, an Einherjar who looked barely twenty years old and whose hair was more carroty than her own, peered at her through the crack. "Sorry to wake you, Charlee, but he's insisting on talking to you."

"He?"

O'Malley stepped aside and jerked his head toward the other side of the corridor.

Asher leaned against the wall, his arms crossed, his expression grim.

Her heart squeezed, stealing her breath. She gripped the edge of the door. "It's okay, Eugene," she told O'Malley. "He's pretty harmless."

"Not with a sword in his hand."

"It's in my belt and it'll stay there," Asher growled. "Let me in, Charlee. Please."

She nodded to O'Malley, who stepped away from the door reluctantly. "Call if you need anything," he said. Like most of the Einherjar, he was very protective of the Amica, and Charlee's informal alliance with Roar was well known. Even though nothing had come of it, no Einherjar would pre-empt an earl's choice. She was forever marked as unavailable, so Asher's demand to speak to her made O'Malley uneasy.

"I'll be fine," Charlee assured him.

He moved away from the door, clumping down the corridor to where the stairs to the lower levels began, where he leaned conspicuously against the wall there. He was going to stay close by, just in case.

Charlee pulled the door open. "You make friends wherever you go, don't you?"

"The Alfar just love me," Asher agreed. He stepped inside and looked around. "This place is hard to find."

He looked so good! Now that *laun* had been lifted and he was free to be who he really was, Asher had peeled away the human layers and was more Einherjar than ever before. He wore leather armor and his weapons openly, and from the rumors and gossip Charlee had heard, he was fighting in the front lines nearly every day.

"He's one of the strongest stallari out there," Eira had said in passing. "I would not have wanted to meet Asher on the battlefield when I was human." Then she had laughed. "I didn't get the pleasure, for Roar found me first. Asher has honed his skills since then, as he was required to do, so now he is one of the Kine's sharpest instruments."

Asher looked the part. He looked strong and enduring. Charlee pressed her hands together to stop herself from reaching out to touch him. "My room is hard to find for several reasons, including determined Einherjar. Why are you here, Asher?"

"Shut the door."

She hesitated. "That's probably not a good—" It was all she managed to get out. He pressed her up against the wall beside the open door and kissed her. She heard the door shut. Then his hands were in her hair, around her, pulling her up against him.

The kiss was achingly sweet, hot and good. She sank into the power of it, letting it steal conscious thought. She clung to him and her conscience did not issue a single warning or whisper of concern. All she could process was an incoherent sense of *rightness*. That this was good, natural.

It was very good, indeed.

When he finally let her go, she leaned back against the wall, propping herself up with her trembling knees. Her gown had come open. She tied it closed with shaking fingers.

Asher rested his head against the wall next to hers and closed his eyes. "I couldn't get the thought of kissing you out of my mind." His voice was rough and low. "Since I saw you yesterday. No matter how much I drank. I just wanted to kiss you and that was all."

He had neatly pinned the thing that had been driving her, too. She slipped her hand into his and his fingers curled over it. He looked at her.

"Now what?" she asked softly.

He hesitated. "Now I go back to war. You go back to the hall."

Something invisible grabbed her throat and tightened painfully. "Isn't everything different now?" she asked. "Humans know; *laun* is gone."

"Roar still has claim on you," Asher said. There was a bitter light in his eyes. "He won't do anything about it until the war is done, but that is a law I can't break, not if I want to keep my place in the hall." His mouth turned down in a sour smile. "I dare not even linger here in your room for too long, or the Irishman out there will become suspicious."

She cast about for a solution, *anything* that would break this dreadful deadlock on their lives. But she had been over this ground so often and had never found even a chink of hope. "You said, once, that you would give up the Kine."

"Not while the war goes on," he said flatly, "and after that, where would I go once I left the hall? Humans know what I am, now. I would not be Einherjar, but I wouldn't be human, either. I don't even have the luxury of *that* escape, anymore." He pushed himself away from the wall, breaking her hold on his hand. "I should go." He sounded infinitely bitter and very tired.

"One more minute," she begged, reaching for him.

He kissed her again and this time, it seared her heart with sadness and pain. Then he let her go. The door shut softly behind him.

* * * * *

Unnur touched her temple as the headache threatened to swamp her thoughts. She needed to keep a clear head so she could get through the next few minutes, although she really wanted to climb the stairs to her little-used apartment and drop onto the bed and sleep for twelve hours.

Angelina didn't seem to be suffering, despite the ill feelings swirling about the room. She stood behind her desk, one hand at her throat, the long fingernails stroking the chain there. Her answers were all calm and reasoned, which was probably as it should be. Angelina had been managing Unnur's day-to-day affairs for years now and was confident in her ability to keep things on the rails while Unnur took care of her commitments.

But this was different. This was a shift in priorities, which Angelina didn't seem to be grasping.

Unnur said a silent mantra, reaching for calm. Then she tried again. "What I would like is for you to take over more of the creative side of the business. The classes, the training school for the Method, the running of the store—all of it, instead of just the administrative responsibilities. Media, too." The media, in particular, Unnur wanted off her plate. Of late, the media interest in her method and classes and her abilities had taken a sharp turn upwards. She spent more time handling media inquiries than she could really afford.

"If you want to delegate some of your less important responsibilities, I can help sort that out," Angelina replied. "But only you can talk to the media, if they want to see you. They would never be satisfied with press releases and statements. You are the brand, Unnur. It must be you."

Unnur pressed her hands together. Hard. "You don't seem to understand. I don't want anything to do with it. None of it."

Angelina's smile didn't quite fully form. There was a wrinkle between her brows. "Not talk to the media at all?" she said slowly. "Perhaps in a year's time, when you're more firmly established—"

"No! *None* of it. Not the store, not the media, not the classes, not the Method. All the Internet businesses and sites. The personal appearances, the public speaking…*none of it.*"

Angelina's fingers gripped the chain. Her eyes widened. "But you can't! The business is based on you and your…abilities. If you don't perform, sales will slump. And these days, the Internet is everything. The Alfar can't use it, so everyone is on it. If you shut them down—"

"I didn't say shut them down. I said I didn't want any part of them," Unnur corrected.

"If you're not involved, they'll shut down anyway!" Angelina stepped out from behind the big desk. She was a trim, pretty blonde woman of forty-two, who looked like she should be attending a women's league meeting before picking up the kids from soccer practice, but in moments like this Unnur knew she was seeing the reason why Angelina had never had children, and why her marriage had only lasted a year. The wrinkle between her brows had become an unattractive scowl and her lips had thinned.

"I don't understand how you could turn your back on the business you have struggled to build for over twenty years," Angelina said. "You're just starting to break into the big time. Mainstream media want to do serious interviews with you. Five years ago, it was the *National Enquirer's* local hack wanting to write a filler sidebar. Why now?"

Unnur still had her hands together. Now she twined the fingers and pressed her palms together hard. "My powers are growing. They have been for nearly a year." She thought of the large Tarot layouts that she had been directed to read lately, and the excessively detailed predictions she had written down. They had come true. Not just in a vague way. Not just part of them. But all of them. In exact detail. Her abilities as a medium had expanded. What had once reached her as a trickle from a garden-hose had grown to a raging torrent.

Her dreams had become more and more vivid and specific. They hadn't directed her to take this step with the business, but they had been guiding her away from it. This was a natural step.

"Your powers," Angelina repeated woodenly.

"I need time to develop them properly and I can't do that when I have three interviews a day, including *The Tonight Show.*"

Angelina rolled her eyes. "You want to walk away from a five million dollar a year business, because your 'power' is growing stronger."

Unnur sighed. "I know that to you it sounds a little bit crazy. You don't have any supernatural talent. That's why I hired you. I wanted someone who wouldn't be distracted—"

"Like Penelope?" Angelina asked dryly.

"What about Penelope?" Unnur asked, confused. Penelope worked in the store and was one of their most popular staff members. Customers liked her, because she was empathetic. She was happy to listen to their troubles and their experiences, her big green eyes full of sympathy and understanding.

"She started spouting Herleifr nonsense, months ago," Angelina said. "How her 'aura' was building, that she could see the future. She spent hours with the cards, until I directed her to not touch them during business hours. Last week she tried to convince me that she could tell the history of an object and the person who owns it, just by touching it. That she's getting 'readings' from the money and credit cards customers hand her."

"Psychometry," Unnur whispered. "And you didn't think it was important to tell me about her?"

"Tell you what? That she is a confused young girl who has been over-influenced by your propaganda?"

Unnur stared at her, as understanding finally dawned. "You don't believe paranormal talents are real."

Angelina laughed. "Of *course* I don't believe in the paranormal. I'm a mature adult. I left fairy tales behind long ago." She walked back behind her desk. "If you want to move away from the businesses you have already set up in order to concentrate on something else, then we can work around it. Somehow." She picked up her pen and tucked her skirt under the back of her knees to sit down.

"Wait," Unnur said softly.

Angelina looked at her, her professional smile back in place.

"Have you always felt this way about my abilities?"

Angelina's smile broadened. "God did not give out special abilities to a chosen few. He made man in His image. We are the children of God and have no unnatural abilities, only those He chose to give us." She sat down and pulled a file out of the wire tray on her desk and opened it.

"Then you believe I have been lying, all along?" Unnur asked. Her headache was coming closer now. The thudding reverberated against her skull, warning her she would have to lie down very soon, no matter what.

"I believe that *you* believe," Angelina said with a gentle tone. "We each have our faith." Her smile was beatific. Enraging.

"I think you should leave," Unnur whispered.

"Excuse me?"

"I said, I think you need to leave. Now." She spoke louder, even though it made her temples throb.

Angelina's smile slipped. "Leave?"

"I'm firing you."

She got to her feet, the movement making the crucifix at the end of the chain she was wearing slip out through the opening at the top of her silk designer shirt. Her smile had evaporated and the slash mark between her brows was heavy. Her cheekbones seemed very high and sharp. "You're firing me because I refuse to believe in demonic practices?"

"Demonic!" Unnur's mouth opened.

Angelina threw down her pen. "The only other supernatural power in this world besides God's is the Devil's."

"And what about the Alfar? The Kine? What about their portals, and the swords that disappear, and the tower over London that all the architects say shouldn't stand on its own?"

"The Devil's creatures, one and all, and their houses of corruption, too," Angelina spat.

Unnur shook her head. "How have you lived with the hypocrisy you have been practicing all these years?"

Angelina's eyes widened almost comically. "How *dare* you! I am not a hypocrite!"

"You have run my business, planned media campaigns, advertising and marketing, talked to customers, built business strategies and only now I learn that you haven't believed a word you were saying."

"I *believed*," Angelina said, with heavy emphasis, "that we thought alike, that it was all just business."

Unnur laughed, but the strain of laughing ripped at her head, making it feel like flesh was being torn from the inside of her skull. "Anything for a buck, huh?"

Angelina's face had turned a pasty color. There were slashes of high red across her cheeks. "God helps those who help themselves."

"With a quote for every occasion." Unnur sighed. "Please leave."

"You'll regret this," Angelina told her. "No one can run your business better than I can."

"I already regret it," Unnur assured her. "I regret meeting you five years ago."

Angelina flinched. She pressed her lips together, fastened the buttons on her jacket and walked toward the door.

"Send Penelope back to see me," Unnur told her.

Angelina hesitated, her hand on the doorknob. "Of course," she said evenly. "You two can keep each other company on the way to hell." She opened the door.

"You wouldn't have been keeping up with the war, as it's between ungodly creatures," Unnur told her, "so you wouldn't know that the citizens of Hel are on Earth now. The day of judgment is here for all of us."

Chapter Thirty-Five

Alfheimr.
One of the occupants of the nine worlds, from Alfheim. The Alfheimr (Alfar) have three major races, the Lajosalfar (Lajos), commonly called light elves; the Myrakalfar (Myrakar), commonly called dark elves; and the Blakalfar (Blakar), called black elves. The Blakar homeworld is Svartálfaheimr.

——

From *The Complete Kine Encyclopedia*, by Darwin Baxter, PhD. 2019 Edition

Asher had never particularly liked Øystein, but once the Einherjar had finished his litany of criticism of Stefan's leadership, Asher nudged it up to active dislike. The man was almost glowing with enthusiasm, and was indeed slightly breathless by the time he finished his diatribe.

Silence fell over the assembled council. Was everyone staring at Øystein as if he were an obnoxious bug? Asher hoped so. This meeting, like nearly all the council meetings since the war had begun, was well attended. If there was a battle in progress, or an offensive that would call away earls and stallari, the meeting was postponed. Asher had seen Einherjar walk into the council chambers still dripping blood from their swords and wrapping cloth about wounds to staunch them, having come straight from the battlefield.

But they attended, if they could possibly make it, and most meetings barely contained the attendees now. Øystein's critique had been heard by nearly everyone who had a vote in the matter.

Stefan and Eira sat looking at Øystein. Their faces were neutral. Neither of them could afford to say anything. But no one else was saying anything, either.

"This is bullshit," Asher said loudly.

The men around the table stirred uneasily. Roar gripped his wrist and squeezed, a silent way of telling him to shut up.

Stefan glanced at him. "Anyone has the right to speak, here. Anyone can bring grievances to this table. That is why it is here. Øystein has a complaint. We must consider it fairly."

"*Fairly?*" Asher almost choked on the word. "Because Øystein has tabled a most considered and fair analysis, after all." Øystein's criticism of Stefan's leadership had been full of rhetoric and bloated negatives like "failed" and "weak".

"Asher," Roar whispered. "Be careful."

Why be careful? Asher looked around the table at the expressions on the faces there. "You're not taking this seriously, are you?"

Again, the uneasy stirring.

"Fuck." Asher pushed back from the table, utterly disgusted. "This is a farce."

"The process must be followed," Eira said, her voice easily reaching the back of the room. "It has worked for us for centuries. We do not abandon it now." It was a subtle way of reminding all of them there that Stefan had maintained peace for at least three of those centuries.

"Bring in the traitor," Eira called.

The door swung open and heads turned to watch the two guards, with Sindri between them, as they stepped through. Sindri wore the black robe he always had, but it was splotched with dust and grime and the hem was dirty. His wrists were chained together. His ankles were similarly bound, for he walked with a strange shuffling motion and the clink of chains could be heard as he moved slowly down the long room, to the head of the table where Stefan and Eira sat.

Like every Einherjar in the room, Eira also wore battle gear. Eira's sword had seen as much action as anyone else's and for that reason, Eira had generated more goodwill in the last year than she had in all the previous years she had been Regin. But if she sided too strongly with Stefan, she would lose that edge. She had to appear to be even-handed and considerate.

The guards placed Sindri at the corner of the table, the supplicant's position. Øystein had stepped away to make room. He stood closer to the wall, wearing a small smile.

Sindri bowed his head toward Stefan, then another, deeper bow to Eira. The difference was noted by everyone and there was another ripple of reaction.

Eira scowled and looked around the room. "Someone other than Stefan should question this man. I will not. Nor do I think Asher should."

It was a fair assessment. Just looking at Sindri roused Asher's anger. He had his hands held in tight fists, fighting the urge to leap over the table and strangle him for the grief he had delivered upon Midgard, and for his part in this sham taking place now. Øystein would never have thought to raise a vote of no confidence on his own. Sindri had either suggested it or outright directed it.

Roar stood up. "Stefan, may I?"

"Please," Stefan said stiffly.

Roar pressed his fingertips into the tabletop, looking at Sindri. "Øystein has raised a concern that Stefan's rule has weakened us, left us exposed and vulnerable. He says it is connected with auras, but cannot explain it to us in a way that makes good sense. As you are acknowledged to be an expert in the use and nature of auras, we request that you explain this theory to us."

"I would be most happy to explain the matter," Sindri replied. "But may I request a cup of mead? The cellar where I now reside is dusty and dry."

Eira motioned to one of the Amica standing in attendance against the wall behind her. The taller of the two moved to the corner where jugs of mead stood, freely available to anyone who wished to partake. She poured a cup and brought it to Eira.

Eira took the cup and pushed it across the table, past Stefan, toward where Sindri stood. The base of the metal cup shrieked across the stone tabletop, making Asher and others around him wince at the sound. Eira sat back, leaving the cup a foot away from the edge of the table. Stefan made no move to lift it closer.

Sindri reached for the cup awkwardly, the chains clinking and scraping across the tabletop as he picked it up. He lifted it toward Eira. "My thanks."

She turned her head away.

Sindri took a sip from the cup and put it down. His thirst had been less urgent than he implied.

"Tell us about the magic," Roar demanded. "Why has it weakened us?"

"Magic." Sindri sneered. "A human word. Most of you understand the auras as well as any human."

"Granted," Stefan agreed with a reasonable tone. "We have deliberately withheld from using the auras since the Descent, to avoid drawing attention to ourselves among humans. It is an integral part of *laun*."

"There are among the Kine many who believe that the laws of *laun* outgrew their usefulness several decades ago," Sindri replied.

Asher kept his gaze steady upon Sindri, fighting the need to glance at Stefan or Roar. He knew that Sindri was referring to him in particular.

"The politics of *laun* are not a part of this discussion," Roar replied. "We want to know why the auras are dangerous to the Kine."

"But that is exactly why the auras are your undoing."

Was Sindri aware that he was referring to the Kine in the second person? Asher studied him, wondering.

"The auras are power itself," Sindri continued, apparently oblivious to the consternation he was creating around the table. "Power is the basic commodity of politics. By denying the use of the auras, you have removed yourselves from that which gives you the control you seek."

It was almost heresy, yet Sindri was speaking the words as calmly as if he were explaining the making of mead. Asher glanced along the length of the table, tallying reactions. Sindri had their full attention, and no one seemed to be finding this as difficult to swallow as he was.

Stefan spoke, his voice ringing around the room. "Are you saying that the discipline of *laun* itself has weakened us?"

Sindri spread his hands, the chains making an almost musical sound. "You failed to understand the nature of the auras. By denying the Kine the use of them, you have weakened the Kine unnecessarily."

"Even though the use of the auras was prohibited in the sixth century?" Stefan asked politely. Curiously.

"Explain their nature," Roar demanded. "Why is not using auras dangerous to us?"

Sindri seemed to almost roll his eyes. Asher sensed his impatience, but he spoke in the same measured tones that everyone around the table was using. "Would you expect a fully licensed electrical engineer to be able to teach you the nature of electrical currents in a sentence or two?"

Roar smiled. It was a predatory expression. Asher knew that expression. Roar was as repulsed by Sindri as he was. It let him relax by a degree or two. He wasn't the only one who found this hearing completely ridiculous.

Sindri spread his hands again. "Have any of you noticed what is happening among humans lately?"

Silence was his answer.

"Every week, almost every day, another human with psychic talent is discovered, or declares themselves."

"Charlatans and con men," someone muttered.

"Humans have had psychics and mediums peddling their talents forever," Stefan pointed out, in a more reasonable tone.

"A Christian bishop?" Sindri asked, a dry edge to his tone. "The Republican senator in the United States who fell down and began to prophesy on the House floor? These are not small people looking for fame and fortune. They are public figures with their lives, their fame and their finances already established. But they are not the only ones discovering they have supernatural abilities. Search the Internet and you will find that psychic talent is appearing everywhere. Humans are finding they can prophesy and foretell, read the future in their neighbors' palms, read their co-workers' thoughts, and levitate garden tools. The smallest, most insignificant human and the most famous human…the auras are not particular about where they channel themselves. Anyone who is vulnerable to their power is beginning to feel their influence."

He paused, his gaze flickering around the room as he assessed the impact of what he was saying upon his audience. Apparently, he was happy with the uneasiness he was spreading, for he continued. "When the Herliefr chose to not use auras in 535, the bivrost was collapsed and you cut yourself off from a power as natural as the electricity the humans cannot live without. But the auras are not electricity."

Roar rolled his eyes. "Get to the point," he growled.

"I am, indeed, drawing close to my point," Sindri assured him, with a silky tone. "The basic fact you forgot, when you established *laun*, is that the auras don't *give* their power. Electricity will race along whatever channel it is provided, even through humans and into the earth itself. It runs, it disperses, it showers everyone with its power. But the auras…they are passive conduits that contain whatever power they have in a quiescent state, until someone with a talent for tapping into them draws on their power. That is why, despite *laun*, your portals have continued to maintain themselves throughout the centuries. Once they were established, they simply remained as they were."

Eira sighed. "You presume to teach us lessons we learned long ago."

"I merely remind you of what might have been forgotten," Sindri replied gravely.

Asher sat forward. "If the auras are quiescent and humans are drawing upon them more frequently, now, then won't the auras be drained?"

Sindri smiled. "Are you familiar with the human term 'feedback loop'?"

Asher stared at him. He did know the term and he understood exactly what Sindri was saying, now. He couldn't help glancing at Roar to see if he grasped the implications. Roar was frowning, his gaze on Sindri.

"The auras are biofeedback loops," Asher told Roar and anyone who was listening. "The more humans, Herleifr, anyone taps them for their power, the more powerful they become. They draw their power from those who use them. That's why not using them diminishes them. They have no power source to draw from if they are abandoned."

Sindri's small smile didn't shift. He gave Asher a shallow bow. "You now understand."

"Is that why humans are suddenly discovering talents they didn't know they had?" someone asked.

"They had the talent, always," Sindri said. "But the auras have been weakened for centuries, so humans stayed ignorant of their natural abilities. When the bivrost opened, the Alfar descended upon Midgard. They have no reticence about using the auras as they should be used, and the auras awoke and grew."

Silence filled the room as they all stared at him. Everyone got it now. Everyone understood.

Sindri's smile broadened. "Now the humans are finding that their Tarot cards really do speak to them. Their tea leaves do, too. Divination is particularly common, which makes me wonder if humans are not somehow linked to the Vanir."

There was another shuffle and shift of bodies at the table. Sindri's observations would feel almost blasphemous to some of them.

"Of course, this is of benefit to the Herleifr, too," Sindri continued. "The auras were dying. That is why swords would sometimes not appear upon command and why portals would mysteriously become inoperable. It is why you have all believed there have been no great Valkyrie since the Descent, because their healing powers seem to have diminished and become chancy, but it was merely the strength of the auras failing them. The Valkyrie have remained as powerful as they have always been and perhaps have grown stronger thanks to the challenges they have faced on Midgard." His gaze flickered toward Eira.

Eira cleared her throat. "How, then, were you able to open the bivrost if the auras have been essentially dead for centuries?"

Sindri's smile shimmered. Asher realized with some amusement that Sindri was trying to look modest. The little man simpered. "There is natural energy in many things. Humans have learned to tap into geothermal energy, the flow of great rivers, even the separation of nuclei, to generate their electricity. The power that drives auras is also natural. The alignment of planets, the change of seasons, the psychic energy of crowds, the focused concentration and emotions at a popular concert…these are all generators of power that the auras can use, for they are weak auras of their own. There are many others, if you know where to look. I merely collected their energy and focused it properly."

"And you used *my* torc to do it," Eira added.

"Yes," Sindri said simply.

The silence this time was more thoughtful. Now, the implications of *laun* were fully realized.

Roar waved his hand toward Sindri. "Get him out of here," he said, his expression one of disgust.

The guards stepped forward and tugged on Sindri's arms. Sindri lowered his head in a short bow toward Eira. It was a surprisingly regal expression. Then the guards pulled him away from the table, and he shuffled toward the doors between them, the chains clinking.

Roar looked at Asher as he sat back in his chair. He grimaced and spoke softly, just for Asher to hear. "You have been insisting for decades that *laun* was harming us in the long term. Apparently, you were more right than even you knew."

Eira and Stefan were looking at him from across the table, their expressions thoughtful. There was still a vote of no-confidence to be decided, he realized with another start.

He stood up abruptly, his chair scraping across the stone floor. It drew attention to him. "Let's get this stupid vote out of the way," he growled. "It's distracting us from focusing on more important issues like defeating the Alfar and their allies. So *laun* weakened the auras. So what? No one could have anticipated that. Not even me. I thought *laun* was unnecessary, but I followed Stefan's lead. I still do. I vote we dispense with this nonsense now."

"Aye," Roar said instantly and loudly, only a fraction of a second before a full-throated roar of approval sounded around the table.

Øystein slipped out of the room, unnoticed by anyone but Asher.

* * * * *

The alarm came without warning. It arrived when Charlee was inspecting a writhing, deep sword cut on the arm of an Einherjar she had treated a week before. It was exactly like someone was shouting at her, but the words boomed inside her mind.

They're coming! They waited until you were gathered and now they spill upon the landscape! Hurry!

Charlee jerked back in reaction, wincing at the volume. She clapped her free hand to her ear. The other hand was holding the bandages aside and as she recoiled, she tugged on them. The Einherjar hissed as the bandages rubbed across the raw wound.

"Sorry," she said, but she didn't look at him, because the images spilling through her mind were too powerful to ignore. She closed her eyes and held her breath, watching hundreds of Myrakar and thousands of Blakar spread out across open prairieland. Among them, and in front of them, the land was thick with Sinnar and Asmegar, running in their peculiar loping way. The location was unmistakeable, for among the hordes of Alfar, elephants trumpeted in confusion and alarm. Thorn trees dotted the mara, while Mt. Kilimanjaro rose up into the upper atmosphere, indifferent to the drama playing out on the plains below.

"Charlee, are you alright?"

Charlee swallowed and opened her eyes. "I have to go." She held out the ends of the bandage. "Hold this for a second. I'll get someone to re-wrap these for you. I have to...I must go."

"If you must, you must," the Einherjar said placidly. "Did I see AnnaJo out there, earlier? Perhaps you could ask her to finish up?" He winked at her.

"Sure," Charlee told him, already moving out of the cubicle. "Stay put, I'll send her to you."

She moved out into the hall, looking around for the Amica with the golden hair that the Einherjar had requested, and beckoned her over and asked her to finish dressing the wound.

Then Charlee hurried down the long length of the narrow aisle, moving faster and faster. By the time she emerged from the hall into the rotunda, she was almost running. Halfway across the rotunda, she did start running. It didn't occur to her to question the warning. The fear that had accompanied the shout had been distinct and highly motivating, pushing her into reacting without thought.

By the time she reached the boardroom doors, she was almost sprinting. She straight-armed the door, the heel of her hand thumping against the aged wood. Agony flared in her elbow and her wrist but she shoved the door aside, throwing her full weight into getting it swinging slowly open. Once the door was moving, it was easy to open, but getting it swinging took effort.

Charlee stepped around the Einherjar standing at the back of the big, long room, pushing her way through to the open space at the end of the table, murmuring apologies as she forced her way in.

Stefan was standing at the head of the table, speaking. Eira looked at Charlee sharply and got to her feet, too. "What is it?" she demanded.

"The Serengeti," Charlee said, breathless. "The Alfar are invading Kenya."

Heads were turning to look at her.

"Why would they invade Kenya?" someone asked, sounding amused.

"I don't know, but they are," Charlee snapped. "I saw it. West of Kilimanjaro, right on the border. They took over the hall at Amboseli and they're pouring out of the portals there. Alfar and vast numbers of Nare. They're killing anyone they come across, taking the men for slave fighters and stampeding everything else that moves."

Heads were turning as the Einherjar checked with each other. Charlee saw amusement on same faces and disbelief on others.

"There's nothing in Kenya they could possibly want."

"We voluntarily abandoned Amboseli, nearly a hundred years ago."

The sound of a phone ringing was almost lost among the murmuring around the table, but Charlee stared at Stefan, for the sound was coming from him. Stefan slapped his hand over his hip where the phone had to be, then grimaced and pulled it out. "Stefan," he said shortly and listened.

Then his gaze lifted and he skewered Charlee with a sharp look. "We'll be there as soon as we can." He lowered the phone and spoke to the whole room, his voice lifting. "That was Nairobi. The Alfar, I'm told, are invading in mass numbers, all across the Serengeti." He lifted the phone back to his ear.

Roar got to his feet. "All hands! Now!" he shouted.

Charlee was almost knocked over as Einherjar began to stream past her, heading for the door at high speed.

"Charlee."

She looked around as she tried to move closer to the edge of the table and out beyond the tide of men without tripping any of them up. Eira was looking at her and when Charlee's gaze turned to her, she beckoned with her finger. Charlee patiently moved down the length of the long table, working her way along against the flow of traffic. Finally, as she neared the end where Eira stood the traffic eased, and she stepped up to the end of the table and faced Eira.

Eira tilted her head. Her eyes were narrowed. "Who told you about the Alfar invading Kenya?" she asked.

Charlee pressed her lips together, trying to find a phrase that would make the truth sound less fantastic than it really was.

Eira shifted on her feet. "Come, come. The battle is raging. I should be slaughtering Alfar, not standing here discussing your personal network." Her hand, Charlee noticed, was resting on the hilt of her long sword, which Eira wore almost every day. She strapped it on when she rose in the morning and it hung from her hip while she worked in the hospital, attended meetings and performed the many administrative duties that were her lot. No one doubted, however, that when a battle began, Eira would be ready. Charlee was holding her up now so she blurted out the frank truth, regardless of how it would be received.

"I heard it in my head and I saw it in my mind."

"You imagined it?" Eira asked, her voice quite neutral. "A prophecy?"

Charlee shook her head. "Someone spoke to me. There was a personality driving the shout."

"Personality?" Eira looked thoughtful. "What did they tell you, exactly?"

Charlee described the words, the thoughts that had been behind them and the images she had seen.

"Cognition and clairvoyance," Eira murmured, staring right through Charlee as she considered the matter. "Do you realize, Charlee, that whoever sent you that warning can reach into the minds of the Alfar and read their intentions?"

Charlee pressed her fingers to her throat as it seemed to dry up. "Who would have that ability?" she whispered, fear rippling through her.

Eira smiled. "For now, it doesn't matter. They're on our side, Charlee." She moved passed her. "We'll talk about this later. For now, do tell me anything else your guardian angel shares with you, hmm?"

"Of course," Charlee said quickly, as Eira strode toward the big doors and slipped through them, leaving her alone in the long, narrow room.

* * * * *

Unnur lifted herself up from the table where she had slumped over as her vision blurred. The pick-axe in her head was pounding away at the soft matter that made up her brain, each beat of her heart driving the sharp point deep inside her skull. She moved slowly, straightening out the cards she had disturbed with her droop, and looked around her little lounge room. It was still daylight outside, and there were even birds twittering just beyond the window.

But in her mind, she saw once more the dry Serengeti plains, pock-marked by thousands of Alfar, their long swords and knives glinting in the sharp, crystal air. Unnur smelled the dust and could feel it on the back of her throat and how the dry air made her nostrils flare as the moisture inside evaporated.

The air there was thinner, for the plains were well above sea level. She had felt the Alfar's collective satisfaction at the lack of oppressive moisture and the thick air that they struggled with when they battled for possession of sea-level halls.

Unnur had spent the morning laying out spread after spread. She had begun with the critical question—*Tell me*—and followed up with more and more specific questions as the details seem to paint themselves in her mind with each succeeding spread, filling in like the paint-by-numbers murals on her shop walls had, inch by inch and square by square.

The thought, the alarm—the vision—had arrived without warning. Unnur didn't know what to call it. She had shuffled the cards one more time, while holding her next question in her mind, meditating on it with a finely held focus that had been stronger and steadier than she had ever been able to achieve in the past.

What does your enemy intend? She had kept that question front and foremost in her mind as she shuffled, then split the deck and restacked it, her hands moving smoothly.

Then she had turned the first card. The King of Wands.

The pain had struck sharply right behind her eyes, making her cry out and her vision fade. She dropped the cards and covered her eyes, slumping over the table, as the images and thoughts/feelings had pummelled her mind. There had been no need to focus or maintain a meditative state. The vision had encompassed her consciousness, ejecting any thoughts of her own. For the few seconds (*centuries*) the vision had lasted, Unnur had ceased to exist. She had become a vessel. A channel in truth.

She had never been to Africa, but she had known without doubt the location of the vision. She had known it with the same certainty with which she knew her name. She knew it was the Serengeti, even though the Alfar had another name for the place. They revered the mountain on the horizon for its solitary splendor.

As the power of the vision waned, Unnur became aware of the sharp edges of the cards under her hands, pressing into the sides of her fingers and with almost the same degree of urgency, she thought of the Queen of Wands.

Warn her.

The thought barely formed in her mind. It was more like an instinct, and without consideration Unnur hurled the essence of the vision out toward the Queen, wherever she may be. Unnur *felt* the warning leave her, tugging at her mind and her chest like a spirit leaving the body.

Then it was gone.

She looked down at the scattered cards, blinking, as she considered what had happened. Would she ever know if the message had been received? Probably not, for this was a new aspect of her talent. It would require a lot of thought.

Was the Queen one of the Valkyrie? Was that why she had immediately thought of her when she had seen the Alfar advancing?

Unnur moved the cards until the Queen of Wands was revealed. "Be safe," she whispered. "Whoever you are."

Chapter Thirty-Six

On day five of the Battle of the Plains, the human military machinery reached the Rift Valley and caught up with the human and Herleifr armies that had been attempting to dam back the Alfar offensive spreading across the plains since their incursion, but by then, it was too late.

The Amboseli hall, which had remained empty for the last one hundred and seventeen years, had two portals—as did all the minor halls, including New York. The first portal connected Amboseli with the hall in St. Albans, just outside the shield that protected the London tower. St. Albans had been seized quietly and quickly by the Alfar, who then poured their masses through the portal to Amboseli. They had raised no alarm in St. Albans, as their intention had been purely to gain access to the portal. They had killed no humans. Their approach to the hall in the quiet suburb had been completely covert, so no alarms had been raised. It was only after they had captured the hall that their presence became known and by then, the Alfar had built a shield protecting the corridor between St. Albans and the tower.

Thousands of Alfar and their Nare cohorts were streamed through the St. Albans portal to spread out upon the Serengeti plains, heading for the capital. Sheer numbers made them an overwhelming force that every able-bodied Herleifr and the handful of human forces able to mobilize quickly enough to join them tried desperately to hold back. The Alfar drove them steadily backwards along the Rift Valley, almost herding them back to Nairobi.

On day four, Nairobi fell.

For the entire day, fighting around the edges of the city raged as the Herleifr held the line, to give the humans in the city time to escape to the north, and to protect the portals in the Kine hall there, for they were the main portals the allies were using. Many Nairobi citizens used the portals for their escape, too.

The Alfar progress was slowed by the buildings and city structures they encountered, for the allies could use the protection the buildings provided to set up blocks and barriers.

Finally, on this last day of the Plains Battle, the human forces' traditional method of fighting became useful. Their guns were able to hold back and pin down the Alfar. On the plains, where the fighting had been one-on-one, the human forces had found themselves ill equipped, especially without the computers and armored vehicles, helicopters, and tactical long-range weaponry that usually supported them, for that was still en route. They had been forced to fight using hand-to-hand combat and personal weapons only.

But once they were among the buildings on the edge of the city, the human cadre could call upon their rifles and snipers, hand-held rocket launchers and grenades to dig themselves in and make a stand.

Asher found himself at the south end of the city, watching a dozen Israeli and Arab soldiers who were part of the third Arab Israeli Federal Army battalion as they launched grenades, systematically bombing the street two hundred yards away. In the space of thirty minutes, they dug a cratered trench with their bombs. The trench ran for dozens of yards and was an effective barrier halting the Alfar.

Then the AIFA settled in with snipers and lookouts, to pick off any courageous Alfar who tried to cross the divide.

Asher sat with his back against a mud-brick house, just behind the AIFA lines, and let himself feel the exhaustion that was turning all his muscles into concrete. He was far beyond tired and right now, he had nothing to do except clean his sword.

Then he heard a series of low whooping sounds to the north-east, and sat up. The Israeli captain sitting against the wall beside him lifted his head. "That's minigun fire," he said. "The transports have arrived."

Overhead, a helicopter streaked past them, low and loud, confirming his guess. They watched it bank toward the east, then straighten up and head north. Hanging from the open doors of the helicopter were two soldiers, each of them behind mounted miniguns. The soldier on the east side of the helicopter fired steadily, picking his targets, as the helicopter headed north.

The thwock-thwock of the blades faded as it floated north.

"American," the Israeli captain decided with a sniff.

The arrival of armored back-up only held the Alfar temporarily. Nightfall provided the Alfar with the cover they could not manufacture for themselves. Asher was woken from an uneasy doze against the wall by a barrage of artillery fire and the light pop of handguns and rifles. It sounded like a New Year's firework display going off.

He got to his feet as shadowy figures streamed over the debris walls lining the trench and rushed past him in the dark. Dozens of the Alfar fell as they were picked off one by one, but there were so many of them, the small arms fire couldn't hold them back. It was the equivalent of holding up a hand to halt the tide.

The Alfar did not engage. They dodged and ran at full speed, which was faster than humans could manage with their shorter legs and heavier bodies. A few were brought down as they passed, but not all of them. Not nearly all of them.

"Fall back!" Asher shouted, already knowing it was too late. "Back to your transports."

The Israeli captain was somewhere nearby because Asher heard his shout picked up and re-shouted, this time in Hebrew.

By the time the moon rose, around ten that night, Nairobi had been taken by the Alfar, along with the prize they had sought all along: the hall with its bank of portals, for Nairobi was a busy junction point.

Asher made his way northeast, along the same general line the helicopters had been taking. He moved slowly, checking for Alfar, and scrambling through the bombed and battered homes. After midnight he finally reached the American outpost. It only took five minutes to be allowed through, although one of the sentries escorted him to the command post.

The harried lieutenant wrinkled his brow as he studied Asher. "I know you. You're the lieutenant from New York," he said.

"And my route home was just swamped by Alfar," Asher told him. "I was hoping I could beg a ride with your men, when you head back."

"There's a Hercules going through pre-flight right now, on the military strip. I put my walking wounded on it." The lieutenant dug in the big pocket on his thigh and pulled out a cellphone. "I'll phone ahead and let them know you're coming." He started dialing. "Washanski!" he yelled.

"Sir!" came the reply smartly. Then a corporal appeared from outside the tent and saluted.

"Take this officer to the troop transport McLean is on, ASAP!"

"Sir, yessir." The Corporal saluted again, and glanced at Asher. "This way, sir."

Asher made the transport with bare seconds to spare. The stairs were folded up behind him and the door dogged down, even as the engines revved and the big plane began to slowly trundle down the hard dirtpan that was the surface of the airstrip. Asher watched thorn trees whip by as the plane built speed.

The transport was full of injured soldiers and medical aides working on the worst of them. It landed at the Ramstein airbase in Germany ten hours later. Asher had slept for nine of them and stepped off the plane feeling more alert. He desperately wanted a shower.

His cellphone, which had been out of range of a tower for five days, suddenly vibrated against his hip and he fished it out. It was Roar.

"I'm alive," Asher assured him.

"I'm in New York, holding the portal closed. How fast can you get here?" Roar sounded stressed.

"Not that fast. The closest portal is Munich, and that's an hour's flight from where I am and I don't think the US Airforce will give me another ride." He frowned, thinking it through. "I can't use a commercial flight. I'm geared up." They would never let him on with the full body armor and all his weapons, and he needed to keep them with him. Besides, he didn't have a passport. "I'll figure it out," he added.

"Keep me posted." Roar disconnected.

Asher looked around. Everyone at the base had something to do. Everyone looked busy.

Then he heard his name being called and turned toward the big hangar where the hail was coming from. Lucas Montgomery was standing at the doors of the hangar, in full battle gear, his helmet swinging from his fingertips. He beckoned.

Asher hurried over to him and they shook hands the way Asher had taught him. He ran his gaze over Lucas, looking for injuries.

"My unit is heading back to the States for a debrief and R&R," Lucas told him. "We've been sneaking around London for weeks, keeping tabs on what happens behind the shield." Lucas cocked his head, looking Asher over. "I heard Nairobi has been taken."

"You heard right," Asher said heavily. Behind Lucas, his men were sitting on anonymous crates or sprawling on the concrete floor. A couple of them looked like they were sleeping, curled up on their sides, their heads on their arms. Snatching sleep whenever the opportunity presented itself had become Asher's life, too. "I'm trying to get home without using human international borders. One of the portals in New York is directly connected to Nairobi."

Lucas blew out his breath. "Isn't the other one directly connected with your HQ?"

Asher grimaced. "That's why I'm hurrying. The Alfar are one degree away from home base. I just need to get to Munich."

Lucas grinned. "I can get you there, for a price."

Asher just looked at him.

Lucas' grin broadened. "I wouldn't mind an instant trip back home. Neither would my unit."

"If you can get me to the hall in Munich any faster than a donkey cart would manage it, you're welcome to use the portals, too," Asher told him.

Lucas laughed. Then he whistled a two-note sound that made his men sit up immediately and look at him. Lucas turned to them. "Wanna get home pronto?" he asked.

A smile streaked around the group, lighting up the unshaved and grubby faces like sunshine.

"Meet Asher Strand, Einherjar and Stallari of the New York hall," Lucas said. "He's going to get us home faster than you can imagine. Remmy, figure you could scare up seats for us on a chopper to Munich?"

One of the men who had been resting on his back on the concrete got to his feet with the lithe flexibility of a cat. "Prob'ly," he replied laconically, and strode out of the hangar.

Lucas turned back to Asher. "Park your butt," he suggested. "Let's see what Remmy digs up."

* * * * *

It took three more hours to reach the base in Munich and another hour to find cabs to take them all to the hall in the heart of Munich's old town. Lucas' group and Asher were the only ones on the helicopter that flew them to Munich and when Asher asked about the purpose of the flight, Remmy had winked. "Better to take the favor and not ask," he said.

Lucas grinned. "You're pretty well known, you know."

"They're doing it for me?" Asher was astonished.

"Not too often we get a real live Einherjar to talk to," one of the others chimed in, his voice tinny over the headsets they were all wearing.

It seemed that the military—or at the very least, Lucas' unit of SEALs—were rabidly curious about the Einherjar, their weapons, tactics and more. For the last year since the Herleifr had revealed themselves, they had been a fast-moving target. Every Einherjar fought in nearly every significant battle, then dashed on to the next one, so time to chat with anyone, let alone curious military personnel, was limited.

Lucas' team made the most of the two hours, asking Asher question after question about the Einherjar life and way of fighting. As a stallari, Asher had the experience to answer most of their questions. With only a small qualm he handed over his sword for them to examine, one after another, passing it on to the next like the bottle of tequila that was making the rounds. The SEALs, unlike other military units, used blades a lot in their own work and they seemed to appreciate the subtle advantages of a sword.

Lucas patted the Luger strapped to his hip. "Better to use a pistol when silence isn't an issue. Then you don't have to get within reaching distance of them."

The man next to Asher was just handing him his sword back. Asher took it and without shifting his position, threw the sword. It flashed across the cargo area and thudded into the insulated wall just over Lucas' head, and hung there, quivering. "You mean, like that?" Asher asked.

The men laughed loudly, as Lucas pulled the sword out with some effort and handed it back. "A parlor trick," he added.

"A trick perhaps, but not just for the parlor," Asher replied. "The Einherjar did most of the fighting on the plains, the last few days. Guns and rifles don't work that well in running battles, and the Alfar specialize in running."

"I bet you I could have made a dent," Lucas replied.

"Me, too," Remmy murmured.

"Then it's a pity you weren't there," Asher told them gravely. "If we had had every useful soldier with us, it might have made a difference."

The Munich hall was well guarded, especially the portals. Asher vouched for Lucas and his team and walked them through the hall proper to the portals, while Lucas coached his men on how to use the portals.

"This is going to take longer than usual," Asher warned Lucas as Lucas gripped his shoulder from behind. Lucas' men were lined up behind him, each gripping the shoulder in front of them. "There's no direct route to New York from here and we can't take the shortest route, because the portal it uses has been taken by the Alfar."

"Anything is better than sitting on a cargo plane for twenty freaking hours," Lucas replied.

It took five jumps to make it back to New York, and Asher was pleased to see that every single hall they passed through was closely guarded, the guards alert and watching everyone who stepped through. New York was no exception. As he stepped through, using the heavy towing stride he needed to haul all the humans behind him through the portal, the guards greeted him with raised swords and shields, only relaxing when Asher spoke their names.

"*Seven* humans, Stallari?" one of them questioned as the line of men behind Asher pushed through the portal and straightened up.

"He always was as strong as an ox," the other said with a grin.

Lucas and his men were spreading out across the hall, looking up and around curiously. There were more guards and more Einherjar sitting around the hall, their weapons at the ready, than Asher had ever seen except on feast days. Roar had whistled up just about every Einherjar who was attached to the New York hall. There wasn't a single woman in sight.

"Welcome home, gentlemen," Asher told Lucas' men.

It was perhaps the stir of interest surrounding their arrival that distracted the guards from the other portal and it was sheer bad luck, for the Alfar tested the other portal at that very moment.

Three Blakar leapt through the portal, their long knives raised over their heads, and fell on the two closest guards. Asher reached for his sword as the third leapt at the guard nearest him. He took out the Alfar's throat, then used the power of his swing to rotate him around in a full circle, which put his sword within reach of the other two, and gave him the impetus to strike again.

The two revolver shots were loud in the enclosed hall, smothering the startled cries of alarm from the Einherjar as they leapt to their feet. The remaining two Blakar were yanked back by the impact of the bullets that hit them. They landed heavily on the floor and lay motionless.

Stillness gripped the rest of the hall. Shock, Asher figured. It had ended even more quickly than it had begun.

Asher lowered his sword and looked at Lucas, who was holstering his pistol once more. Lucas grinned at him. "And sometimes a gun is better than a sword."

"Sometimes, yes," Asher agreed.

* * * * *

Lucas sent his men home, and he and Asher settled at the kitchen counter in Roar's apartment. There was a new piece of furniture in Roar's place: a big-screen TV was tuned in to CNN, where the war seemed to be the only topic anyone was talking about. The battle on the Serengeti was the major focus. Already they were calling it the Battle for the Plains. The loss of Nairobi was being reported in sad tones, accompanied by footage of thousands of Kenyans fleeing the city.

Asher introduced Roar to Lucas, and Roar silently poured them each a large helping of scotch from the bottle sitting on the counter. Roar had dark circles under his eyes, and he moved with the slow deliberation of the very tired.

"Can we hold the portal?" Asher asked.

"With constant vigilance, yes, I think we can." Roar held up his glass. "To victory."

"Hell yeah," Lucas muttered and took a big mouthful. "Do you have enough people to guard the portal twenty-four-seven?"

"We'll manage," Roar said. "Now that Asher is back, I'm happy." He grimaced. "Well, as happy as you can be with the Alfar kicking your ass."

"Are they?" Lucas asked curiously. "Kicking your ass, I mean. You guys look pretty invincible."

"Even the invincible can be overwhelmed by sheer numbers. There are so few of us to begin with and we can't be everywhere at once. In the twenty centuries since the Descent, the Alfar have been breeding themselves an army while we have grown weak and our numbers depleted...." Roar pressed his lips together. "Never mind. I am speaking out of turn. It has been a long few days."

"Have you slept at all?" Asher asked.

Roar's shoulders lifted fractionally. "I've dozed."

"I can take over here. You should sleep. Real sleep, I mean," Asher told him.

Roar nodded. "I'm too tired to even try to argue."

Lucas stood up. "I should let you get your sleep." He put his glass down.

"It was good to meet you at last, Lucas. I've heard a lot about you over the years," Roar told him.

"Really?" Lucas grinned, as if he was genuinely pleased. "I, of course, had no idea you existed until a while ago."

"That was the nature of our life then," Roar agreed soberly.

After Lucas had gone, Asher poured Roar another drink. "Finish that, then go and sleep," he said.

Roar hesitated, then reached out for the glass. "I should remain sober," he muttered and drank deeply.

Asher studied him. "You're being gloomy."

"I'm not gloomy." Roar finished the glass. "I'm far beyond that." He grimaced. "I didn't know I was a pessimist until today."

"You said the portal will hold," Asher pointed out.

Roar stood up. "Do you know what I've been doing while you were in Africa?"

Asher shook his head.

"Disaster planning." Roar's grimace this time looked like he had bitten into something noxious and rotting. "Do you know what will happen if the Alfar make it through to New York City?"

"I have a general idea," Asher said gently.

"Well, I know every last possible scenario. We've been figuring out how bad it would get, and exactly how to deal with them if they break through." He laid the flat of his hand over the now-empty glass and deliberately pushed it toward Asher. It scraped harshly across the counter.

"I won't let them through, Asher. They *must not come through*. It's that simple." His gaze met Asher's, and he held it.

Cold, hard fingers walked up Asher's spine and he shuddered. "You've got a doomsday plan?" he asked Roar softly.

Roar's nod was infinitesimal. "If I pull the plug, you don't want to be within a city block of here."

Asher knew that if the Alfar were pouring through the portal, into New York itself, he would be right there, doing his best to slow them down. They wouldn't get New York without a fight. But he wouldn't say that because Roar would argue with him. "You need to go and sleep," he told Roar instead. "Go on. Go. I'll do the rounds and make sure everything's closed tight. You'll feel happier after six solid hours of sleep."

Roar shook his head. "If you believe that, then you don't understand how precarious our position is. We're holding on with our fingernails. All it will take is one good shove…."

Asher reached for the bottle. He hated scotch, but it suddenly felt like a good idea to drink more of it. "What do you want from me? You want me to join you? Beat my chest and wail?" He took a big mouthful of the scotch. "The Americans say it best. It's not over until it's over. The humans might decide that an atomic bomb dropped on the Serengeti would end this war as neatly as it ended the last world war. The Alfar might all curl up their toes and die because they can't handle our common cold. You don't know how it's going to go. Anything could happen to turn this around. So go and get some sleep, and stop whining like a little girl."

Roar grinned. "That sounds just like you. You've always been stupid about playing the odds."

"So go away and let me play them," Asher growled.

Roar lifted his hand up to signal defeat, and headed for the bedroom area. His shoulders were bowed, and his head lowered. Asher watched him go, his heart thudding unhappily. He could talk about playing the odds and fighting to the end, and he would refute every negative thing Roar said, using sheer bluff and bravado, because to admit how close to defeat they were felt like giving in. But that didn't stop the slow trickle of hope and the drain of courage it took with it.

He finished the glass of scotch, then headed out to the hall to see to the placement and strengthening of the guards around the portals and the public entrance to the hall.

He kept his shoulders straight and his head up. It wasn't over until it was over.

Chapter Thirty-Seven

Casus belli is a Latin expression meaning "An act or event that provokes or is used to justify war".[1] *Casus* is a 4th declension masculine noun. Related to the English word "case", *casus* can mean "case", "incident", or "rupture". *Belli* is the genitive singular case of *bellum, belli,* a neuter noun of the 2nd declension. *Belli* means *of war.* A nation's *casus belli* involves direct offences or threats against it, whereas a nation's *casus foederis* involves offences or threats to an ally nation or nations — usually one with which it has a mutual defence pact, such as NATO.
Wikipedia

Ten days after the fall of Kenya, England was lost. The Alfar, who had systematically overcome hall after hall by pouring through the portals and overwhelming the Einherjar they found with sheer numbers, did a very unexpected thing: they didn't use the portals and they didn't attack the Einherjar. Instead, they dropped the shield that had been protecting the tower straddling London, and Myrakar, Blakar, Sinnar and Asmegar poured out in all directions. Thousands upon thousands of them spread across greater London and southern Britain in overwhelming waves, attacking human centers of authority and reaping slaves as they went. As they conquered, the aura was expanded to shield their new territory. By sunrise the morning after their coup, the southern portion of the British Isles was occupied, the northern portion in complete disarray and panic, and the shield continued to push steadily north, claiming mile after mile of countryside.

Charlee heard the rumor of bad news when she entered the small boardroom that had been assigned to the stallari and his men for training purposes. As all the Einherjar and many of the Valkyrie were fighting in the war, there remained only Amica and a few Herleifr to keep the hall operating. None of them were excused from daily practice, but Charlee would have continued to train on her own even if the training had been abandoned. The stress relief and reassurance the training gave her was beyond price.

She slipped between the open doors of the boardroom, her long knives balanced on her shoulder, and looked around curiously. She was a few minutes late, but no one was actively training, which was what she had expected to see.

Gerda, the most senior Valkyrie still resident in the hall, was surrounded by Amica and one or two Einherjar, including Bahram, the head of security, who was acting as stallari for these training sessions, as Howard was away fighting.

Charlee walked over to the tightly gathered group. "What's happening?" she asked, lowering her knives.

AnnaJo looked at Charlee. "Britain has gone."

Charlee's heart leapt, and cold fear threaded through her veins. "*All* of it?"

"Almost," AnnaJo replied in a whisper. "They're saying it's only a matter of hours. They just crossed into Scotland, half-an-hour ago."

"They're going overland, instead of bulldozing their way through the portals," another Amica said. "They learned from the Plains Battle that they're strongest that way."

"You don't know that," Gerda said disapprovingly. "Facts are hard enough to establish in wartime. There's no need to add to the chaos by speculating on what you do not know."

Scotland. A hop and a skip across the North Sea and they would be in Norway. Charlee took a deep breath, trying to calm her jangling nerves. "Can they cross open water?" she asked. "They don't have vehicles of any kind."

Gerda looked at her sharply, then straightened. "That is enough discussion for now," she said with the same final, inarguable tone in her voice. "Our duty is to keep the hall operating smoothly. Return to your duties. Bahram, please begin training. We all need to occupy ourselves with priorities, not speculation."

Slowly, Charlee moved to a clear space in the small boardroom, which was large enough to hold all of them once the table had been removed, and settled into her training routine. She understood that Gerda was riding hard on everyone in order to kill any hint of panic before it could blossom and infect everyone in the hall. They all needed to keep their heads. Stefan and Eira would not allow the hall to go unprotected, and besides, the Alfar had not shown they were capable of crossing seas. They used the portals, and their new conquests always stopped at the waterline.

Worrying about how close they were to Tryvannshøyden wouldn't benefit anyone. The portals were the most secure sections of any hall, with an overabundance of Einherjar protecting every single one of them. Besides, the Alfar had no idea where the Second Hall was.

But knowing it was pointless to worry, and not worrying were two completely different things. And where was Asher? In the thick of things as usual?

* * * * *

"As long as the location of the Second Hall remains unknown to the Alfar," Stefan said, lifting his voice so that humans and Einherjar at the back of the hall could hear him, "then doing anything overt, like increasing our land-based defenses in the country where the Second Hall is located, will tell the Alfar where it is."

The roundabout reference to Norway was because of the number of humans in the room. Most of the humans were high-ranking military, with a scattering of politicians and other power-wielders and civil servants. Journalists had been carefully screened out of the meeting, although Asher had already been told by the handful of men he had brought over from New York that the media had set up outside the hall and were waiting for an update.

They had stepped over to the Isle of Man as soon as the alarm over Britain's occupation had gone up. Asher had doubled the Einherjar guarding the New York portals, then picked six to take with him to the hastily called meeting.

Roar stayed back at the hall, only after Asher had argued him to a standstill. Roar had still not recovered his usual robust energy, even after two weeks of lighter duties, and Asher refused to let him step onto the field of battle until he was completely his old self once more.

The hall on the Isle of Man was a tiny one and barely contained the assembled heads. It had been abandoned for decades and the smell of mold and dust was strong, even though Amica had been contributed from dozens of halls to clean the building before the heads of state descended.

The meeting had been set for noon, GMT, and the humans given full use of the portals and accompanying Einherjar guides in order to make the meeting in the few hours' notice given them. Some of them had arrived looking sleepy, and some annoyed, but they had come.

An Einherjar tapped on Stefan's shoulder and passed over a scrap of notepaper, then stepped off the dais and moved away.

Eira read the note over Stefan's shoulder. Her face did not move by a millimetre, but Asher had a feeling that the news was not good. She resettled her sword and spread her feet into a ready stance, staring out at the attendees. The knuckles on the hand curled around the hilt of her sword whitened.

Stefan looked up from the note. "Scotland has fallen. That puts the main island of Britain completely in the hands of the Alfar."

Asher held back his surprise, struggling not to show it on his face. The Alfar had moved across the land, conquering it faster than the average human train could travel. He had seen how fast they could move in Kenya, but this was unprecedented. He made a mental note to check with Roar and Stefan afterward—had the Alfar used auras to speed their progress? Was this something they had developed? They had spent centuries honing their use of the auras while the Kine had avoided using them at all. The Kine were paying for that discipline in all sorts of ways, now. The Alfar didn't seem to care about the impact of anything they did upon anyone, or the land itself.

He sighed and refocused upon Stefan, who was standing silently, waiting for the reaction to the news about the fall of Britain to die down.

Someone in the crowd with a rich British accent spoke up. "This is worse than the Second World War. We held back the Germans. They never set foot upon mainland England, but we paid the price for that success. This, though…it's a bit rum, wouldn't you say? How could they possibly move so fast? Is it more magic you haven't told us about?"

"If it is, Minister," Stefan replied, "then it's magic that we have no knowledge of either. The Herleifr have been completely frank about the Alfar."

"But not about your own situation, wouldn't you say?" the same voice shot back. "Why this panicked reaction to the taking of what amounts to a land mass about the same size as Kenya? Are they getting a tad close to home, perhaps?"

It was a shot in the dark, but it was a finely aimed one. Stefan shifted on his feet, a telling movement that nearly everyone in the room would interpret correctly. His normally steady gaze flickered sideways. Asher gritted his teeth, silently urging Stefan to hold it together.

"The time has come to look to our home defenses," Stefan said. "That is what this meeting is for."

"What do they want with England, anyway?" The question came from someone Asher couldn't see between all the heads in the room, but the accent was western European. French or Danish perhaps. It was a good question, but one that Stefan couldn't afford to answer. Not in this room, not to these people. The real answer was, they didn't know. The Alfar were one step ahead of them and had been since Kenya. All the Einherjar seemed capable of doing was defending and retreating, to defend again, only to retreat yet again. Human military technology seemed to have no effect. But hand-to-hand combat with blades did slow them down and that was all the Kine were doing. Slowing them down.

Britain gave the Alfar nothing. Neither did Kenya. The Alfar did not know where the portals they now controlled would take them to, and as they had discovered in New York, trying to find out for themselves was costly.

Asher drew in a slow breath, hiding his reaction as ideas and facts coupled up in his mind. Fear exploded inside his chest, stealing his breath and making him almost dizzy. He bowed his head, struggling to stay calm, on the outside at least. When he thought he could move without stumbling, he pushed his way through the people standing around him, heading for the exit. As he weaved his way out of the crowd, he pulled out his cellphone and thumbed out a text message.

alfar plan to take 2nd hall - from both sides

He hit send just as he reached the big doors, and he looked over his shoulder as he pushed his way out. Eira was reaching slowly for the phone on the pouch at her hip, making it look casual, not drawing attention to herself.

It would have to be enough. Asher stepped outside into the foyer, and sprinted for the portals, calling for his men as he went.

* * * * *

Run! They're coming! Hurry! Get out! Get out! Get out!

The words roiling in her mind barely registered as coherent thought, but the pulsing urgency driving them pushed Charlee to her feet and into a pounding run, heading for the hall doors without thought or consideration. The communication held the same overwhelming compulsion of the one that had warned her about Kenya.

Charlee threaded her way through injured, wounded and dying. Most of them had stumbled or been carried into the Second Hall from Britain, and they filled the main hall, their vacant and shell-shocked expressions and their shaky movements telling a profound story of the speed and effectiveness of the Alfar attack.

She ran past them all, with her dress hiked up in her arms, freeing most of her legs of underskirt and hem so she could run. Some heads turned to watch her go, but not the wounded.

Charlee slammed her full body weight up against the door, getting it to swing open more and let her around the steady stream of people moving in and out through the narrow gap already opened.

She looked around the rotunda, trying to assess where the threat was coming from and which direction she should take. Who could she warn? Gerda was in Britain with Eira....

Her breath caught as movement by the portals, tucked away behind the big pillars, caught her eye.

Einherjar stood by the portals, as they had since the Alfar had taken Ganxiao. But these men were standing over the bodies of other Einherjar.

Their swords and knives were red with blood.

One of them turned to look over his shoulder and Charlee recognized him. Øystein, Sindri's best friend and confidante.

She reached for her long knives, strapped to her hips just as Eira had worn her long sword by her side every day since war had broken out, and withdrew them. "I'll have your betraying entrails, Øystein!" she yelled as she broke out into another run, heading straight for him.

Øystein smiled and turned to face her. At the same moment, Sindri strolled into the hall from the long passage on that side. The passage led to, among other places, the old stone stairs that gave access to the basement cellars where Sindri had been held. He wore a smile of satisfaction, and he looked dirtier and smaller than ever before.

Charlee altered her direction, aiming directly for the little man.

Øystein looked startled, then uncertain, but Sindri's smile broadened even more. He lifted his hand, palm out toward Charlee, then swiped it sideways, like he was cleaning glass.

Charlee rammed into an invisible wall. Her knee flared deep agony as it was popped backwards, then her chest and shoulders and hips slammed into the barrier. She had been moving so fast that she bounced off the wall like a rubber ball and staggered backwards. Her momentum was too much for her to keep her balance. Her feet went out from under her and she just had enough time to bring her knives up and out of the way of her body as she fell back on her butt and her shoulders. Her head rapped the shiny tiles with a knock hard enough to make her dizzy.

She forced herself to keep moving, propping herself up on one elbow and shaking her head to clear the muzziness. There was a heated spot on the back of her head and she felt it delicately. Her fingers came away bloody.

Øystein was smiling once more. The men around him were dragging the fallen Einherjar back down the passage. On the other side of the rotunda, more of Sindri's men were doing the same.

The hall was vulnerable.

There were a few humans and Kine milling in the middle of the hall, trying to understand what was happening, for Sindri's men looked just like any other Einherjar and Sindri was staying back in the shadows. Charlee realized that there was a lot less traffic passing through the rotunda than usual.

She slowly hoisted herself to her feet. Blood dripped to the floor by her feet and she shook her head again to clear it. With effort, she leaned over and picked up her knives again, and spun them, feeling their weight. "Call security!" she screamed as loudly as she could, hoping it would alert someone in the hall, or that the people standing frozen with surprise and uneasiness in the middle of the rotunda would put together that the threat was coming from within the Kine and act.

She headed for Sindri again, where she could see him standing beside the last portal on that side. When she reached the place where the invisible barrier had halted her the first time, she hesitated.

Go forward! came the mental command. *I can defeat the shield.*

Charlee stepped forward. Her skin prickled almost painfully, but she was not halted. She smiled at Sindri and headed for him, picking up speed.

Sindri scowled and muttered something in a language she didn't know. His hands were waving, moving faster. Moving with haste.

But nothing stopped her.

She gripped her knives firmly, feeling the calm of endless training sessions descend upon her, coating her thoughts and directing her movements. She knew she was the only one who could deal with Sindri and halt whatever plans he had put into action. This would be her only chance.

She lifted her knives to the ready position as Sindri screamed at her—a spell or incantation -- but the voice in her head was protecting her.

"No!" Sindri screamed in pent-up denial as she stepped past the big pillars.

"Charlee, to your left!" The warning this time came from behind her. It was Asher's voice, and it was full of some emotion she had no time to analyze. But the fear in his tone was enough for her to whirl to the left, throwing her knives up so that the blades crossed.

Øystein's sword rammed into the vee formed by her knives and she barely—just barely—stopped the blade from burying itself into her head. Øystein looked triumphant, though. He grinned at her. "He's too far away to help you, Amica."

Which was true. Charlee nodded in agreement, an odd calm filling her. She knew that this was probably the moment when she would die, but Øystein didn't seem to understand that it didn't matter.

He lifted the sword, swinging it fast, bringing it around for the blow that would either decapitate her or spill her innards out upon the floor. She dropped her knives low, to block his blow, wondering if her strength would be enough.

The three gunshots sounded very loud in the room, which had fallen almost completely silent. Øystein jerked and staggered backwards, his sword flailing. Red flowers blossomed on his jerkin. He looked in Asher's direction, his expression puzzled.

Charlee looked around, her breath escaping her. Asher stood fifteen yards away, almost in the center of the hall. His sword was in his belt, but there was a gun in his hand, pointing at Øystein.

"I'm close enough for this," Asher told him. He fired again.

The bullet punched into Øystein's forehead, almost dead center. His puzzled expression faded and he toppled backwards, like a felled tree.

Sindri laughed. "It's too late. You can't stop it!"

"Stop what, Sindri?" Eira asked. She had stepped out of the portal behind Asher, and now she walked across the rotunda, which had cleared of people. They had scattered from the field of fire and were now ranged around the edges, too interested in events to scurry away from danger.

Sindri's eyes widened as he looked at her.

"Tell me what you have done," Eira told him, moving slowly closer.

Sindri pulled himself together. He straightened up and bowed low. "Mistress. You will forever have my respect and my love."

"Tell me," Eira snapped. "Have you exposed us to the Alfar?"

"Did you know I was once King Cnut's advisor?" Sindri asked her. He spoke with a tone that made it sound like they were conversing over mead. Two friends, enjoying a moment of each other's company. "I would sit on his white silk banner—no one had a banner so fine or so expensive. Silk was nearly unheard of then."

Charlee stared at him, confused. What was happening here? Why was Sindri speaking so oddly?

Her phone buzzed like a demented mosquito against her hip, and she pulled it out and read the text message.

Guard the ny portal

It was from Asher. She looked over at him. He was holding the gun on Sindri, but his phone was in his left hand, down by his thigh.

Slowly, trying not to draw attention to herself, Charlee side-stepped and shuffled until she was hidden from Sindri by one of the enormous pillars. Then she moved silently across the rotunda, using the pillars on the other side as a guide, trying to keep the pillar behind her between her and Sindri. Behind her, Sindri was still speaking. He had not noticed her movement.

"I would sit upon his banner and scare his enemies with my flapping. Cnut listened to me. He believed me. I won for him the largest empire any king had ever aspired to, in all of Europe." His lip curled into a sneer. "Then the stupid fool tried to renege on our deal."

"You killed him," Eira said softly, as if she understood exactly what Sindri was talking about.

"I ruined his life, first. His life and his kingdom, so that none of his heirs could claim it. Then I ate his heart and took his soul and all his knowledge."

"Is that the price we pay for refusing you, Sindri?" Eira asked. "You

449

will ruin us and destroy our world, because of a lost kiss?"

"I was never truly a part of your world." He seemed almost sad. "I saw what you did to outsiders, to anyone not Herleifr, who got too close to you."

Eira withdrew her sword, slowly. "You know we cannot allow a traitor to live, don't you?"

Sindri spread his hands. "In my heart, I did not betray you. Never you."

"If we survive what you have done, I will remember that," Eira assured him. She moved very fast. Charlee could barely follow what she did. Her whole body leaned backwards, and then swayed forwards as the great sword swung. There was a wet swishing sound that made Charlee swallow.

Before Sindri could drop to the ground, though, he seemed to fold in on himself. His features melted, then ran like hot wax, down into the black robe, which crumpled to the ground slowly, as if all the supporting bones beneath had abruptly disappeared.

As the robe sank to the floor, one wide sleeve lifted up into the air. The arm that had been in it seconds before was gone, but it looked like it was being raised by an invisible arm, nevertheless. Eira stepped backwards, her sword at the ready.

The sleeve jerked and then slid backwards and a bird emerged. It was a raven, pitch black and huge, its small black eyes—so similar to Sindri's—taking in everything around it as it cocked its head from side to side.

Everyone still in the hall murmured and stirred uneasily. The Kine considered ravens to be very unlucky, for they were the birds that most often brought a Valkyrie to the battlefield to collect the dead.

The bird hopped away from the black robe and then with a loud caw, flapped its wings and launched itself into the air, lifting higher and higher until it reached the narrow windows at the top of the rotunda. The bright sunlight pouring through them dazzled Charlee, and she blinked, clearing her vision. When she could refocus on the light and the windows once more, the raven was gone.

Asher ran toward Charlee while Eira lifted her voice. "All hands! Everyone! Einherjar, answer the call! To me! To me!"

The cry was picked up inside the hall itself, and down along the wide corridors leading off the rotunda, where the meeting halls and common rooms were. Movement sounded: running feet, calls, the unmistakeable sound of steel being drawn. The people around the edge of the rotunda moved toward the center.

Asher reached Charlee's side and picked up her arm. "I need you to step through to New York. Now." He was pulling her like he expected no argument, or would consider none.

Charlee resisted his pull. "Are you kidding me? I'm staying here!"

Einherjar and Valkyrie came running into the rotunda. All of them were armored. All carried weapons.

"Everyone who is not of the Kine, leave now—use the New York portal!" Eira cried. "Amica—evacuate the wounded. Hurry! The Alfar will be here in moments."

Charlee looked at Asher. "I want to stay and fight," she told him.

"This isn't your fight." He wasn't even looking at her.

Charlee lifted her knife and prodded it in his side, just enough to get his attention. Asher turned back to her, surprise skittering across his face.

"Of course this is my bloody fight!" she told him. "It's my world they're trying to destroy—or take, or whatever it is they think they're doing! Do not send me through that portal, Asher. I'll die holding my ground before I'll meekly let you and the Kine protect me and mine."

Watch out! The cry came in her head, loud and urgent.

Charlee whirled. They were three feet away from the portals on the west side of the rotunda. The portal right next to the New York one shimmered slightly, the only warning that someone was stepping through from the other side.

Then the Alfar leapt out into the rotunda, from portals on both sides of the room. Charlee heard their battle cries, but she was too busy getting her knives up into a defensive posture, and holding off the first wild charge of Blakar as they poured through all but three of the portals on this side. The New York portal, closest to the main hall doors, was still. Abruptly, she was fighting. Actually fighting. She had no time to fear or worry.

Nine portals were vomiting their alarming cargo out onto the rotunda floor and abruptly, the circular hall was filled with fighting bodies—the human-looking Kine, the brown-skinned Blakar and the lighter flesh of the Myrakar. There were no Lajos or Nare here—the Lajos were the commanding race, and wouldn't appear while their cannon fodder did the work.

"Charlee!" Asher looked over his shoulder, even as he thrust his sword into the stomach of a Blakar. "Evacuate the hall. Get them out. Portals, doors. We'll hold them as long as we can."

She whirled and ran for the main hall, to do as he said. The next fifty minutes were a nightmare filled with panic as Charlee ordered, begged, cajoled and sometimes pushed people through the New York portal. For each human, she found a Valkyrie or Einherjar to escort them. For the wounded, she found stretchers or Kine carriers. For many of the humans in the hall, she simply sent them around the fighting and into the extensive workways and passages that connected the public rooms with each other, so that the Amica and other staff could service them. Charlee appointed Amica to guide the humans through the workways to the only access to the outside world. She told the humans to find shelter anywhere they could once they were outside the hall, but to keep moving as far as possible. Remember London! she urged them, and the fright on their faces assured her that they understood the danger that was being barely held at bay in the rotunda.

On one of her trips through the hall doors, to lead more walking wounded through the New York portal, Charlee saw that there were many more Einherjar fighting to hold back the Alfar, now. She spotted the tall, spare figure of Stefan, deep in the middle of the roiling battle.

Asher and his men were still holding open the New York gate, forming an almost solid wall shielding the portal, and dealing with any Alfar who came through the next portal or tried to demolish their line.

"This won't last much longer!" he called to her sometime later. He was bloody, and there was a cut across his shield arm, oozing more blood. But he was standing and showed no signs of weakness.

Charlee held up a finger. "One more group. The rest I'll send through the tunnels."

"Make it fast!" he warned and stepped forward to clash with a Myrakar who had launched himself from several feet away with an inhuman, ululating cry.

Charlee hurried. The last group she wanted to push through the portal were too weak, too injured, to face Oslo in the depth of winter. She found them halfway to the doors, already heading in her direction, and urged them to hurry, hurry.

She saw Gan-shu, a fellow Amica, across the hall. "Gan-shu! Take everyone out through the workways. The hall is about to be overrun!"

Gan-shu glanced at her, her eyes huge. But she nodded and instantly began to round people up, pushing them toward the service doors.

The injured that Charlee was shepherding along began to shuffle and limp along even faster, encouraged by her call to Gan-shu. She pushed open the big door to get them through. There were five of them, all Einherjar, so they could step through the portals without companions. She guided them along the narrow path to the portal that Asher and his men were holding open, and waved them through.

Behind her, more Einherjar assembled, ready to step through. These men were fit, but breathing hard, their swords and blades bloodied and covered in gore. The fighters were falling back, they were all falling back, to retreat through the one portal they held.

One of the Alfar cries went up, triumphant in its volume and glee. Charlee looked up, just in time to see Stefan standing among a tight circle of them. He was clutching his stomach. As Charlee looked up, one of the Myrakar whirled his blade in a wide arc, slashing viciously.

Charlee bit back her cry of protest as blood spilled from Stefan's throat. He fell among them and disappeared.

"Einherjar! To me! To me!" Eira cried, her voice strong enough to be heard across the hall. It was the voice of a commander, a leader. She was moving across the hall, fighting her way to the portal. She was among the last of them.

"Charlee, go through," Asher snapped.

"Not until you do," she cried back.

He swore, and turned back to fight off the overwhelming waves of Alfar. Charlee stood at the very brink of the portal, her knives up, watching the Einherjar retreat. It was a bloody few minutes' work, as they battled to hold the portal and push everyone through.

Eira drew level with Charlee and looked over her shoulder. She was almost breathless and sweat gleamed on her arms and her face. She glanced at Asher. "Retreat, Stallari!"

He nodded without looking around. Eira jumped through the portal and his men shuffled around, forming an arc to protect the portal, as one by one they leapt. Charlee realized with a start that as their numbers diminished, the more dangerous it became. But Asher had clearly thought of that ahead of time, for when four of them were left, standing shoulder to shoulder, their swords whirling, he yelled: "Now!"

All four of them turned at once and jumped for the portal. Asher wrapped his arm around Charlee's waist and she was yanked through with him.

The Second Hall had fallen.

* * * * *

They fell into a rolling sprawl across the tiled floor, unable to keep their feet. Charlee felt skin scrape and joints jar, but let herself roll as Howard had taught her.

As she came to a stop, face down on the floor, she heard Roar's voice, a bellow of command. "Blow it!"

Asher threw himself on top of her, and she turned her face away from the portal as a great explosion rent the room behind them. A hot wave of air pushed against them, then debris: pieces of brick, mortar and splinters of timbers.

Asher was up on his feet, pulling her up onto hers, before the debris settled. "Fast, fast, faster," he told her. "Hurry. Onto the street and as far as we can get." His fingers were gripping her elbow again, but this time she didn't mind. Her hearing was fuzzy and her mind was having trouble making connections, but she did understand his urgency. She let him drag her into a run, following the many Kine who were sprinting from the main hall, down the wooden stairs and out into the foyer. They were a fast-moving stream.

"How long?" Asher called out ahead of him.

"Three minutes!" Roar called back, although Charlee could not see him over the heads and shoulders of those who were just ahead of them.

They took the emergency exits, running and often stumbling down the iron stairs, gripping the bannisters to keep their balance. Time beat at them, the seconds ticking down.

Then they burst out onto the street and Charlee blew out what was left of her breath in relief.

"Keep running!" Asher urged.

They ran across the street, dodging cars. Eira and Roar and many others were calling out warnings to New Yorkers who were on the sidewalks and they turned and ran with them, trying to get as far away from the Pearl Street building as possible.

Then it blew. There was a deep rumbling sound. Charlee had to fight her need to look back, but instead keep running. Then the rumble was overtaken by one of the loudest noises Charlee had ever heard. It made her clap her hands to her ears. She was aware that she was screaming her fright and panic, but she couldn't hear herself because the explosion was swallowing everything.

Then the blast wave reached them and Charlee was knocked off her feet. She rolled and kept rolling until she was halted by something soft. She looked up, briefly, and saw black rubber and a name outlined over it. *Pirelli.*

Saved by a low profile… she thought disjointedly, as blackness took her.

Chapter Thirty-Eight

Eira stretched as she walked over to the dining table, then unbuckled her sword belt and dropped the weapon on the table. In the two hours it had taken them to deal with human authorities and make their way through the panicky lower Manhattan streets to Asher's apartment, the blood on her sword had dried to a scaly, dark film and was flaking away.

Roar eased into the easy chair over by the window.

Asher dropped his key onto the plate next to the door. "There's a shower through there," he told them, indicating the bedroom. "I'll order a pizza."

"Dibs on the shower," Eira said, her hands on the small of her back. "Do you have a shirt I can use, Asher?"

"In the closet. Help yourself."

"Thanks." She headed for the bedroom, shedding armor as she went.

Charlee eased herself around Asher, who was standing just inside the door, watching Roar.

Roar pulled in a gigantic lungful of air and let it out. He leaned forward, his fingers entwined. "So that's that," he said.

"We're as isolated now as any humans," Asher said. "We have to depend upon their means of travel."

"Why?" Charlee asked, even though she had intended to stay silent and small and unnoticeable. "There are the other halls." She knew there was one in New Jersey, although she had never visited it. There was another in upstate New York and that was three of them, just in this state.

Roar glanced at her. "All the halls are gone."

"*All* of them?" she asked, startled.

"All the halls still held by the Kine. They were all destroyed at the same time." Roar spoke heavily. Slowly. "The Alfar were using them, using

455

the portals, to their advantage. They had to be taken out of their reach."

Charlee realized she had sunk down onto the nearest surface—one of the dining chairs. She gripped her hands together much like Roar was doing. It seemed impossible that all the halls, every last one of them, had been deliberately sabotaged, and blown to splinters, just like the New York one. It was incomprehensible that they had all gone. "But…what will you do?" she whispered. Where would they live? How would they organize themselves without a central hall to gather within?

Roar glanced at Asher.

Asher stirred, shifting his feet and dropping his hands to his sides. "How soon?" he asked.

"Six hours. Let them find some sleep, if they can. Lieutenants only."

Asher nodded and reached into a pocket on his trousers and pulled out his cellphone and began to thumb through it, as he moved over to the sofa and sat down.

Roar gave Charlee an effort-filled smile. "We can't use Kine technology anymore, but humans have tools that will substitute just as well."

"A cellphone network won't deliver you to the next Alfar invasion inside ten minutes, if it's anywhere but Manhattan."

Roar nodded. "We are all scattered. Each of us will have to do the best they can, with what they have to hand. Humans, now, will become our critical ally." Then he grinned, his teeth very white against the dirt and sweat on his face. "Anywhere but Manhattan would be fine by me, though."

* * * * *

Renmar found his gaze drawing back again and again to the image hanging in the middle of the room, even when his advisors were speaking. It was a fascinating image, and each time he let his gaze fall upon it, a sensation would ripple through him, filling him with uneasiness. He didn't like how it made him feel, but he seemed helpless to stop himself from looking at the image yet again.

The picture had been captured by humans, as the Alfar had taken the Herleifr hall. The Second Hall, as they called it. Sindri had been very frank about every aspect of Kine life, and some hidden aspects of human life that they had failed to notice before now. The image hanging in the air behind all his advisors had been extracted from the entity they called Online. Renmar did not understand Online at all, but the Myrakar, who were such good interpreters and diplomats, seemed to grasp the concept quite well. Those who were fluent in the humans' principal languages had conveyed the fact that the humans were speaking among themselves about the Alfar victory, only heartbeats after the fact. They had presented this image to Renmar as evidence, shortly after Renmar climbed the steps to the high dais at the end of the big hall and looked around.

The hall and the complex of connected lesser halls and living quarters were surprisingly grand and elegant. Renmar had trouble believing the brawling, uncivilized Kine had built it, or that they were even capable of conceiving such grandeur.

He looked at the image once more, and his chest tightened. It had been taken out in the round room, beyond the doors of this hall, minutes before the Alfar victory. The Kine had been holding open the portal for their companions to retreat through. There were Blakar and Myrakar bodies at their feet, and more of them clashing with the line of Einherjar holding the gate.

Renmar picked out the tall one again, the Einherjar in the middle of the group. Askr, son of Brynjar. Asher Strand, as he was known to humans. This was the first time Renmar had seen what the Einherjar looked like, although he already was very aware of his fighting prowess, for Asher Strand had been a prickly thorn in his toes for quite a while and the Myrakar had built up an impressive dossier on him for the Lajos to study and absorb. Understanding one's enemies was always desirable.

Then Renmar shifted his gaze to the woman standing behind him. A human, but she stood with very Alfar-looking knives, held high in the attack position. The Myrakar who had taken the hall had assured him she had been fighting almost as effectively as the Einherjar in front of her. She had been the one who had moved behind the Einherjar front line, ensuring the residents of the hall escaped. It was because of her work that the hall they stood in now had been virtually empty of either Einherjar or humans.

That was another oddity. Renmar had been surprised to learn that the Einherjar gave the humans what appeared to be unfettered access to their halls and portals. It didn't seem possible that they could be working with the humans, but the evidence suggested that they were partners and did not make use of the hierarchical structure the Lajos employed to organize the Myrakar and Blakar. It was a very strange arrangement indeed.

But that wasn't what was squeezing at his middle each time he looked at the image. He made himself look again, to sample the feelings it provoked. He didn't know why, but he knew the answer would be important.

"Has the traitor been found yet?" he demanded.

Pernon broke off, staring at him. He had been saying...something. Renmar dismissed the matter with a wave of his hand. This was too critical. He must follow the line of reasoning through. His instincts were demanding it. "The one called Sindri. Has he come forward for his reward?"

Morolab, standing next to Pernon, touched his eyes gravely. "We believe Sindri may have transitioned, great one." Renmar knew Morolab took great satisfaction in seeing Pernon upset, but he was hiding it.

"Transitioned?" Renmar repeated, prompting Morolab to explain.

"We questioned one of the few humans we found in the passageways. It was injured, so the questioning did not last long. But it said that it had seen Sindri…fly away." He added the last with an apologetic simper.

Renmar's torso seemed to shift and squeeze harder. "He saw a bird?" he pressed.

Morolab didn't hide his surprise. "Why yes, great one. A big, black bird."

Renmar couldn't help it. He turned to look at the image once more, his attention fully upon it, the rest of the room fading away. Was it possible? Could it be…?

"The human, there," he said, pointing. "I want to know more about her."

"She is connected with Sindri, great one?" Pernon asked.

"No one was connected with the traitor," Renmar told them. "Do you not remember your history? Sindri was a Valravn. The Valravn do not make friends, or choose allies. They cleave to their own kind, except there are so few of them left. Sindri may be the last."

"Then what is the significance of the woman, great one?" Morolab asked. "A human?"

"Find out more," Renmar demanded. "I want to know everything about her."

There was a murmur and shuffle among the senior Myrakar who stood at attendance behind his advisors. One stepped forward to speak softly to Cison.

"What is it?" Renmar asked impatiently.

Cison touched his eyes. "Great one, the Myrakar have found other images of this woman, possessed by the Online."

"Show me," Renmar snapped.

The Myrakar rushed to obey. Very quickly, a new image took the place of the other one. This image was of the woman's face. She was looking over her shoulder, at something that was not in the image. Wind was pulling at her hair, drawing it over her throat. But her face was not hidden and the image was very clear. Renmar was unable to tell if she was one of the more desirable human women. Human esthetics, just like their Online, was incomprehensible to him.

But the image made him draw in a breath that seemed to sear his throat. Now he knew what the first image had provoked in him and why. It was fear. Genuine fear, such as he had not felt in a very long time. "The first image," he said.

The original image was returned. He looked from the tall Einherjar to the human behind him and thought of Sindri. Renmar stared, feeling almost ill with fright. "Everything," he repeated. "I want to know everything about her."

* * * * *

Darwin tiled the pictures on his screen so he could look at them all at once, and sat back to consider their implications. They were all still photos taken from security footage in the Second Hall, shortly before it had been taken by the Alfar.

Oslo. Norway. Why hadn't he guessed that was where the headquarters for the Kine would be? And under a bloody mountain, to boot. A mountain that sat almost in the heart of the city. It seemed poetic. But when Darwin had wondered where the Second Hall would be, he had only vaguely considered Scandinavia and that was a big place. If he had thought of it at all, he might have guessed Iceland was the location, for that was the other country with the Viking-rich history.

But that was a question that had ceased to be important now. Someone had hacked into the cloud-based archive of the Second Hall's security cameras and had captured and uploaded a collection of images to their Flickr account. Darwin had caught a hint of their existence only this morning, when someone on one of the Yahoo groups Darwin monitored happen to mention it. It had taken Darwin less than sixty seconds to find the images.

He had picked out the more interesting of them and now had them arranged on his desktop. The monitor was a big one, and Darwin was glad now he had plunked down the money for the bigger size and higher resolution screen. It made the grainy photos look clearer.

Darwin considered the first of the images: Charlee's tall, slender figure. She wore a traditional apron dress that came down to her ankles. But there were belts strapped around her waist and hips, weighed down with pouches and pockets. And there were two long knife/sword things in her hands. Darwin had never seen anything like them, although ancient weaponry was not his specialty. The most fascinating aspect about the knives—he settled for "knife"—was the expert way Charlee appeared to be holding them. It spoke of practice. Training. She had mentioned that the Einherjar were training her, but she hadn't revealed that the training was with weapons.

In this first photo, she was facing a small man—he was shorter than her by at least four inches. He was quite bald but had complex tattoos on his head. He was staring at Charlee, and Darwin could feel the menace.

The second photo was only a few minutes later. Charlee and the little man again, but this time, there was another woman in the image. The woman was even taller than Charlee, who wasn't short. She wore the leather and metal-plated armor the Einherjar favored, her hair was pinned to the back of her head and the long sword she held made the biceps in her arm flex. She looked strong, and she looked very capable. Darwin was reasonably sure that this was Eira, whom Charlee had spoken of, the leader of the Valkyrie, who resented that she could not be a warrior as she had been when she was human. She was staring at the little man, too, and Darwin shivered. If she had been facing him with that expression and those eyes, he would have turned and run like hell. She looked like she was ready to kill him.

Which must have been exactly what she had done. The images the hacker had cropped had missed the vital moment that must have happened between this photo and the next, for the next photo was Charlee and Eira again. They both stood at the foot of what looked like a puddle of black. It had taken Darwin a moment to put together what it actually was: the little man's clothing, lying on the floor. But where was he if he was not inside his clothing?

The next photo could only have been a few seconds later in the footage. Charlee and Eira had not moved, but they were both looking upwards. Caught in a shaft of light from somewhere overhead was a bird. It looked big and black, and mean, with a long beak....

Something stirred in Darwin's memory. He frowned and moved onto the next picture. Fighting—lots of it. The Alfar and the Einherjar. In the middle of the round room, Darwin spotted Stefan. He knew who he was from CNN broadcasts and online news sites. Stefan was the leader of the Kine, but he looked like he was surrounded and fighting hard to escape. In the background, Darwin could see Asher and a line of Einherjar, standing in front of one of the milky, cloudy doorways that lined the round room. They had to be the portals that everyone was blathering about online. Darwin was fascinated by the mechanics and possibilities of portals, but he put aside that interest. It wasn't pertinent to this current search for answers. He glanced at Asher's face, at the heavy concentration that marked it. His sword was a blur in the image, caught in mid-swing.

Darwin moved on to the next image. Stefan had fallen. There was a tight, dense knot of Alfar—the almost human-looking ones that they called Myrakar—in the place where Stefan had been standing. The Myrakar seemed to be superior to the darker-skinned Blakar, but it had taken dozens of them to take Stefan down.

"Rest in peace," Darwin murmured. He stirred and looked at the next image. There were very few Einherjar left in the room, which was thick with the light and tan Alfar fighters, who were trying to press in upon the portal Asher had been protecting. Asher stood there, shoulder to shoulder with the few Einherjar left, holding the doorway open against the Alfar. So was Charlee, and Eira, who was just stepping through the portal.

There had been many more images after this one, but Darwin had not downloaded them. They were images of more and more Alfar, filling the round room, with no Kine to be seen. The hacker had logged the last of the security footage at about three minutes after this last image Darwin had taken. Then the feed had simply stopped. But one thing Darwin *had* noticed, beyond the clearly jubilant Alfar crawling all over the hall, was that the portals had no longer been milky white. They had all been coal-mine black.

He reconsidered all of the photos again, his gaze flickering over them, moving at random. What was the thought that had nearly surfaced, a few moments ago? Why were these images pulling at him, demanding he pay attention? Quite apart from the fascinating fact that Charlee could fight like an Einherjar? He pushed aside his pride in her, and considered the photos yet again. *What was it?*

The strangest photo in the collection was the one with the bird in it. That just didn't make sense at all. Never mind that portals and elves and magic had been the stuff of fantasy for most humans, a couple of years ago. The bird thing didn't fit in with what he knew of the Kine, and all modesty aside, he was probably one of the top ten experts on the Kine these days.

So what was it about the bird? He studied the image again. Looked at the wings, the way they flapped. The elongated beak. The shape of the head. The pure black of the wings. It looked like a crow, or....

Darwin jerked forward, his breath bellowing out in shock. He straightened up on the chair so fast that the wheels nudged backwards under the impetus of his shifting weight, and he grabbed at the edge of the desk to hold himself in place. He stared, but not at the photo. His mind was racing, coupling up facts.

"Fuck me standing...." He whispered it and his lips felt numb. Rubbery. He pressed the back of his hand against them, unable to look away from the photo.

Then he shook his head, trying to clear it, and grabbed the mouse, and clicked through his files until he found what he was looking for. Word opened up and the document displayed.

Ouerþrowe þe sayntful kynge and mercyful queene

Þe rauyn kynge shell

To bringe withine þe kynge ou kynges wyþ þe markd blowan

To face þe raþ ou þe worldes.

Underneath it was the modern English translation.

Topple the saintly king and merciful queen,
The raven king shall.
To usher in the king of kings with the branded bloom,
To face the wrath of the worlds.

He looked at it, marvelling. "She was right all along," he said to himself. Saintly king...St. Stephen. Stefan. Charlee had pointed out that connection, months and months ago.

He shrank the window so that the photos were showing underneath it and looked at the bird picture once more. "The Raven King," he pronounced.

He reached out for his cellphone, moving slowly, feeling stiff and achy, like he'd done ten rounds with Muhammad Ali. He thumbed out the text, fumbling and having to delete and re-swype. He didn't use acronyms or the peculiar shorthand that long-term texters used, because on this occasion he didn't want her to misunderstand his question.

Hey. Charlee...what is your full name?

It didn't take long for her answer to come back. It *felt* like a long century or two past, while Darwin sat listening to his heart thudding too fast and too loud in his ears. But after a minute, her reply popped up and his phone buzzed in his hand, announcing its arrival.

Charlotte Montgomery... :) ...Y? U didnt no that?

Darwin patiently swyped out his response, trying to steady his heart.

No middle name?

He waited. It was the longest wait of his life, and it lasted all of ten seconds.

Rose. My mom's name. :(

Charlotte Rose Montgomery.

Charlotte Rose.

Darwin rubbed at his neck as his windpipe seemed to close down on him. "Oh god..." he said, but the words all choked up in his tight throat.

* * * * *

Unnur studied the image on the screen, unable to tear her gaze away. The cards had directed her to buy a computer, so she had shelled out hard cash for the best money could buy. Why not? She had more than enough to afford it. Her businesses were booming in a way that was nearly frightening. Penelope, as her new manager, was doing marvelously shepherding them along. Distancing herself from them had not slowed business by one jot or tittle. In fact, business had picked up. That would have made Angelina sniff disdainfully, if she had still been around to see it.

So Unnur had set up the computer with Penelope's help, and the cards had directed her to this place. It was a news site based in New York, and the current news was about the destruction of the Kine hall, right in downtown Manhattan. The article's subtitles blathered about danger to residents and the Mayor's disapproval of the reckless disregard for public safety that had been displayed. But there were plenty of comments from readers stoutly defending the Kine's radical solution to halt the invasion of the Alfar. If they had not blown up their own hall, the Alfar would be streaming into the city right now, enslaving everyone like they had with London....

But it was the photos that accompanied the article that had her attention. They were very good photos—crystal clear and focused. They had been taken by a professional photographer, or at least someone who knew something about photography, anyway, minutes after the explosion. Dust and debris were still settling down over the cars and witnesses in Pearl Street. But the subjects of the photos were the fully armed, dirty and blood-caked Kine who stood in the street looking at what was left of their hall.

The caption underneath identified the woman with the sword and the man with the square chin, who were at the front of the photo.

Eira, Regin and Valkyrie, and Hroar Brynjarson, Einherjar and Earl of the New York Hall, consider their next defensive moves...

Unnur's mouth had curled down when she first read the caption. They were clearly *not* considering defense at all. There was vulnerability in their expressions as they contemplated all they had lost. It was perhaps only a momentary thing, but the photographer had caught the moment. In all her reading online about the Kine and their bravery, their courage in the face of overwhelming odds, their expertise in battle and their ability to bring the Alfar to heel, Unnur had never seen anyone consider the personal cost to the Kine. The loss of their long-lived friends, the loss of home and property, so carefully built around the structure of human communities so as not to disturb them. Now, with the destruction of their halls, they were essentially without a country to call their own, but still the war went on, merciless in its demands.

Roar and Eira were not the only ones in the pictures. There were two other people, standing just behind them. The tall man—the Einherjar—was supporting the woman, a lovely redhead wearing the clothes that Unnur had learned were the Amica uniform. She was human, then.

The man was close enough in appearance to Roar that Unnur guessed he was a relative. She glanced down at her journal and flipped back to the page where she had begun to build a complex tree of Kine names and relationships, and the hierarchy that governed them. She had recorded the brother's name there.

Asher. Called Asher Strand by most, but his real name was Askr. Askr Brynjarson. The son of Brynjar, but not the oldest son. Roar was the first-born. The leader.

Unnur studied the woman again. She didn't know her name, but she knew who she was, and that was why she couldn't pull herself away from the photo. She had enlarged it until it filled most of the screen and studied it. Mostly, she studied the woman's face. The pale scar that ran along her cheek.

Unnur touched her own marked cheek, marveling. They were both branded. She was looking at her Queen of Wands, standing in the arms of the King.

This was the woman Unnur had been talking to. There had been someone to hear her warnings, after all.

Delight filled her.

"Hello," Unnur murmured, smiling at the woman. "It's very nice to meet you, at last."

* * * * *

As the sun set, the senior Einherjar who found themselves marooned in New York trickled into Asher's apartment at the hour he had dictated. There were many of them, for the last defense of the Second Hall had brought many of them rushing to aid the fight, and the only exit had been New York.

They arrived limping, some of them still dirty and many of them hungry, for they had no shelter and no money. Neither did they have human ID that was useful in this country.

Along with them arrived a handful of Amica, the few who had escaped through the portal. Most of the Amica who served the Second Hall were still in Norway.

Charlee found Eira in a quiet moment and pointed this out to her. "We need a kitchen and we need to find the Kine beds. Then we need to think about permanent arrangements for them. Someone will need to speak to the US government about...hell, I'm not even sure what we ask for. Permission to squat in New York while we finish the war?"

Eira shook her head. "I don't have time for this," she said shortly. "This is the end game. Every sword-hand will be needed for the battle ahead. You take care of it, Charlee. Do whatever you need to do."

"Very well," Charlee said, hiding her surprise. She considered the matter for a moment, then fished her phone out of its pouch and dialed. The number was on her speed dial list.

Ylva answered the phone herself, for it was her direct line.

"Ylva, it's Charlee."

There was a momentary pause. "My dear, I've been following your adventures...." Then she let out a little breath. "Never mind. It isn't important. What's wrong, Charlee?"

Charlee laid out her problems. "I need your help, Ylva. You have resources, and we just lost all ours."

"But, Charlee, I'm no longer part of the Kine."

"Yes, you *are!* Ylva, those old artificial divisions are gone. You're as much a part of the Kine as I am, and we need everyone for the battle ahead. Eira says this is the end game. Help us win it."

Ylva hesitated. "Does Eira know what you are asking for, and whom you're asking?"

"Eira will roll with it," Charlee said shortly. Impatiently. "She has more important things to worry about right now."

"I heard about Stefan," Ylva said softly. "Ah well, now Eira can lead as she has always wanted to. There is no time to go through the voting process for a new Annarr."

"And the Einherjar are scattered around the world," Charlee pointed out. "Roar is the most senior Einherjar in New York and this seems to be the new Second Hall...if we had a hall."

"Eira will like that," Ylva murmured.

"Eira is as stunned as the rest of them," Charlee replied gently. "This has hit them hard."

"Yes, I know how it feels to be suddenly without a hall," Ylva said. "Very well. Tell me what your most pressing needs are, Charlee. We'll go from there."

* * * * *

Ylva became Charlee's second-in-command, almost immediately. She arrived at Asher's apartment forty minutes after the last Einherjar had arrived, and she had ten Amica-in-training with her. The women sailed into the apartment carrying heavy bags and backpacks, all wearing traditional apron dresses, and took over the kitchenette and dining table. In ten minutes, a full, very large buffet was spread upon the table, and Roar graciously halted his war council so the Einherjar could fall upon the food and eat like hungry wolves.

While they ate, the women and Ylva moved about the room, dressing wounds and wiping the worst of the grunge from Einherjar flesh. Ylva had thoughtfully acquired dozens of tracksuit pants and sweaters in a variety of sizes, and many of the Einherjar were able to put aside their armor for the first time in days.

Eira kept her armor on over the shirt Asher had lent her. She watched Ylva move around the room in elegant silk pants and a shirt, talking softly to each Einherjar, assessing their needs and arranging for whatever they needed with a quiet word to one of her women. They had not spoken a word to each other, but when Ylva had first arrived, their gazes had met. After a tense moment, Eira had nodded. Ylva gave a stiff smile in return, then turned back to her work.

Later, Eira had pulled Charlee aside. "It was a good idea, bringing her here."

"Thank you."

"Don't let her dominate," Eira said shortly. "You understand the politics of our position. Ylva never did." She gave Charlee no chance to reply, but had returned to the tight group of Einherjar discussing the intricacies of the war effort.

In the next ten days, Charlee used Ylva and her knowledge of New York and Amica traditions to acquire a building in mid-town Manhattan, close to the river. It had been a factory once and the dusty, tall ceilings reminded Charlee of Anja's workshop. The bottom floor of the building was dedicated to the Kine administrative machinery, which evolved around the war effort, rising like yeast. The official red tape involved in negotiating the resident status of the Einherjar stranded in New York would have been enough to keep three legal secretaries busy full time, but the housing, feeding and clothing of over a hundred homeless Einherjar delivered to Charlee a whole different set of administrative problems.

Asher arranged a line of credit with his bank, and she used the power of money to transform the building in a few days. She hired temporary office staff with abandon. Now that humans were aware of the Kine, the security restrictions against hiring human help had dissolved. The new hires were all thrilled to be working for the Kine themselves, and Charlee could have recruited dozens more willing workers if she had needed them.

Ylva's Amica cleaned the building from top to bottom, and the second floor was turned into a dormitory and common room for the homeless Einherjar. More and more of them trickled into New York as they learned where the Regin and acting Annarr were located. They used buses, trains and sometimes hitched to make their way there. Many more contacted Charlee via the Internet, email and phone, in dire straits because they were in a country that was foreign to them, without funds and without contacts to help them get back home. Charlee directed each of them to New York, wiring money and arranging for them to pass through international borders without issue. Each of the homeless had to be processed and fed and a bed found for them.

Not all of them could be housed in the building. More accommodation was found in the homes of the Einherjar who had always lived in the city, including Asher's apartment and Ylva's house. Charlee knew she would have to find more permanent solutions for the Einherjar, but put it aside in the face of more pressing problems.

The top floor of the building, Charlee turned into the Second Hall. She hired carpenters, who were given a bonus for fast work when they built a dais at the south end of the floor where the weak winter sunlight fell through skylights and completed it inside a day.

Then she approached Eira. "Could I borrow your sword for a moment?" she asked.

Eira frowned. "What are you up to?"

"Come with me and see." Charlee held out her hand.

Eira pulled her sword out of her belt and handed it over. It was surprisingly heavy, and Charlee hoisted it in both hands as she led Eira up the stairs to the top floor. As they passed Roar on the second floor, Eira beckoned. "She's planning something, I think."

"Charlee? She would never be sneaky." He laughed and fell into step with them.

Asher was waiting on the top floor, along with all the Einherjar who lived in the building and anyone who happened to be visiting, including dozens of Amica, and Ylva. They parted, moving back along the walls, leaving a path to the dais clear.

Charlee held out the sword to Eira. "There are pegs for this, over the dais. I think that's where it belongs for now."

Eira's frown seemed to deepen. Then her face smoothed out and she took the sword not by the hilt, but with both hands, completing the little ceremony with a nod. "I think you're right," she said, her voice thick. She turned and walked slowly along the space made by the assembled Einherjar, up to the dais, then stepped up and raised the sword over her head and rested it on the pegs the carpenters had driven into the studs at Charlee's request.

Eira stepped back, then turned to face the hall. She beckoned to

Roar.

After a moment, he blew out a slow breath, then walked silently to the dais and stepped up beside her.

Abruptly, everyone in the room began to cheer and clap. They pounded each other's backs. They hugged. They were laughing and smiling and not a few of them were crying.

Asher picked up Charlee's hand and squeezed it. "They needed this," he said softly. "We were leaderless until this moment. You've changed that."

"I just gave them a home once more," Charlee said.

He shook his head. "You gave them hope." Then he dropped her hand and walked back to the dais to take up his position as stallari at the foot of it. Roar caught her gaze and touched his fingers to his lips, in a silent 'thank you'.

Asher saw the gesture and his expression grew stony.

Charlee slipped out of the hall and let them celebrate. She alone of everyone in the hall had no hope at all.

Chapter Thirty-Nine

The Jotnar
Their World: Jotunheim. Singular:
Jotun. Plural: Jotnar. Mythologized as
Rock Giants and Frost Giants, but are
occupants of one of the Nine Worlds.
The Jötnar are an ancient race, being the
first beings created, they carry wisdom
from bygone times. comparable levels
of ability between this ancient race and
the gods. The primary race are the
Valdar. The secondary race, the Megin,
have disappeared from the Nine
Worlds. Their fate is unknown.

——

From *The Complete Kine Encyclopedia*, by
Darwin Baxter, PhD. 2019 Edition

For nearly a month, the Alfar stayed within their newly acquired hall in Oslo, not venturing out to sweep up the humans still in the city. The Norwegians reported that a shield had been built around Tryvannshøyden, but no Alfar had emerged beyond the shield.

Around the globe, all fighting ceased. The Alfar seemed to be busy with their own concerns, and humans were busy licking their wounds and dealing with the Kine, who had been thrust upon their cities and had to be accommodated or otherwise dealt with.

The Kine used the lull to regroup and strategize.

Charlee used the lull to consolidate the Kine in New York and make sure they never for a moment forgot who they were. She worked harder than she had ever worked in her life. She got very little sleep, snatching catnaps on the fold-up bed that someone had found for her that she kept leaning up against the wall behind the desk she used in the corner of the first floor.

Charlee reinstituted morning training, coaxing Asher as the resident stallari to lead the morning devotions to strength in mind and body, peace of heart and renewal. Even if she had not yet been to bed, she joined the Einherjar in the hall for morning training, and she made sure the Amica were also included.

After the first week of the training, Ylva began to attend, too. She would arrive at dawn in yoga pants and a ratty Harvard sweater, to work as hard as anyone else in the room. Eira said nothing about Ylva training with them, but a few days later, she told Charlee to take care of finding

Ylva a suitable weapon to train with, in a curt 'do as I say' tone.

Three days after they had settled into the new Second Hall, a visitor arrived at the front gates, demanding to speak to the Annarr and Regin. The two Einherjar on duty at the gate phoned Charlee to warn her. "If it's who I think it is," Jarl said, "we'd better let him in right quick, and Eira and Roar should be on the dais in full gear when he gets there."

The Einherjar rarely paid much attention to rank and privilege. They had grown accustomed to an absence of gods and voted their leaders from among themselves. It took real authority for them to straighten up and tug their forelocks, even if only in a symbolic way, so Charlee trusted that Jarl was quite serious. "Give me five minutes," she said.

"I'll do what I can, but he's a testy bugger." Jarl's long-time residence in England showed in his speech and his idiom. But he was a competent Einherjar, and Asher gave him a lot of responsibility. It was the other reason Charlee believed him without question.

She bounded up from her desk. "Olivia! Broadcast text to everyone. To the hall!"

"When?" Olivia asked, pulling her cellphone out of the pocket of her apron dress.

"Five minutes ago!" Charlee called as she broke into a run, heading for the upper floors to find Roar and Eira.

Remarkably, Roar and Eira both stood up as soon as she asked and hurried to their cramped quarters to dress presentably and traditionally. Five minutes later, as Jarl escorted the mysterious visitor up to the hall, they both arrived somewhat breathless upon the dais, while everyone else in the building gathered on the old wooden floor below. Eira was wearing the traditional apron dress, which she plucked at distastefully, while Roar straightened up his battle-worn armor.

When Jarl arrived with his guest at the top of the stairs, everyone seemed to exclaim under their breath. Charlee stood well to one side of the dais and couldn't see through the heads of the assembled Kine, but the muttering sounded like the Kine had recognized their visitor.

Then she saw him. He was a freakishly tall man, at least seven feet, and he wore a black coat that swung about his ankles, with big sleeves and fold-back cuffs, and a big collar that was turned up against the cold outside. The collar hid much of his face, but none of the thick, wavy black hair that spilled down the back of the coat.

Eira's mouth opened, then shut again quickly as she studied the newcomer. Her sword hand settled on her hip, even though her sword was bracketed on the wall behind her.

Roar crossed his arms and spread his legs. It was a defensive posture, one she had never seen him take before. She glanced at Asher, where he stood in the stallari's position just at the bottom of the dais, to check his reaction. Asher was watching her and as her gaze settled on him, he raised his brow and blew out his breath silently. She understood. This was a very unexpected visitor.

The visitor looked human, except for his great height, and he wore human clothes, yet there was a presence to him that drew her attention and pinned it upon him, as if he were silently commanding she look only at him. As he drew closer to the dais, she finally saw his face and she was startled. His eyes did not seem human at all. They were blue. Not a brilliant, painted blue like Asher's, but almost a neon blue. It was as if the blue of a cloudless summer sky had been captured just as it darkened toward sunset. The ageless depth of such a sky had been perfectly caught in his eyes. It was a very unnatural color.

His cheeks were thin, with high cheekbones that seemed stark and sharp. Beneath, his face was disguised under a matted beard. Not a long beard—it looked like it had been trimmed somewhat recently, but the impression that the clothes and eyes and beard, and the carriage of the man gave Charlee reminded her vaguely of fantasy movie wizards and magic.

Well, they were living those times now. Perhaps there was a reason he reminded her of them.

Then he looked at her. It wasn't as if his gaze wandered around the room and happened upon her. He turned his head sharply to look at her as if he had become abruptly aware of her presence. His gaze met hers and Charlee felt hot and shivery, like an invisible sun lamp had been turned on her.

His eyes narrowed just a little. Then he turned his gaze back upon the two Kine on the dais, and the heated sensation disappeared. Charlee wrapped her arms around herself, suddenly cold.

The man halted at the foot of the dais. He did not have to crane his neck to look up at Roar and Eira, for he was only a little shorter than them despite the platform they stood upon. Jarl stayed by his side, looking very short next to him.

"Annarr. Regin." The man's voice was deep, one of the deepest baritones Charlee had ever heard. The sound seemed to rumble around the room, and she had no trouble hearing him at all.

"Verlan Seeker," Roar replied. "You honor us with your presence. Why do the Jotnar seek us out at this time?"

Jotnar. Charlee focused on the name, recalling her earliest lessons when she was newly appointed to the Second Hall. The Jotnar were one of the most ancient species still in existence. Their world, Jotunheim, was closed to anyone but the Jotnar. They were powerful, and they focused

471

upon building and increasing their power.

"They are what you would call a wizard," Eira had told her. "They cultivate the auras and the power found in all living things. Of the two races of Jotnar, the Megin are all gone and there are some who think that is a good thing. They were almost invincible, and I suspect the gods did not like the Megin having that much power and dealt with them. The Valdar are all that remains. They are the weaker race—and the shorter one —but I would never want one of them angry at me."

No wonder Charlee had thought of fantasy movies. This man, this Valdar, was essentially a wizard. Had he put that thought into her mind? Was he able to see what she was thinking? He had looked at her in such an odd way!

"We have been watching from afar since the bivrost was restored," Verlan said. "You and yours are running out of time, Einherjar."

Roar didn't react to what sounded like a dire prediction. "Are you offering your assistance, Verlan? Are the Valdar siding with us?"

Verlan considered Roar with a small smile. "We do not take sides. You know that. But we would prefer that Renmar and his kind gather no more power and territory. He is far too ambitious, and such ambition should be curbed soon and early."

"You could not have stepped in to curb his ambition sooner than this?" Roar asked. "Could you not have arrived before we found ourselves landless, leaderless and scattered around the world?"

Verlan Seeker did not seem put out by the complaint. His amusement seemed to grow. "You flail about, telling each other how helpless you are, but lo! Before me is a leader, no?" He turned on his heels, a full circle, and with his hands indicated the hall and the Kine standing in it. "Is this not territory you have claimed as your own land?"

Then he faced Roar once more and dropped his hands. "Are you not gathering your strays into your fold?" And he glanced once more at Charlee—a hot, dazzling glance.

"The portals are lost to us," Roar pointed out.

"You have destroyed some of them, yes," Verlan Seeker agreed. "But the lost can always be found again."

Riddles, Charlee thought. *They like to sound mysterious.* Or perhaps the Valdar always thought and spoke in metaphors and aphorisms.

"Why does our time grow short?" Roar demanded, and Charlee knew he had grown tired of the double-speak, too.

"The Alfar will come for you," Verlan intoned.

Roar began to roll his eyes, before he caught himself and squared off his shoulders again. "And you think an Alfar venture will be a surprise to us?" His tone was respectful.

"They sense you are weak and failing. Renmar knows he has struck a blow. He will drive the wedge deeper and deeper, until your world falls apart around it."

"Renmar underestimates us," Eira said, stepping forward so that she was level with Roar.

Verlan bowed his head slightly in her direction. "Praefectus Castrorum," he said. "It has been a long while indeed, has it not?" *Praefectus Castrorum* had been the rank Eira held in the Roman Legions, one of the highest a low-born centurion could aspire to.

Eira nodded stiffly, acknowledging the title.

"Why has Renmar underestimated you?" Verlan asked curiously.

"We are stronger than he believes, and he had discounted one of our major advantages."

Verlan waited in silence for her to explain.

Eira looked at Asher. He stirred and spoke. "We do not merely fight *for* humans. We fight *with* them. It is a fact that Renmar cannot wrap his head around."

Eira raised her brow. "We have learned much in our time here on Midgard, Verlan Seeker. And my title is Regin, not Praefectus Castrorum."

Charlee could see that the Einherjar in the hall liked her response. There was a sense of resentment building in the hall. They did not like Verlan's disdain, or his assumption that they would fail without Valdar help. The newly minted sense of identity and belonging that had been building in the hall the last few days was in danger of evaporating, the longer they stood and listened to Verlan speak of doom and time running out.

Charlee stepped forward, toward the edge of the dais, on the opposite corner from Asher's ranked position.

Eira glanced at her. "Yes, Charlee?"

"Perhaps Verlan Seeker would feel more comfortable speaking to you in private. There is coffee brewing in the kitchen—" From the corner of her eye, she saw Olivia slip out the hall door, to run to prepare coffee. "—and I believe there is some fresh kornbröd cooling, and I just acquired a jar of raw honey."

Eira just barely prevented herself from wincing, for she did not like the traditional flat cornbread. She was much happier eating wheat bread fresh out of the oven and dipped in olive oil. "An admirable suggestion," she said. "Verlan Seeker, will you join us?"

Verlan nodded his head once more, but he made the movement look less like a man acknowledging someone of higher rank, and more like a nobleman bestowing a favor.

Perhaps he was just that. Charlee itched to pull Asher to one side, or

Ylva, and drain them of any information they had about this Verlan Seeker, and the Valdar.

But as Roar and Eira reached the door, with Verlan Seeker in tow, Eira looked back over her shoulder. "Charlee. Asher." The movement of her head told Charlee she wanted them both to join them.

Charlee suppressed her sigh. Fact-finding would have to wait.

* * * * *

Ylva and the Amica had claimed one corner of the second-floor dormitory, the corner that had working water pipes running through the walls. They had turned the corner into a working kitchen, complete with gas ranges, two heavy wooden work tables, pantries and two big commercial refrigerators. Most of the meals came from this kitchen, and it was possible to beg a bowl of hot soup from the Amica working there at any hour of the day or night. As a result, benches and stools, makeshift tables and odd chairs recovered from places Charlee didn't want to know about had found their way to the kitchen area, and off-duty Einherjar could most often be found at the tables, chatting and teasing the Amica on duty in the kitchen.

Charlee hadn't made it generally known, yet, but she had reserved most of her domestic budget to buy more formal benches and tables for the hall, upstairs. When the winter solstice arrived, she would surprise everyone with a feast in the hall.

Eira led Verlan Seeker to the biggest table in the motley collection and stood back as he seated himself. He dwarfed the table, but settled himself comfortably on the chair at the head of it.

Eira and Roar sat on either side of him. Asher sat at the opposite end.

Charlee moved into the kitchen proper and helped Olivia with the coffee, laying out spoons, plates, the jar of honey, and the bread while she listened carefully to the conversation around the table.

"How is it you haven't been noticed before now?" Asher asked curiously. "New York has some strange people in it, but you would stand out even here."

Verlan smiled—it was a predatory expression. "I tell people I am a professional wrestler. They do not seem to find that unbelievable."

"So you've explored television," Roar murmured. "Just how long have you been monitoring us, did you say?"

"We are fast learners, unlike the Alfar." Verlan's smile faded. "But even the Alfar can learn. They have discovered your Internet and they are learning how it works. The Myrakar are far smarter than you have supposed."

474

Eira sat back with a sigh. "They're adapting," she said softly. She glanced at Roar. "We'll have to let them know the Internet is no longer secure."

Roar looked up at Charlee as she placed a mug of coffee in front of him, and smiled his thanks. Then he looked back at Verlan. "May I speak plainly, Verlan Seeker?"

"You have not, until now?" He seemed surprised.

Roar did roll his eyes this time. "I am not one of the Valdar, but I *do* know what your last name means among your kind. You're dispossessed. Outlawed by your own people. Why would we believe that you offer us aid?"

Verlan did not seem upset at the probing and blunt question. He poured honey onto his oatcake and rolled it tightly, his big fingers moving delicately. "These are very strange times we have lived to see, are they not? An Einherjar that was merely an earl a few days ago is now the Kine's Annarr. Even stranger, he takes orders from the Regin, whom he once slew upon the fields of Germanicus. Humans, who long ago forgot that we ever existed, except in their fairy tales, now are your allies in battle and one of your last sources of strength. The bivrost, which should never have been restored, is rebuilt by a Valravn in love with a Valkyrie, to prove his worthiness. And the Valdar have emerged from seclusion upon their world, to steer the Alfar back to their own affairs. Is it not so very strange, then, that they would turn to one of those among them known for his yearning for outside adventures, one who has never ceased to roam in search of answers, and ask him to deal with humans and Herleifr and matters that they have chosen to ignore and now have little knowledge of?"

He pushed the entire oatcake into his mouth and chewed with obvious relish.

Roar smiled. "And I thought they'd picked you because you had power we could use."

Olivia was refilling the coffee pot, holding the big, heavy kettle in both hands, while Charlee laid out more oatcakes. She felt, rather than actually saw, Verlan's glance in their direction.

Then Olivia swung around, the kettle still pouring sizzling water. She gasped as she swiveled, her eyes enormous.

Charlee tried to move her hands out of the way, but they were anchored over the plate as firmly as if someone had grabbed both her wrists and was hanging on. She shrieked in alarm as the water poured over the back of her hands.

But it never touched her flesh. She could feel the heat of the scalding liquid, just above her skin. She watched in disbelief as the water roiled and splashed above her, as if it were being poured into an invisible bowl held over her hands. Then it calmed, as the kettle emptied. She watched as the water lifted out of the bowl in a long, silvery stream. Olivia swung back to face the worktable and put the kettle down. Then she stepped back, staring at the kettle like it had grown a head and fangs and was spitting at her.

The water flowed silently back into the kettle, making a soft tinkling sound as it hit the metal at the bottom. The room was so silent Charlee could hear every bubble and gurgle.

Her hands were released. She half-fell and half-stepped back, and examined the backs of them. They were untouched.

Verlan smiled. "It's possible I may be of some use."

Asher's face tightened in a way that Charlee recognized. He was angry and hiding it. "We need armies. Weapons. One disgraced Valdar is not what I define as coming to our aid."

"You do not yet know what your future needs will be, do you?" Verlan asked, cheerfully rolling another oatcake.

"Do you?" Roar said sharply, asking the question that had risen to Charlee's lips, too.

Verlan stuffed the oatcake into his mouth and chewed leisurely. Then he swallowed and licked his lips and reached for the fresh stack Charlee had put on the table. "Unlike you, Einherjar, the Valdar have not forgotten the past."

"As cryptic as anything else he professes to know that we do not," Eira said. She sounded just as annoyed as Roar.

"Which particular part of the past?" Asher asked curiously. His attention had been caught.

For once, Charlee knew exactly what Verlan was saying. "The Vanir," she said. "He's talking about the Vanir and their prophecies."

Verlan put the fingers of one hand to his chest and lowered his head briefly in her direction. Acknowledgment.

Asher was frowning, thinking it through. "The prophecies were known to us, too," he said slowly. "They were written down, the first century we arrived on Midgard, to preserve them. We didn't forget them."

Verlan finished chewing his fourth oatcake. "There is much the Herleifr have abandoned, forgotten and lost, in the years since your Descent."

"But you did not?" Asher questioned. "Is there a particular prophecy that you hold in mind?"

Verlan shook his head. "We have long studied the prophecies the Vanir left behind when they departed. They are as inscrutable to us as they are to you, but we hold them in respect, nevertheless, for they have a tendency to live out their promises when you not at all ready for them."

For the first time, Charlee knew that Verlan Seeker had flat out lied. He had avoided blunt talk and spoken in obscurities, used misdirection and drama—like the water thing—to hide his agenda, but she sensed that he had not lied once, not until this moment.

She thought of the night, years ago, when Darwin had shown her the Nine Worlds Prophecy. Was that the one that Verlan was thinking of when he said that the Kine had forgotten their past and that was why they did not know their future? Or was there another prophecy, one just as dire as the Nine World Prophecy, that she didn't know about, but Verlan and his Valdar did?

Once more, Charlee wanted to get Asher, Roar, or Eira on their own, but this time not to learn more about the Valdar. Instead, she felt a great need to warn them.

* * * * *

Verlan Seeker took up residence in the hall, settling in like any errant Einherjar might have. He spent a great deal of time lying on the extra-long bed they had found for him, his boots crossed at the ankles and his hands behind his head, staring up at the ceiling. Thinking, he said. The Valdar did not sleep, Eira pointed out. But they did wander down mental by-ways while their bodies rested, and Verlan would practice his version of sleeping for hours at a time, his gaze turned inwards, the great blue eyes vacant and open.

He also ate like a draft horse, shoveling platefuls of whatever was cooking into his mouth, a spoon held in his fist. He sometimes ate right out of the pot on the stove. Burning his mouth didn't seem to be of concern to him, and Charlee thought of the way he had handled the boiling water with his powers, shrugging it off as part of his mysterious charm. But his appetite created a more immediate and very human problem.

By the second day of his stay, the Amica working in the kitchen reported to Charlee that the pantries were running out of stock. They were out of fresh vegetables, and the oats they used to grind and bake fresh oatbread were nearly out.

"I got in tons of the stuff, barely two weeks ago," Charlee protested, staring at them in disbelief. "Where did it all go?"

They looked at each other.

"The Valdar," Charlee guessed. She got to her feet and pulled her coat off the hook on the wall. "Find Olivia for me and if Ylva is in the building, I want to see her. Today just became market day."

Ylva promised to supply all her garden and pantries could spare, which was a considerable amount and took care of most of their supply needs. Charlee and Olivia walked to the indoor farmers' market to purchase the rest, hurrying along with their coats to their chins, for the day was bitterly cold.

The market was open year round, although at this time of the year, most of the produce available was imported, and there was little of that, for everything was freighted in by air these days. Shipping had halted abruptly and completely after the first wave of Kraken attacks.

Charlee fumed about the prices as they shopped. "Most of the produce was supposed to be for the solstice feast next week," she grumbled as she paid the extra for delivery to the door.

"There'll be a feast?" Olivia asked, her eyes widening. "I didn't hear anything."

"It's a surprise—well, it's supposed to be, but with Verlan Seeker eating anything that doesn't have a pulse, I may have to announce it early, just so I can put a guard on the food and keep him out of it until the solstice."

Olivia's eyes were shining. "I love feasts."

"Doesn't everyone?" Charlee asked dryly, thinking of two or three disastrous feasts in her past. Then she relented, and handed Olivia the money she had been handed back in change. "Go and get yourself something. Have some fun. We'll be back to working our butts off all too soon. I'll see you back at the hall."

"Really? Thank you." Olivia tucked the money in her coat pocket and hurried away.

Charlee wished she could be so easily distracted and made happy. She watched Olivia slow down and bend over a stall selling pretty soaps and candles and sighed.

There was a man coming toward her, carrying a Starbucks cup with a lid in his gloved hand. He was looking at the stalls he was walking past, his head turned away from her. Charlee realized he was going to walk right into her if she didn't hop out of the way, but by then it was too late, for he was walking faster than she had realized. He cannoned into her, and the coffee went flying to splatter on the concrete.

Charlee nearly followed the coffee. She reached out for the nearest stall table, staggering backwards and trying to recover her balance.

The man lurched forward, too. But instead of trying to steady himself, he took another deliberate step forward, not falling, but using the momentum to bring himself closer. Then he whipped his arm around Charlee's waist and held her up as her feet went out from underneath her.

Charlee clutched at his arm, feeling wiry strength through the coat sleeve, while her heart settled and returned to normal. She swallowed, her mouth suddenly quite dry.

He was looking down at her, watching her recovery. "My fault," he said, and his accent was very strong, and nothing that Charlee recognized. "I was not looking." He gave her a very broad smile, showing white teeth that were charmingly crooked.

"You stopped me from falling on my ass, so you're forgiven."

He frowned a little. "Ass?" he repeated and helped her stand up.

Charlee swallowed her little laugh. Smiling, she turned her hips and pointed to her butt. "Ass," she said gravely.

"Ah!" He grinned, delighted. "Very good. I learn another word."

"It's not a word you can use in general company," she warned him. When he looked like he wasn't following, she added, "Some people think it is a rude word."

He laughed again. It was an odd-sounding laugh—sort of a wheezy bellow—but it was an interesting sound and it made Charlee smile. "It is a good word for that." He pointed to his own butt. Then he bent and picked up the Starbucks cup and the separated lid from the middle of the puddle of steaming mocha. She could smell the chocolate in it.

"Hey, let me buy you a replacement coffee," she said. "I owe you that much."

He held up the cup. "Another...one?"

"Yes."

"It would be very well."

"It would be good. Or great," she corrected him. "Well is for when you aren't. When you are sick. Or not sick." She knew she was confusing him with her contradictions so she shrugged. "Coffee?" she asked, pointing to where the Starbucks stall was located.

"Very good," he said and smiled.

* * * * *

His name was Niko, and he had only just arrived in New York, which he confided like that would be news to her, as if his strong accent and weak English hadn't given him away. He was from Latvia, a little province in the north, where it stayed dark all winter. Charlee looked out the window they were sitting next to, at the pedestrians hurrying along hunched over in the cold. This probably felt like spring-time to someone from such a place. No wonder he was in such a good mood. Being happy seemed to be the only emotion Niko was capable of expressing. Sometimes his smile faded, but it wasn't replaced by anything. He didn't frown and didn't lose the happy, sunny disposition, even when he wasn't smiling.

He had black, short but extremely curly hair, and pale white flesh, which fit with Latvia. His eyes were also very black, but enormous in his thin face. They made him look more lost and vulnerable than he already sounded with his thick accent and comic twists of English.

He chattered about the apartment he had found, and from the description, Charlee figured he had rented an efficiency apartment, which he thought was just heavenly, for the bed was soft and the water was hot.

Niko had arrived to start a job he had been offered, but the job hadn't worked out. Now he was looking for another one. He didn't seem to be dismayed by the idea of finding a job in a city where he didn't know the language very well, and that was generally considered to be one of the most expensive cities on the face of the earth.

Charlee sat back and let him talk, sometimes correcting his English, but not always. It was relaxing to not have to do anything but listen, and the sun was nice and warm where it shone through the windows. She turned her face up to it.

Asher was standing across the street, watching her.

Charlee bounced to her feet, knocking the little table into a skittering dance, and making Niko grab for his cup, which was empty, thank heavens. Charlee settled the table and held it steady. "I have to go," she told him. "I'm sorry."

"But Charlee..." He got to his feet, bewildered. "So quickly?"

"Sorry," she repeated, doing up the buttons on her coat.

Niko's smile faded. "You buy coffee again. Tomorrow? With me?"

Charlee glanced out the window again. Asher was still there. Her heart squeezed. "I don't know, Niko. It's not a very good time right now."

He caught her glance out the window and looked out himself. "I see," he said quietly.

She bit her lip. How to explain Asher? Even she didn't understand it. "It's complicated," she told Niko, and wanted to laugh hysterically at the wildly ironic cliché. Instead, she gave him a stiff smile. "'Bye, Niko." She hurried away, heading for the doors out onto the street.

"Thank you, Charlee!" Niko called after her.

* * * * *

"You're following me?" Charlee accused Asher as soon as she reached him.

Asher pulled his hands out of his coat pockets. "You sent Olivia back to the hall. I wasn't going to let you wander around New York on your own."

"I've been doing that for years and years," she told him curtly.

"You're Amica now," Asher said flatly. "You think you aren't a target, Charlee? You think your name isn't on some list somewhere, as a person of influence in the Kine hierarchy?"

"I'm nobody. I wash dishes and clean halls."

"Don't be so modest," Asher replied, his voice low. "You have Roar wrapped around your little finger. Eira thinks you walk on water, and the entire Einherjar complement in the hall thinks so, too."

She shrugged. "Then tell me the angry expression you were wearing while you watched me through the window had nothing to do with Niko."

"That's his name?" Asher took a few steps in silence, then snorted. "It suits him. A stiff breeze could blow him away."

"He's as tall as you," Charlee said defensively.

Asher smiled wisely. "If I stepped into the ring with him, who would you put your money on?"

Charlee gave up. "It was just coffee. I spilled his, so I bought him another one."

"You looked like you were bored out of your brain."

"He's lonely. He has no one to talk to, I think." She stopped herself from adding the other half of that thought. *Lonely, like I feel so often.*

But Asher must have seen something in her face or her eyes, because he turned to face her, making her halt in the middle of the sidewalk. Pedestrians were forced to step around them, but he didn't seem to care. "Charlee...."

She shook her head. "You said it all, that morning in my room. We don't have to go over it again."

His gaze drilled into her. "Do you know how much I sometimes wish we had run away, that day? Gone to live on a deserted island somewhere?"

"The house with the picket fence?" She could barely breathe. The cold biting into her face and hands, the people all around them, the traffic that always sounded so much louder on the streets in winter, it all faded away. It was just Asher standing in front of her, and he was baring his soul.

"The house with the picket fence," he agreed.

"But the war...the Alfar..." She bit her lip. "You would have hated yourself, if we had run away. You would have resented me for taking you away from the Kine."

He didn't answer for a long time, but just looked at her steadily. "You're right," he agreed at last. "I want to believe I wouldn't be that ungrateful, but I couldn't live with the guilt if I wasn't here, now, doing what I'm doing. But I lie awake at night, Charlee, and I wonder if the price I'm paying for not feeling guilty is too high."

Tears pricked her eyes. "I love you," she whispered. "I *always* will, no matter what."

Asher's blue eyes were steady. Bleak. "You should leave the hall," he said at last.

Charlee's lips parted in surprise. She couldn't think of what to say.

"*You* can leave," Asher pressed. "You have that choice." He pushed his hand through his hair. "You can see how it's going with us, just as I can. Probably better—you were always smarter than me. You could find somewhere safe. Australia. Bora Bora. Some sleepy little island that lives thirty years behind the times. Take off and settle down somewhere like that before it's too late."

Charlee tried to smile. "If the Kine fall, *nowhere* will be safe."

Asher blew out his breath, frustrated. "You're unhappy, Charlee. You hide it well, but I can see it. If you weren't here, if you were safe, even if it's for a while…if you're not in my world, then you'll be happier."

Her heart was thumping unsteadily. Unhappily. Charlee tried to smile again, and this time it emerged—weak, but it was there. "I've made my choice, Asher. I would rather be unhappy in your world than unhappy anywhere else."

Asher began to speak. Twice. But in the end, he just picked up her hand and pushed it into his coat pocket, his fingers curling around hers. They stayed that way all the way back to the hall. He didn't even remove her hand when they walked past the guards, who looked away and pretended they had seen nothing.

Inside once more, Charlee slowly took off her coat. She was exhausted and it wasn't even noon yet.

Asher caught her face in his hands, making her breath stall. She yearned for him to kiss her but knew he would not.

He gave her a small, sideways grin. "At the very least, Charlee, you're never bored out of your brain with me."

Then he let her go.

Chapter Forty

For Sale

Lofts for sale, NYC. Genuine
langhause style. Central gas firepit.
Call today. 555-0876.

A week later, just as the activity in the hall reached a crescendo in preparation for the solstice feast, Lucas came home on Christmas leave. Charlee texted him back, standing in the kitchen with sweat on her brow and her sleeves rolled up well past her elbows. The smell of rich meat dishes and sweetmeats was thick in the air.

I can spare an hour this afternoon. It's the solstice, feast tonight. Central Park?

2 pm was Lucas' response. *Bring asher if he is in town*

Charlee sighed and got back to work. Since their conversation on the way home from the market, Asher had been scrupulously avoiding her. It seemed like he was always on duty or busy with something, but no one could be so busy and distracted, even someone carrying the responsibilities that Asher did.

It would have been simple enough to send him a text, or even forward Lucas' text, but Charlee wanted to speak to him face-to-face, to tell him he didn't have to avoid her anymore. He could come with her to say hello to Lucas.

But she didn't see Asher at all and so when one-thirty arrived, she got ready to head out to the park. She left early. The kitchen had been so hot and humid that the thought of walking through the crisp December air, among the trees, seemed delightful in comparison. She wanted to wander the paths for a while on her own. It would give her a chance to think, without someone hanging on her arm, asking another impossible-to-answer question.

It *was* cool and crisp, beautifully so. The sky hung low overhead, steel grey with the promise of snow. The forecast was calling for heavy snow tomorrow, so it would be a white Christmas this year. Charlee considered the sky and wondered if the snow would actually wait until tomorrow.

There were a lot of people hurrying along the sidewalks, getting last minute shopping done, but their numbers thinned out once she stepped into Central Park proper. There were only a few people scurrying across its width, following the paths. The grass was white with frost that hadn't melted under the weak light. The sun hadn't appeared at all.

The trees were bare but their branches were so numerous that the bench-lined walkway underneath their intertwined arms seemed darker than the open areas of the park. Charlee slowed her pace, listening to the creak and rub of branches overhead. It was a curious sound. There was wind moving them, high overhead, but the wind wasn't reaching ground level. It made her feel cocooned and safe, and she lingered.

"Charlee."

Charlee whirled, fright thick in her mouth, her heart leaping hard. "Niko!"

He stood only a few paces behind her. He had been incredibly light on his feet. She had heard nothing. He was wearing the same overcoat, his hair was as tousled as before, but he wasn't smiling.

"Were you heading for the market again?" she asked. "How is the job hunting going?"

He drew closer. "Hunting. Hunting goes well."

Uneasiness touched her, keeping her original fright circling, her heart thudding. "Well, that's good," she said lightly. She turned as if she was going to head off again, and took a few steps away from him. It bothered her that he was drawing closer, but she didn't know why.

Niko lengthened his stride, closing the space between them.

This time her fright was hot and energizing. She deliberately side-stepped to see if he would alter his direction and come closer.

He did.

Charlee let out a shaky breath. "Don't come any closer!" she yelled.

He reached for her and Charlee dodged, turned and ran like hell. "Help me!" she screamed, hoping that the normal New Yorker's indifference to people around them would be absent today. It was Christmas, after all. "Help! Help!"

Lucas would be close by now, too. "Lucas!" she screamed. "Help me!"

Niko landed on the back of her shoulders, and Charlee threw out her hands as she measured her length on the asphalt. Her gloves shredded with a low ripping sound and the skin on the palms of her hands stung. So did her knees, but it was her back that hurt the worst.

Niko's weight was resting on her shoulders, holding her down. Charlee lifted her chin. "Help me! Help! Someone help!"

His hand slapped over her mouth, holding it shut with a painful grip. He hauled her to her feet. "*Very* good hunting today," he told her and looked up at the sky, which was little more than grey diamonds and triangles glimpsed through the treetops. "Don't—"and he shifted his shoulders. "Or this will hurt." *Don't struggle*, she interpreted.

Screw that, Charlee thought. She breathed in a full lungful of air through her nose, centering herself. Howard's and even Asher's soft instructions cascaded through her thoughts quickly, and her body automatically followed suit.

She grabbed his wrist, the one over her mouth, and with her other arm, the one he was gripping so tightly, she rammed the heel of her hand up against his elbow. It connected with the solidness of a baseball bat in full swing. It was a perfect blow.

It *should* have worked. But it didn't. He didn't move an inch, and his fingers merely tightened against her. Niko hissed and shook her. "Still," he muttered.

Charlee stared at him. He had inhuman strength. The blow *always* worked—it was one of the most crippling joint attacks she knew.

Inhuman strength.

Charlee looked at Niko more carefully, taking in the odd details she had merely dismissed as foreign, not alien. The extraordinarily large eyes. The pale flesh. The hair that seemed too thick and glossy to be true.

He was an Alfar.

"Hey, asshole!"

Niko looked around and a fist crashed into his face. Instead of falling backwards, he just blinked and hissed. He spoke words that were unintelligible, and Charlee knew she was hearing the native language of the Alfar for the first time. He was holding on to her so tightly she couldn't turn to see who had hit him, but she recognized the voice. Lucas.

With help so close by, Charlee lost all control. She struggled and wriggled, and flailed her arms and stamped her feet. Anything but stand still and wait for the outcome.

"Lucas, step back. Let me have him."

Asher's voice.

Charlee's breath shuddered in gratitude and relief. She didn't know why he was here, and she didn't care.

Niko spun to face the new danger, and Charlee could finally see properly. Lucas was backing off warily and slowly, his fists held tightly at his sides. Asher stood directly in front of Niko, his sword held with the point reaching for the trees, both hands around the hilt. His eyes were flinty, hard and dangerous.

He attacked with a speed Charlee had never seen before, the sword swinging down in a curve that slid past her torso and buried itself deep.

Niko gave a soft sighing sound, but Asher didn't stop there. He stepped forward and grabbed the Alfar's face, his other hand still on the hilt of the sword that was skewering Niko. Niko's grip on Charlee loosened and she shoved herself away, staggering across the walkway, wiping her mouth and moaning.

"Why did you want her?" Asher demanded, his face barely inches from Niko's. He added something in a different language—the Alfar language, Charlee presumed.

Niko's mouth fell open, as his gaze remained on Asher. Charlee had a feeling that he was offering the Alfar version of a smart-ass smile. Then he grabbed Asher's wrists and yanked the sword blade up and across, opening himself up. Blood that was the same red as human blood spurted from his stomach and he crumpled, until he was hanging from Asher's grip.

Asher threw him away with a disgusted sound.

Lucas grabbed Charlee. "Are you okay?"

She nodded, unable to look away from the body on the ground. "He pretended he was human. To trick me. They know us well enough to pass as human." The idea was deeply unsettling.

"He's Myrakar," Asher said. He walked over to the body and wiped his sword on the coat hems, then let it disappear and put the hilt away. "They're the smart ones of the three races. They've had to spend their lives adapting to the Lajos' demands. But this is a new achievement for them. We'll have to warn the others."

Hot air washed over them, dropping down through the trees and with it came a deep, heavy throbbing that seemed to instill itself in Charlee's ears and mind, making her bones ache with the volume and depth of it. She looked up and realized that she was duplicating what Niko had been doing. "Stay still," he had warned her.

Alarm crashed through her relief. "Run!" she screamed at them. "The Alfar are coming!" Her voice was distorted by the sound overhead. It was a heavy strumming, like the sound of a very large engine.

Lucas looked puzzled, but Asher took her at her word. He grabbed her hand and pushed on Lucas' shoulder. "Sprint, Lieutenant!"

They ran.

As they ran, Asher pulled out his cellphone and dialed with his thumb. He raised it to his lips. "Alfar! In the air! Brace for incoming!" Then he tucked the cellphone away and concentrated on moving as fast as he could, which was faster than Lucas and Charlee could run. For a big guy, Asher was very light on his feet.

Even Lucas pulled away from her and Charlee fell slowly behind. They were in the meadow now, and she could see the street and the sidewalk ahead. People on the path scattered before them, or stood to one side and stared at them curiously, trying to understand why they were running so hard.

Charlee had a feeling that the danger didn't lie behind them anymore.

She risked a glanced upwards, into the iron grey sky overhead.

A diamond-shaped platform hung in the air. With her quick glance, Charlee couldn't determine if the platform was very large, or just very low. The air beneath it was distorted, just like the air behind a jet engine would be. The throbbing engine sound came from it, but there was no engine-shaped anything. It was just a steel-colored platform, sleek and aerodynamic.

A homeless man pushing a loaded shopping cart looked at her indignantly as she ran past. "What'ser hurry, sister?" he called.

She pointed upwards and he lifted his head back. So did the people near him, and a woman screamed.

"Alfar!" Charlee called.

Panic exploded across the park, as everyone turned and bolted—most of them heading for the west side, away from the Alfar. Only she and Lucas and Asher seemed to be trying to catch the platform, which was now crossing Fifth Avenue, ahead of even Asher.

Now it was ahead of her, Charlee could see the Alfar standing on top of the platform. There was even a very ordinary-looking chair in the middle of it, with an Alfar seated comfortably. She guessed the one doing the sitting was a Lajos. Even from where she was, the Lajos looked extraordinarily tall.

The hall was seven blocks away, on the south-east side of FDR Drive, close enough to the Queensboro Bridge that if they stepped outside the hall, they could hear cars clunking over the joints in the bridge surface, overhead. Charlee knew she would never be able to run all the way. It was a long, brisk walk as it was. And now that the platform was skimming over Fifth and Park Avenue, New Yorkers were streaming west, escaping. The sidewalk suddenly became clogged with people all moving in the opposite direction to Charlee, a sea of panic that it was almost impossible to swim against.

Asher was out of sight, and Charlee could barely see Lucas ahead of her. He had stepped out onto the street, where so far, no one was running. She copied him, and immediately began to make better time.

The first low booming sound didn't register as anything other than more noise. Then the ground seemed to shiver under her feet and Charlee looked up, alarmed. The platform was hovering and as she looked, a streak of almost invisible light left the platform, leaping for the buildings below. Then came the same muffled booming and the shudder of the earth.

They were firing on the hall. They were right over it.

Charlee came to a halt in the middle of the street. All the vehicles had stopped, too, so there was no danger of being run over. Their drivers were hanging out their windows and looking up, or else they had stepped out of their cars altogether.

Then the throbbing, low bass beat sounded, but this time from behind her. Charlee whirled. Another platform was zooming in from the direction of New Jersey, heading for lower Manhattan. The Alfar on it looked smaller, which told her it was higher up, but it was dropping altitude. As it dropped and arrowed into the downtown area, the same barely seen light shot from the tip of the platform and a more distant booming sounded.

Lucas jogged up to her, his gaze on the platform over Wall Street. He pointed over Charlee's right shoulder. "Three!" he called.

There was another, more distant platform and behind it, smaller still, even more of them.

"We have to get off Manhattan!" Lucas said. "The Lincoln Tunnel."

Charlee turned him so he could see the phalanx of platforms over New Jersey as they headed for Manhattan. "Too late," she told him.

Lucas considered. "The archway bridge tunnel, then," he said and picked up her hand. "C'mon. Back to the park."

She had rested enough to gain back her breath so she let Lucas lead her at a steady jog down the side of the roadway, between the cars and the pedestrians. When they got to the tunnel that would shelter them from the overhead strikes, she would think about what they should do next, and how to get back to the hall. They had phones. They could network and figure out what they should do next.

She and Lucas hurried into the pretty tunnel under the bridge and made themselves comfortable. They weren't the first there, and they wouldn't be the last. Charlee had no way of guessing that this was the beginning of what would be called the Rout of New York, and that they would end up staying in the tunnel for two more days.

That was how long it took New York to fall.

MIDGARD

Chapter Forty-One

There was a shelf on this level that thrust out into the air, so that an Alfar could walk to the edge and look out upon the realm below. Renmar studied the effect. His tower in London did not provide such a viewpoint. He used images that were instantly transferred to his preferred work level instead. But this idea had a simplicity that was appealing.

He stepped out toward the edge of the shelf and felt the cool, thin air that eddied around the towers at this level brush against his face. He looked down.

It was quite easy to see where the shield wall ran, for on the other side, where humans were still free to adjust their environment in the way they did, the roads and buildings were whole once more. Cars moved in the narrow streets, although not many of them dared to come close to the shield.

On the inside of the shield wall, there were few whole buildings. No cars moved and the streets were deserted. Alfar craft floated here and there—patrols that Renmar was quite sure had taken to the air only because of his visit.

Human cities were branded by their control of green spaces, which were limited, but in the three years since the Alfar had won New York for themselves, green had been creeping back in. London was very similar, for the surface of the roads had crumbled without constant human vigilance, and plants had thrust up through the cracks and holes. In a year of growing, the plants had torn the surfaces up even more. After three growing seasons, the city landscape was quite different.

The wreckage their pulse cannons had created when they took New York was softened and disguised by mosses and mold, bushes and small trees that were reclaiming the land and converting it back to what it once had been. Renmar found it calming to see the world taking back what once belonged to it.

Soza hurried into Renmar's presence. "Great one, I apologize for my delay appearing in front of you. Your visit is most unexpected."

"You had a day's warning," Renmar pointed out.

"Yes, but a day is not nearly long enough to make preparations worthy of your visit." Soza belatedly touched his eyes. "But your presence alone makes up for my lack. You grace any event you care to be a part of."

Renmar waved away Soza's gushing. "Your report, Soza."

"Great one." Soza touched his eyes again. "It is very quiet here. There is nothing unusual to report that I have not included in my weekly missives."

"I have read your missives. Lately, they have been missing vital information, which is what brings me here to see for myself."

"Great one?"

Renmar liked the fear he heard in Soza's voice. The doubt. It was useful to keep commanders unbalanced in this way, so that they would question everything before them.

"When I appointed you to control this tower and the humans inside it, I gave you specific ambitions. I stressed how critical they were. Yet for the last seven reports you have failed to address these ambitions."

Soza stared. "The Einherjar and his woman?" he whispered.

"The Einherjar called Asher Strand and the woman we believe is his. You have failed to report progress on my desire to capture this Einherjar. You have omitted any mention of them in your reports. This is a sliding of attention I do not appreciate."

Soza swallowed. "Great one, it is precisely because of a lack of progress on that ambition that it was omitted from the reports. My desire to provide you with what you seek is ever fresh."

"So you have continued to fail to meet my expectations," Renmar interpreted.

Soza's gaze darted around the room before settling back upon Renmar. "I...I have failed you, great one."

Renmar considered him. "Describe your current efforts to find this Asher Strand."

Soza prostrated himself on the floor. "It is as I described in my earlier reports, great one. There is no word of the Einherjar on the streets. My spies hear nothing of him or the woman at all. The others, yes. The Valkyrie and the Einherjar that lead them, we hear of at all turns. They are ever a thorn in our toes. But there is nothing of Askr Brynjarson."

"Hroar and the Valkyrie do not concern me," Renmar pointed out. "They are toothless while they are inside the shield. They can growl as loudly as they wish, it is nothing but noise." He hissed. "You irritate me, with your face placed so. Get to your feet."

Soza scrambled to his feet and bent forward in obeisance. "Great one, after such efficient and concentrated effort, after so many years, perhaps it is time to consider that both the Einherjar and his woman died in the original capture of the city. Our pulse cannons were very effective and the human population so perfectly contained on the central island, it was considerably easier to capture New York than London, but the destruction was widespread."

"Because the humans would not yield," Renmar snapped, his irritation building. "I remember the reports. The Myrakar estimated there were nearly eight million humans living within the borders of the shield, including the island. Even if half of them died in the original capture of the city, that leaves a very large number of humans, and Einherjar disguised as human, still within the shield. How many humans have the Myrakar collected as slaves?"

"They were most efficient, Great one. There were too many slaves for this tower alone. We have given slaves to the other towers and even to help with the running of your own palace, in Oslo."

"How many?" Renmar snapped.

"The last report from the Myrakar put the number at just over one million, great one. They have stopped actively recruiting slaves, as there is simply nowhere to house and feed them, even with minimal rations. The humans are quite weak. Without continual nourishment and several hours of sleep, they grow even less efficient."

"Find fresh slaves and replace the weaker ones," Renmar said. "I should not have to point out such administrative simplicities to you, Soza."

"The Myrakar have researched this method, oh Great one. Their conclusions are simply inarguable. It is cheaper and less troublesome to provide basic resources to the slaves we have already acquired than to find, subdue and train new ones. After a period of adjustment, older slaves are far more compliant. I can show you the research and the analysis, Great one. The economic savings alone are very pleasing."

Renmar considered the matter. "Very well," he said. "I am open to change—it is my reasonableness and ability to adapt that has made this venture to Midgard successful to date. Provide the data to my wife. She will check the findings." He turned away from the shelf and the meditative contemplation of the reclaimed human city below and faced Soza for the first time. "I want my ambitions obeyed, Soza. Renew your efforts to find the Einherjar and his woman. If the Myrakar estimates are evenly loosely accurate, and I agree with you that they are very good at gathering information about the humans, so their estimates are likely correct, then that means there are better than two million humans still inside the shield. I doubt that even when you were fresh and zealous about your work, you scanned more than a tenth of that number."

"Yes, Great one." Soza kept his head close to the ground.

"I know he is still alive," Renmar added. "I want you to find him and bring him to me. I hope I do not have to reinforce my request more than this one occasion."

"No, Great one. But, if you would be so generous as to allow a question?"

Renmar considered the top of Soza's head. The Alfar had been highly effective in bringing the population in the shield under control. There had been very few major outbreaks, despite having caught the Kine's Regin and the new Annarr located within the shield where they could stir up trouble. Renmar didn't underestimate the Valkyrie and Hroar Brynjarson. For one, Eira was a noble warrior, who had led one of the strongest human armies ever assembled. And Hroar was Asher Strand's brother, and would have learned the same battle skills, and would think in similar strategic ways. Both of them together—Hroar and the Valkyrie—were potentially a lethal spearhead at the front of the Kine war machine.

But it was far more critical he find Asher Strand *and* the branded woman. Both of them had to be permanently removed from the battlefield. He would not consider victory over this muddy and violent world his until they were accounted for.

"Do you remember your childhood lessons about the Vanir and their prophecies, Soza?" Renmar asked.

"The fairy tales, Great one? My mamman would relate them to me, to entertain. But…." Despite Soza keeping his head down, Renmar could sense his puzzlement. "They are just stories," he added carefully.

"Ragnarok was real enough," Renmar pointed out. It felt good to be so expansive and generous with his knowledge.

"Well, yes," Soza agreed hesitantly.

"Do you remember the Many Worlds poem?"

Soza was silent for a moment. "I remember," he said at last. "Kings, all losing their heads. A great disaster. It was not about the Alfar," he added stoutly.

Renmar sighed. "They are all about the Alfar," he said stiffly. "Alfheim and Svartalfheim are ours. Midgard is nearly ours. They are all part of the nine worlds, are they not?"

"Yes, Great one."

Again, Renmar sighed. Why had he thought sharing his knowledge was such a pleasant thing? This was like pulling the essence from trees. "Any prophecy that speaks of the nine worlds involves us, and this one speaks of a king of kings, who will win the nine worlds for himself."

Soza lifted his head to look at Renmar, momentarily forgetting himself. "Asher Strand? The *Einherjar*? A former human is to defeat us?" He was offended and rightly so. Renmar realized with a little jolt of pleasure that sharing knowledge had a wisdom he had been unaware of. This was much more effective than merely declaring his ambitions.

"He will not defeat us," Renmar pointed out magnanimously, "if he is no longer alive to lead them."

* * * * *

Charlee stopped weeding long enough to look up at where Fudge sat at the top of the broad steps up to the street level. He hadn't moved and he hadn't made a sound.

"Still clear?" Charlee asked.

Fudge yipped shortly, then returned to scanning the empty shell of the building, the windows, the exits, and the street beyond. Satisfied, Charlee went back to weeding. She looked up at the patch of blue sky overhead and the outer curve of the tower visible from here. The tower blocked the morning sun, but the dazzling hot light that reached down here to the cellar was more than enough to grow two crops each season. The proximity of the tower kept nearly everyone away, so her garden had not been discovered.

Yet.

She had started the garden three years ago, and at the time she had not expected she would ever see a harvest—the Alfar had been merciless in their patrols and roundups, and she figured that sooner or later the garden would be discovered. Then the patrols had slackened and become a once-a-night circle around the tower on arrowheads, but there was always the possibility that it might yet be found. She continued to work on it anyway because the garden had become one of their major sources of food and the all-important medicines of which she was constantly in need.

Either Fudge or Torger kept guard while she worked. Fudge hadn't been out of the home base for a few days, so Charlee had ordered Torger to watch over the house. Fudge was very well trained. Asher had seen to his training, patiently weeding out his bad habits and attitudes, while Torger had kept him in line and obedient with nips and snarls, as necessary.

Torger was incredibly old for a dog. He had lived long beyond a dog's usual life, although in the last year or so he had finally begun to show signs of age. His chops were grey and he moved slowly on cold days, if at all. Charlee had wondered aloud if Torger's long life was linked to Asher's and he had shrugged. "The Amica live longer than usual. Even the Eldre linger on. I suppose a faithful animal might benefit in the same way."

Torger was still the smartest dog Charlee had ever met. A day at home, for him, would be a chance for him to rest. However, only having one dog on watch was risky, so Charlee kept straightening up and checking for herself.

It was such a nice day. It was very easy, down here, to forget about the tower rearing over them, or the occupation that shaped their lives. It was easier to listen to the trickle of the little stream that had been created when the Metropolitan Museum had been destroyed—a pipe or drain, or a cistern had been broached and the water ran across the torn-up earth that was all that was left inside the shell of the museum, cutting from north to south. Charlee would never drink the water because she couldn't find the source, but it was potable enough for the vegetables to thrive.

Fudge growled, low in his throat. It was a warning.

Charlee looked up at him, then ran her gaze along the bombed-out window arches and the big dormers. No shadow fell across them. Nothing appeared to be moving out there, but that could be deceiving, because the tower cast a shadow across front of the building in the morning. It wasn't quite noon yet, but at this time of year the sun would be almost completely overhead.

"What is it, Fudge?" she asked, just as softly as he had growled.

His ears were up and he was scanning the front of the building just as she was, his sharply pointed nose wrinkling.

Charlee waited, watching him. Her bow and quiver were leaning against one of the pillars, half a step away, so she took the step and reached out her hand for the bow, keeping her gaze on Fudge. He would tell her where the danger came from, as long as she watched him.

Fudge stood up, and turned in a circle, almost like he was chasing his tail. Then he stood quivering at the top of the step. He gave a little whine and his tail wagged furiously.

He was looking down at her.

"Fudge?" she asked. He wouldn't leave his post without her permission, but it was clear that if he hadn't been on duty, he would have dived down the steps to where she was.

There was a clink of stone, behind her. Farther along the passage. Charlee snatched up her bow and notched an arrow. She drew the bow, watching where the opening of the passage drilled through the compacted earth that had been behind the cellar walls before they had collapsed. The rubble around the passage mouth had been left in place and weeds hung over the top of it. It wasn't hidden, but it did look abandoned and disused.

The clink sounded again. There was a lot of debris still scattered along the maw of the passage and a good way inside it, from when the wall had collapsed. Charlee drew the bow tighter, holding it steady at just under the full pull she would need to release the arrow cleanly.

"It's me, Charlee." The voice issued from the passage, soft and wary. "Put down the bow."

"Asher!" She dropped the bow and picked up the hem of her skirt and skipped over the rows and mounds and the scattered rubble that framed it, heading for the passage at a speed that wouldn't turn her ankle. "You're a day early!"

He ducked under the weeds and stepped out of the passage, then leaped down to the turned earth, landing just in front of her. The long tails of the overcoat he wore flapped around his ankles. She threw herself into his arms and heard him gasp, even as his arms came around her. He chuckled, pulling her up off her feet, then kissed her thoroughly.

Charlee clung to him, reacquainting herself with his size, his warmth, his scent. "Gods, I missed you!" she murmured against his lips. "A whole week!"

"A lifetime," Asher agreed.

She wriggled out of his arms and patted his hip, where one of the handguns he always carried was clipped to his belt. "Ouch," she told him.

"It's been a week. I've got used to not having women throw themselves against me." As he spoke, he unclipped the gun and thrust it into one of the spacious pockets of the coat. The coat wasn't a heavy one, not at this time of year, but it hid weapons and the hood would hide Asher's face if he needed the camouflage. Being the most wanted people in occupied New York brought challenges that sharply dictated the shape of their day-to-day lives.

Charlee helped him remove the coat, then threw her arms around him again and kissed him. Her enthusiasm wasn't just because she had missed him. Whenever he returned from one of his journeys, a deep relief that she refused to voice aloud would drive her to get as close to him as possible, to inhale his presence and revel that he was here once more, in her life. That he had survived.

Asher didn't lift her up on her feet this time. He was kissing her with a heated impatience that always colored his kisses when he returned. He was grateful to have returned safely, too, and that also remained unspoken.

His impatience blossomed into heated wanting. Charlee's fingers scrabbled at his shirt, impatiently tugging at the buttons. His hands were in her hair, running along the backs of her thighs, cupping her bottom.

Asher lowered her into the soft dirt that smelled of green growing things, that reminded her of life itself, and spread himself over her.

* * * * *

Asher stroked her back, but there was no serious intent behind it. He was doodling, a physical man's form of idling. The sun had moved away from the noon brightness, and shadows were creeping across the cellar. It was growing cold, but Charlee didn't want to move just yet.

She lifted her head off his chest and looked at him directly. "How did it go?" she asked. "Did you have to go very far?"

"Almost to the shield," he said and flexed, stretching himself, and lifting her at the same time. "But let's talk about that at home. I see you've been decorating while I was gone." He shifted his head to look at the section of basement wall that remained. There was twenty feet of it, where concrete daub still clung to the bricks that had made up what must have been the original part of the building. The brick foundations had withstood the Alfar's pulse cannons better than the newer poured concrete walls.

Along the only intact section of concrete rendering was a series of rows and columns, painted with a liter of white satin gloss that Charlee had found in the back of a closet in the wreckage of an apartment building she had been scouting for supplies.

Charlee couldn't meet Asher's gaze.

"Just a moment." Asher sat up, bringing her with him, his hands holding her steady. It was one of those impossible-to-imitate movements he made that took pure muscle and strength she did not possess. He held her against him as he examined the wall, and her new decoration, then held her away from him so he could look at her. "It's a picket fence."

She shrugged and pushed herself all the way up onto her feet, using his shoulders for leverage, and reached for her overdress. It had been too risky to undress completely, but that made the coming night something to look forward to.

"Charlee, are you blushing?" Asher asked softly.

She held out her hand. "Come on. I'm hungry and if I'm hungry, you must be starving. I have soup ready at home, and bannock."

Asher laughed and stood up, fastening his clothing. "You really do know how to seduce a man."

"If you're very nice, I have some honey for the bannock, too."

Asher groaned. "I surrender!" He clutched his stomach.

"Idiot," she told him, grinning.

"If I am, it's because of you." He kissed her, then picked up her bow and put it in her hand. She lifted up his coat for him and called Fudge to her with a short whistle.

Fudge bounded down the stairs and took the four-foot drop at the bottom where the stairs had crumbled away with a flying leap. His tail was wagging, but he didn't make a sound, for he was still technically on duty and would be until they reached home.

Charlee picked up her quiver and pointed to the passage. Fudge trotted over to the gaping maw, climbing the rock-fall with sure-footed ease. At the top of the pile, he looked back. His tongue was hanging out of the side of his mouth, pink against the deep, dark brown of his fur. It made him look cheerful.

Charlee waved him on, and Asher clipped the gun to his belt and picked up her hand. "Let's go home."

As she stepped into the passage, Charlee looked back over her shoulder to check that nothing was out of place, that there would be nothing to alert someone who glanced down into what was left of the building that there were green, edible things growing down here. Her tools were all put away, and the plants she tended were scattered carefully among grass and weeds, looking like weeds themselves, most of them.

She looked up at the tower overhead, which was more visible from this angle than anywhere else in the cellar. There were dozens of arrowheads out today, flitting around the tower in almost ostentatious display. She wondered if someone important among the Alfar was in the tower. That would explain the sudden scurry of patrols.

"Patrols are out," she observed as she climbed carefully over the rubble to where the passage was clear.

"I noticed. I would have been here two hours ago, if not for the arrowheads."

"Do you think they're planning to do a roundup?" The last roundup had been over a year ago, and the Alfar had paid heavily for the few slaves they had captured. These days they contented themselves with the few humans they gathered when they dared set foot on the ground. They would only touch down and walk the streets when they had heavy armor and outrageous numbers. Three arrowheads of Blakar at least. With such numbers, human resistance wisely melted away and hid.

"I didn't hear anything about a planned roundup," Asher said, "but I've been traveling for two days. We can watch them, see if they look like they're forming a phalanx, and send word if they do descend."

They were drawing close to the end of the passage. Daylight showed ahead. Asher dropped her hand and pulled out his sword and gun. He left the sword furled. There was no chance the sword would fail to obey his command, for the aura that generated the shield wall around the tower was so powerful, it bled off power that ran to any auras nearby, feeding them. It was one of the very few advantages of living inside an Alfar shield.

Asher inched his way to the jagged crater overhead and looked up. Then he put the sword away and beckoned her closer.

Charlee hurried past him and clicked her fingers to call Fudge over to her. Then she picked him up and tucked him under her arm. Fudge gave a single soft whimper, for he did not enjoy this part of the route at all. Torger was far more stoic about being lifted and carted about.

Charlee grabbed the bent and twisted rebar that emerged from the earth around the edge of the crater using her free hand. The rebar made useful hand and foot holds, once Asher had beaten a few of them into more convenient angles. From long practice, she climbed until her head was at the top of the rubble that surrounded the hole and looked around. The dank alley was deserted.

Moving quickly, she climbed out of the hole and stepped over the rubble to the street itself, avoiding the carcasses of dead rabbits and cats, birds and more. Their entrails had been tossed aside, their bellies disemboweled and the meat gnawed off their bones. The poor creatures had not died in this alley but were the victims of the numerous dogs in the city that had turned feral and hunted in packs. Asher and Charlee had carefully draped the carcasses and the entrails to make the pit look like a dog-pack lair. If the smell of rotting meat did not deter the curious, the idea of facing feral and possibly rabid and very hungry dogs did.

It was also why Fudge didn't like the hole. His sense of smell was so much stronger. As she reached the top he began to kick and wriggle under her arm, so she stopped, and lifted him up to the lip of the hole where he scrabbled with his forepaws until he could get a grip, then pushed off from her shoulder with his rear paws, and scrambled out of the hole.

Asher followed Charlee out of the hole, moving as quickly as she had. He kept the gun in his hand, but let his hand hang by his side. "It's not as offensive as it was. We should find another animal." He spoke softly. It wasn't a whisper, which would carry, but a low murmur.

"I saw a dead falcon in the park a few days ago," Charlee said just as quietly. "I'll bring it over tomorrow."

They walked down the alley. On the wall where the sun fell were the two Norse runes that had popped up all over the city in the last few years, spray-painted with more enthusiasm and relentlessness than any graffiti artist of the past had shown.

The first, Asher had explained, was a Valknut. The three intertwined triangles were a symbol for death. The pentacle next to it wasn't just a human symbol for witchcraft, but a powerful protector against elves. The Alfar.

Death to the Alfar and victory for humans. It was a simple idea that had spread like a virus across the city. On the one occasion that Asher had agreed to take her on an expedition to the shield wall, to study the land beyond for messages or people, Charlee had seen the two symbols everywhere; they were painted on walls facing the outside of the shield, covering almost every inch of it—it was a declaration of resistance to anyone who saw them, including the world beyond the shield.

They pattered down the alley past the runes and on toward the street, their footsteps almost silent. Fudge was like a shadow, hugging the walls as he trotted ahead of both of them.

Asher had refined Charlee's guerilla skills over the years. She could move as silently as he did, now. She fell into step behind him and they both remained silent. *Use your ears and your nose and your intuition*, Asher often said. *They'll warn you well ahead of when your sight will serve.*

So it was the sound of a misstep on loose and dried out shingles, overhead, that alerted her. Instead of looking up, she slapped Asher's shoulder and spun to flatten herself against the side of the building itself. Whoever was on the roof would have to lean well over the edge to spot them there, and that would give them a fat target to shoot at.

Fudge turned to look at Asher, for instructions. Asher waved him down and he sat, his head cocked, listening.

Charlee notched an arrow and lifted the bow to aim upwards, waiting for the target to show itself.

Asher already had his gun aimed at the gutter, but he wouldn't shoot unless he had to. The gun would draw attention to them. He would leave it to her, instead.

They waited. Waiting was another skill Asher had imparted, and it had been one of the hardest to learn. Waiting for five, ten or even thirty minutes for the enemy to take the next step because they were more impatient was a way of exposing them.

So they kept their backs against the wall, their weapons aimed generally at the roof, and waited. It was pleasant with the sun bathing their faces, but Charlee steeled her mind against the pleasure. She stayed focused, scanning the roofline, but listening all around her, for the enemy could move as easily and swiftly as they could.

Almost eight minutes later, there was a scrape of a window against a frame, a sharp squealing sound of neglected, rain-swollen wood on wood that made them both spin to face to the south. Charlee was in front of

Asher, which was perfect positioning. She aimed the bow along the street.

After a few seconds a hand emerged from the window. There was a pistol hanging from the very tips of the finger and thumb, swinging freely by the trigger guard. Then a head emerged.

It was Lucas. He put his fingers to his lips, then disappeared again. A few seconds later his dusty and worn boots pushed through the window and he slid out and onto the pavement with a little hop to keep his balance. His smile was huge.

Charlee lowered her bow, relief trickling through her. She glanced at Asher over her shoulder and he rolled his eyes and started forward down the pavement, heading for Lucas where he stood dusting himself off with one hand.

The other hand was tucked into the opening of his denim shirt and held stiffly at his side. Concern touched Charlee and she hurried after Asher. "What have you done to yourself?" she murmured when she reached Lucas.

Lucas and Asher hugged, banging each other on the back, then Lucas stepped back, wincing. "One of those long knives the Myrakar use. It's just a scratch."

"You need it looked at?"

"Why I'm here." They kept their talk short and to the point. There was no need to draw attention to themselves, and on empty streets sound could travel an astonishing distance.

Asher tilted his head wisely. "Not for the food?"

Lucas grinned. "That, too."

Chapter Forty-Two

They continued to move swiftly through the streets at a speed that let them maintain silence and caution, all of them strung out in a line with distance between them. Asher set the pace. They had to travel three blocks to reach the subway and most of that travel was in view of the tower rising above them, so Asher always chose the north or western side of the streets, and they flitted across exposed intersections only after checking for arrowheads or foot patrols.

There were no other humans on the streets, not this close to the belly of the tower, although as they passed windows and doors, Charlee sometimes caught a whisper of sound—people watching them go by until they were safely beyond their shelter, most likely. People did live here because weatherproof shelter was hard to come by, but they only moved outside under cover of night.

They hurried down the steps into the subway entrance, maintaining silence until they were at the first level. At the bottom of the steps, as Fudge trotted down into the dark on the next level, Asher lifted the hood of his coat up and slid it over his head until his face was in shadows. Charlee was less well known than Asher was. There had been no images of her in the media before the occupation, while Asher had been in the news almost daily, his name and his image spread around the globe on TV and the Internet.

The rendering of Charlee's face above the offer of freedom for whoever led the Alfar to her had been odd and looked quite unlike her, as if the artist had been looking through a warping lens. Asher had nailed it: "A Myrakar drew this, and they see human faces through the same perspective you would look at, say, fish faces. You interpret according to what you have been looking at all your life."

"This is how the Alfar see me?"

"It would be close. We're lucky they didn't think to make it a color picture. Your red hair would make you instantly recognizable, even with this distortion."

So Charlee could move more freely around the city than Asher could, even though the Alfar were offering to escort the informant to the other side of the shield as a reward for the capture of either of them. Even though Asher's likeness was just as distorted as hers, everyone knew his name and knew the real face that went with the name.

Here on the first level, humans were to be found, which had been why Asher had raised his hood. They sat against the walls of the level, watching the three of them with curious eyes. But curiosity was as far as it went. The sort of crimes that had once plagued New York had almost completely disappeared. Humans did not steal from humans or the odd Kine still surviving in the city. Everyone helped everyone else as much as they could, paying it forward in a barter system that used goodwill as valuta, more often than not.

As they reached the top of the motionless escalators down to the subway level that Fudge had already climbed down, Charlee picked up her feet and drew level with Lucas. They climbed down the escalators into a thick, orange-lit atmosphere. Down at the bottom level of the subway, there was no light but what they could create, and that was usually a fire of some sort. The venting of the tunnels was passive, the smoke and heat generated by the humans in the tunnels passing through ducts to the surface that had been in place since the nineteenth century. There were no fans anymore, not since the power had failed. The tunnels grew warmer in summer, although they never became uncomfortably warm, and they were freezing in winter, but were warmer where humans congregated the thickest.

They walked out onto the platform, Fudge moving up next to them, weaving between the shakedowns and sheet tents, sliding along the narrow path that had been left for pedestrians. At the edge, Asher climbed down from the platform onto the rails below via a set of informal stairs that had been built there, using objects of diminishing height including a high chair with no tray, a coffee table and a 1950s vintage television, the curved screen still intact. The wood cabinet was scratched and pitted, but it was still sturdy.

The track closest to the platform was clear except for people picking their way along the ties, their heads down. There were quite a few walking the tracks, for the subway lines had become the major arteries of human movement in the city. They were below ground and out of the gaze of the Alfar above.

As a small bonus, it had been discovered that the Lajos and Myrakar were uncomfortable with spaces that were belowground. Only the Blakar seemed at ease underground, and it was rumored that on Svartalfheim, their home-world, they lived in caves and holes in the ground. As the Blakar were dark of skin and the tallest of them was only five feet high, humans had decided that they were the origins of the fictional dwarves that populated so many human stories. Blakar differed from the story dwarves, as they were not able to grow beards and like their Myrakar and Lajos cousins, they preferred knives in battle. Charlee had never seen an axe wielded by a single one of them.

However, as stout and hardy as the Blakar seemed, even they were reluctant to come into the subway tunnels. A long, slender and fully enclosed area with only one entry point was considerably easier to defend against unwelcome intrusions than any spaces aboveground. Like the Alfar's roundups and patrols, the battles to penetrate the subways had petered to a rare attempt at breaking through the front lines. With each successful defense of the subways, humans grew even more fiercely determined to hold the territory, no matter what.

So the subways had become their roadways. They had also become a busy thoroughfare that provided more than just safe passage.

From custom and hard experience, one track in each tunnel was kept clear for foot traffic. Sometimes the through-track switched over, snaking around stationary trains, which had become the new apartment buildings for the lucky few who managed to claim a car or a section of a car. No matter which track was the through-track, the other track provided commerce.

Stretching along either direction for as far as the eye could see, between the rails of the other track, were people displaying their wares for sale or barter. Barter was the usual coinage now.

Anything and everything was available for haggle and swap, although food items were the most common. Charlee set up shop every few months, selling off the herbs and medicinals she had prepared. Basic medicines and preparations were highly sought, and Charlee was often paid in real coins and notes. A single dollar had a far greater purchasing power than pre-occupation money, but Charlee stashed the money she earned and used the same food, medicinals and cosmetic preparations to buy what she needed. Her moisturizers and lip balms and pretty makeup items were never refused.

It was the middle of summer, so food was in abundance. Charlee didn't know where they grew it all, for the roofs and streets were only green with wild plants and weeds. Perhaps like her, the gardeners had found undiscovered patches of ground where they could safely grow crops.

There were also the crops and trees that had been growing in Manhattan before the occupation. Ylva's house had not been the only one to sport a rooftop garden, and potted vegetables and herbs were everywhere. There had even been miniature fruit trees. In the first year of occupation, Charlee and Asher had raided the ruins of Ylva's house four different times. On the fourth and last occasion, vandals and the hungry had picked through the ruins, too. However, Charlee knew exactly where the most valuable items had been kept. They had systematically stripped the house of anything useful, and most of the goods they had taken with them were still serving them well, two years later.

One of the items Charlee had spent the better part of day looking for among the rubble was seeds. She had found the remains of the antique apothecary cabinet with most of the little drawers still intact and had carefully sorted, repackaged and indexed the seeds and taken them with her.

Seeds had become almost as good as grown food when it came to barter. The collection of seeds and the raising of them was a major preoccupation, and Central Park had become an overgrown jungle of edible plants, bushes and trees where scraps were scattered, letting nature take its course. There were small apple trees growing wild there and sometimes Charlee ventured out into the park to pick strawberries and mushrooms, along with the chickweed, dandelions and thistles that were threatening to take over. She stayed at the edges of the treeline, and kept her head and shoulders covered. The tower overhead was an oppressive reminder to be cautious.

The three of them walked carefully along the track, with Fudge moving in slow circles around them. In the tunnels, Fudge stayed close, but there were friends here who sometimes held out morsels to eat.

Custom dictated that everyone still walking stay on the right to minimize collisions. By unspoken arrangement, Asher trailed along last and Charlee led the way. She was known to many people along this stretch of the subway and would draw attention away from the shadowy figure behind her. She also made her progress look casual, stopping occasionally to inspect goods or to ask after the stall owner. When she did, they would all step onto the middle concrete divider between the tracks, to make way for travelers behind them.

It took forty minutes to reach the end of the tunnel and the next station. They passed the tunnel guards, and Charlee greeted them and waved as they stepped up onto the platform itself. This time, the stairs were made out of hand-sawn logs settled into the earth on their ends.

The same tent-and-blanket city populated both levels of the platform. Those who had been living on the platform the longest had graduated down to this level, while newcomers took space on the upper level.

They made their way up to the surface, their heads lowered. The streets here were just as deserted as those underneath the belly of the tower. They were only a quarter of a mile away from the northwestern foot of the tower here. The foot was monstrous in scale. The base of it rose sixty feet into the air, before it curled in a graceful arc up into the soaring leg, one of three that supported the tower itself, which rose nearly a mile into the air. The tip of the tower couldn't be seen from here, for the wall of the foot dominated the view.

Lucas glanced at it as they hurried across the street. "I still can't get over how fucking big the thing is."

"It's bigger than the London one, we think," Charlee murmured.

"Save it," Asher said harshly and Charlee grimaced, for he was right.

They pushed on, moving back into the strung-out, single-file line, with Fudge back on point. Charlee removed the bow she had strung over her shoulder and walked with an arrow loosely tucked into the string, held between her two fingers, the bow itself hanging from the notch in the arrow. A quick flip would bring the bow up, and the movement would finish with her pulling on the string. It was a quick draw position that didn't tax her arms and fingers by keeping a constant pull on the bow.

They were heading northeast, drawing closer to the wall of the southwest foot, which loomed larger and larger as they progressed. Even the foot itself was home to a small city of Alfar, for windows and white space dotted the surface. They had conjectured that the Blakar lived in the lower levels, along with humans who had been imprisoned and put to work to run the Alfar's tower for them. The higher up the tower, the higher the class of Alfar—the Myrakar would live at the base of the tower itself, while the imperial Lajos would keep the loftier levels for themselves.

As they walked, Charlee could see that Lucas was staring ahead, taking in the impact of the tower on mid-town Manhattan. There were two other triangular feet, just like this one, and Asher had used trigonometry and a scale map of the greater New York area to plot where the three feet were placed. They were heading for the northwest corner of this foot, which neatly cut off 9th Avenue. The northern side of the triangular foot underlined Central Park and the northeast tip ran across Park Avenue, almost to where the Kine hall had been. The hall was there no longer. It had been completely obliterated by the arrowheads on the first day of the occupation. Asher had never made it back to the hall. It had been on fire and crumbling when he arrived. There were too many arrowheads and Alfar on foot for him to risk staying in the area, but he had returned a week later and a month after that and found no one.

"It doesn't mean a damned thing," he'd pointed out to Lucas and Charlee. "If they've got any sense at all, they'll have gone to earth, just like we have. We'll find them eventually. In the meantime, we stay out of Alfar hands while causing them the most inconvenience possible." But it was around then the flyers with Charlee's and Asher's faces on them had begun to circulate, sometimes raining from the tower itself like a paper snow storm, and their priorities had abruptly shifted.

When the wall of the foot was all they could see ahead without lifting their heads, Lucas stepped closer to Asher and Charlee closed the gap so she could hear what he said.

"How much farther? We're going to hit the wall itself in a minute."

"Afraid?" Asher asked.

"You're not, you freak?"

Asher pointed ahead. "That crack there."

"*Which* crack?" Lucas demanded. "There's only, like, a bazillion of 'em. The Alfar didn't exactly clear out the space when they took over."

All three of them had watched the frightening, quite awful construction of the tower, which had taken nearly a full year. The bases, however, had been built within a week, for they arrived prefabricated. They were airlifted by dozens of the bigger workhorse arrowheads the Alfar had developed, brought in from some far-flung, Alfar-held location, sending shadows across the landscape that had darkened the day.

The three of them had sat at the windows of the top floor of Asher's bank building on Wall Street, which was relatively untouched and completely deserted, for there was no food to be found there. From there they had watched the southwest base make its way from the north of the state, coming in over Hackensack, unable to properly absorb the size of the thing. It had taken hours of hovering for the arrowheads to position it in exactly the right place.

"They're very close," Lucas had said, his voice tight with concern.

"And very high. They're going to have to start lowering it soon, aren't they?" Charlee had asked Asher.

But he had watched the tight maneuvering silently, his face a mask. She could feel the tension in him and left him alone. Later, when they were alone, she would ask him what had troubled him.

Then Charlee had noticed something. "The platforms. They pulling away!" It would take several weeks for the nickname of arrowheads for the irregular diamond-shaped platforms to come into common use.

Lucas pressed his hand against the glass, like he could reach out and stop everything. "They can't!" he breathed. "The people, all the survivors, beneath…" He glanced at Asher. "They wouldn't, would they?"

Charlee understood, then, what was troubling Asher. "They are," she said softly and bit her lip. They could do nothing to stop it. Asher had already considered it and knew they were helpless.

The big base began to drop as the arrowheads all pulled away from underneath it. It seemed to sink slowly, which told her how truly large the thing was. Charlee drew in a shaky breath and tucked herself under Asher's arm, clinging to him. His grip on her was tight.

They stood silently, watching the base descend. When it landed, the tremor ran through the building, making it sway, and dust began to billow in clouds that didn't properly disperse for another two days. But even by nightfall, they could see clearly enough how the base had landed.

"Everything…is just…*flattened*," Lucas whispered, his face drawn. "Buildings, trees, houses, everything. It's just gone, like an elephant stepping on an ants' nest."

They stayed at the windows for another day, paying silent tribute to anyone who had been caught beneath the base, too horrified to leave the view.

Now they were standing only a few dozen steps away from the very bottom of the base wall, and here the damage from the base's landing was emphasized. Buildings were cleaved sharply in two, as if a giant chef had chopped through them with one blow. The remains of buildings that had been sliced had most often collapsed and rested against the base like forgotten toys flung against the wall. Some of the buildings had slid down the wall, sagging like candles left too long in the sun.

The strangest and most disquieting, though, were the remains of buildings that had stayed standing. Perhaps their construction had been stronger, the engineering better, or perhaps the section that had been removed by the tower base had not removed vital support with it. Whatever the reason, there were some buildings that hugged the base wall itself, looking like they were completely intact, making Charlee feel like if she blinked and cleared her vision, the rest of the building would appear. It was eerie to look at the remains of buildings still perfectly whole, that had been home to humans not so long ago, pressing up against the Alfar symbol of conquest.

Of course, there were cracks everywhere, where buildings had collapsed, where others had sagged and still others had fallen in upon themselves. It was toward one of these that Asher strode, where timber framing was propped up against the base wall.

The wall was a charcoal grey—almost black, except when the sun shone directly on it; then Charlee thought the color shimmered like a rainbow. Or perhaps it was the building itself that shimmered. Magic was everywhere these days.

The remains of human buildings were all a dusty dun color, regardless of what they had once been. In comparison to the wall, the rubble looked utterly lifeless. Windows with broken panes gaped like mouths with missing teeth.

Missing from this area were the Norse runes, the Valknut and the pentacle. No one ventured this close to the tower voluntarily.

When Asher was ten yards from the crack, he whistled softly and pointed. Fudge raced ahead, diving through the crack.

They waited.

Twenty seconds later, Fudge stuck his head out. He was panting and grinning again.

They stepped forward and slipped through the gap between the framing and the base wall. It looked like the section of building would slide down the base wall if so much as an errant breeze caught at it, which discouraged anyone crazy enough to get this close to the base wall to even consider venturing under the wreckage. But Asher had spent days shoring up the remains from underneath, where the support would not be noticed. It was as sturdy as a well-constructed roof.

The crack was deceptive. It was possible to walk through standing upright. Ten feet inside, where the light failed, Asher reached behind a beam and flicked a switch. Dull LED lights began to glow, giving enough light to see the way ahead in the gloom. The path twisted around the beam and disappeared.

Charlee nudged Lucas forward, encouraging him to follow Asher, who had stepped under the beam and moved on. Lucas ducked under himself and stepped forward. Charlee dipped her head under and followed. The path was wider on the other side of the camouflaging beam, and here, the light from the LEDs seemed brighter without the sunshine to compete with. The path was clear of rubble and four feet wide, leading right up to a panel door that rested on beams and sections of collapsed walls. One of the sections still had a clock hanging from a nail, but the glass was broken and the hour hand was missing. There were also several hundred pounds of drywall fragments and dust, which stirred in the breeze created by their movements. The dust and the ruined vestiges of human occupation, like the clock, gave the space an abandoned feeling.

Asher waved Lucas forward and pointed at the door. The handle had been wrenched from it and had left behind a circular hole.

"Put your fingers into the hole. Carefully," Asher told Lucas.

Lucas gave Asher a look that was his equivalent of raising a brow—dropping his chin and looking directly at him. He gave it two seconds, then reached over to slide his fingers gently into the hole left by the doorknob. Then his fingers grew still. "Trip wire," he said.

"There's enough slack to open the door a few inches," Asher explained. "Then you unhook it from the latch on the inside of the frame."

Lucas grinned. "You devious bastard."

"Forget to unlatch the wire and you'll blow half a block out. There's twenty pounds of C4 hooked up to it."

Lucas pulled the door up and open the required few inches, then reached inside and around the frame that had been hidden beneath the door. He grunted his satisfaction and opened the door all the way, until the hinges wouldn't swing anymore. The opening was door shaped, but it was at an angle. Stairs led down from it. They were quite normal and horizontal.

"Basement?" Lucas asked.

"Several of them," Asher agreed. "I'll go first. I know where the light switch is. Fudge."

Fudge hopped through the doorframe and trotted happily down the stairs into the dark. Asher stepped through and climbed down the stairs, ducking carefully under the top of the door.

"Light switch?" Lucas asked Charlee, clearly expecting an explanation.

"It's complicated," she said. "Go ahead. I have to secure the door behind us."

Lucas walked down the steps and Charlee followed him, tapping his head just before he rammed it against the top of the door frame.

He ducked and kept climbing down, moving out of the way. Charlee followed, bringing the door swinging over the top of her and backing down the steps until it was lowered into place. Then she dropped the black masking patch over the hole in the door. "Lights," she called softly.

Ahead of them, Asher flicked the switch. Naked, low-wattage, incandescent bulbs glowed overhead, the wire between them pinned to whatever would hold a nail. Lucas stared at them. "It's not a generator," he decided. "They're not flickering. Not a bit."

"I told you—" Charlee said as she slid the locking bar into place and the bolt over the top of it to secure it.

"Complicated. Yeah."

The steps led straight down, with a short landing halfway down. The basement at the bottom had once been a studio apartment. There was carpet, wallpaper, and furniture, but all of it was covered in a thick layer of dust. On the west wall, there were twin rock-falls in each corner.

Lucas stared at the wall there, which was pitch black and didn't reflect any of the light at all.

510

"Is that…?" he asked, pointing.

"The base wall, yes," Charlee told him.

The base wall had cut off a thin triangular section of the corner of the room, which left the rest of it looking oddly shaped, as if a giant had wrenched the square out of shape.

Asher walked around the sofa, over to a standalone black wooden closet that Lucas thought he might have seen advertised in an Ikea catalogue once. "Don't touch anything," he told Lucas.

"Don't leave dust prints telling someone people have been here?" Lucas clarified. "Would anyone survive the C4 upstairs, to make it down here?"

"I can't think of a way they might," Asher admitted, sliding his fingers along the crease between the wall and the closet. "That just means I haven't thought of all the ways someone might end up down here."

"You've grown cautious in your old age," Lucas teased him.

"Absolutely. Charlee lives here, too."

There was a click and the closet swung forward a tiny fraction of an inch. Asher opened it the rest of the way. "Charlee first."

Charlee stepped across the room, unstringing her bow. "I'm dying to take a shower," she confessed and stepped through.

"Shower?" Lucas repeated, sounding startled.

Charlee held out her hand. "Torger," she called and reached for the main light switch, turning it on. Lights came on, brighter than the ones illuminating the basement steps.

The passage they were in ran straight ahead and Torger was standing in the middle of it, sniffing at Fudge's tail. His own short tail was wagging.

There were doorways along the length of it. The Alfar's base wall made up the right-hand wall of the passage. Even with brighter light, the wall did not reflect anything back.

"You're living right up against the wall?" Lucas asked, astonished. "Christ, I knew you both had balls, but this is…." He shook his head.

"Thanks, I think," Charlee told him dryly. "We've discovered the outside of the tower has some useful properties. Here, put your hand against it."

Lucas laughed nervously, so Charlee picked up his hand. She put her own hand flat against the black wall and pressed his next to hers.

He spread his fingers, exploring the sensations under them. "It's warm," he said, surprised. "And sort of…it's very faint, but it feels like it's…pulsing or something." He pulled his hand away and looked at Asher, who was fastening the closet door behind them. "Is it living?"

It was an astute question, one that Asher and she had considered at length.

"Not if you're using the scientific definition of 'life', which includes the ability to procreate," Asher answered. "We're pretty sure it's a highly complex, self-contained system, and one thing we do know for certain is that the tower is generating the shield aura."

Lucas rubbed his hand. "Out of what? Thin air? You don't get something for nothing."

Asher smiled. "Auras aren't electricity. They keep using that analogy because it's a useful way to explain alien concepts, but the auras behave quite differently." He put his hand on Lucas' shoulder. "Come and have a drink, and I'll explain as well as I can."

Charlee headed down the passage, but Lucas stopped at the first door on the left. "There's bright light coming from under the door. What's in here?"

"Have a look," Asher offered.

Charlee turned back patiently. Lucas had always been this way, exploring every inch of a new environment. Becoming a SEAL had cemented the habit—he had explained once that knowing the layout of any indoor area was a basic survival skill in his work.

Lucas pushed down on the lever handle and let the door swing open.

The rush of warmth fanned Charlee's face, and the aroma of green, growing things. She noticed that Lucas didn't step straight into the room. Instead, he scanned the interior for a second, from outside the door. His mouth fell open. "I'll be…." he murmured and walked inside.

It was very warm. The overhead lights provided a lot of that heat. Lucas looked up at them. "Full spectrum light," he judged. "Of course."

The room was big—twenty-five feet by twenty. There were no outside windows, and if there had been they would have been buried under rubble. The walls were bare concrete. Everywhere were trestle tables, made of rough materials: pallets and framing studs, pieces of drywall, and more, all of it recovered and brought back here. The objects holding the tables up at a useful workbench height were equally as creative: dining chairs, boxes, ladders, roughly cobbled together A-frames made out of more recovered timber. There was even a battered electric stove holding up one end of a table. The oven door was a useful under-shelf.

On every flat surface were tubs, pots, half-barrels, boxes and yet more boxes, made of anything able to hold soil and that was mildly water-proof. Every container held plants.

Lucas walked along the rows of tables, examining the plants curiously. "I thought you used the art museum for this stuff," he said, his voice remote. He was absorbed in exploring.

"I still do," Charlee replied. "When we were living in the Strand Manhattan, it was my only source of soil for growing things. But after you found your old team members and went off to reconnoiter the shield, I started to look around for alternatives. The garden at the museum can't be relied upon. It might be discovered at any time. I only plant herbs and crops there that I can afford to lose. These," she waved her hand around the room, "are the vital supplies."

Asher leaned against the wall just inside the door and crossed his arms. He wore a small smile, like he was very pleased about something.

Lucas stopped where he was, in the middle of the second row, and began to turn slowly around. As he turned, he named what he recognized. "Potatoes, lettuce, tomato, cabbage, cauliflower, strawberries…is that kiwi fruit?"

"Very high in Vitamin C," Charlee replied.

"Lots of herbs…and what are these scrungy looking things?"

"Turmeric, mustard, kale."

"Is there anything you *don't* grow, here?" he asked.

"Protein," she said flatly. "I dream about chicken breasts, sometimes. I think I've forgotten what they taste like. Whenever I see the golden arches on the corner of 42nd Street, my mouth starts watering, and I used to *hate* hamburgers. Squirrel doesn't even come close."

"I brought you a hawk last month," Asher pointed out.

"He shot it down with his pistol, he says," Charlee told Lucas and rolled her eyes. Asher just grinned.

Lucas straightened. "So what surprises do the other rooms hold?"

Charlee showed him around the rest of their living quarters. In New York terms, it was a spacious apartment, hacked out of three adjoining basements. There was a bedroom, a large kitchen/workroom that also doubled as their relaxation area, when they had time to relax. Two of the smaller, irregular rooms created by the base wall chopping rooms down a size or two were used for supplies. The smallest triangular room, in the far corner of the kitchen area, was the walk-in refrigerator.

Lucas backed up as the cold air brushed his face. "A fridge? A fucking *fridge*? I thought you were pulling my leg when you mentioned a shower, but the greenhouse was *hot*. You have running water, too?" He looked almost offended.

"I told you, there are advantages to living right beside the base wall," Asher told him. "Come and sit down. You look like you need to." He closed the door on the cold room and pulled one of the chairs out from under a small square dining table pushed up against the opposite wall. Most of the space in the middle of the kitchen was taken by Charlee's big work table.

Charlee tended to Lucas' wound. It was a shallow cut running the length of his biceps, a scratch in comparison to what the Alfar knives could do to a human body. But the edges were inflamed and the flesh on either side red and puffy. "I have home-grown penicillin I can put on it," Charlee told him. "You'll have to change the dressing in a couple of days, but the penicillin will take care of the infection."

After she had finished dressing the wound, she set about preparing a meal. There were three hearty servings remaining of a savory soup she had made from some wild mushrooms and onions from the garden, and cheese she had made from milk she had bartered for. The goat that had lived on the roof of Ylva's house had long gone, but the milk-giving animals living on the island when the Alfar had arrived had been recovered and cared for. Charlee made cheese from goat's milk and gave half of it back to the woman in the tunnel who had started with a pair of goats and created a milk industry by breeding them.

There was plenty of salad, which would round out the meal. As it was a special occasion, Charlee used some of her precious supply of oat-flour to make and cook some flatbread. While it was cooking in the oven, she put honey and jam on the table, along with dressing for the salad, also made of goat's milk, and salt and pepper.

Lucas touched his stomach. "Whatever you're cooking, it smells heavenly," he told her.

Asher put a mug of mead in front of him. "This will take the edge off your appetite."

"It will, indeed." Lucas picked up the mug. "Who made this?"

"I did," Asher said, "but Charlee taught me how to do it."

"Did she now?" Lucas asked. Then he took a deep, gulping swallow of mead and came up for air, his eyes widening.

"Been a while since you had a drink, I imagine," Asher said, refilling his mug.

"A bit," Lucas agreed. He looked at Charlee. "Where on earth did you learn to make mead, and all the rest of this stuff?"

"What stuff?" she asked curiously.

He touched the board holding the cheese. "This and the jam and the whatever-it-is that is cooking in the oven and making my mouth water. All the medicines you make. And I couldn't help noticing you're wearing makeup, and I don't think I've seen a woman wearing so much as lip gloss for a year or more. I was told all the makeup has been used up. I've seen women mixing ash with water to try and create eyeliner and that looked, well, weird. But you look freaking marvelous, if Asher doesn't mind me saying so."

Asher chuckled.

Charlee had a few minutes to spare, waiting for various items to come to boil or finish cooking, so she sat on the edge of the office swivel chair that served as their spare seat. Fudge pushed up against her knee, his tail thumping happily.

"The Valkyrie taught me nearly everything useful," Charlee said. "First, living in Ylva's house, where the training was incredibly thorough. Then afterward at the Second Hall in Oslo, where all that training was put into practical use, which polished everything off." She gave Asher a small smile. "I had no idea at the time, but everything I learned as Ylva's apprentice has been so incredibly useful the last few years. There are people inside the shield who live hand-to-mouth, begging for scraps and shelter, and living the most desperate lives. There's very little meat, no power for most people, and there are no viable medicines left on the shelves anywhere. A single Tylenol capsule can buy you a full meal *with* bread. But Asher and I have thrived, with barely a snivel between us, thanks to Ylva's training."

"If I ever come across her again, I'll kiss her cheek," Lucas said.

"I imagine she's busy keeping together the Kine who survived the initial wave," Asher observed.

"Do you still think she might have survived?" Lucas asked curiously.

Charlee got up to stir the soup. "We never see them in the tunnels, trying to barter, but I think Ylva and her girls are alive and using all their abilities to provide for the Kine inside the shield."

Lucas glanced at Asher. "Still keeping your distance?"

"It's still too risky to contact them. The Alfar have learned how to pass as human, and that means they've learned the art of spying. They will have tabs on the Kine inside the shield. If I contact them, the balloon goes up." Asher shrugged and looked down into his cup of mead. "They'll have to do without me for a bit longer."

"Until when?" Lucas asked.

"Until something changes."

"Something will change," Charlee added softly. "It always does."

Chapter Forty-Three

Asher pushed open the bathroom door and stood back. "Take as long as you like. Hot water isn't in shortage around here."

"And a flushing toilet?" Lucas blinked. "Now I really do know I've died and gone to heaven."

"Valhalla," Asher corrected, with a grin. "The toilet was already here. I just adapted the water supply. The water comes from the Alfar, and it's purer than anything you would come across in nature, with no nasty chemicals to get it that way. That's all they drink so they know something about purification."

"They haven't figured out you've tapped into their water lines?"

"They don't use pipes. They use...well, the ancient Arabic qanat is the closest you'd get, except they build theirs indoors instead of across the desert."

"Doesn't say how you tapped it." Lucas plucked at his shirt. He had been wearing personal armor, and the denim had become wrinkled and sweat-soaked underneath. The shower beckoned like a siren, but the mystery of power and water was too strong to leave unanswered, especially after years of bucket baths and flickering firelight, to say nothing of the stench of old-fashioned outhouses.

Asher blew out his breath, soft and slow. "Okay, I'll break it down to very simple. You'd have to become an Einherjar and work with auras for a few centuries to really understand the details, and a few snotty Valdar lecturing over your shoulder would help a lot, too."

"You saying I'm stupid?" Lucas kept his face deadpan.

Asher gave him a quick smile. "The Alfar draw the water up through the earth, right here in the feet. The process creates energy as a by-product, which they feed back into the aura that creates the shield. That's why the base wall seems to throb. I syphoned off some of that power, and used a transformer to create human electricity from it. Voilà, lights, power, a water heater—"

"The heater doesn't use gas?"

"It's one of those instant hot water things. I lucked out on that one. But if it had been gas, I could have used the heat that bleeds off the base wall instead. That's what I use for the cold room—"

"Now you're bullshitting, man," Lucas complained.

"Look up how refrigerators work next time you're near the library. Push the heat through a small enough aperture with enough pressure, and what emerges is icy cold air. It's basic physics."

"You're a fucking freak, you know?"

"So you've told me." Asher didn't seem to mind the description in the slightest. "I lived through the development of all these inventions—power, refrigeration, the flushing toilet. I got to see each stage, so I know by experience what you can only learn through books and only if you specifically need to know. Everything is specialized these days."

"Survival ain't," Lucas pointed out. "You're ahead of everyone on that, too." He straightened up, cocking his head to listen along the corridor. Charlee was still banging around in the kitchen.

He looked Asher in the eye. "I've never seen her look so happy, man."

Asher's expression didn't change. "The occupation wiped away all the politics that said we couldn't be together, that's all. As long as we can both pretend I'm not Einherjar, we get what we want."

Lucas pursed his lips, considering. "She's not the only one who's over-the-moon happy about it."

"Glad I have your blessing."

"I was talking about you, stupid. You think I didn't notice that what you've got set up here is a throwback to the way you used to live? A few modern conveniences like hot and cold running everything, and this is an apartment, not a longhouse, but she's still keeping the homestead while you head out to do whatever Vikings used to do."

Surprise flittered across Asher's face. "I hadn't thought of it like that. And how do you know how I used to live? Have you been talking to Darwin?"

"He still hasn't shown up. I look in on his house every now and again, but the north foot of the tower is awfully close."

"You think he bugged out somewhere?"

"All his books are gone. What do you think?" Lucas raised a brow. "And don't think I didn't notice the change of subject there."

"It wasn't deliberate." Asher waved toward the waiting bathroom. "I'll dig up some spare clothes. Charlee is a damned fine dressmaker, too."

"Thanks."

Asher took a few steps away then turned and looked back. "And you're wrong about the homestead thing."

"I am?"

"I was never a Viking. Only those who went out on sea raids got to call themselves that."

"But didn't you die in battle?"

Asher nodded. "Leading my father's army, defending our land against the neighboring king's attack."

"Did you win?"

Asher's mouth lifted in a small smile. "I wouldn't be here if we had."

"What is it like, dying?" Lucas asked, then felt his jaw slacken. Where had that come from?

"Painful," Asher replied, as easily as if Lucas had asked him what it was like to drink mead.

"Did you...were you scared?"

"Are you scared when you're on a mission?" Asher asked curiously.

"Sure, when I was younger. Now, not so much."

"What are you, then?"

Lucas laughed. "Concentrating, mostly."

"Yes," Asher agreed. "And when the moment came, all I felt was anger, because I had failed. Because they were going to win, and I had run out of time to stop them."

Lucas drew in a breath. "You're still doing it, too."

"Doing what?"

"Getting pissed about running out of time to do things like wipe the Alfar from the earth. And here you are with eternity to get it right."

Asher shook his head slowly. "I don't get eternity."

"Yeah, but—"

"Yes, I get a very long time. A lot longer than a human life. But eventually, everyone runs out of time."

"Like Stefan?" Lucas asked softly.

"Like Stefan," Asher agreed, with a sigh.

"Is that why you're here with Charlee instead of with the Kine?"

Asher opened his mouth, but didn't answer. He pushed his hand through his hair. "I ... guess, yes." He gave a shrug that seemed almost embarrassed.

Lucas let out his breath. "Thank you. I really had trouble believing a price on your head would send you of all people diving down a rabbit hole, no matter how comfortable the hole was."

Asher nodded and headed back toward the kitchen. Lucas shut the bathroom door and almost tore his clothing off, so anxious was he to get beneath hot running water. When he found the gently scented shampoo in a glass jar on the shelf he mentally kissed Charlee for her vast talents and Asher for being Einherjar enough to know how to make a shower work.

It was the best shower of his life. Period.

* * * * *

Charlee shaded her eyes against the western sun and watched Torger trot among the thigh-high grasses and bushes that were once the Meadow. Central Park was becoming wilder each year. Central Wilderness would be a more appropriate name for it now.

She kept her back to the tower reaching up into the sky behind her. Doing so was automatic. From the middle of the tower upwards, where observers might be located, she and Asher would look like small dots, but they remained cautious anyway. She kept her hair covered with a straw hat she had found on a model in Neiman Marcus a few months ago. The scavengers had gone for food, tools and equipment. Clothing was a distant fourth on everyone's list of priorities, and pretty accessories were ignored.

Asher was keeping a careful eye on Fudge, who was still young enough to break out and do something silly. The dogs knew that when they reached the park, they were allowed to roam and play, one at a time. Torger was taking full advantage of the opportunity even though he couldn't move as fast as he once did, now that arthritis was stiffening up his back legs. But his instincts as a working dog were still exceptional, and he didn't mind pulling Fudge back into line as needed.

Charlee had bought several bags to collect anything ripe and edible. It was late summer, and all sorts of goodies could be found growing wild now, if one knew where to look.

Most of the trees in the park had grown completely out of hand, their leaf litter turning the paths underneath into soggy, unrecognizable tunnels, while the benches had faded and warped, the wood turning green with mold and the seats covered in a blanket of leaf litter. But deeper in, there would be ripe herbs and juneberries, and wild raisins. Rosehips were in season, and they made a delicious dessert, and they had medicinal properties as well. There were crab apple trees all over the park, and native persimmons to be had.

There was also a tree that provided berries that could be dried and ground to make a naturally decaffeinated coffee, the closest they would come to real coffee while caught behind the shield.

There was wild ginger growing in the north of the park, and there were all sorts of greens that would make good salads, including wild spinach, chickweed, sorrel, garlic mustard and field garlic. It was as bountiful as any supermarket would have been, and it was fresh and organic, to boot. Because the park was so close to the tower—almost tucked underneath the northwest curve between the north and southwest feet—most humans tended to shy away from it, using the smaller parks and gardens that had gone wild to forage for food. Central Park was just too much of a risk.

Asher was keeping an eye on the sky overhead. Because it was late summer and ripe food was simply hanging for the plucking, birds tended to circle endlessly when no one was around. A hawk or an owl would be a real treat. Unfortunately, seagulls were virtually inedible, even though there were more of them every year, along with the squirrels, which they ate whenever they could trap them.

Torger's slow meander brought them closer to where Asher and Fudge stood guard. "Can we head into the trees for some nuts, later?" she asked Asher. Neither of them went in among the trees unless they were together and fully armed. She had her bow over her shoulder and Asher was carrying everything including his sword, which was fully extended and pushed into his belt.

"Sure, but let Fudge stretch his legs for a moment," Asher said.

Charlee looked at Torger. "Front, Torger!"

Torger took up position next to Asher and sat, his tongue out and panting. He began to scan the park.

"Off, Fudge," Asher said softly.

Fudge gave a little yip, then took off, instantly at full speed as he took the gentle curve of the footpath. Then he dived happily into the grass and weeds, startling the insects and making the grass sway as he pushed through it.

Asher pulled Charlee closer, dropped his arm around her shoulders, and kissed her temple. He wore a small smile.

"Something on your mind?" Charlee asked. He had been quiet all morning, even though he had come to bed with her after they had pulled the sofa bed out for Lucas and wished him good night. Even Lucas had not insisted Asher stay up and drink with him, which had become something of a tradition with the two of them. She guessed it was Lucas who got poured into bed more often than Asher, for Asher had centuries of practice drinking mead. But last night they had both been quite sober and didn't seem inclined to change that.

They had crept out of the warren mid-morning, leaving Lucas still passed out on the sofa. Charlee wanted to collect whatever she could from Central Park while Asher was at home.

"You've been very quiet all morning," Charlee pointed out. "Did

Lucas say something to you last night that got too deep?"

"Yes." Asher's gaze wandered around the park. Even when he was relaxed, he was on guard. Charlee stayed silent. She had learned long ago that it was better to let Asher get to his point at his own speed. Battering him with questions wouldn't produce his answer any quicker. He was too used to keeping his own council.

"You painted a picket fence on the wall in the museum," he said.

Charlee frowned. "That's what Lucas said?"

"No, but it made me start thinking. Then last night...." He sighed and looked down at her. "Lucas said you were happier than he's ever seen you."

"Yes, I am," Charlee said instantly. Truthfully.

"Is that why you painted the picket fence?"

She hadn't been aware of it when she painted the silly fence image, but now she realized that it had been in the back of her mind the whole time. The picket fence Asher had spoken about. Their dreams of happiness, that had always seemed to be just out of reach.

"I suppose, yes," Charlee answered Asher. "Do you mind?"

"That you're happy?" He smiled and shook his head.

"That I'm happy in the middle of all this. All the human suffering and chaos."

Asher's smile faded. "Lucas asked me last night if I had deliberately chosen to cut myself off from the Kine not because the Alfar want us both, but because it was the only way we get to be together."

"That's a devious thought," Charlee breathed.

"He was right, though. I didn't know it until he asked, but he's right." He lifted her chin with his finger. "I could stay right here forever, Charlee, as long as you're right here with me. I can't even begin to think of what life would be like without you. Just trying makes my blood run cold."

Charlee gripped the edge of his armor, wanting to pull him even closer, but it would take their attention away from their surroundings. So would kissing him, and she wanted to do that, too. "Are we both completely insane to be blissfully happy living right beneath the Alfar themselves?"

"If love makes you mad, then yes." His voice was rough. Thick with emotion.

Charlee drew herself up so that their lips were nearly meeting. The need to kiss him was overwhelming, but the danger was too great. "How long will this last, Asher? How long until you have to leave me?"

He brushed her hair away from her face, then cupped it again. "It doesn't matter. Time doesn't matter. Only now matters and you're here, now. I think that's the one thing I've learned as an Einherjar that really matters. Now is all the time anyone gets."

Charlee nodded. "No matter what happens, then?"

"No matter what happens." He touched his lips to hers, then stiffened. "There's someone in the trees. Behind us."

Charlee's heart leapt. "My bow is over my shoulder. I can't get it off without them seeing it."

"It's your right shoulder. Your left is toward the trees." Asher's eyes had taken on the distant, flinty expression they did when he was thinking hard and making decisions. He pulled at the string of the bow, bringing it down her arm. "Slide your arm out and take it," he said.

Charlee gripped the center of the bow so the string lay against her forearm. "I'll have to shoot left-handed."

"I've seen you use your left. You'll be fine." He reached around her thigh and withdrew an arrow from the quiver that hung along the back of her hip, bringing it up under her right arm and easing the notch against the string. The arrow hung vertically, but as soon as they moved apart, she would be able to bring it up to bear on the treeline.

"Ready?" he asked.

She nodded and stepped away, bringing the arrow up to target the trees. They both moved forward, walking fast, drawing closer. Then she heard what Asher had heard: a distant crunching of leaves. She glanced at him. "They're not even trying to hide their approach."

"Torger, point," Asher said quietly.

Torger ran toward the trees silently, his tail up and the coarse, grey hairs fluffing out in the ancient canine instinct to look as big as possible.

Charlee gave a soft whistle, and Fudge came slinking out of the grasses right next to them. "Fudge, point," she breathed. Fudge stepped up beside her thigh and kept pace, his snout pointed ahead.

Asher drew out his sword and the pistol that lived on his hip.

Someone was walking along the same path they were following, but deeper inside the trees. They were making no attempt to move silently. The leaves crunched under their steps, which were regular. They weren't running or hurrying. They were strolling, almost.

Charlee looked at Asher. He shook his head. He had no idea, either.

They crept closer to the treeline. Now, Charlee could see the bend where the path turned and disappeared, perhaps twenty yards inside the trees. She could only pick out the path because the thick leaf litter was flat and undisturbed between the trees.

She saw the flicker of movement and lifted her bow, pulling it almost all the way back. She could see Asher's gun aimed from the corner of her eye. His finger was on the trigger, too.

Torger growled, somewhere ahead.

"Good dog! Good doggie. Gonna let me through? I gotta talk to your fellow."

Torger's growl rolled like miniature thunder, a continuous rumble.

"Hey! Wanna call your dog off?" The hail came loudly through the trees. "I just wanna talk!"

Asher whistled, a short, sharp, two-note sound. Torger barked once and came hurrying out through the trees.

"Torger, point," Asher muttered, and Torger turned and placed himself next to Asher.

They kept their weapons trained on the path, watching.

The man who appeared was short and middle-aged. He was greying around the temples. He lifted up his hands when he saw they were aiming at him and gave them an easy smile. "Really, you ever seen an Alfar my height, with my color skin?" he asked reasonably.

An Alfar as short as him would be considerably darker-skinned—a Blakar. This man had clear white skin and dirty blond hair, where it wasn't grey.

"Name three of the Seven Dwarves," Asher told him, not lowering the gun.

"Happy, Grumpy, Dozy, Sleepy, Doc and the little one with the big, red nose." The man grinned again. "I haven't seen Snow White since I was a tyke."

The Alfar—the Myrakar in particular—had tried to infiltrate human enclaves more than once, but they were easy to detect once humans had figured out they didn't understand humor or story-telling. A joke or a question about Grimm's fairy tales would confound them.

Asher lifted up his gun, and Charlee relaxed her pull on the bow string and straightened up. "You're alone, this close to the tower?" she asked.

"Figured you'd be more comfortable if I came alone."

"You're looking for us?" Asher asked sharply.

"I've had scouts watching out for you for a few weeks now," the man said. "I heard you'd walked through the tunnels yesterday, coming from this direction, so I put a couple more scouts on the tunnel and they let me know when you headed out to the park." The man lifted his brows. "Most of the old gang managed to make it through the slaughter when the Alfar first descended. They're good, reliable soldiers now."

"Gang?" Charlee repeated. "Is that just a figure of speech?"

"No." The man held out his hand toward Asher. "You're Asher Strand, also known as Asher Brynjarson, or Askr, son of Brynjar. You're the top Einherjar around here, and I've been waiting to talk to you for a while now."

Asher didn't take the offered hand. "And you are?" It didn't show, but Asher was on full alert and would switch into lethal action with little more prompting.

Charlee lifted the bow and the arrow that rested notched against the string up under her elbow, so she didn't have as far to lift it if she needed to shoot quickly.

"You don't know me."

"No," Asher said flatly. "And if you know who I am, then you know the Alfar are looking for me. The clock is ticking. Who are you?"

"About twenty-five years ago, there was a punk kid who thought he was hot shit because he controlled some little turf sitters up in the Bronx. He came down into my territory. Did the right thing. He negotiated passage and all, and that got my attention. He was all hot to deal with a suit working in a bank on Wall Street." The man's language had changed, even his posture had shifted. He looked like he had put on an invisible swagger. "Guess who the suit was?"

"Me," Asher said flatly, standing up and lowering the gun. "You controlled the Comanches."

Comanches? Charlee tried to put it together, but she had too little information.

"Very good," the man said. "You know more than I thought you would." Then he shrugged. "That was a long time ago. Whole world has changed since then. Except for you. I've been watching you since then. Laughed myself into a hernia when it turned out you were one of the top Einherjar in the world. Should have figured that out after you dealt with Sergio." He shook his head admirably and his gaze flickered toward Charlee.

Sergio? Charlee started at the name. That had been…that really had been twenty-seven years ago. For the first time in several years, she was reminded of the scar on her face, and it seemed to pulse with heat the way it had when she had first got it.

She studied the man. He had deep wrinkles at the corners of his eyes. Smile wrinkles, or perhaps he squinted a lot. His face was very tanned, which spoke of long hours outdoors. She put his age at around fifty, although with the leathery complexion it was hard to be very precise.

Asher held his sword point down, both hands fisted around the hilt. He didn't quite rest the point on the ground. It would drag if he had to pull it up quickly. He was still cautious, but he had put the gun away as a signal to the man in front of them. "Do you have a name?" Asher asked him.

"Koslov." He held out his hand again. "It is very good to meet you face-to-face after all this time."

Asher shook his hand, but Charlee could see that he was still wary. "And why have you been looking for me, if it isn't for the free walk out of here?" he asked.

"Because you're Einherjar and as far as I can figure, you're pretty high up in the command chain."

"I might have been, but I haven't been in contact with the Kine since the occupation."

Koslov studied Asher frankly. "You know that your leader died, right? Stefan?"

"Yes."

"I figure you're not too many places away from the top. You were always on TV, leading the charge. And I figure not too many Einherjar made it through the occupation, either. So you're probably top dog now."

"Go on," Asher said warily.

"Well, man, we've been waiting for you!"

Charlee could feel her mouth trying to open, and kept it shut with effort, staring at him.

Asher's face tightened. "No," he said flatly, clearly understanding more than she did and not liking it, either.

Koslov took a step closer to them. "Look—"

Torger growled deep in his chest. It was an unsettling sound. Koslov looked at him and took a hasty step backwards. "Look," he repeated, spreading his hands for emphasis. "You're the only Einherjar around. You're the only one I know of, anyways. I don't know where you live or nothin' but you walk through the tunnels, so you know what it's like for most people. They're dying. Bad food, no food, no heat, no medicines. I ain't seen nothing like it since I was a kid and I thought we had it bad back then, but it's nothin' like it is now."

"I know," Asher said tightly.

"So, you could be leading them, fighting to take out the Alfar!" Koslov made it sound like it was the most natural thing in the world. The most obvious thing.

"Lead humans?" Asher clarified, sounding winded.

"They want to fight, man," Koslov said earnestly. "They just don't know where to go or what to do. You could show 'em. You lead them and they'll fight to the death, because if they don't, death is all they have left. But that death is slow and miserable, and hard." His jaw flexed. "They don't want that. No one wants it. They're angry and getting angrier." He looked Asher in the eye. "They're ripe, man." It was one leader speaking to another. He had made an assessment about the caliber of the potential fighters.

Asher shook his head. "They don't know how to fight. The Alfar would slaughter them."

"Anger overcomes most shortcomings," Koslov said flatly.

"You have no weapons, no training and as you say, everyone is weak and getting weaker and sicker. How are they going to go up against the Blakar, who are bred to be slaughtering machines without mercy? What about the Myrakar, who make a dozen Blakar look weak? The Asmegar and Sinnar will eat them for dinner, probably literally." Asher shook his head. "You can't win. What would be the point of trying?"

Koslov took another step closer and this time he ignored Torger's growl. His jaw flexed again. He was angry. "The point of trying is to try," he said flatly. "We should just hunker down inside this fucking shield and die? Christ!" He whirled on his feet, his wound-up emotions sending him three paces down the path. Then he turned back again. His fists were tightly held at his side. "I'm not talking about a dozen boys from the 'hood. Do you know how many people live in the tunnels and are scattered through what's left of New York? Thousands of them! And I'm not talking about men now. Women and kids and old folk. Thousands and thousands. If they thought there was even a tiny chance they could get out of here, they would fight with teeth and nails and bad breath and they would never give up." He threw out a hand. "They just need to know what to do."

His chest was heaving.

Asher swallowed. "It would be suicidal," he said, his voice very gentle.

Koslov took another deep breath. "Are you telling me that even with thousands and thousands, that sheer numbers wouldn't do the trick?"

"The Alfar have sheer numbers," Asher pointed out. "Even if you could round up hundreds of thousands and could coordinate them all, the Alfar would still have you outnumbered."

"We got a TV station," Koslov muttered. "We could coordinate them that way."

"It's working?" Asher asked, surprised.

"Nah, but I gotta guy that says he could run it if it had juice."

"And who has working televisions to listen?" Asher asked gently.

Koslov slammed his fists against his thighs. "There has to be something!" he raged.

Charlee bit her lip and looked at Asher for guidance. Koslov's fury over his helplessness and that of his friends was painful to witness.

There was a fluttering sound overhead and all three of them looked up sharply. The sky overhead was filled with fluttering, turning, drifting sheets of paper.

"Christ!" Koslov muttered.

"The Alfar are dropping notices again," Charlee muttered. She reached up to snag a sheet and had to jump sideways as the breeze pushed it southward. She reached for one that was closer, flipping it over and turning it around.

The writing was ill-formed, as if it had been carefully imitated, and the English was strained, but it was quite understandable.

TOMORROW AT NOON,
HROAR BRYANNARRSON, ANNARR OF HERLEIFR,
TO BE EXECUTED
BASE OF NORTH FOOT OF EYRY,
UNLESS ASHER STRAND IS TO ALFAR IMMEDIATELY,
OR HIMSELF IS AT PLATFORM TOMORROW.
ALL HUMANS FOUND BY ALFAR WILL DIE
UNTIL ASHER STRAND TO US GIVEN.

Koslov looked up at Asher. "Why are they so hot for you?" he demanded. "They've got themselves the real leader of the Kine, but they want you instead."

"I don't know," Asher confessed.

Charlee stayed silent, her heart aching.

Koslov grinned and jerked his head toward the flurry of sheets that covered the sky wherever they looked. "Word is going to spread, man. You thought you were hot before this. If the Alfar kill a single human after the deadline is over, they'll tear you apart themselves, then go after the Alfar."

Charlee fought to stay silent. She had no idea things were so bad.

Asher crumpled the sheet in his hand. "How do I contact you, Koslov?"

"You'll do it then?" Koslov's expression brightened with hope.

"Something has to be done." Asher shook his head. "I don't know what, yet, but I don't want your people going off half-cocked either. I need to consider this, to talk to some people." His gaze flickered toward Charlee, and she knew that she was one of the people.

Koslov started explaining where he was located and how to reach him, and how to pass through the layers of security surrounding him and the people living with him. Charlee let Asher take it in, while she thought about the relentless Alfar search for her and Asher.

Noon, tomorrow.

Time always runs out.

Chapter Forty-Four

"You can't possibly be considering doing it?" Lucas asked, sounding stunned.

"Handing myself over? No," Asher said flatly, looking down into the empty mug cradled in his hands.

"Leading untrained, unprepared phalanxes of human cripples, women and children on some stupid crusade to give them meaning in their life," Lucas shot back.

"The Alfar have Roar," Asher pointed out. "I don't know where Eira is, but the rest of the Kine will be with her. She can lead—probably better than Roar. But she would want to fight. Koslov should have asked her."

"Eira has always felt betrayed because she was made a Valkyrie, not an Einherjar," Charlee added. "She led armies of men in Roman times, when women fighting was absolutely unheard of. She has never adjusted to life as a Valkyrie, even as the leader of the Valkyrie. She would absolutely fight, if she had an army at her back."

"The humans inside the shield are not warriors," Lucas replied. He pulled the big pitcher of mead closer to him with a sigh. "Asher is right. Any attempt to storm the tower would just be a pretty form of suicide." He poured. "That doesn't solve the basic problem. They have Roar." He filled Asher's mug. "*Why* do they want you so bad?" he asked.

Asher shook his head and drank deeply.

Charlee shifted on her chair. "I think I know why."

Both men looked at her.

She pressed her lips together. "Darwin told me about a prophecy a long time ago. The Nine Worlds Prophecy."

"Prophecy?" Lucas repeated, sounding stunned. "You're saying the Alfar are turning heaven and earth over looking for you two because of some stupid tea leaves?"

"Prophecy is a serious matter in the other worlds," Charlee said gently, trying not to laugh at Lucas' outrage.

"You haven't noticed how many soothsayers have been discovered among the humans since the auras were opened?" Asher asked. "There's a reason why, of all the talents the auras can enhance, prophecy is the most common among all the worlds. But the Vanir were the best at it, and everything they saw and predicted has a way of coming to be. Most of their predictions were lost when the Herleifr descended upon Midgard, but we tried to write down the ones we remembered the best. The Nine Worlds Prophecy was one of them. Something about a saint-like king and queen." He drank again.

Charlee recited the prophecy she had memorized long ago. "Topple the saintly king and merciful queen, the raven king shall, to usher in the king of kings with the branded bloom, to face the wrath of the worlds."

"Gibberish," Lucas shot back.

Asher was staring at her. "Sindri…." He said slowly.

"The Raven King," Charlee said in agreement.

"Then Stefan was the saintly king." Asher sat up and rubbed at his mouth with the back of his hand. "Gods," he whispered.

"That makes Eira merciful?" Lucas asked. "How? You've both always talked about her like she was a complete ball-buster, and if she was leading a Roman legion back in the dark ages, she would have to be. There's nothing merciful in a queen like that."

"The prophecies can't be taken literally," Charlee told him. "They've been interpreted and re-interpreted. The original version was in Old English."

"How does it connect to you and me?" Asher asked softly, watching Charlee. "You've thought it through. Tell me."

"This is the awkward bit," she confessed. "It's so hard to believe." She sat up, too, and pulled the empty mug Asher had put on the table for her closer and reached for the mead. "Darwin asked me, one day, quite out of the blue, what my name was. My full name."

"Charlotte Rose Montgomery." Lucas shrugged.

"Rose," she repeated for emphasis, then touched her cheek. "A branded rose."

"The branded bloom," Asher said softly.

Lucas laughed. "So that makes you…what?" he demanded of Asher. "The king of kings?" He thrust to his feet with a jerky movement. "This is crazy! The Alfar are going to commit genocide because they think you're going to live up to some prophecy made when the British were wearing woad?"

"Actually, the British didn't start speaking Old English until the Anglo-Saxons invaded, about three hundred years later," Asher said mildly. His gaze was unfocused. He was back to thinking hard.

"I don't give a fuck!" Lucas cried. "This is so fucking crazy I want to shoot myself so I can wake up in the next life and get away from it. Shit!" He threw his hands up.

Charlee tugged on his belt. "Sit, Lucas. Have a drink."

Asher topped up his mug, and Lucas blew out his breath and sat down heavily. Reluctantly.

"It doesn't matter whether you believe in the prophecy or not," Asher said, still speaking quietly, contemplatively. "What matters is that the Alfar believe it. They believe it, and it makes them afraid enough to happily exchange the current leader of the Kine for me, because they think taking me off the board will abort the prophecy."

"He's not the current leader," Charlee pointed out. "He wasn't appointed by acclaim. Eira coaxed him to take up the responsibilities, but he's not officially the Annarr."

"It still doesn't matter," Asher said patiently. "The prophecy itself doesn't matter except that it explains why the Alfar are so determined to find us. That puts this thing tomorrow into context. Otherwise, we can forget about the prophecy."

"But you said these things are taken seriously!" Lucas cried.

"They are, but…." Asher sighed. "Prophesy is slippery. Let's say I was a seer, and I told you that tomorrow, you're going to step out onto the road and get hit by a bolt of lightning. What do you think you would do?"

"Think you were soft in the head," Lucas replied instantly.

"But you wouldn't go outside if there were thunderclouds, would you? You'd play it safe. Just in case. Even though you don't think the prophecy is real and I'm a charlatan. Because of my prophecy, you would change your future behavior."

Lucas squinted his eyes at Asher, thinking it through. "Reading the future changes that future?"

Asher nodded. "But sometimes you can change your behavior so much, you put yourself in the path of the prophecy."

"Do you?" Charlee asked. "Or are you simply doing what the prophecy predicted?"

Asher looked at her. "You believe you've lived your life according to someone else's predetermined course, Charlee? Or would you prefer to think you have free will?"

"I am self-determining," she told him. "But because I am, I am becoming what they expected me to be. If I had not controlled my own future all these years, then that could not have happened."

"You're saying you have free will at the same time you're saying you're living according to a prediction," Lucas pointed out.

"It sounds like a contradiction, but it's not," Charlee assured him.

Asher considered her. "Something is bothering you," he said softly. "Koslov?" he guessed.

Charlee pressed her lips together. Then she sighed. "He was old."

"That tends to happen to people," Lucas pointed out.

"Yes, I know," she said patiently. She touched her cheek. "I got this twenty-seven years ago. *Twenty-seven*," she repeated slowly. "Koslov would have been in his twenties. I was in junior high and you were in high school, Lucas. I looked at Koslov today, and it reminded me of something that I have forgotten in all the years that I lived with the Kine." She reached out and touched the hair at Lucas' temples. "You're going grey."

"True," Lucas agreed.

"You turned forty-four this year."

"Forty-three, thank you very much," Lucas said gruffly.

"Asher, look at him," Charlee urged. "Really look at him."

Asher shook his head. "What should I see?"

Charlee sighed. "While you were away, I ran into an old friend of mine, from when I was in high school. Elizabeth—do you remember her?"

Both of them nodded. Lucas grinned. "I thought about trying to go out with her once or twice. She was a pretty thing. But she favored the rich kids with prospects."

Charlee nodded. "She knew her family wouldn't settle for less. Elizabeth was very smart in that regard. She survived the occupation and she is just barely hanging on. She was driving in from Long Beach when the Alfar invaded and was caught inside the shield." Charlee pressed her hands together. "Asher, she was, gods, she was *old*. Her hair was salt-and-pepper, and I know there's no hair dye left, but that wasn't all of it. She had wrinkles. Her skin was sagging, and I swear she was shorter than I remember. I didn't recognize her. Not even after she said who she was and started talking about high school and her ex-husbands." She reached up and undid the clip that was holding her hair in place and shook her hair out. "*Look* at me. How old am I?"

Lucas sat back. "Nu-uh. I'm not playing that game. Last time a woman asked me to guess her age I ended up with a black eye."

"Asher, you've spent a long time watching humans age," Charlee told him. "Look at me. Really look at me and tell me how old you would think I was if you met me in the street and didn't know my past."

Asher's gaze flickered over her face and her upper body. He glanced at Lucas. "She looks like a very young twenty year old," he said.

"I don't have a wrinkle. Not a grey hair, nothing is sagging," Charlee said.

Asher smiled and she hit his arm. "Behave," she told him and Lucas snorted.

"Both of you," she added and pinned up her hair again. "I know you barely keep track of such stuff, either of you, but I turned thirty-nine last birthday."

Lucas sobered. "I'd say impossible, except I know how old *I* am, every freaking decade. I can tell when I get out of bed in the morning." He glanced at Asher. "She's right. You're right. She doesn't look a day over twenty-two. Fresh and dewy. What gives?"

Asher shook his head slowly. "I don't know. The Amica do enjoy a long life, generally void of sickness. But it's not an extraordinarily long life."

"The Eldre live much longer than normal humans," Charlee pointed out. "But I am not a Valkyrie."

"Is that why the prophecy talks about you?" Lucas asked. He licked his lips. "Not that I'm saying I believe it or anything, but if the Vanir really do know their stuff, why did they single Charlee out? Because she's, I dunno, not human?"

"Charlee is very human," Asher said. "We aren't going to get answers to this tonight. Let's move on."

"No, let's go back," Charlee insisted. "What are you going to do tomorrow, Asher?"

Asher pushed his hand through his hair. "What do you want of me? You want me to lead a poor man's army on a quest that will most certainly fail? That will make you feel better?"

"It will make them feel better," Charlee replied. "But I don't think you should do it."

"Why not?" Lucas asked curiously.

Charlee kept her gaze upon Asher. "The Alfar *want* you to make a move. They want to locate you. Dangling Roar is one way. If you make any overt move against them, they will get what they want."

"My location," Asher said.

Charlee took a sip of her mead and wished briefly they had equipment to make long mead. She liked the bubbles. "You have to look at this from thirty thousand feet. We don't know what is happening out beyond the shield."

"For all we know, humans have been completely overwhelmed by the Alfar, who now rule the world," Lucas said.

Asher shook his head. "They would have dropped the shield, if they controlled all of Midgard. They would have nothing to shield against anymore." He looked at Charlee. "You think they're losing."

"I think they're hurting," Charlee said. "The Kine outside the shield and the human armies—I think they got together and for the last few years they have been kicking butt as hard as they can and the Alfar have been forced to take a step back. Not defeat—not yet. But they can see how they might lose. It's on the horizon of possibilities. So now they're covering all the bases. Anything that will help them, and that includes getting rid of the Vanir's king of kings."

"Listen to her," Lucas breathed, sounding very proud.

Charlee grimaced. "I learned a lot from Eira."

"I don't think you learned it all from her," Asher said. He looked at Lucas. "Charlee has had a varied and deep education. It shows in unusual ways."

"Tell me about it," Lucas agreed with feeling. "So, what would you suggest Asher do tomorrow?" he asked her.

Charlee looked at Asher and lifted her brow.

He nodded. "Tell me what you think."

She took another mouthful of the mead, giving herself a few seconds to consider. "I think you should be at the north foot at noon tomorrow. But not just you. I think anyone who can walk should be there. No children, but the more adult humans, the better."

"More witnesses," Asher guessed.

"It's a pity the world isn't hooked into television waves anymore, or I would suggest that Koslov's TV studio be fired up."

Lucas sat up from the slump he had fallen into. "Shit on a stick," he said. "Someone has a TV studio up and running?"

"They think they can run it, if they have power," Asher said. "Why?"

"The fighters that went through the shield in London—remember the footage, Asher?"

"What of it?"

"They analyzed the spine out of that footage, along with every monitor, meter and scale the fighters carried and they were loaded up with everything they could carry, so it took a while. I remember the Rear Admiral bitching about the final analysis. He said that the only radio waves that came through the shield while the fighters were inside it was anything between one hundred and fifty megahertz and about two hundred and seventy five. Which was useless, as nobody was set to receive that frequency anymore, except maybe in Australia."

"Australia?" Charlee asked.

"One of the last countries in the world to adopt cable for television," Asher said absently, staring at Lucas. "They're still mostly using broadcast bands. Television will get through the shield?" he said, speaking to Lucas.

"*If* the studio broadcasts at that specific megahertz range, and if a power source can be found or invented to drive it, then possibly. If the guy who says he can run it isn't full of smelly brown stuff."

"That's a lot of if's," Charlee pointed out. "We know light can travel through the shield and certain sound frequencies, but nothing within human hearing range. Nothing physical can get through."

"What advantage does pushing TV frequencies through give you?" Lucas asked, and this time he was looking at Charlee.

Charlee looked at Asher. "I said get everyone to the north foot tomorrow, as witnesses. Television will give us the entire world as witnesses. Human technology—the Alfar have always had trouble with it. Let's use that to our advantage. We can talk to the rest of the world and they won't know it."

* * * * *

There was no sleep for any of them that night.

Charlee loaded up a backpack of food and supplies for Lucas, and he shrugged into it and glanced at his watch. "Seven p.m. This is going to be close."

"You're a ruggedly fit SEAL," she reminded him.

"Who has been eating squirrel droppings for three years, and he's getting old into the bargain." He kissed her cheek. "Be careful, 'kay?"

"Always," she assured him.

"Make sure the big guy doesn't do anything stupid, too."

"I'll try. But it's Asher."

"Yeah." Lucas grinned at her. "I'll see you there. Noon tomorrow." He hitched the backpack into a more comfortable position.

"Fudge!" Charlee called.

Fudge trotted over to her.

"Go with Lucas," she told him.

Fudge looked at Lucas, who held out his hand. "You're sure about this?" he asked, for the third or thirtieth time.

Fudge licked his fingers and seated himself at Lucas' side.

"Apparently Fudge is," Charlee said.

"Okay, then," Lucas said with a heavy sigh. "On point, Fudge," he told the dog, who moved out ahead of him. Lucas waved to Charlee and stepped out, too. He was going to look for Koslov in the places Koslov had said he could be found, and go from there.

An hour later, Charlee and Asher were ready to go. They had always kept themselves ready to ship out at a moment's notice, so the preparations they had to put into place did not take more than twenty minutes, but there was one last thing Charlee needed to do before they could leave.

She found Asher in the small workshop where he repaired and built everything, including their weapons. He had worked furiously up until Lucas had been ready to leave, and inside Lucas' backpack had been the portable transformer Asher had built, that could convert the energy of the auras to direct current and then into alternating current, for human technology. Bits of wire and mysterious pieces of metal littered the bench.

Charlee took the screwdriver from Asher's hand and turned him to face her. He gazed at her, his blue eyes in the low light looking darker than usual.

She kissed him. "One last time," she murmured.

Asher drew her to him. "There will be others," he assured her, his lips against her throat, his hands sliding over her body in the way he had that made her shiver and throb with impatience.

"No, there won't," she whispered. "Not here. We've run out of time."

He didn't dispute her.

* * * * *

They came from across the shielded city. Some were drawn by the leaflet alone, wanting to witness their fate first-hand. Others had heard rumors, in the wind, on the breeze, muttered and passed on from one human to another, using every communications device they had discovered or reinvented since the occupation, including old dial telephones, and Morse code sent by flickering light. But mostly, word passed from mouth to mouth.

As Charlee and Asher traveled north toward Harlem, Torger by their side, others materialized around them, emerging from rubble, from cellars and the occasional untouched building. They emerged in greater numbers from train stations. Their numbers built the closer they got to the base. People moved silently through the night, walking, rolling or hobbling as they needed to. Everyone carried possessions on their back or over their shoulders. Clothes were dirty, torn, and worn.

But this was not a mob. There was a single-minded purpose driving them all northwards, and while they rarely spoke, when they did there was a grave courtesy used. The idea that they might be marching toward their deaths pervaded the atmosphere, and made most issues seem petty and not worth wasting what little time they had left.

Once the train tracks moved from under the earth to the surface, then to the overhead platforms, the stream of humanity flowed beneath them.

It was well past midnight when they drew level with the south end of the northernmost foot. The south end of the foot was the blunt end. Silently, the river of people bent around the corner and followed the monstrous foot toward the north point, which ended in Harlem.

Sometime during that unending night, Charlee reached out and grasped Asher's hand, careless of the fact that she was holding his sword hand. He didn't seem to mind. He kept quiet, his face hidden behind the deep hood, his gaze on his feet. Once, he drew their linked hands to his mouth and kissed the back of her hand.

Charlee was glad of the dark, for it hid her face from him. She kept her chin down, tucked between the upturned collar of the coat that she wore for the same reason Asher did—to help disguise who she was, and to carry her weapons discreetly. The bow was too long, and she had left it behind in the warren. But her long knives were hanging from under each arm, within easy reach. There were other blades and weapons scattered about her. Asher carried even more, simply because he had more pockets and most of his weapons unfurled, like his sword, the last vestige of auras that the Kine had continued to use.

Charlee thought of the time they'd had together and tried to be content. It had been stolen time. If peace still reigned, if the auras had not been opened, if the Alfar had not descended, that time would never have happened. She might be bonded to Roar by now, her unhappiness cemented in place by a contract and the rigid rules of the Kine that had preserved them throughout history.

Things change, she told herself. *Things always change.*

* * * * *

They reached the northernmost tip of the north foot mid-morning. The day had dawned with grey overhead and a small breeze that smelled of rain. The chill gave Charlee and Asher a good excuse to huddle inside their coats, their heads down, as they made their way closer to the tip of the triangular foot.

They were not the first there. Humans had been gathering for hours. The northernmost section of the shield cut through Englewood in New Jersey and the north end of the Bronx, before curving to slice through Forrest Hills and southeast Brooklyn, then out across mid-New Jersey on the west. Humans in the northern quadrant had a shorter journey to make.

The area in front of the tip of the foot was not level, nor was it very clear. There were the same bulldozed mounds of rubble up against the base of the foot, and most of the buildings in the immediate vicinity had been squashed by the initial concussion when the foot had landed. There were not many buildings still standing with their middles sliced through the way the southwestern foot had left them.

People sat on top of rubble, after carefully clearing a space. Others cleared out road surface or sidewalks. There were more people who had climbed to the roofs of the nearest buildings, which were thirty yards away. Most of the buildings in the area were only two or three floors high. Some people found windows with a clear view, inside the buildings.

Asher picked out a building on the far side of the point from where they had arrived. "There," he said. "We'll find space on the roof."

They made their way along, following the hundreds of rivulets of people passing between those who had already settled. Many people were sleeping, secure in the knowledge that the Alfar would not touch them until the noon deadline.

The stairs in the building Asher had selected had collapsed, leaving the mid-point landing thrusting out into mid-air, a long gap below to the cellar. It was a thirty-foot drop, and the landing was fifteen feet away from where the last of the solid floor ended. "No wonder there are so few on the roof," Charlee said. "Fire escape?"

They went around to the side of the building. The strap for pulling down the lower level of the fire escape had broken off. The ladder hung twelve feet above, out of reach.

Asher threaded his fingers together and bent down. "I'll hoist you."

Charlee knew he was more than strong enough, so she settled her foot on his fingers and her hand on his shoulder to steady her balance.

"One, two, three…!" She pushed off with her other foot as Asher lifted her, fast and high, and reached for the small section of leather strap that remained hanging from the lip of the ladder. She curled her fingers around it and hung for a moment from one arm, wincing at the strain in her shoulder.

Her weight was more than the counter-balance, and the ladder slowly dropped to the ground. Asher grabbed the first step, and Charlee let go of the strap thankfully. He leapt on to the lower steps and gave the short whistle for Torger to go ahead. Torger scrambled with his short legs and hauled himself up onto the top step, then climbed the iron stairs, panting heavily. Asher pulled her up onto the steps and they climbed swiftly to the roof, three floors up.

There was only a handful of people already on the roof and they huddled against the wall of the stairwell, which protected them from the breeze.

Asher kept his hood up and strode over to the corner closest to the tower and stood looking out. "This will do," he told Charlee when she stepped up to his side.

She looked over the sea of people below, for there were no more whole buildings between this one and the tower. The rubble and the street were almost completely covered by humans sitting and lying, waiting for noon, while others walked carefully between them. The flow of humans between those who were already settled made Charlee think of blood flowing through veins and capillaries.

It was a silent scene. No one was speaking above a murmur. No one was enjoying themselves. Tiredness and dwindling hope seemed to hover over them like a miasmic, invisible cloud.

Overhead, the clouds rumbled warningly.

Asher looked up. "How fitting," he said.

They sat down to wait, their backs against the low parapet. Torger pressed against Charlee's arm, a warm half-wall protecting her against the breeze.

After a while, Charlee pulled food from her backpack, and they ate and drank slowly. She realized that Asher was studying her with more than the usual closeness. "What's on your mind?" she asked. "Have you decided what to do?"

Asher shook his head. "There's too many variables. I'll have to make decisions on the fly and probably change my mind as often as I make it up."

"You mean, you're going to go by your gut?" She laughed. "That doesn't sound like you at all."

Asher smiled. "I usually left the heavy strategy stuff up to Roar, or Eira." He glanced toward the tower and sighed, his smile fading. "I don't know where Eira is. It's up to me, now."

Charlee glanced toward the tower, too. "Do you really think they have Roar?" she asked him. "I mean, are the Alfar capable of bluffing?"

Asher pursed his lips for a second. "They have him," he decided. "There's no possible way they could pull this off if they don't. If they didn't have him, they would never have thought of trying to pretend they did, just to reach me. It's like stories—they just don't understand fiction."

"But they can lie, can't they?"

"They will distort the truth, but they can't fabricate a story to save their lives. So yes, I think they really do have Roar." He reached over and picked up her hand. "Do you want to know what's on my mind, Charlotte Rose?"

His fingers were stroking her palm, making her skin tingle. "You mean, beyond the obvious?" she asked.

Asher smiled, but it was small and faded quickly.

"Tell me," Charlee said.

Contrariwise, he fell silent, staring down at their hands.

Charlee gripped his hand with her free one. "It's alright," she assured him. "You don't have to say anything."

His jaw rippled. "Yes, I *do* have to say it. In Norway, when I was still human, it was understood that when men went away to war, they might not come back. It was important to settle up debts, to mend rivalries and solve any bitterness. No tears, but no regrets, because it had all been said and nothing was left undone."

"You're not going away to war," Charlee whispered.

"I have no idea what is going to happen in the next few hours." His voice was as quiet as hers.

"But you're already at war and I'm right here."

It was his hand over hers that halted her, this time. He looked at her very steadily. "But not everything between us has been said."

Charlee swallowed. Her heart was aching. She didn't want to do this. To say everything was a way of acknowledging Asher could die soon. To wind everything up into a completed package, tied with a neat bow…it was giving up. But instinctively, she knew that Asher needed to do this. It would let him get through the next few hours, no matter what occurred.

"What haven't you said?" she asked.

He was back to studying her hand. For Asher, with his ancient upbringing, speaking of what was in his mind and heart, speaking of emotions, came harder than for some.

"Do you remember the day we met?" he asked.

Charlee couldn't help smiling. "Of course. You were my own personal superhero. You rescued Chocolate. How could I ever forget that?"

Asher's mouth turned up in a small smile. "Superhero. I remember when you first called me that to my face. It shocked the hell out of me." He glanced at her. "It took me days to realize that I liked being thought of as a superhero, especially by you."

"I hate to let you down, Asher," she said gravely, "but I haven't thought of you in that way for years and years."

"Not since our first argument, I'm guessing."

She laughed. "That certainly cracked your pedestal for me." She stroked his fingers with her thumb. "In many ways you're a man just like every other human, only more so. I don't notice your Einherjar qualities nearly as much as I used to."

"Especially not the last few years."

"No, barely at all since the occupation."

Asher's gaze dropped down to her hands again. "I don't know if I've ever told you how close I was to the end, when I met you."

"The end?" Charlee's heart gave a hard little knock.

He shrugged, making it look casual, but she knew, suddenly, that this was terribly difficult for him to speak of. "Ending it. One way or another. Drink seemed like a viable option. But there were other, quicker ways, and in the years before I met you, I had been toying with them." His blue eyes flickered up to her face, to check what her reaction was to such a confession.

Charlee schooled her face into neutral lines, hiding her shock. "I figured out, after a few years, that your life wasn't a bed of roses. But I didn't know you were so…desperate."

"I wasn't desperate. I was bored. I have been alive for over fifteen hundred years, Charlee. I can't begin to explain to you how draining that can be. After a while, everything repeats itself. After a few centuries, nothing humans do surprises you anymore. After five centuries, anything even remotely novel becomes your whole life's focus. But staying human, pretending this was our first time experiencing *anything*—that made it harder. I waited, hoping for something to come along that would give me a purpose, a reason to get up in the morning, because protecting humans from a threat that was less real than a fairy story had long ago lost all meaning."

Charlee bit her lip. She had always suspected that Asher's life when she had first met him had been crumbling around the edges. She hadn't understood, at ten years old, exactly why and how that might be, but she had instinctively known that in some way he needed protection of his own. "But you were there every single day, once you knew I was coming to the restaurant. Almost without fail, you were there."

"Because you wanted me to be. Four o'clock every afternoon was the only bright spot in my days." Asher let out a heavy breath. "Do you know how much difference you've made to my life, Charlee? Do you begin to see?"

She couldn't think of an answer that would give his declaration the honor it deserved. "I didn't know. I thought I was a nuisance. Like a millstone around your neck. You saved my life, more than once, and then you were stuck with having to watch out for me."

"You *were* an obligation. It was exactly what I needed. It was the best thing to happen to me in centuries, even though I resented it at first. You were interfering with my drinking." His smile was more natural and relaxed this time.

"Prickly gruellies," Charlee said softly, remembering.

Asher laughed softly. "*Yes*," he said firmly. "Exactly."

Charlee gave a soft laugh. "Then I grew up and really complicated things, I guess."

"You grew up and I fell in love with you."

Her heart gave another heavy beat. "I have always loved you. *Always*. I knew, even in junior high, that I only wanted one man in my life. I painted the picket fence because that was the dream, wasn't it? We would get to live like humans and that would make us completely happy." She swallowed. "But you're not *just* human, and I've spent my entire life learning what makes you different. I love the Einherjar part of you as much as anything else you could give me. I don't want you to give it up, like you once said you would."

"I couldn't anyway," he told her. "Not anymore. You're as entwined in my world as I am, now. I don't know what happens next, Charlee, but…" He swallowed and his grip on her hands grew tighter. "I want you in my life. *Really* in my life. However that works out." He gave a tight smile. "Even if my life only lasts the next few hours."

Her eyes prickled with hot tears, and she blinked hard to get rid of them. "I'm not going anywhere. Not if you aren't with me."

Asher pulled her over to him so that she was lying against his chest and her arms were around his neck. His kiss was hard and brief. "I'll do better next time," he murmured against her lips. "This is just a promissory note."

"No debts, remember?" she whispered back.

"A sweet inducement to return." He touched his lips to hers again. "I would fight every last Alfar standing to come back and claim this debt. Let it stand."

He held her against him, then, his hands sliding restlessly against her, as the morning lengthened around them. Charlee fell into a hazy reverie, where she might have slept, or might have simply wandered back into the deep recesses of her memory, bringing forth every happy moment with Asher. There were many of them, and she replayed them all. As noon approached, she wound her arms around Asher even more tightly, and even his hands grew still and he simply held her.

She could feel his heart beating beneath her chest. He was real, he was here, and he was hers.

They could hear the almost silent mass of people around them getting to their feet, brushing themselves off. Murmuring and soft rustles filled the air.

It was time.

Asher pressed his lips against her forehead. "*You* are my purpose, my sweetest one. You are the reason I am here."

Chapter Forty-Five

The clouds overhead had grown thicker and darker as the morning had wound down. Now they seemed to hover so closely overhead that they could be touched. The thunder had rumbled deep inside them on and off all morning. The cool breeze had evaporated and now the air was still and stifling.

Charlee and Asher stood up behind the parapet and looked out toward the tower. Torger took his place next to Asher, propping himself up with his forelegs on the parapet's thick top and sniffing the air, his nose wrinkling.

All around them, everyone was shifting uneasily on their feet. There were still people arriving, even now, but they did not work their way through the crowd already assembled. Instead, they were gathering at the edges of the available viewing area, a thick border of humanity. Charlee considered the mass of bodies. If they needed to move away from the tower quickly, for whatever reason, the sheer mass of people would make it difficult. Had the Alfar planned on that?

She also noticed something else about the crowd that made it utterly different from any Fourth of July or Christmas event she'd ever attended, quite apart from this crowd's silence. There were very few children in the crowd. People had arrived singly, or in twos, threes or big groups, but very few of them had children with them. Charlee was glad of that. If the children were tucked away somewhere safe, hopefully deep inside a tunnel and guarded by caretakers, then whatever happened here would not be a total disaster.

A mutter seemed to sweep through them all. It was a running whisper.

"Blakar!" she heard, just as she spotted them herself. Hundreds of Blakar were marching out of a portal in the base wall. They were fully armed, and although they were shorter than the average human, their spears and long knives moving between the humans marked their passage.

542

After the first alarm, a thick, tight silence held the crowd almost motionless, everyone watching the Blakar progress among them with intense wariness. Charlee thrust her hand into Asher's, seeking the reassurance his touch always gave her. His grip was hard.

The Blakar were spreading themselves out among the crowd, concentrating on the edges, where the humans were thickest. Charlee watched several of them make their way to the base of the building she and Asher were standing on, then spread out. They were dark-skinned. Their stature and the sharp angle at the top of their ears—it was not quite a point—distinguished them as Alfar. So did their eyes, which, like the other two Alfar races, were large. But the Blakar showed nothing in their eyes. There was no spark of feeling and very little sense of intelligence. They radiated a cold indifference that would switch to raging fury when they fought. There was no reasoning with the Blakar. They were the fighting machines that Asher had so aptly described them as.

The border of Blakar around the fringes was thicker than elsewhere and it made Charlee lick her lips. "They're penning us in."

"It's what I would do," Asher said. He was concentrating, his brows drawn together. Then he lifted his head to look sharply upwards, causing Charlee to look up, too. She hadn't heard anything, which told her exactly how keyed up Asher was.

There was a platform overhead, one of the larger workhorse arrowheads. Charlee watched it slowly sink down over their heads, aiming for a position directly in front of the rounded point of the base. As it drifting down past the top of the base wall, she realized that this was a different sort of arrowhead. It was even larger than the workhorse platforms that the Alfar used for everything from construction to (*dropping base feet on top of humans*) troop transport.

As it slowly lowered down to a level just above the heads of the people standing closest to the tower, another mutter of concern rippled through the humans. There were a dozen Myrakar on the platform and three extra-tall, very pale Alfar that Charlee knew must be Lajos. She had never seen one before, for they usually kept themselves safely ensconced in their towers.

The two Lajos on either end of the trio were half-turned toward the one in the center. "Is that Renmar?" Charlee whispered.

Asher nodded. His expression was hard. "I would give anything for you to have your bow here right now."

"My bow, and a guaranteed escape route. If I were to draw an arrow on him, the Blakar would swarm this building in a heartbeat."

Just to one side of the trio of Lajos was a small man—a human—standing very still and looking straight ahead. Charlee looked at him and gasped. "Roar!" she breathed. He was barely as tall as the Myrakar standing all around him, bristling with weapons held at the ready. It told her exactly how tall the Lajos were. "Why is he standing so still? He doesn't even look like he's blinking."

"He's bound by an aura," Asher said stiffly. "I've heard it could be done, but I've never seen it before." His jaw tightened briefly. "He must have fought them every step of the way. Fought even when they restrained him. That would explain the overload of Myrakar guards around him, and the aura."

Pride touched her. Roar had not fallen into their hands easily. Good.

The platform halted. Overhead, with perfect timing, thunder rumbled once more.

Behind the platform, the air seemed to flicker and shimmer, as if thousands of fireflies were hovering in one large rectangular area. Then the shimmering intensified and an image formed. Charlee gasped, for now hanging in mid-air, part of the air itself, was a close-up picture of the platform and the Alfar standing upon it.

"A megatron," Asher said, his tone a mix of disgust and admiration. "Well, they've learned a thing or two from humans, after all." Then he looked up again, this time over Charlee's shoulder. "Koslov," he breathed.

Charlee whirled to look at the back of the building they were standing on. A small arrowhead was hovering just above the parapet. It was filled with humans, all of them men, and a single Blakar who stood at the controls of the arrowhead with a human guard right next to him.

There was also a dog—dark brown and panting. "Fudge!" Charlee called, and heard a soft yip in response. The dog trotted over to the edge of the platform and looked down at the six-foot drop to the roof.

Lucas strode to the edge of the platform, scooped up Fudge and jumped without hesitation, watching his landing. He let Fudge go as his feet made contact, and bent his knees, absorbing the impact. One hand thrust out to keep his balance.

Fudge ran toward them and thrust his nose into Charlee's hand with a small whine. Then he flipped himself around and sat at her feet, panting.

Lucas hurried across the roof and gripped Asher's hand. He was smiling. "Made it, by the skin of my teeth. Those arrows can really move."

"The studio?" Asher asked.

Lucas pointed to the arrowhead, which had lifted up higher and was stationary. The arrowhead was drawing attention, but it was too far away from anyone for details to be clear. "There's a guy with an outside broadcast camera on his shoulder, and a wireless feed back to the station.

It worked. Koslov's guy was a fucking genius."

"Let's hope the rest of the world is paying attention," Asher said, and turned back to face the tower. So did the rest of them.

* * * * *

Pete Shawman was the news director for WLMB-TV, a CBS affiliate in Washtok, Pennsylvania and today, like most days, he was living on the edge of an acute angina attack, as he juggled the multiple information streams coming at him every second. Decisions, decisions, decisions…that was his life, especially when the news was airing. He lived on a diet of antacids and Pepsi, and was chewing a Tums anxiously when he noticed the affiliate feed monitors over by where one of the interns was working.

"What the fuck is that?" he demanded, pointing. For three years, four of the monitors had displayed greyed-out snow, but no one had had the courage to physically switch off the feeds from New York and New Jersey. It would have been the same as burying someone you weren't sure was entirely dead.

One of the monitors was showing images of something that Pete had to turn his head sideways and squint to make out. "Is that…fuck, is that one of their towers?" he breathed and strode over to the monitor to look closer. "Jesus H. fucking Christ," he cried. "That's Harlem. Fucking New York is broadcasting!"

His assistant, who had ice for blood and steel for nerves, switched his board to his other hand. "Run it live?" he asked quickly.

"Fuck yes! Break into the news—no, break into *everything*. Send it global. Phone everyone! Fucking sprint, people! This is Pulitzer territory!"

The control booth, which was already frantic with activity, instantly became a crisis center at full strength. Someone threw the feed up on one of the bigger screens that covered the back wall, and Pete squinted at it again. "It's grainy. What's the issue?"

"Looks like the signal is pretty weak, boss," someone called.

"Juice it up before you pass it on. We can't clear the haze, but we can stop it dropping out. Look lively people. This is…" He turned his head sideways again to actually study the picture. "Fuck, isn't that one of the head Viking guys the elves are holding there?"

His assistant was right by his elbow. "Hroar Brynjarson," he said quietly. "He was earl of the New York hall, and the one most likely to succeed Stefan as Annarr. He and Eira, the Regin, were both in New York when the Alfar took it. He has most likely been leading the Kine inside the shield since then. He's smart, but he was pro-*laun* and pacifist by nature."

545

"You say that like it's a fucking weakness, Nelson."

"We're at war with four alien species that we know of," Nelson replied calmly. "Peaceniks just gunk up the machinery."

Pete shook his head. "Whatever. Make sure that feed is clear and clean and uninterrupted, or you'll wish *you* were a hippy out on the street holding a sign." He lifted his voice. "Please tell me someone is talking to L.A. about this?"

He looked back at the arrowhead on the screen, and the figures standing on it. The Einherjar was the only one among dozens of Alfar. Three of the Alfar looked like they were over seven feet tall. He squinted his eyes again. "Can anyone tell me who the lily-white dudes are?"

"Lajos!" came the call. "We've never seen them before. They don't match any images we have on file."

"Whatever," Pete muttered, studying the feed. It didn't look good for the roar-guy. Not at all. The controlled frenzy of the control booth felt comforting and homelike in comparison.

* * * * *

When Renmar stepped forward, his long legs flowing beneath the white robes he wore, the hush that gripped the area seemed to intensify. Tension crackled. Charlee heard one of the women standing along the parapet on the other side of Lucas draw in an unsteady breath, for it was that quiet. All the people who had been sheltering against the side of the stairwell were up on their feet and standing with them, now.

One of the Myrakar stepped up with Renmar to stand behind his shoulder.

Renmar spoke. The Alfar speech was airy and pretty, but Renmar's voice was the opposite: harsh, like broken bottles rolling about in a tin can.

Charlee glanced at Asher. "What did he say?" she asked, for Asher understood enough of the Alfar tongue to make sense of it.

"Listen," he said, and lifted his chin to indicate the Myrakar standing next to Renmar.

The Myrakar lifted an arm, the one not holding his long knife, and spoke in a voice that carried easily across the open area. "It is gratifying to see so many of you care enough about your future to gather here at this time. Have you brought the Einherjar to me?"

Silence.

Charlee gripped Asher's hand and he squeezed back.

Renmar looked behind him and gave a signal. Four of the Myrakar moved in around Roar. Then from within them he staggered forward and would have fallen to his knees, except that two of them caught his arms and held him up. His head hung between them.

Charlee bit her lip. Had the Alfar beaten him? Tortured him to learn where Asher was?

The Myrakar marched him to the front of the platform and Roar's feet tried to keep up, but they were almost completely holding him off the ground. They settled him on his feet again.

Renmar looked at him and spoke.

"Speak, Herleifr," the interpreter said and pushed at the back of Roar's shoulder, making him stagger and thrust out a foot to hold himself up. The two guards hauled back on his arms, righting him once more.

Roar lifted his head and looked at Renmar. His face was calm, although there was dried blood on the corner of his mouth and along the side of his face where it must have run from an injury on his head. "I speak only because I wish to."

An almost soundless sigh washed over the humans watching. The faces turned up to toward the platform were all pale and strained.

Roar looked out at the people below. "The Alfar want me to plead with you, to beg you to turn over my brother in order that I might live." His voice was strong. Confident.

Behind him, the Myrakar was murmuring to Renmar, translating.

Roar leaned sideways and spat. The bloody spit landed close to the foot of the translator, who stepped back with a grimace. The long line of guards at the back of the platform shifted uneasily

The crowd reacted. Some smiled. Others leaned to speak to companions in a low voice.

Charlee caught her breath. Roar was winning their sympathies. He was surrounded by Myrakar guards, bloodied and bowed, yet he was still the earl who had led an army for centuries.

Roar gave a grimacing smile. "I know why they want him. Perhaps you do, too."

There were some nods. Just a few. Charlee saw someone waving their hand as they spoke, far away across the open area. It was a familiar gesture, and her heart squeezed as she studied the man speaking. Was it Darwin? He was wearing a coat with the collar turned up, and a battered cowboy hat, which disguised most of his face, but the way he had waved his hand....

"Would you turn your brother over to the Nazis?" Roar demanded of his audience.

Renmar was starting to scowl as the translator passed along Roar's words. Clearly, Roar was not saying what he had expected to hear. Renmar waved and spoke, and half a dozen Myrakar stepped forward from the file of motionless guards at the back of the platform.

"Oh gods, Asher!" Charlee breathed, her heart stopping as the guards stepped around Roar, caging him in on all sides except the front. That way, there was only the long drop to the rubble-covered earth below.

Roar glanced at the guards around him and drew himself upright. He lifted his chin.

"No," Asher whispered, his fingers squeezing Charlee's like a vise. "Don't do it..."

"I speak to the king of kings," Roar said, his voice rolling across the densely packed humans.

The Myrakar around Roar lifted their long knives high, ready for the downstroke.

Asher drew in a sharp breath.

"Do as you should!" Roar cried. "Lead as you should. You are Einherjar first and last. Show them what that means!"

The knives came down in unison, all of them skewering Roar from both sides, and his back. He snapped taut, his mouth opening wide and soundlessly. Fresh blood trickled from the corner of his mouth.

Charlee moaned, and Asher reached over and covered her mouth, holding the sound in. His eyes were stormy and pain-filled. "Don't cry out," he whispered urgently. "Don't react. They will be watching for the slightest hint of where we are. Do you hear me?"

Her eyes stung with tears, blurring her vision. She nodded and his hand was removed. Charlee looked back toward the platform, making herself stand still and silent. She let the tears course down her cheeks, not wiping them.

Roar fell to his knees, his body still upright despite the many blades piercing it, and it sounded like everyone watching drew in their breath at the same time. The collective gasp triggered a ripple of movement through the audience. People were stepping backwards, sideways, away from the platform. But the Blakar were scattered like pepper among them, and the instinctive impulse to turn and run was aborted as they brought up their knives and swords. The blades glinted in the low light.

Overhead, thunder rumbled long and loud.

Roar drew in a gasping, shuddering breath and Charlee pressed her lips together, holding in her need to cry out her alarm and her sorrow. She knew it would be one of his last breaths.

"Don't let them win," Roar said, and even though he could not raise his voice, his words were heard by everyone, for an utter silence and stillness gripped the area.

Renmar turned and plunged a knife directly into Roar's heart.

Charlee turned, too, and gripped Asher's coat with both hands, her back to the platform. "Don't move," she said and used one hand to turn his face inside the hood so that he was looking only at her. "Don't react. They *want* you to react. They'll cut you down in a heartbeat."

Asher closed his eyes, his jaw working hard. One hand was fisted at his sides, his sword hand thrust under the coat and curled around the hilt of his sword.

Lucas gripped his shoulder. "She's right, Asher. You'll play right into their hands."

Charlee kept whispering, kept forcing Asher's attention back to her, until his iron-hard stance relaxed. He drew a deep breath that shook much as Roar's last breath had. Then he nodded.

Lucas patted his shoulder and relaxed his grip.

From the other side of the arena came a long, drawn-out scream. It was filled with pain and fury, and sounded almost inhuman. Heads snapped around to see who was making that unearthly sound, and Charlee turned on her heels, too, scanning the crowd.

There was movement within the crowd, a swirling of bodies and cries and exclamations.

Then a hooded and cloaked figure surged from among the huddle of heads and shoulders, leaping onto a pile of rubble. They climbed it with gymnastic sure-footedness and gained the top. There was a long sword in their hand, and the blade was dripping blood. They flung the cloak aside, and it swirled like a flag as it floated away.

It was Eira. She stood on the top of the pile of debris, dressed in full battle gear, a knife at her hip and another in her boot. Charlee knew there would be more blades hidden away. She raised her sword high over her head. "Einherjar! To me! To me!"

As more hooded and hatted figures turned and began to surge through to crowd toward Eira, Asher straightened and drew his sword.

Charlee arrested the draw using both hands and all her bodyweight to hold the sword still. "*No*," she said. "If you join them, the Alfar will see you. They'll slaughter everyone to get to you."

I can see you! I can see you now!

Charlee whirled to look over her shoulder as the urgent mental voice spoke.

There! You're on the roof. With him.

Charlee pressed her fingers to her temple. "Where are you?" she demanded.

Watch out! Behind you! Behind!

"Behind!" Charlee screamed, and both Lucas and Asher whirled as the rest of the people on the roof cried out and scattered. Four Blakar had crept onto the roof, perhaps drawn by their reactions and movements after all.

Asher shrugged off the coat. Both he and Lucas pulled out their guns and fired quickly, two shots each.

The Blakar dropped to the ground, but Asher didn't wait to see it. He turned back to the parapet, one boot propped on the lip as if he was about to jump down to the ground, and leaned far over the edge, his gun in his fist. Lucas joined him.

Charlee pulled out her long knives and dropped her coat, too. No one was looking at them. All eyes were on the swirling fight at the foot of the small hill that Eira stood upon. Eira's sword was whirling as she took on every Blakar and Myrakar who challenged her, and both she and the stones at her feet were splattered with blood.

Don't go down there! The mental voice held the same urgency as before. *There are too many of them.*

Charlee flung back her own thought angrily. *That's exactly why we need to go!*

And she *felt* the speaker's hesitation and doubt. And to her surprise, Charlee knew it was a woman, instinctively and without doubt.

"You heard me," Charlee thought and whispered.

Yes! There was fierce satisfaction in the single word.

Charlee grabbed Asher's arm. "I can speak to someone on the other side of the shield."

Asher's lips parted in surprise.

Lucas stepped closer. "Tell them to send in the military. Any military. All of them! We're about to be overrun!"

Asher's fingers curled around her wrist. "Do you trust them?"

Charlee nodded. "She's saved my life at least twice before today."

"She's using the auras to reach you," Asher said urgently. "Like the Valdar do. Tell her to bring down the shield."

"Did you hear that?" Charlee asked. Articulating her thoughts aloud made it easier.

I only hear you. Tell me what to do.

"Bring down the shield."

How?

Charlee bit her lip, her first reaction one of disbelief. This was not her sphere of expertise. She could stitch wounds and heal, she could and had done thousands of other things that had kept them alive, but she was not powerful, not the way Verlan Seeker was, or even Eira with her Valkyrie abilities.

But an idea was nagging her, calling for attention. She considered the tower and the idea bloomed properly. *"The tower,"* she said and thought. *"It generates the aura. We interrupt the generator, make it hiccup, and the aura will drop."*

I feel it. I feel the tower.

Charlee could feel her attention being pulled toward the tower. Not her gaze, not her normal eyesight, but she could feel her focus being turned toward it. She saw the tower in her mind, as if she was standing very high up, floating over it. It looked small.

Yes, with me.

She/they reached down to the tower and…encompassed it. Immediately, Charlee could feel it throb in her hands like a living thing. It *was* alive, but it wasn't life.

Take it in. Stop it spreading.

Charlee wasn't sure who said that. It might have been her idea or not. It didn't matter. She drew in the power. It felt like drawing liquid through a straw, as if she were inhaling it. But her whole being was absorbing the power. But not for long, for the aura was too powerful. They just needed to hold it still inside for a few heartbeats, but it was too strong.

As she held her breath mentally and physically, Charlee could hear war raging around her: the clash of metal, the sound of gunfire, and the screams of people injured and dying. But they were fighting. Humans. Einherjar. Both.

Together.

Yes, together, Charlee murmured. She sent out the mental call before she had fully thought it through, too hurried to worry whether it would work.

To me! To me! All who hear me, gather to me!

The mental cry echoed in her head, unanswered.

Then a thought appeared in her mind, strong and well-formed, as if the sender was practiced at this. *So, you have found your purpose at last, branded one.*

Charlee gasped, for the word-thoughts had a character to them that she recognized at once. Verlan Seeker.

We need more, the woman declared.

Much more, Verlan agreed smoothly.

Together, Charlee told them, making her word-thought clear and inarguable. *Reach for others.*

She sent her cry out once more into the world within her mind. So did Verlan and the woman, and this time there were responses. Many of them.

Charlee pulled them toward her. *To me! To me!* Then she turned her attention upon the tower once more. *Take the power within you.*

This time, she could feel the power coursing through her and she realized that she was a junction, a focal point for the others to use to reach the tower itself. The power of the aura fizzled through her, pulling faster and faster until—

The shield stuttered. And failed.

Charlee blinked, drawing her attention back to here and now. Asher and Lucas and a dozen more humans were fighting off more Blakar who had gained the roof. They were standing in an arc around her, keeping her protected.

"The shield is down!" Charlee cried.

Lucas glanced at her, the only reaction to her cry, but on the ground below them, she heard the words repeated.

"The shield is down!"

"Someone brought down the shield! We're free!"

"The shield, the shield!"

Word was spreading.

Asher used his sword to bring down the last Blakar on the roof as Lucas whirled and pulled a cellphone out of his thigh pocket.

"What the hell?" Charlee demanded.

"I charged it at the station last night, when the power came online." He grinned as he held the phone to his ear. "Sir! Lieutenant Montgomery reporting in." He turned away, speaking rapidly, his left hand holding a bloody knife. "The shield over New York just popped and we're in a bit of a squeeze…."

A collective cry of rage and despair sounded, mixed with the inhuman cries of triumph from the Alfar. Charlee spun once more to look out across the swirling, surging sea of humans, Einherjar and Alfar down below.

Eira still stood upon the hill, but she was clutching her side, her sword at her feet. As Charlee saw her, Eira folded forward over her hands.

A Blakar climbed up to the top of the rubble, his long knife over his head and an expression that looked gleeful to Charlee. Eira's back was exposed.

As the long knife came down, Eira picked up her fallen sword, straightened up and thrust the blade through the Blakar. He squealed, clutching at the steel. Eira withdrew the sword and shoved him. He tumbled down the rubble and disappeared from view beneath the fighting bodies at the foot of the hill.

Eira dropped her sword again. Blood covered her side, and it was dark and thick. Charlee recognized the fatal wound and drew in a steadying breath, pushing her sorrow deep and burying it.

Eira was looking up at the roof, toward Asher. She brought her hand up and pointed at him.

Heads turned. Among them, Charlee saw familiar, dear faces.

Eira fell. She did not crumple. Her body, held in disciplined tension until the last, toppled backwards. Hands reached up and caught her and lowered her to the ground.

Asher caught at Charlee's arm and pulled her away from the edge of the roof, toward Lucas.

"Take her and go," he shouted at Lucas.

Charlee caught her breath, horror spilling through her.

"They'll come after me with everything they have, now," Asher added. "Get her somewhere safe, so I can concentrate."

He turned and kissed her, hard and fast. "Don't argue," he said roughly. "Let me do what I'm supposed to."

Charlee nodded.

His thumb brushed her scar, then he turned and strode to the edge of the roof and raised his sword. "Einherjar! To me!"

Lucas tugged on Charlee's elbow. "Come on, I'll get you on the arrowhead and out of this."

"Wait," she said, watching Asher, and the reaction of the people below.

"Einherjar! Humans! All of you, to me!" Asher shouted.

The fighting paused, just as the aura had stuttered, interrupted by a stronger force. Silence and stillness gripped the arena.

Charlee could feel the tension. The moment teetered upon a knife-edge.

Slowly, she moved toward Asher.

"Charlee, what the hell...?" Lucas protested as she shook off his grip once more and moved to the parapet next to Asher, where everyone could see her.

Renmar still stood upon his own platform, but it had been lifted a few feet higher, safe from the fighting below. Now he pointed at them both with a long finger. "Bring them to me! Bring them both! Bring them and no one else has to die here today!" The interpreter's voice rolled over the hushed arena.

Asher held out his sword to one side, point up. It wasn't surrender, but it was a neutral position. "Choose!" he demanded, his voice harsh. "You want choice. You want freedom. It is yours. Choose wisely."

The tense stillness ticked on, marked by Charlee's heartbeat, which echoed loudly in her ears.

Then the silence was broken by a single hoarse cry. "Freedom!"

To the left, by the farthest reaches of the arena, a man held up his fist, a rough and ready shiv in it. He turned to the Blakar next to him and rammed the shiv into the Blakar's chest.

The Blakar grunted in pain, then thrust his long knife into the man's stomach and wrenched upwards. As the man fell to the ground, the

Blakar plucked the shiv out of his chest and tossed it away.

Instantly, a dozen more humans leapt upon the Blakar, attacking him with hands, knives and rocks. The Blakar disappeared under the attack.

Catalyzed, the arena again became a roiling battlefield, but with a difference. This time, the humans were not merely defending themselves. This time they were attacking. They were fighting for themselves.

Asher turned and ran for the side of the building. "Come on!" he urged to everyone on the roof, who turned and followed him.

"No, you're coming with me," Lucas said, holding Charlee back.

Charlee smiled at him. "Wanna bet I won't put this long knife through your thigh if you don't take your hands off me?"

Lucas held up his hands. "You're not thinking of going with him, are you?"

Charlee rolled her eyes and ran for the fire escape and the stream of people running down the stairs.

Lucas swore. "Then I'm coming with you!" He caught up and ran beside her.

Once they reached the pavement, Asher began to swing his sword, taking down any Alfar near him. With his other hand he pushed humans aside, clearing a path. "Follow me!" he cried. "Everyone, follow me! To the tower!"

His cry was picked up and repeated, passing on. "The tower! The tower!"

Go with him. The words were cool. Calm.

Charlee had no intention of letting Asher out of her sight. She raised her knives to the defensive position and forged ahead, through the path Asher was clearing.

By the time they reached the base wall, hundreds of humans had coalesced around them, fighting with bare hands, homemade weapons, and the long knives they had taken from the fallen Alfar.

Asher had been moving diagonally across the open area, and now they were paces away from the door that was set into the base wall. Here, the fighting became heavier and their progress slower, for the Alfar were defending their tower, desperate to prevent invasion.

But Asher urged everyone on, shouting his encouragement and directions, and the mass of Alfar defending the opening fell under the overwhelming number of humans and Einherjar.

A cry of jubilation went up as the door was cleared.

"Onward!" Asher cried. "On and upward!"

They poured into the tower, a steady stream of ragged people buoyed by hope, determined to win their freedom.

The tide of people swept Charlee and Lucas along. Even if they had wanted to withdraw, they could not. Not now.

Lucas lifted Charlee up, his hand on her arm. "Stay on your feet," he warned, shouting in her ear. "You'll be trampled, otherwise."

They pushed through the door, a thick bottleneck of people, many of them screaming and shouting, roused to a rare fierceness. There were so many of them pouring through the door that the Alfar could not contain them. They had fallen back and the humans streamed into the tower, a rushing river of bodies.

The Alfar did not attempt to halt them on that level. Charlee looked around as they pushed through the door into a wide, level, cool and dim area with a high roof. Light seemed to emanate from the walls themselves. The floor beneath was polished like black marble, but not slippery. Grit ground beneath their feet, tracked in from outside.

The air was cool and refreshing after the humidity outside.

The shouting cries were even louder in here, and from among them, Charlee heard a common thread.

"Up!"

"Upwards!"

"Up to the top. Drive them out!"

There were stairs ahead, very wide and open, and the mass of bodies was climbing them. At the edge, at the top of the stairs, Asher stood with his sword raised, point upwards. He was urging everyone onwards, and scanning the heads and shoulders below.

Charlee waved, catching his attention, and he straightened. She could see his chest lift. Relief? Or vexation?

"There she is!" came a shout behind her.

"Charlee, watch out!" Lucas screamed.

Charlee whirled, bringing her knives up, but the Blakar was too close. The tip of his blade slid in over the top of her crossed knives. It pushed into her with a sharp, ripping sensation.

Someone gasped heavily.

I'm making that sound! Charlee realized.

Then the pain hit and she groaned. The world lifted up around her and she realized that it was her; she was sinking to the ground.

The blade pulled upwards. She could feel it in her body, tearing through her, a hot, slicing sensation. Heat seemed to be pouring out of her.

Her vision was fading. She couldn't make sense of what she was looking at, but she could hear the oddest things from among the noise around her.

Lucas grunting. Swearing.

"Charlee! Charlee!" That was Asher's voice, from far away.

Lucas laid down beside her. He dropped down tiredly. Charlee drifted her gaze over to where he laid. His eyes were open. There was blood on his face.

The noise was fading. Going away. There was relief in that.

Then something shook her and Charlee blinked.

Asher. Asher was in front of her.

Charlee forced herself to focus. It meant riding over the pain, fighting for clarity. But for Asher, she would do anything. She looked at him.

He was touching her face. His hands were trembling.

The need to leave, the urge to drift away, swelled up in her once more. It was like a tide, pulling at her, too strong to fight against.

"Lead them," she whispered.

Then she let go and embraced the darkness.

Chapter Forty-Six

Blankness held his mind. The blankness kept his body still. He didn't want to move away from this moment. He could feel the weight of her lifeless body in his arms. She had been so very alive only a moment ago.

Somewhere deep inside, a keening set up, a long, undulating cry of pain and rage and abject grief.

Asher bowed his head over hers, letting the pain fill him.

A hand gripped his shoulder, hard, heavy and demanding. "They need you, Annarr. If you forsake them now, they will be lost."

Asher shook his head. No, he couldn't do this. Not now.

Lead them. Charlee's last words.

Hands were on his arm, pulling him up. "Get up on your feet, soldier! Now!"

He looked up. Ylva stood before him, her hair cut short, her figure heavy with armor and weapons. As he looked up, she bent down and picked up the long knives still gripped in Charlee's hands. She slipped them out of Charlee's loose grip and swung them. "Freedom or death," she said. "I chose freedom. You?"

Lead them.

Asher climbed to his feet. His body, like his heart and mind and soul, was heavy with the darkness. He looked around at the people standing guarding him while he selfishly took these moments for himself. They were Einherjar and human, both.

Asher took a deep breath. And another. He unfurled his sword and held it up. "To the top," he declared.

* * * * *

Charlee rolled over with a groan, feeling an ache over her entire body. Carefully, she opened her eyes.

Sunlight played on her face, and cool air brushed over her skin. There were trees all around her, and close-cropped turf beneath her. She pushed up with her hand, lifting herself into a sprawled sitting position.

Lucas laid next to her and as she saw him, he rolled over with a groan of his own and shook his head to clear it as he lifted his upper body and propped himself up with his arms. He looked around and saw her.

"Charlee." He swallowed and looked around again. "I think...I think we're dead."

Charlee got to her feet. She was wearing the same clothes that she had put on last night, to journey to the northern foot. Her hair was loose and lifting in the soft breeze. Apart from the sound of the wind in the tree tops, it was silent. Peaceful. "I don't think we're dead," Charlee said, looking at the trees. They looked oddly familiar, but she didn't think she had ever seen them before. Yet a memory was prodding her. Something to do with a photograph....

"Then where are we?" Lucas got to his feet. He was wearing the ragged shirt and cargo pants she had last seen him in, but he carried no weapons.

Charlee turned slowly, taking in the trees. They were all around them, as far as the eye could see, except for this little clearing they had found themselves in. At the very edge of the horizon, though, there was a dark, uneven line that made her think of mountains in the far distance.

"There's something nearby," Charlee said.

Lucas stepped up beside her, peering ahead. "No, it's a long way away, but it's..." He shook his head. "Calling?" he asked.

"Waiting," Charlee decided.

"Yes, waiting."

"If there's somewhere for us to go," Lucas said slowly, "then perhaps we *are* dead, or nearly dead. Perhaps this is..." He hesitated.

"Purgatory?" Charlee asked. "Do you think that's where we are?"

He gave the trees and the uneven horizon another baffled glance. "No," he said shortly.

"I think we should go there. To where we're expected."

"We could just stay here."

"We could," Charlee agreed. "But that's not what you do. You have always fought for what you wanted."

Lucas gave her a smile that lifted one corner of his mouth. "So have you, in your own way. And you fought harder than I ever did."

Charlee turned to face the ragged horizon once more. "Somewhere over there," she decided.

"There's no path. No trail," Lucas pointed out.

"We don't walk there," Charlee said firmly.

Lucas studied the skyline. "Then how...?" He turned to her. "You brought down the shield."

"It wasn't just me," Charlee pointed out.

"You touched the auras. You shaped them."

Auras. Charlee faced the horizon once more. High up in the sky, she saw two black dots. Birds, very far away. But they were getting closer.

"Is that a goose?" Lucas asked, shading his eyes with his hand and squinting.

The long neck of one of the birds was growing more distinct. "A swan," Charlee murmured.

"The other is a crow," Lucas decided.

Charlee shook her head. "A raven." She could feel the rightness inside her, agreeing with what she had said. A swan and a raven. Why did that stir something in her?

The two birds were flying together, the swan dipping and lifting as the powerful wings worked to carry the heavy creature. They were very close now, and quite low above the tree tops. They arrowed directly toward Charlee and Lucas in the middle of the clearing.

The raven gave a hoarse caw, then both birds streamed past. Charlee and Lucas turned to keep watching them, and the birds banked, circling. With slow flaps of their wings, the birds flew past them again, this time so low Charlee could hear the wind in their wings and the rushing sound they made as they passed by.

The two birds headed back the way they came. Back toward the mountains.

"They want us to follow," Charlee said. She didn't know where that knowledge came from, but it was true. She felt it in her bones.

"How?" Lucas asked reasonably.

Charlee picked up his hand. "I'm not sure."

"You know everything," he pointed out.

She shook her head. "I could live as long as the Kine and still not know it all." She looked ahead, feeling the pull, her gaze drifting back to the mountains. She tried to feel ahead, like she had felt and encompassed the tower. But there was no one to help her this time. It was just her, and the little bits she had learned about the nine worlds.

"Hurry," Lucas urged. "We need to go. Soon."

"I know." She felt ahead, groping blindly. When Verlan Seeker had reached her, his imprint had been steady. Confident. Then there was the silvered rush of power from the aura running through her.

Through her.

Charlee recalled that sensation once more. It had been a pure, cool feeling. The auras were inhuman. Alive in their way, and with a literal intelligence, like a computer was intelligent. Complex. Ethereal. Strong.

She felt the brush of one against her mind and turned to it. Facing it. Embracing it. It passed through her, and Charlee gasped.

"I can *feel* that," Lucas whispered, his eyes wide. His hand gripped hers tightly.

Charlee studied the sensations swirling through her as the aura pushed through. It was too wide. Too generalized. She grappled with it, feeling the aura pulse and respond. She had to narrow the aperture that it was passing through. But how?

Focus...like a magnifying glass focused light in a pinpoint....

Charlee stared at the distant peaks, shutting out all thoughts, all distractions. She shut down her hearing and lost sense of Lucas' hand in hers. There was just the place ahead, the place she must reach.

Everything she had learned since Asher had come into her life, every skill and the sum total of her experiences, had prepared her for this. By accident or design, everything she had learned had shaped her and honed her for this moment: her stolen knowledge of the Kine and learning their ways; training as an Amica, which was the closest a human woman could come to being a true Valkyrie; her healing skills, which had prepared her for dealing with auras; the unknown woman in her head; and finally, Verlan Seeker himself and his dry mental observation that Charlee was about to fulfill her purpose.

Charlee felt the rise of confidence that this was true. With that confidence came the knowledge she needed. She tightened her grip on the aura, channeling it, narrowing down her focus until the aura burst through her, honed to laser-like power.

The air opened in front of them, dazzling like a sunrise and crackling with energy. As the aura settled down, lengthening and forming, Charlee shaped the opening into an upright rectangle.

"A door," Lucas murmured. He looked at her. "A portal." His hand squeezed again. "Can we go through, do you think?"

Charlee let out her breath. "You know the answer."

"Yes, we can," Lucas decided. He moved forward and Charlee went with him. They stepped through.

* * * * *

The hall was very large—larger than any Charlee had ever seen before. It echoed emptily as they stepped from the portal and looked around. Ahead, doors stood open, and through them an ethereal white light

560

poured.

Without speaking, they moved across the silent hall and through the doors. The light was coming from overhead, falling through a roof made of high, arching beams of stone, with patterned glass between them.

At the far end of the hall was a dais, with two grand chairs upon it. Behind the dais, higher still, was another platform with a single chair upon it, bigger than either of the pair below.

Charlee glanced at them, but her attention was drawn to a table sitting in the middle of the hall, halfway between where they stood just inside the door and the dais at the other end.

There was a pitcher and a cup sitting on the table. Both were made of a metal that might have been bronze or gold. They were quite plain, but very beautiful.

Charlee walked to the table, her footsteps echoing. Somewhere high overhead, a bird fluttered restlessly, disturbed by her steps. But otherwise the hall was silent.

Moving by instinct, Charlee picked up the pitcher and poured. The golden liquid flowed into the cup and its distinct scent rose up. It was mead.

Lucas came to the table. Silently, Charlee held the cup out to him. He took it and drank, then gave it back to her. Charlee sipped the cool liquid, feeling it slide down her throat.

Lucas looked around. "Are we where I think we are?"

"Where do you think you are?" Charlee asked, putting down the cup.

He looked at her. "Valhalla."

Charlee sampled the air, looking for the rightness inside her that would confirm his guess. "Yes," she said at last.

With the acknowledgment came a sense of urgency. Of business unfinished.

Lucas frowned, as if he had abruptly grown aware of the same urgent call.

Charlee gasped. "Asher!" she cried as the memories rushed back in like the returning tide.

* * * * *

They found the Lajos cowering at the top of the tower, for the humans still fighting for access to the base had sabotaged what they had been using as their stage, and they had scrambled into the tower at a mid-point doorway and raced to the top just ahead of Asher's army.

The tower narrowed at the top, but it was still a massively large construction. The level they found when they fought their way up the last set of stairs was open to the air on all sides and soared up to the tip of the tower, many feet above.

Renmar stood behind the ranks of his Lajos, who had arranged a phalanx of Myrakar as protection in front of them.

Asher's people spread out across the level, facing the Myrakar line. Asher walked into the middle of the clear space between them. He glanced behind him, and Ylva and Darwin stepped out to stand just in front of the line. Koslov made his way to the front, far to one side, and waved someone through with him. A man with a camera on his shoulder, his eye to the viewfinder, walked out into the open. The camera moved around the level, then pointed at Asher.

Asher mentally sighed over the camera. He looked past the ranks of Myrakar and Lajos to where Renmar stood outlined by the grey sky visible through the big open arch behind him.

"Come out from behind your men and finish this with no more bloodshed," Asher told him.

One of the Myrakar leaned to whisper in Renmar's ear, but the Lajos waved him off. He looked at Asher, his large eyes filled with a very human emotion: bitterness. He pushed through the line of Lajos. The Myrakar parted to let him through, and he stepped out into the empty space between the two armies and turned to face Asher. He was taller than Asher, but not by much. For a Lajos, he was quite short.

Asher rested his sword point down, the blood running the length of his blade and pooling on the floor at his feet.

"You think you have won," Renmar said slowly, his English ill-formed and hesitant, but intelligible. "You cannot win, even if you cut me down right here and now. You are a dying race, soon to be interred within the earth of your lesser cousins, bereft of a world to call your own. The branded one is dead. The prophecy is broken. You have failed, even as you have won."

The reminder of Charlee caused the blackness in Asher to rise and try to break free. He fought to keep it contained. "I would not speak of her at all, if I were you, Renmar." He waved around the tower. "Surrender, and we will negotiate terms."

"Surrender?" Renmar smiled, and it was an odd expression on his face. It seemed to be skewed, just like his English. "We have not lost. Once I am gone, another will be here."

Asher switched to the language of the Alfar. He did not want Renmar to misunderstand him. "No human will suffer another Alfar to control their world, Renmar. They will rise up as they have today and topple whoever dares try. It is over. All that remains is for you to save what is left of your people."

Renmar's face worked as he struggled to deal with Asher's words.

Asher chose his next words carefully, for he was at the limits of his knowledge of Renmar's tongue. "You did not kill her soon enough, Renmar. Everyone saw her standing by my side. They will remember that forever. They will remember that humans stood with Herleifr on this day, and they know that the Kine will always stand with them."

Renmar howled in protest. It was a wordless battle cry that lifted the hairs on Asher's neck. He brought his sword and knife up, just as Renmar's long knife materialized in his hand and came down to cleave Asher's skull in two.

The three blades locked with a ringing sound, and everyone in the hall took a step forward in alarm.

Renmar hissed, the fury in his eyes revealed at last. He had played his last hand and lost.

Ylva ran forward, her long knives up. "Arsenios!" she called and Arsenios jogged over. The two of them wrenched the long knife out of Renmar's hands and wrestled him to his knees on the floor in front of Asher. His robe fell into the pool of blood and it began to soak the cloth, spreading upwards.

Asher stared at him, the blackness threatening to break through. "The misery you have caused," he muttered. "Returning you to Alfheim isn't enough." He lifted the sword again and Ylva stepped away from Renmar quickly, anticipating his blow.

"Asher, no!" came the cry from behind him.

It was Charlee's voice.

Asher halted his sword at the very apex of his swing, his heart squeezing and his breath rushing out in a heavy gasp.

Ylva's eyes were wide, her mouth open as she looked past him.

"Charlee!" Darwin called from his place at the front of the lines, and there was delight in his tone.

Asher spun to look.

Charlee and Lucas stood together, and behind them was a shimmering, unframed portal.

Charlee stepped forward, slowly, her hand up toward him. "It's really me, Asher," she said softly.

He remembered to start breathing again, but it was hard to inhale because of the tightness in his chest.

Ylva moved closer, studying Charlee and Lucas. "I can see it for myself," she whispered. "You're Valkyrie."

Ylva's words let Asher acknowledge the difference in her and Lucas. The familiar sensation one of the Kine felt in the presence of another. It was true.

"We're back," Lucas said in confirmation. "From Valhalla."

The reaction in the hall was compound: surprise and pleasure, consternation among the Alfar who understood English, and whispers as the implications behind Lucas' simple words were understood.

Directly behind Asher, Renmar screamed out his fury.

Lucas lunged forward. "Asher, watch out!" He leaned over Asher's shoulder as Asher spun out of the way of danger. Asher saw the sword appear in Lucas' hand. The blade buried itself in Renmar's chest with a wet sucking sound that came from the sharpest of edges sliding through flesh and bone.

Renmar staggered backwards two steps. Lucas' sword was pulled out by the movement, and Renmar grasped at the wound and dropped to the ground.

Immediately, Asher's people swarmed forward to surround the Alfar on the other side of the room. Swords and guns hemmed them in, holding them at bay.

The room became still once more.

Asher looked at the Myrakar. "Put down your weapons," he told them in Alfar. "You do not need to die today."

The Lajos among them were weaponless, but one of them, whose sense of self-preservation was stronger than his leadership instincts, lowered himself to his knees and bent forward, placing his face on the ground. The remainder of the Alfar followed, silently and meekly.

Darwin looked at Asher with a sideways grin. "Victory is yours, king of kings."

Charlee hurled herself into his arms, making Asher stagger a little. He didn't mind at all. He dropped his sword and picked her up, and with a deep breath of anticipation, he kissed her.

She was warm and pliant and soft in his arms, and Asher touched his forehead to hers, profoundly simple happiness blooming in his chest.

It was then he realized that everyone was cheering and clapping around them. He looked around, feeling oddly bemused.

Ylva raised her brow at him, her arms propped up by the long knives resting pointed down in her hands. But there was a silly smile on her face.

Darwin was grinning hugely, and so was Lucas.

Asher held out his arm toward Lucas, who took it with the warriors' grip.

Charlee looked into Asher's eyes. "I have something to show you," she whispered. "Once the world lets you be for a moment."

Chapter Forty-Seven

It took weeks before the world was ready to leave Asher and Charlee alone for a few hours of private time. Ylva, Darwin, Koslov, and many others who had helped with the overthrow of the Alfar found themselves equally in demand, for media interviews, debriefings, conferences, summits, and endless numbers of formal inquiries.

The Alfar had fled Midgard, but the bivrost was still open, the nine worlds free to mix and mingle as they dared. Humans needed to learn and come to terms with their new reality now the war was over and they had time to heal and grow. The Kine would be the facilitators of the education humans faced, and all of them faced intense scrutiny, at every moment of their days.

But eventually, the intensity of the interest faded and Asher was finally free to deal with Kine business, away from the harsh glare of lights and microphones.

At the first opportunity, Charlee delivered her promise. She opened a portal and invited Asher, Ylva, Darwin, and Lucas to step through. Verlan Seeker had invited himself along once he heard where they were going. After consulting with Asher, Charlee had agreed to him tagging along.

They stepped through the portal Charlee made, into the front hall and looked around at the soaring walls and glistening floor. "This isn't the same as I remember," Ylva said. "It *feels* the same, but it isn't the same place."

"Yet it is the same place, anyway," Asher said, looking upward.

"It only looks different," Verlan said, his hands on his hips. "And it is in a different place now, but it *is* Valhalla."

Charlee gave them no more time but led them through the dazzling doorway, to the main hall.

The table was still sitting in the middle of the hall, but this time, there were six cups sitting next to the pitcher. Charlee filled four of the cups, then handed the pitcher to Ylva, who poured the remaining two.

Charlee handed Lucas and Verlan a cup each and Ylva gave Darwin another. Then Charlee held a cup out toward Asher, both hands around the stem. "Welcome to Valhalla, my Annarr."

Asher drew in a deep breath. Slowly, with a bow, he took the cup. "My thanks, Regin."

Charlee had been reaching for her own cup, but her hand stilled. "No," she said quickly.

"Yes," Ylva said firmly. "You are going to argue with the prophecy? With the Vanir? With Verlan?"

Verlan bowed his head. "You are supposed to lead. With Asher."

"Who opened the portal?" Lucas asked. "Who found the way back to Valhalla? It wasn't a simple Amica, Charlee."

Darwin took a deep swallow of his mead. "The Vanir were right all along. You are the ones to lead, you and Asher. You already are. Everyone looks to you for answers, for direction. You have been guiding the Einherjar and the Valkyrie—purely by example, if not actively giving directions. The world is watching you, taking its cues from what you do. You *have* to lead."

"Only by acclaim," Asher insisted. "Only if the Kine agree."

"No." Verlan shook his head. "Your place is preordained, Asher. The Kine must adapt to this new reality, just as humans must."

Ylva put down her cup. "Odin is not here," and she glanced at the big chair above the platform, "but this is Valhalla. You stand in his hall, Charlee. Would you gainsay the gift Valhalla has bestowed upon you?"

Charlee swallowed. "But...I'm just...Charlee." She reached for Asher's hand and he took it, a rare public demonstration. When they were in public he was usually stiff and formal—a most proper Einherjar.

"Yes, but you are Valkyrie now," Ylva insisted. "Asher, demonstrate, please. Draw your sword."

He frowned and reached for his pocket.

"Not like that," Darwin said. "The way Lucas does it—thrusting with his hand."

Asher's brows lifted and he glanced at Lucas.

"I can't explain it," Lucas said. "I just do it and it's there."

Asher put down his cup, then turned so that the space in front of him was clear. He stepped forward and thrust...and the sword was *there*.

He looked down at it, at the runes running the length of the blade, and the iron and silver of the hilt. It was a huge sword, made for a man of his height and strength.

"I have never seen this sword before," Asher said, "but I know without question that it is mine." He stood up and raised the sword, studying it carefully. Then it disappeared. "Just as I intended," Asher added. He looked at Charlee. "You try."

"The Valkyrie are not warriors," Charlee pointed out.

"In their own way, yes they are," Darwin replied.

"You died in battle," Lucas pointed out. "Try it."

Feeling self-conscious, Charlee copied Asher's movements. She thrust forward with her foot and curled her hand around a hilt that was not there, pushing it forward like she intended to skewer an enemy.

The hilt filled her curled fingers, and the sword glittered under the light from the roof overhead. It was an odd color, not at all like Asher's silvered steel and iron blade. Charlee lifted it up in both hands, just like Asher had, examining the very fine writing on the spine of the blade. It was a language she didn't know. Not yet.

"The metal...it's strange," Asher murmured, stepping closer to examine it.

"It's red," Darwin declared, tilting his head to study it. "Red for the red-headed rose. Very appropriate."

Charlee moved the sword about. The metal really was red and very beautiful. It wasn't too heavy, and it was perfectly balanced.

"Do you doubt anymore, Charlee?" Verlan asked quietly. "Do you think Valhalla would bestow such a symbol upon a mere Amica, or a mere human, or even just-Charlee?"

Charlee shook her head. "No," she said, her voice trembling. "I suppose the prophecies know what they're talking about. I'll just have to catch up with them." She let the sword vanish.

Asher pulled her against him, his arm around her. He kissed her temple. "We both will," he said gently.

"The whole world is going to have to catch up," Darwin said, and his voice had taken on its professor tone.

"Uh-oh, lecture on the way," Lucas said with a grin.

Darwin rolled his eyes. "Prophecies just deal with the end of things. The results. After that, everyone has to clean up the mess and figure out how to go on now life has changed directions on them. That's where you and Asher come in."

"I must be missing something," Charlee said. "For the first time in a long time, Darwin, I don't know what you mean."

Ylva smiled. "He's been talking about this for weeks. I think he forgot to explain the steps in between."

Darwin put down his cup and pressed his hands together. The professor was in full spout. "Charlee has spent her life choosing her own path, or thought she did. Because of Asher, she learned about the Kine at an early age. So did Lucas, indirectly, and a bit later. Charlee immersed herself in the Kine world, even though it was a secret world then. She lived and breathed the Herleifr life. And because the Kine maintained *laun* so strictly, Charlee's education was unique. No one learned as much as she did, not even the Amica who are trained to the life."

"The Amica learn from infancy that they are human and will always be so, despite the Kine world they were born into. Charlee doesn't have that bias," Verlan said. His voice had taken on the same flat, lecturing quality as Darwin's. "Both Charlee and Lucas have believed without a shred of doubt that Valhalla is real, that the Kine are real. Humans who know about the Kine, who believe in self-determination, who believe absolutely in Valhalla...that hasn't happened since the Kine descended to Midgard."

"The prophecy accounted for that," Darwin added. "It *needed* Asher to reveal himself to a human and break *laun*. The Vanir knew Asher's rebellious ways would make Sindri feel even more isolated and unloved and coax him to open the bivrost, opening Midgard up to the nine worlds once more."

"It also took in account," Verlan said, "that Charlee's influence on Eira would make Eira pause long enough to let Sindri live, once he had revealed his betrayal to her. And through Eira's mercy, the prophecy tightened its hold."

"Who is telling this story, anyway?" Darwin complained.

Verlan frowned. "You seek to dispute one of the Valdar?" he asked, his voice cold.

Darwin considered him. "You're my first wizard," he said. "Is the big ol' stick up your butt common to all of you?"

Lucas snorted and raised his cup to drink and hide his expression.

Ylva squeezed Darwin's wrist in warning.

"Let it go, Seeker," Asher said, his voice soft. "Remember, we are all learning, here."

Verlan bowed his head in Asher's direction. "Annarr," he acknowledged.

Darwin lifted his cup toward Charlee. "You are the only one who could find the way back to Valhalla. You might think you weren't born to it, but your entire life has been leading to it."

Charlee sighed. "All I wanted was a picket fence."

Asher's fingers tightened around hers.

* * * * *

After the Alfar occupation of the Second Hall, none of the Herleifr were comfortable with the idea of it becoming the seat of Kine power once more. So Charlee worked with Verlan Seeker to build permanent portals to key locations around the world, and the new Valhalla, which was also increasingly called the First Hall, became once more the home and headquarters for the Kine.

She also worked with engineers and builders to adapt the hall for human and Kine occupation, as the mystical designers had overlooked some practical necessities. After the war, she and Asher had moved into a suite in a hotel on Long Island, but after three months, they moved the extensive operations and personnel that had coalesced around them to Valhalla.

Charlee showed Asher the quarters she designed and had built. They were large and airy, and there were many rooms—with the public rooms at the front end of the suite and their private rooms deeper within.

"All these formal meeting rooms..." Asher began, sounding doubtful.

"There will be lots of meetings," Charlee told him. "We can't use the big halls for small occasions, or they will lose their majesty."

He kissed her. "I will trust you in this." He looked around. "There is something missing though."

"What?" she asked, wondering what she had overlooked.

"I'll have to think about it," Asher decided. He glanced at the digital clock on the desk. "I have a meeting. In one of those public rooms, I suppose." He kissed her and left.

Asher's days swiftly filled with many meetings and commitments. The public rooms at the front of their quarters were well used.

One of those meetings was with Ylva, who went through formal channels to set up an official appointment. She and Darwin arrived together, Ylva wearing a business-like and very elegant skirt suit, and Darwin in a new and modern suit of his own. He smoothed down his tie uneasily as Asher asked them to sit.

"Are you nervous, Darwin?" Charlee asked as she and Asher sat on the sofa opposite the pair.

"Like a cat in a room full of rockers," Darwin said. "Although you can probably guess why we're here." He reached out and picked up Ylva's hand.

Ylva wore a small, warm smile.

Charlee looked from one to the other, delight filling her. "I had no idea," she breathed. "But this is wonderful!"

Ylva looked at Asher. "You're my earl and my Annarr," she said. "I didn't ask for permission last time, but to not ask this time would set the wrong precedent. So I seek your approval to marry Darwin Baxter, a human with no allegiance to any hall."

Asher studied Darwin. "Would you be willing to swear your allegiance to the Kine and to me, Darwin?"

Ylva caught her breath, but Charlee just smiled.

"He can't," Ylva protested. "Darwin isn't Kine."

"Ways change," Asher said evenly. "The Kine must change with them. There's no reason why a human cannot serve a hall, just as the Kine do."

"I'm no warrior," Darwin pointed out. "And I'm too old to start being one."

Asher nodded. "But you can serve in many other ways. You studied the Herleifr for years. Your knowledge will be useful. And you can teach others, too." He looked at him sharply. "Do you believe you are too old for that?"

"Hell, no," Darwin said.

"Then welcome to my hall, Darwin Baxter. I heartily approve your coming nuptials and if I don't get an invitation to the wedding, I'll crash it, along with every media camera following me."

Ylva paled. "You'll get an invitation," she assured him.

Another meeting was one that Charlee had arranged with Verlan Seeker some weeks before, sending him out on a mission that only he could complete. He stood waiting in the room when she and Asher entered, a slender woman standing next to him. She looked like she was in her late fifties. She had long hair pinned neatly at the back of her head in an old-fashioned bun and plain clothes. From beneath her well-tailored pants a steel brace peeped.

There was a terrible scar upon her right cheek that radiated out across her face in angry red weals that drew the gaze and did much to hide the fact that the woman had the loveliest eyes—wide, grey and almost limpid, with thick lashes.

"My work is completed to order, as you can see," Verlan said dryly. "I found her in a place called Lakelands—a hot, fetid swampland I have no wish to return to."

"Thank the spirits for that," the woman told him and looked at Asher. "Your forgiveness, Annarr, but I was under the mistaken impression that wizards would be interesting company."

Asher managed to hold himself to a mere smile although Charlee could feel the tremors from silent laughter rippling through him from where her thigh touched his.

She studied the woman. *It's you*, she thought/whispered.

The woman gazed at Charlee. "I have known you nearly all my life," she said. "I never thought I would meet you, though."

"We have much to thank you for," Charlee said. "Most especially for what you did to help bring down the shield around the New York tower."

The woman blushed and the scar reddened even more. "I wanted to," she said. "It was little enough."

"Then there is more you can do?" Charlee asked.

The woman looked startled. "I...er...."

"She has appreciable abilities, for a human," Verlan said dryly.

"I'm not...people don't think of me as...well, talented," the woman said. "I got used to being alone at an early age, you see."

"Clearly," Verlan said.

She looked at him. "I'm an introvert because lightning hit me when I was twelve. What's your excuse?"

Charlee struggled to hide her smile, then settled for not laughing aloud. Verlan Seeker's expression was so comically surprised. "Perhaps, if you don't mind," she told the woman, "we can start with your name."

The woman's eyes widened. "Well, yes. My name is Unnur. Yours, of course, is Charlotte Rose. Everyone knows who you are."

Charlee hid her sigh. The long form of her name and both names hitched together had become the most common form of reference to her in the media, especially once the Nine Worlds Prophecy had been explained to the world at large. "We have something in common, Unnur," she said.

Unnur touched her scarred cheek.

"That, too," Charlee agreed. "But you will find that here, scars are honorable markings. I would like you to stay in the hall. You have skills I can use and that you can teach to others."

"Really?" Verlan asked, and rolled his eyes.

"Verlan," Asher said warningly.

"He's quite harmless," Unnur told Asher seriously.

Charlee dug her fingers into Asher's knee, battling the need to bray her laughter out loud. When she thought she could speak once more, she cleared her throat and glanced at him, then back to Unnur. "Would you be willing to swear allegiance to this hall and its earl, the Annarr? To serve the Kine and in turn, help them to serve humans?"

"Me?" Unnur whispered. Her eyes filled with tears, and she nodded.

Verlan considered her, his expression thoughtful.

As long as he *stays far away from me*! The thought slipped into Charlee's mind, shaped and shaded exactly like Unnur. She would recognize the thought as hers even if Unnur were not standing in front of her.

Verlan looked affronted. "I heard that."

Unnur smiled sweetly at him.

Another meeting was held several weeks later, once the initial rush of mundane administrative tasks had been taken care of in between the hungry world media's demands for news and more news.

"We'll need a communications division," Charlee told Asher, after working her way through draft press releases for more than an hour.

Asher laughed.

"I'm serious," Charlee said, lifting the pile of papers.

His smile faded. "Very well. Put Darwin on it. He's the only man in the hall with a formal human education and degrees after his name."

So Darwin was tasked with hiring communications people and setting up the division, and much of the delicate public relations work shifted from Charlee's desk, as did many other areas of concern to a big organization, leaving them with more time to consider the important aspects of the Kine: their future and their priorities.

Asher requested that Lucas attend him in the great hall, and he and Charlee dressed in traditional Kine clothing. But they did not sit in the great chairs. Not yet. Asher had insisted that they not take the symbolic seats until the right time. Instead, they stood at the foot of the dais, while the full assembly of Kine who were aligned with the First Hall stood in attendance.

Lucas presented himself at the appointed time. He wore full Einherjar plated armor, and his extended sword was thrust into his belt. The traditional battle gear looked good on him, and Charlee let the warm happiness fill her at the idea that Lucas would be a part of her world for the foreseeable future.

"Annarr," Lucas acknowledged, bowing his head.

"Einherjar," Asher returned gravely. "I have need of your services."

"How can I assist?"

"You were human such a short while ago that you have not forgotten what it is like to be truly human. I can use that knowledge. I can use you to help forge a bridge between the human military and the Einherjar."

Lucas frowned. "All of them?" he asked.

"You can hire humans and assigned Kine as you need them. You will need the help, because I also want you to control the New York hall."

Charlee gasped, for this was news to her. "There is no hall left," she said quietly.

Asher nodded. "We will rebuild it. This time in the open, in full view of humans, and proudly so." He looked at Lucas. "I believe a native New Yorker would be the best person to figure out how to go about doing that."

Lucas grinned. "With pleasure."

And so Lucas had moved to New York. Charlee ensured there was a permanent portal between the First Hall and New York, and she thought herself content, even though her life wasn't anywhere close to how she had imagined it might be.

Chapter Forty-Eight

It had only been four years since the last reaffirmation, but it was fitting that all Kine everywhere renew their commitment, so on a night several months after the end of the war, when most of the mopping up had been completed and the Kine had a semblance of organization once more, representatives from each hall assembled in the great hall to swear their oaths, a glass of mead in hand.

The preparations had taken weeks, but finally, Charlee and Asher stood at the threshold to the hall, her hand in his, ready to walk the length of the hall and for the first time take their places on the dais.

The assembled Kine bowed and stepped aside as they walked slowly down the length of the hall. Charlee realized that she knew almost everyone, if not by name then at least by their faces.

The hall blazed with light. It was part of the mystery of this new Valhalla that the sunlight never failed to shine in upon the great hall, no matter what hour of the day it was. The temperature never varied from a comfortable degree and rain clouds never darkened the blue above, which meant that lights and warming fires were not needed.

Charlee lifted the hem of her long evening gown as they stepped up onto the dais, Asher holding her other hand. Nervously, she stood in front of the slightly smaller chair and looked out upon the sea of familiar faces. She spotted Darwin, Ylva, Lucas, and his new stallari, a woman he had chosen who was human and had once been a member of the U.S. Army Rangers. Asher had approved the choice and caused more ripples of interest and concern to run through the halls, but like most of the new ideas he had introduced, this one had eventually been accepted with cautious approval.

Charlee picked up the two glasses of mead sitting on the tray waiting their arrival, and handed one to Asher.

Asher held the glass, but did not lift it. "Tonight, I want you to forget all that has gone before. Tonight, we start again, but this time, we begin in a world that is vastly different from the one that we knew before." He glanced at the rank of media people and cameras that stood at the side of the hall, watching silently. This had been one of Darwin's suggestions, which he had argued for with unusual insistence. Charlee was suddenly glad they were here to see this.

Asher continued. "We have a time of peace ahead of us. A time we should use to clean out our stables, shine our shields and prepare. Our purpose is and always has been to defend humans, and now we know that our purpose is not an empty one. Does anyone doubt that others of the nine worlds will not try to conquer small and weak Midgard?"

He paused, and the hall was utterly silent. "We have been reminded of this and by the barest good luck, we triumphed. Now, we can never forget." He raised his glass high. "We swear fealty to Odin—" he began.

Their voices rose to meld with his, including Charlee's. "—the first among us, whose wisdom and strength is our guiding light. We swear to protect humanity, whose care was given into our hands. We will remain upon this path, forsaking all others, and forsaking our own humanity in order to provide the strength and valor that Odin has granted us. So say we all."

Charlee sipped and threw her glass down on the floor, where the shards scattered and mingled with Asher's.

He turned and kissed her, right there in front of the assembled Kine and the world's media. "Now our secret is really out," he whispered.

* * * * *

No one knew where Valhalla was, physically, although Darwin kept arguing it was sited within another dimension and could never be found. Because there was no geographical time zone they could call their own, the clocks in the hall were kept on Greenwich Meridian Time, or ground zero, as Lucas called it.

Asher found Charlee just after midnight and picked up her hand, tugging her toward their suite. The party was still in high gear, but Charlee didn't mind at all. She was floating along, buoyed by more than the two cups of mead she had drunk.

Inside the suite, Asher closed the heavy door, and the noise in the hall dropped to a murmur. "At last, I can think," he said and picked up her hand again. "I have something to show you."

Curiously, Charlee allowed him to lead her through the rooms into their private section and then into the small sitting room just off their bedroom. "Close your eyes," he warned as he pulled her into the room.

She shut them. He led her carefully around the coffee table and stood her between the table and the sofa, turning her to face the table.

575

"Now look," he said.

Charlee opened her eyes. The room was a mess. There were work tools all over the coffee table, and drop cloths on the floor. The furniture, including the big TV, had all been pushed to one side, leaving the stone wall bare.

But it wasn't bare anymore. Charlee stared, her heart doing a little rapid patter. Carved into the stone, so that they stood out in relief, were slim vertical lines. Planks, even with little bolts holding them together, and slimmer cross-braces running horizontally.

"A picket fence," she breathed.

"I spent the last three days ripping my fingers to shreds," Asher said. "And lying my head off to you about it."

"You did this? Wait, this is what you've been doing whenever you skipped out on the organization committee meetings?"

"Guilty," he agreed.

Charlee stared at the stone-carved fence. "It's wonderful," she said.

Asher turned her to face him. "It's the only picket fence I'm ever going to be able to give you. You know that, don't you Charlee?"

She pressed her lips together and nodded. "But I don't care," she whispered.

"We've been looking for the way out all these years. Looking for the place where we can build the picket fence and have what we want. But we were looking in all the wrong places."

His gaze wouldn't let her go. Charlee caught hold of his lapels, happiness spilling through her.

"We can build the picket fence right where we want it." He glanced at the wall. "I did build it."

"Yes, you did," she agreed.

He dug in the pocket of his suit jacket and then held out his hand. There was a gold ring on his palm. "From now on, we're going to steal the best of the Kine and the best of human ways. Marry me, Charlee. No Kine-negotiated contracts, no agreements, no verbal understandings. Marry me the human way, be my Regin and help me keep humans safe for the rest of time."

Charlee closed her hand over his. "I will."

THE END

Author Notes

I have taken liberties with some of the landmarks and features of New York city in particular... there is no Mercy General in the Bronx, for example, except in my imagination, and some of the features and locations mentioned do not exist. For fictional reasons, some world events that are part of our history do not happen in this story, for instance, the 9-11 attacks, for their world-stopping scale would have distracted readers from the story in this book. If this omission bothers you, please think of Charlee and Asher's story taking place in an alternative universe that looks very much like our own.

More epic romance by Tracy Cooper-Posey

Diana by the Moon

He is Arthur's man. His duty is his life. She fears and mistrusts him. The only way they will survive is to work together.

Britain, 469 A.D.: Shortly after the Roman legions returned to Rome, leaving Britain open to Saxon attacks, Diana's abusive parents die during a Saxon raid on their villa farm, the same day her brother takes most of the male slaves and servants to join the rebel Celt, Arthur.

Diana, who no longer trusts anyone, must find a way for the women in her household to survive after the enemy has stolen everything. They struggle to eke out a living from the meager provisions remaining.

Alaric, proud Celtic warrior and trusted lieutenant to the upstart British leader, Arthur, has been sent by him to establish and maintain a line of signal beacons — one of which must be built on a strategic hill on Diana's property.

His mission is critical to the security of Britain. Alaric must overcome his hatred of Romans if he is to fulfill Arthur's ambitions in the north. He forces Diana to agree in return for the protection of Alaric and his men. Diana is pulled into a deadly political net, when Roman British enemies, including the Bishop of Eboracum, take exception to her new Celtic allies.

A haunting tale of two lives touched by the coming of King Arthur, and two hearts and souls struggling to come together against odds as great as those against Britain itself. Only together will they survive, or else be sundered…forever.

Diana by the Moon is part of the Jewels of Tomorrow series.

—

Reviewer's Top Pick, Romantic Times Magazine
Night Owl Reviews Reviewers' Top Pick

This novel drew me in so completely, so thoroughly, time just simply faded. Diana by the Moon is a work of written art. Tracy Cooper-Posey has penned a beautiful story; of one woman's courageous journey of self-discovery amidst turbulent times. *Love Romance Passion*

With her dedication and sheer will, Diana is an enthralling and moving character. Alaric and Diana's hot and delicious romance exceeds expectations. Another "can't miss" by Cooper-Posey! *Night Owl Reviews*

It's Alaric's deep sense of honor and goodness that makes this sensitive tale so appealing. It's a beautifully written novel with a distinctly different plot than most Arthurian books. I highly recommend Diana by the Moon. It's well researched with two very strong and appealing lead characters. *Romance Reviews Today*

Stay Up To Date

Subscribe to my mailing list and join the hundreds of readers who are the first to hear about my latest books. You receive two free stories when you subscribe, and occasional discounts on new releases. http://bit.ly/dkc9Yu

Or you can subscribe to my blog feed for more frequent news. To subscribe to the RSS feed via an e-reader, click here: http://bit.ly/VDrFUA

To subscribe so the posts are delivered to you via email, click here: http://bit.ly/UtFGFk.

About the Author

Tracy Cooper-Posey is an Amazon #1 Best Selling Author. She writes romantic suspense, paranormal and urban fantasy romances. She has published over 70 novels since 1999, been nominated for five CAPAs including Favourite Author, and won the Emma Darcy Award.

She turned to indie publishing in 2011. Her indie titles have been nominated four times for Book Of The Year and Byzantine Heartbreak was a 2012 winner. She has been a national magazine editor and for a decade she taught romance writing at MacEwan University.

She is addicted to Irish Breakfast tea and chocolate, sometimes taken together. In her spare time she enjoys history, Sherlock Holmes, science fiction and ignoring her treadmill. An Australian, she lives in Edmonton, Canada with her husband, a former professional wrestler, where she moved in 1996 after meeting him on-line.

Her website can be found at http://TracyCooperPosey.com. Tracy appreciates hearing from readers and can be reached at Tracy@TracyCooperPosey.com.

Other books by Tracy Cooper-Posey

Blood Knot Series (Urban Fantasy Paranormal Series)
Blood Knot
Southampton Swindle
Broken Promise
Blood Stone
Blood Unleashed
Blood Drive
Blood Revealed (Upcoming)

Beloved Bloody Time Series (Paranormal Futuristic Time Travel)
Bannockburn Binding
Wait
Byzantine Heartbreak
Romani Armada

Kiss Across Time Series (Paranormal Time Travel)
Kiss Across Time
Kiss Across Swords
Missing
Kiss Across Chains

Guardian Bonds (Gargoyle Paranormal Series)
Carson's Night
Beauty's Beasts
Sabrina's Clan (Upcoming)

Destiny's Trinities (Urban Fantasy Romance Series)
Beth's Acceptance
Mia's Return
Sera's Gift

Short Paranormals
Solstice Surrender
Eva's Last Dance

Guns 'n' Lovers Series (Romantic Suspense)
Red Leopard
Black Heart
Blue Knight
White Dawn (Upcoming)
Silver Noon (Upcoming)
Golden Day (Upcoming)

Go-get-'em Women (Short Romantic Suspense Series)
The Royal Talisman
Delly's Last Night
Vivian's Return
Ningaloo Nights
Sian's Run (Upcoming)

Jewells of the Morrow series (Historical Romantic Suspense)
Diana By The Moon
Heart of Vengeance
The Perilous Maiden (Upcoming)
To Soothe a Savage Heart (Upcoming)
The Heart of the Enemy (Upcoming)
The Cherlebury Rose (Upcoming)
The Duchess of Winter (Upcoming)
Despite The Sands Of Time (Upcoming)

Scandalous Sirens (Historical Romance Series)
Forbidden
Dangerous Beauty
Rhys Davies' untitled story (Upcoming)

Romantic Thrillers Series
Fatal Wild Child
Dead Again
Dead Double
Terror Stash
Thrilling Affair

Contemporary Romances
Lucifer's Lover
An Inconvenient Lover

The Sherlock Holmes Series
Chronicles of the Lost Years
The Case of the Reluctant Agent

For reviews, excerpts, and more about each title, visit Tracy's site and click on each title in turn: http://tracycooperposey.com/books/tracys-trilogies-series/

Made in the USA
Middletown, DE
05 October 2021